AMMANI AMMAL VA VE SU IYER SUBRAMANIA BHARATI
AA MADHAVAIAH SELVAKESAVARAYAR V VISALAKSHIAMMAL
PUDUMAIPPITTAN MAUNI KU PA RAJAGOPALAN RASIKAN
NA PICHAMURTHY CI SU CHELLAPPA KUMUDHINI S V V
KA NAA SUBRAMANYAM KALKI DEVAN THI JANAKIRAMAN
A SA RAMAMRUTHAM KI RAJANARAYANAN VAASANTHI
KU AZHAGIRISAMY SUNDARA RAMASWAMY ASHOKAMITRAN
G NAGARAJAN AA MADHAVAN SAARVAAGAN AMBAI
INDIRA PARTHASARATHY KRISHNAN NAMBI C N ANNADURAI
NEELA PADMANABHAN JAYAKANTHAN T K SEENIVASAN
RAJAM KRISHNAN R CHUDAMANI SIVASANKARI SUJATHA
NA MUTHUSWAMY SA KANDASAMY S RAMAKRISHNAN
K VITTAL RAO AADHAVAN POOMANI VANNANILAVAN

The Tamil Story

ANNADASAN PRA... HAN SIVAKAMI
BALAKUMARAN SUBRAMANYA RAJU JEYANTHAN BAMA
MAA ARANGANATHAN C R RAVEENDRAN GANDHARVAN
NANJIL NADAN DILIP KUMAR SURESH KUMARA INDRAJITH
IMALADHITHA MAAMALLAN THOPPIL MOHAMED MEERAN
THILAKAVATHI EGBERT SACHIDANANDAM PAAVANNAN
HENBAGAM RAMASWAMY SUBRABHARATHI MANIAN
KANCHANA THAMODARAN DHAMAYANTHI SA TAMIL SELVAN
MA KAMUTHURAI JEYAMOHAN KONANGI IMAYAM
SU VENUGOPAL PERUMAL MURUGAN UMA MAHESWARI
ELA RAMAMOORTHY G MURUGAN GOKULA KANNAN
N SHRIRAM S RAMAKRISHNAN AZHAGIYA PERIYAVAN
ANMANI GUNASEKARAN MEERAN MAIDEEN CHO DHARMAN
VIZHI PA IDAYAVENTHAN SUDHAKAR GHATAK KUMARASELVA

The Tamil Story

Through the times, through the tides

Edited by
Dilip Kumar

Translated by
Subashree Krishnaswamy

TRANQUEBAR PRESS
An imprint of westland ltd

61, II Floor, Silverline Building, Alapakkam Main Road, Maduravoyal, Chennai 600 095
93, I Floor, Sham Lal Road, Daryaganj, New Delhi 110 002

First published in TRANQUEBAR PRESS by westland ltd 2016

10 9 8 7 6 5 4 3 2 1

ISBN: 978-93-85152-75-7

Printed at Thomson Press (India) ltd.

Book design by Art Works

To

the pioneering stalwarts of the Tamil short story

and

all the other writers who have kept the tradition alive

ACKNOWLEDGEMENTS

Our deep sense of gratitude to Meenakshi Mukherjee, who sadly is no longer with us today. The fruition of this dream project owes much to her – when we were scrambling around trying to get support, it was she who saw value in such a project and persuaded us to write to CIIL.

Prof Uday Narain Singh, the then director of CIIL, appreciated the significance of our proposal and responded immediately. If this project has seen the light of day, it is because of him, for not only sanctioning a grant but also ensuring that the process was smooth and efficient. We are immensely grateful to him. Our thanks also to Prof K Ramasamy, the then deputy director of CIIL, and his able staff.

We couldn't have found a more discerning publisher than Gautam Padmanabhan of Westland Ltd, who saw the literary value and historical importance of this project much before the book was ready. His commitment to and interest in such works was evident even several years ago when he published a seminal anthology of contemporary Tamil short fiction. We also thank Jayanthi Ramesh, Westland Ltd, for her prompt and efficient coordination at every stage.

We are indebted to our resource persons who gave invaluable suggestions and insights – Ramakrishan of Cre-A, senior writer Ashokamitran and Kannan M of the French Institute, Pondicherry.

If this book is a pleasure to read, it owes much to the sharp eye and meticulous reading of Aruna Nambiar, who untiringly and unhesitatingly went over the manuscript a few times, insisting that she thoroughly enjoyed each reading afresh. We owe a deep debt to Vidya Mani, who, despite her busy schedule, offered with great alacrity to pore over the proofs, asserting that nothing gave her greater pleasure. We are also thankful to Varsha

Natarajan, who volunteered to read the final proofs. However, mistakes, if any, are entirely ours.

If this book is a pleasure to hold, it owes to the creativity and aesthetic sense of Malvika Mehra, who immediately agreed to design the book. We also thank her able assistant R Venugopal. For the beautiful images on the cover, we have to thank the gifted artist, K R Santhanakrishnan, who readily gave us permission to use his paintings.

We are also deeply grateful to Gita Krishnankutty for her meaningful and perceptive comments. Our sincere thanks to A R Venkatachalapathy, who spared no efforts to provide us with an informative bio-note of writer Visalakshiammal.

A project of such a scale would not have been possible without the help and support of friends and well-wishers. We would like to particularly thank Ahana Krishnamoorthy, Bava Chelladurai, Janaki Neelamani, Kannan Sundaram, Kutty Revathi, Padma Narayanan, Prapanchan, Rajagopal, M Ramanathan, Ravi Subramaniyan, Sadiq, Selvi, Sendhooram Jagadish, Shailaja, Sri Kumar, Dr P R Subramanian, Thiruppur Krishnan, Seeni Vishwanathan, Dr Ganesh Kumar, Dalavai Sundaram and Nagam Muthu.

That this project took the avatar of a book is entirely due to the dedicated efforts of computer expert Ambika Dilip Kumar, who not only kept the manuscript scrupulously in order but also kept us replenished with endless cups of tea and snacks. Our very special thanks to her.

CONTENTS

FOREWORD

Modern prose in Indian literatures is barely a century and a half old. As is well known, the first inheritance from the West was the novel; the short story trotted a little behind. In the initial decades, because of its huge popularity and entertainment value, the novel held sway in Tamil. However, the lengthy, tiresome ramblings of social and moral issues never allowed it to achieve literary compactness or depth (even today the novel remains as deceptive a form as earlier). But with short fiction there was hardly a dull moment. It attained remarkable literary success and maturity no sooner than the form was adopted, with the perfect short story appearing quickly, all its elements intact. It is perhaps the short story that corresponds to and reflects the Indian perspective of life quite convincingly – the glimpses may look scattered on the surface but are well bound beneath. Only the craft of the short story seems to have the benevolence to accommodate the fragmentary realities and truths of our existence.

In 1999, Manas published the anthology *Contemporary Tamil Short Fiction* (edited by me and translated by Vasantha Surya), covering three decades between the 1960s and 1980s. The translator of this anthology was the in-house editor at the time. The critical success and the readers' response to that effort not only made us aware of the need for such a volume, but also goaded us to explore further possibilities in that direction. This comprehensive collection is the pleasant consequence of that understanding and process.

Unlike the earlier volume, which featured only stories that appeared in little magazines, this collection seeks to represent almost all the aesthetic and political perspectives that define and characterise the movement of the Tamil short story. The focal point, therefore, is more on the art of the short story than the diverse streams that converge towards it. There was a danger that such an inclusiveness might lend a brittleness to the nature of this volume, but a sense of evenness soon played itself out, and the stories, particularly of the popular genre, managed to transcend the literary inequalities by firmly demonstrating the strengths and traits they are known for. The newness of the genre resulted in a flood of fictional imagination and it was interesting to observe how a society conditioned by various religious, cultural and political influences negotiated the form of the short story to convey its own experiences, ideas and dilemmas. The short story, as well-known Tamil writer Sundara Ramaswamy once rightly observed, is 'the last child of literary creativity', and Tamil writers – each according to his/her sensibility – constantly attempted to either trespass or conform to this imaginary literary bar. To put it more vividly, the Tamil short story for a brief moment wore the look of a person who had paired a shirt, necktie and coat with a traditional veshti, resulting in an exotic but a truly happy marriage of the New and the Old, (or the East and the West). But when viewed from a historical perspective, the ever-evolving Tamil short story soon outgrew this illusory dichotomy and attained a seamlessness, providing for a wholesome literary experience. These little aberrations were not at all unpardonable.

As we embarked on this very complex task we set ourselves three vital principles to attain the larger objective of this collection and guide us through the selection. First, apart from all the conventional elements of the short story, we wanted the selected pieces to possess a very strong sense of 'story', so that they would survive the conflict of nuances between languages during the process of translation. Second, we decided to choose stories that reflected diverse geographical, professional and social backdrops that are a composite of Tamil life and ethos. Finally, the commitment of the writer to the form of the short story and to the truthful narration of the depicted experience was crucial. These parameters instilled clarity of vision in the work at hand.

Here, for the first time, the Tamil short story has been studied very carefully from its origins and through all its ascents and descents. This compilation is a result of reading thousands of stories written not only by the authors who are included here but also by those who have not found a place in this collection. There are eighty-eight stories in all in this anthology, spanning nine decades (1913-2000).

Any discussion on the Tamil short story always begins with the three stalwarts – Subramania Bharati, VaVe Su Iyer and Aa Madhavaiah of the 1910s and 1920s, who are considered the chronological pioneers of the Tamil short story. However, during that time many other writers too published stories in magazines and also as anthologies. Hence, we decided to explore a bit beyond the three established names. Following the references made by Tamil critics Chitti and Sivapadasundaram in their book *Tamil Sirukadaiyin Varalarum Valarchchiyum* and the Tamil short story writer Pudumaippittan's essay on 'Tamil Short Story' we managed to locate three very important stories of that period – 'Sankalppamum Sambavamum' (1913) by Ammani Ammal, 'Subbayyar' (1921) by Selva Kesavarayar and 'Moondril Edhu' (1924) by V Visalakshiammal. These stories, thematically interesting and technically superior, are being published in translation for the first time in this anthology.

It is in the short story, undoubtedly the major medium of literary expression in most Indian languages, that the link between modernity and literature best manifests itself. This highly nuanced genre, constantly explored and experimented with, has always provided ample scope for a wholesome literary experience. It convincingly captures a startling range of human responses to the struggles and complexities of modern life. The art of the short story challenges the writer to attain the acme of perfection within a very limited space, at once imposing discipline and granting freedom. The essence lies in its precision and unity, revealing in the process the concerns of the writer and his fidelity to the form. Therefore, a good story – old or new – is always ageless, forever fresh.

It's almost a century now since the short story made its appearance in Tamil. Contemporary Tamil prose is believed to have evolved from its rich oral tradition of storytelling. But this genre, introduced from the West, was a distinctive, fresh literary form. Unlike the novel, the modern Tamil short story could rely very little on the oral tradition; instead, it had to invent a tenor and sensibility that was compatible with, conducive to and reflective of the grammar of the new genre.

Tamil is a classical language which has a long literary heritage backed by a strong grammatical tradition. The Tamil short story, therefore, had to journey through several stages before establishing itself, taking shape only after much deliberation among the writers. The pioneers who were quite familiar with Tamil's classical heritage first encountered the short story in English and as translations of Western and Bengali literature. Enthused by the new form's possibilities, they looked for various ways in which it could be teased out in terms of their own milieu and ethos. Naturally, the newly introduced genre threw up several challenges with respect to logic, convention, choice and treatment. Tamil writers are wont to compare the novel to an epic and the short story to a lyric. It is very rarely that so much informed debate precedes the inheritance of a new literary form in any language. The grammar of the form has been so efficiently imbibed that a Tamil writer today is unafraid of flouting convention, without, however, forsaking the literary spirit. Consequently, for the past hundred years or so, self-critical Tamils have been snipping experience to the easily digestible bite-sized slice of the short story, highlighting the uniqueness and universality of life and language in the microcosm of Tamil Nadu.

As previously mentioned, Subramania Bharati, VaVe Su Iyer and Aa Madhavaiah took to this form with great zeal. A great poet and essayist, Bharati was inspired by the folk and panchatantra tales. Aa Madhavaiah, who had written many novels, is usually pegged as a writer who used that form as a good vehicle for social reform. He, however, disproved this perception and wrote a brilliantly nuanced short story titled 'Kannan Perunthoothu' (1925) just before his death. Freedom fighter and nationalist, VaVe Su Iyer, more than anyone else, was the one who seriously contemplated the aspects of form in the short story. His story, 'Kulathangarai Arasamaram', published in 1915, might remind us of one of Tagore's stories, but it was fused so seamlessly into the Tamil milieu that it marked the beginning of the short story in Tamil in the real sense.

The modern Tamil story, as it is understood today, truly blossomed only in the 1930s. It was the literary journal *Manikodi* that promoted the short story and played a major role in its development. Three important writers, Pudumaippittan, Mauni and Ku Pa Rajagopalan earned their fame through this magazine. It was Pudumaippittan who honed the idiom of the modern Tamil short story; the stamp of his influence is seen even today. The *Manikodi* writers borrowed merely the form and its finer aspects from the Western short story; the themes and language were deeply rooted in their own milieu, resonating the pulse of the Tamil experience, lending a fresh literary vibrancy. If Pudumaippittan turned an ironic gaze on society in his starkly realistic accounts of rural and urban life and retold myths inventively and often shockingly, using even history as a backdrop, Mauni plumbed the psychological depths of his characters, subjecting them to philosophical scrutiny and in the process often twisted language into new, impossible shapes. Ku Pa Rajagopalan focused on the simmering cruelties underlying the man-woman relationship with great sensitivity. However, it must be said that it was Pudumaippittan who gave a fresh impetus to the Tamil language, boldly investing his wide canvas with the spirit of rebellion, experimenting successfully with a variety of narrative styles, setting the tone that the short story was to follow.

The modern movement, which stemmed from little literary magazines, has always configured itself as a parallel counterpoint to the popular magazines and their outputs. The serious writers associated with it never bothered to defy the ''other'; they just got on with their experiments in literature. They shared a collective identity, primarily based on certain literary perspectives which neither approved of any kind of glorification of the past nor indulged in literary complacency. Making a selection of stories from this era was a thoroughly rewarding experience.

The pre-Independence writers combined in equal measure the nationalist cause and the human predicament, underscored by a noble idealism but without sacrificing art. In the forties, with the advent of popular periodicals, the short story became a form of entertainment and reading a pastime. Serious writers such as Ka Naa Subramanyam opposed this popularising of the genre. Besides advocating good literature, he translated innumerable Western classics into Tamil, contributing immensely towards creating an awareness of modern literature.

In any language, there always is a link between the short story and magazines. While literary journals strive to uphold the sophistication and the literary value of the story, popular magazines, on the other hand, unwittingly simplify the form for the sake of readability and appeal. The flurry, therefore, in short-story writing in the thirties and forties attained, in the fifties, a hue that was popular and in a way insouciant of literary values cherished earlier. The post-Independence fifties, the decade of a young nation filled with hopes and aspirations, saw a proliferation of magazines which not only drew in new writers but also spawned many a new kind of writer, subscribing to the spirit of the magazine he/she wrote for. Writer Jayakanthan's appearance and growth is demonstrative of this interesting and complex phenomenon. He started his writing career in the 1950s by contributing to left-leaning little magazines and re-emerged a decade later in the popular weekly *Ananda Vikatan*. His progressive and unconventional themes, his earthy characters from all walks of life and his somewhat dramatic and loud but engaging style captured the imagination of a large readership. The aura of his persona and stories was so intense at the time that it not only reshaped the image of the Tamil writer but also reinterpreted the notions associated with light reading and popular magazines.

The fifties also saw the rise of the Dravidian movement, ushering in a new kind of writing, both popular and influential. These writers reinvented and emphasised the grandeur of the Tamil language, the Tamil way of life and its people. The tenor of the writing was oratorical, borrowing heavily from the classical usage of Tamil, skilfully melding it with the modern idiom, highlighting a new political consciousness that appealed to a generation of new readers. C N Annadurai and T K Seenivasan, featured in this anthology best exemplify this kind of writing.

In the sixties, the trickle that began with writers like Jayakanthan, Sundara Ramaswamy, Ki Rajanarayanan, Ashokamitran and Thi Janakiraman (all of whom started writing in the fifties) became a flood that swept the Tamil short story into its next phase. Influenced by Marxism and by translations of Russian and Western classics, these writers successfully enriched the form and experimented with the content, probing and depicting the political and social changes in post-independent India. The Tamil short story shifted its focus from the idealism of the Manikodi writers, and emphasised instead strong storylines, well-defined narratives and sharp social criticism. Realism reigned supreme. Like their predecessors, these writers too expressed themselves through literary magazines. Over the years they allowed creativity a free rein, using even fable and fantasy to structure their story. This entirely flexible approach helped them retain their sanity, to make the most of even the wretchedest situation, and to evoke a rationale of survival and acceptance. Journals like *Ezhuthu, Saraswathi, Deepam* and *Ilakiavattam*, which appeared one after another, made all this possible.

Wading through the stories of the early decades after Independence was the most challenging part of this endeavour. This was not only the period when Tamil politics, films and magazines piled layers and layers of illusions on Tamil life, but also the time when the middle-class took to reading with passion. It was the heyday of the popular magazines, which propped up a pretence of seriousness. At the same time, various literary orbits floated around, each connected to a magazine and represented by a set of writers. Celebrated within their spheres, these happy and complacent writers never believed in introspection. The reputation of these writers invariably outweighed the literary value of their works. Whenever such complexities threatened to blur our judgment while selecting the stories, the guidelines we had set for ourselves helped steer us to the right course.

Konalgal, an anthology of short stories by four young writers, Sa Kandasamy, Ramakrishnan, Ma Rajaram and Na Krishnamurthy, defined the new sensibility that was to shape the stories of the seventies. Freudian psychoanalysis, existentialism, and the ideologies of various political movements, impacted, in a large measure, the writing of the time. The shifts in Tamil Nadu politics, the break-up of the left parties, the degeneration of social and cultural establishments, thoroughly disillusioned the writers. The aspiration, or even the ire, which underscored the works of the earlier generation was noticeably missing. Cynicism set in and the thrust moved away from the story, making way for detail. Simple phraseology, sketch-like characterisations with bold or subtle strokes and intricate background details became the norm. Loneliness, individual angst, ignominy, all these were reflected in a dispassionate, impersonal tone. These stories never claimed to voice strong social concerns, but they nevertheless made crucial statements about life.

The mid-seventies and the eighties saw another important body of literature making a mark on the short story. Many urban middle-class writers such as Vannanilavan, Rajendra Sozhan and Prapanchan, who had rural beginnings and scant acquaintance with the English language, brought in fresh perspectives. The quotidian happenings in villages and small towns interlaced with precise geographical detail were narrated with great compassion. These stories brought to sharp relief the contradictions of the Indian existence without being vicious and shrill.

The 1990s marked the emergence of a strain of writing which has come to be known as Dalit writing. The Dalit writers were from the oppressed and disadvantaged castes and also first-generation learners. Inspired by the stalwarts of Marathi Dalit literature who pioneered this literary genre, which in a way resembled African-American literature, the Tamil Dalit writers enriched the world of the Tamil short story in their own special way. Their writings justifiably exposed the hitherto suppressed social realities and ripped the veneer off middle-class writings. Tamil Dalit writings are remarkably nuanced. Ever since the 1930s, contemporary Tamil literary tradition had imbibed the spirit of social realism and had honed the short story in a manner that was capable of conveying a modern political idea or a position convincingly. This background perhaps inspired the Dalit writers to venture into the sphere of writing more confidently and shape their narratives with literary sophistication. Today, after centuries of oppression, we have Dalit writers like Bama, Sivakami and Azhagiya Periyavan who have broken their silence to write in a rich, earthy dialect. Their searingly honest tales often shame us into taking stock of our complacent little lives. For these polemical writers, form too was as political as the content, as is evident in the doing away of the formal language for the authorial voice. By ironing out the direct and indirect speeches, they jolted the aesthetic comfort of the average reader, who was unaware that the voice of dissent was encapsulated not only in the content but also in the narration. Tamil Dalit writings have always revealed a refined sagacity without forsaking their political edge, thanks to the modern Tamil literary consciousness which has steadfastly encompassed a world view in all its expressions.

It must be emphasised that ever since the short story made its appearance in Tamil, women have always played a significant part. In fact, two of the earliest stories featured in this collection – both well delineated and nuanced – are by women. The stories by Ammani Ammal, Rajam Krishnan, Ambai, Dhamayanthi, Uma Maheshwari, R Chudamani, Thilakavathi and Shenbagam Ramaswamy span a range of concerns, displaying great sensitivity and a remarkable mastery over the form.

Our collection tries to be as representative as possible, primarily focusing on literary achievements that stand the test of time. But we have taken care not to overlook some of the cherished pieces of popular writing. Popular writings in Tamil, always distinct, attempt to discuss and expose topical conflicts and human folly in a way that never breaks any convention nor hurts any tradition. A notable exception is the gifted writer Sujatha, who appeared on the writing scene in the early nineteen seventies. An engineer by profession, he was immensely talented and well read. He invented a fresh, racy style all his own. His stories and novels, which trammeled all the elements of popular culture, redefined conventional styles of narration. Not surprisingly, his crisp, lively prose, interspersed with intelligent humour, was lapped up by legions of readers. Though less complex and less nuanced, popular writings wielded a great influence on middle-class readers. We have chosen here some of the finely crafted stories that try to reach out, defying their very categorisation. In the process, we have demonstrated how the short story can be effortlessly tuned to voice even clichéd sentiments in a novel way and provide light entertainment. The approach of many of these writers to the short story may seem naïve to some, but the writers themselves firmly believe in their relevance and function.

We were forced to exclude some of the experimental writing. Mainly because there are not that many and the few that are there are deliberately audacious and creatively insufficient. These writings failed all the hopes the initial post-modern years had generated. And the advent of Dalit writings with their raw experiences rendered these luxurious formalistic journeys totally irrelevant. A few favourites we genuinely wanted to include, but we were hindered by their resistance to translation and hence had to regretfully leave them out.

A few words about the authors in this anthology. Most are not full-time writers and are engaged in a variety of arduous professions to sustain a livelihood. It is astonishing that they have crafted such chiselled gems in such adverse circumstances, defying the perception of leisure and comfort commonly associated with literature. Such is their commitment to literature and their faith in the act of writing.

Tracing the Tamil short story from its origins and through all its phases and stages was an exhilarating experience. But it must be said that even a mammoth project such as this is confined by the restraints of space. We could have added a few more stories, but they would have been included more for their historical value than for their literary merit, the main thrust of our anthology. We are, however, confident that almost all the writers we have chosen will find a place in any anthology that attempts to represent the Tamil short story. But of course the stories may differ since choice is often subjective.

We have made a slight departure in the arrangement of stories too: we have relied on the writers' chronological emergence on the literary scene rather than the year of publication of the stories themselves. The short story, as we have said elsewhere, is a form unbound by time; hence a chronological arrangement wasn't a strict necessity. With such unique voices and world views, an eclectic collection readily fell into place.

By stringing together these finely etched stories from various decades, we have tried to represent Tamil life in all its manifestations and resplendence. This anthology not only records the evolution of the Tamil short story but also documents the changing landscapes over different periods, straddling a range of social concerns relevant to the times. Similarities and dissimilarities notwithstanding, these stories encapsulate the Tamil experience in its entire glory, marked by the dominant impulse of the human predicament and the triumph of dignity.

Dilip Kumar

A Note on the Translation

Translation is not an unfamiliar term or activity in these modern times; however, despite the excellent translations and translators in Tamil, the translations of Tamil's classical works seem to garner more attention. This anthology is one more attempt among the many to restore the credit due to contemporary Tamil fiction. One of the very first stories that I read and attempted to translate was Ammani Ammal's 'Expectation and Event'. It begins much like a parable, and I settled in for a comfortable read, a smile very much on display. But the intelligent and unexpected end shook me out of my complacency. This nuanced piece, written in 1913, at a time when the short story as a genre had barely reared its head in Tamil, revealed the sure hand of a skilful writer. It was then that I fully comprehended the magnitude of the decision I had made: I, a poor swimmer, had audaciously plunged into the deep end. Smooth, effortless strokes were going to be few and far between; instead, I had to brace myself to flail around, gasping and spluttering. Not surprising that I took on this endeavour with a lot of humility, with one thought playing like a refrain at the back of my mind: I must not let the writers down.

A close reading of merely a handful of stories by the early writers revealed that the short story had been quickly adapted and seamlessly subsumed into the rich Tamil literary tradition. The writers had clearly mastered the grammar and craft of the short story in a short span of time. They effortlessly situated the stories in their milieu to reflect the concerns and issues of their society. Perhaps the brevity of the form proved to be a perfect vehicle to capture the immediacy of modern life.

We had planned to translate the stories in chronological order so that we could also systematically trace several things at the same time: the changes in written and spoken Tamil over the years, the trajectory of Tamil social life not only through the years but also through the different landscapes of Tamil country, the responses of the people to different situations in the various decades and how they negotiated and fitted themselves into social and political spaces that have changed drastically through the years. But like most plans, this was unmade too. For one, the editor could not access the stories in strict chronological order; hence it was impossible for the reading and selection to be linear. However, despite such inevitable deviations, we could easily uncover the gems in this anthology.

Leaping back and forth in time was one of the biggest challenges: we were steeped in the idealistic fervour of the early twentieth century one day, only to be confronted with the cynical eye of an author writing in the late decades of the twentieth century the very next day. Or, in a flash, urban dialect and angst had to be supplanted by a raw, earthy Dalit voice. Also, once you are deeply entrenched in the process of translation, a few methods that you invent and adopt permeate all the stories. But this also ushers in the inherent danger of flattening out the distinctive voices of the writers, lending a sameness to all the stories. Hence I had to ensure with utmost care that whatever the author intended – humour, pathos, irony, to name just three – was captured convincingly. The style of the narrative too had to be replicated as far as possible. Short, staccato sentences or rich, descriptive passages were conscious decisions taken by the authors and it was imperative that I not only retain them but make sure that they read well in English.

Translation is a tricky terrain, forcing one to perform many a precarious balancing act. Of course mere proficiency in both the languages is simply not enough. One must possess the sensibility and the ability to capture the spirit of the original. When you translate a story, you dismantle it piece by piece and reassemble it in another language. In the process, the writer's approach to language and literature is laid bare. And the literary success of the writer hinges on his/her relationship with the language. As for the translator, one brings to the table all the knowledge and resources one possesses, without ever calling attention to them or proclaiming them. In many ways it is a self-effacing task. Oftentimes I did feel like the protagonist in the story 'The Key' who enthusiastically took on the job of picking a lock, only to find that it wasn't easy at all. The excitement and zeal slowly gave way to frustration, despair and anger. But unlike him, I didn't abandon the exercise altogether but ploughed on tenaciously.

I kept these important things in mind when I finally chose a story: one, the story had to have a universal appeal, despite its unique cultural specificities. But that doesn't mean that we settled for simpler stories. A challenging text which would prod me to bring out the beauty of the source language in English was what we looked for. It was also vital that the translated text retained almost all the nuances and the natural flow of the original, overcoming the inevitable losses that happen during any process of translation. A few translations had to be abandoned since they didn't stand up to scrutiny after translation. Some stories hinged totally on local dialect, while a few were riddled with too many linguistic impossibilities, which when elaborated upon within the text made the reading experience cumbersome and laborious. Besides, a few stories that resonated strongly among readers in Tamil quite simply didn't work with readers of the translation. Including such stories would have shown the authors in poor light.

Several stories come to mind, but just one story, the delightful 'Godavari Gundu', will suffice to illustrate the decisions we have taken. Set in the 1960s, it bristles with small human desires and lively day-to-day exchanges that so mark life in small-town Tamil Nadu. Yes, it is deeply rooted in a local milieu and culture where a married woman will go to great lengths to buy a heap of jasmine offered to her, even pawning a vessel. The other woman, never one to miss a good opportunity, shrewdly hopes to appropriate the vessel by doling out just a rupee. Simpleton Dattu, the ever-smiling indigent priest, is happy enough to escort his wife – decked with jasmine flowers of course – to a film and patiently wait outside to fetch her back since there is money enough for just one ticket. As for the harried man of the house, who has run out of money as early as the tenth of the month, he is forced to sell his old newspapers to meet his day-to-day expenses. The deft hand of the author transforms all these ordinary people, fraught with petty yearnings and frailties, into enchanting characters who make the story come alive with their sparkling speech and irrepressible humour. But it is the philosophical dimension which dovetails the different strands of the story in the end that lifts it to a universal and sublime level, effortlessly transcending all the cultural specificities.

This anthology, which traces the evolution of Tamil short fiction, is perhaps the first collection which systematically chronicles the art of the Tamil short story, irrespective of its lean and fertile patches. It is a social and cultural history of sorts, spanning the entire spectrum of the Tamil society over the decades.

As with any piece of writing, we, above all, wish to immerse readers in the world of the author, which though deeply rooted in its own distinct milieu oversteps all cultural barriers. But, at the same time, we didn't want to give the mistaken impression that they are reading the original, by ironing out all the peculiarities of the Tamil text so that it better suits English. On the other hand, we are more than happy to constantly remind readers that they are reading a translation – a world removed from the English-speaking one – which hasn't sacrificed the nuances of the original, and which perhaps adds an enriching dimension to English, and also opens up newer possibilities. But we were always conscious of the conventions of English grammar. We did keep in mind that English is the target language, a language completely different from Tamil, which is bound by its own rules and grammar, which must be adhered to and respected if our task is to be deemed meaningful. We were conscious that the essence of the original must be retained. We wanted the intonations of Tamil to come through – the slang, the idiomatic usage, and even the swear words, if possible. We would like the readers to experience the Tamil culture, the Tamil language. We have taken great care to retain the authors' distinctly diverse voices from different regions, strata and times. We hope that the reader can perceptively sift the ironic gaze from the comic and the metaphysical. We also hope this text, a different avatar from the original, will usher in a new readership for the writers and introduce to the readers an entirely fresh world.

As we had mentioned earlier, we did certainly keep in mind that the translation had to work in English. But when it came to dialogues, we gave a free rein to Indian English, which is really the English spoken in India. But even this, we know, varies from region to region. We have attempted to capture the English spoken in Tamil Nadu, which carries with it inflections of Tamil. Correct English might appear somewhat stilted, especially in conversations, and, given the backgrounds of the characters, something they would never use. We are of course always aware that the characters do not speak English in the original, but if it is informal speech in Tamil, we must strive for it to be casual and natural in English too. We hope the readers' sharply tuned ears will allow them to engage with the text imaginatively. For example, if it is a casual conversation, we haven't hesitated to use: 'Just like that only I came.' Perhaps a native user of English wouldn't speak like that. But all Indians who speak English have a lively register. For example, in 'Godavari Gundu', the wife doesn't hesitate to tick off her husband: 'You don't have any compassion at all, is it?' The tags – is it or isn't it – are typically Indian. So is the continuous verb, as it is used in this sentence: 'If her husband is smart, will she be suffering like this?' But if the person uttering the words wasn't given to chattiness or was terribly uptight, we have used a more sedate English. We have trusted our ears and hope that the cadences flow unobtrusively.

We have also used kinship terms unapologetically in many places because not only do they give the flavour of the original language but also because most of us do address our kith and kin by these terms, even when we speak to them in English. Besides, there aren't equivalents in English. When we have used a kinship term which cannot be easily understood, we have done so with a non-intrusive interpolation. For example, at the first instance it is used, we have said, as we have done in Ki Rajanarayan's 'The Chair': '… to churn curd, Paati, our grandmother, would sit only on it.' Of course the words 'our grandmother' were not there in the original. There is yet another reason for using kinship terms: it has become highly fashionable of late, especially with urban Indians, to call their parents 'Mummy', 'Daddy', etcetera. But if it is a little girl toiling in the fields in the interior south, she cannot call her father 'daddy'. She would sound as if she were asking for a pizza, not a serving of the humble gruel.

Besides kinship terms, in our societies that are strictly graded by social order, there are other forms of address that denote status, gender, age, etcetera. They can reflect many things, from reverence and obeisance to familiarity and derision. For example, someone in a higher social scale would be addressed as ayya, appa or amma depending on the gender, often shortened to 'ya, 'pa or 'ma. But these terms can also be used by anyone to convey kindness. Da and di, which express familiarity, contempt or chumminess are freely used since they are now part of the Indian English lexicon of Tamil Nadu. Of course, the English 'sir' is 'saar', but has assumed inflexions which can be obsequious but also jocular. Sometimes in public places, a spouse is often referred to as 'they', the third person plural. Which is why in Jeyanthan's, 'Bonds of the Day', we have used: 'What? 'they' are not here today?' Likewise, children are affectionately called 'it' and oftentimes spouses refer to each other as 'it'.

The colourful expressions in our languages convey outrage, insolence, scorn, anguish, playfulness, sarcasm and what have you, and we use them naturally even in Indian English. So we have used: 'Chee! Is this any way to hold a lantern?' 'Ayyo, where is my husband?' 'Adei! Rascal!'

As mentioned earlier, we have used unobtrusive interpolations which we hope will meld naturally into the text. We did this because it is tiresome to keep going to the glossary. But we have provided one at the end of the book for the interested reader.

As far as possible, we have kept idioms, proverbs and other local expressions as they are. They might, at times, need to be delineated a bit more, but they are fresh and reflect the beauty of the language. For example, in Si Su Chellappa's 'The Village Road', the master tells his employee: 'You have no right to twirl your moustache and call yourself a Naicken proudly.' Twirling one's moustache signifies taking up a challenge in a manly fashion. Or as the mother admonishes the son in 'Dhavamani' by Kanmani Gunasekaran: 'I must beat my brains only with a slipper.'

We have used certain Tamil words unabashedly because they not only have a charming, rhythmic ring to them but also convincingly illustrate the meaning, despite their alienness in the target language. And quite simply, there aren't English equivalents. For instance, in Thi Janakiraman's story 'Godavari Gundu', we kept the word 'gundu' as it is, and any reader can understand the meaning from the context that it refers to a vessel which is huge, hollow and fat.

In a few instances, we have also used the suffix 'aa' quite unapologetically since that is the way Tamils speak English too when posing a question. For instance, usages such as 'For six months paper-aa?' ('Godavari Gundu') are pretty common. Also in Vannanilavan's 'Jackfruit', we have said: 'Come "condition-aa" this evening.' Now condition may be an English word, but it has different connotations in Tamil. In this case, it means definitely. We have left the word as it is, but from the context, the reader will certainly get the meaning.

If the titles of some of the stories read a little quaint, it is with reason. Authors usually choose titles with great care and thought; so, as far as possible we have stuck to the original titles, consciously giving 'catchiness' the go-by. Spellings of Tamil words too may seem a little unusual, but we have retained them to approximate the Tamil pronunciation. As for the spellings of the authors, we have gone by their preferences. As also the date of publication of the stories.

It is also with reason that throughout the note the 'I' and the 'we' have been used interchangeably. This is very much a collaborative effort and

I have worked closely with the editor, relying on his mastery over the Tamil language and his vast reading and scholarship in both the languages.

As we all know, the process of translation is dynamic and there are ever so many possibilities. Hence there can be no one conclusive approach or theory. Each text poses a new challenge and demands a focus entirely unique and in the process a lot of decisions are taken, which though small are significant. It must be emphasised that traditional tools such as the dictionary or thesaurus are seldom of much use in such situations. Mere proficiency in two languages can never ensure a good translation. We have to invest all our expertise and literary insights in the process, but refrain from looming large over the text. Translating these stories was a painstaking, arduous, yet pleasurable process. And above all, a humbling experience.

Subashree Krishnaswamy

Expectation and the Event 1

Ammani Ammal

There was once a casuarina tree in a forest. It was thriving comfortably, lush and green, with enough rain and sunshine. Children sang and played joyously under its shade; birds nested in its branches and cooed melodiously. Squirrels jumped so playfully on its branches that merely watching them evoked a feeling of briskness. Even though every creature that benefited from the tree was lively and contented, the tree itself was never satisfied. It always felt that it could be something else. It wanted to be put to use for something famous in the world. Knowing this, a tree beside it said, 'Good, one day you will become the mast for a ship. What could be more special than that?' But the tree didn't like it: 'Pooh! What, did you say the mast for a ship! I would like to be more special than that, thank you very much!'

Every year, the men who measured trees would mark out the tall ones in the forest; the woodcutters would then arrive, fell the trees, chop up the branches and deliver them to the shipbuilders. The tree thought all this was too demeaning.

One day the tree was marked to be cut. 'Aha, the time has come for you too, is it?' remarked a nearby tree. But the tree laughed it off. 'I'm much smarter than them.' It got the mark rubbed off with a squirrel's tail.

The weaver birds who came back the following year exclaimed, 'O! You're still here!' The tree replied haughtily, 'O, yes, they tried to chop me off. But you think I'll give in to them?'

'But don't you want to be tied to a mast of a pretty ship, travel the seas in style and see new-new ports and people?' asked a weaver bird.

'No, I'm not at all interested,' said the tree. 'The sea looks the same everywhere. I want to be of use to the world, that's my aim.'

'You are talking senselessly. We have no time to chat with you now,' said the birds and went about their work.

The time came for the tree's wish to be fulfilled. One day, a few other woodcutters came to the forest. Instead of picking the tallest and the most upright trees, they earmarked trees at random and started cutting them down. The weaver birds remarked to their old friend, 'Be careful. Whether you like it or not, these people are sure to chop you today.'

'I quite like the idea,' replied the tree. 'I wish to be of use to the world.'

On hearing this, a woodcutter said, 'Good, as you wish.' With a chop of his axe, he pulled it down. 'I don't think you will work as a ship's mast. Don't worry, you aren't suitable enough to be put for such use. They will use you to make paper.'

'What is paper? ' asked the tree to the weaver birds who were flying here and there on its branches. 'We don't know. We'll ask the sparrows.'

The sparrows said what they knew: 'Paper is the white thing on which people write and read. Earlier they were making it with rags. Nowadays because trees are so easily available, they are making it with trees.'

'O, people will read me, is it?' enquired the tree eagerly. 'Yes,' they replied. The tree lay spellbound, its happiness knowing no bounds. Aware that there was little reason to be so joyful, the sparrows cautioned: 'Ayyo, wait a minute. They are going to turn you into newsprint, not paper for a book.'

'Whatever it is, they will write only interesting, good things on me, isn't it?' said the tree. 'Perhaps,' said the sparrows. 'But, generally, they don't always write good things.' A few men then came to drag away the tree. Poor thing, the tree went through such ordeals. First they chopped it into bits, then pushed it into the grinding machine along with the others, pounded and squeezed all the juice out of its body to make it into mush, torturing it in ever so many ways, before finally turning it into paper. What was the point in having such thoughts while undergoing such torment? And what use thinking of days of pleasant sunshine in the sloping hills of the forest, when birds cooed in the branches and children scampered about in the shade and when you proudly watched them all? 'I never imagined the world would be like this,' mused the tree aloud. The other trees, also turned into paper, concurred in one voice: 'Whatever has been said of the world is all highly exaggerated.' Then they wound the tree into a roll, five miles long, and loaded it into a ship. There, poor thing, it suffered from ailments such as seasickness for a week. A fierce wind blew over its head. When they heard the noise, all the trees that were turned into paper sighed about the days spent so pleasantly in the forest, when they had so fearlessly braved the winds. Our casuarina tree (turned into paper) had the misfortune to be piled at the bottom of the mast of the ship.

Not only that, the mast also happened to be its old friend. The mast told the tree with satisfaction and pride: 'There is no greater life than being a mast. Under the sunshine during the day and under the stars and the moon at night, we take people and goods to new-new countries, see so many ports – I can't tell you how much use we are to the world.'

The tree started to cry. 'Are you telling me that a mast is as important as a newspaper?'

The mast shook with laughter. 'Well, this is what I like. Why, the life of a newspaper is just one single day; it's of no use at all even the very next day. A mast, on the other hand, is of use for several years. O, I forgot another thing. Sometimes the captain of the ship leans against it. Just imagine how proud it feels.'

The tree was engulfed in immeasurable sorrow. On reaching the port, the rolls of paper were unloaded on the shore. In the end, it reached the godown of the city's newspaper. It would have been so breezy in the forest; it was so different being shut inside the airless godown. Every roll of paper that lay in the room lamented with great sorrow. One night, our tree (the paper) was taken to the printing place, where under the press, unable to breathe, it lost consciousness. When it came to in the morning, it found letters imprinted on its body. What the sparrows had said had come true. What was printed on it were advertisements with crude illustrations – 'Fragrant snuff', 'Sparrow virility potion', 'Hypnotic aromatic tobacco', 'Sixteen expensive things for a rupee', 'Novel hair remover', and things such as 'Broad-daylight Murder in Chinglepet', 'Man Dies Climbing Tree', 'Trains Collide', 'Yogi Living on Air', 'Flying Baby', etcetera. There was not a single thought-provoking word to be seen.

Oh! Even the all-knowing Lord of the Serpents, Adhiseshan himself wouldn't be able to express how sad the tree was when it came to know what was printed on it; it bemoaned the fact that it hadn't become a mast. It took a vow that if only it could somehow escape from this predicament, it would never let its mind wander. But ayyo, it was all over. Then the tree and others like it were cut up, folded, and bundled off in the early-morning cold to be sold in the railway station. A man bought it for half an anna, read the entire contents, announced that there was nothing worthwhile in it, and flung it under his seat. Another man picked it up, read it, and on the way back home when he bought some fish, he wrapped them in it. Stinking of fish, it spent the entire night thinking about life in the forest. The next day, when the stove didn't light up, the maid flung the fish wrapping into the fire. In a minute it was burnt – 'busss…'

Forgetting that it was a story that they read, the students pondered on both the joys that the tree could have experienced and the turmoil it was subjected to in reality.

The teacher who was considered a great enemy and nicknamed 'Teacher Never-to-Die' asked: 'What is the moral of the story?' 'Man proposes, god disposes', or 'you can't beat fate' or some such grandiloquent philosophical statements were what he expected from the children. But one boy, whose mind was still on the story, uttered: 'The moral is, these wretched newspapers should be banned!' Taken aback by the unusual response, the teacher didn't know what to say. Just because he was a young boy, we shouldn't presume that he answered in jest. Moreover, we elders are tortured daily by many such newspapers which give us error-ridden information, poorly printed on shabby, dirty paper, yielding nothing in return for the effort we put in. Shouldn't we then endorse this view?

Original title: Sankalpamum Sambavamum
1913

Peepul Tree by the Tank 2

Va Ve Su Iyer

Coming to think of it, I'm only a tree. But if I were to tell you whatever there is in my heart, it would take more than a day. How much I have seen, how much I have heard, in this life of mine! I've seen with my very eyes your grandmothers' grandmothers crawling and playing about. You might laugh, but there's no lie, not even the size of a sesame seed, in what I say. I'm an ancient tree. I've never learnt to lie. It must be about ninety to hundred years ago. Your great-great grandmothers used to come to this tank only, pot and all. Some used to bring even children along. How cute the children used to look. Leaving them on the bank, the ladies used to wash their saris and bathe gracefully, smearing turmeric on themselves. Like little Krishnas, the children used to crawl towards the jasmine bushes and chuckle at the buds. In those days there was a coral-jasmine tree in the corner, with blooms like pearls. A sweet fragrance used to waft across the banks. But now, without anyone to tend to it, it has all withered away. The slightly older children used to pick the flowers and lovingly smell them. Aah, how pleasing it is to think of those days.

But now I'm not going to tell you a tale from those years. When I'm happy in mind, I will tell you. For the past seven-eight days I've been thinking of Rukmini. It's been fifteen years, but it seems like yesterday. None of you know

Rukmini. She looked like a golden doll, that child. If I think of her smiling face, I feel as if she herself is before me. You can look at the beauty of her forehead for a whole day. She was tall, with limbs like lotus stems. Her body was as soft as jasmine. But her beauty was in her eyes. What sagacity, what clarity and what intelligence! If you looked at her eyes, clear blue skies and a crystal-clear pond would come to mind. What affection and sympathy in her gaze! Every new-moon Monday, she would circumambulate around me, praying to god. How can I explain the affectionate gaze she bestowed on me at that time? Even my withered-away tiny branches would spring new shoots! Ayyo, my darling Rukmini, when will I see children like you again?

Ever since she was a child and till the day she died, there wasn't a day when she didn't come here. When she was about five or six, she would be forever playing here. There wasn't a person who didn't want to gather her and kiss her. However busy our Venugopala Sastry was, he would never fail to pluck flowers by the handful and give them to her after he bathed. Our town's calves, however boisterous they may have been, would turn docile on seeing her, and wait to be stroked by her little hands.

I've always loved children, but if she came, I would forget myself. Not a sliver of the sun should touch her. Even if she was a little away, I would stretch out my hands and unfurl an umbrella over her. After I saw the face of my lord Sun with devotion, the thought of baby Rukmini would come to mind. I would eagerly await her visit. An unbounded happiness would fill me as soon as I saw her. One shouldn't play favourites with children, but it must be said that I never felt the same about anyone else's visit. Was it only me? Why, even the other children would play with fullest joy only after she came. She was the queen among them, she possessed such magnetic charm.

In those days, her father, Kameshwara Iyer, was comfortably off. He was very fond of the child. He never tired of doing anything for her. Whenever he spotted new varieties of silk in the bazaar, he would immediately buy them, thinking to himself, 'It would look lovely on our Rukmini.' He made a lot of jewels of top-quality diamond and red stone. When she was about ten years old, he bought a paavaadai and half sari for a kolattam performance. In the moonlight, how majestic her adornments and her beauty looked! What majesty! An eye-catching spectacle it was! I forgot to tell you about her voice. What is a koel in comparison! Her voice slithered like a golden strand. You wouldn't be bored with it even if you heard it the whole day. I heard her songs only at dance gatherings. But even if I think of them now, the sweetness and fineness of her voice resound in my mind.

As she got older, what can I say about the ever-growing grace of her affection? Even as a child, she was close to everyone. This quality increased day by day. She never differentiated between herself and her friends. She held the same affection for every friend, rich or poor. Why, she showed more love for the poor. She couldn't bear it if anyone suffered. She gave beggars handfuls of rice. How often I've seen tears pouring down her eyes when she saw blind beggars. She would give more alms to them. Because she possessed such boundless compassion and sympathy, whenever I think of her, I experience the great joy that one feels on seeing rain after a harsh summer.

Should such a fate befall a child I looked after like my very eyes? What a sinner I am! Should my affection go to such a waste? Does the creator have no eyes at all? But what can god do for the treacherous acts of human beings?

When Rukmini turned twelve, her father gave her hand in marriage to Nagarajan, the son of our town's revenue collector Ramaswamy Iyer. The wedding took place with great fanfare. At the pre-wedding festivities when friends gathered and on the day of the wedding procession, I saw her go round the village in full finery. Eyes would be cast on her, so beautiful was she! When I saw her among her friends, it looked as if strands of lightning were in prayer before their glittering goddess.

Kameshwara Iyer had offered a lot of dowry and gifts at the wedding. Rukmini's in-laws were very satisfied. After the marriage, her mother-in-law would often take Rukmini away to her house. She would fondly plait her hair and decorate it with flowers. She would never forget to take her when she visited relatives. In many such ways, Janaki (that was Rukmini's mother-in-law's name) showed her affection for Rukmini. The bridegroom Nagarajan too was very intelligent. He too was extremely fond of Rukmini. There was no one in the village who didn't speak of how suited they were in beauty, brains and wealth.

Three such years passed by. So many changes in these three years. Kameshwara Iyer's earnings became lean. He had invested all his money for interest in some Arbuthnot bank or something. It swallowed four crores of money and gave out a belch. In a single day, Kameshwara Iyer became a pauper. Only the jewels that Rukmini's mother Meenakshiammal wore were left. He could clear his debts only by selling off his ancestral house and lands. He moved to where Kuppuswamy Iyer now lives, near the canal bank. Meenakshi also used to look like Goddess Mahalakshmi. She had infinite dignity. Such a big tragedy had befallen them, but she was not broken. She used to say, 'We lived so happily for all these years. Did god ask someone and give it to us? What he gave, he has taken away, so what? As long as he and Rukmini are alive, I have no complaints. This coming month of Thai, if I perform 'shanthi muhurtam' for Rukmini and send her away to her in-laws, then we have no worries. We'll drink kanji or something and spend the rest of our days thinking of god, as always.' So sad. How could she have known what was going to happen?

When Ramaswamy Iyer realised that nothing of Kameshwara Iyer's wealth could be salvaged, his friendship towards him turned cold. Earlier, he used to often visit Kameshwara Iyer. If he met him somewhere, he would never fail to chat with him for over ten minutes. Now if he saw Kameshwara Iyer at a distance, he turned the other way hastily, as if he had an urgent errand to run. You would have already guessed without my telling you that a man who behaved like this would stop visiting Kameshwara Iyer's house. His wife Janaki too kept away from Meenakshiammal. But Kameshwara Iyer and Meenakshiammal never made much of this. When there is wealth, relationships flourish. When it disappears, relationships too go away like strangers. Would you consider all these real bonds?

But they started distancing themselves from Rukmini too. A few months before Arbuthnot bank dissolved, every Friday Janaki would send her maid for Rukmini after the morning meal was done. That day she would plait her hair, put pottu and mai, dress her up, take her to the Akhilandeshwari temple for the darshan and keep her with her for the night and send her back only the next morning. But once it was known that what was lost in Arbuthnot bank was completely gone, the very next Friday she sent word to Meenakshi, 'I have a lot of work at home. I will send for her next Friday.'

The next Friday she didn't even send word. This deeply saddened Meenakshi and Kameshwara Iyer. Rukmini too felt sad: Even my mother-in-law seems to be snubbing me.

A few days thus passed. The whole town started speaking in whispers. All the secrets were discussed on the tank's bank only. But I heard them only in bits and pieces; the full story never reached me. It had never happened like this in our town before. My heart was pricking. I knew that when such secrets cropped up something evil would happen. But to whom and what, I did not know.

In the end, sifting this and that, adding up this and that, I slowly understood what the matter was. Ramaswamy Iyer and Janaki had decided to abandon Rukmini and had arranged another marriage for Nagarajan. What could I do? My heart was broken. How could anyone forsake little Rukmini? Janaki, what a sinner you are! Isn't she also a woman like you! What did she do to you? Even stone would melt at the sight of her. Is your heart more hard than even stone? Kameshwara Iyer and Meenakshi sat stupefied. If I myself felt like this, do you have to ask how the parents would have felt?

Hereafter, the only hope lay in Nagarajan. He was studying in the city. The month of Margazhi began. I counted the days for him to come. At last he came. The face, full of laughter and cheer the morning he came, suddenly changed. His parents started poisoning his mind. Day by day, he looked more and more disturbed. Those who are clever at melting can even melt stone. Whenever I saw his confused face, my stomach would churn. What was left now? There was just this hope, and now even that was gone. I thought, Rukmini's fate is over and done with.

The month of Thai dawned. It was spoken about openly. Some girl from the east, it seems. The father had wealth worth four lakh rupees. Had no sons. Had another daughter besides this one. In due course, Ramaswamy Iyer's family would get two lakhs. It was awful to hear all this. But what could be done? It was my fate to listen to all this.

As soon as the talks began, Meenakshi stopped coming out in the daytime. She would come to the tank before sunrise, bathe and fetch water. Her face looked ghastly. No proper sleep or food. The distress of having lived well and now fallen to penury had robbed her of her beauty. She never regretted that she had lost her home and jewels and was reduced to wearing a mere string for a thaali. But day and night, the only regret she had was that Janaki had decided to get her son married a second time in front of her eyes when she had a daughter as pretty as a parrot at home. Even Janaki's heart would have melted if she had seen Meenakshiammal's face, but where would the queen give her a look!

I don't know how Rukmini felt or what she thought when all this was going on. She was an innocent girl. Perhaps she felt that her mother-in-law would not betray her completely. Or did she think that Nagarajan would not agree to whatever his mother said? It was not even five years yet since they had played as children together on the tank's bank. Even after marriage, when they met alone, how often had Nagarajan spoken to her with love and affection like earlier days! Rukmini would have thought that he would never let her down.

But as the days went by the talk of Nagarajan's wedding firmed up. No one knew the goings-on in Nagarajan's mind. No sign of him after he had paid respects to the in-laws the day he had arrived from the city. There was no sign, not even the size of a sesame seed that he thought of Rukmini at all. But the carefree cheer seen on his face the first day had left him forever. He never spoke to anyone and had a sullen face always. In the end, a date was set and the girl's people came and read out the marriage invitation. Ayyo, hearing the sound of the melam that day, the very elements of my life twitched. How would Kameshwara Iyer have felt? How Meenakshi's heart must have fluttered. How did Rukmini bear it? God alone knows.

There wasn't a day when I didn't weep thinking of how Nagarajan too didn't have an ounce of compassion or sympathy for Rukmini. Oftentimes, I'd even remarked: will he ever have a peaceful life after doing all these things? When my heart was thus grieving and grappling, one day I heard a piece of news, much like milk being poured into my stomach. A certain Srinivasan, believed to have studied with Nagarajan, came to visit him. They wanted to talk in secrecy. What better place than the tank's bank?

One evening after everyone had left, at about seven or eight, the two of them came. Srinivasan was a good chap. He came from a place fifty or sixty miles away. It seems someone had written in saying that Nagarajan who already had a girl waiting for him was getting married to someone else. He came at once like a mail van. When he came to the bank, he asked Nagarajan if all that was true. Nagarajan said, 'If Amma and Appa have already decided, will I accomplish anything by refusing? Besides, I believe the girl is pretty. It seems her father has written out a lakh of rupees in her name. In later years I believe she will inherit another lakh. Why should I refuse such a goddess of wealth who came of her own free will?'

How can I describe how Srinivasan looked when Nagarajan uttered these words? When he finished, for over half an hour Srinivasan advised, 'How many ever lakhs you may get, should you heap on yourself the curses of a girl like this? Can you erase the promises you made in the wedding pandal to the chant of mantras?' In many such ways Srinivasan explained dharma and nyaya on Rukmini's behalf, to the point of melting hard stone. Every minute of the half hour, I wished him well: that he should live long, have a happy life, without any troubles.

After he finished speaking, Nagarajan replied, 'Srinivasa, whatever I have told you till now is all in jest. Do you think I will stoop so low for money? I wanted to keep it to myself, but since we've spoken so much, there's no point in keeping it from you. But one thing: don't tell anyone. Since they've decided to behave so cheap, without any justice, I have decided to disgrace them thoroughly. Despite my protests, Appa and Amma are adamant. So I'm going to Mannar Koil. Even there, I will refuse. But they are going to force me. I will sit in the marriage pandal. Whatever it is, I only have to tie the knot in the thaali, isn't it? No one else can do it. At that time I'm going to say 'no'. Let them all blink like monkeys who have eaten ginger. Do you think that this hand which has touched Rukmini will touch another girl?'

'But did you stop to think how Rukmini and her parents would feel if you left for the marriage?' asked Srinivasan. Nagarajan replied, 'Yes, I've thought over it. But when they think that they've lost everything and are in utter disappointment, I will suddenly rush in at that exact moment and bow before my in-laws, "Don't worry. I will never let my Rukmini down. I've insulted all those mad after money and come here." When I say all this, how happy they will feel. I want to experience that.'

Srinivasan said, 'But think of how they will suffer till that day.' Nagarajan said, 'Only five days now. Today is Friday. On Sunday all of us are going to leave. The next day is the wedding. We'll start that very day and be back the next morning. They who have put up with so much for so many days, won't they bear with all this for another five days?'

'I don't know 'pa. This doesn't sound right to me,' Srinivasan said as they started moving away. I couldn't hear anything more.

I couldn't sleep at all that night. I told myself, 'See how you cursed Nagarajan. Is there a better boy than him in this world? There is no need to fear now. What is five days or even ten days? Nagarajan is a determined fellow. He will do as he says. Rukmini will have no more sorrows in life.' I puffed up with satisfaction.

Sunday: there was such a hullabaloo in the town that they were leaving for Mannar Koil. There wasn't a person who didn't curse Ramaswamy Iyer and Janaki, but none to give them good advice. Even if at all anyone attempted, they weren't the type to listen.

Since it would surely burn their stomach were they to stay back and see them starting from the village, Kameshwara Iyer and Meenakshi left for Manapparai on Saturday afternoon itself. At home, her aunt Subbalakshmi Ammal was Rukmini's caretaker.

It was Saturday night. The town had quietened down. It was about nine, nine-thirty. Nagarajan came to the tank's bank alone and sat down in contemplation under the neem tree. In a while, at a distance, a figure of a girl could be spotted coming towards the bank. But the figure kept looking back every once in a while. Only when she came and stood near Nagarajan, I realised it was Rukmini. I was startled. But I shook myself immediately, wiped my eyes and looked intently to see what would happen.

For five minutes Nagarajan didn't notice her at all. He was in deep thought. Rukmini stood still. Nagarajan casually lifted his head, saw her. He too was astounded. But he immediately recovered and said, 'Rukmini, how can you come here alone at this hour?' 'The day hasn't come for us to be together, that's why,' said Rukmini. For a couple of minutes neither of them opened their mouth. Both their hearts were in turmoil. But they didn't know where to begin and what to say.

In the end Nagarajan said, 'If people come to know that we are here at this hour, they will say something. Come, let's go home.' Rukmini replied, 'The past one month I've been wanting to say something to you. Only today I got the opportunity. You must give me permission to say it.' 'Say it,' said Nagarajan.

Rukmini started: 'I don't know what to say to you. Only Goddess Akhilandeshwari knows how my mind has suffered the last three months. I thought all my worries would vanish once you came from the city. I thought you wouldn't let me down, whatever Maama and Maami may do. But if you also let me down, on what hope will I live? If the fence itself destroys the crops, what will happen to the crops? Whatever has happened so far has broken my heart. Only you can mend it. Otherwise, my life will be over. No doubt about it.'

Tears poured down Rukmini's eyes when she uttered these words. She stopped there. Nagarajan didn't speak. Rukmini waited for a while and asked, 'They've arranged for the travel tomorrow. You are going, isn't it?' After thinking for a while, Nagarajan replied, 'Yes, I'm thinking of going.'

When she heard him, Rukmini's chest tightened with sorrow and her body trembled and tears filled her eyes. But she bit her teeth and didn't show it out. 'That means you've let me down, isn't it?'

'Will I ever let you down, Rukmini? But it is also my duty to please my parents, isn't it? That's why I'm going, listening to them. But you don't worry. I will never cast you aside.'

Rukmini couldn't bear it. 'You are going to marry again, I shouldn't be worried, you won't let me down ever! But you will never go against your parents' wishes! What is there for me to say now? This is my lot in life, that's all.' She sat down.

Nagarajan didn't say a word. Only the words 'I will stop the marriage' would assuage Rukmini's heart. But he didn't want to say it now. So he showed his love and support through gestures. He took her hand in his, placed it on his lap and pressed it softly. As if pacifying a child, he stroked her back affectionately. He felt her hair on his hand. He was startled. 'What is this, Rukmini, you hair is all matted. Why are you behaving like this? I can't bear to see you so unkempt. Let's see your face. Ayyo, your eyes are all red. Your face has lost its glow. My darling, please don't be like this. I won't let you down, believe me, truly. Don't be afraid. I'm telling you from the bottom of my heart that I can't see you like this. Don't even think in your dreams that I have forgotten our childhood bonds. Come, let's go, it's late. We shouldn't stay here anymore.' He finished speaking.

Rukmini didn't get up. She sat down dolefully. Looking at her, Nagarajan's eyes were wet with tears. At that time it appeared as if his brain nudged him to tell the secret. But did he say it, the useless fellow? To him his game seemed more important. So he didn't utter a word. But how would he have known that all this would happen. Even I, with all my age, didn't know. How would that little fellow have known?

Nagarajan lifted the limp Rukmini gently like a flower and clutched her to his chest and said with compassion, 'What, Rukmini, you're not saying a word. What can I do?' Rukmini lifted her head and saw him. How can I describe the look? Like one who has been swept away in a stream and whose hands have become tired; when such a person spots a log of wood at a distance and tries to swim anxiously in its direction, full of hope, thinking 'Appa, I'm saved now', only to find that it is garbage – think of how his mind will be torn to pieces. And how his face will change. That was how Rukmini's face looked, with her heart reflected on it.

Boundless sorrow, boundless grief was seen in her eyes. When she saw that Nagarajan was silent even on seeing that look, Rukmini moved away and said, 'I don't have anything more to say. You are not saying that you won't go to Mannar Koil. My fate is sealed now. When you have decided to leave me like this, what can I believe now, and for whose sake should I keep my life? I don't have any grudge against you. I know your heart would not have agreed to such a thing. My fate and the troubles of my parents is making you do all this. In future, once in a while think that there was a girl called Rukmini, who loved you with all her heart, and who even breathed her last only thinking of you. That is what I would like to ask you finally.' She fell on Nagarajan's feet, clasped them tightly and heaved uncontrollably. Nagarajan lifted her up immediately and said, 'Foolish girl, don't do anything like that. If you leave, my very soul will leave. Then who will think of whom? It's drizzling now. The skies have turned dark. In a while it will pour heavily. Come, let's go home.' He clasped her hand and took a few steps.

No moon or stars in sight in the skies. Darkness everywhere. Once in a while creepers of lightning glittered, as if cutting the skies with a sword. But the next minute it turned even more dark. Thunder rumbled, as if splitting the skies, shaking the earth. Winds swirled like a hurricane. The sounds of the faraway downpour were closing in. I couldn't catch the words of Nagarajan and Rukmini, spoken at such an apocalyptic moment. They were going homewards swiftly. One could see Rukmini flinching, reluctant to go home when lightning flashed, but Nagarajan urged her home. I could hear only one or two of their words. '... won't be alive... Amma's heart is satisfied... Friday morning... girls'... break... don't say that... that's all my fate is... keep at least that girl happy... I wish you with all my heart... you will come to know on that day... final namaskarams... bear with it till I come...' These were the only words I could hear amid the rumblings of thunder, the sound of the winds and the noise of the rains. Rain fell down in torrents. Rukmini and Nagarajan disappeared from my view.

That was it. The next day dawned. The rain had abated, but the sky wasn't clear. The blackness of the clouds hadn't faded away. The wind was wailing like a child not having anyone to console it. I can't explain the confusion in my mind. However I tried to steady my mind, my heart could find no peace. 'What is this? Today my heart is filled with a sorrow that I have never known. Don't know the reason,' I thought to myself, when Meena cried out, 'What is this? A sari seems to be floating here.' Immediately I turned towards that side with great trepidation. All the women who were bathing in the tank turned around and looked. Then they started whispering among themselves. My very soul left me. It looked like Kamakshiammal's sari. It was Rukmini who had jumped into the tank, hurling a stone on her parents' heads. That's it, after that I fainted.

After a while I regained consciousness. By then a crowd had gathered by the bank. There wasn't a soul who didn't curse Ramaswamy Iyer and Janaki. What did it matter now if they cursed or not? Taking away the grace of the town, the lives of her parents and my happiness, my dear Rukmini was gone in a flash. They had laid her down near the jasmine creeper. How many times she had picked the jasmine flowers with her golden hands. When she was a child, there wasn't a place on the banks where her feet hadn't trod, a tree or a plant that she hadn't touched. Ayyo, the more I thought, the more my heart churned. Those beautiful hands, feet, all wilted away. But the lustre of her face hadn't changed. Her earlier sorrows had vanished, and an astonishing peace prevailed over her face.

There was little time to note all this. By then a buzz rose in the crowd, 'Nagarajan is coming, Nagarajan is coming.' Yes, it was true, it was him, rushing in panic, not knowing head nor tail. As he reached the jasmine bush, unmindful of the crowd and his parents there, he wailed, 'Rukmini, what have you done, Rukmini!' and fell down like a log. The din in the crowd died down in a second. Everyone looked at Nagarajan.

For a long time he lay on the ground, lifeless. When the scared Ramaswamy Iyer sprinkled water on his face and fanned him he at last regained consciousness. He opened his eyes, but never said a word to his father. Looking at Rukmini's lifeless body, he said, 'Destroying all my plans, you've flown away like Juliet, Rukmini. What Srinivasan said has come true. What a sinner I am! You died because of me. I'm the wretch who killed you! If only I had told you this secret yesterday, such a fate would never have happened! Kusuma satrusam… Satya: pathi pranayi hridayam* – I only read these profound words playfully, never realised the truth of it! What is there for me now? Rukmini, you have left me in haste. I don't want a married life now. I'm going to take sanyasa.' Thus saying, he tore up his veshti and the upper cloth before anyone could say anything. His parents didn't open their mouths. Before they could recover from the shock, Nagarajan fell full length on their feet, and left in his loincloth, without speaking a word to anyone.

This is how my Rukmini's story ended. My dear children, please think of this story whenever you feel like doing something that will hurt a girl's heart. Don't even in jest crumple a girl's heart. Who can tell which game will lead to what grief?

Original title: *Kulathangarai Arasamaram*
1915

* The love-filled hearts of women is as delicate as a flower. If the love is harmed, it will wither and fall off.
Meghasandesham by Kalidasa.

Railway Junction 3

Subramania Bharati

Spring. Early morning. Tenkasi station. It belonged to British India. To the west, the next station, Senkottai. It belonged to the province of Tranvancore. To the south, about two miles away were the famous Kuttralam falls. Mountain slopes all around. If you went a little to the west, only ten stations between Senkottai and Thiruvananthapuram. On either side, steep mountains and deep gorges. Splitting the mountain was a tunnel for the train to pass through. Beyond that, on either side, nature draped in the lushest of greenery was an unforgettable sight to behold.

On the outer platform of the Tenkasi station, at the time of the arrival of the train going east towards Thirunelveli, around a hundred people had gathered.

A few were orthodox Brahmins. Their bodies draped in old white clothes, faded to the colour of mud after repeated washing, they sat sweating, chatting about this and that – like who was going to perform the seemandham ceremony, on which date and where.

Brahmin widows were talking among themselves on one side, while young married Brahmin women stood on the other, heads bowed, looking at passers-by from the corner of their eyes.

A few working men walked up and down leisurely, turban, coat, watch-chain and all. The policemen marched like kings, heads held upright. A few veiled Muslim women sat, heads and faces covered, each facing a different direction.

Selling betel leaves, betel nuts, tobacco, cheroot, snuff, snacks like murukku and thenkuzhal, coffee, etcetera, a few Brahmins and non-Brahmins were indulging in daylight robbery – selling worthless things at three to four times the price.

That day the train was late by an hour. I was bored, so I took a stroll within calling distance towards the south, close to the rails. There under a tree sat a handsome Muslim gentleman. Zari cap, zari-bordered muslin kurta, zari-bordered pajama, zari slippers, a face like a full moon, a luxuriant moustache. As soon as I saw him, I knew for certain he belonged to a rich family. Tears poured from his eyes and I felt sad for him. I never gave it any thought that he might get angry if he were questioned; I just walked up to him impulsively and asked: 'Why are you crying, thambi?'

He looked me up and down for a moment. He couldn't have been more than twenty-five. Even when he was crying, head bowed, he looked handsome. When he wiped his tears and looked me in the eye, he seemed like a veritable Manmathan, the god of love.

From the way he looked at me, I felt that he had formed a good impression of me. Without getting annoyed, he asked me, 'When is the train coming?'

'It will be late by an hour, the station master said,' I said.

I knew Hindustani and Urdu rather well. So I started speaking to him in Urdu straightaway.

'How do you know Urdu?' he asked. 'You look like a Hindu.'

I replied, 'When I was young I studied in Kashi. So I know Hindustani well.'

'Don't they speak Hindi in Kashi?' he asked.

I said, 'Hindi, Urdu, Hindustani, all are one language only. In the beginning, the Mughal kings conducted their affairs in Persian. Later they and their descendants adopted Hindi, the language of this land. Hindi sprung from Sanskrit. It is a distortion of Sanskrit. The Hindus wrote in Devnagri and spoke the language naturally. The same thing the Musalmaans wrote in Farsi script, adding many Farsi and Arabic words, and started calling it Hindustani or Urdu. Urdu means language of the camp, the hybrid language which sprang up when the Mughul soldiers set up camps in several countries and mingled with locals. I know Hindi very well. But since Urdu or Hindustani has only extra Farsi and Arabic words, I'm quite conversant with it as well.

'Anyway, why are you upset?' I asked again, impulsively.

The Muslim gentleman replied: 'Swami, just looking at you fills me with trust. My heart tells me that you might be able to solve my problem. It's not a predicament which I can tell everyone. Still, I feel like telling you. You will earn merit if you can solve my problem. I will never forget it all my life.'

'First tell me what is troubling you. If I can help you, I certainly will.'

Then the Muslim gentleman started his tale: 'You know, perhaps, that in my community cousins can marry. I was born in the north, in the city of Hyderabad. Not the Hyderabad of the Sindh, but the Hyderabad of the Nizam. I'm my father's only child. When I was born my father was extremely poor. A few years after I was born they started a big lottery in our province. My father borrowed ten rupees from someone and bought a ticket. He was lucky. Allah must have decided to end our poverty. His ticket earned him one crore rupees. He used that to start a few businesses. He earned huge profits and in a few years his worth became seven-eight crores.

'After that, a few losses. But my father was smart. As soon as he started incurring loss, he sold off all his businesses, bought a lot of lands, built himself a mansion and did as much social service as he could. He died when I was fifteen. Since I was his only child I inherited all his money. It fell on my father's younger brother to oversee our household. At the time of his death, my father had not only gifted him lands worth lakhs of rupees but had also left me under his care.

'The first thing my uncle did was to marry me off to his girls. This happened within two years of my father's death. My uncle doesn't have a son. Only three girls. He did this so that my wealth won't go outside our family. My mother wasn't for my marriage. She wanted me to marry a pretty girl from her family. Besides, she said if I have to marry, I must marry only one of them, not all three. Because of this there was a disagreement between my mother and uncle. My uncle took me away to another city and without my mother's permission got me married off.

'Unable to bear the grief my mother passed away soon. What my uncle said became the law in my house. I didn't bother about my inheritance. I left it all in his hands. In two-three years he had wasted about a crore on prostitutes and liquor, and in the end, because of alcohol, died of a rupture of the intestines. Then it fell on me to manage all my wealth.

'Ok, I don't want to go into the details of all this. I wasn't troubled by the loss of some of my wealth. But I can't tell you how much of torment I undergo because of my three wives. See there – can you see? Can you see a group of veiled women at the end of the station? The ones in the middle are my three wives. The ones around them are servants. Can't you see, the way each one is sitting, faces in different directions, that they are not at all united. The eldest one is Roshan, she is twenty-two. The second one is Gulab biwi. She is nineteen. The next one is Ayesha biwi. She is sixteen.

'Gulab wants to chop me if I speak to Roshan. Ayesha doesn't like me talking to Gulab. If I buy her a jewel, she will break one of hers. If I buy her a silk blouse, she will tear up another one. Like this, with every little thing, they take my life out. And what, is it just for a day? Or two days? For a year? Or two years? My entire life is going to be hell. What will I do?

'Last night I had a dream. Mohammed came to me and said: "Ade, Ismail Khan! How you are suffering with your three wives. Divorce two of them and allow them to get married outside. Just keep one girl. Your sorrows will end." I believe that dream to be god's words. I think what one feels appears as a dream. And since Allah lives in our soul I think this dream is Allah's decree. I like all three equally. All three too love me equally. Who will I shove aside and who will I keep, I don't know. That's why I'm so sad.'

I could hear the noise of the train arriving. He quickly said 'Salaam, salaam' and ran towards the station. I too went to catch the train thinking 'thank god the train came before I could give a solution to such a difficult problem.' I think he would do as Mohammed decreed in his dream.

Original title: *Railway Sthanam*
1920

After this story was published in the newspaper *Swadesamitran*, a Muslim reader pointed out to Bharati that it wasn't the custom among Muslims to get married to sisters. Bharati apologised to the editor and readers and explained that he wrote such a fictitious tale only to propagate progressive ideas.

Kannan's Grand Mission 4

Aa Madhavaiah

Five Brahmin ladies took a sunrise dip in the Tamaraparani river and returned to the bank. Four of them – Meenu, Ammaalu, Anandavalli, Thiruvi – were middle-aged. Meenu's daughter-in-law alone was a twelve-year-old girl. All five were wrapped in wet saris; a damp blouse hung from the daughter-in-law's shoulder. The older ladies performed their morning japa. Filling their gleaming brass pots, copper chembus and pooja pots with river water as sweet as sugarcane juice, and dabbing turmeric on the cheeks and dots of kumkumam on the foreheads of their glowing Brahmin faces, they made their way towards the city. And what city was that? The one to which Namazhvar sang: Mada kodi mathil thenkulanthai. It was about two miles to the north of the river, and the thoroughfare was common to all. A few 'untouchables' who crossed their path, obligingly stepped aside on their own. But if they didn't oblige even after fervent pleas, the ladies themselves ran into the fields on either side. And they would also abuse them: 'Curse you! Hope you drop dead.' The scene of these five family goddesses returning home early morning reflected both the good and the bad of the orthodox Indian way of life! That aside, let us now hear a bit of their conversation.

Thiruvi: What di, Meenu! Didn't you say you learnt the song 'Krishnan thuthu' from Ekamma Patti from Arumangalam? Why don't you recite it – let us at least earn some merit while we walk home.'

Meenu: Why not? I don't know it all that well, but what I know I will tell you.

Ananda Valli: 'Krishnan thuthu?' What song is that?

Thiruvi: You dumb thing! You haven't even heard of it? In the Mahabharata, didn't Krishna on behalf of Dharmaputra go as an emissary to Duryodhana? The song about that!

A Valli: I see. Ok, Meenu, let us hear it.

Meenu: Shall I start? 'Kannan Perunthuthu Kelaai Ni Karigaiye – *Kanna's grand mission! O listen to it, my darling girl!'*

'Di, Ammaalu! Hadn't your husband gone to Allikulam? He's back already?'

Ammaalu: He came back last night. After the temple was shut. There wasn't even rice left over at home. Woke up next-door Seshi, borrowed a pot of rice. By the time I got to sleep, it was after ten.

A Valli: I see. O that's why Ammaalu has come so early in the morning to bathe in the river!

Ammaalu hung her head down in embarrassment while the other four heaved with laughter. The little girl blinked, not understanding a word.

Thiruvi: This Ananda Valli, forever making fun. Nothing else she knows. Continue with the song, Meenu.

Meenu: Where did I stop? *'Kanna's grand mission! O listen to it, my darling girl!'*

'Ananda Valli, then why are you coming so early to the river bank even when your husband is not in town? Even when he had gone to Kulasekharapattinam? What about that then?'

Ammaalu: Yes, yes, ask her, ask her. You are the right one who can match her teasing.

Meenu: Enough, enough, 'ma! Here I am taking up for you and you are calling me a tease! That's what they say: in these times no use doing good for others!

'Kanna's grand mission! O listen to it, my darling girl!'

Daughter-in-law whispered to Thiruvi: What is this '*O my darling girl*'? Who is saying this to whom?

Thiruvi: Come on, Meenu, answer your daughter-in-law!

Meenu: What is she asking?

Thiruvi: O my darling girl! She is asking who is calling whom that?

Meenu: Let her think that I am only telling her.

Thiruvi: Ok, tell. Now look here, all of you, if anyone interrupts once again I will really get angry. Shouldn't the song finish by the time we reach home? Begin, Meenu.

Meenu: If I keep on reciting, as if I can't finish by the time we reach home.

Thiruvi: If you tell more only can it finish, no? If you keep on saying the same thing, how can you finish?

Meenu: Ok, I will tell you further. *'Kanna's grand mission! O listen to it, my darling girl!'*

Thiruvi: Ade, ade! Please move a couple of paces. A thousand blessings on you! You are a good man, no? Look, there is fresh shit everywhere. And my chappals are also worn out. So please move a little, 'pa!

Passerby: Go, Paapaathi, you go to the side. Where do you want me to go and fall?

Thiruvi: Ada, curse be on you! May you die of plague! As if you can't go four paces away. See, I've got a thorn in my foot. Meenu, please take out this thorn.

Passerby: Why, Paapaathi, that disease won't befall you, is it?

Meenu: It is bleeding, so don't worry. Anyway, as soon as you go home, just close that wound with a dab of lime paste. Is it hurting?

Thiruvi: No, it's not. Don't know whose face I got up to today. Bleeding on a Friday and all.

A Valli: You said no one should talk! But you can, is it?

Thiruvi: Yes, yes, if you were pierced, you will know! Such a fat, long thorn it was too!

A Valli: Let that be. Meenu, why don't you recite the remaining part?

Meenu: Where did I stop? Ah, yes, *'Kanna's grand mission! O listen to it, my darling girl!'*

Thiruvi: I think he's an outsider. If he was from our town, he wouldn't have behaved like this.

Ammaalu: He moved away, no?

A Valli: Yes, she shouted, and so did he!

Thiruvi: Yes, yes, I shouted. As if Meenu praised him or what.

Meenu: It's all in the way you say it. There is a sea of difference in saying a cow-like Brahmin and an animal-like Brahmin. Listen now, I'm going to tell the song:

Kanna's grand mission! O listen to it, my darling girl!

'What, di, Andhuvalli, do you know who Kannan is?'

A Valli: I may not know as much as you, but don't mock too much. As if I don't know Kannan and all.

Meenu: Ok, come on, tell, let us see. Is he your servant Mookan's younger brother or what?

Thiruvi: Or is it the mirasdar's farmhand Kannan?

A Valli: Yes, yes, to you all, I'm a dull-head only. I don't know how to speak like you all. So you are saying what you want!

Meenu: Why all this? Just tell us who Kannan is.

A Valli: So what, let me be foolish. Now that you people have gone on and on, I will definitely not tell...

Ammaalu: Kekkelo blah-blah, maakolam blah-blah! You really don't know, that's why you are saying all this.

A Valli: Ok, let it be. Tell the song, Meenu. I can see our street.

Meenu: *'Kanna's grand mission! O listen to it, my darling girl!'* O, we've reached home. I will tell it another day.

Original title: *Kannan Perunthoothu*
1925

This story appeared in the last issue of *Panchamritam*, a journal edited by Aa Madhavaiah, He had edited the entire issue but unfortunately died before it went to the press. Though the issue didn't credit Madhavaiah with the story, scholars are of the opinion that only he could have written the story.

SUBBAYYAR 5

SELVAKESAVARAYAR

Peddanaickan Pettai to the east, Vepery to the west, salt pans to the north, Poonamallee High Road to the south; right in the middle of Chennai is a park. Locals usually refer to it as Rani Park, Victoria Park or Singara Park. Those who have studied English call it People's Park. Manmade mounds, lotus ponds, little islets with spaces for eating; and in between all these are trees brought from various countries. The town's municipality maintains it beautifully.

Though the park is only a mile long and a quarter mile wide, the paths criss-crossing inside are at least four to five miles long. Between the paths you can find lush grass. Lining the paths on either side are kamuga trees, kaattu vazhai, punga, and poovarasu trees, providing shade so that you never feel the heat. Between the grass are beds, circular, square, triangular, all shapes, really, with flowers blooming in every colour. In some places, low platforms are seen, where small and big flower pots are kept on steps in rows. To take you to the flower pots and beds, small pathways two to three spans wide lead from the main paths. Edging those small pathways are varieties of bushes, neatly trimmed. In places, crotons, bamboos, etcetera, have grown into bushes. For the morning and evening visitors to sit on so that they can enjoy the breeze and the scenery are benches and planks here and there under the shade of the trees.

In two or three spots are huge cages where pigeons, parrots, peacocks and various small and big birds are found. In one place can be found a group of deer, fenced off by iron railings. In another can be found a crocodile in a water body. In yet another you can find an elephant tied.

In the middle of the northern half of the park, in a space surrounded by a circumference of four furlongs, enclosed by zinc sheets on three sides, taller than man can see, is a water body twenty feet wide. In it children can row little boats. Visitors to this enclosure pay a fee of an anna to the man at the entrance. In the upper half, here and there are big iron cages. One has a lion, others a tiger, a bear, a cheetah, a giraffe. Beyond the pond on a platform are all species of monkeys. Onlookers usually feed them bananas, groundnuts and fried gram.

In the southern half, in a piece of land measuring a hundred-odd cents is an enclosed dome of teak beams and planks; inside, in big pots, leafy plants from hilly places, which are watered at least twice or thrice a day, are grown, and kept cool. In this fernery, on summer evenings you can find couples sitting on benches and chatting among themselves. Some read the papers, novels. If you go in you will never feel like coming out. As long as you are there, you will feel as if you are in Bangalore or Wellington, so cool it will be that you will never feel the heat.

Within shouting distance of that place is the bandstand on a platform. Around the platform is a pathway, one foot in height. Surrounding the pathway, an iron fence. To enter, on four sides are six-feet-wide gates with iron railings. On which grow creepers of Rangoon jasmine, champaka flowers and kaakkanam, forming a canopy. Around them, a big pathway.

Once a week the army band plays on the platform. To enjoy this music Englishmen and locals gather. The English youngsters dance to the music and enjoy themselves. Because of the light, the colourful clothes of the people and the cool breeze, that place is very pleasant.

Thirty-five years ago this park was even more beautiful. Then the town hall wasn't there. Moore Market came after that. The municipal office came into being only then. Other than the small bungalow for the overseer of the park, there was no other building. You could sleep and sit anywhere, without a mat, so clean it was. However sad anyone was, this park would take it away and give happiness. It was like an elixir, everlasting. Affluent couples chatted happily in the secluded islands, without embarrassment.

The old ones sat on the benches and recounted the good old days. Children learning English used to stroll, talking about this and that. Villagers used to be astounded by the animals. They would bring sweetmeats, sit by the pond and enjoy. On holidays and Sundays, teachers and office-goers would stroll around and relax.

In the year of Dhathu (1876) and before, how the people in the province of Chennai suffered without rains, many don't know today. After the disaster abated, a few important Englishmen and locals in Chennai and big officers sat together and decided that in December, during Christmas time, when there would be holidays in English companies, big business houses, schools and colleges, they would hold a carnival in Rani Park to entertain the masses. All the arrangements would be made by a committee constituted by them.

People from out of town could only visit the zoo during the day with their families. Because other than that nothing special would happen in the northern half. People would come and go. The southern half was where the carnival was held. Beyond the paths around the bandstand were circular pandals made with bamboo and coconut fronds. As specified by the sellers, the thatch was divided into stalls. Some sold sweets, others bread, biscuits, bun, soda, lemonade, betel leaves, etcetera. Some sold attractive foreign and Indian goods. A few numbered the objects, wrote the numbers on pieces of paper, put them in a box and cried out to people to try their luck. Those who wished gave some money, put their hands in the box, took out a ticket and got the object marked by that number. Such raffles were in plenty. In those stalls stood pretty English girls near the boxes to hand over the things. One of the stalls was meant for the committee. After dusk, the electric lights around the bandstand looked like many moons lit together at the same time, filling people with joy. You could also hear strains of music now and then. To enter there were four entrances and entrants had to pay four annas. To prevent crowds from getting out of hand were a few policemen here and there.

Only a few came to buy things in this enclosure. Many came just to take a look at the grand clothes and the accessories worn by people who gathered there. Plenty came to admire the natural good looks of many. A few came to look at the latest fashions. There were many women who came to admire the designs of jewellery so that they too could make such special things. Some came to meet the ones they rarely visited. A few came to salaam the big bosses. Many came just for fun. Even if they were hungry, they didn't leave, telling themselves they would go in a little while; such people increased by the hour. Even those wearing ochre robes never left the place early enough.

At the time of the carnival, there would be dance tents, drama tents and wrestling rings. Stalls for freakish things could also be found.

In those days, in the eastern half, the athletic association stadium, where they honour the silambam artistes today, was not there. There used to be poles joined by ropes. Inside which horse racing, rekla racing, running race used to take place. The crowds would burst into laughter when the runners with water-pots fumbled, or those in the gunny-sack race jumped haphazardly and fell. There, so that onlookers didn't jostle each other, mounted police would control and shoo them. Police would threaten the crowds. Sometimes the crowd would push them off. Those who were not tall enough looked at the spectacle from the tops of vehicles. Some would clamber up trees, looking like tailless monkeys.

The crafty ones who didn't have work at that time in the Gujili bazaar found the carnival a favourable ground to exhibit their skills. Notes from pockets, coins from hips, angavastrams, the necklaces of women, they would disappear like magic. Like stealing the hen and then commiserating, these men would say 'catch the scoundrel', 'there he is running', 'beat him up, beat him up'.

For four-five days this beautiful park would be full of such ruckus and hullabaloo. On the last day, after ten in the night, there would be fireworks. People would marvel at the unusual spectacle. The carnival would end with that.

In 1886, in the month of December, i.e., the Tamil year of Partibha in the month of Marghazhi, they had a carnival. For two-three days the funfair went off smoothly. On the fourth evening at seven, there was a wail, 'o', from the stalls. Five or six stalls were on fire at the same time. In minutes, the fire spread everywhere.

Those near the exits cleverly ran away. Where there wasn't any fire, a few boys and strong men survived, breaking the bamboo and tearing apart the thatch. In minutes, a few died in the stampede at the exits. A few who escaped from the thatch and the bamboo sustained scratches, bled and ran. Because of the surging crowd, some were stamped upon. Arms and legs broken, a few people limped on shouting 'ammadi, appada'. In a while, even that place was engulfed in fire. The exits too. Those who were trapped inside could be heard shouting, 'ayyo, where's the child, where's the father, where's amma, where's the husband, ayyo, the fire is coming close – what to do? Ayyo, can't bear the heat'. In ten minutes, the stalls were burnt to the ground. A few ran, hair, moustache, beard burnt, and face blackened. A few threw away their clothes and ran naked and survived. Among the rest who lay unconscious, only a few survived. Those dead amounted to a few hundreds, they said.

In half an hour, in the whole of Chennai, in every street, was complete mayhem. 'Ayyo, did you see my son?' cried mothers. 'Ayyo, where is my husband?' cried young women. 'Go and search for your brother,' said a few to the elder brothers. 'Nephew hasn't come back yet,' said a few, searching the streets. 'Ayyo, he went without listening to me. What happened to him?' said a few. 'The wretch of a neighbour took him away forcibly. Neither can be seen,' wailed a few. 'Some friend, dressed tip-top, came, and dragged off my son. Is he alive or dead?' cried many. Those who lost children, brothers, daughters, women, hit their mouths and chests, squeezing their hands and stomach, shouted, 'ayyo, appa, kanne,' and ran to Singara Park.

Meanwhile the police doused the fire and lined the corpses in a spot. Those injured were taken to the General Hospital. A few identified the bodies and took them away in vehicles, saying 'this is my brother, this is my son, this is my uncle, this is my brother-in-law'. There were a lot of mistaken identities too. Many bodies could not be identified at all. They were taken away and cremated by the police.

Among those who came to claim the bodies were two traditional Brahmins, Appa Sastry and Gopal Iyer from Muthialpet. Appa Sastry lived in Ramaswamy Street. Gopal Iyer in Pavazhakara Street. Their two sons had been friends from childhood. In leisure time, the two visited each other and chatted about this and that. For any function or funfair, they always went together. Gopal Iyer's son was Nagaswamy Iyer. Appa Sastry's son was Subbayyar. When they searched among the bodies, they found Gopal Iyer's son. Gopal Iyer took him away in a vehicle and performed the last rites.

Poor thing, Appa Sastry. He didn't even get the body. 'Ayyo, what misfortune has befallen my son, I'm such a sinner. He ought to have performed the last rites for me; instead of which I'm doing for him. What will I do?' he lamented. Except cremation and last rites, he did all the other rites. If this is God's wish, what can we do? He gave the child, he took it away, what is the point in feeling sad? he thought and gathered strength. He resolved to spend the rest of his life doing good things close to his heart. His daughter-in-law, Kamakshi Ammal, was twenty. She took off the maangalyam and ornaments, had her head tonsured, threw off all signs of a married woman, put on the garb of a widow, wept, thinking of her husband again and again. Her mother lamented, 'Ayyo, I went on a pilgrimage, observed fasts, prayed, and after many, many years of waiting my darling daughter was born as a gift from god. She has come to such a state. What sins did I commit in my previous birth, I don't know. She would have been better off dead. Now how I can I bear to see her as a widow? Oh god.'

In the nights, Kamakshi Ammal lay sleepless, lamenting. At times when she dozed off a bit, she would dream of cooing with her husband and get up with a start, full of tears and with a running nose. Her mother, looking at this, would also cry. At times she would console her. Like this, twenty days passed. The festival of Shankaranti came and went.

On the twenty-first day, at eleven in the night, there was a knock on the door. Appa Sastry had gone to listen to the religious discourse at the Krishnaswamy Temple. His wife was in the kitchen, having dozed off while thinking of her son sadly. Her daughter-in-law and her mother too had just nodded off. They had slept after locking the hall door. Kamakshi Ammal woke up with a start, hearing the knock. The father-in-law who had gone to the temple had come, she thought. By the time she could get up, there was yet another hard knock on the door. Her father-in-law would never knock so hard, she thought. Before she could even think, 'Adi Kamu, open the door,' came her husband's voice. Meanwhile, her mother too got up and called out, 'Who is that?' Because it was the mother- in-law, the voice replied, 'It's me Subban, ask them to open the door.'

Hearing this, Kamakshi Ammal and her mother shook as if thunder had struck them, clasped each other and stood without speaking. Again, a shout could be heard. 'Amma, open the door, Appa, please open the door.' Gathering courage, Kamakshi's mother said: 'Appa, it's twenty days since our lives were finished. We have been lamenting since then – how did you have the heart to leave us? Which world did you go to? Is this the time for you to come and test us?'

'What is this, have you gone mad? Where is Amma? Appa? Kamu?' said the voice. No one opened their mouths.

In a minute, one could hear knocks on the next door and the opposite house. On being asked who, a voice from the outside said: 'Me only, Subban.' It was Subbayyar's voice. Everyone was scared: ayyo, he had an unfortunate death, his soul is wandering around, not knowing the house. No one opened the door.

At that time a purohit in Thambuchetty Street had finished a ritual for Parthasarathy Chettiar's son and was returning with a new veshti and dakshinai. Thinking that someone was approaching, the purohit checked to see if the dakshina was safely tucked in his waist. He tucked the bundle with betel leaves, coconut and banana under his armpit tightly. He walked step by step, without hurry. Feeling that the figure two-three houses away had the look of Subbayyar, the purohit trembled and almost died. The person approaching him said, 'Oi, Kuppa Sastry, the bundle looks heavy. Where are you coming from?' Hearing this, the purohit fell flat, unconscious.

In a minute, two people came from the corner of the street, towards the north. One of them was Narayanaswamy Ayyar. He was the English teacher of the Christian College High School, Chennai. He had a BA. The other was Krishnayyar. He had finished the old UCS and was a writer at the accountant general's office, earning a salary of fifty rupees. They were coming from a music concert on the occasion of their friend's son's marriage. That Narayanaswamy Ayyar was so brave that even if he confronted the lord of death Yaman, he would dare to ask, 'Are you the old Yaman or the new Yaman?' As for Krishnayyar, even if there was a battle in faraway Arcot, he would cower in the kitchen. They saw the man coming towards them. Since he had the look of Subbayyar, Krishnayyar hugged Narayanaswamy Ayyar in fright. Hence Narayanayyar could not walk fast, so he stood looking at the man intently. The man opposite also stared as intently and asked, 'Where are you coming from? Isn't it Krishnayyar with you?'

Instantly Krishnayyar shut his eyes firmly and clasped Narayanayyar even more tightly. Narayanayyar tapped the man in front of him on the shoulder. All flesh and blood, a sandal pottu on his forehead, a zari upper cloth and an ordinary veshti below, pearl studs in the ears, he stood, disappearing into the dark, only his white teeth flashing. He thought for a moment, concealed his surprise, and asked: 'We are coming back from a music concert. Haven't seen you around for days. Where had you been? When did you come?'

Subbayyar said, 'I just got back. It's been twenty days since I left. I went on business.'

Narayanaswamy replied, 'You are saying you just got back. Why are you walking past your house then? Where are you going at this hour?'

Krishnayyar wasn't aware of the conversation between the two. He stood dumbstruck, pasted on to Narayanaswamy Ayyar as if they were one body.

Subbayyar said, 'Nagaswamy and I went to see the carnival. On the way, I saw the businessman Ramaswamy Chetty. He urgently wanted two hundred tins of ghee from Salem and gave me the money. I asked Nagaswamy to inform people at home and immediately boarded the train. I don't know what's happened in my house and the houses nearby. In my house, only my mother-in-law called out. Didn't open the door. Even the neighbours, nobody is opening the door. I'm going in search of Nagaswamy.'

Narayanaswamy Ayyar, who listened to all this patiently, glad that what he thought was right, said, 'Let's go to Nagaswamy's house in the morning. Come.' Even after being patted comfortingly, Krishnayyar's fear didn't leave him completely, though he recovered somewhat.

It was at that time the purohit regained consciousness. When he saw the three approaching, he plucked up some courage. When he saw that it was Subbayyar with them, he didn't get up and just lay there. Subbayyar knew a bit of English, so he told Narayaswamy in English that the purohit got frightened after seeing him.

Knowing the secret, Narayanswamy Ayyar made Subbayyar stand at the back and said, 'What swamy, have you passed urine? Why don't you wash up in the tap outside the next house? Let's all go together.'

The purohit asked, 'Is it Narayanaswamy Ayyar? Wait, I'll come.' He went towards the tap, washed his hands and feet. Thinking that he would somehow reach home with the help of Narayanaswamy Ayyar, he walked a step ahead cautiously.

Making everyone sit in the pial of the fourth house, Narayanaswamy Ayyar said, 'Wait a while. I'm also going to the bathroom.' Saying thus, he went to Appa Sastry's house. Subbayyar noticed this. The purohit and Krishnayyar shut their eyes and leant against the pial. Appa Sastry had come a little while ago, heard the story, felt sad and sat on the pial. His wife and Kamakshi's mother urged him to come in.

Looking at Narayanaswamy Ayyar coming up the steps, Appa Sastry asked, 'What brings you here at this hour?'

'Sastry, I have some good news. Your son had gone out of town. The message that he gave Nagaswamy didn't reach us. Don't be scared. I'll go and bring him,' said Narayanaswamy Ayyar and left. Hearing this, the women peeped out in surprise.

Appa Sastry went behind Narayanaswamy Ayyar. Looking at them, Subbayyar asked, 'Appa, where were you? I knocked and knocked, nobody opened the door. Where's Amma? Where's Kamu? Maami gave a shout, but kept quiet and never opened the door.'

Embracing him, Appa Sastry said, 'Subbu! What a thing you did! Couldn't you have written a letter? How you will bear to look at Kamu, I don't know.' So saying, he turned towards home. Kuppa Sastry and Krishnayyar walked behind as if they had had a nightmare. Mother on one side, wife on the other, came running, embraced him, kissed him all over the face. Mother-in-law experienced boundless joy. On seeing Kamakshi, bald head and all, embracing her husband and kissing him, Krishayyar, who until then had drooped like someone who had succumbed to fever, laughed inside. Kuppa Sastry, who felt his hip to ensure that his dakshina was intact, sniffed a pinch of snuff, and blessed Kamu: 'May you have a long married life.'

In a while, as the news spread, the entire neighbourhood came in hordes, and felt happy looking at Subbayyar. In the meanwhile, Subbayyar's mother-in-law adorned Kamakshiammal with every ornament and put a kumkumam on her forehead.

The next morning Appa Sastry invited all friends and relatives and gave them a feast. Looking at Kamakshiammal, all the little children teased, 'You went to Tirupati and gave away your hair, is it?' Subbayyar often visited Gopal Iyer to console him.

Original title: *Subbayyar*
1921

The exact year of publication of this story is unknown. It, however, appeared in a collection which was published in 1921. We have gone by that date.

Of the Three, Which One? 6

V Visalakshiammal

'Amma, Amma, Vedu was peeling the banana stem and now she's cut her hand,' said a boy, running towards the kitchen.

'What is this, can't keep quiet even for a minute. Why did you allow her to pick up the kitchen-blade? Aren't you old enough to know that?' said the mother. Vedu herself came running in, crying loudly.

Kamalambal picked up the child. 'Show me, where did you hurt yourself? Such a fuss for such a small thing! Just a little scratch, that's all.' She picked up a bit of paper, wiped the blood off Vedu's left thumb and said, 'Don't cry, here is some sugar.' She then looked at her son and said, 'And you, Seema, you look after the baby carefully. I have some work to do.'

Kamalambal was about twenty-four. Seema and Vedu were her children; Seema was seven years old, and Vedu, not yet three. Her husband Sundaramayar was a clerk in the railways. He had got transferred to Kumbakonam four months ago; ever since, the family of four were living there by themselves. Kamalambal had never lived alone; either her mother-in-law or her aunt was always around. So Kamalambal found it very difficult to manage both the housework and the children all by herself.

That night Vedu groaned and moaned and didn't sleep at all. By the morning her finger had swollen up and reddened, and she kept crying in pain. Before leaving for office Sundaramayar said, 'Just grind and boil some turmeric and ripe chilli and smear it on the finger, it will be all right.' Concerned that Kamalambal might find it difficult to cope with the child, he returned home at two in the afternoon. Vedu had high fever. The entire palm had swollen. The child was crying non-stop in pain.

'Just a scratch. It didn't even bleed much. Why should it swell up like this? I'm scared. Nowadays they say that the poison enters even the blood. Shall we take her to a doctor? What do you think?' asked Kamalambal.

'Okay, there's a Dr Menon who has come newly to the next street. Studied abroad it seems. Capable man I believe. I'll go and bring him,' said Sundaramayar and left.

Dr Menon came. He was only twenty-eight. He was an FRCS from England. So he didn't believe too much in the power of medicine. He believed that chopping off troublesome organs was the answer. His opinion: the kitchen-blade may have been rusty; since they hadn't put any 'poison stopper' (antiseptic) immediately, the poison had spread to the entire hand. It would be better to chop off the hand at the wrist. Otherwise her life itself might be in danger. Saying that he would bring a few medicines in an hour, he left. Sundaramayar too left for the 'shop' to buy a few other medicines the doctor had prescribed.

Poor thing. Kamalambal didn't know what to do. If the child's life itself was in danger, it would be better to chop off the hand, she thought. She stood there dazed.

'Andi pandaram! I pray to you!' sang a mendicant on the street. Seema pulled his mother's hand to give the mendicant some alms. Tormented by the threat to her child, and hence not knowing what she was really doing, Kamalambal went to the front of the house and related the entire predicament to the mendicant. He gave her some vibhuti and medicinal leaves. Saying, 'Just smear the vibhuti on the forehead, crush the leaves and apply on the hand. Everything will disappear like magic. Don't worry, ammini, Lord of Palani will protect you,' he left, taking the coins Kamalambal gave him. She smeared both the vibhuti and the juice from the crushed leaves on the child and sat restlessly next to her. She hugged the child's hand to her cheek. She moaned, 'Ayyo, the hand is so nice and plump. I wanted to make a bracelet. Now they are saying they are going to chop it off! Ayyo, Goddess

Mangalambigai! I can't turn to anyone but you. I will make a gold bracelet for you. Please save my child!' Copious tears flowed from her eyes and wet the child's hand. In an hour, Sundaramayar and the doctor returned.

'What is this, 'ma! What are you doing! If your tears fall, won't it turn more 'septic'?' said the doctor. He gave some medicine for the night and left saying he would get all the things for the operation in the morning. The next day he brought along with him an anaesthetist and a helper.

'The child slept well. The fever has come down,' said Kamalambal eagerly. Not hearing a word, the doctor got everything ready for the operation. He felt the child's pulse. With a surprised look, he placed a thermometer. He unwound the bandage. The swelling had come down, and so had the fever; Vedu had recovered almost seventy-five per cent. 'What is this miracle! Yesterday it was difficult to tell if the child would be alive; I was sure I would have to cut off the hand; today everything is fine. I've never seen a case like this,' exclaimed Dr Menon, FRCS.

'Amma! Mangalambige! My goddess above! Cure her completely and I will perform the milk abhishegam,' said Kamalambal.

Seema, who had been shooed away and forbidden from entering the room, tiptoed inside when no one was looking. He wanted the dapper doctor, dressed in boots and hat, to know that he could read; so he picked up a Tamil magazine and read in a loud, booming voice:

'Tears – it is well known that diseases that people suffer from are caused by poisonous creatures not visible to the human eye. One of the things that can suppress these creatures is human tears. A drop is believed to kill millions of creatures. But these creatures have not yet been isolated from tears. Once that is done, it will become one of the most potent things to destroy the poisonous germs.'

'*That is it! Out of the mouths of babes and sucklings*, Mr Sundaram,' exclaimed the doctor. 'Yesterday, her tears that wet the child's hands must have killed the poisonous creatures, 'bacteria', and cured the hand. Otherwise I've never seen a case like this. An American doctor has written about tears as 'antiseptic', but I never believed it. Nature is really amazing. I am going to write about this in the magazine *Lancet*.' He left with his things and the men he had brought.

'Do you think it could have been those mendicant's medicinal leaves that did it? Perhaps these mendicants with medicinal leaves know something that the doctors don't. Why shouldn't that have cured it?' said Sundaramayar.

'Tears it seems! And medicinal leaves! That cured it! If the child's hand is fine, it is because I prayed to Goddess Mangalambigai and said that I would make a gold bracelet. It is all because of her grace. Go, fetch that goldsmith Chokkalingam in the evening,' replied Kamalambal, tears of joy flowing down.

Original title: *Moondril Ethu?*
1924

The Great Graveyard 7

Pudumaippittan

Once it turns evening, the city transforms into a crowded thoroughfare where etiquette and culture either means jostling yourself forward or getting jostled in return. And if it happens to be a junction of four-five big roads criss-crossed by tram tracks, much like the knots of nerves in the human body, the chaos is even worse. Completely wrung-out office-goers, fashionably dressed elite out to relish the gaiety of the night, and clumsily dressed, gaudy bats who can't afford motor cars – all of them coalesce into an indistinct whole; shoving and jostling each other, they go their separate ways. That day too it was much the same.

Ever since the one-way traffic rule was introduced, if you stand at the top of a high-rise building and look down, you can see civilisation swirling along. Like gushing waters bursting the banks viewed from the top of a dam.

I am also talking of such a place. The Mount Road round-tana. A row of women selling mangoes and bananas from their baskets. Behind them, the low-caste women of the city, sucking on the mango seeds thrown away by others, wiping their soiled hands on their saris. A kabuliwallah walking around, waving a stick, a Muslim beggar, a lame beggar, a leper. A young thing primping herself for the 'night job', sitting at the edge of the road and combing her hair unhurriedly.

And then there were those: 'What, Saar, long time since I saw you'... 'The bus has come'... 'Get in, get in.' Hurry, hurry, hurry, they seemed to be in a flurry.

It was at such a moment that he lay on the footpath at the edge of the road, dying leisurely.

It was a good place to die. Soothing shade. Against the setting sun, spent of its heat. A swirl of humanity. Must say it was a real festive moment.

He was dying, leisurely dying.

People were going to and fro. They didn't know. And many didn't want to know.

He was an old Muslim beggar. His beard had turned really grey. He was covered in dirty rags. Arms and legs emaciated by old age and lack of food. Callused feet.

By his side sat another beggar. He was trying to give him water from a tin cup; he didn't succeed and only managed to wet his lips. Placing his hands under his head, he tried to lift him. The old man, the one who was dying, tried to lift his head, clutching the tin drum placed on the road by a charitable trust. The light had died down in his eyes. His lips had turned blue. In a little while, his story would end. Even so, he didn't let go of the tin drum. There was a certain solace in the grasp, also a certain strength. But he didn't seem to be aware at all that someone was giving him water. Water was given, it had to be drunk; that was all he felt. He couldn't think beyond that; it wasn't necessary, and neither did he have the stamina.

At the time two people came to take the tram. Both waited. But the tram never came. One was a father, around thirty; the other a little girl of four or five. By the look of him, the father didn't seem to be one who struggled to make ends meet. The child looked ordinary. But it was evident that the mother was a meticulous person. The child was dressed neatly, though not flashily.

The two still waited for the tram. The child was clutching the father's index finger. The mangoes sold on the opposite side of the road looked fresh.

'Kunju, dear, you must stand here itself. Appa will go to that side and buy ripe mangoes for you, okay,' said the father.

'All right,' said the child.

'You should not step on to the road, okay. If you do, no mango for you.' But he felt a bit uneasy – perhaps he ought not to leave the child alone.

'I will stay here only, Appa,' she promised her father, urging him to go to the other side.

His love for mangoes prompted him to cut across the road, leaving the child alone.

The child was brave. Perhaps used to being left like this. The child's gaze which at first followed the father in fear later got absorbed in the goings-on around.

A red motor car caught her eye, she kept looking at it. A person in a hurry – thinking god knows what – jostled the child. The child tottered. Forgoing her desire to see the red car, the child stood by the wall at the edge of the footpath so as not to be knocked aside. Leaning against the wall, hand in pocket, she looked around in all directions.

Her eyes fell on the man who was dying and the man who was helping him to die. 'What kind of spectacle is that,' she wondered, and very hesitantly made her way towards them.

If she said, 'I won't drink milk,' her mother would cajole her, tumbler in hand, and somehow make her drink it. If Appa said, 'No,' the mother would keep quiet. She knew that elders had the right to say, 'No.' The child held the belief that even though she was an amma, she was afraid of Appa. She found it funny – would anyone feed a grown man from a tumbler?

To watch the fun the child went towards the beggars. She stood near the old man's head.

The younger man once again tried to wet the old man's throat. He wasn't very adept. Either the water fell out in a gush, drenching his neck or not a drop came out.

Clutching the tin drum, the old man was dying.

Pouting her lips as if to drink water, she said, 'Slowly, slowly.'

The man giving water looked up. 'Child, you shouldn't stand here. Go that side.'

'Why?' asked the child.

'He's dying,' said the beggar.

'What is that?'

'He's dying, 'ma, dying.' He demonstrated, slumping his head.

The child found it amusing. 'Do that once again,' she said.

Afraid that a crowd would gather, the beggar closed his mouth and gestured with his hands.

A few coins had been thrown near the old man, as if for his last rites.

The child spotted the coins. 'Why don't you buy him some fried gram,' she said, pointing to the old man, confident that whatever she liked would be liked by others too.

Fearing that someone might accuse him of cheating a child, he looked on all four sides and asked the child, 'Do you have any money?'

'Here, take this new coin.' The child held it out to him.

He quickly took what the child gave him. It was a newly minted coin. Like millionaires hoping to end all starvation and poverty by building just one free food distribution centre, like dissolving a tiny bit of asafoetida to make the vast sea aromatic, the child too did her bit of charity.

Eyes dim and lifeless, the old man was dying, clutching the tin drum. People kept passing by, up and down.

A one-anna coin slipped from the hand of a man who was hurrying by. Unaware, he walked on and disappeared into the crowd. He was in such a hurry. The beggar who was sitting pounced on it, looked around and made sure no one noticed him.

'Go away, child,' he tried telling her again.

The child said, 'No,' standing firmly, feet spread out, making a face.

'Bawa, I'll get some milk for you.' The younger beggar rose and walked towards the hotel on the opposite side.

The old man didn't hear a word. Clutching the tin drum, he was slowly dying.

The child could now look at him properly. She went near him to watch the fun. That young bogeyman was no longer there to shoo her away, no? The old man wasn't aware of the child standing near him. He was clutching the battered drum. He himself was a battered creature, wasn't he?

The child found his face, his beard and his gaping mouth fascinating. A fly came and sat on his swollen blue lips. Yet another one came and sat too. When he pursed his lips and tried to shoo them away, the child found it funny. For some odd reason, she called out softly, 'Bawa,' like the other beggar had done. She was scared deep inside if the 'old-bogeyman' would suddenly get up and sit.

The old man's eyes opened out widely. A fly came and sat on his pupil...

'What is this, di? Why are you standing there? Where all I searched for you!' said a stern voice. It was the justified anger of a man who had haggled long and hard for two mangoes and got the seller to agree to his price.

'No, 'pa, that Bogeyman-Bawa, no… I just was watching him,' said the child running towards the father.

Only a few passersby looked up.

The father carried the child. With some difficulty she held the mango and smelt it. 'It smells very nice!' she said, and rubbed it to her nose.

Original title: *Mahamasanam*
1941

8

TRANSFORMATION

MAUNI

He had sent them the telegram last evening itself. But he didn't inform anyone in the neighbourhood. No one knew. They could come only by the nine o'clock morning train – what difference would anyone's arrival make now.

Yesterday, perhaps in anticipation, he had been in a good enough frame of mind too. He had slept well in the night and woken up only after sunrise. He realised that he was lying very close to her. He felt a small surge of happiness. He saw her lying next to him. Taken aback, he got up with fear and went to the front door. He stood for a while by the pial, looked up and down, went in, but without even crossing the inner passage, came out again. Blocking the entrance, he stood on the steps gazing into the street.

Somehow going past him, she stood in front of him. She appeared to be flitting here and there. His pupils followed her languorously, now and then tucking into the corner of the eyes and disappearing. As if pulling at her, they would gradually return to the centre. His ideas and thoughts soared higher and higher, then melted and vanished.

Immense alertness and serenity brimmed over uncontrollably, swaying this way and that, creating a feeling of restlessness within him. As if at peace with the situation, he stood there calmly, gazing into the street.

A crow flew in, sat on the front slope of the thatched roof of the house opposite. Hopping around, it sat on the parapet wall of the terrace. Cawing loudly, it seemed to foretell the arrival of the expected visitors. 'Yes, they are coming only by the nine o'clock train –' It flew a bit and sat on the middle of a frond of the coconut tree. Then it immediately flew away and disappeared.

Again, only the empty street in front of him…

A man from the northern parts drove along a cart of casuarina wood. The heavy cart dragged by, the rolling wheels, reluctant to spin around the axle, groaning annoyingly. Two hornless bullocks pulled the cart. Indifferent, weary, they tossed their heads and inched along. What appeared before his eyes was the noiseless movement of the bullocks – necks without bells, hoofs without jingles – pulling at the load, swaying their heads. The weighty logs were stacked at the back. He saw the cartman sitting in the front, legs hanging on either side, whip in hand, a small piece of cloth tied round his hips, chivvying the animals along with kicks, calling out, 'hai-hai'.

'Why does he have to appear before me? The bullocks, their nods which seem to call out to me, the heavy logs, the revolving wheels – are they not enough? Are they not enough to see sense? But who will take on my burden? He? Or that one? Who then?

'She is lying inside. Waiting to be one among the shadows of the immense universe…

'The nodding bullocks which seem to beckon. The wailing sounds and rotations of the greaseless, annoying wheels, jolting along with the wheels sinking into the earth. O cart, from where did you come? How far, and how many people have you helped perceive your philosophy as you inched along? Just get out of my sight! You, who announces events and disturbs thoughts, your disappearance can only bring happiness.'

A goat sauntering, hidden by the passing cart, could be seen again down the street. He stood there looking at it.

He felt no hunger.

A mud pot hung from either end of a bamboo pole which grazed and wobbled lightly across leathery, withered shoulders. Now appearing, then disappearing, the man walked between the pots, calling out his wares. The pot in line of his vision seemed to be empty. Just at a little distance from where it hung, he balanced the pole on his shoulder. The pots bobbed up and down, gently dipping and nearly grazing the ground. Although it was an empty pot, he watched over it carefully because should it break under pressure of touching the ground, the other one would topple over too and shatter. He walked quickly as if wishing to catch up with the empty pot. The other pot, which followed him without ever touching his feet, was valuable and very precious to him. Yet, it wasn't within his vision. Wasn't it comforting that the pot which he could see was empty!

He still felt no hunger. The man selling sweet toddy too was gone, appearing and disappearing between his pots. 'Why is she still standing there, refusing to disappear? Can't she disappear? She seems to be fading away ever so slightly, but never completely going away. She doesn't seem to disappear like she appears. She seems to just show herself in another form. The wood-cart, the goat, the man selling toddy, one after another. No one speaks. Nothing makes a sound. Yet emotions seem to surface, breaking through – is this all a dream?'

A man walked along the street, past his house, flaunting his leather belt, his art-silk shirt tucked into a freshly laundered veshti. He folded the veshti up to his knees, holding the ends in both hands, displaying his two and a quarter rupee boots, which he wore with socks. He walked briskly, looking this way and that ever so often. Over his shoulder he had carelessly tossed a green shawl, which looked as if it would slip off any moment.

He had come from Singapore. And only just then! 'His shine will surely vanish soon enough. Let him be. Chee, chee, it's so funny!'

'In front of the eyes tiny glass-like flies swirl upwards. There, there! Is it the top of the coconut tree? Or is it the mango? Down below. Chee, chee! Only the terraced house stands there. Tree tops are always like that! Those little black clouds, are they not standing above the trees? Or have they left them, painting the in-between spaces blue? They all seem to join in a conspiracy. They seem to drag me in too. Now appearing, then disappearing – transforming, perhaps like an illusion.

'Yes, she is right in front of me, standing. But she seems to be moving. Will she disappear into the wings, away from my vision? And be transformed? No, she never moves from side to side. Only up and down.'

Opposite him, that house. And its eaves sloping down. The parapet wall of the terrace. Below the wall, window holes. Above, the tops of trees, and still above, tiny clouds scattered in the blue skies.

In front, only the street.

'The freight cart, the pot of sweet toddy. At the time of loss, only that house opposite stands. She also disappears – she whom I saw in front of me.

Wait! Wait! Don't disappear. Chee, chee, no, she transforms herself. Is it in my mind – that she changes? The transformation… She moves to one side, as if about to disappear.'

His eyes looked steady. His pupils, which followed her, slipped into the corners of his eyes. He stood blocking the doorway, waiting expectantly – for how long? Pulled back again, his pupils appeared.

There she lay inside. In front, the street…

His mother came. So did his father. They also came. They all came by the nine o'clock train all right, but were different selves, each engrossed in his own thoughts, heartbroken and silent. He stood blocking the doorway, his dark pupils countering their gaze.

His mother reached out for him, hugged him and cried out, 'My dear son, that this should happen to you also!' She wept, embracing him.

The pupils which had slid into the corners hurried back to the centre. With a forlorn face, he gave a foolish laugh, the one which usually precedes tears. 'How… did she change… did she disappear?' Perhaps thinking of this, he laughed aloud. His mother too stopped crying. She looked at his face and stood frozen.

His in-laws disappeared into the house next door. They found that they could neither face him nor bear the loss, so they retreated indoors in grief. He hugged his mother and took her in. He pointed to her lying down. Trying to nudge her awake with his foot, he laughed. Only for a moment. His mother fell upon her and wailed.

They, who had hidden themselves away, came and sat either inside or on the pial. Holding the upper cloth in the hand, they covered their faces and looked on sadly.

He wept. He talked and talked and wept non-stop, saying all sorts of things. But he didn't say a word about how he had perhaps seen her and that she had disappeared, and had perhaps transformed.

Thc following year on the last Friday of the month of Thai his mother performed the sumangali prarthanai. Wearing a wet sari, she observed the rituals conscientiously till noon. She did everything herself, even if she was stricken in years.

After placing a new sari on the plank by the first banana leaf, all the women sat down in their places. It was then that his mother started sobbing. She hurriedly went in and disappeared. She wept copiously, hugging the calf born the previous year. Her wet sari too had dried on her body. The calf too twisted its neck, placed its face on her back and stood calmly.

When the married women sat down to eat, she came back in to enquire if they had all been served…

He was in the city, at work in his office. He was writing something in the books that lay in front of him. When he looked up, he saw a tree at a distance through the window. A tiny cloud which sat on top of it floated up and disappeared. Heaving a deep sigh, he bent his head and began to write. 'Am I rewriting my destiny? No, I'm only writing my destiny.'

In front, lay the street. But he didn't look at it then.

Original title: *Marudhal*
1937

Desperation 9

Ku Pa Rajagopalan

'Why don't you sit, di? You can go later. What's the hurry?' Savitri, who was lying down, asked her, turning over.

'No, it's time for him to come home. If I go and heat up the water for coffee, it will be just right,' said Kamala, getting up.

'Come on, how long it will take to make coffee? You can do it even later. Just sit. Time is just not passing for me.'

Just then Raghavan returned, calling out, 'Kamala.'

'I told you, no. See, he's come back,' said Kamala and ran towards her room.

Savitri lifted her head and looked up; Raghavan entered the room, smiling at his wife. Kamala went in after him, uttering, 'Is it time already?'

The room was a little away, but not that far that you couldn't hear people conversing. Sometimes young couples don't remember where they are, do they?

'Go, what is this. What are you playing at? Someone will come.' Savitri heard Kamala's playful words faintly. The joyous air that filled the room wafted across to Savitri, choking her. Sorrow wracked her mind and body; she turned on her back, letting out a deep sigh.

Savitri's husband was in the 'military service', somewhere in the north. For the sake of custom, he had stayed behind for three days after the shanthi muhurtam and then left hurriedly. It had now been two years. Letters arrived. But not the man.

People would remark, wouldn't they, if shanti muhurtam hadn't been observed? So the two families performed the function. After that it didn't really matter how long the boy stayed away from the girl. No one would open their mouth.

Savitri likened that shanti muhurtam to Yama, the god of death. She could control her mind somewhat, like she used to earlier. But not her body. It constantly needled her mind. It couldn't forget the blissful touch it had experienced those three days. It screamed out.

Savitri was blessed with a healthy body. Robust youthfulness glowed all over her. She couldn't bear its incessant desire.

What cheek of this Kamala! Just because her husband is around, should she keep jumping like this? What is there to come and show off to me? I'm lying here all withered up. What is there to come and romp around? No, she's doing it purposely. I think she's doing all this just to torment me. Forever singing her husband's praise! Did she bring him to life? Why won't she stand on her head – looking at me languishing all alone like this while she is so happy is what perhaps makes her so conceited! I'm broken. But did she even think of that? How will she – only if she undergoes this, she will know.

Savitri slept, muttering to herself.

'Why, di, couldn't you have got up and fetched water from the tap outside? Here is your coffee,' said her mother.

'Ok, ok, it will be done. That's why you gave birth to me. I will do it. Go.'

'Here is your coffee. I'm going to that house. Don't know if I'll be able to come back in the night…'

'What are you going to do coming here? Stay in your brother's house itself and come.'

'Lock the door carefully in the night.'

'Ok, ok, go!'

Her mother adjusted her sari, smeared some vibhuti and left for the street. Savitri's coffee turned cold. But not her heart.

Kamala came after her husband left for office. 'O, Ammami has not drunk coffee, is it?'

Savitri looked at her enviously. 'It's cold, I didn't drink it.'

'Shall I give you some? I've kept some in the flask for him for the evening. I will give it. I can always make some more.'

'No need. I don't feel like it. My chest is burning.'

'I asked him if we can go for a film today. Tomorrow, he said. You'll also come, Ammami?'

'Wonderful. You two want to have fun, and I'll be there in the middle…'

'Go, Ammami!' said Kamala, really pleased. To Savitri her joy seemed like poison.

'What Ammami! You're not feeling well?'

'What is wrong with me? Nothing.'

'He's brought a novel called 'The Wilted Bud'. Shall we read it?' Kamala got up and sat down with the book.

There was a picture on the cover. Kamala showed it to Savitri, coyly smiling.

A fellow was sitting on a chair, deep in thought. The book in his hand had fallen down. Unknown to him, his wife was standing behind him with a smile.

'What is the meaning of this, Ammami?' asked Kamala.

'The husband is deep in thought. Looks as if the stupid wife standing there smiling is not aware of his mood.'

Kamala's smile vanished. 'Do you think it's like that?'

'What else?' asked Savitri cruelly, although she smiled.

'No, Ammami. It can't be.'

'Then what can it be?'

'See, see… the husband is reading it, thinking of her. The book falls down because he's dozed off. She didn't come for a long time, and then, at last…'

'O, that's always there.'

'Shall we read?'

'Read.'

Kamala read for a while. But how much did Savitri hear?

'Ayyo, it is so late. I kept on reading.' It was five in the evening; Kamala got up and went to her house.

Savitri didn't get up. The sweeper woman came.

'I will sweep it myself. Go.'

The flower woman came.

'I don't want any flowers today.'

It turned dark. It was now hours since it had turned dark. She couldn't bear to hear the fun that Raghavan and Kamala were having.

Weren't they aware that there were others too in the house? She got up angrily, switched on the light and lay back again.

'I've laid out the leaf for dinner. Come to eat,' said Kamala.

'So quickly… after eating so early, what…'

'I'm sleepy.'

'Sleepy?' Raghavan said smilingly. Savitri heard it all.

As Kamala threw away the leaf outside and locked the iron door and the verandah door, she saw Savitri lying down drowsily in the opposite room. She asked, 'Ammami, have you eaten?'

'Finished.'

Kamala went in and locked the door.

The house looked like a marriage hall. Tenants on either side. Doors on either side of the hall and the verandah.

It was only about eight in the night. Even the town's noise hadn't died down. But the noise in Kamala's room had died down. Savitri never even got up.

'Raghavan! Is he there?'

'He's there!' Savitri opened the verandah door and turned around.

A young chap stood hesitantly.

'Just tap lightly on their door. They'll open,' she said with somewhat cruel happiness and went inside her room and sat down. She waited expectantly for the proceedings.

The young chap tapped the door. 'Raghavan.'

After a while a murmur was heard, 'Who is it?'

'Me!'

'Me who?' hissed Raghavan, opening the door to peep out.

'Me, Seenu – Madurai.'

'O… come in,' said Raghavan, a bit perplexed. Leaving the door open, he escorted him through the verandah and took him outside.

A sight flashed for a second before Seenu's eyes. The light was on. Kamala, who was lying dishevelled facing the door, jumped up with a start and ran towards the wall when Raghavan's frame moved away from the doorway.

Savitri saw it even more clearly. A bunch of flowers were hanging from Kamala's hair. The smell of jasmine and agarbathis wafted strongly across from the room.

She couldn't bear to see any more of the room which lay exposed, its privacy invaded. The glow from the light, lone and naked, blinded her. Noiselessly she closed the door.

Suddenly she was consumed with sadness and pity.

'What a thing I did! God knows what sin I committed or who I separated, I'm all alone now, suffering. Ayyo…'

The two hearts which had engulfed each other with great ardour were thrown far away in pieces in just a moment. Kamala, almost in tears, adjusted her clothes angrily, switched off the light and lay down on the bed.

Raghavan came back, after sending off Seenu.

He climbed gently on the bed and touched Kamala. Kamala snatched his hand and flung it away.

'What Kamala?'

'Why didn't you open the other door as well?'

'O, I forgot, Kamala!'

'Why will you remember?'

'Why are you blowing up such a small thing all out of proportion?'

'Small thing-aa? All my dignity gone.'

Raghavan began to get angry.

'How much of it gone?' he hissed.

'Just shut your mouth. People around can hear you,' she also hissed back.

Savitri heard this too. Lying prone, she wept, heaving uncontrollably. 'What is to be done with this cruel creature?' she cursed herself.

She could hear Kamala blowing her nose.

'Happy, aren't you, you witch!' Savitri asked herself loudly.

Original title: *Aatraamai*
1943

The Surge 10

Na Pichamurthy

On this side of the river bank, the steps couldn't be seen. On the other side, the bent tips of the tender reeds dipped again and again in the waters of the river. Palm shells, jackfruit leaves and dried garlands floated on the waves swirling against the banks. It was the festival of the eighteenth day in the month of Aadi on the banks of the gushing Kaveri.

There's no doubt the Tamils have poetry in their hearts. Why else would they liken the River Kaveri to a pregnant woman in bloom? Don't the waters of the Kaveri gush through mounds and troughs, riverbeds and farmlands, turning the earth into gold and bringing so much joy to one and all? Don't the cadences of the waters remind you of the graceful movements of a pregnant girl?

If you stand on the terrace of the house at the end of the street and look northwards, this joyful spectacle will greet your eyes. If you look east, the road hitting the banks stretches out like the tongue of a snake, disappearing into the south. Like the surging waters of the river, this street too is always overflowing. And on a festival day, one doesn't have to ask about the teeming crowds.

It was the eighteenth day of Aadi. The street was packed. People selling black beads, jostling girls pushing flowers into your face, enticing you to buy, people rushing back and forth to buy vegetables.

Everyone speaks highly of solitude. But not everyone can relish it. Not even a few can live alone. To be frank, solitude is dangerous for an ordinary man – for the body and mind. How would it be if a horse rushes away with the cart, with neither the bridle nor the cartman? Only if he is surrounded by people will an ordinary man behave right and proper. Have you noticed how your mind gets exhausted when you are alone? In a moment, it will leap-frog and go off into the universe. In the next moment, it will get buried firmly like an anchor in the oceans of your mind. Sometimes it will tread on a pure and selfless path, at other times it will pounce like a beast on all fours, the tail touching the head. It will rush unfettered, like a bull. The life's force will never remain still – forever troubling you, slithering around like mercury. One who can handle solitude is a yogi, a sage.

He was neither a yogi nor a sage. A very ordinary man. Like the Vedantists say, he was an unevolved creature. Full of flaws and shortcomings that befall the male.

He had a holiday for the festival. No one was at home. It had been two or three months since his wife had left for her mother's place. He drank coffee at the hotel and came and sat on the pial. Time moved like a rock snake. He was irritated by the noisy dragging of the toy-chariots by young boys. He closed the front door and went upstairs and ambled around.

On the one side, he saw the Kaveri gushing. Along with it, his heart too. In the end it had to join the sea. Why so? Is it destined that one should mingle with the other? Or is it the secret of pleasure? Perhaps. Kaveri is going to marry the sea. That is why she gracefully takes along with her the frothy flowers, the tender reeds, the colourful blooms of the trees. But when will she meld with the sea? he mused.

On the other side, a rush of people. Without being aware that it would join the sea, the river flowed on. But not so the people, who knowingly rushed to pay their respects to Goddess Kaveri. But within him arose very different thoughts about this surging crowd.

One can get crushed in a crowd, but can one really enjoy a crowd? One cannot view anything with delight. In an ocean-like crowd individual faces lose all their charm. Even the most beautiful woman loses all her magic in a crowd, dimming away like embers in ash. Yes, a crowd is something where solitude dies and expansiveness begins. Had his wife been here, she too would have been a part of this herd.

The teeming waters and crowds affected him; yearning and loneliness shook his mind. Exhausted, drained, he spread out the towel and lay down. Across the deep blue sky a cloud sailed across, like a crane that had lost its way. 'Ada, the same plight for you too?' He turned to one side. His eyes faced the wall. Since the wall was unevenly whitewashed, several patches appeared like waves, and even strange animals and trees.

For a while, his mind thus was occupied. Suddenly a squirrel appeared from nowhere and huddled near the wall. Its eyes shone with desire and cunning. At the same time, another squirrel was screeching from the roof, voice brimming with desperation. He got up and looked at the roof. A squirrel, tail held high, swivelled around and squealed. Suddenly it stopped its cries and jumped down near the wall, in a flash. It ran behind the huddled squirrel. Then, they chased each other, and finally one grabbed the other with the front paws. The game of lust. The roguish eyes closed with ecstasy. Only for a moment! By then, another squirrel peeped out slowly from the hole at the bottom of the wall. No sooner had it witnessed this drama of love, than it pounced on the male squirrel in a trice. The two of them wrestled. The female stood in a corner, front paw held high, wondering who the winner would be. Then the new arrival ran away. A few drops of blood from the bruises of the male one hit the ground. But it was unruffled. It inched towards the female lustily. His thoughts drifted off somewhere, pleasurably.

'Amma!... Amma!' The tapping on the front door shook him.

Leaning over the banister, he asked, 'Who is it?'

'It's me,' said a honey-toned youthful voice.

'Me means who?'

Stepping back from the doorway, a girl stood looking upstairs. A bit baffled, he came down and opened the door. A young girl. Brown. Body taut and shining like an Arabian horse. Though she possessed a queenly beauty and majesty, her clothes betrayed her poverty.

He looked intently at her. It was a face he had seen before. But didn't know where.

'Who are you?'

'Don't you know me... I brought pumpkin flowers here in the month of Margazhi last year? Where is Amma?'

He remembered. She had been a young girl then. Now a nubile beauty. She had completely changed. He looked at her once again. Yes, it was the same girl. Her lush youthfulness sliced the roots of his heart.

'Isn't Amma there?'

One had to reply, however confused one was.

'No. She's gone to her town.'

'Why?'

'She's carrying… Okay, why have you come?'

'Just like that.'

'Who'll come just like that?'

'No, it's the festival. I thought I'd get some rice from Amma. But Amma is not there…'

'So what if she's not here.'

She was touched when she heard those words. She lifted her head and looked at him. He too looked at her. For a fraction of a moment a tacit silence. Then he went in and came back with a measure of rice and a four-anna coin. She collected it in the ends of her sari and stood looking at the floor silently for a moment. He looked blankly at the wall of the hall. A big spider stood still. A little distance away, a smaller spider stood staring at it.

'Shall I take leave and come then?' she asked.

He didn't know whether he hadn't heard properly or if he replied thus since he couldn't help himself. 'When?'

'Late in the evening.' She left the house and became one with the crowd.

The moment she left, he was deeply bewildered.

In the woods of desire, he saw a tiger prowling in lust. In the slush, a fish revelling. 'Thoo!' he cursed, resolving to push aside this episode. He sat down on the pial.

Women, freshly bathed, arrived in hordes. Wet clothes sticking to their body slopped noisily when they walked. Their hennaed hands and feet shone brightly. Several had turmeric smeared on their forehead and sandalwood paste on their neck. They walked on, laughing fearlessly and chattering like mynahs.

His mind keenly captured the snapshots of such images. In the hope that no thoughts of her would enter. But those images didn't interest him. Like the breeze swallowed by a grove, they too died away. Like a bee shunning a resplendent garden in bloom and hovering around a single rose meant for the market, his heart too steadfastly thought of her. However much his intellect demurred, there was a certain kind of pleasure in thinking of her.

Till midday this excitement didn't spend itself. More than sorrow, it was these kinds of sweet torments that were unbearable. Need you ask if the intellect too intervened in such matters and made things worse? Thank goodness he got some respite in the afternoon. Courtesy card games. He plunged into the game. Even so, he played badly. When he forgot to ask for the trump card on more than five or six crucial occasions, his friends were surprised.

It was evening. Like a gorgeous woman lifting herself from the tank after a bath, a figure appeared in his heart. His mind drifted away from the card game. Would she come – that thought gnawed him.

He left the game and went to the river. It was dark. The bank was strewn with offerings of rice and leaves. In the dark, the waters sliced through like the flash of a knife. Fireflies buzzed around trees on either bank. The star-studded sky glittered like the silken drapes of a Muslim queen.

Yes. Even the Kaveri flowed on in the night in search of love. Would she merge into the sea or would she get exhausted on the way…

When a bunch of such thoughts gave him pleasure, he deemed that there was nothing wrong in succumbing to nature's temptations. He then left for the hotel, ate his food and came back home. He latched the front door, spread out his mattress in the corner of the front yard and lay down. Pleasurable thoughts filled his mind.

A couple of minutes passed by. A sharp tap was heard from the front.

Excited that 'she' had come, he opened the door. But there was no one. Perhaps it was his own desire that had echoed as a sound and fooled him. He latched the door again. Again a clear noise could be heard. Even as he reached the passage, he understood – it was not properly latched. The noise was due to the latch falling on the wrong side. Even so, he couldn't help opening the door and looking.

He came back to the bed, his mind restless.

A single desire had created so much madness! Like a ravaging flood how it had dragged me into slush and thorns. Am I a beast? What should I do now? She might come in half an hour… if I were to meet her alone, who knows what would happen? Thinking so, he locked the house and went out.

As he took a step, a girl's voice called out, 'Ayya!' He was shaken. Even if he wanted to tread the straight path, it looked as if fate wouldn't allow him. Come what may. Determined to enjoy the pleasure here and now, he looked in the direction of the voice. That voice was from the third house. It wasn't calling out to him. 'Chee! Is my mind that scared?' he muttered and walked towards the railway station. On the way, when the shadows of the trees moved, he had visions of her suddenly appearing behind him every ten steps or so. Even if he knew it was only an illusion, he couldn't help turning back and looking.

He came thus to the Ayyanar temple. There the divine vehicles of Lord Ayyanar – stone elephant and mud horse – were ever ready to make their nightly rounds around the town. Usually, he took the stretch between the temple and the divine vehicles. That day he went around them because the elongated shadows of the statues had somewhat darkened the street. He wanted to walk in the dark and avoid known faces. As a consequence, his agony lessened a little. As he strode on, a honeyed tone called out, 'Saami!'

It was her voice. He was stunned. He felt a frisson. Like the wind rustling in the casuarina grove on a moonlit night in the month of Margazhi. He felt the familiar thrill. He suddenly decided against going to the station and turned back home.

As he reached the front of his house, he didn't know what to do. More than the agony of vanquishing a desire pouncing on all fours, wasn't it sweeter not to restrain it at all, but enjoy it? His mind was engaged in a philosophical battle. Without opening the door, he stood looking out, engrossed in thought.

By then she had come. But not the confident Arabian horse of the morning. Now she huddled, wanting to dissolve like a shadow in the dark. The way she cowered pierced his heart. All the old desires disappeared in a flash.

In the next moment, he went in, brought a rupee and stuffed it into her hand. She was shell-shocked. He didn't look back, locked the door and went upstairs…

She turned back silently. Behind her, her elongated shadow swayed. Till she disappeared out of sight, he kept looking at her and her shadow from upstairs. Then he started pacing up and down…

But the River Kaveri, without a care, lush with froth-blossoms, surged towards the sea in search of love.

Original title: *Pathinettaam Perukku*
1936

VILLAGE ROAD 11

CI SU CHELLAPPA

The tree-laden road widened and wound its way through the gorge between two small mounds. The branches of the monstrous tamarind and banyan trees cupped the road, nest-like, not allowing a clear view of the sky. As if the road was a dug-out tunnel. Like strands hanging from above, the aerial roots of the banyan trees swayed in the gentle breeze.

Pushing aside the waves of clouds bumping into each other, the beams of the moon slipped through the leafy gaps and scattered like slivers of silver all over the path. Since the traffic had died down for a long time, only one or two shadows could be seen moving, of people returning at this unearthly hour. Besides the faint echoes of the songs of workers in the betel garden and the sudden shrieks of the monkeys in the branches, no other sound could be heard.

In the dark abyss of the road, a pair of bullocks rhythmically walked in the middle, their hoofs clip-clopping on the tarred surface. Every now and then, as they grazed the gravel, tiny sparks flew. The wheels of the cart slowly wound their way as they returned to the village, slightly afar.

'Veerasami, isn't it time yet? It's already ten o'clock. No sound of the cart yet, da?' asked a voice authoritatively from inside the cart.

Veerasami replied humbly. 'It's almost time, master. Only a couple of hours after dusk will the weekly fair wind up. After that only they have to get the cart ready and travel six miles, no?'

'Perhaps he didn't go to the weekly fair?'

'What are you saying, master? I myself saw the cart go.' Veerasami stopped himself suddenly. 'I think I can hear the sound of the cart.'

'Yes, it's the sound of the wheel. But it's very faint…'

'Yes. But will the Gounder's cart come like this? As soon as they enter this road, they will start bucking up. After that, for the rest of the three miles, only breakneck speed.'

'Okay, drive carefully. The sound of the cart is getting stronger. Don't be duped. Then you don't have the right to twirl your moustache and call yourself a Naicken proudly.'

Chuckling loudly, Veerasami nudged his foot between the legs of the bulls and urged them to run faster. He glided his hands over the reins and slung them over his shoulder. Taking out a bit of betel nut from his small cloth bag, he popped it into his mouth. He then took the betel leaves and lime which were tucked into the sides of the cart. He was also watchful of the carts behind them.

'Did you hear them say anything about us buying new bulls?' asked the master.

'Yes, I did. That day the Gounder's cartman…'

'That Mookan? Just because they've got an Edakadan bull, he's talking, is it? That he will give Iyer's cart a licking.'

'Yes…' Before Veerasami could add further, they could hear carts rushing amid the shouts of the cartmen a little behind them.

'Dei, somebody is trying to overtake. Be alert,' said the mirasdar Iyer.

'It's our Veerannan's cart. He brought corn to the weekly fair. Let him go. Forgot to tell you this… That fellow Mookan said, "This Iyer has also gone to the Veerapandi cattle fair and got a pair of bullocks, just to pit them against our Edakadan bulls. If you have a bull and a cart, there will be challenges, no" – it seems he was saying this to Velu.'

Iyer laughed. 'Let's see today. More than Gounder it's him who's more agitated.'

'Yes. Before they had all sorts of able breeds, no – koodu kombu savalai, neerkalu karambai, virikombu?'

'Yes, da, with our tiny pair, how we licked them one day…'

'From then he's fuming. Somehow we must beat Iyer's cart...'

A cart overtook them. After that, one or two more.

'Let them go,' continued Veerasami, chewing on his betel leaves. 'He wants to wipe out the talk that is doing the rounds – that in these parts there is no cart that can beat Iyer's cart. He's itching to put an end to all this.'

'Even Gounder feels the same way, I think,' said Iyer.

'Yes, what you say is right, master. Gounder feels the same. This year he's made a lot of money selling cotton. So it seems they've given two big notes to get these. But do they look as if they are worth two notes?'

'So what? Even we bought that bull that runs on the left hand side for a three-quarter big note because it took our fancy... Dei, the sound of the cart is echoing loudly. Be careful!'

Even as he engaged in this conversation, Veerasami never let his attention wane. He kept track of all the carts that passed them by. Since he was familiar with the shadows of every bull and cart, he was confident that his eyes wouldn't let him down.

He allowed several other carts from the fair to pass him by. 'Gounder will come only in the end, till he touches this road. He'll allow every vehicle to pass him by and make sure there is nothing behind him. Then only he'll pick up tremendous speed in these two-three miles.'

The bulls themselves prick their ears once they hear the sounds of carts rushing behind them. Without being spurred by the cartmen they themselves pick up speed. When carts arrive at their side, they leap even faster. Just as man believes that nothing should surpass him, animals too feel natural to behave in the same fashion.

'Master, look at the left bull! If it hears some movement, then this is how it will get agitated. It will try to rush and leap. It's a bit of a ruffian, this donkey.' He smeared the lime paste in the corner of the hood of the cart.

'Then slip one rein through the nose-bridle of the left one. The ropes on the horn alone are not enough. It's night time – it will drag the cart astray during the race.'

Veerasami stopped the cart and slipped the reins through the nose-bridle to have better control. He adjusted the ropes on the horn. He tested out the reins once and let the bulls run. Now the left and the right bull were in tandem.

At that time, a few more vehicles passed them by.

'There are a lot of vehicles coming from behind, da. Spur them on,' said the mirasdar.

Thinking that Gounder's cart too could be one of the carts, Veerasami readied the bulls for a race. The whole road resounded with the shouts of 'Hai, hooi, don't stop, buck up!' The wheels churned noisily on the road. Racing against one another, the carts rushed from behind. Looking at the bulls straining at the leash, Veerasami loosened his reins to allow them to go fast.

'How is the Pillai breed doing?' asked Iyer, looking at the way the newly bought bulls ran.

'It's not like the mixed-colour Mylai breed. At the start itself it goes into a quick trot. But it takes a while to gallop. But it's not as alert as the Mylai. If you give it two lashes, it becomes okay. It will adjust to the yoke perfectly without any sluggishness. You can't say the same thing about the right bull. It will never allow you to beat it. Just try it once, then holding the reins, your palms will get bruised, as if sliced by a saw.'

The cartman who went alongside informed him enthusiastically, 'Anney, Gounder's cart is coming at the end. Don't let it pass.' He tapped his cart and moved on.

Veerasami elbowed the bulls on their sides a couple of times and goaded them on.

'Okay, let's have this idle chat later. Now concentrate on the job on hand.'

Veerasami pulled out with a swish the whip tucked in the hood. He upturned the whip, ran the cane handle across the running wheel a couple of times, making a clackety noise. He clasped the split ends, ran his fingers across the whip firmly, straightened the knots and tested the sharpness of the whip. Getting ready for the big fight, he tigh ly wound his head-cloth. Rapping the flanks and the backs of the bulls, he pulled the bridle with a sudden jerk, teasing them. He then whipped their legs sharply and the noise echoed. All heated up, the bulls sprang forward. Veerasami contained them. Pulling them back from going astray, he steered them on to the main road. The bulls flew, their feet barely touching the road.

Waiting for the Gounder's cart, Veerasami allowed all the other carts to pass by.

'Karupannan's open cart is trying to overtake on the right,' said the mirasdar.

The open cart leaped sharply ahead like a cicada. That didn't worry them too much today since they had a big moment ahead.

'Veerasami!' shouted the mirasdar urgently.

'From where is it coming?' asked Veerasami, all revved up.

'He's coming from the left. Can't you hear the bells! Pushing aside all other carts, look how's he's speeding forward. You keep ahead firmly,' said the mirasdar, hastening him.

'Let them come,' said Veerasami nonchalantly. For a moment he wondered which side he ought to take.

'Are you also going to take the left and block him?' asked the mirasdar into his ears.

'That side is full of dust,' said Veerasami, tugging the bridle and steering the bulls to the right. Within the next few moments, he overtook all the carts that had passed him by earlier, one by one. The bulls ran at breakneck speed, leaping on all fours.

'Master, can you see from where they are coming?' he asked.

'Coming straight behind us on the left, he's trying to get ahead. Can you not hear the whip's loud lashes? Hmm! Buck up! Go at full speed!'

Gounder's cart to the left and Iyer's cart to the right surged ahead to reach the middle stretch of the road, leaving behind the other carts. Only four or five carts remained to be overtaken.

Suddenly Veerasami shouted angrily, 'Dei, who is trying to overtake? Keep to the middle.' The next moment, he had to pull the bridle and contain the bulls. Otherwise the four or five carts would have moved left, crashing into one another. Since one of the carts had blocked the way for a few seconds, the Gounder's Edakadan bulls surged past them.

'O no… Okay, keep behind them. Let us cross the bridge. If you lose today, then this Iyer will have to sling the plough-log around his neck and totter around, crestfallen. And the Gounder – his head will soar beyond his neck!' said Iyer anxiously. In that voice resounded the pride of one whose bulls had never been vanquished in these parts.

Veerasami laughed heartily. 'This Veerasami Naicken will not allow that to happen, master,' he said strongly. 'Then what is the point of me holding the whip,' he added.

He pulled back the bulls straying to the side of the road and lashed them. The bulls shook. It looked as if their focus was on rushing ahead. Whenever he raised the whip, they leapt. The faces of the bulls almost touched the edge of the Gounder's cart. Gounder, who sat with his legs swinging outside, pulled them back with a jerk.

'Mooka, speed forward,' he spurred his cartman on. The Gounder's two Edakadan bulls were lusty and strong, as the breed was wonted to be. They measured more than fourteen spans. Curved horns to complement the sharp face. When they ran, the roads shuddered. As they trod the gravel stones, sparks flew. Mookan lashed non-stop, as if he was trying to split their skin. Pushing and shoving the bulls, he made a ruckus, shouting, 'hai-hooi!'

Veerasami's style was in total contrast. He never beat the bulls roughly. He knew where to poke them to get a rise out of them. He had the skills to handle the cart and win races. He never displayed any anger, impatience or anxiety. His two bulls were country breeds. Good, strong horns. They looked similar, in body and face, as if they were born together. Obedient beasts. Had short tails. They came from proud breeds that didn't need more than one lash to spur them on.

'Look how Mookan is going!' said Iyer.

'Let him go. So what? Is it a plane to fly? He has to still go two more miles. Without a hitch…'

'Okay, we're nearing the bridge. After that…'

The carts behind disappeared from view.

No sooner had they crossed the bridge than Veerasami pulled back the bulls, whose breaths nearly touched the cart ahead. He pulled the Pillai bull and spurred the bull on the right by patting it.

'Dei, he's coming on the right,' said Gounder.

Mookan twisted the tails of the bulls and poked them with a prod.

'Veerasami, take them on with one breath,' Iyer shouted anxiously.

In a few moments, both the carts ran side by side, neck and neck.

'What, da, why aren't you ahead?' asked Iyer, since the cart was a few paces behind.

'The Pillai bull is not bucking up. It's slowing down,' said Veerasami, cracking the back of the whip on the Pillai bull. He then kicked its butt and poked it with a prod. He hit the other bull too a couple of times. The two bulls pounced with a frenzy. Now the fronts of the carts were abreast.

'Mooka, don't let go, prod them on,' shouted Gounder. Then he himself heaved forward and fisted the right bull.

As if they were frustrated by the way they had been used less by man to quench his beastly instincts, the bulls scurried along, overturning their innards. Froth gathered at the ends of their mouths, dripping down in strands. The hoofs clattered vigorously. Eyes burned with rage.

The two carts ran yoke to yoke, without giving in. Mookan and Veerasami could look at each other. The two of them kept looking at each other's bulls and goaded their pairs to run faster. They ran abreast like this for a furlong.

'Hustle them on! You think you're playing a game or what?' Iyer admonished Veerasami. Only if you go past and take the centre of the road is it considered a victory.

Veerasami laughed. 'That's it, it's all over now.'

'Why, have we beaten them?' asked Iyer tensely.

'No, Edakadans can only do this much.'

Iyer's face lit up. 'Why, is it trailing?'

'No, but it won't go any further.'

'That's okay, da. Have you gone past them?' poked Iyer.

'Just see now,' he said. 'Dei, Mooka, why don't you drive them on? Look, your right bull is trailing,' he mocked.

Mookan retorted sharply, 'Why don't you try overtaking me if you can, annen.'

Veerasami laughed at Mookan. 'What do you mean "can"? Come, let us see.' He parted the bridle, poked his hand between the legs of the bulls and made them run faster.

'Mooka, look, the yoke of Iyer's cart has inched forward. Poke the bulls to run faster,' shouted Gounder.

Mookan bent down swiftly. He grasped the tail of the right one and bit it sharply a little above the end. He did the same with the left one. The bulls jumped up in pain. With one leap they were neck and neck with Iyer's cart. Both the carts were in tandem, again.

'Why, annen, why don't you race ahead?' Mookan laughed.

Veerasami too smiled. 'And beyond that?'

'Here, take the spur,' said Iyer, taking it out from where it was tucked in the hood.

'No, no need.'

Iyer fisted the right one on its belly harshly. A frenzy possessed him and he wanted to lick the other cart at one go. Both the bulls ran crazedly.

Mookan understood. He had already tested the maximum speed of his bulls. They weren't capable of going any faster. Gounder asked from inside the cart, 'What happened, da?'

'The left bull is tired,' said Mookan. 'Let them go.'

'What do you mean, let them go? Pull the neck of the right one and beat the left one. Do you understand? Fast, they will overtake us.'

Mookan grasped what his master had said. A cruel smile touched his lips. In the next moment, Gounder's cart, running in the middle of the road, suddenly veered, its yoke starting to graze the neck of Iyer's Mylai bull. In fear, the Mylai bull slowed and pushed towards the right.

For a moment, Veerasami was taken aback. He guessed Mookan's intention. Ashamed that he would lose, he tried to take revenge on the bulls themselves.

'Dei, the wheel is going over the bull's leg. Control them and move a bit!' said a tense Iyer. 'He's taunting it.' His voice was filled with seething rage and ire.

No sooner had he said this than Veerasami jerked back the bridle and tried to move away. Spokes invisible, the wheels rolled speedily, but in the clackety sound could be heard a rasping graze.

'The wheels are grazing the bull,' shouted Iyer.

One after another, four monstrous lashes fell on the right Edakadan bull. The bull that was banging into them now moved away to the middle of the road.

Mookan shouted, restraining the frightened animal, 'Why are you hitting my bull?'

Veerasami replied in a mocking tone, 'You tried to run over my bull's legs. So have you won? Is this any way to ride a cart? Sell them off tomorrow for whatever price you get.' He then shouted, 'Come now, let us see.'

The two bulls sped like the devil. In one leap they went past and came to the middle of the road. Behind them, Mookan was trying to control his bulls.

'See if the bulls are hurt. Pull aside and see,' said Iyer.

Veerasami peered out and checked the sides of the left flank of the Mylai bull. The wheel had grazed the frantically running bull. The skin had split under the white hairs and blood oozed out.

'Master, he's been bruised badly. We'll check him out after a bit.' He let the bulls run on.

'Go, go, only a mile left now. We have to watch out for Gounder's cart. See it and go,' Veerasami said to the bulls and tapped them on their backs.

'Stop the cart and check the wounds,' said Iyer.

'Then Mookan will beat us and go past.'

'Never mind, da. The donkey has already lost. What does it matter even if he flies now. Stop the poor voiceless beings by the pond and soothe them.' Veerasami turned around and looked. No sign of the Gounder's cart as far as the eyes could see. 'I think they've stopped,' he said, bringing his own vehicle to a halt. The two bulls burned when touched. Their whole bodies dripped sweat. They gasped, their breaths coming out like hissing snakes, as if their innards would splatter out. Their legs trembled and the whole body shuddered, froth dripping at the corners of their mouths. The two men got down.

Veerasami searched for some dung and applied it on the wound. Blood oozed and dripped from the underbelly. To staunch the blood, he applied more and more dung. Every time his hand touched the wound, the animal flinched.

Iyer's face reflected the raw frenzy of victory and compassion at the plight of the bleeding bull. 'Hmm… cart, bull, pride, all this is part of the game. How many times we ourselves have toppled over, the nose-bridle falling off and the axle breaking,' he said, patting the bulls.

'It's all the same, master. For both man and beast, rage and pride are the same only, no.' Veerasami affectionately scratched the bulls and patted them.

'Let them go slowly,' said Iyer, getting into the cart.

The cart went slowly on the road.

At the same time, Gounder's cart too appeared.

Unable to overtake, it followed behind. As they neared, the bridge of the river appeared white in the moonlight. The two carts rolled along calmly, one behind the other, as if nothing had happened.

Original title: *Koodusaalai*
1945

Kannan, My Friend 12

Ka Naa Subramanyam

When the ten-year-old boy picked up his mat and said that he was going to sleep alone on the pial, Paati, the grandmother, grew really afraid.

She came to the entrance with a kerosene lamp. 'Nicely dust out the mat. Why aren't you listening to me – wanting to sleep alone on a desolate road? What will I tell your father?' Paati asked, almost in tears.

'Just say, I told him, but he didn't listen. Your responsibility is over with that,' said the boy, talking firmly, beyond his years.

'Why are you talking like this, Kanna? It's not good.'

Paati heard someone bursting into a laugh, so loud that the whole world could hear it. But did she really hear that laugh? Or was it a delusion? Was it her grandson? She looked at him. He was dusting out the pillow. She lifted the lamp and peered. She saw a dark figure at the edge of the glow. The same age as her grandson Kannan. But only for a second. Then the figure seemed to disappear into the dark.

Does man ever remain alone in this world, asked Paati to herself. Then she loudly said, 'Who is this new friend, da? Looks like as if I've seen him somewhere before?'

Kannan spread out the mat and with a start looked around. He was about to utter, 'Krishnan.' But he quickly said, 'There's no one here except you and me, Paati.'

Paati felt as if her doubts and fears had disappeared. It seemed as if someone once again burst into a loud laugh. She was of the age when her eyes and ears fooled her. Holding the lamp tightly, she stood for a minute. The boy was a stubborn fellow. How long could she manage to argue with him? 'God is there,' she said naively.

'Yes, He is there,' said Kannan.

'Your mother and father have left you in my charge. They'll be back in four days,' said Paati.

'Don't worry, Paati. Go and sleep.'

Was it Kannan who spoke, pondered Paati as she went in. After she locked the door, as soon as she lay down, she fell asleep soundly. She woke up once during the night. The boy was sleeping peacefully.

She kept looking at her grandson in the glow of the lamp and then went back to sleep.

The next morning it was her elder grandson Shama who questioned Paati, 'The mat is rolled on the pial. Where is Kannan, he is not to be seen?'

The same fears that she had had yesterday surfaced again. As she went out asking, 'Where is Kannan,' Kannan appeared at the doorway. His face looked so radiant. The sandalwood paste and kumkumam looked unusually bright. His dripping hair conveyed he had just had a bath. His eyes flashed with keenness.

'Where did you go, da, so early in the morning?' Paati's voice tried to hide her anxiety.

'Went to the temple, Paati,' said Kannan innocently.

In these parts a temple meant the Iswaran temple. It was about two miles away. With a river in between. In these months the river swelled. If you crossed the river, there was a burial ground. Beyond that you had to walk a full mile on a narrow desolate path to reach the temple. Though this temple had been sung about by great saints, now no one cared. At exactly eleven in the morning, the priest came to the temple, presented a steaming hot neivedyam, which was nothing but a hot stone covered in a damp cloth. He immediately locked the temple and went back. In all her lifetime, Paati had never heard of sandalwood paste being given as prasadam from this temple.

'At this hour the Iswaran temple would not even be open, da, Kanna?' said Paati.

'It was open, Paati. This sandalwood paste is from the temple. The priest also gave some tulsi leaves. Look, here it is.'

'Crossing the river in the dark alone – should you be doing that, Kanna?'

'I didn't go alone, Paati. He also came.' Kannan went in to study his lessons.

Paati didn't know what to say and how to say it. Kannan was never going to listen to her, whatever she said. She just wanted to hand over the child safely when the parents came.

Kannan's parents who had gone to Chennai for a wedding came back to Puliangudi only after a week. Anxious, Paati spent that entire week carrying live charcoal in her belly. Even though she believed that no evil would befall Kannan, she was afraid.

That entire week Kannan slept only on the pial. Every morning the mat would be rolled up on the pial. He would be back only an hour after sunrise. With sandalwood paste and kumkumam glistening on his forehead. Beyond that nothing unusual happened.

When her son returned, Paati told him about Kannan without making much of it. Ramanathan was a patient man. Besides he was very fond of Kannan. He knew that Kannan wasn't given to lying. Paati knew very well that her son wouldn't reprimand Kannan violently.

When Kannan came back from school, Ramanathan called him and asked, 'What is this I hear, Kanna?'

Kannan knew his grandmother well. It took him only a moment to realise what his father was referring to.

'Daily he and I go to the Iswaran temple, Appa. For about a week to ten days now,' said Kannan meekly. His look seemed to imply that surely there was nothing wrong with it.

'Who's he, da?' asked Ramanathan a little sternly.

The boy was a little hesitant. He said, 'His name is Krishnan. Appa, he must be my age. He is not from our town. But he's a nice chap.'

Ramanathan knew that a boy who had impressed his son must be a good boy. 'Where is he from? How long do you know him?'

'He said that his hometown was Brindavanam. On the first day itself when I saw him I liked him, Appa. He said that he would be in our town only for ten days. "Let's go to the temple early in the morning. Will you come?" he only asked. I said I will come. We bathe in the river and take the boat and go to the other side. On the way he tells lots of stories. Such wonderful stories he tells, you know! If you also hear him, you will keep listening to his stories the whole day.'

'I would like to see him,' said Ramanathan.

'By the time we reach it is always time for aarthi with camphor. No one is usually there in the temple but us and the priest. We have a good darshan and come back. He comes back only halfway with me. After that he takes the path by the sluice-gate, saying that his house is on the opposite side.'

Ramanathan knew that his son was incapable of cooking up so much detail. Even so, he asked, 'The boatman will never come that early. Also the temple is never open at that hour.' But his voice didn't sound as assured as it did earlier.

'When we are bathing itself the boatman arrives, Appa.'

Ramanthan decided to go with Kannan the next morning. He too spent that night with Kannan on the pial. He was usually a light sleeper. But that day, without his knowing, he fell into a deep slumber. When he woke up, Kannan's mat was rolled up, as usual. No sign of Kannan.

Ramanathan was anxious. It wasn't untrue to say that his second son was his life. Just looking at his very face, hunger, thirst, everything would fly away, he would say. With a worried heart, he himself went to the river bank to receive Kannan returning from the temple.

At the free-boat-service jetty, boatman Murugayyan was brushing his teeth. The boat, unmanned, was on the opposite bank.

'Ele, Murugayya? Did you see my son?' asked Ramanathan.

Ramanathan was in charge of the free boat service in Puliangudi. So Murugayyan replied respectfully. 'It is time for the little master to come back. By the time I brush my teeth and swim to the other side, it is time for him to arrive.' He washed his face, tied his head-cloth and towelled himself.

'Who accompanied Kannan, Murugayya? Is he a boy from our parts?' asked Ramanathan, without sounding unduly anxious.

Murugayyan lifted his head and looked at him. 'How do I know? I've just got up. For the past week to ten days, every morning the boat is tied on the other bank. When I swim across and reach the boat, the little master will come from the temple. If you look at the sandalwood paste on his forehead, all your sins will be washed away.'

'Where did you tie the boat last night?'

'Here, in this corner only, as usual. Why do you ask, ayya?'

'Then how did the boat go to the opposite side?'

Murugayyan scratched his head. 'The little master…'

He couldn't believe it. A ten-year-old boy, all alone in the dark, taking a big boat meant for thirty people single-handedly… Ramanathan exclaimed to himself.

By that time, Kannan, who stood on the opposite bank, called out, 'Murugayya!' Ramanathan was overjoyed when he heard that voice. On hearing it Murugayya too jumped into the waters without seeking permission and started swimming across. On seeing this, Ramanathan couldn't but be proud. When his son got down from the boat, seeing his peaceful face with sandalwood paste on his forehead, Ramanathan's worries flew away. He reverently touched to his eyes the tulsi leaves his son gave him. 'Did you go to the temple today too, Kannan?' asked Ramanathan. 'Couldn't you have called me? I too would have come.'

'I will ask Him,' answered Kannan in a ringing voice.

When he uttered Him, Ramanathan's old doubts resurfaced. 'Who rowed the boat this morning, Kanna? Murugayyan didn't come it seems,' said Ramanathan.

'What, he didn't come? He only rowed,' said Kannan without hesitation.

'Was it me, saami?' asked Murugayyan looking intently at Kannan.

Ramanathan felt that both were telling the truth. 'Did that Krishnan come today too?' asked Ramanathan, trying to change the subject. He felt that he understood the whole thing.

'He came!' said Kannan, eagerly recounting his friend's prowess in storytelling, his radiant face, his grace, his intelligence. Enthralled, Ramanathan reached home, feeling as if he was reading an epic.

If anything unusual happens, intelligent people usually don't have the sense to deem it unusual. It didn't take much time for Ramanathan to understand that there was something beyond his reach in Kannan's tale. But he kept digging into it, determined to unravel the truth.

That very evening he went in search of the Iswaran temple's priest. Like the fox of a palmyra grove, unafraid of any rustling, the temple priest was neither afraid of god nor would yield to devotion, as goes the proverb. The priest made fun of Ramanathan.

'In the morning? Pooja? What are you saying? Here we are scraping and struggling even for one high-noon pooja! There's no way for even a morsel of offering. As if for a ten-year-old I will open the temple in the morning and perform a pooja and all. Are you mad? Go, go!'

Not to leave him in any doubt, the priest offered further testimony. 'I get up only at eight every day. I light the fire and ready the water for coffee decoction, and then wake up my wife, calling, "Adiye." She will get up only with the third "adiye".'

All this was known to the entire village. Going to verify this merely earned Ramanathan the title of 'mad man'. Without giving up, he also enquired with two passersby. One said that he had seen the two boys walking along to the temple, hand in hand, chatting away animatedly. One even knew who Kannan was. But he said that the other boy was dark and charmingly attractive and his voice too was very sweet. He wasn't a boy from these parts. He also said that he had a flute in his hand. After that Ramanathan didn't have any doubts.

Ramanathan returned home anxiously and immediately asked Kannan if his friend played the flute.

'O, yes. He plays very well,' said Kannan. 'Since Paati had seen him on the first day in the glow of her lamp, he stopped coming here. Every day he plays the flute at the end of the street. When I hear the music, I get up and go.'

Beyond that Ramanathan didn't ask his son anything. The next morning Ramanathan was ready to hear the melody of the flute. He too heard the flute a couple of hours before dawn. But it mesmerised him and made him feel even more sleepy. He couldn't follow his son, as he had planned. He watched his son rolling the mat, as if in a dream.

That morning he didn't go to the jetty in search of Kannan. He went in and asked his mother, 'Why, Amma, it seems you saw Kannan's friend the first day?'

'What?' asked Paati.

'The first day when Kannan slept on the pial...'

'Yes, yes!' replied Paati. 'He stood merging into the dark.'

'What did he look like?' asked Ramanathan eagerly.

'He looked like Kannan only. If you looked at Kannan, you don't have to look at him.'

It would have been like that. If you attempt to reach for something you can't reach, then you have no go but to rely on what is close at hand. As

Ramanathan came out, he spotted Kannan. His forehead was bereft of the sandalwood paste. Even his face looked downcast. 'What, Kanna? What happened?' asked Ramanathan concernedly, hugging him close.

'Appa,' said Kannan, but couldn't talk beyond that. His voice quavered and his lips quivered.

Ramanathan felt as if the whole universe had exploded. He embraced his son even closer and asked, 'What happened?'

'Appa…he… he…' he fumbled. 'He's going back to his place,' he said, sobbing inconsolably.

Ramanathan felt that there was no need to ask for details. He understood everything. He didn't know what to say and how to console the young boy. His guilt-ridden heart felt as if it would burst.

'I am the sinner who refused to believe. I'm the reason for His going away,' Ramanathan lamented. 'Don't know what good fortune you were born with to see and be with Him for ten whole days. But… I…I…' Ramanathan started to weep.

The boy didn't know why his father wept. Forgetting his own sorrow, Kannan began to console him.

Original title: *Kannan En Thozhan*
1961

The Passing of a Day 13

Kumudhini

You could hear the sounds of bhajans at the end of the street. Seshi Paati, asleep on the pial by the doorstep, got up quickly. She lit the extinguished hand-lamp in the hall, went to the back of the house, drew water from the well, sprinkled cow-dung in front of the house, peered with great difficulty in the dark and swept the front of the house, taking care to push the rubbish on to the road and not into the neighbours' houses. Seshi believed that if you knew your neighbours for a number of years, it wasn't wise to push your garbage into their front yards.

The sun hadn't risen yet in the east. The bhajan singers neared, lanterns in hand. From a distance, Paati folded her hands in reverence and looked with lowered eyes. It was the time when only Venus was shining, and despite being seventy-odd years, she noticed that the Brahmin who sang the bhajans hadn't shaved for quite a few days now. Is his wife pregnant? Must find out. They haven't had children for fifteen years now. She tucked away a note to herself in her mind.

What a surprise as she turned to enter the house! Paati got goosebumps! Suddenly, her blood chilled! She saw with her very own eyes a man coming down the stairs of her neighbour's house and entering inside. She felt as if someone had slapped her. She even tottered for a second.

She somehow managed to regain her balance, resolved not to think about it, locked her house and started on her morning round of the streets.

As she walked along on East Street, Koma's new daughter-in-law was drawing a kolam in front of the house. That pleased Paati to no end. Such a young thing up so early, sweeping the front and drawing a kolam, she thought. In South Street, in front of the house of the big landowner, stood a hired vehicle. The driver unloaded the last piece of luggage, a mattress, and carried it inside.

Who could have come? The son? Didn't they say the son was working in Calcutta? The girl was here for the past six months! Would the son-in-law have come? If so, it would be a miracle only.

Kanaka Paati lived next door to the landowner. She was scraping the pial, 'suruk suruk', with a stubby broom.

Seshi approached her softly and asked, 'What, di, Kanakam, didn't see you yesterday in the temple. Did you pray when the thirumanjanam was performed?' Not that she cared a bit whether Kanaka Paati prayed or not. But she wasn't one to ask baldly about who had come to the landlord's house. Yes, unlike some people, she wouldn't stick her head into someone else's affairs.

Kanakam replied, 'No Seshi. I ground some flour yesterday and my back ached. So I lay down quietly.'

Flour-aa? Who did she grind it for? What was the occasion in that house for which they had to grind flour? How much did they give her? Seshi had to know all this. They say that there is propriety among thieves too. In much the same way, there are conversational gambits among grandmothers as well. Rule number one: only if you divulge something interesting can you expect to gather in return something equally interesting. This system, much commended by economists, is known as bartering.

'Kanakam, I'm going to tell you something. Let it be a secret. Don't tell anyone else. Go, I don't know what to say! From then it's been tormenting me! The people in town think that we like to gossip and take pleasure in making up stories about others! I'm not made that way at all. Ever since I saw it, my stomach is churning! How many times have I told you that Bhooma is a nice girl! Just listen to this! Today, someone wearing a zari angavastram came down the stairs and went inside – I myself saw it. My body trembled,' she described.

'Maybe it's her husband or something!' said Kanakam placatingly.

'Not at all. She only told me, "My husband has joined the military. No leave from now on"!'

Hearing this disquieting piece of news, Kanaka Paati looked suitably astonished. She had a lot of work to do, so she said quickly without Seshi's prompting, 'I pounded the flour for the lawyer's house only. The lawyer's wife wanted to send murukkus to her sister's children. Somebody is going to Delhi, it seems. She is going to send it through them, she said.'

Seshi asked, 'Looks like someone has come to the landowner's house.'

'No one special. That brother of hers only, the one who was studying in the city. I believe he's got a job now, seventy rupees salary. She told me yesterday that she wants to find a nice girl for him.'

The two grandmothers parted ways, extremely satisfied. Seshi finished her round of the streets hastily, went home, picked up her pot and left for the River Kaveri. Her mind was often tormented by Bhooma's problem. But that didn't mean she forgot about other things. She had to praise Koma's daughter-in-law at suitable moments, 'What a young thing and how well behaved she is!' The lawyer's wife was always full of her sister. Her feet didn't touch the ground because her sister's husband earned three hundred rupees in Delhi. What was there to be proud of that? Every year, without fail, her sister bore a child, dark and fat. She had seen that brother-in-law of that landlord. Good-looking boy. No parents. So what? He had a sister to pamper him.

Janaki was dipping her pot into the Kaveri. Seshi asked, 'Has the marriage been fixed?'

'Don't know what to do, Paati. Can't get sleep in the night,' Janaki sighed.

'Why don't you give her to that landowner's brother-in-law? The boy looks like a king. Got a job now, it seems. Think the salary is seventy or hundred. His sister will keep her on her head and look after her. No kitch-pitch. I know her well. If you like, I myself will speak to her,' said Paati.

'They will ask for dowry, no?'

'They won't ask for much. If you do for five hundred to thousand rupees, it should do.'

'Where will I go for even five hundred rupees, Paati? Only if you give me,' said Janaki, with a faint smile. Paati had put away a small amount. She would lend it out to her friends on a suitable pledge. Now and then if someone referred to her as 'rich', she felt immensely satisfied.

'Of course I will give it to you wholeheartedly,' she said, feeling quite proud. As she spoke, she calculated in her mind the worth of Janaki's house and how much she would lend, keeping it as a pledge.

On her return from the Kaveri, she quickly made some food and left for the temple, to the goddess's shrine since she knew very well that the landowner's wife came every day to pray there at ten. She now forgot about Bhooma and was solely immersed in Janaki's daughter's marriage.

When she saw the landowner's wife Lakshmi Ammal in the goddess's shrine, she casually exchanged greetings, as if she had come upon her by accident. She then asked, 'What, 'ma, I believe your brother has come.'

'Yes, he arrived only this morning.'

'Any plans for marriage this year?'

'If we get a good girl, we will.'

'Our Janaki's daughter is a good girl. She is pleasant-looking, I'd gone to their house just the other day. In a fraction of a second, she whipped up some food. She will give dowry too. Not less than five hundred. It's your wish, of course!' said Paati.

'Let's see,' said Lakshmi Ammal and slipped away from her.

Deep in thought about the marriage, Paati completely forgot about Bhooma. What a surprise! When she neared her house, she found Bhooma's husband standing there, as big as a log. He had cropped his hair... it was all too much... how could she explain it? Paati felt odd.

'What, 'pa, Ramasamy, when did you come? Bhooma said you'd never get leave,' she asked.

'No, Paati, I came only last night,' he said.

'It looked like someone was coming down the stairs in your house this morning – it was you only, is it?' asked Paati with anxiety, and a fraction – you can say about one in a hundred – of chagrin.

'When? When the bhajan group came? Yes, that was me only, Paati.'

Paati was filled with happiness. What else but happiness. For one who had been so sad that such a nice girl had turned so bad, such news could bring only happiness. Nothing else!

When she finished eating, she left for the lawyer's house. Had the murukkus been sent? What else had she sent? Paati was a little eager to know all this.

Etchumu came towards her. Paati didn't like Etchumu. Forever she gossiped. She always spoke ill of others. She could utter hundred when it was really one, without her mouth pricking her.

Etchumu asked, approaching Paati eagerly, 'What Paati, I came to ask since I thought you may know. I can't believe it at all. Tell me if it is true. That Bhooma who lives near your house, they are saying all sorts of things about her, I believe.'

Paati asked emphatically, 'What are they saying? What is there to say?'

Who knew better than her about Bhooma? What right did the others have to speak about her!

'Her husband has joined the military, no? They are saying all sorts of things about her.'

Paati began. From morning, she hadn't yet picked a quarrel. 'Which wandering gypsy came and told you all this? How can she say that? What cheek to say all this! Isn't she scared she will go to hell if she speaks like this. Sin, merit, hasn't she heard of all this?'

Without let-up, Paati lectured for half an hour with great emotion and expression about the good character of Bhooma, the wickedness of the people of the town, their bad habit of gossiping, and the punishment they would undergo in hell. She also hinted at one or two doings of Etchumu's maternal family.

'I don't know, amma! Someone saw it with their own eyes, it seems,' mumbled Etchumu.

Seshi uttered a few more words, as hard as nails, completely wiping out the rumours, and left for the lawyer's house, immensely proud of herself.

She knew very well that the cause of this rumour which had taken such a monstrous form was no one but herself. And it was she who had sneaked the information to Kanakam. So she was doubly satisfied that she had contained it in such a fashion.

There was no time to go to the lawyer's house. It was already dark. She had to go to the temple. Paati turned back, thinking that she would see the lawyer's wife tomorrow. At that time, Vedantam came running. 'Paati, please come. She has poured hot oil on her foot.' Paati hastened and went inside his house. She forgot everything – Bhooma, Janaki's daughter's marriage, the lawyer's wife's sister in Delhi. She cried in panic, 'Silly girl! What have you done, di?' Vedantam's wife Shanbagam was sitting in the kitchen, holding her foot. Thankfully the hot oil had fallen only on her toes. There were boils around her nails. Paati washed them with limestone water, applied coconut oil and strapped them with available bits of cloth.

'If you touch me, you have to bathe again, Paati. No need, I will tie it myself,' said Shanbagam, but Paati wouldn't hear of it. She then washed all the vessels that lay in the wash area, stacked them on the shelf, served both of them the remains of the meal, wiped the stove, drew a kolam and readied the things for Shanbagam to cook in the morning. Only then she left.

It was nine in the night. Seshi Paati didn't feel like bathing and having dinner. Not bothering with anything, she went to sleep on an empty stomach. She knew how to contain hunger. But unlike others, she wasn't one to follow conventions merely for the sake of appearance.

Tomorrow, she must pursue strongly the business of Janaki's daughter's marriage. She also had to investigate the lawyer's wife's Delhi sister's matter.

Like a child who goes to sleep clutching to her chest two new dolls she had got that day and looking forward to playing with them the next day, Seshi Paati longingly held to her chest these two matters. She swept the pial and lay down.

Original title: *Oru Naal Pozhudhu*
1946

Milk Account 14

SVV

'What is the milk account for this month?' I asked, with the intention of tallying the accounts between the two of us before the milkman came home.

'What big account? It's like this – till the thirteenth, three-fourths ollock cow's milk and three-fourths ollock buffalo milk in the morning; in the evening, one and a half ollocks cow's milk, two and a half ollocks buffalo milk. And on one of these days, he said the animal kicked him and gave only a quarter measure.'

'About cow's milk – remember one day we went for a film? That day he came and went. That day of course we didn't buy milk. Besides, the previous month he owed us seven ollocks. What account? This is the account! Till the thirteenth these are the calculations…'

'Every month I tell you! Jot down in a notebook every day whatever you buy. How easy it will be then to quickly do the accounts!'

'What is there to write? Daily we are buying the same quantity only!'

'What same quantity? One day you are saying two ollocks less, another day three ollocks more. Even if the late Ramanujan reappears, he won't be able to do your accounts! Ok, ok, tell me, till the thirteenth…'

'I told you, no! See, in the morning, three ollocks cow's milk, three ollocks buffalo milk for thirteen days. What is thirteen into half? Six and a half…'

'Ok, tell me.'

'Cow or buffalo?'

'Tell cow's milk separately and buffalo milk separately. Cow's milk is two and a half padi for a rupee. Buffalo is two and three quarter. The two accounts should be calculated separately, no?

'Ok, do it that way then.'

'Ok, tell me cow's milk first. How much in the mornings? And in the evenings?'

'I've already told you, no?' Three ollocks in the morning. In the evenings one and a half ollocks. Total four and a half ollocks. For thirteen days. Just minus one and a half ollocks for the day we went for the film. Last month he owed us seven ollocks…'

'Let's add and subtract later. Let's tally this first. Four and a half ollocks for thirteen days, is it? Thirteen into four is seventy-two.'

'What, thirteen into four is seventy-two? O, a maths whiz! Fifty-two!'

'Yes, yes, fifty-two. The brain splatters just doing your accounts. Thirteen fours are fifty-two…Thirteen halves are six…'

'Six and a half.'

'Yes, yes, six and a half. How much did we calculate earlier? Fifty-two? Fifty-two plus six and a half is fifty-eight and a half. How much for this fifty-eight and a half now?'

'We went for the movie, no? We have to minus that one and a half ollocks, isn't it?'

'Fifty-eight and a half minus one and a half is fifty-seven.'

'Last month he owed us seven ollocks. Minus that too.'

'Ok. If we minus that as well, we can say till the thirteenth it is fifty ollocks. At the rate of two and a half padis, how much for fifty ollocks?'

'Convert the fifty ollocks into padis; eight fives are forty. No, no, eight sixes are forty-eight. It is eight padis and two ollocks.'

'Eight padis? Say six padis. Eight ollocks for one padi, isn't it?'

'Yes, six padis and two ollocks; that is six and a quarter padis. How much it comes to? For five padis two rupees. Then there is the one and quarter padi. For that it is half a rupee. Total two and a half rupees.'

'Let that be. Now tell me the buffalo milk account.'

'What buffalo milk account? It is known only, no. Morning three ollocks. Evening two and a half ollocks. Two days the milk was very watery.

I won't count that. I told him then itself I will not pay money for that. Just minus that.'

'Let that be. Tell me the account. How much did you say for buffalo milk?'

'In the morning three ollocks, in the night two ollocks. No, no, two and a half.'

'Tell both the wretched things together. How much daily?'

'Why don't you add it and see. Three plus two and a half is five and a half.'

'How much for thirteen days? Thirteen fives are sixty-five; thirteen halves are six and a half. Sixty-five plus six and a half is seventy-one and a half.'

'Minus from that two days of watery milk.'

'As if he will agree just because you want to deduct?'

'What "not agree"? That day itself I told him I will not pay for that watery milk.'

'Leave it. Continue.'

'What "leave it"! You should definitely not pay for that milk. Because you keep on giving like this only he takes advantage. If you give him today, that's all, he will give you only watery milk from tomorrow.'

'Ok, ok. We'll minus that in the end. Totally, how many padis buffalo milk, did we say? Seventy-four ollocks or what?'

'Seventy-four-aa? Seventy-one and a half, didn't I say?'

'How seventy-one and a half?'

'For thirteen days, five and a half ollocks means…'

'Yes, yes, seventy-one and a half. How many rupees? Two and a half padis for one rupee. For seventy-one and a half…?'

'First convert all the ollocks into padis. Eight nines are seventy-two. Nine padis minus half an ollock.'

'Let that half an ollock be. Count for nine padis. Two threes are six, three three-fourths are two and a quarter; if you deduct eight and a quarter padis, three-fourth padi remaining.'

'Shouldn't we deduct half an ollock from that? Six ollocks for three-fourth padi; if you minus half an ollock, five and a half ollocks. Three rupees and five and half ollocks. How much did we calculate cow's milk for? Two or two and a half?'

'Two and a half. Three plus two and half is five and a half. Above that, five and a half ollocks. O, we forgot something. The day the animal kicked. Only quarter padi he gave. Shouldn't we subtract that?'

'There are five and a half ollocks above. Deduct from that.'

'How can you deduct from that? That is cow's milk. This is buffalo milk.'

'See how she buys milk. She buys milk it seems, milk!'

'Why are you getting so angry? If you don't want me to buy milk, I'll stop it. As if I'm buying milk only for myself!'

'Who said not to buy milk? Can't you write down how much you buy?'

'What is there if you write or tell it through your mouth? Everything is calculation only. As if the account is going to run away!'

'It won't run away anywhere. Now tell me the accounts from the fourteenth?'

'How many days did Chellammal and her husband stay with us – five days or six days? When they stayed, we bought quarter padi extra buffalo milk in the morning and one and a half ollock cow's milk extra in the evening.'

'For how many days?'

'For however many days they stayed. Just see, no.'

'Yes, yes, I'll see and be damned.'

'And then when Kunju was sick, for kanji, curd and all, I bought an ollock extra every day. He had fever for four days, no? And then we also went out of town for three days – we didn't buy then. And we returned only in the evening on the third day, isn't it. I had instructed Mangalam well before: "We will be back in the evening, so get milk and keep." She had bought three-quarter padi milk. How much is all that, calculate and see.'

'Yes, yes, I will see and be reduced to rack and ruin. Wonder if that milkman has kept accounts?'

'Of course, he would have. But just because he keeps, we needn't calculate or what? We should just give whatever he asks, is it?'

'No, no. We'll pay him according to our calculations only. But first let our accounts tally.'

'What tally? What I told you only is the account.'

'Yes, yes, your account only. I don't have time now. There is an accountant in my office, very clever with calculations. I will bring him with me when I come home in the evening. We'll check the account then.'

I then left for the office.

Original title: *Paal Kanakku*
circa 1949

A Slice of Jackfruit 15

Rasikan

Sitting in the front courtyard, Thangammal scooped out the segments from the jackfruit. A good Tanjore jackfruit; big segments, gold in colour; probably twenty to a portion. Vaidyanatha Iyer had bought it for the death anniversary of his father when he had gone to Tanjore for a court hearing. One half of it had been used for the ceremony. The following afternoon the lady of the house herself was leisurely plucking out the pulp to relish it. A small bowl of oil lay beside the chopping blade. Now and then she dipped her fingers into it so that her hand wouldn't get sticky. A big banana leaf was spread out on the other side; she heaped the segments at one end and the seeds at the other. But only one in two segments reached the leaf; the other was absent-mindedly popped into her mouth midway.

As her hand and mouth were thus busily working, she heard the noises of children outside. Thangammal hurriedly upturned a cooking pot over the leaf. Two children came running inside. Both were around the same age. Just running four or turned four. 'Amma, I can smell jackfruit. Isn't there any for me?' The child who asked was very fair, full of smiles. A silk cord with gold jingles was tied around his waist. Silver anklets on his feet. A gold chain with a talisman around his neck. The child who followed him had nothing but a worn-out pendant – an imprint of a dog – tied to a black thread around his waist.

He didn't climb in to the courtyard with his friend but stood back, holding on to the knob of the outer door. Thangamma gave a couple of segments to her son and said, 'That's all. Shouldn't eat more. Not good for health, Kanna.' The child asked, 'For Narayanan?'

'Yes, yes, they are buying fruit every day in their house!' she mumbled and clucked to herself, choosing two of the smallest segments half-heartedly. She called out to Narayanan. 'Here, take this, da. Now run, it's already dark. You can play tomorrow,' she said a bit sternly.

While the child was on his way out, Vaidyanatha Iyer, who was reading a book on the pial, called out to his wife, 'Can't you give four more to the child? Do we only have stomachs? We've eaten our fill yesterday. Give him a heap.' The child went back into the house eagerly. Picking out a portion from which she had already plucked most of the segments, she covered it with a piece of banana leaf. 'Here, take this, 'pa. The order has been passed… As if we have plenty!' She handed it over grudgingly, escorting him up to the door so that Vaidyanatha Iyer wouldn't know how much she had given.

Vaidyanatha Iyer was a rich man in the Thethaarampatti agraharam. The precious child had been born after many years of marriage, after several temple visits and fasts. He, who was always fond of children, became doubly affectionate towards other children after his child was born. As for his wife, she always cursed children. Because she got a child after so many years, she was so pleased with herself, as if she had accomplished an extraordinary feat. She believed that only her son was a divine child and the rest were fashioned out of mud and stone; so she cosseted Krishnamoorthy and didn't allow him to mingle with other children. She, who visited no one, on good or bad occasions, tried her level best to prevent her child from visiting others when he turned two or three.

Vaidyanatha Iyer didn't much like her ways. 'Are you trying to make him a vile creature like you?' he would fume. She would reply contemptuously, 'There is no dearth of envy and jealousy in the wretched creatures of this town. They will burn the child with their eyes only. Ayyo! Children, it seems, children! They're nauseating – noses leaking and mouths drooling! Grime will stick on you if you just touch them.' But Krishnamoorthy couldn't be restrained. He and Narayanan from the thatched house at the end of the street were bosom friends. Thangammal didn't like this one bit.

But she couldn't say anything. Because Narayanan's father was Vaidyanatha Iyer's cousin, once removed. Besides, at this tender age itself, Narayanan was well behaved and understanding. Because of these reasons, Vaidyanatha Iyer was immensely happy that his son had befriended him. Thangammal too let that be, since because of this friendship, Krishnamoorthy didn't seek other children.

Carrying the fruit, Narayanan hastened towards his house. On the way, he popped into his mouth one after another the two segments that were given to him. They tasted like honey. Till then he hadn't known the taste of jackfruit.

His parents were terribly poor. And his father was utterly useless. Though he had enough capacity to earn, he was bone lazy. He wandered around from place to place, looking for marriages and functions to earn free meals. He also appeared as a false witness in several cases to make enough for coffee; the rest of the time he gambled. It would be unusual if he made it home for even half a day in a month. He might give a quarter or half a rupee if he felt like it. Even if he didn't, his poor wife never opened her mouth. If she did, she would get slapped for sure.

That good woman spent her days foraging to get enough for herself and her son, somehow or the other. She was extremely intelligent. Even though she came from a poor family she never sought help from others. Her hands could perform several jobs. Even for a while, she never remained idle. She neither had the time nor the wish to gossip. That was the very reason for Thangammal hating her.

Thangammal believed that all the women of the town were slaves to her and her money and had to comply with her wishes. 'Only if one answered when called, would one feel like giving some curry or vegetables.' She who uttered these words always had about ten women to attend to her. The women who spent the entire day patting out appalams, making murukkus, grinding batter for dosais or doing whatever she ordered were happy to receive half a litre of stale buttermilk, withered brinjals, a banana flower or some such thing. Thangammal commanded these poor women like King Sugreeva of Ramayana.

That all this never worked with Radhai was the main reason she hated her. She never visited Thangammal's unnecessarily. She didn't expect any help just because they were related to her husband. But if Vaidyanatha Iyer offered something in an emergency, she never refused. Thangammal didn't have the guts to stop her husband. But she would tell her slaves out of Iyer's earshot, 'No end to arrogance for the daughter of a "club lady". Wants to eat even husk daintily!' She assuaged the fire in her belly by using these harsh words.

The child entered the house saying, 'Amma, they gave jackfruit in Krishnamoorthy's house. It's very nice.' When he didn't find his mother, he went searching for her in the kitchen. The rice was boiling on the stove. A tin lamp flickered. His mother sat still, looking intently at the burning stove. Not wanting to disturb her, he too leant against a pillar. Though he wanted to give the jackfruit to his mother, his hand automatically groped for a piece. Since there were just one or two segments, he couldn't find them quickly. In his hurry, he tore the long, thick paper and put a segment into his mouth.

'Che, this is not sweet at all. What that maami gave was like sugared candy,' he said disappointedly. His mother, who was sitting silent in deep thought, turned towards him and said, 'Bring it here. Let me see.' She took the jackfruit and looked at it in the light. Two or three small segments, badly squashed with the hand, lay hidden in the paper. The rest was mere paper. She looked at her child's face. His eagerness for the fruit and his faith that his mother would put into his hand tasty segments shone in his eyes. Her stomach curdled with grief. 'Ayyo! What a sinner! Would anyone cheat a child like this!' she said. She dropped the jackfruit and hugged Narayanan. Tears flowed down like streams.

Stunned, Narayanan didn't open his mouth. Even at such a young age he knew very well the harshness of poverty. He didn't mind starvation or hunger. Even so, when one day Krishnamoorthy had given him half a cashewnut toffee ball, he had yielded to the taste. He had come home and asked his mother, 'Amma, why don't you ever make cashewnut toffee ball? They make it in Krishnamoorthy's house. It's very nice.' When she had replied sorrowfully, 'They are rich. They have cashewnut groves. Where will we get, appa?' it had been imprinted on his mind. From then on, he had stopped asking his mother for this and that. Even today, when he realised that there was no jackfruit, he didn't open his mouth. Lying on his mother's lap, he fell asleep. Radhai pulled out the fuel-log to put off the stove and lay down near her son. With tears and sobs, she bemoaned her fate for a long time and then fell asleep.

She didn't know how long she had slept; she suddenly woke up. She heard someone knocking on the door urgently. She carried the lamp and opened the door and was startled to find Vaidyanatha Iyer standing there.

He, who never spoke to her directly, said, 'The child is ill, amma. There's vomiting and loose motion. I don't know what to do. Please come.' It was late in the night, and the child was sleeping alone at home. She looked at Vaidyanatha Iyer again. She couldn't bear to see the sorrow and fear on his face. The old lady next door was lying on the pial, coughing fitfully. She asked her to keep an eye on the child and hastily followed Vaidyanatha Iyer.

It was the month of Margazhi; it was drizzling irritatingly. She could hear whispers from every house. But no one opened the door or lit the lamps. Only then she realised why Vaidyanatha Iyer had come seeking her. This was the reason: since cholera was prevalent in the town, when Krishnamoorthy started vomiting and had diarrhoea, the woman next door managed to spread the tale, in a trice, as if by air mail, and even 'confirmed' that it was cholera. When Vaidyanatha Iyer knocked on a few doors of Thangammal's cronies, they all feigned deep sleep. Only when Iyer saw through all this, did he approach Radhai.

The whole house was in disarray. The doddering old cook was dipping flannel in hot water, squeezing it out and fomenting the child's stomach and back. Tossing and turning, the child moaned and screamed, eyes wide with fear, 'Ayyo, can't bear the stomachache.' Leaning against the pillar, hair unkempt and hanging loose, Thangammal was mournfully blabbering whatever came into her mouth, 'God knows which sinner cast their evil eye on my child! God knows whose curse has come true. Will I see my son again? Oh god, can't you grant me death and make my child well?

On seeing Radhai she said, 'Adi amma, Radhai! You are a good woman. People say that you know all about treating sick children. Please tell me if my child will survive.' She asked Radhai so piteously and humbly, almost to the point of touching her feet.

Somehow swallowing the disgust which erupted doubly in her heart, Radhai said, 'Put your trust in god and keep calm. Nothing terrible will happen.' She looked at the child's condition. She recalled the days before her marriage, when her mother (she was the 'club lady' so derogatorily mentioned by Thangammal) made a living nursing sick people. Since Radhai had carefully watched her mother handling such situations, without fluster or a fumble, she attended efficiently to the child with the help of the old cook. As she surmised, it was jackfruit indigestion. She took medicinal ingredients like vasambu, charred them and gave them to the child. In a while, he felt better. He closed his eyes. When his moans and grunts quietened, Thangammal too nodded off, snoring. Iyer in the verandah and Radhai in the hall kept vigil.

Dawn broke. When the townspeople came to know that the child was well, they hastened to enquire about him. The village doctor sped in to examine the child, felt his pulse and pronounced, 'Nothing to worry. Just a bit sluggish. Just two doses of medicine will do.' As if he was the one who breathed new life into her son, Thangammal gave him a rupee and a measure of rice. When Radhai thought it was no longer necessary for her to remain there, she started for home. Spotting her, Thangammal said, 'Wait a bit.' She ran into the courtyard and brought the remaining jackfruit. 'Here, take this. I kept this good fruit only for you,' she said in a generous and affectionate tone.

'Don't want ammami. After eating the fruit you sent through the child yesterday, my stomach is full.' Radhai gave a knowing laugh.

'Adi, that wasn't for you. It was only for the child, no…' When Thangammal started to cover up, Radhai didn't allow her to speak further, 'Let that be. It's getting late, I'm going home.' Radhai rushed back home.

The next week there was a sumangali prarthanai in Vaidyanatha Iyer's house. Thangammal bought a six-yard sari as an offering, and do you know who she gave it to? Yes, the day Krishnamoorthy was ill, she had decided to give it to Radhai. But the one who actually received the sari was Dosai Kuppan's wife Logammal, who constantly buttered her up. It came to light that Thangammal gave a reason for this too to her gang. 'Because her tongue was dying for good food, I gave a full portion of the best jackfruit, di. About twenty segments. You know what she did? She just refused and strode away. What arrogance! What pride! Only because of her son's evil eye, my child fell sick. Thank god, only because of the merits earned by our forefathers, the danger to the head just flicked off the turban, and nothing more.'

Original title: *Palaachulai*
1938

Police Feast 16

Kalki

'Chee, chee! What kind of world is this? Everything has turned upside down these days,' said Kandasami to himself.

'Then what, ayya? Can it be considered a world at all if there's no way to get two pooris and one cup of coffee?' he questioned himself, and spat out a 'thoo' in reply.

At the time Kandasami's finances were pathetic. He opened his wallet. Found only three quarter-anna coins. He took them out, peered longingly at them one by one, wondering how nice it would be if at least one of them turned out to be a half-rupee coin. 'Quarter anna, half anna, three-quarter anna,' he counted in three different octaves and flung them on the street. Walking a few paces, he turned back, and on second thought retrieved the coins.

Kandasami was usually never in such dire straits. His smart brain always looked for other ways to earn money if something failed. How our finance ministers get into a tizzy, worrying about how they will balance the accounts if they remove the taxes. If only they would call Kandasami, give him two pooris and one cup of coffee and consult him.

That was the problem: there was an intimate relationship between Kandasami's brain and his stomach. If you asked for his advice after he downed a cup of coffee, his brain could solve any fiscal problem, however tricky it might be. But if there was no cup of coffee, his brain would go on strike.

That morning Kandasami went into a saloon without taking proper stock of his finances. When he looked into his wallet soon after his hair was cropped, he found only six and three-fourth annas. He didn't want to owe a debt to a saloon! It would be quite demeaning. Besides, he visited the shop every day for free grooming. So he gave away six annas and came out. What remained in his hand were three quarter-annas.

Kandasami's latest effort to juggle his finances was to dabble in palmistry. He had come upon a book by a North Indian who had certificates from bigwigs attesting to his expertise; Kandasami simply swiped his ideas. With that he had led a very comfortable life for six months. He earned well then. Had he so wished, he could even have saved money. But he had no belief in savings. 'He' who planted a tree would surely water it. Why bother to save? If there was money on hand for today, why worry about tomorrow?

You might ask why Kandasami gave up such a lucrative trade like palmistry. First, he didn't believe in sticking to any job for a long time. Second, because of an incident that had happened at the fag end of that career. It had put him in such a resolute frame of mind that he had even vowed to become a sanyasi! He had gone straight to the Peraananda matham, but the chief saamiyaar there who had heard him out had said that he had enough disciples already and that the financial situation of the matham didn't allow for the purchase of saffron robes for the initiates. He had flung the thought away thinking, Chee! Useless! Wherever I go, the same wretched financial plight.

The incident that had determined Kandasami's aforementioned resolve was as follows:

As a palmist he had observed that anyone, big or small, was immensely flattered if you said nice things about his love life. He would spin a yarn after assessing the person's age and wealth. If he said, 'Saar! You ought to be married by now. If not, you will be very soon,' the man's face would bloom, whatever kind of person he might be. Or he would tell someone with hesitation, 'You shouldn't take it amiss just because I'm telling you. But you have two wives.' Immediately a smile would appear on the face. Taking note of a person's dress, grooming and style, he would say, 'Saar!

You have one lawfully wedded wife. But you must be also having one or two in "private". No point in getting angry with me. Your lines reveal so.' Immediately the fellow's mouth would be full of teeth. He wouldn't accept anything less than a rupee from them.

To another one he would say: 'Your wife is very lucky. Wherever she sets her foot, everything will flourish.' To yet another one: 'Your wife will give her life for you. But you won't be so fond of her.' Saying all this, he would extract a silver coin, however miserly the person might be.

But one time this strategy hadn't worked. There was nothing wrong with the strategy, but it was the target that had been wrong. Showing his palm, a man had learnt everything about himself and had then asked for his wife's palm to be read. Without realising what he was saying, Kandasami had blurted out, 'Amma! You have one lawfully wedded husband. And you have another one or two in "private".' That was all. The lady had taken the form of Goddess Kali and cursed, 'May they set your body on fire, and may a snake bite you!' And then she had given it to her husband too, 'And this lifeless moron asked me to show my palm!' The man had even beat up Kandasami.

That day Kandasami had been well and truly trapped. Besides getting pulped till his back was swollen, he had been set free only when he had given a statement that he had tried to steal a silver vessel from their house, for which act he had humbly begged their pardon.

All this was an old story. After the aforesaid incident, Kandasami had vowed to not even blink in the face of palmistry. That was the reason that he was walking around with only three quarter-annas in his pocket.

A blind beggar was sitting at the edge of the road, an old cloth spread before him. There was one one-anna coin and two quarter-anna coins. Kandasami's hands itched to take away the one anna. He took out a quarter-anna from his bag (so that he could feign to put that in and snatch away the one anna). He had a suspicion and looked around. He noticed a policeman peering at him intently from the corner of the street. He dropped the quarter-anna that he had in his hand on to the beggar's cloth and walked away. A little distance away he spat out 'thoo', venting out all his anger.

Even a blind beggar had one and three-fourth annas. His fury spluttered when he counted that he had only two quarter-annas left. Fearing that even that would be in danger, he went to Saibu's tea-shop and bought a cup of tea. Once half a cup of tea went in, his brain started functioning. As soon as he finished drinking, he decided, 'Sabash! That is what I call work! No wonder tea is advertised so widely!'

It was largely the middle class who lived in Nellipakkam. Tiny bungalows in the middle of tiny gardens. The residents, office staff and clerks, earned between sixty-seventy rupees and three hundred-four hundred rupees. A few were retired officials and businessmen.

At eight in the morning, Srimaan K Ramakrishna Iyer was sitting in the main hall, newspaper in hand, when someone called out 'saar' from the corner of the window in the front. Iyer raised his voice and asked in irritation, 'Who is that, da?' When Kandasami replied, 'Police saar,' Iyer lowered his voice a bit and asked, 'What?'

'Rounds duty, saar.'

'So what about it?'

'All of us are going to celebrate Pongal, saar.'

'So? What should I do about it?'

'You can give how much ever you wish, saar.'

Ramakrishna Iyer thought for a minute. When he heard the word 'police' his heart had skipped a bit, but he had regained his composure. That Kandasami had come only to solicit funds made him glad. 'Yes. So much thieving going on these days, it's scary. Police protection is so necessary.' He thought a bit about how much to give, opened his wallet and took out four annas. 'Six of us are doing the rounds, saar!' He took out another two annas.

That day, by ten-thirty, Kandasami had earned twenty-four rupees and a bit. Since it was already hot, he decided to stop for the day. But he wanted to round it off to twenty-five rupees and then stop. If he were to wake up ten days in a row to the same auspicious face he got up to this morning, it would be enough. Then he could open a soda shop and make a living. Why, he could even get married!

He entered the house with the name-plate which said: 'Mr K Senapathy, GDA'. A man was sitting in the front hall. It was unfortunate that Kandasami didn't know that he wasn't Senapathy but his son Theerthapathy.

'Who is it? What do you want?' asked Theerthapathy calmly.

When Kandasami said, 'Police, saar,' there was a glow on Theerthapathy's face. But Kandasami didn't understand the import of it.

'Which police?'

'Town police only, saar.'

'What do you want?'

Kandasami parroted his usual spiel and said, 'You can give how much ever you like.'

'Okay, wait a bit,' Theerthapathy said, called out to a servant boy, wrote out something on a piece of paper and sent him away. He continued writing something else. Kandasami waited.

In a little bit a uniformed policeman appeared, stood in front of Theerthapathy and saluted.

Theerthapathy looked at him and shouted, 'What kind of job are you all doing, da? Lazy donkeys! Go and stand outside.' Kandasami who was standing by the steps whispered to the policeman, 'Who's this lordship?'

'Don't you know?' replied the policeman, 'Sub-inspector ayya.'

Only such tight situations reveal how valiant Kandasami was. He wasn't one to cower in front of any danger. He hastened towards the inspector, took out all the rupees and coins from his shirt pocket and placed it on the table. 'Lordship should forgive me,' he said.

'Is that all, da? Do you have anything else?'

'Not a paisa, your lordship!'

'Okay, get lost. If you do like this again, I'll finish you.'

'Lordship…'

'What, da?'

'My stomach is hungry. Something for a snack…'

'Okay. Take something and get lost.' The inspector took out two annas and flung them at him. Kandasami took it, went out, looked at the policeman and said, 'Lordship has asked you to go, brother. No work for you here now.'

Sub-inspector Theerthapathy immediately wrote out a letter to Circle Inspector Malayaperumal:

I hereby enclose rupees twenty-four as my contribution towards the dinner that we are hosting for Deputy Superintendent who has been transferred.

Your most obedient servant,

Theerthapathy

As he walked down the road with two annas in hand, Kandasami muttered to himself, 'The world is moving on the right track, all right. What belongs where, goes there.'

Original title: *Police Virundhu*
1935

The First Cheque Arrives! 17

Devan

When he began to pursue a career as a detective, Saambu actually brimmed with enthusiasm. His belief was all fired up because in novels he had read ever so many times that every clue and evidence was always unearthed only by detectives and while the police fumbled and floundered on the streets, it was they – the detectives – who came home with bouquets and bags of cash. But as the days went by, his ardour waned. The reason: no murders or robberies took place in the city, as he had expected. He bought newspapers and combed through them, not leaving a line. Hoping to find news of some mystery or two. But it wasn't to be.

All right, one wouldn't come by a case if one went about in such a fashion. Hence he decided to walk around in disguise, without anyone knowing. But Saambu in disguise attracted attention even from those who normally ignored him. And many of those whom he stalked protested vociferously. When a man with a stout stick ticked him off, 'If your face pops up in any place I go, this stick will split into pieces!', Saambu got nervous. Knowing fully well that his face would splatter into pieces before the stick split, Saambu stopped shadowing people. One evening, his enthusiasm completely dead, he leant against a park bench, eyes closed.

It was darkening quickly. Had he been in that position a while longer, he would have even nodded off. He got up with a start when he heard a couple of voices from behind. But he closed his eyes the next minute.

He heard a woman's voice: 'I didn't like the way you chopped it off like that.'

A man's voice asked, 'I did as you asked only. You are saying this because the body is full of blood marks, is it?'

'Who cares about that! I'm only worried now that we have to hide it without anyone knowing. Ayyo! Why did I ever say that! Just like that you've chopped it all off.'

'So what if I chopped it off? Who will do anything to me? As if I won't put it on someone else's head. If our police inspector hears of it, he won't leave it that easily. If nothing else works, I will tie a stone and drop it into the well in our backyard, all right?' Saying so, they started to move away slowly. Saambu, who had with great difficulty feigned sleep till they went some distance, opened his eyes with alacrity and sat up. His heart thumped. Aha! Here is the case which I've been waiting for all this while. A man and a woman are going to dump a body into a well. It has been hacked. Full of bloodstains. The police inspector is not going to leave it easily. What more proof do you want? 'Go behind the murderers, come what may!' exhorted his conscience. Saambu started off immediately, dogging them a hundred yards behind.

It didn't look as if they had noticed Saambu. They walked down the road. For about fifteen minutes, never turning back even once. Saambu too plucked up courage. Now the path crossed a bigger road. As the couple reached the junction, the tram arrived and they swiftly got into it.

Saambu, who was walking behind, never expected them to get on to a tram. When the tram started moving slowly, he reflexively ran behind it. Even today Saambu can't fathom why and how he ran. Running till his guts split, Saambu grasped the handle of the tram, but it never stopped. He ran along with it; it picked up speed and so did Saambu. Onlookers on the road raised a cry; the tram conductor shouted, but Saambu paid no heed to it. An unknown power entered his body and, in the end, with a giant effort he managed to leap into the tram.

Passengers in the tram stared at him, but an unfazed Saambu looked intently at the couple he had followed. Only when he noticed that they were facing away from him did peace descend on his heart.

The couple got down after a fifteen-minute journey. Since it had already become very dark Saambu boldly got down at the other end. It was easy now to follow them. Saambu worked tirelessly and was duly rewarded: he noted the bungalow that they entered.

He waited a while, groped his way to the gate and noticed a brass name-board beside it. When Saambu peered to decipher the name, an unexpected thing happened. A hand grasped his neck and shook it and a voice admonished: 'Adei! Rascal! What are you doing there? Come to snoop around, is it?' Saambu froze. He didn't have the courage to look back. His instincts informed him that it was the murderer who had grasped him. It would take two minutes to narrate all that had happened. But it all happened in just two seconds. Saambu felt as if he had been lifted to the sky and dropped to earth with a thud. When he came to, he realised that he was lying in a dark room, legs and arms tied tightly.

Somewhere a clock chimed ten. The door to Saambu's room opened. Within half a minute he heard a 'click' sound and a light, bright as milk, filled the room. Saambu rubbed his eyes. The lady stood in the middle of the room, a revolver in hand. Her freshly draped georgette sari and diamond jewellery glinted in the light.

She pressed her finger to her lips and signalled, 'Don't talk!' Then she neared and said, 'Oi! You foolish fellow! Your life will be over in an hour!'

Saambu's heart beat loudly. His lips twitched. And he was about to cry. The lady added, 'It's my husband who caught you. He's now adamantly insisting on killing you. If you harbour any hope of escape, drop it. Because Mangudi Mundan is on guard outside. He will squeeze you in a single grasp.'

'Mundan-aa?' mumbled Saambu. At that moment a terrifying laugh was heard outside.

'Did you hear that? That is Mundan. But I am determined to save you. So I will brave it even if my husband shouts at me. Because I don't want an innocent like you to die unnecessarily. Now I'm going to untie you. What do you say? If you get up to tricks after I untie you, look here, this revolver will drink up your life, do you understand?'

Saambu trembled at the sight of the revolver. In the next two minutes, he was untied and the ropes lay on the floor. Saambu flexed his arms; meanwhile the lady went out and was back with two cups of sherbet on a tray.

She said, 'You drink one and I will drink one.' It seemed to Saambu that she drank from one of the cups to instil confidence in him. But at the same time a big doubt consumed him. Poison! His cup may contain poison; her cup may not contain it. See how she has decided to kill me in such an easy fashion. And saying that she will save me! Saambu hesitated. He had just escaped from one danger, only to fall into another one.

At that very moment, Mundan arrived like a godsend and hastily called the lady outside. She put her cup down and went out hurriedly. Saambu quickly put down his cup and picked up the other. The next minute the lady appeared and took the cup that was on the floor, unaware of what had happened.

'Umm. Still not drunk it, is it? I'm going to drink it, see!' She quickly tossed it down. Saambu's heart fluttered, wondering what would happen. But the effect was seen earlier than expected. The lady fell down in a heap immediately.

Saambu thought, 'If I had drunk it, I too would have fallen like this!' His legs refused to cooperate. Knowing that danger was nearing every minute, Saambu summoned up courage, snatched the revolver from her hand, climbed out of the window and went near the gate. He heaved a big sigh of relief. 'Thank god! I escaped!' At that very instant, a policeman pulled Saambu's arm tightly and said, 'What, 'pa, what are you doing here?'

Not only was Saambu determined not to get caught this time, he was also ready to put the revolver to use. He heard a 'click' sound. But that policeman didn't die and fall down. He grasped Saambu even more tightly and dragged him into the bungalow. 'Ayyo, am I being thrown to the monsters again?' Saambu turned lifeless.

That man was sitting in the hall.

The policeman began to tell him, 'This fellow jumped from your house and ran out. Saar, I've caught him.'

Saambu wailed, 'Ayyo, police, saar! Let us run away from here. This man is a murderer. You don't know! He's committed a murder in this house and put the body somewhere. He'll kill us also!'

'Ei, shut up!' When the policeman sharply twisted his arm, Saambu piped down.

The man looked at Saambu and said, 'Adede! Uncle escaped, is it? Now only we shut him up in the room upstairs and closed the door!'

The policeman asked, 'This is your uncle, is it?'

'Yes, yes. You should have heard by now that we shut him up in a room. He's a bit…' The man tapped his finger on his temple.

'Okay, okay, I understand. Mad, is it?'

Saambu screamed, 'Ayyayo! I'm not mad. Not his uncle either. He's a murderer, a murderer!'

'See for yourself,' said the man.

'Yes, yes. But he's playing around with a revolver.'

'Revolver? That is a toy gun. We've given it to him simply. It's not dangerous.'

The policeman turned to leave.

Saambu hollered, 'Ayyo! Please don't leave!' It seemed as if the house would crumble down.

'I see, looks like a real hardened case!' Mumbling, the policeman hurriedly made his way out.

No point in shouting anymore, thought Saambu and gave up. But another surprise awaited him.

A lady came from inside the house. It was none other the one who he thought he had given the poison to. But now she was wearing an ordinary sari. Till now a fear had gripped Saambu. The fear that the man would finish him off for killing his wife.

Inappropriately, laughter welled up within Saambu. Why, at a time of such danger. Because only then the goddess of fortune began to shower her grace. Saambu laughed uproariously. He didn't stop even after ten minutes.

The deadly murderers looked at him astonished. Saambu stopped laughing, looked at the lady's sari and asked, 'Madam! Did you think that I would be taken in by a mere sari?' If you asked him now why he said such a thing, he wouldn't be able to answer.

Startled, the couple looked at each other. The man asked, 'Sit down, saar! You know everything already, is it?'

Saambu didn't know anything before. Yet he remarked, 'Uncle, is it? Fine uncle! Why don't you write this as a story, ayya, immediately!' They say that even the foolish are sometimes overcome with courage; it was such a courage that visited Saambu.

She said, 'What? You know everything, is it? Astonishing!'

Saambu didn't understand what she said as well. 'Like a fine cinema! A first-rate cinema. This is how a film should be!' Raising his voice, he said it to himself, shaking his head.

The man got up and grasped Saambu's hand. 'I thought you were an idiot. You behaved like one too! Now I know that you knew everything beforehand and purposely put on an act!'

The lady interrupted, 'How did you know that when we mentioned "kill", "bloodstain" and all in the park that it was all about my sari?'

There was only a muddle in Saambu's mind. He didn't know a thing about the sari. So, unable to utter a word, he only managed to nod his head.

The man said, 'Hearing you speak, I thought we had fooled you. But you seemed to know that I was writing a story for a film and that we used you as a test to find out if such a thing could happen in reality. You behaved like a fool who didn't know a thing till the end in this drama I staged. Now you are saying, the story is fantastic, it will make a very good film. Astonishing! Who are you? Please tell me your name first…'

Finally Saambu began to understand. He realised that a cinema writer had rattled him only to put his story to test. Something he had blabbered in the end seemed to unexpectedly yield good fortune.

It wasn't as if Saambu didn't know that the game would be over if he spoke more. So without opening his mouth, he handed his visiting card from his coat pocket.

The couple were stunned. The man said, 'Aha! Only now I understand. If you are a detective, you should be able to act till the very end, no? Because you are a pro, we didn't know that you were putting on an act all the while.'

Saambu's mind drifted off somewhere. His mouth muttered, 'Mangudi Mundan.'

'As if you won't know that. When you were acting, I only pretended to be Mangudi Mundan outside. My native place is Mangudi. My name is 'Mangudi Maharajan'. I write stories for films. That policeman who came now is my brother-in-law only.'

Saambu smiled. Everything seemed like a dream. That day Saambu returned home only very late in the night. The couple put him in a rickshaw with great ceremony.

Two days later a cheque arrived for Saambu. Mangudi Maharajan had sent it and had enclosed a letter: 'I've enclosed a cheque for hundred rupees. Day and night we are marvelling at your astute performance. A cinema company has bought my story to make a film. I'll never forget your help regarding this matter. I will definitely recommend you to my friends.'

Saambu bought a file and tucked in the first testimonial. He had earned success and money. No wonder he was elated!

Original title: *Mudhal Cheque Varukiradu!*
1942

CLAY

18

LA SA RAMAMRUTHAM

I sat in the pial of a hut, the thatch of which sloped so much inwards that it almost touched the head. He was sitting on his haunches on a grinding stone embedded in the earth.

'Just look at this heat! What can survive in it? Only in this Chinglepet district you will find such heat and such a rotten neighbourhood. Just keep walking on the road, and you will find in the middle, here and there, ten-fifteen houses with mere walls – all dissolved in the rains and withered away in the heat.

Water never remains here. They keep saying proudly, the rivers Palaar, Vegavathy and all, but I've seen only sand here. Ten months of the year, what I see is only sand. Whatever gathers in the ponds and lakes in the scanty rains, that's what is used for bathing, washing, drinking and even for the fields.

As for the grains, what sort of grain is that? The wind blowing through the tamarind trees is like fire, making you giddy. No dearth of firewood to burn the corpses. Arid earth. Even if you plough till you pull out the intestines of the earth, only the iron blade will get blunted, hitting ever so many rocks. A story here goes like this: a fellow said he was going to dig a well here. He kept on digging, no sign of water at all. The fellow never came out at all. This place's water situation is such!

There is no shortage of wisdom and penury in this place. If you say a tamarind fruit is hanging from a tamarind tree, no one will believe you. But if you say that a ghost is dangling from it, everyone will readily believe it. No one should wear a shirt on their body; if you do people will burn you with their very eyes. Any fellow who can string four words and read four letters is considered Lord Adhiseshan, known for his extraordinary intelligence.

Whatever it is, you must agree on this: everyone should survive, both the literate and the illiterate. Hunger is common to all.

As long as this life exists, we have to feed this one-span stomach and somehow survive, no? A human being gets together with four people, leaves them, fights with them, makes up with them; in between chicken pox, cholera, if nothing, then old age, all this sweeps him away. Even then there is so much desire for life, desires – what can one say? Everything is contained in that only – god, demon, even ghost, everything. If the saplings dry up for want of water, they take effigies in procession and cry. If there is too much water, a blouse piece, turmeric and lamp for the river goddess Ganga – all this placed on a winnowing tray and set afloat on water. Your anger should abate, you must protect us, Mother – thus he prays to Goddess Yellaiamman. Why I am telling you all this is because there is so much contained in this thing called hope. What is in this body is not life. Hope only is life.

It is only from such hope that this place itself came into being in the beginning. What else would they have had in mind, the four-five people who built their huts here all those years ago? As far as I can remember this place has always been cast aside. We have to buy everything, from salt to camphor, in the weekly market that takes place every month eight miles from here. Yet, by the time I was old enough to understand, the four huts had grown into forty, just on hope alone.

At that time a man and woman came to live here. I don't know if they were husband and wife. The woman didn't have a thaali around her neck. Had a bundle on her back and a child on her hip. That's how she came. He came pushing a potter's wheel. Just see there – on the incline there, where the thatch has fallen in, that hut only was theirs. Can you see the pit in front – there was a drumstick tree there. She tied a sari to a branch, put the child in that makeshift cradle, kneaded the clay, and he himself built a wall, wove the thatch from the palm leaves to make the roof. Then he set up the wheel in front and started making pots.

I must admit one thing: there isn't a single good-looking person in our village. No one has the time or the means to dress up. Should they doll up, there are no eyes to see it anyway. Even so, I've never seen three such ugly people, he, she and the child. If someone curses someone in the village, they will say: did he leap from a branch or what? If you saw these three, they looked like as if they leapt from a branch only. Do you understand what I'm saying? Yes, you're laughing, you understood, no?

Her teeth didn't fit into her mouth; they jutted out, stained with tobacco, red like blood. Two slits for eyes, slashed, as if for form's sake. Hair plaited. Two holes for a nose, just so she could breathe. If she was like this, to him she was the apsara Ramba herself. Torn lips hanging to the stomach. Yes, like that only. You yourself imagine how bad she looked. On top of it, a scar running down her cheek.

Sheer beasts.

Their behaviour too was as if they were from the wilds. Terribly rough. One day I happened to pass by that side. They were both arguing. He had heaped clay on the wheel and was spinning it. Suddenly a leap, a pair of feet springing from the ground, as if flying, and the way he slapped her against her mouth with the back of his hand, I was dumbstruck. What a blow! Like a shovel. Blood spurted out from her lips.

She saw me. It didn't matter that her husband had hit her. She was furious because I saw her. She abused me in the filthiest of language and hurled a stone at me. I ran for dear life. I was a small boy then.

Their affection too was like that only. I told you they had a child – what to say of its beauty? What can I say – can tuvaram paruppu sprout if you sow avarai bean? Even so, it was their child, wasn't it? Their entire lives centred on this fellow who had a head like a palmyra-seed. At the lamp-lighting time of dusk, joy would fill the yard. My throat would ache, spitting out in disapproval.

The little Manmatha was never to be seen around. They themselves didn't have a friendly nature; they would look as if they would bite us. Even we villagers didn't take to them. Just one good thing. If you needed to buy a pot and pan, you had to go to the weekly market and trudge back eight miles with them. But this time we could buy the Pongal pot in our own village. There's a thrill in that, no? Days went by and Pongal too neared.

The month of Aipasi went away, the month of Karthigai was half over, and now if we crossed Margazhi, it would be Pongal.

But by then something happened: the child died.

Would you need a reason for a child's death? Big-big men too suddenly croak. The cold would have settled on the chest. Perhaps the gruel would have gone up the nose. Just telling you how it can all be.

Placing the child on a sheet in front of the house, the woman lay beside it, curled up. He stood beside her, hands folded on the chest. He didn't weep. Eyes were red, as if he had drunk toddy. Two-three people in the neighbourhood went to their house out of kindness. Death, big or small – a man can't cope with it alone.

'Ayyo, so sad. You came to make a living here, and look what happened,' said one of them. One had to say something, no?

You should have seen the way the man growled in anger.

'Enough, enough. Who asked you people to come? You and your village…'

Who could do anything with a man like this? As if it was our fault that his child died.

I've seen it once – there was a cat in our village. Its kitten died. The cat just sat next to it. Didn't allow anyone to come near it. The dear kitten lay there for three-four days, stinking.

At high noon he slung the shovel over his shoulder, snatched the corpse from her forcefully, clutched it in one hand and set off beyond the village. The child's legs and arms dangled loose.

Who could do anything with a man like that?

We never heard the sound of crying after that from their house. Even so, at times, she, who would be at work, would suddenly lift her head and stare at the path he had taken, shovel and baby in hand. Standing on the heap of clay she had gathered. It could be seen from that tamarind tree beyond.

Once two-three of us along with a couple of children walked along the road to the weekly market. She walked up to us, a basket of clay on her head. She also had a dry lump of clay in her hand. The children who were looking this way and that playfully dashed against her. The way she looked at them – the eyeballs rolled in the white of her eyes. God knows what fury she suppressed. The lump in her hand got crushed to dust.

But would the stomach obey if you melt for a child? One had to get on with one's work. That too the festival of Pongal was nearing. The conch you blow for death, if you blow it at the crack of dawn with joy, wouldn't you feel happy? The conch seemed to say: Pongal is here, so near. Shouldn't we make the Pongal pot?

You people who ink white paper always look down upon labourers. You will easily say that the hands can do what the eyes see. Take this clay business. Do you know how difficult it is? You have to collect it, legs and arms aching, then you have to knead it and stamp on it carefully. Do you think it is easy to make a pot? How many fall apart at the wheel! And then when you have to close the bottom you have to tap it with a wooden plank, then tap it thrice to shape it, and then when you leave it to dry in the sun, do you know how many get cracked? And how many get cracked when you put it in the kiln. For the labour involved, the price you pay is nothing. People say it's only clay – if you say that, then everything is mud only, no? I am clay, you are clay, everything is clay.

In the teeth-chattering cold of the early Margazhi morning, when you hear the sound of pot-making 'lottu, lottu', every pat will seem to whisper into the ears of those sleeping: 'Pongal is nearing.'

Of all of our festivals, Pongal is the one dear even to the poor. The rest are all only for the rich. In any poor household, the pongal has to be cooked only in a new pot. We are all poor.

We dig a hearth in the middle of the yard, make the pongal boil over, then put it in a leaf, make a hole in the middle, pour milk, show it to the sun and shout: 'Pongalo pongal!' Whether good times begin or not, the month of Thai begins. Besides, hope dawns for a new beginning.

Everyone in the village is united in this thought. Even if they make rice every day in a bronze pot in the village chief's house, on Pongal day it is always made in a new clay pot.

If it is Pongal tomorrow, only this evening they will buy the pot. There are some who buy the pot on the day of Pongal also. A new life dawns. This time no one went to buy the pot at the weekly market in Margazhi. This time no pot from the market place; the pot will be from our own place. This itself made us so happy, you know.

I'm not that educated. But our village, our country, our nation, it's all one and the same, isn't it?

Setting off to buy a new pot itself is like a festival for the womenfolk. They may just take ten paces, but they will gather in crowds of four and five, tuck a drawstring purse in the waist, suck on tobacco in the sides of the mouth, make merry, chatter away and walk towards the potter's place. I saw it all standing far away.

The pots were placed beautifully, one on top of the other, fenced off by a rope on all sides in front of the house. He had made so many pots, enough for three Pongals. Pongal pot, water pot, vegetable pan, row pots, they were all there.

The two of them were waiting for everyone, smiles on their faces. It was a wonder to see them smiling.

The bargaining didn't begin immediately. The woman said, 'Let everyone come. We want to see the entire village together.'

In a while a crowd gathered, children and tiny tots, youngsters and elders, in front of the potter's house. There was a buzz.

The woman asked in a loud voice, 'Has everyone come?'

'Yes.' Just imagine this one word coming out of the mouths of about hundred people at the same time.

The woman, laughing, kicked at a row of pots stacked in front of her.

It was only a single kick. But that row toppled over the next, those two over the next, and the next... Have you seen pots breaking row after row? Have you at least heard of it? How many pots!

We didn't know what to say or do. When the pots broke, something in our gut too shattered.

'You and your village.' The woman hissed like a snake. She hastily bent down, picked up a fistful of mud and blew it into the air. 'Our child is gone. We too are going. You all be happy.' Both of them strode away hurriedly. They disappeared from our view. We turned into stone, standing where we were.

Not even one pot was spared. In a moment, the place had become like a graveyard.

After that the village never prospered, dogged by something or the other. Even the usual rains failed. All the crops died. Cholera swept away whoever it could. Of those left, many started leaving, one by one. Everyone was possessed by fear.

What is left if there is no new pot in the village for Pongal? You yourself tell me. What is there after hope itself is gone?

Original title: *Maan*
1961

Godavari Gundu 19

Thi Janakiraman

The scales of the wastepaper man were the handiwork of a goldsmith who made ornaments for the gods. It would show six palams even if you placed an elephant on it. So what chance did a six-month bundle of newspapers have? Applying castor oil to my eyes and not looking this-way-that-way even for a second, I watched over the needle intently.

'Is amma there?' asked a voice at just that moment; I lifted my head. The woman stood there grinning from ear to ear. Her name was Ganga or Godavari or something – couldn't remember properly. Some river's name, of that I was sure. She had something stuffed on her hip, hidden under the ends of her sari.

'She's inside. Go in,' I said. The pleats of her sari rustling, she crossed the hall and went in, that woman.

I peered at the needle of the scales. It was a divine needle, after all! Sixty newspapers or even half a newspaper? Would it falter? Uuhmmm… When would the time dawn for me to get my own scales? Ishwara!

I uttered the last sentence loudly. Which worm would put up with such swindling?

'What, saami! You are saying such things about these scales. It will show the difference between a blank card and a written one, saami. If you have doubts, go fetch a pair of scales from the shop... why should I earn a bad name from you?'

Where was the time to go to the shops? And at nine-thirty in the morning, would a shopkeeper attend to his business or lend his scales? Not even half an hour left for me to start for office – I had yet to bathe and eat! Enough if I saw a few rupees, I felt. Otherwise why would I have left a Sunday and chosen a 'home says go-go office says come-come' of a Thursday to sell old newspapers!

Darkness seemed menacing in two or three ways. It was two months since the last date for payment of electricity bills. If left unpaid today, darkness would envelop us. Who could wrestle with that hurricane lamp, which would jump up and down 'tak tak' and would be snuffed out in a minute?

The daughter was sitting inside with a long face. Wouldn't go to school, she said. Some priest had to be given eight annas. This was another nuisance, the convent nuisance – as if the school fees weren't enough, money was collected in the name of every saint. If she didn't get the eight annas, she would not be in peace today.

Six months' daily newspapers, weekly magazines, all of them amounted to six and a half rupees.

'How much did he give?' asked Gowri, as soon as the paper fellow left.

'Six and a half rupees.'

'For six months paper-aa?'

'Why are you fretting now? Should have done it when he was here.'

'I was talking inside.'

'Then don't come here and nag.'

'I won't say anything. I need two rupees.'

'Two rupees? What for?'

'I need it.'

'The electricity bill is three and a quarter rupees, an eight anna for your daughter, for you two rupees. What will I do with the remaining three-fourth rupee – tiffin, betel leaf, areca nut shavings, bus fare!'

'I have packed tiffin for you – peppered beaten rice. '

'Coffee?'

'I've kept some in the thermos flask.'

'Betel leaf?'

'That also I've folded and kept.'

'Ok, I have enough bus fare for Thursday, Friday, Saturday, those three days. What about Monday?'

'What about it now? We'll see about that later.'

'How will we see?'

'Ask that singer Subramaniayyar.'

All the seven chords of my voice died down. It had been Gowri's habit for the past two years to use Subramaniayyar's name to seal my lips. In the year nineteen hundred and fifty-six, the singer Subramaniayyar took ten rupees from me, saying that he would return it the next day. He engraved the word 'tomorrow' on the wall of the mind. Because it is said that you would never recover your loan if you didn't ask for it, I began asking from the year nineteen hundred and fifty-nine. He ran and hid, smooth-talked, begged, but money alone he never parted with.

In the end, he came one day. 'It seems you know the manager in the Talaivaasal office. My son has finished his studies. For the past year he has sent out a hundred applications. No job... Will you please see him and...' 'Ok,' I replied. Now I hid from him. As soon as he'd see my head, he'd start, 'Did you see that manager in Talaivaasal...' Seeing his tuft and his green cycle, even a mile away, I would enter into any nearby street as fast as my feet would allow. The words 'did you see that manager in Talaivaasal' rose in my mind and chased me.

'Why do you need two rupees?'

'Gangabai wants it... Come here,' Gowri said, raising her voice.

Gangabai came. A double barrel. Hair half grey. A Maharashtrian-style sari tucked between the legs. Black beads on the neck. Well-combed plait twisted into a wheel at the back of the head. About fifty years of age. She took out a bronze vessel from the ends of her sari and kept it in front of her.

'She wants us to keep this Godavari gundu and give her two rupees,' said Gowri.

Godavari gundu was a huge vessel. You could cook two big measures of rice in it. Scrubbed with tamarind, it shone.

'Weren't you the one who kept a bronze vessel a couple of months ago and borrowed a rupee?'

'Yes. That was the Nachiar Kovil vessel. A one-measure pot!'

'You haven't even redeemed that yet!'

'I will redeem this one and that in a month. I am terribly short of money now.'

I had seen that Nachiar Kovil pot just half an hour ago. It was kept upturned in the mango-wood loft above the kitchen shelf. I had been looking at it for the past two months. When a couple of guests arrived for the Ganesha festival, Gowri even cooked rice in it, if I remembered right.

'It's been two months. And you couldn't even redeem for one rupee that small pot. And now this?'

'Don't think like that. In fifteen days if I don't come take these two, then you ask me.'

'No, 'ma… Just take it and leave. Our own necks are choked with lack of cash. I am not in a position to give you.'

'You mustn't say that.'

'What do you mean, mustn't say! You yourself saw, no? That I gave papers to that paper fellow and got some money,' I replied, my footsteps guiding me to the backyard to bathe. In a minute Gowri followed me.

'If you don't have two rupees, why don't you give at least one…' she dragged on the words.

'No rupee or kupee.'

'She's begging, can't you see?'

'And whom will I beg from…' I rolled my eyes. 'If I want even a 'single tea' at four in the evening, I have to jingle someone else's pocket. One-rupee loan she will give, it seems. Don't ask me anything now. It's late. I have to bathe.'

Even after I came back from the bath I saw Gangabai standing in the hall.

Frowning, I went into the kitchen.

'What?'

'Why are you snarling? She doesn't have, that's why she's asking.'

'Even here we don't have.'

'Mkum… We don't have! As if she's asking you simply? She's pledging something and then only asking for money. If she goes to the shop he will give her thirty rupees for that Godavari gundu. If she pledges such a big thing for just a rupee, it must be a head-rolling crunch, no?'

'Yes, yes.'

'You don't have any compassion at all, is it? You will give that Singer Subramaniayyar tens and twenties and don't mind running after him. But this innocent thing, this poor creature is asking for just a rupee, keeping a three-measure bronze vessel as pledge… For that you are making such a fuss.'

I came to a decision in a flash. 'See here, if she wants, ask her to take a rupee. And it should be returned in ten days.' I handed over the rupee.

She who went to the hall came back in a trice. The Godavari gundu shone brightly in her hand.

'You know, if she had kept it at the Sait's shop, he would have given her ten rupees.' Gowri kept it on the floor, lifted it up and swirled it around, as if fondling a child.

'M…m. Ten rupees, it seems. He will also charge fifteen rupees interest.'

'Poor thing. Don't know what difficulty she is in. Kept this and took a rupee. If she has to pledge something, she must be in a terrible state, poor thing. If her husband had been smart enough, will she be suffering like this?'

'Dattoji Rao is not a man without any means. He also earns something, no?'

'What kind of earning he does? Like a seasonal bird. He has to run here and there, and push ahead and earn. They need one full gunny bag of red gram alone for three months.'

'For his brains and education, that is all he can earn.'

Gowri kept looking at the Godavari gundu again and again when she served me food. Navarathri was round the corner. At least on one of the nine days if she didn't put it on the fire she wouldn't have any peace.

On my way to the office I kept looking at the entrance of the Konganeswaran temple. As was his wont, Dattu was sitting there. The perennial smile on the face. You ought to draw a portrait of Dattu. Such a fine face and body. A chest neatly split into two. A child's stomach. Broad shoulders. Medium height. An old Peshwa regal look. A drooping moustache. He was about fifty-five. But you would think he was about forty. Not a single grey hair. One look at Ganga and you would guess she was fifty. Only because he was her husband you would presume he would be above fifty. Otherwise you wouldn't put him beyond forty.

Dattu wouldn't budge from the pial of the Konganeswaran temple. They always came there to fetch him. The priests who belonged to his community. He neither had the learning nor the capacity to mug up the chants necessary for a priest's profession. He went as a helper. He would hold out his hand for a dakshinai of one or two annas. If you asked him to eat, he would. He usually sat in the temple pial, one leg over the other, grooming his moustache with his middle finger.

If there was a bhajan in any matham, he would go there, clutching a mridangam in his right hand. With just a single beat 'dhim-dhim-dharu dhim-dhim-dharu' he would keep the beat to all the tunes. Besides that, he could bang 'thakajunu thom' three times for the finale. Otherwise he didn't know anything more about beats. But there was something pleasing about his music – like his smile.

The man never got angry. Even if you scolded him. Always a smile. Never walked fast. Never in a flutter. Never raised his voice.

His house was ten houses away from the temple. His own house too. How could he afford to pay rent? It was a house that he had inherited. But to recognise that it was indeed a house you needed a research-oriented mind. A big platform four feet above the street. Must have been part of the base of a big house. At the back end of the platform you could see a black and grey wall. The only sign that revealed that there must have existed a house earlier was this: the wall of the single-roomed tenement. That was where Gangabai did everything, including cooking and sleeping; the rest of the time she sat on the steps which led into the street at the end of the platform. When I crossed the house, she was opening the door, clutching some packet… The rupee I had given hadn't been wasted, after all. I don't know why I had haggled so cheaply for just a rupee! Does meanness need a time and place to descend on a human being?

Gangabai's sari had at least fifteen patches as far as the eye could see. Dattoji's dhoti would have a few more, not less. It was a good thing that Dattu had taken on a job that involved eating – at least he had that much luck. And that job actually came with money. But even that seemed to have slackened now. Who fed the priests like in the days of yore? The days of giving veshti and towel on ritual occasions too were gone. Why else would Dattu have a sieve of a veshti? At least if the priest knew mantras and stuff there was a chance of getting by. Of what use was an unskilled person?

I couldn't fathom why people believed that the creator would provide for the stomach. But here, the pot meant for feeding the stomach itself had been pawned.

Why had I created such a fuss to give a single rupee? Why hadn't I given a rupee without taking that Godavari gundu? As usual, these questions popped up in hindsight.

All the places where I usually saw Gangabai came to mind. Wherever there was a marriage, an annadhaanam or a ritual such as samaaradhanai, you could find her. Big or small, in any wedding she would wait for the hosts, VIPs and friends to eat, a Poona tumbler in hand, seated on the pial, for the last round of eating when they would serve the dregs of the food. In the temple samaraadhanai during Navarathri, however, you would see her in the first round of eating itself. If there was nothing, you would find her wandering around with a tin dabba, trying to sell puffed rice or beaten rice which she herself had flattened. Today it looked as if she didn't have even that.

Dattu's forefathers were believed to have been priests in the palace. These vessels, Nachiar Kovil pot and Godavari, all of them must have been amassed by the family at that time. Dattu's education wouldn't even earn him an iron pot. Also, looking at him, no one would want to give him such a cheap thing. Why, he looked so regal, moustache and all! Oh lord, you made him poor, yes, but couldn't you have at least made him decrepit and dark, like something a dog had torn apart! Did you have to make him tall and handsome, moustache and all? To give alms one ought to feel a hint of pity and compassion. You created him to appear rich, but you omitted to bestow him with luck and brains… che! Was god such a below-average creator?

'What, ayya! So deep in thought today! You're looking at the wall! At the floor! You scribble something! You get up and stand!' commented his colleague Pakkirisami loudly.

'Nothing. You mind your own business!'

'Tell me, no. Let me also know what it is.'

'What are you going to do, knowing it? You're going to give me ten rupees or what, saying "here 'pa, don't struggle so much"?'

'Oho – it's like that, is it? Why? It's only the tenth of the month! What 'pa, you started moaning already! I can't give five or ten. Just wait for two days! I'll start moaning along with you!'

'Why? You give your newspapers every month, is it?'

'Oho, even that you finished doing, is it? You're a smart fellow!'

The peppered beaten rice wasn't good at all in the afternoon.

As usual, the office closed shop at six. The afternoon tiffin had burnt off in a trice, like grass in a forest flame, and my stomach was still on fire.

I walked, thinking of the clock-tower hotel. I was just about to enter the hotel when there was Dattoji standing in front of the betel-leaf shop, looking up at the clock's hand! There he was, moustache and all, dressed in a patched-up dhoti, when the world, full of cars, buses and pedestrians, whizzed past him southwards and northwards. He stood looking at the clock leisurely. What was the occasion to look at the clock? Or did he merely stand there marvelling at the extraordinary thing called a clock tower?

'What, Rayarvaal?' I called out. A slight surge of compassion poured out of my mind.

Dattu turned around. Saw me. Widened his smile. 'Last-house saar-aa? Namaskaram, saar. Can't get your audience these days.' He walked towards me.

'What, you've come so far? And looking at the clock too! What's the matter?'

'Just like that only I came. She asked me to come.'

'Who?'

'My wife only. She's gone to the bioscope – the three o'clock show. She'll come at six-fifteen, it seems. She asked if I could pick her up. That's why I'm here.'

'She's gone to the cinema-va?'

'Yes – in this theatre only.'

'Why didn't you go?'

'Had money only for one ticket. That too she would have got it only by chance.'

'But shouldn't you go along with her…?'

'No saar. Listen, I'll tell you. Early in the morning a woman brought jasmine from Reddypalayam. Rare to get jasmine in the month of Purattaasi, no? Immediately, my wife bought a heap. She gathered the flowers in the ends of the sari and went in. Didn't have any money. Will anyone return the flowers bought in the morning? She asked the neighbour. Didn't get anything. Then she took a pot, kept it in someone's house and came back with a rupee. The jasmine cost only ten annas. She had six annas remaining. "What to do with it?" she asked. "Some new film is coming today. Why don't you see it," I said. So she said "yes" and she came. And now I must pick her up.'

'Shameless creatures!' I wanted to shout out.

'Shut your mouth, you insensitive creature,' said a voice, grinding its teeth. I didn't turn around to see who it was. It was my voice only from deep within.

'What a stupid brain,' said the mind, tapping the cheeks in remorse.

'Join me for coffee?' I asked. Dattu came without hesitation.

When I returned home the jasmine string on Gowri's hair cast a romantic spell. It seems Gangabai had given it saying, 'I've brought for you, maami.'

No other jasmine in the world has the aroma of Reddypalayam jasmine. Appa! What fragrance!

Original title: *Godavari Gundu*
1961

THE CHAIR 20

KI RAJANARAYANAN

A house without a chair?

Suddenly everyone in our house began to feel this way. That was it: it was put on the family 'agenda' and discussions began.

The day before, a family friend had paid us a visit. He was a sub-judge. Couldn't he have come like one of us, in a veshti and shirt? No, he arrived in 'suit-boot' and all. There was only a three-legged stool in our house. It measured a mere three-fourth foot; to churn curd, Paati, our grandmother, would sit only on it. She was quite heavy. Our grandfather had asked the carpenter to make it somewhat broader.

The sub-judge too was a little portly. Since we didn't possess any other furniture, we brought that for him. Placing one hand on its edge, he made to sit down. One wretched thing about this stool: if you didn't place the weight exactly above the legs, it would topple over. Ever so many times we had fallen down when we stood on it carelessly to steal ghee from the rope-net. Poor thing – just as we were about to caution the sub-judge, he fell down with a thud and rolled over. Me, my brother and my littlest sister couldn't contain our giggles, so we ran to the back garden. Just as we thought our chuckles had subsided, our sister would mimic the sub-judge, leaning her hand and rolling on the floor. Our laughter only lengthened.

There was another reason for our giggles – the memory of our parents suppressing their giggles in front of the guest who had tumbled over.

So when we finished laughing on everyone's behalf and pussyfooted into the house, the stout guest was not to be seen. And neither was the stool. 'Did he take it away with him?' asked my sister to me.

After this incident, it was decided that a chair would be made for our home. The one practical difficulty in getting it made was that there wasn't a single chair in our village to show as a model. Besides, there wasn't a single carpenter either who knew how to make one.

'No problem. We can buy one from the town,' suggested my brother, Pedanna. Our father rejected it, saying it wouldn't be sturdy.

Athai, our aunt, said that there was a skilled carpenter in the neighbouring village. That there wasn't a chair he hadn't made. And that the governor himself had praised him.

When my mother heard my aunt's second sentence, she turned her face, as if to say, 'Yes, yes, she's seen everything!'

My father called a worker, despatched him to the carpenter's village, and came and sat with us. Now there was discussion on the kind of wood to be used for the chair.

'Teak is the best. That's what will be light to lift and carry around and be sturdy at the same time,' said our grandmother, pressing her stretched legs. (Our paati was extremely fond of her legs. She was forever stroking them.)

At that moment, our maternal uncle, Maamanaar, walked in. Pedanna ran and brought the stool. For a while, the whole house spluttered into giggles before things settled down.

Maamanaar himself had chosen a spot to sit whenever he visited our house. Chop off his head, and he'd still sit there and nowhere else. He would lean against the pillar adjoining the wall to the south of the storeroom. The first thing he would do as soon as he sat down was to loosen his tuft, give it a good shake, scratch his head and tie it back tightly. He observed this ritual unfailingly. Then he would inspect the floor around him. 'Didn't see any money falling from your head,' Anna would say with an impudent smile.

He would always be pierced with such paper arrows whenever he visited us. He would sit mum with a smile, like a stone Pillaiyaar, as if to say, 'You are my relatives – if you don't tease me, who will?' When our ridicule overstepped the limits, Amma would pretend to chide us. The last word always ended in 'you donkeys'.

As soon as Maamanaar sat down, Amma went towards the kitchen. Like a lamb, Appa followed her. In a while Amma appeared in the passage, a silver tumbler of buttermilk seasoned with asafoetida in her hand, followed by Appa, who, unseen by her, aped her movements for our benefit, as if to say, 'Her brother has come, it seems. Look at her taking buttermilk for him with so much care.'

The aroma of the buttermilk and the asafoetida made us want to drink it right away.

We believed that Maamanaar visited us mainly to drink buttermilk. The buttermilk from our cow was that divine. Besides, we thought that our uncle was the stingiest person in the village. We firmly believed he never gave away anything to anyone.

He himself had gone to Kannaavaram to buy this famed black-tongued milch cow for his sister. My younger brother and sister doted on its calf. Whenever he came over, and just before he left, he always went around the cow, gave it a pat (he was afraid his own evil eye would fall on it!), and uttered words of praise, even if he was thrifty with them. My little siblings always had this big fear that once the milk dried up, the cow would be taken away to his house, along with the calf.

The anticipation of this imagined separation only increased their fondness for the calf and their bitterness towards Maamanaar. Whenever he relished the buttermilk, these small children punched and pinched with their very stares.

Maamanaar showed interest in the debate about the chair. He let it be known that he too would like one to be made for him. We too were glad to have a partner in this enterprise.

Maamanaar said that the neem tree was the best. It would keep the body cool. And keep off piles.

When he expounded on the neem tree, Appa looked at him with round-eyed astonishment. Only the day before Appa had been talking to a farmhand about cutting down an ancient, diamond-hard neem tree in our cattle-pasture and laying it out to dry. Pedanna said, 'Making it out of poovarasu wood would be really good. It's a fine-grained wood, without knots. And glossy and strong too.'

Our elder sister said, 'All these are light-coloured woods. Ugly to look at! After a while, we'll begin to even detest them. I'm saying it will be best to make it the colour of ripe sugarcane or dark like sesame oilcake. But it's your wish...' The vision of a highly comfortable chair – in black wood with a mirror-like gleam, with perfectly shaped front legs, and curved back legs, yawning languorously, to match the recline of the chair – flashed before our eyes.

Everyone felt that she was right. So it was arranged for two chairs to be made immediately, one for us and the other for Maamanaar.

When the two chairs arrived, we didn't know which one to keep and which to send to Maamanaar. If you looked at one, you didn't need to see the other – they were like Rama-Lakshmana. We kept one and sent the other to Maamanaar. We had a doubt: had we sent the better one to him?

One by one, we took turns to sit on the chair. Never felt like getting up from it. But had to because others too had to be given a chance. Pedanna sat and exclaimed appreciatively, 'Ah...ha!' He ran his hands over the arms of the chair. He sat cross-legged on it. Athai said, 'We have to stitch a cover for it. Otherwise it will get soiled.'

My little sister and brother fought over it frequently. She would shout at him, 'You've been sitting on it for so long, get up. I want to sit now.'

'Ayyo, I've just sat down. Look at her, Amma,' he would say, his face puckering, as if about to cry.

The news of the arrival of our chair spread like fire around the village. People – children and adults – arrived in hordes to see the chair. A few even stroked it. An old man lifted the chair. 'Quite heavy. He's made it sturdy,' he commended the carpenter.

A few days passed by.

One night, someone knocked on the door. Pedanna, who was sleeping in the inner pial, opened the door. They said that an important person had just died in the village and that they needed the chair.

Since the deceased was also known to us, we too attended the funeral. It was on our chair that they had propped up the eminent person!

Till now in our village they always seated the corpse only on the floor. A grinding stone was laid on the floor and propped up to keep the corpse from rolling away. A gunny sack stuffed with millet straw would be rested against it. Against this bolster the corpse would be placed, as if reclining on it.

From where our townspeople picked up this new fad of propping up a corpse on a chair, we had no clue, but from that day troubles began for our chair. (They had moved from floor-tickets to chair-tickets!)

When the 'occasion' in that household was over, they left the chair in our front yard. The children of the house were scared even to look at the chair. We had the servant take it to the well and give it a good, hard scrub with hay, and wash it down with fifteen big buckets of water. Even after several days, no one had the guts to sit on it. We didn't know how to bring it back into use.

Fortuitously, a guest visited our house one day. We had the chair brought for him. 'Don't bother, I'll sit here,' he said, and went towards the cloth-mat. We were afraid that he would sit on the floor. The whole family persuaded him to sit on the chair. As soon as he sat down, my little brother and sister fled to the garden in the backyard. Now and then, they peeped in to see what happened to the man on the chair.

The next day a local elder dropped by and chose to sit on the chair on his own, bringing us even more relief. ('He's rehearsing on the chair now itself,' whispered Pedanna in my ear!)

This is how we 'seasoned' the chair. First the elders in the family sat on it. The children were still afraid. My little sister would beg my little brother, 'Why don't you sit on it first, da?' He would retort instantly, 'Why don't you sit and see?'

Suganthi, from the neighbouring street, came by and put her baby brother on the chair. It was only from then on that the children of our house sat on the chair without fear.

Again one night someone died and they took away the chair. This happened ever so often.

We sent away the chair with sadness. The mourners who came interpreted our sadness differently. They assumed that we too were mourning for the dead.

We were irritated that our sleep was being thus disturbed. Akka remarked one day, 'God knows why these wretched people have to go and die at such unearthly hours!'

Anna said exasperatedly, 'Good chair we made. For the corpses of our village to sit on. Tchai!'

'All because the chair was ordered at an inauspicious time,' said our aunt.

Pedanna finally thought of an idea. We kept it to the two of us.

Amma sent me on an errand to Maamanaar's house one day. When I entered his house, there he was, sitting in splendour on his chair and popping betel leaves into his mouth. It was an interesting pastime in itself to see him prepare and chew the betel leaves. Carefully, with utmost gentleness so as not to injure it, he would open his beloved betel box. A span wide, an elbow long, and four fingers high, he would clean and burnish it every day till it shone like gold. He would reverently take out his paraphernalia, as if taking out things from a pooja-box. Though he wiped the betel leaves clean, he never pinched off the stalk. (So thrifty was he!) If he found a coarse leaf, he would strip the veins off. Which always made us think of the old riddle-chant about betel leaves:

Catch hold of Muthappan, strip off his spine,
Smear him with fresh butter…

He would sniff the broken arecanut. Sniffing was supposed to ward off 'intoxication'. Then he would blow on the nut. To get rid of invisible arecanut worms, that's why. This sniffing and blowing, slow to begin with, would increase in speed, hand moving from nose to mouth, until with great noise, oom oosh, oom oosh, it was popped into the mouth – tabak!

To find out how tidy a person is, all one has to do is to look at his lime-paste dabba. Where this was concerned, Maamanaar was unmatched. Even the excess lime-paste on his finger wasn't wiped off unnecessarily on other objects. You could press his lime-paste dabba to your eyes with reverence. His Eveready torch, bought fifteen years ago, was still in use, bright and spanking new, as if bought just now. The one bought by our family at the same time had sprung a leak. Dented, yellowing and pitiable, it looked like a chronic patient about to die.

No one but him could use the chair in his house. The first thing he did as soon as he got up every morning was to wipe it. Had it to be shifted, he himself carried it and put it down carefully, as if placing down gently a mud pot brimming with water.

As soon as he saw me, Maamanaar greeted me, 'Welcome, dear nephew! Won't you have some betel?' Then he himself answered, 'If schoolboys start chewing betel, chickens will start butting!'

I conveyed to him what Amma asked me to and returned home.

At an ungodly hour in the night, there was a knock on the door. Everyone at home was fast asleep. I woke up Pedanna.

A few people from a house of bereavement stood outside for the chair. Pedanna took them into the street. I too followed. When they finished telling us what they came for, Pedanna replied patiently, 'Chair only, no? It's in our Maamanaar's house. Go and ask him, he will give it.' After sending them off, we returned home, chuckling noiselessly.

Tossing, Appa asked sleepily, 'Who was it?'

'What else – some fellows want our bullocks for threshing.'

Pulling the bedsheet tightly over him, Appa turned and went back to sleep.

Now it was raining in Maamanaar's forest!

After many days, when I visited Maamanaar, he was sitting on the floor preparing betel leaves. He greeted me with his usual smile and banter.

'What is this? You're sitting on the floor! Where is the chair?' I searched around. Smearing the lime-paste on the back of the betel leaf, he looked intently at me and smiled. He then said calmly, 'I asked them to keep the chair for that purpose alone. Anyway, you need one for that too, no?'

I didn't know what to say. I hurried home to convey this news to Pedanna. But gradually, my steps slowed to an ordinary gait.

Original title: *Naarkaali*
1969

Two Different Estimates 21

Ku Azhagirisamy

Nammalvar Naidu died yesterday in his seventieth year. A ripe old age. A grand life, lived to the fullest. Owned over three hundred acres. He saw grandsons and granddaughters and closed his eyes, satisfied. His last journey too was seen off with great fanfare. His passing away was not merely a disappearance of a physical self, leaving behind fame in its wake. It seemed as if an era, an entire world had died along with him.

Shanmugam hadn't been aware that Naidu had passed away yesterday. That fact grieved him more than Naidu's death. He'd got the news only this morning and had come running from his town. He went straight to the burial ground, prayed in front of Naidu's ashes and came to the town to see me.

He asked the reason for his sudden death. 'Can't see a blessed soul like him these days,' he lamented. He was sad that he hadn't been fortunate enough to see his face before the cremation.

It was at that moment that I asked him, 'Shanmugam, are you maintaining those four acres carefully? Is it giving good yield?'

'By the blessings of ayya, in these ten years there's always been good yields. Last year I bought two more acres.' As he said this, I saw tears welling in his eyes.

'Really?' I asked, my eyes welling up too.

After that, praising Naidu in his own way, Shanmugam left for his village.

Exactly ten years ago, around the same time on a morning like this, I first saw Shanmugam.

That day Naidu and I were chatting, sitting on his pial. His nine-year-old grandson and eight-year-old granddaughter were playing in the shade of the neem tree in the courtyard. In the cowshed on the right-hand side, ten or fifteen cows and five-six buffaloes were munching on fodder. No one else was at home. Everyone had gone to the fields.

I casually mentioned to Naidu that I would be going to Thirunelveli in four or five days. Just as he was telling me to get a good bedsheet from Thirunelveli, we heard a voice: 'Ayya, my respects to you.' We turned around and saw Shanmugam standing in the courtyard.

'Come, 'pa, Shanmugam!' Come, sit here,' Naidu said, pointing to the other pial.

But he didn't sit down. He stood respectfully in the courtyard.

I asked Naidu, 'Where is he from?'

'Mandi Thoppu,' said Naidu.

It was a village six miles away from our place.

Shanmugam started speaking about what he came for. 'Ayya! I have come to see you about the promissory note.'

'What about it? Only the month before last you cleared your interest dues. What now?'

'Ayya! I don't think I can redeem the note even if it takes ten more years. I'm trying my best. Income and expenditure remain the same. I spend as much as I earn. Can't save even a paisa. In two more years, I don't think I can even pay the interest dues. My family is also getting bigger. Last month I had a child…' he said embarrassedly.

Naidu smiled a little and asked, 'What child? Boy or girl?'

'Boy child, ayya.'

'Okay, okay. How many children do you have?'

'By the grace of god, I have five. Four boys and one girl.'

'Okay, if you can't redeem the note, what are you going to do?'

'I have come to talk about that only. Take my land,' he said succinctly.

'You are a smart fellow, da. Very smart. Who else could think up such a thing?' Naidu turned towards me and told me about Shanmugam's loan.

Three years before he had borrowed five hundred rupees from Naidu for his sister's wedding and for his own family expenses. No one had been willing to lend so much money against his four acres in his village. So he had travelled six miles, given a note to Naidu and borrowed the money. He had unfailingly paid the interest every year. Now, since he had no means to pay off the interest, he'd come to ask if Naidu would take his lands.

I don't know if his land would have fetched five hundred rupees. I hoped he wouldn't take advantage of Naidu's goodness and cheat him. I couldn't covey this to Naidu tactfully. Perhaps the land wasn't yielding enough, which was why he couldn't pay off the debt. So I asked, 'How's the land?'

Nammalvar Naidu intervened, 'How else will the land be? He has only four acres. With his heart and soul he would have tilled, ploughed, and fertilised the land. Will a poor man's land ever be barren?'

'If you give away the land to me, how will you look after your children?' asked Naidu.

Then Shanmugam explained his calculation. 'Ayya! If I toil in the four acres, I can feed the family only for six months. For the remaining six months, only by taking on work for daily wages, I am supporting my family. If I give away my land to you, I can go for work throughout the year. It's all the same to me, having the land or not.'

'So you're saying if you give away your land to me, there's no loss for you.'

'Yes, no loss. And at the same time my debt also will be cleared.'

Naidu laughed once again after listening to Shanmugam's calculations. I too couldn't help but admire his intelligence and honesty.

Naidu bent his head and thought for a while. As if he had remembered something, he looked at the cowshed from one end to the other.

'Shanmugam! Untie that grass bundle there and put it in front of the white cow at the end of the shed. Since it has nothing to eat, it is craning its neck, trying to take the grass from the next cow.'

Shanmugam did as he was told, and placed the grass in front of the cow. 'There's lot of grass in front of it. It is simply stretching its neck to the other side.'

Then Naidu's grandson came and sat beside us. We were all silent for a while.

'Ayya, what do you say? It's getting late for me,' said Shanmugam, reminding him about his matter.

Laughingly, Naidu asked Shanmugam, 'Shanmugam! Do you know to read and write?'

This irrelevant question surprised me.

'Where have I studied, ayya? Even in the note, I have only put my thumb impression.'

'That's why I asked. You can't even sign. But I can. If a fellow like you who can't even sign can make such a calculation, then what about me who can sign – what all calculations I can make. Have you thought of that? If you keep the land or give it to me, it's all the same to you. No loss at all to you. I agree. But, if I take the land, it should be profitable for me, no? Your land – that too four acres six miles away in the next village. If I get this, how prosperous and well fed will I get? How many palaces will I be able to build?'

'What, ayya? How can you say this?'

'How else can I say it? By your calculation, if you give your land, there's no loss for you. By my calculation, if I take the land, there's no gain for me. What do you think of my calculation?' he asked like a small child.

'What can I say? If you don't take my land, I can't clear my debt. I thought of selling it within my village to give you the money. But when they know that I'm desperate to sell, they are not offering even fifty rupees per acre. They want it for an atrociously low price!'

At that moment Naidu's granddaughter too came to the pial.

Without saying anything, Naidu went in to the house and came back in five minutes with Shanmugam's promissory note. 'Shanmugam! Come here,' he said. As soon as Shanmugam came near, Naidu tore the note into two and put it in his hand.

Shanmugam's hands trembled. Lifting his hands above his head, he struggled for words, 'Ayya…'

Naidu looked at his granddaughter and said, 'Rukmini, go and get some buttermilk for Shanmugam. Didn't you see, he fed our cow and all? Go, bring it quickly.'

Without looking at Shanmugam, he turned towards me and said, 'Thambi, don't forget what I said. It should be a good bedsheet. Check properly.' He changed the topic.

At that moment Rukmini came in, struggling with a big brass pot, and gave it to Shanmugam. When he took it, he found that it wasn't buttermilk, but milk.

By mistake, the child had dipped into the milk pot.

'Thambi, what do you think of my granddaughter?' Naidu laughed.

I was overwhelmed.

'It looks as if your granddaughter too has learnt your calculations.' When I said this, I remember distinctly that Naidu had pulled the child into his lap and cuddled her.

Had Naidu known that Shanmugam had bought two more acres of land? I never asked Shanmugam about this; I don't know why.

Original title: *Irandu Kanakkugal*
1960

Peacock 22

Sundara Ramaswamy

An incident that I saw in my twentieth year. It happened in front of my eyes. It's been fifty years now. It ought to have been forgotten. But, like a scar from a slashed cut, it remains in my mind. However, if readers think the way I relate all this is just a narrative technique and appreciate it, I have failed. On the contrary, if they think that it has failed as a story, yet carries the stench of fresh blood, then I have succeeded.

My readers know fully well that I was unwell for a number of years in my childhood. I've said it often enough. Then I was an oppressed child, cheeks sunken with yearning. Half of it could be my imagination. Imagining the sorrow to be more than what it really is and wallowing in self-pity does fill one with a kind of pleasure on the inside.

This incident happened in those days. Inside the precincts of the Suseendram temple. Just beside the place where the incident happened was the sanctum sanctorum of Lord Thaanumalaya. Since the piercing screams of the child wasn't heard by lord Thaanumalaya, the women who cursed the deaf Lord from the pits of their stomachs that day couldn't be faulted. When that woman wailed, I started running unthinkingly towards the vaidyar's house. You don't know what a big coward I am. In any emergency, cowards are given to only thinking of themselves. That's the characteristic of cowardice. You cannot blame them.

There was a famous vaidyar in Suseendram then. His family still lives there, so I don't want to mention his name. Since it was a name much tossed around my tongue and very familiar, I cannot bring myself to call him by any other name. I often went there to get medicine. The senior vaidyar would never be seen in the front pial or in the front rooms lined with medicine almirahs. You could not see him that easily. You could see him sitting in an easy chair in the sunlit central courtyard of a traditional Kerala house, drowned in medical studies. To those patients who complained that it was impossible to see him, the junior vaidyars would remark that his one hour in the easy chair could save one more life. That might have been true. What do I know of medical science? But one thing happened before my eyes. That day they brought the child, face full of blood, dripping profusely from the chin, and when the big vaidyar urged that the child be speedily taken to an English doctor, I was astounded. Why then call him the reincarnation of Dhanavantari, the god of health?

In my eighteenth year as I had lain confined to bed for three years in a row, the senior vaidyar had visited me out of compassion, felt my pulse and prescribed some medicine. From that day it was the same medicine for two years. A bedridden fellow earlier, I now started moving about. Only a slight limp remained. If anyone asked, I always said that a thorn had pricked me. The junior vaidyars held on to the senior vaidyar's prescription. Soiled with sweat, the smudged letters looked like six-legged insects and tiny stars twinkling in the sky. The dust-laden oily stains gave a decrepit look to the slip of paper. To even make a copy of it seemed like sacrilege to the junior vaidyars.

That day, when the junior vaidyars gave me the medicine bottle and the powders wrapped in tiny packets of newspaper, I, as usual, returned them, saying that I would come back and collect them. My heart would have been troubled if I had gone and returned like a robot from Suseendram with merely the medicine. It would have been saddening that I had done nothing pleasant on my own.

Those were the days when the mind longed to carry out several naughty pranks without my mother's knowledge. Desires loomed ahead, nipping in the bud thoughts of any disastrous consequences that reared their heads.

My dreams too realised beautifully my various desires, without danger or exposure. In the hope of this, the mind too began weaving the innermost desires in silken threads. What couldn't be accomplished if god desired? God can even make our movements visible only to the women we desire. We ought not to brush against anyone when we walk on the streets. But that's no big feat. One ought not to talk to oneself. That's the difficult thing. Thaanumalayan – Thaanu (Siva), Mal (Vishnu), Ayan (Brahma). Each one had inordinate love for his wife. Even in old age, don't they look at them, speak to them, full of passion brimming over? They show all this in films, quite openly. If it is like that for them, how would it be for us mere human beings?

That day I went in search of Comrade Chandran. A hot and cold relationship with him. Despite moving closely with him for four or five years, I never had the feeling that I really understood him. But I would get the urge to see him. The reason: Chandran had been a whiz in English from a young age itself. How he tamed such an audacious language was hard to even imagine. I could have learnt English from him even in those days. I could have read a few books. Since he assumed that I knew English, my telling him otherwise became a hurdle.

Owing to his prowess in English, Chandran was able to enter the house of the lady who had all the men in Suseendram in thrall. Under the pretext of giving tuitions to her child, he was able to enter that home which never had even a whiff of male scent. Even now, fifty years later, when I think of the fire of envy that it aroused in our hearts, I feel it was justified. If there is a girl such as this, fire is bound to erupt. All we friends had a secret desire gnawing at our hearts that this relationship should break. Not only break, but Chandran would also have to be humiliated, said friends now and then. Even if we doubted that it would happen, we wanted it to.

Even that day Chandran spoke with a sleepy face and a hoarse voice. He was running a slight temperature, he said. Putting his arms across his chest, he held his shoulders so tightly that the flesh was squeezed. Before immersing ourselves in our desires, we always had to preface our talk with general chit-chat. Unable to contain my eagerness, I asked before waiting for an appropriate moment: How is it all going? Got closer? Is Thaanu studying well?

Chandran smiled. Chandran had just joined as a tutor in a venerable college. He had come second in the state in MA English. And he was teaching ABCD to a mere child! I didn't know how to deflect the talk in Kolammai's direction. Is everything getting closer, I asked again. He said that to put up with Thaanu's face was the most difficult thing. Even now the sheen of blood had not healed. Perhaps it never would. The child wasn't aware that he had lost an eye. He was forever playing on the streets recklessly. He was forever shouting. He even became used to the street children calling him 'one-eyed fellow'. But when it fell on his mother's ears, shadows, like those of moving clouds on grass, would fall on her face. Chandran went on…

My heart twitched to ask him whether his relationship with Kolammai was on track. What words would I have to use so that he would feel that I hadn't lost my manners? As if he knew my yearning, Chandran said: 'It's difficult to bring it on track. Like the waning moon that moves ahead of us when we walk, she too strides ahead. (How well he put it in English!) She too is brimming over with desire. There is no doubt about it. It's unfortunate that such a thing has happened to the child. I ought to have got closer a little earlier itself.'

I didn't understand. What was the connection between this and that, I asked. Don't know how to say it. But there is a connection. That's what is holding her back. I'm able to look at her, that itself is my good fortune. When she smiles, her neat teeth, the twitch of her lips transport me somewhere else. Through her body language and mind, how cleverly she expresses herself in myriad ways. Thus Chandran went on glorifying. Earlier, I also used to go to the temple regularly to see her. When gossip spread in the town, I stopped, he said.

I never ever garner the glory due to me. No one in the town, including Chandran, was aware that I had been the only witness to the incident that had happened that day. I was tired of forever demanding the respect due to me.

That day too I had been circumambulating the temple's precincts. My mind was anxious that she shouldn't disappear like lightning before I completed one round. With every completed round, I peeped at the entrance. Were I to stand in the same place, everyone would be suspicious of me; I knew this through my experience. For some, moral values should never be diluted – what concern! What responsibility!

Everything Chandran had said was imprinted in my mind. Even though I hadn't seen her, I felt as if I had. There wouldn't be any difficulty in identifying Kolammai. The moment I spotted her, my mind would place her. As if such intoxicating beauties are strewn on the streets. She was only medium-complexioned. You could also say she was short. Eyes the colour of aubergine flowers. A brisk stride which didn't sway this way or that. Bringing to mind a peacock with plumes. A restless peacock without the plumes fanned out, Chandran had said, and it all came to mind. My mind befuddled by the thought, I stood at the entrance, looking at the peacock confined in a wide cage. The floor was full of white bird-droppings, as if splashed with lime paint. The light passing through the colours of the moving neck enhanced their shimmer. Burdened by the plumes, yet shouldering them, the peacock went round and round, spreading its exquisite pride. Since it was the main entrance, everyone had to pass that way. My mind said that she would appear in the next round. Were I to return that day without seeing her, then my life would have left me before I crossed the temple pond.

God's grace. As I came to the end of the northern passage, I made her out faintly, sitting on her haunches in front of the cage. Her small boy next to her, a red silk veshti tied tightly to his stomach. With broad lines of vibhuti smeared on him, he looked absolutely divine. Fluffy like the nei appam they give at the temple. In a new sari that she had unfolded only that day. For a moment I felt as if the cloud-coloured sari bristling around had slipped off her body.

Not wanting to stand near her, I sat on the steps behind her, as if I was casually looking around. Her thick hair sat like a burden on her folded knee. The dampness from her hair spread across her blouse, stretched on her taut, wide back.

In his enthusiasm at seeing the bird, the child jumped uncontrollably and she too was immersed in the joy. That was when the incident happened. I couldn't see what she placed in the child's hand to feed the bird. The peacock stuck its neck out of the iron bar and plucked it in a moment. The mother and child couldn't contain their joy. When he stretched his hand out for the second time, in the twinkling of an eye the peacock plucked out the left eye of the child. When the child screamed, I saw his eye hanging out like ice-fruit.

∾

Chandran stayed in East Germany for several years. At a young age itself he had earned the reputation of being a Communist intellectual in Travancore.

He was the pet of EMS Namboodiripad. Namboodiripad's rightful recommendations saw him through, said the Communists themselves. When East Germany fell, Chandran came back to India and joined the Jawaharlal Nehru University in Delhi. At the time of the Left's rule in Kerala he got a top-level post in the education department. When he was in office, there wasn't any contact between us. Even if they are our friends, if we go to see them when they hold high office, there is bound to be disappointment. We may perhaps nurse a secret desire to be humiliated. If such a thing never happened to Kuchelar, it was another story.

In old age Chandran anchored at the shores of Suseendram. At the time our friendship sprouted in no time. We mostly spoke about the health we didn't enjoy. Twice we each had heart attacks. Chandran was a little envious of me. Every morning, I had to swallow eight tablets, one less than him.

Even if he was still shy to reveal it, Chandran could never forget Kolammai. Her suicide had left a deep slash in his heart too. I told him that Thaanu earned handsomely from astrology and had bought himself a house. He had matched the horoscopes of all my children. His house was just opposite to the bus stand, I said. In Chandran's mind, Thaanu was still perhaps a tiny boy. When I said that he might be around fifty-five, Chandran exclaimed loudly.

When I went to visit Chandran, I was captivated by the cover of an English book lying on his table. The title: *Doubt and Certainty*. A science book co-authored by George Sudarshan and Tony Rothman. When Chandran said that Sudarshan was from India, I opened the book eagerly. My eyes fell on mathematical formulas, and I quickly shut it.

When I asked Chandran about the book, he said: in essence, you could say that for every incident there are reasons as yet unknown to us. A bus accident occurs in a busy place. Only a single life is taken. The question is: why that life alone? Research goes on in the hope that reasons can be explained in the future. Underlying all this is the basic question, 'why'.

What immediately came to mind was Thaanu's accident. What would Thaanu think today of the accident that had happened to him? I thought I would visit Thaanu on my way back home.

When I went to his house, Thaanu was taking lessons for his grandson Thaanu. He had placed a rough stone on the horoscopes which fluttered near him. Just a minute, he said to me. He signalled me to sit down. I sat on the dilapidated armchair. Grandfather Thaanu asked in a loud voice what the national bird of India was.

Grandson Thaanu replied, 'Peacock.'
What fans out its plumes and dances?
Peacock.
When I heard the sound of the bus, I came out hurriedly.
When I crossed the road, the voice wafted from behind.
What is the vehicle of Lord Muruga?
Peacock.
I couldn't hear any more of the lesson.

Original title: *Mayil*
2002

TIGER ARTISTE

23

ASHOKAMITRAN

Our tiffin recess is between one and two in the afternoon. They say that in the old days it used to extend till two-thirty. But then work used to begin only at eleven. For eleven o'clock office, if one ate one's morning meal at home at ten-thirty or ten-forty-five and came in at eleven-thirty, then a round of snacks at one o'clock would have been a bit impossible. That's why the cafeteria swarmed with people only at two. Now from eleven it has become ten-thirty; and for the past month they have even changed it to ten. The office which closed at five is now extended until six.

Work, however, has always remained the same. Those in the 'factory' department – carpenters, electricians and technicians in the labs – have always worked eight hours. Likewise the accounts department – whether work happens or not in other sections, they have to keep writing accounts right through the year. Then the telephone operators: there has never been respite or holiday for the telephone. So, only those who do not belong to the above departments find leisure during office hours now and then. Many a time for days, for weeks and even months. Why, I once remember our studio not making a film for almost one and a half years. And for the whole year and a half, you could draw a salary without doing a jot of work; put your feet up on the table during office hours and sleep blissfully; allow your hair to turn grey; allow your belly to gather flab, paving way for diabetes; allow your eyes to dart here and there since you have nothing to think about; allow your tongue to babble. Then after one and a half years if real work came your way, putting an end to your forced leisure, you could be all fired up. At the same time, because you had lost the habit of working, you could flounder.

It was on one such day, as we were waiting for all this to happen, that he walked in. When we had just finished our tiffin in the afternoon and were savouring a round of betel leaves and tobacco.

'What do you want, 'pa?' Sharma asked him. There was a time when Sharma used to be seen only in half-trousers. He used to be a police sub-inspector. Having written and published plays and stories and having made a name for himself, he joined our story department and became a key figure. In the good old golden days, he had even scouted for outdoor locations on his motorbike, with our boss on the pillion, no less. Now he was well used to wearing a veshti and munching tobacco. Only the square set of his shoulders when he stood up revealed that he had been once used to a regimen of exercise.

A small room. With three antique desks of different sizes. Seated behind the largest desk, Sharma was the Speaker of the House, in a manner of speaking. Besides the chairs we sat on, there was one extra. All ours were old and mismatched, but one of the legs of the extra one was shorter. Whoever sat on it tilted to one side, and was scared out of his wits. The visitor stood holding the back of that chair.

'What do you want, 'pa?' asked Sharma again.

'I came to your house on Saturday, ayya,' he said.

'I wasn't even in town on Saturday, 'pa,' said Sharma.

'I came in the morning, ayya. You were repairing an umbrella too, ayya.'

'O, you are that chap. Velayudam, right?'

'No, ayya. I'm Kader. Tagar-Foight Kader.'

'You came, is it?'

'Yes, ayya. Vellai only sent me. He said: Go and meet ayya at home.'

'Who is this Vellai?'

'Vellai, ayya. Agent Vellai.'

Sharma now seemed to understand. It was Vellai who rounded up men and women by the hundred and brought them to our studio whenever a film required a 'crowd' scene. They had to just stand around; they didn't have to act. Each one was given two rupees plus food for a day's work. Vellai would pocket one rupee out of that.

'We are not taking any crowd scene now, 'pa,' said Sharma.

'I know, ayya. But he said if I go and meet you, you'd give me some role.'

'Said who?'

'That Vellai saar only, ayya.'

Sharma looked at the two of us. We in turn looked at that man. He was a bit short. Must have once had a well-toned body. Now his collarbones poked out; his jutting jaws made his dark cheeks appear even more sunken. But then, almost everyone Vellai brought looked like this. Even if we were to make a film on the prosperous days of Ramrajya, the citizens would look so emaciated, as if struck by the famine of the year Dhatu.

'I'll send word through Vellai,' said Sharma. We leant back once again. The interview was over.

He said, 'Okay, saar.' Then he said in a feeble voice, 'If you can give me something immediately, it would be very helpful, saar.'

'Shooting work hasn't started, 'pa. They'll take the 'crowd' scene and all only towards the end.'

'That may be, saar. But please give me some role now, saar.'

'What role can we give you, 'pa? Look, there's the casting assistant. Give him all your particulars and go.'

I was the casting assistant. I had noted down particulars such as name, age, height, address, etcetera of thousands of fellows like him. If we dropped letters to four of them from the list whenever we needed, three would come back saying that the addressee had moved. Then it was all up to Vellai again.

But he didn't turn towards me. He seemed quite certain that of the three of us Sharma was the important one.

'Only if you say a word, something will happen.'

'Do you know to swim?' asked Sharma.

'Swim...?' he asked and hesitantly said, 'Little bit, saar.'

'A little and all won't do 'pa. We have to take a scene where a man has to dive from top and swim across a river. You won't be able to do all that.'

'I can do tagar foight, saar. My name itself is Tagar-Foight Kader, saar.'

'What's that tagar foight?

'Tagar foight, saar. Tagar... Tagar, you don't know?'

All of us grew attentive. But it made no sense at all.

He said in Tamil, 'Puli, saar, puli. Puli Foight.'

'O Tiger fight-aa? Tiger fight. So you can fight with tigers, is it?'

'No, saar. I wear a tagar costume and perform, saar. They call that only tagar foight, no?'

'O, you're a tiger artiste, is it? Why do we need a tiger-artiste for a film, 'pa... So you're a tiger artiste... Okay... okay...let Vellai come. I'll send word through him if there's any chance. Definitely.'

'I am very good at tagar foight, saar. It will be like a real tiger.'

'If we need a tiger, we can always get a real one, no?'

'No, saar. What I do will be like the true tiger, saar. Shall I show you now, saar?'

'No, no. No need.'

'Just watch for a bit, saar. Where would a big man like you have got a chance to see a tagar act?'

'Why, on every Muharram and Ramzan, there are lots of tiger acts on the streets.'

'But mine is very different, saar. Will be like the real tiger.' He pulled out a tiger mask from somewhere. Made of tiger skin. Only then did we notice that he had brought a cloth bag with him. In a second, he wore the mask over his head, drew it at his chin for a tight fit. He transformed into a tiger with human eyes. With a darting glance or two, he made a survey of the room in a second.

'Besh,' applauded Sharma. We looked at him, transfixed.

He lifted his arm high and flexed his body. Then he bent down, got on all fours, and rolled his head this way and that.

'Besh,' said Sharma again.

Like a cat he raised only his back, tilted his body and shook himself. Then he opened his mouth. We were startled. We had never heard such a terrifying tiger's roar at such close quarters.

He roared once more and shook the back of his body. He leapt on all fours and deftly huddled himself on the vacant chair. The chair shook violently. I shouted out, 'Ayyo!'

He then jumped on to my table. In the blink of an eye he leapt on to Sharma's table. Papers, books, betel packets and all lay strewn. But his feet didn't touch any of them. He crouched on the table and, looking at Sharma, let out a blood-curdling roar. From there, he sprang upwards. All of us yelled out, 'O!'

It was an old building. Ten feet high from the floor, a two-inch wide ledge ran around the walls. On one side of the room, a little above the ledge was a single-rod window which served as a ventilator. It was covered in dust, dirt and cobwebs.

On his fours, he sprang higher than a man's height and planted himself on the two-inch wide ledge above our heads. Then, clutching the iron railing of the ventilator, he let out yet another roar.

'Careful, 'pa, careful 'pa,' Sharma shouted. At that height, just in front of his face, the ceiling fan whirred away with demonic speed. Not even a few inches separated him and the blades of the fan.

From such a height he jumped on to the chair in one leap. And then made a perfect landing on the floor.

We were still in a stupor. Through the mask his eyes shone like a tiger's. The tiger once again roared fiercely, mouth wide open. The next instant his body slackened and slumped. He rose and stood up.

Even Sharma couldn't bring himself to utter 'besh'. He removed the tiger mask. We stood still, speechless. He was the one who became his old self first.

'I will definitely try to do something, 'pa,' said Sharma. His tone had totally changed. Kader folded his hands and paid obeisance.

'Where do you live?' asked Sharma. 'Mirsahibpet,' he said, and mentioned a number and the name of a lane. I noted it down. He said hesitantly, 'But I don't know how long I'll be there.'

'Why?' asked Sharma.

'No, saar…' he began and then suddenly fell at Sharma's feet.

'Get up, 'pa, get up 'pa, Kader,' said Sharma, highly disturbed. We had all got up. Kader too stood up and wiped his eyes. 'My wife has asked me not to come anywhere near our house, saar.' This was the man who had been a tiger a few minutes ago.

'It's been so many months since I earned anything, saar. What can she do? We have four children. All small, small things.' By now he was weeping.

Struck by a thought, Sharma asked, 'Did you eat anything today?'

He said, 'No, saar.' We didn't need to ask if he had gone hungry only on that day or for several days.

Sharma put his hand into his pocket. We too dug into ours. It all added up to two rupees. Sharma said, 'Look here, take this. Go first to the canteen and eat nicely.'

He said, 'Don't want, saar.'

'What "don't want"? Go first and eat, 'pa.'

'Get me some role, ayya,' he said tearfully.

I had never seen Sharma so angry. 'How dare you say that you won't take the money that is given to you? If you refuse money, how will you get it? Even if it is a mere coin, it's Goddess Lakshmi, 'pa. How will Lakshmi ever come to you? Go, take this and eat first,' shouted Sharma.

After his crying stopped, he took the money. Sharma said comfortingly, 'Role and all isn't in my hands, 'pa. But I'll do my best for you. Go, first fill your stomach.' He then looked at me and said, 'Take him to the canteen and make him eat something.' I stood up at once.

Kader said, 'No need, saar. I myself will go and eat. I will go and eat.' He once again folded his hands to us in obeisance and left.

We all stayed silent for a while. Overwhelmed, Sharma spoke to himself in a slightly loud voice, 'What can we do for him? What we are filming now is a king and queen story, no?'

But he didn't forget. After two weeks, when the story department met, he obtained permission for a scene where the hero would slip into the enemy's fort in the guise of a tiger. For the tiger act, Kader could be used as a 'dupe' for the hero. We could get him at least a hundred rupees for that.

I sent a letter to Kader. In four days, it came back as usual. The addressee was not to be found.

Sharma took Vellai and searched for Kader. We too enquired about him everywhere. The day for shooting the scene when the hero enters the enemy fort kept getting closer. Kader could not be found.

Even if they had found him, it wouldn't have been of much use. In that month was released a film where the hero did a kaavadi dance to a folk song. That film drew huge crowds all over Tamil Nadu.

It was decided that in our film the hero would perform a karagam dance.

Original title: *Puli Kalaignan*
1973

IN DARKNESS

24

G NAGARAJAN

'You are your dreams. If your dreams go away, you too are finished.'

The young couple standing at the bus stop laughed loudly. Madanan looked at them again. A kind of sturdy city bus turned the corner of the street and halted, letting out a heavy hiss. Its slightly red lights blinked pathetically in the moonlight. As soon as the young couple scurried into the bus, it started, kicking off dust. Madanan looked at the bunches of cloud above and turned his eyes down once the dust settled. Every house was enveloped in lush darkness. A blue light from a half-open glass window of a single-storey house spread out diffusedly, losing its way. Jaya came to the balcony. Her body touched his.

'How beautiful it is!'

'Yes.'

Madanan left her in the balcony and turned into the bedroom.

A tubelight shone, cursing the solitude. Jasmine buds had drawn a kolam on the mattress. Grapes, bananas, betel leaves, scented betel nuts on a stool. A steel chair which ought to have been near the table, stretched out its legs like a lame fellow in the middle of the room. Whiffs of fragrance curled up from the corner of the table. On the table, sat their photo with pride. An indelible proof. He and she. He controlled his laughter. As he sat on the bed, the light from the hall next to the balcony got switched off. She came inside.

'Why did you come home so late today?'

She sat near him and put her hand on his shoulder.

'I went to see the engineer. It became late.'

Lies. Utter lies. You went to Coronation theatre. You knew that that SIT manager and his lady-friend Manorama would come if there was a new film. That's why you went for the film. To see that Manorama, two times you threw away two and a quarter rupees. What is there in it? Didn't she dedicate the usual look to you? You've seen her for ten years. It's such a body, is it?

'Tomorrow is Saturday. Shall we go for a film?'

'I'll tell you tomorrow morning. Looks as if I will have work in the evening.'

'Then shall we go for a night show?'

Like those youngsters!

'Let's see.'

She stretched out a half-peeled banana to him. *She expects you to playfully bite it with your mouth.* He took the fruit in his hand and bit it. *Banana is good for health. A ripe one.* She dangled a bunch of grapes in front of him.

'I'm allergic to these grapes,' he said.

'What allergy?'

'Doesn't agree with me.'

He ate another banana, stretched out on the bed and lit a cigarette. When she leant against him and kissed him on the cheek, he shouted, 'Ayyo, wait.' Her hand came towards the burning cigarette tip. His hand which held the cigarette was trapped against her pressed body.

'Look here, this is a cigarette,' he said.

Ayyo, what a pity. Her face cleared.

'Ok, shouldn't you give the betel leaves?'

She sat up and started giving him the betel leaves. They were good. One of the things he loved was to smoke a cigarette while chewing on betel leaves.

'Shall we go up to the terrace? The moonlight is beautiful.'

'No, it's beautiful here only. You and me on this bed.'

She bent her head. *Good idea only. She and her lover-husband outside in the moonlight, deep in love-thoughts.*

'Why are you laughing?'

'Didn't laugh.'

'Looked like laughing.'

Madanan didn't say anything.

'I don't think you like me.'

'Who said? I like you very much.'

He held her close and kissed her cheek. *Then her eye. All these problems are not there if you visit a prostitute's place. That too if they are a bit high-class. If you give a little more money, how civilised they are. That Rohini! What a girl she was! Poor thing, she had fallen in front of a train and died. She wanted to clear all her sister's debts and become a nun.*

Jaya was leaning against him. He held her close, arm around her.

'What are you thinking about?'

'Nothing. Just how pleasant it is when you smoke.'

He stubbed out the cigarette in the ashtray and held her close. He pressed his mouth against her lips and sucked her breath. *Yes, it's like that only. Not kissing with feeling but with strength. That's enough for those girls. They fall into your hands. They shut their eyes. Give out deep breaths. Struggle hard. They don't have to kiss with their heart. Just with the lips. An embrace without blood boiling? Umm... all that can't happen now. That dung-swept house, what a tumult it gave you. The moment she closed the door you jumped on her with frenzy and tore her up. She doubled with laughter, slapped you on your back, disentangled herself and floored you.* He pushed Jaya roughly on to the bed. His hands burned with frenzy. He got up and switched off the light. Moonlight filtered in through the half-open window and formed a long rectangle on the wall. Darkness.

Madanan continued. His hands and feet knew the usual tricks. *Bhagyam, Bhagyam! The smell of garlic. A body like banana stem. O Bhagyam!* Both of them were in a tight embrace. She was throbbing. *Yes, she's trembling. Good, good. The fervour is rising. Not much work for your imagination.* There was a film of sweat on her body. A new odour hit his nose. He continued. 'Ayyo, I feel strange. You are killing me.' *This is the right moment.* He fumbled a bit. Soon he was ensnared. Completely, wholly. Thoughts emptied. The body, yearning to recreate itself, was consumed by an animal passion. He pressed her lips with desire. The tongues swirled. It seemed as if a current had suddenly swept into the room. Like the scream of a neighbour's child when it was stung by a scorpion. In a while a stillness, a silence. Then thoughts surfaced. Slowly he drew himself away from her. She blabbered, 'You are everything to me. You are my life. Don't let me down. I will die if you leave me.' He turned on his back and lit a cigarette. She clasped him with her arm and curled up close to him.

'Are you sleepy?'

'Yes.'

'Then you are satisfied, isn't it?'

'What is the connection between that and sleep?'

'My friend said that if men are satisfied, they will immediately fall asleep.'

'Is it?'

'Yes, darling. Yes.' She nipped his lips playfully. 'Will you eat something before you sleep?'

'No.'

'Take a little bit of milk. I've kept some bananas also.'

'I don't want.'

'Eat a little.'

'Okay, I will eat.'

In the dark, she went towards the table, tripped on the steel chair and fell down. He jumped down from the bed.

'What, 'ma, are you hurt?'

'I stubbed the little toe against the chair.' She sat where she had fallen down, her feet stretched out. After a while she got up and fetched the milk and fruit from the table.

'You are limping, 'ma. Are you badly hurt?'

'No.'

Both sat on the bed. He drank the milk and nibbled on the fruit.

'I don't look good, no?'

'Who said that, Jaya? Ayyo! I agreed to the marriage only after seeing you.'

'Yes, that's the done thing now. But...'

'But what?'

'But even when I fell down you didn't think of putting on the light.'

'Ayyo, what nonsense are you talking? When you said it was just a small bruise, I kept quiet.'

He put his hand on her back and tried to embrace her. But by then she had fallen on the bed like a corpse.

Original title: Iruliley
circa 1953

THEFT

25

AA MADHAVAN

Dim nightfall.

The street lamp stood alone, spreading light in the narrow street. Swarms of insects buzzed around in the circle of light. The thief nonchalantly took a last puff on his beedi, flung it in the gutter and walked down the street. Not a soul around. All the houses were sleeping. In the silence, the whir of the fans could be heard clearly through the windows. A huge bandicoot slithered out of the drain of a house and scurried past his legs. A small child was bawling from some house in the corner. Beyond an open window upstairs, even the dim red light decorating the god's picture appeared bright.

The thief stood near the street tap in contemplation, sized up the length of the street from one corner to the other. A dog came up panting, looked at his shadow, turned back unconcernedly and scampered away with a 'what is it to me?' look on its face. A mango tree stood beyond the wall adjoining the tap. The branches, holding an umbrella to the dull light, had donned dark clothes for the night. Very convenient for the thief. Placing a foot on the tap, he limbered up by the wall. When he stretched up, he was able to reach the edge. He clambered up the wall. From the height, the next street's lights too appeared like a picture. Within earshot, the sounds of the oil mill running. He quickly jumped down on the other side. A small bushy garden. All kinds of plants grew wild in the shadows. Some burr-like odour wafted. From the corner of the wall, the smell of shit and rotting fish pierced his nose. Hastily, he walked up and looked at the low wall. Some ten feet away a light shone inside a house. The window of the kitchen was open, welcomingly. The iron grills were threaded closely. The thief held the grill to test the strength. His foot hurt slightly from something that had poked him a while ago. In the dark, near the mud wall the insects sang a happy chorus… despite that, his ears pricked up for the slightest sound. Nothing anywhere. It was safe. And sound. In the distance, the noise of a lorry rattling on the road rose and fell. In the skies plenty of stars sparkled.

The grill was stronger than he thought. The strength of his hands lost to its power. His body broke into a sweat. He tied his veshti a little more tightly. He mopped his chest hair and flicked the sweat away. When he wiped his arm and massaged away the strain, a new idea flashed. He ran his feet over the ground. Kling – a long thing touched his foot. When he bent down and picked it up, it was a grinding stone with an iron pestle. Lifting the iron pestle, he prised the grill away with effort. A small rustling sound, and the deed was done. He noiselessly placed on the ground the pestle and the grill bar. Since the window was a little above the level of his hip, he first put one leg and then pulled the other leg in and got inside. That he had conveniently landed on the kitchen counter made him happy. He blew away the cobwebs from his head and face. He slowly came to the storeroom.

A couple of rats and cockroaches scampered into the cracks of the almirah recessed into the wall. 'Nungg' – an aluminium vessel fell down from the loft.

A child cried from the room in which a light was on. 'Keep quiet, you wretched thing,' said a woman's voice and smothered it with something.

The thief advanced fearlessly. A light shone brightly inside the room. Everything was seen clearly. On the bed, a man and a woman were in a tight embrace. A little distance away, a child was sleeping in a crib, thrown there willy-nilly. The child which had wept a few minutes ago! Its chain shone in the light, pendant and all.

'Heard some noise.'

'Ada, just keep quiet. Thinking of all this at this time!'

'Shall we at least put off the lights?'

'The only thing I want to do is hold you, can't do anything else.'

'Ayyo, you have no shame. Even he doesn't take such liberties or licence. Ayyo, leave me. It will all be finished if the child wakes up...'

'Look here, it is a big thing to even get you when 'he' is not there. On top of that you are saying you are scared. You are saying "switch off the light", then saying "o the child"... If you are this scared, you shouldn't have sent out signals for such a thing... ok, ok, come here... that's it...'

'Ammaadiyo, you are a terrible fellow...'

It was very convenient for the thief. Without allowing himself the time to rejoice that he would surely accomplish what he came for, he went quickly by the crib and pulled at the chain on the child's neck. The child squealed. That was all. 'Ayyo, thief,' she cried. She looked clearly at the thief. Assessing intently her unclad state, the thief half ran this time, not towards the back, but quickly to the inner hall and opened the front door locked from inside and climbed on to the road slowly. He knew very well that no one would come after him or even shout out. In the glare of the street lamp, he walked nonchalantly on the main road. Coolies were asleep on the pials of shops.

This was one of the many thefts he had accomplished. When the police dragged him to the house with the stolen chain in order to be identified, the man of the house was there.

'This chain belongs to your house, isn't it?'

'Yes.'

'Why didn't you give a "complaint" to the police that it was stolen?'

'I wasn't there when the theft took place. Only the wife and child were there. In the morning, they found that the child's chain wasn't there and that the window at the back of the house was broken. It was deduced that a theft must have taken place. A woman's mind must have said "why police and all unnecessarily?" I am very sorry...'

'It's only because "educated peoples" like you are so careless that petty cases like this are increasing... despite this our department won't let these matters be...Ok – just get a signature on this form, after that when the "court summons" come, your wife can come there and "give witness" that the jewel is yours only and take it.'

The police inspected the place and the broken window and asked him to re-enact the theft. As they were noting down his confession, the thief saw her again in the bedroom. When she saw his gaze she hastily went in, as if she had been cornered. But the child, on seeing him, bawled loudly.

The thief laughed to himself.

'You are laughing, is it, you rascal,' said the policeman and lifted his fist.

'Come on, saar, I know everything,' said the thief and dodged him.

There was a good crowd at the court. All the cases were brawls, illegal chit funds, gambling and bootlegging. Then the policemen who had booked them took the witnesses to a corner and instructed them on what to do once they went into the witness box – 'Don't blabber once you get on to the box. You have to say exactly what we have taught you. Otherwise, you will be counting the bars inside... Look here, you chit-fund gang, they will question you thoroughly. Turn everything inside out and ask you. Don't falter. You don't know about chits. Tell you haven't set eyes on chits. Look here, be careful...'

She sat in the car with her husband. She took everything in – the melée, the noise, the warnings, the court attendants who loudly called out the names, and the red-capped men who were running here and there. Two gun-toting policemen escorted a couple of shirtless roughnecks in handcuffs into a room stacked with papers.

The policeman who made out the 'charge sheet' came near the car and said, 'They will ask you to identify the jewel. Tell properly. They will ask how many blue stones in the pendant. How many...'

'Seven,' she said.

'No, isn't it nine?'

'No, only seven.'

'Yes, say like this only, emphatically. Why hesitate to tell the truth... You are an educated lady...'

Her mind churned. She felt odd with her husband near her.

'What, Nirmala, one night I wasn't there. This unfortunate thing has happened. All because of carelessness. See, even if we don't mind our stuff is gone, the policemen won't let go. That fellow, the rascal, is a real thief. I think thieving is his profession. Whatever it is, is it easy to flick sand into the eyes of the police, court, law and order?'

She thought she was going to cry anytime now. 'Stupid idiot, you have such a tender heart. Why are your eyes wet? They'll ask you a couple of questions...What is it to us, as if we stole... you have to tell them about the chain and get down, that's all, no?'

She was dressed daintily. She had tied her hair into an Ajanta bun and stuck a single red rose in it. She had darkened her eyebrows. Had put on a tight-fitting blouse. High heels. A handbag and a little dot of a 'pottu'. Dignity sat on her, or beauty itself sat on dignity.

The attendant called out her name loudly. 'Go bravely,' her husband said reassuringly.

When she stood in the witness box she felt as if her make-up, elegance, status, personality, modernness, everything had been shed. The judge presided over regally, spectacles, bald head, tip-collared white shirt and all. In front, amid the policemen, he, the thief, stood tall – unkempt hair, matted hair on the bony chest, crumpled veshti, and round red eyes. She looked at him once. Was he smiling slightly?

...That night's ecstasy, the sudden appearance of the thief, her dishevelled state in haste...

The judge asked, 'This is the fellow, isn't it, who came to your house in the middle of the night and stole your child's chain with a pendant, breaking the grill of the back window?'

It was he who looked at her.

'... Saar, I have something to tell you... I'm not the thief who entered their house,' said the lean, tall, thin thief, breaking into loud laughter.

The policemen twisted his arm and shook him...

'You thieving rascal, keep quiet,' they threatened. He laughed even more loudly.

The crowd in the court buzzed like a disturbed beehive.

She, who stood in the witness box, started to swoon.

Original title: *Thiruttu*
1975

Flag Hoisting in Chinnoor 26

Saarvaagan

When Narasimman got up in the morning, he remembered that they had to go for the flag-hoisting ceremony at seven o'clock. He hastily brushed his teeth and drank his coffee in one gulp and came to the hall. His father, Ramanjulu Naidu, was waiting there, all ready. 'Come, let us go,' he said, and walked towards the gate.

Ramanjulu Naidu was an old Congressman. Now he ran a small grocery store, and he was a homeopath on the side. He had some land, which included a tiny bit given to freedom fighters. Having participated in anti-toddy agitations and been beaten up soundly, he had spent a year in jail in those times. After Independence, he had slowly withdrawn from politics. The reason could be that he was dejected that his party hadn't given him a ticket in the first general elections after Independence. Or it could have been that he magnanimously thought that 'now that Independence has been achieved, my role is over.' Whether he stepped aside or was asked to step aside, in any case he wasn't in politics. That is, till recently.

When Narasimman came to Chinnoor on his annual vacation, he was taken aback to see that his father had been appointed as the head of the Town Congress Committee.

'What, Naina, why all this headache in this old age?' Narasimman advised. Because Narasimman was an idealist – first a follower of Gandhi, Ramakrishna and Vivekananda, then a Communist sympathiser, and then after 1956, a follower of Nehru, but not of the Congress party. In the end, he concluded that political affiliations weren't for idealists like him. He didn't like his father being chosen for a party post by the ruling party, much less six months before the elections. He not only thought that the wily politicians would use and throw away his father but was also of the opinion that after sixty-five, there was no need to indulge in politics.

But Ramanjulu didn't quite agree. 'If honest people always shy away from politics, then this country will only go to the dogs,' he argued. Narasimman couldn't refute this logic.

The previous day itself Ramanjulu had informed his son, 'At seven tomorrow morning, the flag should be hoisted. It's our Independence Day, you see.'

Narasimman readied himself to start the car. Why did his father have to walk when Narasimman had brought his car to Chinnoor? Besides, he also wanted to see his father hoisting the national flag in the heart of the town as the head of the local Congress committee.

Just before starting, Krishnaveniammal asked Ramanjulu if she too could come along. She was Ramanjulu's younger sister. She was his father's second wife's daughter. Years earlier she had lost her husband to cholera and come back to live here. Ever since, she had become Ramanjulu's right hand. When Ramanjulu had gone to jail in 1932, it was she who had brought up the motherless Narasimman. Today she too yearned to see her brother hoisting the flag like in earlier times.

Narasimman brought the two of them to the heart of the town. Since the road had been muddied in the previous day's downpour, his car tyres left a trail of 'mud kolam', much like an aircraft leaving a jet trail in the sky.

In the town's centre, there were four or five flag posts with the flags of the different political parties hanging red, white, green and black. In the middle was a bust of Gandhiji, imported from Italy for five hundred rupees. It was fixed on a high stone platform. Along with Gandhiji, the ones who unveiled the bust twelve years ago – district collector, A P Venkateswaran ICS, municipal chairman, the honourable Rao Sahib Sundara Murthy Mudaliar, municipal commissioner Mr David Paul BA – too had attained eternity, consigning their names to the slab below the bust. Circling the bust, an iron-grilled fence. Perhaps to prevent Gandhiji from running away from Chinoor if ever he came to life.

When they reached, it was sharp seven. Parking the car in the corner of 'Rangaraj Building – 1945', they got down.

'No one has arrived,' complained Narasimman.

'They will come, they will come,' said Ramanjulu, adjusting his old handloom towel which doubled as an angavastram over his shoulder.

Both of them looked around. Rajagopal Mudaliar emerged from a small lane nearby.

'Welcome, welcome. What is this, seven means you've arrived exactly at seven,' he said, unloading the chewed-up betel remains from the mouth on to the street.

'Who is this, saar?'

'My elder son, Narasimman.'

'Oho, the one in the city? Vanakkam, saar. I'm so glad.'

'Where are the rest?'

'They've gone for tiffin to the hotel. They should be back now. Come into the shade.' Courteously uttering these words, he went to a nearby shop and opened the door. Only after it was opened, did Narasimman realise that it wasn't a shop but the Town Congress Committee's warehouse for flags.

At that moment Kanniappan and Idli-shop Venkatramayyar (earlier he was in the idli business, but now he was the checking inspector in buses) came. A few others too joined them. There was a babel of voices. 'Come on, take out the flags. We need seventeen – Chinna Kadai Street, Ranga Pillai Street, Dharmaraja Koil Street, Kosavar Street…' Narasimman listened with interest to all the flag hoistings that were to take place after this main event.

He was suddenly startled by a sound. It took him a while to figure out what the noise was and where it came from.

Near the Gandhi statue an English band with a traditional Tamil drum accompaniment was playing with gusto. A crowd had gathered around.

Everyone, including Krishnaveniammal, made their way towards the Gandhi statue. Narasimman and Krishnaveniammal stood a little aside, while the others stood around the flag post.

'Quick, let the job get done quickly,' hurried Ramanjulu.

Deaf Kannaiyan removed the party flag from the Congress pole and tied the national flag and readied it for hoisting. Then he ran to the shop opposite. The English band was playing a line of a song – Narasimman couldn't make out what it was – over and over again. About ten-fifteen urchins gathered around. There were a few people standing in front of the tobacco shop. By now V G Krishnasami Mudaliar (secretary of the Town Congress Committee) and Rangayya Bhagavathar had joined the crowd. Also squeaky-clean Sundaram Chettiar.

'How he used to look, Rangayya Bhagavathar! Look how he has gone down now!' whispered Krishnaveniammal into Narasimman's ears.

'That's how all the men from the weaver community become,' answered Narasimman listlessly. He considered the weaver community as the lowest of the low among all humans, but he held nothing personal against Rangayya Bhagavathar.

Kannaiyan stood on the fence and placed kumkumam on Gandhi's forehead.

'Wretched fellow! Can he not use his right hand to place the kumkumam?' openly scolded Krishnaveniammal. Neither Deaf Kannaiyan nor any of the others paid much heed to this stricture.

After smearing the kumkumam Kannaiyan jumped inside the fence. He lit some camphor in front of the statue. He took the coconut handed to him over the fence by V G Krishnasami Mudaliar, broke it at the edge of the pedestal, waved his palms over the camphor flame and reverently touched his eyes. He climbed over the fence. He looked so happy, as if he had returned from the jail once again.

'Hurry up, 'pa,' said Ramanjulu. Kanniyappan and Rajagopal gestured to the band to stop playing. The English band came to a halt. At that moment, the Chenganoor bus, which until then was speeding along, inched its way on seeing the crowd, as if caught in a funeral procession.

Just as Venkatramayyar cautioned, 'Be careful, the mud will splash,' someone from the bus blew his nose loudly.

V G Krishnasami Mudaliar spoke in a voice that seemed as if his head was trapped inside a lead vessel, 'I hereby invite the great nationalist and freedom fighter and our town's Congress chief Ramanjulu Naidu to hoist the first flag in our town on this Independence Day.'

Ramanjulu turned towards Narasimman and said, 'Did you see, only the old hands have come.' He then went to the flag post and hoisted the flag. Even if there was a hitch at first, the flag went up smoothly. Narasimman was disappointed that the flag didn't flutter as there was no breeze, but all the same he was happy that it shone brightly in the morning sun.

Just as Ramanjulu started his speech 'The esteemed people of Chinnoor,' the English band played the same refrain and the bearded Subramanya Achari started distributing the sweets. Kannaiyan shouted at the band and asked them to stop. Ramanjulu resumed his speech.

'The esteemed people of Chinnoor, the reason we fought the British under the leadership of Mahatma Gandhi was to hoist this flag. For the last nineteen years we have earned the right to do it. Even so, our struggle for freedom should never stop. We are now threatened by other countries. We are also facing many problems within the country. Prices rise like poison…' At that moment there was a commotion in the crowd.

Since Subramanya Achari was distributing tricoloured sweets, people, young and old, jostled around him, stretching out their hands and yelling, 'Saar, saar.' No one heard Naidu's speech.

Only when Rajagopal growled around twenty times, 'Go further and distribute, Achari,' did the crowd move away along with Achari.

Engrossed in this melée, Narasimman missed his father's speech. By the time the commotion died down, he had finished his speech.

The band resumed again, circumambulating the fenced Gandhi statue.

'So now you all take care. I'm leaving,' said Ramanjulu, wiping his neck with the towel, and walked towards the car. Narasimman and Krishnaveniammal followed him.

'We will take care of everything. You don't worry. Okay, saar, vanakkam, saar,' said Kanniappan, V G Krishnasami Mudaliar, Kannaiyan and others. They walked towards the bus stand. Perhaps the next hoisting was there.

As Narasimman started the car, Krishnaveniammal exclaimed, 'They were simply playing "pee…pee…" Can't they play our national anthem?'

Narasimman peeped out of the car.

The English band was still circling the statue, playing the same line. At the far end, Subramanya Achari, a plate on his head, was dancing around distributing the tricoloured sweets. Twenty feet ahead, V G and others walked briskly, their veshtis folded up. The clock at 'Rangaraj Building – 1945' showed quarter to eight. Narasimhalu was opening his petty shop. Narasimman remembered with a flash what the band was playing. 'It's a long, long way to Tipperary…,' the first line of an Irish song.

'Start the car. I'm hungry,' said Ramanjulu Naidu.

Original title: *Chinnooril Kodiyetram*
1968

Husband, Hunger, Human Bonds

27

Indira Parthasarathy

Gopalan woke up suddenly. He saw his wife sitting on the bed.

He knew the reason. He wondered if he ought to ask her yet again in the dead of the night.

Four days ago, Kamala had informed him, 'I had a dream yesterday.'

'What dream?'

'A girl seemed to come and whisper in my ears.'

'How old?'

'Don't joke. I can't seem to make out if it was a dream or true. So real it was.'

'What did she tell you?'

'That's what I can't make out. It seemed as if she was moaning.'

'Maybe you yourself moaned. And it would have been just the echo.'

Kamala had glared at him. Then, turning her face aside, she had said, 'Hereafter I'm not going to tell you a thing.'

'Kamala, listen to me! If you start thinking about this ghost, goblin and all, I can't stop you. But I don't have to believe all that.'

'No ghost, no goblin, nothing. I don't have any fear. It looked as if that girl had some grievance. That was what all that moaning was about.'

'Ok, let's exchange places and sleep. I will find out about her grievance.'

That night they had switched places.

He, who had fallen asleep at ten in the night, got up only in the morning. No girl had moaned in his ears.

When Kamala had woken up, she had said, 'That girl knew that we had switched places. She came even yesterday and moaned in my ears.'

'Why didn't you wake me up immediately?'

'I didn't know if it was dream or reality. It seemed as if I was conscious. And also not really conscious. I couldn't make out.'

Without saying a word, Gopalan had started to read the papers.

'Why don't you say something?'

'I think...' He had stopped himself.

'Yes, tell me.'

'I think it would be good if you saw a psychiatrist.'

Kamala had got up in a huff and gone into the kitchen.

The next day Kamala hadn't told him anything about her dream.

She was now sitting on the bed.

'The same dream?'

Kamala went into the hall and sat on the sofa. He became aware of this when the sofa protested with a 'creech' sound.

That the sofa was not repaired was one of Kamala's grievances. She rejected his suggestion of selling it and getting a new one. 'After retirement, what is this talk of new-gew and all. As if we are new! I'm asking you to find a fellow to repair it, that you are not willing to do. You want to buy a new one. If you spend all your money like this, what will we do in old age?'

'So you are saying we are not old now or what? How nice to hear that.'

'You don't seem to have the seriousness of old age. All the time you are talking like a child.' This was her usual assault.

Why had she gone and sat on the sofa now? What was the time?

He picked up the timepiece from the dressing table. The light from the lamp post by the window revealed dimly that it was two.

Gopalan got up and went into the hall and switched on the light.

Kamala screwed up her eyes when the light came on suddenly. 'Why are you switching on the light?'

'What is this? It is only two. Why have you got up so early?'

'I can't sleep.'

'Why, you dreamt again, is it?'

Kamala remained silent.

'Tell me.'

'What is the use of telling? You are not going to believe anyway.'

'What should I believe?'

Kamala got up and went by the window.

Gopalan went near her, touched her shoulder and asked in a soothing tone, 'What should I believe now?'

'I think it would be good if we performed a sumangali prarthanai.'

'Sumangali prarthanai?'

'Yes. Someone in our family must have betrayed a girl. That's why she is coming and moaning to me every day like this.'

'So you finally understood what she said?'

'Is there anything to understand? Can't you make out from the moaning?'

'In your family or mine?'

'My family means yours only. After marriage where's the question of "my family".'

'Just because it is betrayal, you are trying to lay the blame on my family saying that a girl has no family after marriage and all.'

'Just think about it. You wouldn't have done it. Not your father either. Such a nice man he was. But your grandfather?'

'That I wouldn't have done is your belief. Then…'

'If you've done it, tell me.'

'In my grandfather's days, all the grandfathers of people of my age had a 'keep', according to their status. And if they happened to be mirasdars of Thanjavur district, then you can't call it betrayal. It was the norm.'

'You don't call this betrayal, is it?'

'If this is betrayal, then some girl or the other must come and moan into the ears of all the women of your age. But that doesn't seem to be the case, no?'

'No need for all these cheeky retorts. We must perform the sumangali prarthanai. It's good for our children also. Each one is in one place, somewhere abroad. Please don't be stubborn about this.'

'Look here, I'm not telling you not to perform the sumangali prarthanai. Let that happen on one side. But if you feel someone is coming and moaning in your ears, it's better we see a psychiatrist.'

'See one for yourself first. I don't need one,' said Kamala, and went back to the bedroom.

That Gopalan gave the nod for the sumangali prarthanai made her face bloom with happiness. She never expected victory to come by this easily.

You couldn't say that Gopalan was an atheist. He didn't believe in rituals. He used to think that if only he could bring himself to believe, how comforting it would be psychologically.

He knew very well that Kamala firmly believed that some girl had moaned into her ears. She wasn't given to lying.

But how did the notion that someone in his family had betrayed a girl take root in her mind? That was what he couldn't understand.

When he lay on the bed, he asked Kamala, 'How did the thought take seed in your mind, that someone in our family had betrayed a girl? And why did that girl come only to you and moan?'

Kamala interrupted, 'You need a subtly sensitive ear for all this. And the wavelength should match.'

'What is the meaning of matching wavelength and all? When have I ever cheated on you?' he asked somewhat angrily.

'Che, che, I didn't mean it that way. Maybe the girl believed that this woman would understand her grievance.'

'In what way will she benefit from a sumangali prarthanai?'

'It's not for her. It's for us. For the well-being of our children. If we give a sari to a poor old sumangali, and if she blesses us, that's enough. We won't have any troubles.'

'Then that girl won't come and moan, is it?'

'Definitely not. There's so much power in the blessing from an old sumangali.'

'This is your blatant selfishness speaking. In the guise of pitying that girl, no need for all this nonsense about "subtly sensitive ear" and "same wavelength" and all,' said Gopalan.

'Say what you like. Only the remedy is important to me,' said Kamala. She turned and closed her eyes.

The next afternoon, as Gopalan was wondering whether to lie down on the bed or read a book reclining on the easy chair, the doorbell rang.

He was a little irritated. Who could it be in this scorching heat? Wasn't there a time to visit people? He went to open the door.

An aged woman stood there. Her hollow cheeks seemed to touch each other. An emaciated body, with skin hanging loose in waves. Eyes seemed to be dug out. It looked as if it had been several years since her teeth had waved her goodbye. A big circle of kumkumam on her forehead.

It is said that there is a special charm to a toothless smile. Gopalan understood that only now. He, who had been so angry, asked politely now, 'Who do you want to see?'

Meanwhile Kamala came in saying, 'Come in, please come in.'

The old lady came in hesitantly.

'This maami must have come regarding the sumangali prarthanai. I'd mentioned it to the priest who had come this morning to the house downstairs. He must have sent her. Sit, maami. Wait, I'll bring a mat,' said Kamala.

'No need, 'ma. How smooth the floor is. Why do we need a mat?'

The old lady sat down. But Gopalan felt that she sat herself down with great difficulty, clutching on to her hip. He wondered how old she was. Eighty perhaps. Had she been even ninety, he wouldn't have been surprised. She must be Kamala's dream sumangali.

'What is your husband doing?' asked Gopalan. It was only after he uttered the question, he realised how foolish it was.

'What can he do? He's lying down at home. He's eighty-three. I'm seventy-five. I'd like to go before him. Who knows what 'he' has written for us? It will happen like that only. Can you give me a little rice, 'ma? We both have been starving since morning. They say that you never feel hungry when you are old. Perhaps it's like that for rich people. It's not at all like that for us. We have a fire in our belly all the time. Only when the final fire consumes us, maybe this fire will die down.'

Kamala went in saying, 'There's plenty of rice. I'll bring it.'

'Don't you have children and all?' asked Gopalan.

'We have. Three children. No education, nothing. Flying hither-thither in search of Brahmin ritual food. We don't even know where they are. When you starve where is the question of affection, family bonds and all?'

Kamala brought rice in an aluminium vessel. 'You don't have to return the vessel. Come next Friday for the sumangali prarthanai.'

'Next Friday? Not tomorrow?'

'Can't do it tomorrow. Come next Friday,' said Kamala decisively.

Disappointment was clearly evident on the old lady's face. 'All right, as you wish.' Saying so she got up.

After she left, Gopalan asked Kamala: 'Why, can't you do it tomorrow? That paati looked so pitiful.'

Kamala replied, 'There's so much work. You will say all this easily. Only those who have to do the work know. I'm not going to call anyone to cook. I'm going to do it all by myself. I have to shop for so many things. Buy a good sari. See how we've got such an old starving sumangali. We are so lucky.'

'What, you call it luck to find an old, starving sumangali! Wonderful. No one will say that you don't have sympathy or compassion,' said Gopalan.

'You are always so perverse. So many fool us saying they are poor. That is what I meant.'

'Okay, let that be. You can call that old man too, no, serve him food and give him a veshti? Why didn't you think of that?'

'You seem to have thought of it. Why didn't you say something?' asked Kamala.

'All right, let that go. Next Friday, send that paati off with some food and a veshti,' said Gopalan.

The following Friday when Gopalan woke up from his sleep it was six in the morning. No sign of Kamala beside him.

He went to the kitchen. Freshly bathed and draped in a traditional sari, Kamala was busy at the stove. 'The aroma of cooking is choking my nostrils.'

'What lies. I haven't even started cooking. Just making coffee for you.'

'What time will paati come? She didn't tell us the time.'

'She'll come only at ten. As if they are all breakfast-eating people like you. One more thing: no breakfast for you today. At eleven itself we two will eat. After the paati has eaten and taken the sari.'

It was eleven. No sign of the paati yet.

'What Kamala? Paati hasn't come yet. I'm hungry.'

The doorbell rang.

Gopalan got up and opened the door.

An old man! The skin looked as if it had been draped like a tight dress over a skeleton. Had it been dark, even the skin wouldn't have been visible. Had hunger eaten up even the skin? To Gopalan it appeared as if life clung on to the skin out of sheer habit.

'I'm Mahalakshmi's husband. Is there a sumangali prarthanai here?'

'Yes, please, come in,' said Gopalan.

That old man was used to sitting on the sofa. He sat down and looked around him.

Kamala came out of the kitchen.

'He is…' When Gopalan hesitated a bit, the old man said, 'My name is Selvanambi. Mahalakshmi's husband. I've come with regard to the sumangali prarthanai…'

'When did maami say that she was coming?' asked Kamala.

'She can't come today. She's not feeling well. That's why I…'

Before he could complete, Kamala snarled, 'Then… couldn't she have informed earlier? We would have made some other arrangements.'

Gopalan felt that Kamala needn't have been so harsh. The old man's face looked a bit pathetic. Gopalan said, 'Must have taken ill suddenly. Old age is always like that.' He didn't fail to notice the gratitude on the old man's face.

'Aa…yes…s… She bathed in the morning and got ready. But then she sat down saying she felt giddy. I thought I would come and tell you.'

'What can we do without maami? We'll see about this next week,' said Kamala.

Selvanambi's face shrunk a bit when he asked, 'Next week?'

'Have you bathed?' asked Gopalan.

'Yes.'

'Then you eat. And take some food for maami as well. We'll see about the sumangali prarthanai next week,' said Gopalan.

'Can I take a look at the sari you have bought for the sumangali prarthanai?'

Kamala hadn't expected this. She said angrily, 'Wonderful! What you are saying! You'll only accept the sari after seeing the design, is it?'

'For a long time she's been asking for a red sari with a light yellow border. That's why I asked.'

'All right, you eat now and go. We'll talk about the sari later,' said Gopalan.

'Can I come back and eat after sometime? The fire in the belly refuses to die down. She used to always say "only when the final fire consumes us, maybe this fire too will die down". As for me, only 'he' knows when it will die down.'

'What are you saying?' asked Kamala.

'The fire in her belly has been silenced.'

'Really?' screeched Kamala.

'Yes. As soon as she bathed, she sat down saying that she was giddy. That was it. She died a ripe old sumangali. For a long time it had been her wish to wear a bright red sari. If the sari you have bought is like that, please give it to me. I will drape it over her body. Then her soul won't lament, no?'

Gopalan and Kamala looked at each other.

The old man, who had closed his eyes for a bit, got up.

'All right. I'll take my leave. I only have to light the pyre. As for my eldest son, who knows in which house he is eating the ritual food now? May I come and eat here after the funeral rites?'

Original title: *Pathi, Pasi, Paasam*
1988

The Anthoni Who Got Lost 28

Krishnan Nambi

Old lady Martha was searching for her darling Anthoni.

Where could Anthoni, her precious goat, have gone? Did it have to disappear on the morning of Christmas?

'O Jesus, what a misfortune! Where is my goat?'

The old lady's eyes began to fill with tears. She, who no longer had any peace of mind, paced up and down the kitchen. Her husband Asirvatham hadn't yet got up. Covered head to foot with an old sari, he was curled up on an old cot. It had been really late when he had come home in the night, after a second show. When the old lady had lamented, 'Can't you come home at a decent hour, the same headache daily,' he had lied, 'Coming from Tuticorin, woman.'

'Okay, okay, eat your food. Then go and keep some rice-water for Anthoni and then sleep,' the old lady had grumbled. She had been irritated because her sleep had been disturbed. She had gone and lain down again. Christmas would dawn. If she kept awake, she would find it difficult to go to church, as planned. Even if she did manage to get up and go, sleep would surely press down her eyelashes when she knelt down to pray, eyes closed. She had seen many women nodding off when they prayed.

She could hear the sounds of noisy slurping in the kitchen.

The old man had served himself. Then what? Which woman would feel like doing wifely duties, shrugging off her sleep, if the husband came home at ungodly hours? Martha herself had got up at one or two on many nights, opened the door, fetched water to wash the feet, bent and straightened up ever so many times to serve food to her husband. But that was many years ago, when young blood had coursed through her body, days when she had pined for her husband's love, embraces and kisses.

The old lady had now become truly old. Her lips, which had once yielded to rough kisses from young Asirvatham's black ones, stinking of beedi, now rolled out Jesus's praises. She found pleasure only in that. She didn't have children. She wasn't interested in anything. But was unnaturally fond of food. She would eat till her stomach burst. She took great delight in cooking varieties of food and eating them. But she didn't have the means to do so. The old man had a salary of thirty rupees. He was a peon with a big fish exporter. He had held the same job since he was twenty; his salary too had increased from fifteen to thirty. The old man too had been a sappaturaman, a glutton, for all these forty years. Even the old lady, a voracious eater herself, used to be astonished by the way he rolled food into balls and gobbled them. The echoes of his non-stop belches would bring to mind the demons of the fables.

A half-asleep Martha had turned over on the mat.

The old man had called out, 'Ei, woman!'

'Mmm…'

'Where's the chilli? Just tell me, I will take it.'

The old lady had mumbled without opening her eyes, 'The old fool eats chilli like cake and bread. How will blood stay in his body if he eats chilli like this?'

'I'm shouting and asking where the chilli is and you are lying down like stone.'

'Yes, chilli… I've kept it in the corner, on the pot. Take it and eat it.' The old lady had shut her eyes tightly, as if beckoning sleep.

The old man had washed his hands at the back of the house. He had uncouthly gargled his mouth and spat out, 'Poo…poo!' He had searched for the matchbox, lit his beedi and flopped on the string-cot with a sigh. When he had curled on the bed with a feeble yawn, Martha had opened her eyes.

'Did you keep the rice-water?'

'For the goat? O, I forgot,' the old man had said casually and remained curled up.

A violent temper had arisen in the old lady.

'Will your arm break if you keep rice-water for the goat one day? Will a man be so lazy? When it comes to eating food, no sign of laziness.'

The old man had chuckled loudly. His body had shaken.

'Don't tell me to do all these things. Have I ever kept rice-water for your goat any day?'

'My goat-aa? When it comes to keeping the rice-water alone it becomes my goat, is it... Mmm, just get lost,' the old lady had said and got up.

'Mmm... you only go and keep it.'

'I need your recommendation for that, is it?'

The old lady had flung her white-dotted red sari over her shoulder. She had then pushed back her grey, thinning wispy hair away from her eyes.

She had made her way towards the kitchen, the tips of her ears, with big holes from wearing heavy earrings, shaking. Only a couple of years ago, she had flung away the gold-plated earrings which had adorned her ears for a long time. The useless things, how heavy they were!

The old man, nodding off to sleep, had got up, as if shocked.

'Nowadays my brain has really become rotten. I have slept without taking off my white shirt.'

The old man had got up and looked down at his shirt. Thank god it hadn't crumpled. He had taken it off gently, as if it were a flower, folded it and hung it on a rope.

A chimney lamp in the left hand and a pot of rice-water in the right, Martha had made her way to the back of the house.

A small shelter made of coconut fronds supported by four poles. A small wooden pen inside. Anthoni had been asleep there, tied up. When it had seen the light, it had got up and said, 'mme'.

'Old lady, come, come. I'm very thirsty.'

'Okay, okay, drink it. It's only for your sake I get up even if my body cannot!'

'I know that. If you don't keep rice-water for me, you won't get sleep.'

Anthoni had drunk the rice-water thirstily, slurping up every drop.

The old lady had stood staring at Anthoni in the dim light. How it had grown from what it had been!

Was it the sickly white goat she had bought for seventeen rupees at the Vadacheri Kanagamoolam fair? How plump it had become, so roly-poly. It would easily be worth eighty rupees now.

Under Martha's dedicated cosseting, the goat had grown like a pony, heartily.

Even in the dim light the mat of fair hair glistened, sparkling white. The horns jutted out like curved knives. With firm resolve and overzealous affection, the old lady had lavishly fattened up the goat.

The old lady never allowed Anthoni to graze outside. She only took it out when she bathed it. She would take it to a nearby pond and scrub it tirelessly for hours. She would then hastily drag it home, half-running, fearing evil eyes would befall it. Then she would tie it, fetch the greenest fronds that the goat loved from the hillock at the edge of the village. She would never let Anthoni go hungry, any part of the day.

One day when Martha was on her way back with Anthoni after giving him a bath, a pair of evil eyes had crossed her path. Butcher Peter's eyes they were.

'What, Martha? I didn't know you had a goat like this. Nice plump thing, this goat. Are you selling it? I'll give forty rupees…'

The old lady had shouted like one possessed. 'I hope your eyes catch fire. You've got evil eyes. If your eyes fall on Jesus, he himself will become Satan!'

Peter had laughed heartily and moved away. He was a little afraid of her. Why, the whole world would shiver if she got angry.

After that incident, the old lady had made sure that no eyes fell on the goat. She fetched water to the shed itself and bathed it. Anthoni was raised so affectionately.

Anthoni had made a 'mme' sound again. 'My thirst has been quenched. My stomach is full. Why are you still standing? Why don't you go and sleep?'

'Okay, okay, I'll go. I have to get up very early. So much work I have on Christmas.'

The old lady had made the best arrangements, as far as possible, for Christmas. She had bought on credit a new sari to be worn to church. A lovely red sari dotted with white, costing nine rupees. She had promised the shopkeeper, whom she knew, the money the very next day. She had bought a big cake, decoratively designed, for two rupees; a crown-like yellow cake it was. Written across it prettily was 'Jesus' in red icing. It was safely kept on the kitchen shelf.

A couple of days earlier itself she had bought all the titbits necessary for the meal, everything on credit, of course. Nothing could be achieved with the old man's salary. He would always take one or two rupees on loan, and before the salary date it would all amount to thirty rupees or even more. The old man, what did he do with the money? Did he drink? No, he only took money for the beedi and gave everything else to her. For cinema and coffee, he managed with the tips he received.

The old lady had promised to settle the money for the provisions too the next day.

No new clothes had been bought for the old man. As usual, he had said he didn't want any. 'Why for me, woman? You buy a sari on my behalf!'

When he had said uninterestedly that he didn't want veshti-mundu and all for Christmas four years ago for the first time, the old lady had fought with him. Then she had kept quiet. She had thought to herself, To that extent, money can be saved.

When the church bell had rung majestically, the old lady had got up hurriedly, washed her face hastily, wrapped the new sari and set off for the church, an old Bible in hand. She couldn't read, yet she never ever left without the Bible. That she held it in her hand made her proud. That Bible was an ancestral legacy from her mother.

'Wait, wait, I'll go to church and be back,' she had said, going inside the house.

She had come back from church by six itself. The old man had been snoring. She had kept back the Bible in its place, taken off her new sari and gone to the shed.

But the shed was empty. No sign of the goat. Her insides had collapsed. Pressing her belly tightly, she had run hither and thither at the back of the house. Where had Anthoni gone?

She felt as if a diabolic force had made her crazy and foolish.

Did she expect such a terrible loss on such a happy festival like Christmas? She didn't even dream that such a thing would take place.

Slapped with disappointment, she ran into the street with a dark, gloomy face.

'My goat is lost, ayyo, my goat is lost!' she wailed loudly. The neighbours gathered to condole. Many of them were happy inside.

'Serves this old lady right, serves her right!'

The old lady set off, searching for Anthoni. It didn't occur to her to wake up her slumbering husband and drag him with her. She had lost her mind.

She asked everyone who crossed her path, 'My goat, did it come here? My precious one, did you see my goat anywhere this side?'

The old lady wandered around like a dog. Where had that Anthoni gone? Had that butcher Peter stolen it?

She hastened towards Peter's shop. He was busy selling meat.

'Ele, Peter, you scamp, you thief! Where is my goat?'

Peter's eyes reddened; he bit his lip.

'Look here, old lady, hold your tongue and speak. Do you see what is in my hand?' He lifted his knife up to his head menacingly.

The old lady quietened, cowed. 'Peter fellow won't steal. Will do anything, but will never steal a goat. I asked only in anger.'

The old lady ran from there. She wound through the coconut grove, combed the fields, circled the tank, and investigated all the fences with plants and creepers.

Where had the goat gone?

She ran panting along the bank to the pond. She peered into the waters.

The pond seemed to reply, 'What are you looking for? Peering to see if your Anthoni has fallen in and drowned here? Nothing like that, old thing. Go somewhere else and search. My sympathies to you.'

The old lady's eyes poured out tears.

She flew to the bazaar. No sign of her beloved Anthoni even there. Joseph from the next street crossed her path. 'What Martha, did you get your goat? Hum… everything is gone. I too feel bad.'

'Okay, where are you going, Joseph? Come with me, no, let us search a bit.'

'No, Martha. Plenty of work at home. As if you don't know, today is Christmas, no?'

The old lady felt he was right and said, 'Okay, you go.'

She searched all over the bazaar. 'Anthoni, where have you gone? You ungrateful corpse!'

At the end of the village on the east, within shouting distance from the pond, was a hillock. There were plenty of banyan leaves there. Had that

Anthoni gone there? It was like the old lady and man, that beast, eating gluttonously.

No sign of Anthoni even there.

'Your goat didn't come here. Go and search somewhere else. So sad. You needn't have suffered such a big loss,' said the hillock.

The old lady returned home, tired after searching and searching.

Asirvatham hadn't yet got up from the bed. The snoring pierced the thatch.

The old lady sobbed till no tears were left. She paced up and down the kitchen restlessly.

In a while, the old man got up with feeble yawn, stretched himself lazily and lit a beedi.

Martha sat down in the kitchen, a picture of sadness.

When the old man heard the story, he too hung his face down. Pouted his lips. 'Let the corpse go. What has to go, let it go. What has to go will go only,' he tutted, feigning sympathy. Thank god, the old lady didn't notice it.

'You have searched thoroughly. Should I also search?' he asked, calmly.

The old lady sat still. All her plans had turned to dust. The festival of Christmas had turned into a day of mourning.

Asirvatham paced the kitchen, locking his hands at the back. A listless stride, a waste of a stride, which reflected no aim or purpose.

He, who was pacing up and down, suddenly opened the kitchen shelf, plucked the red letter 'J' from the cake, popped it into his mouth and tasted it.

Head bowed, Martha sat still, her right hand holding her jaw.

'What is the point of feeling sad, Martha? Go, get up, and see if you have any work to do,' said Asirvatham placatingly, his face devoid of any emotion.

At the time, a voice could be heard from the street calling out for the old lady.

The old man went outside quietly. What a surprise!

George, a building-labourer, stood there, holding Anthoni in his hand.

The old man screamed, 'Martha, the goat has come back!'

The old lady came running, her face wet with happy tears. She said a thousand thanks to labourer George. She bent down, touched his feet and paid her respects.

George asked for a reward for finding the goat with great difficulty.

'Okay, come in,' said the old lady.

The old lady came back to life. Jesus had brought back Anthoni. Now her plans would be fulfilled.

'Bring Joseph. He will be at home only,' she told the old man.

The old man was back in two minutes with Joseph from the next street.

'What, Martha? The goat has come back, no? Okay, gain for you and gain for me,' said Joseph laughingly.

'Give me four pounds of meat and take the rest for the price I had quoted. Give me the money by the evening. Give that George fellow also one pound.'

The old lady's dream had come true. A grand feast for the old man and the old lady.

Joseph pulled out the long knife from his hip.

The Anthoni who had got lost got lost again.

Original title: *Kaanaamal Pona Anthoni*
1959

Fight and Resolution 29

Neela Padmanabhan

'Amma…'

Mariammai recognised the clear, soft voice that she heard near her. Even so she couldn't believe it.

Had Chellayya come?

Mariammai's eyes turned heavy.

Going without food for four days, exhausted by the fever and weakened by old age, she couldn't see very clearly. Even so, the faintly visible broad face and the thick, curled moustache helped her recognise him.

As he touched her forehead to check for fever, she grasped his hand desperately, as one would if one were drowning midstream.

Happiness glimmered on her face. Her eyes brimmed. Chellayya didn't say anything. In a hoarse voice, she asked, 'When did you come?'

'I came two-three hours ago. I called out to you. But exhausted, you were fast asleep… Not wanting to wake you up, I went upstairs and was talking with Thangasami.'

'Oho.'

The hope that had flared on her face a moment ago died down. Only to be darkened again by disappointment.

She heaved a sigh.

She, who was aware of neither day nor night for the past four-five days, now looked around her anxiously.

The dim electric light hung pathetically. Against the dark skies, the window bars drew long, distinct lines.

'It must be night now… then the daughter-in-law Tamilkodi must have also come back from school.'

There were sounds of children playing on the street. The faces of one or two women, with infants on the hip, were faintly visible.

House-owner Sornamma, who lived downstairs, quietly came and stood on the verandah.

'Whatever you say, your mother shouldn't be stubborn at this old age. Total starvation for four-five days. Before even the elder daughter could come from Bangalore, she just lay there without a care, not drinking a drop of water or medicine, as if she wanted to die.'

Unmindful of the discomfort of sitting down with trousers and shoes, Chellayya somehow managed to sit beside his mother on the mat.

'Umm… you've been starving for the past four-five days. Shouldn't you drink something…?'

'I don't want anything… If possible, get me some poison… That I've lived for so long is enough…'

That Chellayya had gone and gathered all the details from Thangasami and his dear wife Tamilkodi before speaking to her first irritated Mariammai. She smote herself on her head and wept.

Chellayya was disturbed by this sight.

Chellayya was ten years older than Thangasami. He was now about thirty-five. He was the supervisor at Nagamma Mills, Nagercoil. It hadn't been even three months since he was sent to Bangalore to be trained to manage some new machine. He had come to Trivandrum at the behest of his mother, who had sent him an urgent letter. He was more fond of the mother than the younger fellow. That Mariammai knew very well.

'Okay, you won't drink anything from my younger brother's house… But you won't even drink if I buy something from the shop, is it? Umm… I'll come in a bit…' He got up.

Without waiting for a nod from Mariammai, he walked out but turned back and asked Sornamma, 'Do you have any small vessel to buy some tea? If you do, please give it to me…' She went in and brought back a steel vessel with a screwed-on lid. He took it and walked down into the street.

Knowing full well that the 'case' would be heard only on Chellaya's return, the ladies who were watching the fun returned home, as if it were recess time.

Mariammai lay curled in the corner of the pial, eyes wearily closed.

Had she slept or fainted, she didn't know. The sounds from her younger son's house upstairs... The goings-on from Sornamma's house... The sounds of footsteps from within and from the street.

On the first day of the fever she could feel the hunger very well. But now she couldn't feel the pangs. Yet she had a certain longing to drink something piping hot from Chellayya's hands.

In a while Chellayya returned, his shoes squeaking. He had bread and an orange in a small packet and tea in the steel vessel.

He took out a multicoloured strip of tablets from his trouser pocket and tore out a pill. He propped up Mariammai, and unmindful of her resistance, popped a pill into her mouth and made her drink tea sip by sip. He forced her to eat the peeled orange segments and the bits of bread and then made her lie down. He lit a cigarette and propped himself against the wall in a corner and made himself comfortable.

Now Mariammai felt a little invigorated.

He began slowly, 'Okay, why did you so urgently write to me, asking me to come immediately?'

'Your wonderful brother and his wife would have already exaggerated everything and told you. What is there for me to tell?'

Brushing aside the irritation and the wistfulness in her voice, he insisted, 'Just leave aside what they've said. You tell me.'

He looked and saw the neighbouring women who had once again gathered around the door of the house.

Sornamma understood his look. In the portion downstairs lived her son, his wife and their two-year-old son. To make ends meet, she had let out the upstairs for forty rupees to Thangasami who had recently come to Trivandrum from the Kanyakumari district to work as a clerk at the Inspector General's office. It was through this verandah – where Mariammai lay after quarrelling with her son – that anyone had to pass in order to reach the toilet at the back or the street outside. She had let out only the upstairs to Thangasami's family, so they had no rights to the verandah, except as a passage. She never stopped Mariammai from lying down on the verandah and neither did she now stop Chellayya from sitting there. So she wondered how she could shoo away her neighbours who had gathered to watch the fun.

Since Chellayya too was aware of all this, he simply continued to listen to his mother.

'Ley, Chellayya… you know very well that Thangasami should leave home by nine every morning. And Tamilkodi has to leave by seven to reach the Poondurai school. They also have a baby! At this age, I must get up before dawn every morning and prepare food for her to take. Thangasami will come back only in the evening – so I have to pack lunch for his office. I have to look after the baby, cook again for the night, grind the dosai batter for the next day… all this I'm doing in this old age, working like a buffalo…'

Mariammai's throat choked as she related her woes.

'Amma, who said that you are not slogging?' When Chellayya said this, Mariammai got even more angry.

'If anyone says that, God will not spare them. But… if the two of them think that I'm their servant… The lord and the lady will go away for work, I must slog away at home and do all the work for them. I also take care of the tender sapling. After all this, to celebrate the child's birthday, the two of them left for Tamilkodi's mother's house, without saying a word to me. Why can't they tell me? As if I'm going to go with them.'

Too choked, Mariammai couldn't speak. Sornamma related the rest.

'One day four months ago… When Mariammai finished washing clothes and bathing, she neither found her son upstairs nor the girl. The child too was not in the cradle. When she realised that it was the child's first birthday the next day, she was so disappointed and angry. It wasn't as if she didn't know where they would have gone to celebrate the birthday. Still, she couldn't bear the ungratefulness. She hurriedly bundled her clothes, locked the upstairs and gave the key to me. "I slogged and brought up that child. And I shouldn't know about his birthday. Even a servant will get more respect. Here even a mother doesn't get it. I won't step into a house that doesn't respect me. I'm going to my daughter's house in Panakkudi. When the school opens and both of them return to work, let's see who's going to cook for them." She left for Panakkudi to her daughter's house.'

Sornamma continued.

'When they returned after the celebrations, I only told them that your mother, feeling hurt, had left for Panakkudi. Since the school was still shut, the two of them didn't care much. As the reopening day drew close, Tamilkodi went to Moolamoodu and came back with a twelve-year-old girl to help her out… After the school reopened, for two months Tamilkodi got up early, cooked food, packed lunch and went to school, leaving the child with the girl. I only couldn't bear it and asked Thangasami once or twice, "Can't you write and tell your mother to come back, poor thing."

"Umm... umm... let her come back like how she went... she's not a guest to be invited..." he would simply end the conversation.'

Mariammai calmed herself and continued, 'A mother's heart is truly crazy. I was waiting in Panakkudi in Thayi's house for him to at least come when the school reopened... For two months after the school reopened, he didn't even write to me and kept quiet like a stone. I didn't want to return without him calling. But Thayi's husband got a transfer to Madurai. He didn't want to take them to Madurai before seeing a house, so he sent them away to his parents' place in Thakkalai. Since I knew that he alone was going to Madurai, how could I stay there? Since I had nowhere else to go, I came straight here. If you had been there, I would have come to Nagercoil. Umm... you also went off to Bangalore!'

Letting her talk, Chellayya kept silent.

'When I returned, it was afternoon. Only the servant girl was taking care of the child. I couldn't bear it after I picked up the child... He had become so thin... It wasn't yet time for Thangasami to return from office. Tamilkodi would also come back only after two hours... I was really hungry... When I went into the kitchen, there was just little rice for Tamilkodi to eat after she returned. I took a little roasted flour from a dabba in the loft, prepared a batter, made a dosai and ate. I also drank a little cold water. The lady of the house came back from school and said, "I brought the flour from my mother's house. This one ate it up like a queen, not doing a jot of work...!" After that I didn't even take a sip of water from that house...' completed Mariammai, in tears.

A little emotional, Chellayya asked, 'Didn't Thangasami say anything?'

'Umm... he!' The old lady heaved a sigh. 'Pearls will drop, no, if he opens his mouth! He didn't even lift his head to see me, a mother who has returned after days... He walked out, as if some stranger was being shouted at.'

Chellayya looked at the stairway angrily. It looked as if he was wondering whether to summon Thangasami down or not.

Sornamma said, 'The one who is giving the rent is your brother. So I shouldn't complain about him... But I can't help relating what happened. Is she the mother who begot him or some stranger? The day she came back from Panakkudi, she made some dosai and ate, that's all... after that, complete starvation. Along with that, this fever… her body keeps shivering and tossing. She is just lying here on this mat ever since then. I kept quiet thinking why I should bother when her own son and daughter-in-law don't. They were going up and down, crossing her, but not once they thought of asking. I couldn't bear it anymore. Let him think whatever, so I called him and asked, "Dei, Thangasami, isn't she your mother? She's starving and shivering and suffering like anything with fever… can you not take her upstairs, make her lie down and give some kanji and medicine? You're committing a great sin, da. Don't forget, you too have a son." Like this, I said so many things. You know what Thangasami said? "Why is she behaving like a guest? With full rights, she can always come up and lie down. And can she not ask whatever she wants from Tamilkodi – will her pride take a dent in this old age? You have let out only the upstairs to us… What right has she got to use this verandah? Ask her either to come up, or tell her to go out…" Then he just left for the office…'

Chellayya sprung up agitatedly. It seemed as if he didn't want to question Thangasami in front of everyone. But his face revealed that he was livid with Thangasami. Coming to a decision, he hastily marched up the wooden stairs.

For a while Mariammai could hear his hoarse voice. In between, Tamilkodi's soft tones too… After a while, complete silence.

Sleep and tiredness overcame Mariammai and she dozed off. She didn't know how long she slept. Suddenly, when she heard the wails of her grandson, she woke up. There was no one when she looked around.

Sornamma and the other women had gone away, as if disappointed that there was no big fight between the two brothers.

No one picked up the child for a while. Then one could hear Tamilkodi irritatedly pacifying the child.

After sometime Chellayya came down the stairs softly and stood near Mariammai. The pace with which he had gone had receded.

'You shouldn't be so stubborn in this old age. From what she says, it looks as if you are in the wrong. You don't have any rights here, is it? Why should you behave like a guest? You should help out and share whatever is there… instead of that why all this trouble? In this old age, don't pig-headedly think "me and me only". Try to adjust with her. Who is Tamilkodi? Your daughter-in-law only, no? If she says anything, don't make it a big thing. Just keep quiet… Ummm…That's what is good for you. Okay, I don't have much time. I must catch the next train. I'll go.'

Chellayya's gravelly voice resounded firmly.

Without waiting for her reply, Chellayya reached the entrance. Thangasami entered.

'Going back to Bangalore? A while ago when I left home, I didn't see you here. Where had you gone?'

Chellayya suddenly looked disconcerted when he was confronted with Thangasami. But he managed to say, 'No, I went to buy medicines for Amma… That's when you must have gone out. Okay, I'll leave. I must take the next train. I don't have any leave.'

Without looking into his brother's face, Chellayya hastily marched down the street, his shoes clacking.

Original title: *Sandaiyum Samaadaanamum*
1969

Dissonance 30

Jayakanthan

The toe-rings click-clacked. The bangles jingled.

In the hall, eight-year-old grandson Muthu to the right and four-year-old granddaughter Viji to the left were fast asleep. Kailasam Pillai, who was lying down between them, lifted his head and looked up.

He could see his daughter-in-law Sarasa entering his son's bedroom, a glass of milk in hand. When his gaze fell on her, Sarasa lowered her head.

He did have a naughty streak, the old man.

Kailasam Pillai's eyes followed her as she entered the room. When the door shut with a creak, his gaze, unable to follow her further, butted against it.

A girl's figure appeared like a painting on the closed door. A girl not more than sixteen.

A brooch on her tightly combed hair and another on her lush, long plait, a pearl-studded ornament on her forehead, a nose-ring dangling above her coral lips, a long-sleeved blouse, a swishing silk sari full of zari, under the glistening creeper-like dark brows kohl-rimmed big bashful eyes, youthful radiance melded with disarming coyness, an enchanting beauty…

Yes, a spitting image of Dharmambal aachi in the first flush of youth.

The figure, full of bashfulness, nervousness, excitement, lust, passion and devotion, walked towards him. Kailasam tried to fold her in his arms.

After finishing her kitchen chores, Dharmambal came to the hall and spread out the mat near her grandchildren.

Hearing her movements, he snapped out of his reverie and he looked at his wife. She straightened her grandson who was lying down haphazardly.

'What children! Playing right through the day without a break, bouncing and jumping around. And sleeping like logs in the night, as if knocked out. Adada! What jumping and bouncing!' she grumbled, patting her grandson on the back.

He was the first son of their only son Kannan, wasn't he?

'He's eight. But he doesn't seem to look it at all. Never eats!' she sighed with worry.

The four-year-old granddaughter Vijaya, brought up by her grandmother, was also lying on the floor. Dharmambal pulled her too on to the mat.

'Hmm...Paati,' whimpered the child.

'Nothing, Kanna. You were on the floor. Um... go back to sleep.' Paati stroked her back.

Kailasam remained silent, allowing his mind to wander over the lush, green days of his youth.

'Why are you still sitting... Should I sing a lullaby for you also? Can't you drink the milk and go to sleep? How long ago it's been kept there... it must be cold by now...' she said, straightening the rumpled bed.

'Please give me the tumbler with your own hands.'

When she handed him the tumbler, he caught hold of her hand.

'Yes, yes, you are asking me to go to sleep... but which devil's daughter has crushed betel leaves for me yet...' he said laughingly, without letting go of her hand.

'Yes, yes, just can't stop laughing I suppose... as they say, in a house without children the old man is frolicking... let go of my hand.'

'Who is old? Me?' He smiled, patting his wife's cheek.

'No, no, you are just seventeen, going on eighteen... shall I look for a bride for you?'

'Why? You are there for me, no?' he said, tugging the ends of her sari.

'Aiyee! What is this?'

The naughty old man laughed again.

When he had drunk the milk, his whole body sweated. Wiping himself with a towel, he said, 'Uss… how stuffy it is… take the mat and spread it out in the courtyard… I will bring the betel box,' he said.

Dharmambal rolled up the mat and switched off the hall light. She spread out the mat where the moonlight shone brightly.

'Uss… ammaadi… how breezy it is…' She sat, stretching out her legs.

She wiped her hands and the front of her neck with the ends of her sari. She loosened her blouse, lifted it a bit at the back and scratched herself with the handle of her hand fan.

Kailasam Pillai sat next to his wife and gazed at the moonlit sky.

When the wafting clouds neared the moonlight they glinted brightly and as they moved away they dimmed into dark, shadowy patches – a stunning display of colours in the vast expanse of the sky.

In this moonlight… yes, the same moon – time passes by but the moon remains the same. Memories flitted by – of listening to tales on his grandmother's lap, eating milk-rice, of resting his head on his beloved wife's lap, chewing betel, mesmerised by dreams.

Those memories too glistened and dimmed like the clouds and drifted away.

Where are the clouds? Where is the moon? Where are the memories? Where is my place now?

Are they thoughts only if you think of them? Where are they when you don't think of them? Why are thoughts born? And how are they born? What is memory? Does whatever you think actually happen? Don't we also think of things that never happen? Are thoughts really true? Don't lies, desires and meaningless fantasies become true when you roll them over again and again in your mind?

'Todak'…'todak'…

The sound of the nut cracker in Dharmambal's hands echoed in the still night.

Kailasam saw his wife and in her he saw himself too.

Dharmambal scraped the hardened lime paste into the betel leaf along with the betel nut and started pounding it in the tiny mortar and pestle.

Kailasam's tongue combed the place where once his teeth were.

'Umm… I always had weak teeth…'

He stroked his body. He turned his shoulders and arms, shook out his hands and cracked his knuckles. Though the skin on his hairy chest and shoulders had sagged, the muscles still rippled.

Kailasam was a strong man. He once possessed a giant's strength; now he surely had a man's might.

Only last year he had turned sixty. Dharmambal was in her fifties.

She had the sinewy strength of a bamboo shoot. Even though she was lean, she was strong. How else could she have coped with his demands for forty-odd years.

The old man's hands caressed his wife's shoulders…

'What's all this cooing? Take the betel leaves and go to sleep.' She placed some pounded betel paste on his palm, and popped the remaining into her mouth, chewed it and tucked it to a side.

Dharmambal possessed teeth. Even so, she derived a certain satisfaction in sharing the paste she pounded for her husband. It had been like this for the past six years.

There hadn't been the slightest misunderstanding between the couple in all these years. No quarrels either. He'd never said to her, 'Chee, get lost!' Whether she could have endured it was a different matter, but his tongue couldn't bring itself to utter such a thing.

They had spent their lives in fun and laughter.

Could you already say 'had spent'? So far, perhaps.

The moon dimmed; it was quiet everywhere. Muthu, who was sleeping in the hall, rolled over, mumbling something.

From the room, the jingle of bangles, the creaking of the cot and the murmur of a woman…

Somewhere a bird flapped its wings; a bat flew across the sky. A portion of the courtyard was enveloped in darkness.

The moon had sunk below the opposite roof, creating a curtain of shadow where they lay.

Dharmambal giggled softly, as if youth had crept back into her. Her face disappeared into her husband's broad chest. Her gold bangles shone against the old man's back.

Light or dark, day or night, young or old, passion was beyond all this.

Yes, passion, that which is in the heart. It befits anyone, at any time, in any moment. Kailasam and Dharmambal had it in their hearts. So what did age matter?

'Tok'… 'tok'…

Kailasam dragged his mat towards the moonlight and pounded the betel nut.

Dharmambal was sleeping beside him. Perhaps half asleep.

'Aren't you asleep yet?'

'Um… do you want some betel?'

'Um… I've kept a small vessel of water near the pillar. Can you bring it? My throat is parched.' She swallowed her saliva.

'I too want some.' He drank some water and brought it for her.

As he walked towards her in the moonlight, his strapping frame captivated her heart, filling it with ecstasy, as if youth had seeped anew into her.

He came and sat near her.

Dharmambal quenched her thirst and leant on her husband with a deep sigh. Stroking his strong arm, she felt like laughing. And she did.

'Why are you laughing?'

'Nothing. Just thought people will laugh the way we old things are frolicking.' He tapped her head, as if in admonition. 'Who is old here?'

They both laughed.

Dharmambal sat up and helped herself yet again to the betel leaves. Her eyes remained downcast.

The old man caressed her face. She lifted her eyes. He looked deep into her eyes and smiled.

'Che, you are so wicked,' she said bashfully. The pleasure they had experienced a while ago filled her with laughter. The old man burst with pride.

He wanted to say something playful to her. Crushing some tobacco in his palm, laughing to himself, he said, 'What do you know of my escapades in those days?' He popped the tobacco into his mouth.

'Why, did you go abroad or what?'

'Dharmu, you don't know. You've always been a child. I have never told you this. Why not tell you now?'

The old man spat into the gutter and came back.

'Remember Gomathi from our Sannadhi Street?'

An image flashed in Dharmambal's mind – ankle bells on the feet, a slithering snake-like plait, eyes and lips that spoke tales… a golden statue in a dancing pose to the song 'I have a score to settle with him…' Mocking her, the image lingered on…

'What, do you remember her? Was there anyone equal to her in those days? Whatever you say, a courtesan is a courtesan. Can a family woman ever match them in giving pleasure?'

'Um…' Dharmambal's eyes stared at her husband questioningly.

Oho! In those days he was crazy about her dance. Was this the reason? Recalling several incidents, her mind tried to probe.

The old man, oblivious, continued the banter. 'Do you remember? They posted me to Nilgiris once? When you were seven months pregnant with Kannan.'

'Um…' Dharmambal's eyes rolled. Some voice within her said, it is true, it is true.

'Did you think I went alone? You foolish one! That Gomathi only came with me… Her body was like a figurine… You know what she said in the end?' The old man laughed to himself. '"I've seen so many men in all these years. But you are the only real man!"' The old man laughed again.

What kind of laugh was that? Was it real or false?

The rage of betrayal and anger surged like flames within Dharmambal.

'Really?'

'Then what? Do you think I'm lying? Never mind, it all happened long ago.'

You idiot of an old man. What does it matter if it is true or false. Can't you tell something that would satisfy her?

Dharmambal may be an old woman. But she was a woman all the same.

Traitor, traitor! Her heart twitched. Yes, it was the truth. Not a lie. For some reason her heart believed it all. She didn't, even for a moment, suspect that it could be a lie. That was the enigma of marriage.

Dharmambal suddenly got up, groped her way through the dark and flopped down with a thud in the darkness of the hall.

'Adede, Dharmu, you're angry, are you? You mad woman!' he said playfully and spread his towel on the mat.

Playful? What kind of playfulness was this? It was the evil Saturn only that had played on the old man's tongue.

It struck twelve. The old man slept. But Dharmambal didn't.

The next day…

Why only next day? Till the end of her life…

She never gave him coffee; never fetched him water for brushing his teeth or bathing; never scrubbed his back; never served him food; never pounded betel leaf and nut.

Poor old man. He suffered like an orphaned infant.

As far as she was concerned, she behaved as if he didn't exist, as if she had never married him. She never spoke a word, neither to him nor to anyone else.

Her son and daughter-in-law tried to probe.

She remained silent.

The old man? What could he say?

He remained silent too.

That night Vijaya asked, 'Paati, you're not friends with Thaatha anymore?'

She didn't reply.

'Why, Thaatha, Paati is not talking to you anymore? Did you beat her?' pestered Muthu.

The old man couldn't bear it.

'What Dharmu? I lied only in jest. Don't you know me? Do you think I would have ever betrayed you? You've lived with me for so many years, haven't you understood me yet? Dharmu… Dharmu…'

'Chee! Did I live? Ayyo, what a life! I fooled myself thinking that I had lived…'

Of course she didn't utter all this. The children fell asleep.

'Dharmu… won't you believe me?' His hand stroked her head.

Like a hurt animal she flinched and moved away, her body trembling.

'Chee!' she growled with revulsion. 'If you touch me, I will scream and turn you into a laughing stock.'

She gasped. Her whole body broke into a sweat. She had never spoken to him like this. This was the first time. The old man was shocked.

Hurt, the old man walked away.

She doubts me… me… The thought choked him and his eyes moistened. 'Let her go. She won't die in peace.' He cursed her.

Desolate, like an abandoned orphan he slept on the bare floor in the front pial.

Since the day he married Dharmambal, this was the first time tears flowed from his eyes.

'Fate… fate…' he muttered.

It was the time for fate to unfold itself.

Eight in the night. A car at the entrance of the house.

Dharmambal lies on the bed in the hall. Her son, daughter-in-law and grandchildren stand around her. The doctor is giving her an injection.

Kailasam Pillai, who is at the corner of the pial, peeps through the window with a heavy heart.

He isn't allowed to go in.

The doctor comes out. Kannan walks behind him, carrying the doctor's kit.

'Doctor… will my "life" survive?' Kailasam's voice stops the doctor.

Head bent, the doctor walks out silently, trampling over Kailasam Pillai's sorrow.

The old man rushes in in a frenzy.

'Dharmu… Dharmu… don't leave me alone and go… Dharmu!'

Not a movement on Dharmambal's stiff body on the cot.

Life…?

A fly sits on the forehead. The skin on the forehead and the eyebrow twitch.

The eyes open wide and look around once.

With tear-laden eyes, Kannan feeds some milk into her mouth.

'Who… is it, Kannan? The bonds are all in milk. Now this too will break away…'

Now it is Sarasa who gives her milk.

'How will you cope with two children, my dear?'

The grandson sniffles, 'Paati, Paati…' and poured the milk.

Her eyes brighten, as if twitching to hug Muthu.

Viji stands, frightened and confused. When with her tender fingers she pours milk into Paati's mouth…

'…is a there a special sweetness to this?' An unusual glow spreads over Paati's face and the milk goes down effortlessly.

Covering his face with a towel, Kailasam comes in, his whole body shaking.

'Won't she forgive me at least in this state…' he yearns.

His hands tremble when they take the milk tumbler.

'Dharmu… Dharmu… Won't you look at me, Dharmu?'

'Who is it?' Her eyes open and look around.

To the lips that twitch with unbearable pain, Kailasam, mustering up a smile through the tears, brings the milk tumbler.

Clenching her teeth, as if in an epileptic fit, Dharmambal's face moves away and falls on her neck.

The milk drips off the ends of her lips.

'Ayyo, Maami,' Sarasa's voice bursts out.

'Amma…Paati… hmm…' Muthu hugs his mother and cries. Viji stares blankly. Head bent, Kannan weeps.

The old man stands upright. His face swells, and his eyes melded with tears and anger redden with rage.

Kailasam is an old man all right. But he is a man, isn't he!

'I will not even light the funeral pyre for her with my hands.' He flings the milk tumbler and strides out of the room.

The milk tumbler rolls away noisily into the moonlit courtyard.

That night, on that last night, in the place where they slept, the moonbeams shine brightly on the spilt milk, chuckling away.

Yes! It is the same moon.

Original title: *Pinakku*
1958

Dhanabala Chettiar Company 31

C N Annadurai

Of course, all this is imagination. But could the lives of these individuals be any different? The owner Chettiar's pomposity, the labourers' weariness, the contrasting attitudes of the two, only all this I've written. Read it and see. You will never get a lesson equal to this even if you read cartloads of books.

Dhanabala Chettiar's account 7-1-1940

	Rs	Annas	Paise
By interest from Aa mu ka	648	6	0
By shop rent from Kalinga Naidu	68	0	0
To conveyance	0	6	0
To clerk Kumarappan	5	0	0
To household medical expenses	22	0	0
To Lokamrita gurukkal for panchamrita abhishegam	75	0	0
To advocate Sundaram Iyer	32	0	0
To watchman Kandan	2	8	0
To oranges	1	8	0
To Ambika Hotel expenses	2	8	0

	Rs	Annas	Paise
Total Income	716	6	0
Expenditure	140	14	0
Balance	575	8	0

Dhanabala Chettiar was a moneylender and a landlord. He leased out many houses on rent. The above are the details of a day's account written in his account book.

Clerk Kumarappan's account 8-1-1940

	Rs	Anna	Paise
By salary from Chettiar	5	0	0
To rice merchant	1	8	0
To firewood	0	6	0
To vegetables	0	2	0
To temple expenditure including archanai	0	4	0
To cinema	0	8	0
To interest	2	0	0
To soap, ribbon for the child	0	4	0

Earnings and expenditure are equal here!

Kandan's account

	Rs	Annas	Paise
Salary from Chettiar	2	8	0
Arrack	0	14	0
Tiffin	0	2	0
Household	1	0	0
Moneylender	0	8	0

Here too the income and expenditure tally!

Kuppi's account

	Rs	Annas	Paise
What Kandan gave	1	0	0
Rice	0	8	0
Dried fish	0	1	0

Chillies	0	2	0
Oil	0	2	0
Salt	0	1	0
Pujari	0	2	0

Here too the accounts tally!

Lokamrita Iyer's account

	Rs	Annas	Paise
Income from Chettiar	75	0	0
To fruit vendor	15	0	0
By Mr Su Pa Su for panchamritam	6	0	0
To Shama	5	0	0
By Sethji Bansilal	3	0	0
By Muthu Mudali	7	0	0
By Nagalinga Naidu	4	0	0

	Rs	Annas	Paise
Income	95	0	0
Expenditure	20	0	0
Balance	75	0	0

The accounts don't tally, but there is an excess.

Pankajavalli's account

	Rs	Annas	Paise
Received from Iyer	75	0	0
Bombay silk sari	35	0	0
Organdy blouse	6	0	0
Silk pavadai for Janaki	12	0	0
Cuticura soap, powder, perfume, ribbon	5	0	0
Chintamani expenses	2	8	0
Bangalore vegetables	2	0	0

	Rs	Annas	Paise
Income	75	0	0
Expenses	62	8	0
Balance	12	8	0

The accounts don't tally here!

Chettiar's accounts were written in a calico-bound notebook by a clerk.

Clerk Kumarappan wrote his accounts in a pocket-sized diary. Lokamrita Iyer wrote the accounts in a pretty notebook stitched by his daughter Kokilam using the temple festival handbills. Pankajavalli's accounts were written on the back of cinema advertisement bills. Where did Kandan and Kuppi have books to write on!

Kandan came home and gave a rupee.

'What is this nonsense? What can I do with a single rupee?

'Go, di! What do you know how I had to bare my teeth to that fellow to get this money.'

'Tell me, on your father's honour. Did he really give you only one rupee?'

'Yes, di. I tell you.'

'Wonderful. I can see it. What is there to tell? I can see by the way you are staggering. Did you pay off the moneylender?'

'Will he leave? Took away eight annas.'

'The remaining…?'

'I have the remaining…'

'Where?'

'It's there, just leave me. Simply irritating a man!'

'Tell me, where?'

'Won't tell. Go, di! Will not tell! Won't show it even.'

This is how the accounts were sorted out. At the end of the argument, Kandan's fist tested Kuppi's back and that woman's wail pierced the ears of the neighbour. After that, Kuppi settled her account by giving one on the back of her child who asked for sweetmeats.

'That sinner gave me a rupee after spending on the moneylender and the arrack. Half a rupee for rice, two annas for chilli, one anna for salt, two annas for oil, the remaining two annas I tied into the ends of my sari. The pujari said that they were sacrificing a goat for Goddess Moolakaatha and I gave what I had. What else would I have? If you want to eat sweets, I have to steal only. I have bought dried fish for an anna, and I'm going to make it now. If you cry and don't eat that, I'll give you one.' Thus Kuppi recorded the accounts.

Thus were the family's accounts. Leave money matters aside, and see how they labour.

Chettiar's labour:
Morning 7.30 opened his eyes
By 7.45 got up from bed
By 8.30 finished the ablutions
Till 9.30 stayed at home and had tiffin, etcetera
The watchman informed that the cart had arrived.

Chettiar shouted, 'Dei, you fat donkey. Day by day you are becoming very lazy.'

That lazy fellow got up at 4.20 in the morning. After informing the farmer that Chettiar wanted the work in the fields to be finished quickly, he ran to the garden and told them to bring six tender coconuts to Chettiar's shop for the afternoon. On the way back he went to the granary. In order to keep the boss informed, he noted that about only ten carts had arrived. He went to his hut, but there was no firewood. Kuppi complained that the wood from the tamarind tree was very knotty. He split it with an axe, popped a betel leaf into his mouth and made his way to Chettiar's bungalow. After telling the cart-driver that Chettiar would soon start, he went in and told Chettiar that the cart had arrived. Chettiar scolded 'that lazy fellow' and went into his wife's room. He came out at eleven! By this time, the cart had been readied three times. The lazy Kandan watered the crotons, heaped up mud and levelled the holes near the fence, plucked wood apples from the tree and took them inside the house, wiped his sweat, shook out his faded cloth and tied it on his head.

Chettiar asked him, 'What audacity, da, for you. Other than shaking your cloth, tying a turban and strolling around like a bridegroom, do you do any work at all? Day by day you're getting too spoilt. You don't want to stay here and work properly or what?' Kandan bowed his head, bobbed up and down, and displayed his servility.

Completing his task at home, Chettiar started for his shop. There would be lazy fellows there too, wouldn't there? He had to extract work from them too. How did he go? By cart. On the way, the bulls gave some trouble. The cart-driver had been telling for the past four days that there was no horseshoe, the bulls were not moving and that the feet had worn out.

'What da, you son of a thief! It's not even three months since you had fixed the horseshoe and so quickly it has worn out, is it? That horseshoe fellow, he's giving you commission or what! Every month, without fail, you take my life out saying, "Horseshoe, horseshoe!" We'll look at it next month, manage somehow and drive.'

That day too he tried to drive, but the bull collapsed.

After cursing him, 'Useless fellow! Buffalo! You have only clay in your head!' Chettiar hailed a cart for hire and reached the shop. Wasteful expenditure of six annas for the vehicle.

One of Chettiar's clients welcomed him, 'Come, come Chettiar. You look tired and exhausted.'

Chettiar replied, 'Yes, yes, too much of running around.'

'Everyone is now gathering and talking at Ambika's.'

'Who?' asked Chettiar. He looked towards the clerk. The clerk looked at the shop-boy. The boy brought a hand-fan, stood near the boss and commenced his work.

Meanwhile, Chettiar's friend replied, 'Who-aa? What, Chettiar? You're sleeping or what? The three parties have already arrived.'

'Coimbatore or Salem?' asked Chettiar.

'Salem fellows only,' he replied.

'What is happening at Ambika?' asked Chettiar.

'That PV fellow – taking them to Ambika, buying coffee, tiffin and all, and cajoling them to buy stocks from him.'

'Is that so?' said Chettiar.

They both left for Ambika Bhavan. They met the party. PV wasn't there. For the three of them, coffee, etcetera, at Chettiar's expense. The bill came to 2-8-0! Then they all came back to the shop.

The clerk informed, 'The rent money has come.' At that time Chettiar was busy explaining the difference between banana and potato chips to the Salem party. The clerk attempted to convey this twice or thrice, but Chettiar turned a deaf ear. After the Salem merchant left (oranges worth one rupee eight annas were polished off before they left!), Chettiar called the clerk.

'Look here 'pa, I'm telling you nicely only. I'm not at all happy with the way you do things.' The clerk started to reply. Chettiar raised his voice and uttered quickly, 'Don't talk back. Get out of the shop. Behave properly.'

The clerk turned silent. After ten minutes Chettiar started again, 'You get angry soon. Do you do at least one job properly? Didn't I ask you the collect the rent money?'

'You did tell me. I only…'

'I told you and you asked and simply came back. You are a big lord's son! Whose money is it?'

'I told you I received the rent money.'

'The rent money has come, is it! Why are you then standing like a tree? I'm shouting myself hoarse "rent, rent". You kept quiet then, and you are telling me now as if it is a secret.'

'I told you then itself, ayya. That Salem party was there.'

'What, da, you said it in front of them? Should you be saying all this in front of them?'

'That's why I whispered.'

'The devil only knows what you said. Okay, how much did he give?'

'Sixty-eight.'

'What is this – why two rupees less?'

'Two rupees for whitewash it seems.'

'Who asked them to whitewash?'

'The sanitary inspector sent a notice it seems.'

'Ade, what do I care what notice came. Did I ask them to whitewash?'

'No, ayya.'

'Who did they ask and whitewash? How can they deduct two rupees? Fine story this is.'

'I tried to tell them.'

'He said no and you agreed, is it? Why are you betraying me like this? Look here, these two rupees must be somehow collected. Otherwise I'll deduct from you.'

After all this show of affection, he managed to wrench what he wanted. The lunch arrived. Chettiar ate and the boy cleaned up the place. The clerk poured water to wash the hands. Another clerk gave a towel to wipe. In the meanwhile, a mattress had been spread out. Chettiar eased his tired body. The boy fanned him. He got up at about five in the evening. He sent the clerk to the medical shop. He asked the boy to fetch the lawyer's clerk and gave the man some money. After overseeing the work at the field the 'lazy Kandan' filled his stomach with a bit of kanji. Hefting back tender coconuts from the garden, he found the Chettiar asleep. So he went back to the bungalow, busied himself in chores, returning later to the shop. Chettiar threw him some money.

As he started for home, the gurukkal arrived. Chettiar welcomed him with a smiling face. The sacred conversation began.

Chettiar: Come, come, saami. Never seem to get your darshan these days.

Gurukkal: What are you saying? To get an audience with Chettiar only is like a horse's horns.

Ch: Siva, Siva. What saami, talking about me so grandly.

Gu: Do you think it's only me, Mr Chettiar? Why, do you know what Kamala said last evening?'

Ch: Kamala-va? She talks about me and all, is it?

Gu: Besh! Asking if she talks about you. God knows what magic you did. All the time thinking about you.

Ch: Go on! You are saying all this simply.

Gu: I swear to you.

Ch: Siva, Siva. Okay, what did she say?

Gu: She said looking at Chettiar is like seeing the special prayer for Lord Garuda in Kanchipuram.

Ch; Did she say that? That Kamala always talks very cleverly.

Gu: What are you saying? Only in speech?

Ch: No, no, she's smart in all ways.

Gu: Who sings like her in this town?

Ch: Dances too.

Gu: Like the dance of Siva.

Ch: Good-natured, but always an eye on money.

Gu: That's natural, Mr Chettiar. Tomorrow she's also coming for the panchamrita abhishegam.

Ch: Bale. Then you should do it grandly.

Gu: If Brahma wishes, can the lifespan be short?

Ch: Give Iyer fifty rupees (calling out to the clerk).

Gu: Give another twenty-five.

Ch: So much expense?

Gu: Yes, she and I have made the budget.

Ch: Then there's no 'appeal'.

After Iyer left with seventy-five rupees, Chettiar walked merrily towards the bazaar, chatted with friends and then left for home.

Original title: *Dhanabala Chettiar Company*
1945

Beyond the Boundary 32

T K Seenivasan

Unable to bear the darkness of the night, the stars scattered in the sky twitched. From time to time the vehicle which inched along caused earthquakes to those sitting inside, thanks to the small potholes kindly provided by the municipality. But to Chandran who was with her it seemed as if he was circling in an aeroplane.

She…?

She was someone. A feast for the passion of youth. One who surrendered her body to him that night.

The street light flickered on and off her face. The smile on her lips tried to hide the exhaustion on her face, which was lined with a faint hint of coyness. The tremor of her lips created a passionate frenzy in his heart. As if taking a stroll, the soft breeze entered the vehicle; the scent of her jasmine flowers drew him to her. His heart spilled over with a mesmeric joy, much like an enjoyable puff of cigarette that you draw in and blow out.

It's not merely enough to know the tenets and doctrines, one must realise them as well. One cannot accomplish anything by resolve alone. Chandran was a standing example of this.

He had suddenly donned ochre robes and set off in search of god. Somehow god had got to hear of this. He went off somewhere and hid from Chandran's eyes.

What was strange about this was that when Chandran was a young boy, he had tied a thaali around the neck of a young girl, as dictated by the ways of his caste; he had also assumed property rights over her. Suddenly Chandran had shrugged off his interests in land, women and gold, and the marriage had then become a property without proper documents.

He ought to have known that he was searching for the omniscient being who was everywhere; or at least god ought to have compassionately appeared before such a devotee who was searching so hard to find him. But in this game of hide and seek, neither of them realised the torment which seemed to be growing in a young woman's heart. Be it fate, destiny or self-awareness, Chandran had suddenly set himself free of the ochre robes and beard, and gone in search of novelties that life had to offer.

On his way back, it was on the train only that their one-day relationship had occurred.

That night, for them it had been a good night. In the beginning, it was all there – shyness, fear. But it all vanished once passion gradually overtook them, like the incense that wafts out before a play, driven away by the cigarette from the front row. That night – it had come and gone like all other nights. The initial fear which gave way to hesitation, the pleasurable twitches in between, the exhaustion which dragged them to sleep, these were the outcomes of that night.

It was only well after daybreak that Chandran woke up. The open door revealed that she had left. The few withered jasmine flowers scattered on the bed seemed to mock him.

The tenets of his religion seemed to threaten him, 'One of the five great sins is debauchery. You've committed that, you sinner! God will not let you go unpunished.'

'God cannot punish me. He has behaved just like me many times,' he retorted mockingly, driving it away.

Humanity questioned him sternly, 'Betrayer! There is a girl for you, but one who has lost her life because of you. Only because you are a man you have the audacity to behave like this.'

'What can I do? It is youth which destroyed me.'

'Youth spoilt you, did it? Where did your discriminatory powers go? Go, run. Go and ask for her forgiveness.'

Dipping his imagination with colour, an unknown artist had created the joyful scene: a flute-playing Krishna surrounded by dancing gopis.

The joy from Krishna's heart which spilled on to his face melted each and every one of the gopis through the mellifluous notes from his flute. The longing and yearning on the faces of the girls whose sinuous curves were gracefully revealed...

Guided by Krishna, the passion in Chandran's heart swelled. The silk mattress, the delicate flowers strewn on it, the silver plate laden with a variety of fruits, the freshly ground sandal paste, the burning, fragrant agarbathi, tender betel leaves, scented betel-nut powder, the moon which spilled light like milk, the gentle, cool breeze which sent tiny quivers on the skin – yes, raga and tala played in unison.

But...?

It was not his first night, it was his second. He was well aware of the novelties. Had experienced them too.

But what about her?

Yes, what about her who seemed to beckon sleep, tossing this way and that on the bed with a heaving, simmering heart? The mirror on the wall reflected his figure, which was nothing more than a crawling worm.

The door opened. Fair feet with a tinge of red, a thin voile sari draped almost invisibly around her, narrow hips, high breasts, a milk vessel in one hand, beautiful neck, a golden chain glistening in the folds of her skin exposed between the neck and the breasts.

'You?' Chandran shouted.

The milk vessel slipped from her hand.

Tears spilled out.

'You loose woman! You evildoer! You betrayer!'

'Stop it. I am also human like you. I too have the same feelings that you have.'

Chandran felt as if a mike had failed while making an emotional speech.

This was a new lesson to him. He realised only now that there were many things beyond the vedas-vedantas. Ants swarmed around the spilt milk on the floor, as they do always.

Original title: *Ellaikku Appaal*
1950

The Fisher Girl

33

Rajam Krishnan

Bongdo!

Bongdo! Baiko! Bongdo!

A sweet childish voice, as if a yaazh and flute had melded together, wafted in from the street, calling out the wares.

It was about eleven in the morning. Radhabai was busy at the stove, seasoning something. Wasn't that Kaveri Maami's voice calling her in? 'Adi, kutti! Bongdo! Come here, come here!' A little startled, Radha looked out of the window.

'Come here, Bongdo!' It was the same Kaveri Maami who, despite rain and all, would run towards the well to pour water over herself even if a small child accidentally touched her!

The little fisher girl who had reached the end of the street skipped back merrily. A polka-dotted black gown in cheap cotton. Rubber chappals several sizes too big for her feet. She couldn't have been more than ten years old. As she neared, shaking her brass earrings, she said, 'A rupee and a quarter for half a kilo, bai.' Kaveri Maami realised her mistake.

'Ade, karmam,' she cursed. 'Fish? Is it fish? Go, go, jaav! I called you by mistake. I thought "bongdo" meant brinjal. Please go, 'ma. The stench is wrenching my guts.'

Looking at Kaveri Maami shooing her away agitatedly, the little girl stood startled, fluttering her lashes like a butterfly. Even as Maami backed off, the girl walked briskly towards her, put down her heavy basket in the doorway, took out the scales and the plastic cloth. The fish gleamed like silver.

'O… Take! Take! Twelve for a rupee!' The girl not only took out the fresh fish in her hand to show Maami but also reduced the price.

'I'm asking you to go and you are coming! Karmam! She's put the basket on the doorstep! Nako, no, go away, jaav!' She shooed the little girl away with the few words of the local language she knew. Disgusted by the sight that she ought never to have seen at all, she slammed the door.

There was disappointment, disbelief and astonishment in the little eyes. Why did this bai, dressed in the slippery moss-green sari, flashing diamonds on her nose, close the door after calling out to her? These were fresh fish! 'Baiko! This fish is fresh. Just caught this morning by my father. I'm not lying to you. Just name whatever price you want. This will be my very first sale for the day,' pleaded and cajoled the little girl.

What else could she do – she who would insist on performing a cleansing ritual just because a fish basket was placed on the doorstep? Was she being adamant sitting on my doorstep, Kaveri Maami wondered, just because I committed the crime of calling out to her unknowingly? Was this also the way of this town? To call out to that Radha I'd have to shout out from the doorstep. If she'd heard, surely she would have come by now.

'Adi, Radhabai, Radha! Please come for a bit and ask this girl to go away. I called for her, not knowing it was fish,' called out Kaveri Maami in a tearful voice through the window near the door.

Radhabai came down the stairs. 'Ei, little girl, she won't eat fish, go away!' she explained in Marathi.

'What?' As if they'd witnessed some extraordinary sight in the world, the curious eyes widened. 'Why bai?'

'She doesn't eat fish. Don't come and shout here. Go.'

'Really, she doesn't eat fish?'

Paying no attention to the cat which was peeping into the basket, the little girl looked at Kaveri Maami's face framed within the window, 'Then? Prawns?'

Shaking her head, Radha chuckled, 'No, she won't.'

'Little shellfish then?'

'Mm… hmm…'

Thinking for a couple of minutes, the girl asked: 'Chicken?'

Like tiny birds who fly for the first time into the blue sky and wonder about everything in amazement – aha, what beautiful colours – the little girl too eagerly burst into all sorts of questions, making Radha laugh loudly: 'Chicken? I'm telling you she doesn't even eat fish, will she eat chicken?'

'Pork? Beef?'

'Uhuumm... If you even utter these things she'll bring a stick to strip the skin off your back. Go, go, you chatterbox.'

'First take your basket away, di! She's a smart little thing, this one. Che, don't know how many more polluted days I must spend in this Goa.'

Kaveri Maami chided the girl in a strong tone. Stepping for the first time into a world removed from hers, the little girl stood still, puzzled and bewildered, then picked up her basket and left. You didn't hear the shout of 'Bongdo' till she reached the end of the street. Only when she climbed the steps leading to the hilltop you heard her call out.

Heaving and shaking, Kaveri Maami brought a copper pot full of water and threw it on the doorstep. 'Radhabai, what did she say?'

'Nothing, Maami. They don't know anyone who doesn't eat fish in this town. How did you call her? Don't you know that "bongdo" means fish?'

I don't know all this Konkani-Marathi, it sounds like Sanskrit. I thought they call fish "matsya" or "macch" or something. That day in the market you said brinjal is "bongo" or some such thing, isn't it? I thought it was brinjal!'

Radha controlled her laughter. 'That's "baingan", Hindi for brinjal. "Bongdo" is a kind of fish. In this place they don't generally call out "fish". They usually call out the names of the different types of fish. Here you won't get brinjal and all at your doorstep, Maami.'

'It's all bad luck. By mistake we've come and got caught in this place. Even if we want to leave, somebody should come to replace us, no? I was so orthodox, but all that's gone now. Today, it is Ekadasi. And she's bringing fish and telling me to buy! Even now I feel like retching.'

Kaveri Maami poured pots and pots of water on the doorstep. Radha wouldn't have been surprised if she'd poured a potful on her head too by the well. All the neighbours called her 'orthodox maami'. She was the only one around there who didn't know Hindi, Konkani or Marathi. All day long she scrubbed and polished the kitchen, the verandah at the entrance, the stainless-steel vessels, the lead pot and the mud pot. A creature of habit, she remained aloof and rejoiced in her sanctimoniousness and loneliness.

She shunned vegetables like onion, cabbage and carrot, and on half of the days she observed fasts to the point of getting parched. A routine of which she was proud. From the age of fourteen to thirty-eight, this ritual had only got more rigid.

'He bought only cabbage. I have to make something for him to take to the office, isn't it? I shouldn't say it, but cabbage really stinks when it's being boiled. I have to grit my teeth and fling away the water in which it's boiled. I just mix plain tamarind sambar and buttermilk, roll the rice into balls and swallow it. Thank goodness there is no dearth of good water in this Goa.'

Radha couldn't help staring at the diamonds flashing on Kaveri Maami's withered, emaciated face. Not only diamonds, but thick gold bangles as well and layers and layers of chains round her neck. Shimmering silk saris were what Maami wore, each one costing no less than hundred or hundred and fifty rupees. After all, there was only the two of them to spend the good income earned by Varadarajan as a chief accountant. Abstaining from food and observing strict fasts were certainly lofty objectives, but were they geared only towards diamonds, silk and silver vessels?

What else was Radhabai to think, she who could never dream of gold and who wore only a thaali of black beads, earrings of cultured pearls and bangles of glass. She was a mother of four children, and of an age to be still scared of pregnancy. It had been a matter of survival which had made her leave a village called Gokarnam and come to Bombay. They had quit that crowded city and come to this underdeveloped, sleepy town, where her husband got a job as a lowly clerk; they considered it a golden opportunity. For Radha, the housewife, the burdens somewhat lessened. It was the Tamil she had picked up in Bombay which brought her close to Kaveri Maami. She hadn't made a home for herself anywhere. As for Kaveri Maami, she had never seen anything beyond Mayuram and her ancient house in Triplicane in Madras; she had no desire to see anything else either.

The higher-ups in his auditing office saw fit to transfer Varadarajan here, to this place where they neither knew anyone nor the language, and so here they were as if some unknown wave had tossed them into a strange land. Like water not being able to mix with oil, Kaveri Maami, who had led a caged, ritually pure life, found it all a struggle – but was it that easy to get a transfer back?

Varadarajan ate at about nine every morning. Soon after, Kaveri Maami would finish her daily pooja, then sit down to eat at about eleven. That was usually the time Radhabai would begin her cooking after a visit to the market. Today she'd put her infant to sleep and was running back home quickly in the scorching heat, bag in hand. She found the little fisher girl on Kaveri Maami's doorstep, the basket on her head. Kaveri Maami, like she had done before, slammed the door shut and looked out of the window.

'I'm telling her to go, she keeps saying "Baiko, Baiko". What cheek! And she's only a tiny bit of thing! How many times should I shout out that we don't even so much as glance at fish? Stubborn thing, she is, Radhabai. It's Dwadasi today, and it's time to tell slokams, so I came to shut the door. What all terrible things she wants to make me buy from her basket? Rama, Rama!' Kaveri Maami was not only livid but was also hungry.

'What, I told you she doesn't eat fish. Why are you worrying the life out of her?'

'Then what does she eat? If she doesn't eat fish, chicken, meat, pork, what only does she eat?' The girl wasn't being insolent, she was just genuinely puzzled. After all, wasn't she of the age to ask why it rains, why the sea has waves, why it is hot?

'She eats rice and vegetables,' said Radha, naming one or two vegetables.

The little girl picked out some shellfish from her basket and blurted out: 'Aren't these vegetables from the sea, Baiko?'

Radha burst into a laugh.

'What, di, I just want her to take the basket and leave, what is there to talk and laugh?' Kaveri Maami was clearly angry with Radha too.

'Go, go, she won't eat any vegetable from the sea. This bai can be very rude. If you're insolent she'll throw water on you and your basket.'

The little girl moved away, neither able to swallow nor spit out her words. A voice like a low-pitched yaazh could be heard: 'Kuppe, thisri, baiko.'

'Thought I would eat, and this one came and landed here. I don't think I can stomach any food now.'

'Adada! What Maami? As it is this American rice that we get is like some maida mush. Go, go, stop your bathing and wiping and go and eat. You fasted yesterday too.'

Radha looked at her with compassion. Kaveri Maami looked old because she didn't have any flesh on her face, but she was, in fact, only a few years older than Radha. It seems a daughter had been born to her years ago, but she had died. The turmeric on her face and the wet hair knotted low added a certain radiance to her face. Kaveri Maami's eyes which scanned the open skies shone with tears. Like a flower dropping from a tall tree, a drop of water fell down. She wiped her eyes with the ends of her sari.

'It's nearly ten years, she was of the same colour, same voice. If she'd been here, I suppose we would have started showing her horoscope around. Perhaps it was that, she didn't want to trouble us, that's why she went away like a dream. I'm not really superstitious. Don't know what, but since yesterday her face, voice and speech keep coming to mind like a fluttering firefly. This one comes from a family which catches and eats fish, mussels and crabs. Just look at us, our family, why should there be any connection – it's like an illusion. I tried to think and think, but my foolish mind can't make out anything. It was astonishing – I'd just served myself and was about to close the door when I heard "Baiko". It was as if the voice had called out "Amma" – I was jolted out of my skin. I just slammed the door. As if I didn't know it was the fisher girl. She'd been firmly packed off yesterday, then why did she come today to make me buy fish? Though my mouth grumbles, her face structure, jaws, are exactly the same. I think Brahma just changes each mould a bit and creates again, so that we don't recognise them immediately. Making faces, "it" used to make me laugh like crazy; and when "it" left "it" was of the same age. It was a Friday, and "it" made a fuss to have oil-bath. Wretched thing, gave "it" some slaps on the back and somehow rubbed the oil in the end. Developed fever because of that. He'd taken his mother to Kumbakonam for the Maamaangam festival. By the time he came back, the story was over. Why is all this coming back now? My mother-in-law would tell me: "You say you never think of her, what kind of heart you have, di?" I used to reply: "That's all the luck we have. Some debt, we've paid it off, that's all."'

On hearing a soft heart speak from this fortress of orthodoxy and rituals, Radha stood still, oblivious to the wailing child.

The next day when Radha came down for a chat after putting the cooker on the stove, the young girl trotted in, an empty fish basket in hand. A smile revealed a row of rice-like teeth.

'What, for the past three days I'm telling you she won't buy fish; why have you come? She won't eat any of those sea-vegetables!'

The young girl showed the empty basket. 'Meet, meet – salt? Baiko?'

Radha felt as if an arrow which had been aimed with such force had been stopped by mere pollen. Had this girl been thinking only about this all the while?

Radha smiled after a moment. The little girl looked at the silk-clad, diamond-flashing Kaveri Maami with innocent eyes, full of eagerness and naivety.

'What is she asking, di?'

'She asked yesterday: "Fish, mussel, all these are vegetables only, no, from the sea? She won't eat them?" To which I replied: "She won't eat all your sea-vegetables." So today she is wondering if you eat salt. That also comes from the sea, isn't it?'

'Look at her. Even if she eats crabs and shellfish, see how smart she is.'

Radha spoke in another language. 'Yes, no one in this world can live without salt. All right, what's your name?'

'Miri. You know Dona Paula? That's where my house is.'

'Are you coming all the way from Dona Paula daily?'

'My mother is not there. Before, my mother only used to bring fish. You know that big hospital in Panjim, behind the fish market, that's where my mother is lying. Because my mother is not there I come to give fish to the regular customers. In the bazaar, you know that Hedwin Amma, the one wearing full black and selling fish – sitting behind the shop full of mud pots; all that fish is caught by my father only. During the last rains, because Hedu Maama made some mistake, the Sea Raja got angry and took him away, boat and all. Who will catch fish then for Hedu Amma? Little Hedu comes just up to the knee. So my father, now that my mother too is not there, gives the fish to Hedu Amma and lives in her house.'

When Miri, who spoke like the wind rushing out of a bottle which had been unplugged, finished the last sentence in a low voice, Kaveri Maami made out the situation somewhat.

'She's spluttering, saying this and that. Can't understand a word, Radhabai,' said Maami, anxious to know everything.

The girl started again: 'You haven't seen my mother, bai. She's beautiful like this bai. But she doesn't wear gold and diamonds. I believe my father used to tell my grandfather that when my mother is by the shore, she looks like a mermaid who has come floating.'

'O! You have a grandfather then?'

'My Joe Grandpa only, bai. Everyone calls him that. You know the place beyond the seaside bridge in Dona Paula, where the sea looks like a lake? There buried under the coconut trees is Joe Grandpa's boat, Sea Queen. You haven't come to Dona Paula? Many people come there to enjoy the breeze, bai.'

'What is she saying, Radhabai?' Hindered by not knowing the language, Maami was desperate to know what was falling out of those doll-like lips in such a soft voice.

'She's asking us if we've visited her place by the seaside.'

'Is there a bathing enclosure there, Radha? I really want to know. Let's bathe in the sea on an auspicious no-moon day at least.'

Even before Radha could ask, Miri nodded her head eagerly: 'O, in front of Sea Queen the waves are smooth. That's where I learnt to swim, bai. When I went into the water, Joe Grandpa used to wave to me with a smile. When Grandpa was healthy and nice, he used to climb into Sea Queen, catch sharks and give them to the foreigners. Now the Sea Queen can't go on water, and Grandpa's also become old, isn't it? Grandpa just sits now under the tree, weaves the nets, stitches them up and gives them to people. Someone or the other gives him some fish and rice. Grandpa has a nice fishing rod, a nylon one. If you just hold the end and cast it with a swish, a hook will come up. Some days he will sit on the Dona Paula bridge and do fishing. If he catches good fish, he will take it to Johnny's shop, have a drink and come home to lie down and tell stories.'

'Ok, but tell me, do you go with your father to catch fish?'

'Uhmmm, do ladies ever go into the sea? They'll stay by the shore – cook, fetch water, and when the nets come to the shore, they'll put the fish in baskets and take them to Panaji market. My mother remained on the shore only. I too stay only in the shore. Joe Grandpa too, it seems, had a bai in the shore in those days. Then who will light the colour-candles for the cross under the seaside mango tree if Sea Raja gets angry? My mother used to light one every Friday without fail. Now that she is sick in the hospital I light one. If my father caught the big mori fish, my mother used to take one to the priest as well.'

Like a waterfall tumbling down, finding its way between rocks, her words gushed out freely. Radha was eager to listen to her more and more. 'You don't have any brother or sister?'

'Ummm, I have a brother, bai. I believe he will study in a convent. That's what Father says. It seems he won't go near the water.'

Kaveri Maami was a little irritated that Radha kept on listening, without translating anything into Tamil. 'What's this, like some mustard spluttering in a ladle. She won't stop talking, I think. Ask her to go. The smell of this fish basket is tearing my guts. Go, go, di. Jav, jav, aren't you late?

Radha understood Kaveri Maami's feelings and started to explain everything.

The rains had stopped at last, and the moss which had spread all over the wet walls dried up and dropped off. When fresh ladies' fingers, gourd and cucumber appeared suddenly, they, a rarity, disappeared in a flash. Baskets and baskets of fish, big and small and tiny, were being sold in the streets by so many women, calling out in ever so many voices. Small salted fish, bought in bulk for a bargain, were spread out in the sun in every courtyard, while the big fish hung down like festoons, tied in strings from one coconut tree to another. The cats which usually descended on the baskets as soon they were put down, lazed around in the courtyards, eyes half shut, as if they were tired of eating so much fish. The crows too, bored with all the fish, went in search of grain. Even the pigs reared in the Christian homes crossed the yards where the fish were spread out and went in search of vegetable peels.

Afraid that the awful stench of meat which enveloped the entire city would seep into her breath, Kaveri Maami skulked inside, like a snail in its shell. She never opened the door. But the voice of the little girl alone, smooth and mellifluous, evoked an inexplicable feeling in her. Miri stopped shouting in front of her house. But Maami used to wait by the window till her ears could catch Miri calling out as she turned at the end of the street to climb the steps to the main street. As she crossed the closed door, Miri never failed to glance at the face in the window. Her lips would blossom into a smile, revealing the rice-like teeth.

Even Radha didn't know that these days Kaveri Maami sat down to eat only after she heard the little girl's voice. Why, even Maami herself wasn't aware that a crack had developed in that impregnable fort of ritual purity.

It was a Navratri Friday. Kaveri Maami was deep in pooja. It was the time to chant the thousand names of Devi.

'Baiko! Baiko!' It was the voice used to shouting out 'bongdo', a voice which caused a flutter in her heart.

'Baiko, it's Miri, Baiko, Miri.'

God, Maami thought, she's calling out in the midst of my pooja. Why is this wretched creature calling me? Uhumm, she'll stand at the door, her hand full of fish. Feeling disgusted, as if the stench had wafted in, Kaveri Maami lit two more agarbathis.

'Baiko! Miri.'

What a nuisance. Won't Radha come out and ask? Why is this thing calling me? Even if I'm as firm as a diamond, there's a sliver of anxiety – a deep-seated fear curdles my heart.

All her worries, hopes and desires grew around the only pole she leant against. It had been an entirely new experience, that febrile excitement which had consumed her when she was a coy sixteen-year-old. And that love had neither deep roots nor a firm base. Now, of course, the roots were firmly entrenched; but it was a barren tree, one with no hope of sprouting again, despite sucking up the moisture from deep below. Like a banyan tree dropping aerial roots, they supported each other to quench the flame of insecurity with mutual love and affection. But that flame suddenly rose, turning her thoughts into an illusion.

He'd already left for the office – could it be that someone had brought news from somewhere for him. Was that why 'it' was calling without knocking on the door? Her pitiful mind thought all sorts of things in dreadful fear.

Forgetting all about her pooja, she ran to the window. 'What, di, what do you want?'

A fish basket as usual on her head; but in her hand a small basket which held a plantain flower. Showing it to her, she said something which sounded like: 'You'll eat this, no?' But Kaveri Maami's wavering mind hardened.

'What are you saying, you wretched thing? Will I buy and eat something which you've kept in your fish basket? Is that why you shouted bai, bai, as if there's been some calamity. Get out, you wretched girl!'

Angry on the one hand that the pooja had been disturbed and disappointed on the other that she'd yielded to this small weakness, Kaveri Maami firmly shut the door and the window and sat down for pooja. But her mind was elsewhere.

What could 'it' have wanted to say? It's been so long since I ate plantain flower. Even in the market in the city, they usually serve you after eating fish sambar, without ever washing their hands. I usually wash the vegetables as soon as I step into the door. That plantain flower looked so fresh. Would 'it' have brought it specially for me? How her face had drooped, like a flower poked by a needle.

It's been ten years. Has she been reborn here? Ambike, Jaganmatha, is this all your maya? Is Ambike testing me by creating this illusion?

However hard she tried, Maami was unable to focus her mind. Finishing the pooja quickly, she rushed to open the door. There was nothing there, not even a bird or a fly. It was totally bare.

From the minute she got up the next day an inexplicable frenzy consumed her mind. All kinds of people called out – the bread man, the waste-paper man, the alloy man, the ice cream man, various fisherwomen, egg-seller, chicken-seller, and what have you. But that young voice didn't reach her ears.

Would Radha have mentioned that she ate plantain flower? Should I have called Radhabai to find out what 'it' could have said? Why hadn't 'it' come today?

Kaveri Maami couldn't scrub the vessels with care. She found no fulfilment in washing and swabbing the kitchen either.

Of all things, to think of that fisher girl! Che, why did the mind get so disturbed? She, who was born into such a good family, who came from such a great lineage, who was married to such a fine husband, who'd been disciplined at such a young age to serve elders, why had she given in to this senselessness? That too to a fisher girl. And worse still, thinking of that plantain flower she'd brought.

Kaveri Maami felt shy to even ask or tell Radha. She enjoyed a high status as Kaveri Maami. Never mind if she wasn't that much older, or that her hair hadn't greyed, she commanded respect. How could she, who was used to advising others and laughing at their foibles, spell out her grievances?

'Appada! The transfer has been sanctioned, Kaveri, we can leave in a week. You look somewhat strange, why?' This turned out to be totally unexpected news for Kaveri.

Till Radha enquired, 'Maami, I believe you're leaving. You kept saying it, and now all of a sudden it's happened, isn't it?' Kaveri Maami hadn't told her the news.

'It will be so empty without you. Speaking with you my Tamil has improved tremendously. How will I pass my time if you go – it will be so difficult.'

'What difficulty, di? What have I achieved by going on and on about "ritual purity"?'

The entire neighbourhood asked Radha, 'I believe that "orthodox Maami" is leaving, that Madrasi bai is leaving?'

On account of the six-month stint in Goa, Varadarajan had to endure four send-off parties. They always informed that 'Saar, this is only a Coca Cola,' but he said with a smile: 'I have to check twice before I drink anything.'

'This milk-powder tin is new. We don't get them there. But we didn't use it here. Shall we give it to someone there? Or shall we give it to Radha?' Kaveri Maami kept repeating even the most trivial of things. Even after dismantling the six-month household and packing everything, she didn't feel as if she was leaving the place. She felt a strand of regret, as if she was leaving behind something she had earned. Even the fact that she could look forward to familiar situations, and would be greeted in a familiar tongue by known faces, couldn't overcome the niggling feeling inside her.

The same look, the same height, the same voice, the same colour. Why hadn't 'it' come again. 'It' said that 'its' mother was lying sick in Panaji hospital. Would she also be sick by any chance? Radha had said 'it' mentioned some old man who 'it' called grandfather or something. What a life! Wretched creatures, sailing over man-sized waves and bringing back these useless fish!

Adiayamma, what does it matter to which caste one belonged? To be born a girl, getting hitched to a man, delivering children, experiencing the trials of life, is it all different for different castes? If a man who commutes to office by road is late even by five minutes, the mind gets turbulent. What about men who journey every day over seas to places the eye can't see, pledging their lives – is that any less?

As time drew close, the days sped by. Radha rushed down anxiously, leaving behind a bawling baby, when she found out that Kaveri Maami had cooked even on the day of the travel.

Puris and coconut powder, coffee decoction for the journey, everything was ready. They'd sent off their things earlier. They were to take the two o'clock bus.

Dressed in a silk sari which fluffed about her, a plastic basket filled with tiffin boxes and a jug of water in hand, Kaveri Maami looked towards the street and imagined that she heard the echoes of 'bongdo' from somewhere. She had an illusion that she was seeing the figure that was so tightly tied to her pupil. But the one who was shouting out that very name was some woman who was wearing a sari that stopped well above her knees. Taking a puff from her beedi, she put it out, tucked it into her hair, heaved the fish basket covered with a waxy cloth high on her head, and sped by, flapping her chappals noisily and shaking the scales. No sign of the child who used to stroll by, tossing the tiny rings in her ears.

Radha laughed: 'No more darshanams of these fish people for Maami.'

'Di, Radhabai, we haven't see that fisher girl since.'

'Yes, Maami, you're right, we haven't seen her. So many people go by! She did say that her mother was in the hospital; haven't seen her either.'

It was Radha who had stopped her and spoken to her, but so caught up was Radha in the struggle of everyday life that all these seemed to be immensely forgettable conversations which faded away from the mind. How matter-of-fact she sounded when she said 'didn't see her'.

Would her mother have died? Her father would have caught someone else, surely. Would that girl be sitting on the beach with a sad face?

She imagined a shadowy figure of her own child – who was part of her own life and body, who had once joyously danced through life, left a trail of happy dreams and totally disappeared – waiting longingly for someone on the beach.

All sorts of office people came to see them off. The taxi arrived.

Should have gone to that beach at least once. What a miserable being I am, she cursed herself. The wide expanse of the sea where the waves shattered against the shore and an image of a lone girl in a faded dress, crying bitterly, tousled hair, quivering lips and all, came to mind. Travelling further in her tortured imagination and breaking that impregnable fortress of orthodoxy, she hugged the little girl and pressed her cheek to hers. All her orthodoxy withered away. On the other hand, satisfied and at peace, she felt purified.

'Are you leaving, Maami? Do think of me. Satish, say bye to Maami, da.' Kaveri Maami shook Radha's hand mechanically.

The taxi dropped them off at a stand; a luxury bus was parked under a tree. Kaveri Maami, who was about to get in, caught sight of a tinny old bus which bore the letters 'D Paula'.

'Tale gao, Dona Paula, Dona Paula,' shouted out an old man dressed in khaki, in order to rustle up a crowd for the small bus. Poor fisherfolk, villagers, and all sorts of people shoved and pushed one another to get into the bus. A withered, bent old man, a stick in hand, climbed in.

Could this be the grandfather, this old man?

What, 'pa, where's that child? She used to say: 'I'll swim and Grandpa would keep watching me.' Had she drowned? With the mother gone, and the father giving the fish to some woman, she didn't have anyone. Ei old man, has she become one with the water and the waves because of that? The restlessness was dying to burst into words and Maami was overwhelmed. The little bus was bursting at the seams. Though she was seated in plush comfort, she wasn't even aware of it. The old man was the only one who held out any hope to pursue her imagined goal; her weak heart fluttered as the bus moved on.

D Paula – Carrier. Her only link was severed.

They put behind them the shops of Panaji. The groves fed by the waters of the River Mandovi sped by. The bus passed the village of Raibunder, full of fishing nets, which gave out a stench that mingled with one's breath. Coconut and cashew groves, and now and then the tall steeples of old churches bearing a cross came into view.

We're leaving, we're leaving. There's no more connection, no more hope. The sad loss gushed out of Kaveri Maami's heart. She pressed her face against the glass window.

Original title: *Meenkari*
1972

Outside, Pouring Rain 34

R. Chudamani

It was pouring outside. Through the glass window it appeared as if the world had drawn a curtain over it. The vehicles crawled like shadows on it.

In the hall, Ramesh was losing the game of Scrabble. His score didn't usually cross single digits. How did Suresh manage to pick letters that would give him so many points and also form words that would earn him double the score? He suddenly screamed out, 'You are looking at the letters on the sly and choosing them, you cheater!'

'I'm not cheating. I'm in luck. I'm getting the big letters, that's all.'

'How can it happen all the time? Your score is steadily increasing but mine isn't.'

'Even if you get the big letters, your score will never increase. You should know how to form big words!'

'Nothing like that. You're cheating.' In a huff, Ramesh threw away the Scrabble board and spoilt the game. The square letters scattered all over the room.

'You loser! Just because you don't know how to play and can't stomach the fact that I'm winning, you spoilt the game, did you?'

Suresh sprang on his younger brother. Ramesh, who was no match for his elder brother, fell flat on his back. Aching from the blows and kicks from his brother, he ran to his mother, tangled hair, crying face and all. 'Amma, look at this, Suresh, 'Ma, not only did he cheat in the game, but he also beat me up…'

Suresh followed him, his body reddening wherever his brother had pinched him or bit him. 'You are only telling her about me hitting you! He also hit me, 'Ma. See, he has even bitten me like a dog. We should tie him up with our Tiger hereafter…'

'What is this, da, Suresh, beating up your younger brother like this?' Amma pulled Ramesh to her side and wiped his tears. Suresh boiled over with grief. 'Just because he is younger, he can do what he wants, is it? He didn't know many words and so he was losing in Scrabble. Because of that he should get angry and spoil the game, is it?'

He was about to pounce on Ramesh, but his mother stopped him and pacified the two of them. 'No need of that Scrabble. Play something else. Nice children! Because of the rain, just one day you are playing inside, and even that you can't play without fighting! Go and play something quietly. I'm going to rest for a while.'

The two came back to the hall and sat in different corners with long faces, not speaking to each other for a while. Then they put away the Scrabble board in a box but didn't play anything else. Within the house they usually played Rummy, Monopoly, Chinese chequers, Carrom, but they didn't feel like playing anything. All were old, boring games.

Usually, they went out in the evenings to play cricket or something with their friends. Friends also sometimes came home. On regular holidays, they normally made interesting plans to pass their time in the afternoons. Today's holiday was not a legitimate one, an unexpected one declared on account of the rains. And because of the rains, friends couldn't visit each other's houses. Trapped inside the house, the siblings couldn't get along and had broken into a fight.

Suresh came near the window and looked outside. No sign of the vehicles now. The world had changed into rain.

Not wanting to miss the interesting sight that his brother could see, Ramesh too came and stood near him. 'There's nothing there. What are you looking at?'

'Your head.'

'If you talk like this, I'll go and tell Amma.'

'Crybaby. You only know to sneak. What else do you know?'

'Amma…'

'Shut your mouth, da. I'll break you into pieces.'

'Amma, Suresh is beating me, 'Ma!'

'Dei, liar! If you tell lies, the rats will chew up your tongue in hell, da.'

Ramesh looked at his brother in fright. Suresh was looking outside listlessly. It was boring to be trapped at home doing nothing.

What was that in the thick of the rain, something moving? Suresh's eyes peered intently.

Something was moving. Some mass, moving in the rain. It came in as the iron door creaked. It was coming towards them like a small white tent. It was nearing.

The children exchanged glances, wondering 'What is it?', 'Who is it?'

Soon there was a knock on the door. In the noise of the rain it wasn't clear whether it was a knock, after all. Then, another knock, slow, hesitant.

'Who is it?' asked Suresh.

The knocking stopped, like tears after a scolding. Then it was heard again.

'Who is it? Knocking instead of ringing the doorbell.'

'Me… me only.'

Suresh suddenly unlatched and opened the door. His eyes had to peer down. The figure reached only up to Suresh's chest. Would he be five, that boy? He had knocked because he couldn't reach the doorbell. The plastic piece that had covered the head had billowed out like a tent and hung down. On it were drops of rain like glass pieces. A faded blue shirt and khaki shorts with tattered ends. A small puddle where he stood since the rain too had come in along with him. The boy was so dark-skinned that it looked as if the colour would bleed in the rain. Two wide eyes looked up from the dark face. When Suresh and Ramesh peered at him, they appeared to take the vishwaroopam. Their thirteen and ten years seemed to touch the skies.

'Who are you, da?' asked Suresh.

'…'

'Tell, da.'

'Mani.'

'Is it the clock Mani or the bead Mani?'

Hearing the brothers' laughter, the boy shrank back.

'Answer, da. I'm asking you, right?'

'I'm… just Mani.'

'O, just Mani-aa? Where have you come, da, just Mani?'

'I… my mother sent me.'

'Who is your mother?'

'The one who works here…'

'Oho, Nagamma's son, is it? Don't you know that servants should use only the back door? Why did you come in the front and knock on the hall door?'

'What cheek!' said Ramesh.

Mani said tremblingly, 'No, no… I didn't know that I had to come through the back door.'

'Why have you come?'

'My younger sister has fever. My mother asked for ten rupees so she can go to the doctor and put an injection. She has no money on hand.'

'There's no money here also. Go.'

Suresh shut his brother up with a look. The idiot, didn't he understand that here was a new game.

'Let it be, Ramesh. Don't shoo him away. He's a small boy, no. Dei, Mani, who did your mother tell to ask for money?'

'The house-owner lady.'

'She is my mother only. I'll ask her and get it for you. But first you must play with us for a while, okay?'

The dark face bloomed suddenly.

'O, of course I will play with you. Shall I call you both "anna"?'

As soon as he said it, a slap landed on his cheek.

'You're a servant's son. How dare you call us "anna"? I'll break you into pieces. Call us "saar" respectfully, do you understand?'

Suresh's slap, Suresh's face, Suresh's voice – the three knives pierced Mani's gut sharply. He stood stupefied, holding his cheek. Tears welled up.

'I'll… I'll go. I don't want to play.'

'Don't you want the money?'

'Want it.'

'Only if you do what I say, I will ask my mother for money and give it you.'

Mani bit his lip. His cheek still burned. 'Okay.'

'What did you say?'

'I said okay.' In fear the voice didn't rise.

'I told you to call us "saar". Have you forgotten?'

Ramesh, who was disappointed that his brother didn't slap him again, raised his own hand this time. Before he could be slapped, Mani said, 'Don't, don't hit me. Okay, saar, don't hit me, saar…'

'Rascal,' said Ramesh.

'M… come in.'

When Mani took a step inside, Suresh's voice raised again, 'Dei, dei, you dirty fellow. You've drenched our verandah, da. There's mud on your feet as well. Clean up everything properly and then come in.'

'Cloth?'

'We should give you a separate cloth for this, is it? Don't you have your shirt? Take it off and wipe with it.'

'With my shirt?'

'Yes.'

The gaze which looked up pleaded. But Suresh's face remained stern. Ramesh's right fist clenched and opened. Quickly dodging that hand, the boy shifted the plastic piece on his head, took off his shirt and started wiping the floor. Something curled inside his throat again and again and choked him.

'M… Wipe the inside of your feet also properly. Have you finished? Good. Throw that cloth away in the corner and come here.'

Mani came into the room timidly. His chest shivered in the cold of the rain. Suresh closed the door and latched it.

'Let's play ball for a while. Ramesh, go and get our ball, da.'

A light red ball, three-fourth the size of a football, arrived. The sofas and chairs in the room were already arranged in a corner. Calling out to Mani, 'Mmm… come, da, you too come and hold,' the brothers pushed the two tables in the centre to the side.

'Look here, Mani. Go and stand there. Ramesh will stand here. And I will be on that side. When we kick the ball to you, you must kick it back, okay?'

'Okay, saar.'

'You begin, Ramesh.'

Ramesh kicked the ball to Mani's side. Fully alert, with the tip of his tongue sticking out, Mani was about to kick the ball, but Suresh's foot pounced as quick as lightning and pushed the ball to another side. When Mani briskly ran behind the ball, Ramesh intervened quickly and pushed the ball to his brother. Mani chased the ball and even managed to touch it… but the ball refused to roll. Suresh sprang from nowhere and stopped the ball and kicked it forcefully to the opposite side. Eager to play, Mani even forgot the chill and went behind the ball, only to have Ramesh sweep it to the other side. For a little while Mani ran here and there breathlessly and then looked up at them disappointedly.

'What, da, you've stopped? Don't you want to play?' asked Suresh.

'You are not allowing me to kick it at all.'

'A game will be like that only.'

'You should be clever enough to kick it.'

'Are you a fool?'

Mani shook his head to say 'no'.

'Then play.'

The game went on in much the same way for a while. Mani was panting with all the running around. The ball flew everywhere, eluding him.

'Mmm… kick the ball, da, you shortie. You are a dope who cannot play.'

'You should kick like this, da.' Miming a kick, Ramesh swung his foot.

Screaming, 'Ayyo, Amma,' Mani flopped down, clutching his foot. 'You kicked me.'

'What did you say!' Suresh glared at him. Frightened, Mani got up.

'You kicked me, saar!'

'A game is like that only. Blows and kicks will fall on us sometimes. You should play carefully.'

'I don't want to play. I'm going. Get the money from your mother, please.'

'I'll get it only if you kick the ball properly at least once.'

'I don't want the money. I'm going.' Mani walked towards the door. Suresh took a couple of strides and blocked the door.

'You cannot go.'

Mani looked at the brothers with stricken eyes. They were laughing.

Mani shouted, 'I want to go. I want to go!' From the inside of the house a dog's bark echoed.

Mani stood frozen.

'Is there… Is there a dog here?'

'You are scared of dogs?'

'Yes… very scared.'

'Guard the door, da, Ramesh. I'll come in a minute.' Suresh went inside.

'Wait, wait. Because you didn't play well, no, we are setting the dog on you to bite you,' said Ramesh. Mani started shivering. He opened his mouth once or twice but couldn't say a word. Then he stammered, 'No… no, please…'

His eyes widened and filled with horror. His mouth remained agape. His body sank back. In front of him stood Suresh holding a light-brown Pomeranian on a leash. Seeing a stranger, the dog barked and tried to leap forward.

Breaking into a sweat, Mani stuck to the wall. Blood drained from his face.

'Are you going to play or not? Or shall I set the dog on you?' asked Suresh with a laugh.

Mani could not speak. Only his hands moved in his numb body to signal 'no'. As if hypnotised, his gaze froze on the dog.

Suresh patted the dog's neck. 'Tiger, if this boy misbehaves, then I will set you on him. Till then keep quiet.'

The dog gave a faint growl.

Mani's eyes darkened. Outside the rain didn't abate. Even in daylight the lightning flashed now and then like a searchlight. Followed by thunder.

'Dei, Mani, I'm not going to play now. I will stand here holding the dog. Ramesh and you play. Ramesh will kick the ball. You catch it with your hands. Do you understand?'

Mani stood like a stone.

'What, da, I'm asking you, no? Answer me. What cheek! Look here, I will set the dog on you.'

When the dog took a step, Mani instantly sprung to life. 'I will do it, I will do it… Don't leave the dog… Don't leave the dog on me, saar…'

'Right, that's the way!' Suresh pulled the chain back. 'Keep quiet, Tiger. Mmm… the two of you play now.'

Ramesh kicked the ball. Mani didn't move. Looking at the dog, he remained stuck to the wall.

'Dei, Mani, are you going to play now or what? Tiger…'

'I'll play now!'

Dark feet quickened. When the dark hands lowered to hold the ball, Ramesh kicked it to the other side. Mani ran after it. His heart fluttered. His breath stopped and he couldn't even cry. Dog, fear, running feet, pouncing hands, elusive ball – there was no other world. There was no other truth.

'What, da, you fool. You can't even catch it once, you lazy fellow. Shall I leave the dog?'

The dark feet sprinted even faster, the dark hands yearned to hold the ball. Earlier he had tried to kick the ball, and now he tried to grasp it; but bending again and again made his back ache. The pain, however, was forgotten. The same sounds of the rain. The faint growl of the dog was the only thing Mani heard.

Ramesh's lightning kick. The ball bounced, eluding Mani once again.

'You don't seem to run fast, da. You're very lazy. You'll heat up once Tiger comes. Tiger, go chase the boy.'

'Ayyo, please, don't, don't…'

Suresh loosened his grip on the chain. The chain hung loose enough to let the dog run around freely. Tiger pounced towards Mani. Mani jumped around, dodging the barking dog. Eyes popping out, he ran to every corner of the room. His legs became indistinct, turning into whirls of black lines. Spit drooled from his mouth. There was but one goal in his mind: to escape from the dog.

'Ada, Shortie is running fast! Let's see if he can run faster. Tiger, go catch him.'

With wet shorts and legs, Mani ran even faster.

Suresh and Ramesh roared with laughter. 'Good, good, you're a smart fellow, Mani. You run very well. Just run a little faster. Just a little. That's enough. Tiger, mmm…'

'Ei, boys, what's all this ruckus? Not allowing me to sleep in peace even for a bit. And Tiger, why is he barking?' The mother came out.

Suresh quickly pulled the leash and controlled the dog. The bark receded into a deep-throated growl. Ramesh stood innocently. The ball lay under the sofa. The dark little five-year-old huddled against the wall, gasping and eyes full of fear. His body heaved. His lips and chin quivered. Shrinking further, he looked intently in the direction of the dog.

She looked at him and then at her sons. 'Who is this boy?'

'Nagamma's son, it seems,' mumbled Suresh, looking down.

'Why has he come?'

'His mother needs ten rupees urgently, it seems. Sister has fever. That's why.'

'What did the two of you do to him?'

'Nothing.'

The mother looked at them. Then at the dog straining at the leash. And then at the shaking, huddled boy.

'Chee! Aren't you ashamed of yourselves? Get inside, the two of you. Let Appa come in the evening, the belt is going to tear you today.'

The two boys, head bowed, vanished inside with the dog. Mani collapsed on to the floor.

She knelt before him and straightened his hair.

'Did you get frightened, child? The dog won't do anything. I'll see to it.'

His fear-filled eyes looked at her. His mouth twitched. His throat choked with sobs. He then broke into tears.

'Don't cry, 'pa. Will you eat a biscuit? Adada, you've come without a shirt. Never mind. Wait, I'll give you one.'

'… I want to go… open the door, please. I want to go home. I want to go to my mother…'

He didn't even wait to collect the money. As soon as she opened the door, without even picking up the plastic piece or the crumpled rag of a shirt, he ran sobbing and disappeared into the rain.

The mother bolted the door, went in and chided the boys. They heard her out, like always, heads bent. They went back to the hall and sat down. Tried to read the magazine *Ambulimama*, but got bored. Tried to play rummy, and were still bored. They just sat quietly for a while.

Suresh's eyes brightened with interest. 'Dei, Ramesh, did you see how he peed in his drawers!'

Without their mother knowing, the two of them laughed, covering their mouths.

The rain fell rhythmically.

Original title: *Veliye Nalla Mazhai*
1985

JOURNEY 35

VAASANTHI

'Haven't you gone for your bath yet?' A stern voice called out from the doorway.

Nagu Paati, who lay curled up in an old art-silk sari against the wall, looked in the direction from where the voice came. To Paati, Parvathi's physical body appeared as a shadow-like form. Without getting up, she said, 'I'm going now. Is the wash-area around the well free?'

'It's free only. You get up now,' said Parvathi testily.

'Fine then,' said Nagu Paati and got up. She took the towel that pillowed her head and started walking with the cane that had been propped near the corner of the wall.

'What is the time?'

'Nine-thirty.'

'Only nine-thirty?'

'What "only"? Every day you take an hour to bathe, and after that you'll say japam-tapam and all, saying the same things again and again. Going round and round, by the time you come to eat it is always twelve. Today Kamu and I want to go the shops after the food-business is over.'

'All right. What do you want to buy?'

'We must tell this old crone everything! We are going to buy something! She's going to Bombay tomorrow to see the girl. There's so much to buy. Don't take forever, dilly-dallying like every day.'

'No, di, no. I'm just going. I won't take long.'

Nagu Paati walked slowly across the hall and went to the back of the house.

Pattamma was rinsing the clothes in the wash-area near the well.

'What, di, Pattamma? Isn't your work over yet? Parvathi said the place was free.'

'Ei, Pattu, clear the place quickly. The crone has got up quickly today. As soon as I asked her to. Thankfully enough. Let her have her bath. I have to go out.'

'Just finishing. I'll just take a minute to wash off. It's full of soap water, no? If she slips and falls and kicks the bucket?'

'Nothing is lost if she goes. Don't think she'll go any other way.'

Pattamma quickly lifted her head and looked at Nagu Paati.

Paati stood there, as if she hadn't heard a word of what Parvathi said. 'Are you done, Pattamma?' she asked very calmly.

'Finished.' Pattu briskly swept the water away with a coconut-stick broom, stood aside, making way for Paati.

Paati walked very carefully and reached the well.

'She has her tensions to deal with,' she murmured. 'I'm also waiting for thirty years, di, Pattamma. Yaman is refusing to take me away.'

'Maybe your name is not on his list.'

As she loosened her sari, Paati spotted her granddaughter Kamu. She didn't possess Parvathi's crotchety demeanour.

'Sit down. I'll pour water for you.'

A faint glimmer of joy spread across Paati's face. She sat and said, 'Pour now.'

When Kamu drew the water from the well and poured it on her head, Paati asked gently, 'Are you going to see your daughter?'

'Yes, Paati, I'm leaving tomorrow. I asked her to come to me for her second confinement. She said it is not convenient and stayed back in Bombay itself. It's been three months since the child was born. I too couldn't go.'

'How could you have gone? It was at that time your husband broke his leg and was lying flat.'

'See how Paatiamma remembers everything?'

'Kamu, if you keep chattering with the old hag, we'll never be able to go to the shops.'

'Enough, Paati?' asked Kamu.

'Enough, di. Have you brought my madi sari?'

'Yes, I have.'

Slipping the sari off the pole which she held out, Paati slowly wrapped it around herself in the traditional style. Pattamma, who watched this from afar, asked, 'Shall I bring the barber tomorrow?'

'Yes, di, wanted to tell you myself. It's pricking me like thorns when I sleep. It's itching like anything. I kept postponing saying festival, no moon, and all.'

'Paati, finish your japam. Come.'

Paati mumbled, 'Coming, di.' When she entered from the sunlit backyard, the passage inside was dark. Fumbling, she tapped the switch on the wall and went into the pooja room.

Not yet used to this tiny city house. As long as he was alive, I was used to walking freely in the vast traditional house in the village. It was known as the mirasdar's palace. No dearth of light in every part of the house. You didn't have to switch on the lights in the day like this. Those were different days. I lived like a queen. This Parvathi used to tremble to stand in front of me! He went off before me like a king, keeping his dignity intact…

She went into the pooja room and took out vibhuti from a tiny metal pot on the counter. As she smeared it on her forehead with her withered, thin fingers, she uttered, 'O why hasn't my time come yet?'

She sat on the small wooden seat, wrapped her knuckles on her temples, began to recite the first words of the slokam, 'shuklambharataram', but couldn't remember a syllable beyond that.

'Maybe your name is not on his list.'

Yes, of course, it must be so. It's not that Yaman doesn't visit. I'm sitting like a withered, dry leaf on the doorstep, but he doesn't seem to notice. He seems to be plucking away unripened fruits, flowers and tender, green shoots. How many such people – to pour ire into my stomach! Starting with Suppini.

How Suppini used to be. The eldest son of the house, handsome, striding around like a majestic king. Ladled out cash in plenty with two hands, working as a lawyer. Parvathi herself used to be constantly mesmerised by the sight of her husband. All that pride snuffed out in a moment by a heart attack as he was holding forth eloquently in the courthouse.

In that shock he too died. Only I'm sitting around like a lump of pounded tamarind, not moving an inch. Bala, Meenu, Venguttu, Echu,

Ramesh, one by one, all in a row – all of them, hale and hearty, just leaving without any warning and I, the sinner that I am, sitting in the corner of the pial, watching them. Every time they carry a corpse away, my mind is agitated. Ayyo, I writhe, thinking it ought to be me on the bier.

I can only sit and watch, unable to do a thing. My eyesight is good and my ears are sharp. It is as if someone has cursed me: just sit there, look at everything and listen to everything. Only my heart has turned numb. My life really should have sped away in a whir on the day Suppini or Ramesh died – the kind of things Parvathi said.

'Paati, have you finished your japams?'

'God knows for whom this old crone is praying? Only her life seems to be getting longer; it is of no use to the family whatsoever!'

'Keep quiet, 'ma. Poor thing. Even at this age of ninety-eight, she is hale and hearty, of no trouble to anyone.'

'So, of what use is she to anyone? What is the point of being a burden to this earth for so many years. I have lost a sturdy, young bull of a son – to whom shall I pour out my gut-wrenching sorrows? This old thing could have died, no?'

'What can be done, 'ma?'

'Don't say that. She's a sinner of a soul. As long as she is alive, everyone will have to sit clutching fire in their bellies.'

'No, 'ma. I don't believe all this.'

Nagu Paati got up. Someone had switched off the passage light. With eyes accustomed to darkness, Paati slowly walked towards the kitchen and peeped in. Kamu was busy at work.

'Come, I'll lay out a leaf for you.'

'Haven't you eaten?'

'Amma and I will eat together.'

'Where is Parvathi?'

'The vegetable-man is at the door.'

'Okay.'

Paati started daintily eating the food served on the leaf.

'Is it banana-stem buttermilk kootu? Did you make it?'

'Yes, Paati. How is it?'

'Like elixir.'

'Whatever you eat is going down like elixir for you.' So saying, Parvathi entered in and laid the vegetable basket in a corner. Mother and daughter looked at each other and chuckled knowingly.

Not heeding all this, Nagu Paati crushed the banana stem with the tips of her fingers, mixed it with the rice and popped it into her mouth.

The telephone seemed to be ringing in the front room.

Kamu got up wearily. 'It's the third time – the phone keeps ringing but stops before we can pick up.'

'Perhaps Padma is calling from Bombay. Out-of-town calls are not that easy to receive.'

To Parvathi who came in saying this, a rice plate in hand, Paati said, 'Serve me a tiny amount and pour the buttermilk.'

As she was serving, Parvathi called out, 'If it is Padma, ask her without fail what she wants from here.'

As she was mixing the buttermilk, Kamu's high-pitched voice burst in from the hall.

'Who? What? Padma? Ayyayo! When? What is this, son-in-law? You are throwing a big thunder at us.'

Paati's gut wrenched. She looked at Parvathi with dread and blinked confusedly.

Parvathi abruptly left the room and hurried towards the hall.

'What is it, di? What is it, Kamu? What is the matter?'

You could hear Kamu howling.

Nagu Paati's legs and hands shivered.

'Who now?'

'Padma. Died this morning, 'ma. From electric shock.'

'Ayyayo! Oh no!'

What screaming. What wailing. All the world's sorrows boiled into a furious flood.

More than sorrow, Nagu Paati was filled with terror. Sitting like a rock in front of the leaf, hand on the rice, she felt as if she had committed a crime. Her body quivered. In anticipation of what was to come, her brain numbed.

Parvathi entered in fury like Bhadrakali, the goddess of wrath.

Nagu Paati's heart froze. The deaths of Suppini and Ramesh came to mind.

'Leave me, di… leave me…' Parvathi strode towards the kitchen and picked up the bronze vessel. 'Take it, gobble. Gobble it all up!' she roared, tilting the pot over the leaf. The hot grains of rice splattered sharply on to Paati's hands. Paati backed off reflexively.

Tongue dried in fear, she stared, shocked, at the bronze pot and the steaming mound of rice.

'It is to pack off everyone one by one that you are sitting nailed to the ground like this. How many more days you want to gorge? That sinner of a Yaman is not whisking you off. He's plucking off tender shoots and buds.'

Nothing Parvathi uttered fell on Nagu Paati's ears. The fury, disgust and frenzy, all together, stared menacingly at Paati.

'Her disgust for me is more than the sorrow of her granddaughter's death. Next she will even throw the cutting blade on my head. Throw it, let me at least perish like that.'

Someone knocked loudly on the front door. Throwing a fierce look at Paati, Parvathi growled out in a deep voice, 'Padma's gone it seems. A lush child of twenty-four. You're happy now, no? Gorge everything, don't leave a grain.' She went outside.

Nagu Paati looked at the leaf with trepidation. Three good eaters could eat what was on the leaf. Even now the rice was steaming. The ends of the leaf had browned from the heat. The more she looked, strange shockwaves shook her body.

What shall I do with this now, di? You've upturned so much of rice on my used leaf. Would you have had the guts to do such a thing had your father-in-law been alive?

Siva, Siva, it's a good thing that he died. It's enough that I am the only one to bear all this. What's to be done now?

Kamu's wail could be heard from the hall.

The bronze pot was still hot. The old lady turned it up with great difficulty. Little by little, she put back the grains of rice. Her hands tired. She murmured to herself, 'How many mouths I have fed! Such wastage of rice, can it be justified?' After she managed to fill up the pot, she got up. Holding the stick, she tottered. The body was heavy, as if dragging a great weight. She washed her hands and gargled her mouth from the tap at the back of the house and stood hesitantly by the hall. Should she not console that child Kamu…

Not thinking about anything else, Paati stepped into the hall. The hall seemed full. Had all the women in the street already gathered there or what?

Paati's eyes didn't take in anyone. She went slowly towards Kamu. Pushing aside the hold of the consoling women, Kamu sobbed uncontrollably, her face covered with the ends of her sari. Paati bent down a little and asked in a trembling voice, 'What, 'ma, Kamu. What injustice is this, child?'

Kamu removed her hands from her face and looked at Paati sharply.

Along with sorrow, fury too was visible in her gaze. Was this Parvathi or Kamu?

Paati's blood froze. Suddenly Kamu got up with a pounce. 'What Amma says is right. It is this old lady who is turning us into sinners. She's a witch. She will budge only when she has packed off everyone in this house.'

Was it Kamu? Was it Kamu who was talking like this? Nagu Paati's guts wrenched. People around seemed to look at her accusingly.

'What can I do, di?' she said weakly. 'He is not taking me away.'

'How will he take you?' hissed Parvathi. 'Your heart is like iron. A son who was like a king, son-in-law, behind him your daughter, grandchildren, now your great-granddaughter – one by one, everyone is going, and you are still sitting digesting all this. Are you human?'

As if in endorsement of her words, a silence spread.

Parvathi mimicked, '"What shall I do, di?"' Then she said, 'Go fall into a pool or a pond.'

'What are you saying, maami? This is a terrible sorrow. But what can this old thing do?'

'You don't know, Saroja, my belly is burning!' Parvathi spluttered out tearfully. 'One by one everyone is getting snuffed out and this old crone is sitting here, as if seeking vengeance.'

Parvathi wept copiously. 'Paati, go in,' said someone prudently.

Nagu Paati moved away, head hung low. When she reached her room, she silently sat down in her usual place where an art-silk spread had been laid out.

The harsh transformation of Kamu's pleasant face and the words confused her mind.

You too don't join in, di. Don't become like her…

Nagu Paati got up slowly. She walked back silently, clutching the wall and reached the kitchen. The soiled leaf from which she had eaten and the bronze rice pot still lay there. Paati sat down gently and started stuffing her mouth with rice from the pot…

Saroja, who had come to the back of the house, sped into the hall.

'Ayyayo, maami, the old thing has gone mad. She knows that this is a house in mourning. She's sitting in the kitchen, taking rice from the bronze pot, putting it on her leaf and stuffing her mouth with it…'

'What nonsense is this?'

'She's no ordinary woman, di, this one.'

'How did a hundred-year-old thing lift a bronze pot?'

'Yes, an incredible thing, isn't it?'

Parvathi got up in fury.

'She's not going to let me off today. She's out to take my life, this crone…'

The other women went behind her to watch the spectacle.

The bronze pot had rolled away. Half the rice remained. The other half, stuffed down Nagu Paati's mouth and throat, had snuffed out her breath.

Saroja, who gently laid down Paati's body that was leaning against the wall, said, 'Deranged mind, nothing else.'

Original title: *Payanam*
1990

TIME-PASS 36

SIVASANKARI

She was bored. If only she had listened to her husband, she could have saved herself all this bother.

The previous day when he had said, 'I have to go for inspection,' she had said, 'I will also come.'

'*You will be bored,*' he had said in English, 'if I leave you in the traveller's bungalow. I won't be able to stay with you. It will take a long time to inspect four bridges and return.'

'*I don't mind…,*' she had replied in English. 'As if it is great here. *I would like to come.*'

She was a city girl – born, brought up and studied in the city. It was four months since they had married. The elders had fixed the alliance.

He was an engineer. He, who had been working in the Public Works Department in the city, was transferred willy-nilly to this small town two months ago on a promotion as Assistant Engineer.

She had been dismayed as to how she was going to set up a home in this small town.

'Let's go now. After six months let's try for a transfer. How can we refuse a promotion saying we are scared of the place?'

She had joined him as soon as he had found a somewhat acceptable house in this undeveloped place.

It wasn't like working in a city. Forever inspections and tours. Even if it didn't entail staying overnight somewhere, he often left early in the morning and returned only when it turned dark.

She didn't like this place. She didn't like anything.

This town didn't suit her, she, who had done BA English Literature.

Whenever he went on office work to the city, she would go with him and return with books from four libraries. When he wasn't there, she would lock the door and read books and magazines. Or she would sleep.

Because she didn't have any books at home to read and because she liked the breeze on her face whenever she went with him in the jeep, she had adamantly started along with him when he had said he was leaving for inspection that day.

They had started early in the morning and had taken tiffin in a hotel on the way.

Since he had to survey a few highway bridges, he had booked a room in a nearby traveller's bungalow and dropped her off.

This TB belonged to the PWD.

The section officer who worked under him, the peon, the contractor and the TB watchman had been waiting for them there.

'Amma is all alone. Guard the door and look after her without going this side, that side… If she calls, attend to her.'

The watchman had nodded.

'Special food will come from my house at twelve, saar. Don't worry about Amma's food, saar.' The contractor had itched to contribute.

He had gone in. 'Food will come from the contractor's house. The watchman is here. Ask him if you want anything… *I will try to come as early as possible.* Lock the door if you want and try to get some sleep… shall I leave?'

Confirming that no one was looking, he had kissed his wife fondly on the cheek and gone out.

The jeep left.

After locking the gate by the fence, the watchman had started sweeping the garden.

She stood on the verandah and looked around.

It was a tiled building.

A sprawling big garden around.

Huge neem trees. Under the shade, stunted periwinkle plants. The bricks laid in a row at the edge were newly painted white. Wonder which VIP had visited?

To the left of the TB was a badam tree. Beside it a lush manoranjitam bush.

Will there be any flowers?

She got down and went around it twice.

'It won't flower now… only after some days…' She didn't like the watchman's silly laughter. Who asked him?

She went up the verandah again and shut the door of the room.

The room looked big.

An iron cot, mattress, wooden table, chair, some sand in the corner. On it a pot of drinking water.

The fan hung from a long rod…

A bathroom behind. No pipe. Some water in a tin drum.

A strong odour of moss.

A small verandah on this side of the bathroom.

Through the grilled wall she looked at the back garden.

At a distance, she could see a hut. The watchman's hut? No sign of any person. He wasn't married? Looked like an old man. Would the wife have died? What about the children then?

What nonsense! What is to me if he is married, has children, or if his wife is dead? *Why should I indulge in such good-for-nothing thinking?*

Her eyes homed in on a well. A big well, like all village wells. Bricks were visible on the short wall, and they weren't painted.

As she was watching, a blue, brown and black bird alighted on the wall. Long beak. What bird could it be?

Oh, yes. Must be a kingfisher. Didn't it look like this, the picture in her childhood textbooks?

In a flash, the bird on the wall flew into the well.

Goodness! Did it fall in?

Not even twenty seconds would have passed.

'Sarrr'… it came back, sat on the wall and started eating the tiny fish it had caught, holding it with its feet.

Ada! Crafty thing! It *dove* into the well, plucked the fish, and cleverly came out! The well wasn't deep?

In the next ten minutes, it again *dove* into the well, but the third time it flew away with the prey, without eating it.

Was its stomach full? Or was it taking it for the young ones?

Thinking that it would come back, she stood there for a bit; disappointed, she went into the room.

She looked at the clock to see the time, but it had stopped.

Damn it!

What would be the time?

Eleven? Nearly twelve? Would the watchman know? Should she call him?

What did it matter what time it was? What was she going to do knowing it? She started to get bored.

Should she have listened to her husband's words and stayed at home?

Should she send the watchman to buy some magazines from somewhere close by?

What day was it? Tuesday. Not a day when any magazine would appear on the stands.

She opened the newspaper she had brought from home.

The prime minister's picture. The Congress public meeting at Jawahar Nagar was reported.

Whoever it was, the talk was always about the twenty-point programme.

Everyone was talking, but how many among them really practised what they preached?

Three-fourths were frauds. *Hyprocrites.*

What would be the time?

She took out a piece of Chiclets from her bag and chewed it. Sitting on the chair, she looked at the garden through the window.

There was a badam tree just opposite.

The big tree's leaves were large and green.

Remembering how as a child she ate the red badam fruit and broke the seed and ate the tasty kernel, she went to the window and peered to see if there were any fruits.

Mhmmm. Only plenty of white flowers and small green unripe fruits could be seen.

Looking at the tree up close, she could see black bully ants creeping down in a row.

The ants were fat. If they bit, it would definitely bleed.

There was an ugly chameleon at the foot of the tree.

It shook its head like a drunken old man. Sitting at the same place, raising its neck up and down, it swallowed, 'labak', the ants which came near it.

Foolish ants. How easily they fell into the chameleon's mouth.

Couldn't they have gone to the other side of the tree?

Wouldn't the ant know, if it saw the chameleon swallowing the one before it?

In the time it took for the chameleon to swallow an ant, the next ant which crossed escaped. The stupid ant neither realised that it may have been trapped nor that it had escaped by sheer luck!

She was irritated with the chameleon which feasted till its stomach was full without moving an inch. She tore up a bit of the newspaper, made it into a ball and threw it at the chameleon through the window.

The paper ball missed the target and fell away from the tree.

She threw another ball; this time it fell by the window.

Another, another.

Not even one touched the chameleon.

She thought, If the ants were destined to die like this, *why should I bother?*

She was tired. Since she had been standing for a long time, her legs hurt.

When she went to sit on the chair, she heard the watchman talking to someone. She opened the door.

Her food had arrived from the contractor's house.

'Ask them to leave it on the table and go!'

After they left, she locked the door again and pulled the chair to eat.

Adada. I could have asked this boy the time. He had a watch.

She spread the leaf, sprinkled water on it and opened the carrier.

Bright red sambar, rasam, kootu, banana dry curry, potato chips. And was that payasam? Curd rice.

Not bad.

Only when she began to eat, she realised that everything was throat-burningly spicy and full of garlic. She didn't like garlic.

She ate the chips. Then the curd rice. Too sour.

She ate something half-heartedly and got up.

The watchman cleaned the table. 'I will go and eat and be back in a minute, amma,' he said and went off.

She locked the door and slept.

Some odour from the pillow.

She screwed up her nose.

Wonder who had slept there?

She took out a towel from the plastic basket she had brought and spread it both on the mattress and the pillow.

She lay down again.

Now it is better. Can't get the smell.

She closed her eyes and tried to sleep.

The sleep which usually overcame her at home refused to come now.

Was the watchman back?

What a desolate place. It was so silent.

When would he come?

She closed her eyes. *Now I should sleep.*

'Kak kak kak kak.'

Half asleep, she didn't heed the noise.

'Kak kak kak kak.'

What a funny noise... Where was it coming from?

'Kak kak kak kak.' In the quiet, the noise could be heard even more loudly.

She looked around and couldn't make out anything.

She got up and peeped out of the window. She looked at the bathroom and the verandah.

She was a little scared.

'Kak kak kak kak...'

What was this noise, the same thing again and again?

Was the watchman back?

When she peeped out he wasn't to be seen.

She again sat on the bed.

It was clear that the 'kak kak kak kak' noise came from somewhere close by.

Where? Why?

Plucking up courage, she looked around the room.

On the door was a white lizard, neither big nor small, medium-sized.

This side, by the light was another one, exactly like it.

'Kak kak kak kak!'

The sound seemed to be coming from the light.

The light-lizard swung its tail, this way and that way like a snake, and the way its jaw shook, she knew that the 'kak kak kak kak' came from that.

Was it the lizard making the noise? She was a little relieved.

She had heard the lizards making a noise in the city. It would cluck once and that was it! She had never heard it cluck non-stop.

The light-lizard took a couple of steps forward. Again it swung its tail like a snake. Clucked.

Was the lizard not feeling well? Stomachache perhaps?

The door-lizard didn't move.

Little by little, the light-lizard went toward the door-lizard with the same tune and speed.

Was it going to fight?

Was it cowering only to pounce?

She found it funny.

Couldn't it pounce 'gup' and fight? Why all this clucking, tail wagging and cowering?

Time ticked by.

When the light-lizard neared the door-lizard little by little, her interest grew.

That's it. The two came close.

The door-lizard didn't move.

The light-lizard went even closer. More noise, more tail-wagging.

It came very close. Within touching distance.

Suddenly the light-lizard clucked loudly. One leap. The two got entwined. No tune. No tail shaking. Nothing. Just silence.

Male and female?

Was that what she was watching all the while with such interest?

She turned her head, abashed; the sound of the jeep could be heard outside.

Original title: *Pozhuthu*
1977

In Search of Truth 37

Sujatha

Nine years after their marriage, at about eleven on a Sunday morning, Krishnamoorthy and Chitra sat in the hall, face to face. The usual silence. While Krishnamoorthy scanned the papers, Chitra was reading a serial in a magazine, waiting for the pressure cooker to hiss. They could hear the wooden gate opening. Krishnamoorthy peeped through the window. A barefooted man of about thirty crossed the garden, a plate in hand. 'Who is it?' he asked. The man gave a little start and narrated his woeful tale in a 'capsule', 'I'm new to the city, saar. I came in search of a job. But my wife died this morning. The body is still lying there. I don't have money to cremate it. Big people like you must help.'

There were a few notes and coins on the plate in his hand. Strangely, there were a few flowers too. And a joss stick was burning.

'Did you see that, Vimala! The way these children are suffering' – Chitra stopped the story at that point and peeped out.

He had a three-day stubble. Enough pain in his eyes. 'What is it?' she asked.

The man repeated his story, 'I'm new to the city, 'ma. I came in search of a job…'

It was bound to shake anyone immediately, hearing the tragic words 'wife died'. One would rush in and fetch some money. But Krishnamoorthy didn't do that. He wouldn't. Chitra knew very well that he would question everything.

'Where's the house?' he asked.

'Here only, saar, near Gokula. It happened in a known person's house.'

'What's the address?'

'Near the cinema theatre.'

'Ok. Tell me the address.'

'Let it be. Why don't you just give him something and send him away,' she said softly.

'Wait!'

'It's been only three days since I came to Bangalore. She died this morning!'

'Ok, 'pa, tell me the address!'

He thought for a bit. 'Third Cross,' he said.

'Third Cross-aa? HMT layout-aa? Sunder Nagar-aa? Or is it Gokula colony?'

'I don't know, saar. Near the cinema theatre.'

'Why all this argument with him?'

'Will you keep quiet! Which cinema theatre, 'ya?'

'What, saar, you are asking all this? There is only one cinema theatre, no! As if you don't know the name, saar?'

'I know it. You tell me!'

Again he started his chorus. 'It's been only three days since I came to Bangalore, saar. She died this morning.'

'Ok, 'pa. Where is the place? You won't say that, is it?'

'What, saar, I'm so sad that my wife is dead. You are asking all sorts of things like a policeman. Tell me if you can give the money or not. I have to go. The body is lying there.'

'Tell me the address properly. I will give you.'

'I told you, no?'

'Tell it correctly.'

'Ayyo!' he said. 'I don't want, saar. Why you are asking like this?'

Chitra expected it. She very much expected the man to start shouting, 'What a man you are, you have no humaneness or what?' Instead, he started weeping. He changed the plate to the other hand and cried silently. 'I'll go, saar!' He turned and started walking and latched the gate on his way out.

Krishnamoorthy didn't expect this. 'He's gone,' he said.

'Call him back!' said Chitra.

'What for? You know it's all fake.'

'*Please*. Call him back. Please call him and give him something.'

Krishnamoorthy laughed and looked outside. He could see him at a distance. He disappeared from view, wiping his tearful face on his shirt.

'If it was the truth, he would have brightly said the address, no? Why the reluctance? As if I wouldn't have given if he had said the address properly!'

'He said he was new to the city. Perhaps he didn't know the address!'

'Che che! You don't know, Chitra. This is a big *racket*. Did he look like someone whose wife had died? He blinked foolishly!'

'I didn't feel like that. Why did he cry?'

'That's all part of the drama.'

'We could have given something. Poor thing.'

'Again and again you are talking foolishly. Don't you know the world is full of lies. All sorts of frauds… You, you are always at home. How much cheating is happening, do you know?'

'Looking at his face, I didn't think he was lying!'

'You don't have enough brains.'

'Ok, I don't have enough brains! And yes he was lying! So what? What will happen if you give one or two rupees, will we become any the less? How much we spend uselessly.'

'That's another matter altogether. The question is whether we should *help* those who come to our house to cheat us. If he had come and told me brightly and honestly "Saar, I'm poor. I don't have money for the next meal," I would have given two… why, five rupees! Instead, he pulled a fast one saying that his wife was dead… thinking if he said "death" we would give money without questioning. Did you see that? How can we *encourage* this, you tell me?'

Chitra wanted to say so many things. She wanted to say that there were no lies in his statements; that, really, in all this flurry, he may have been confused about his new address; that I don't at all like what you did. If she had said all this, there would have been arguments… fights. He would have said 'go to hell' and left without eating.

The cooker gave a loud hiss. Chitra went in.

Krishnamoorthy went back to the paper. But he couldn't concentrate on the *newsprint*. Why couldn't she understand clearly that he was right? The way she had slunk in revealed her disappointment. What did she know…

He said, 'Like this only, once a woman, yellow sari and all, said she was going to Tirupati and asked for five rupees. What happened? Didn't we see her at the theatre?'

'Yes.'

'Then there was that *notice* which said they were running an orphanage. You remember that man who came with a receipt book printed and all? What happened?'

'What happened?' she asked from inside.

'Didn't I prove to you that there was no street by that name in the city?'

'Yes, I remember.'

'You shouldn't get fooled like that so easily. To get ten rupees, they will say their mother is dead! There are ever so many lies in this world, do you know Chitra?'

No reply from Chitra.

'Chitra?'

No answer.

When Krishnamoorthy folded the paper and walked towards the kitchen, he saw with a start that Chitra was crying.

'Why are you crying now?'

She wiped her tears quickly.

'I'm asking why you are crying?' he upbraided her.

'Nothing.'

'Don't lie. Because I sent him away, is it?'

'No, no,' she said, sniffling. 'Looking at him I thought he wasn't lying… He… The way he suddenly heaved and cried came to mind. An unknown being. Some sadness. It seemed as if he gave me a bit of his sadness and left…'

'How many times to tell you it's all lies?'

'How do you know?' She raised her voice and asked. He glowered at her.

'How do I know? I'll tell you how! Through experience. Experience which I got outside. Chitra, you look at everything with *emotion*. That is what is wrong with you. I look at things *practically.*

'Ok, what you say only is the truth! I won't cry. But…'

'Tell me. Tell me what you are thinking?'

'Like you say, many people lie. Cheat. What if by chance what this man said was true… A grief-stricken man – we made him stand outside, asked him question after question, to which he blinked not knowing how to answer, and we chased him away without giving any money… isn't that wrong? Why should we ask questions… Whether he told the truth or lies, who cares? If only we had given two rupees, all this…'

'Again and again you are saying the same thing. Two rupees is no big deal to me, Chitra! It's the *principle!* That only is important!'

'Ok,' was all she said. He looked at his wife for a while. *'All right.'* You are still not convinced. I'll tell you what – what did he say? Third Cross near the theatre, no? The theatre is close by, let's go and see if he is there, come! Only then you will be satisfied. Come, we'll take the car and be back in a minute…'

'No, it's ok, I'm *convinced* by what you said. Don't know why I started crying foolishly.'

'No, you are not *convinced!* You still don't understand, what I'm saying is right.'

'I'm not coming. I have other work.'

'Even if you don't come, I'm going to see.'

'Why this…? Forget it.'

'No. I want to see who is right in this *case*. You or me.'

'You only are right. I've agreed only, no?'

'You haven't agreed wholeheartedly. You want *proof*, right? I'll go and look.'

'What kind of stubbornness is this? What are you going to achieve by going there, even if you find it is true?'

'If I'm wrong, I'll give him ten, no, fifteen rupees! But that will never happen. I've seen a lot in *life*, Chitra.'

'If you are that *sure*, why should you go?'

'For your sake only, Chitra. You cried like a waterfall, didn't you? To prove that this is wrong.'

'I feel like laughing now.'

'Let's see who will have the last laugh.'

Krishnamoorthy opened the shed, the big gate, and took out the car. He zoomed away. The theatre must be within a mile. Definitely must go and see. Didn't he say Third Cross? What did he think of me? That I'm a heartless fellow? What does she know? As if I'm a fool to give money without asking. Crybaby. Once like this only…

There was a Third Cross near the theatre. Before you could even turn, you could see the whole desolate street. In the middle of the street was a pot, from which smoke arose. Green bamboo poles for the bier were ready. He was sitting in the corner, on the ground, hands on his head.

Krishnamoorthy hesitated, only for a moment – he reversed the car. He started with a hiss towards his house.

'What happened?' asked Chitra listlessly.

He said quickly, 'What I said was right! I enquired thoroughly in the Third Cross that he mentioned. Nothing there.'

'Really? Appa! What utter lies!' said Chitra.

Original title: *Nijathai Thedi*
1980

Yellow Fish

38

Ambai

The sands have already become hot. It's summer. The sands are no longer moist. If you turn away from the shrunken, spent waves of the dull sea, the sands spread out like a desert to the left. Yet the gaze always turns towards the sea. The white boat has arrived. It's the pilot boat, heralding the return of the fishing boats. Floating in like a swan, swaying this way and that. Far away, colourful spots begin to emerge. The fisherwomen ready themselves to receive the boats. Dazzling colours: deep indigo, demonic red, dark green, striking blue. They advance speedily, against the white boat on a faded blue and ash-grey sea.

You can see the other boats now. If you walk down to the boats, you can see the nets full of fish. Bodies and hands darkened by the salty winds, the men will unfold their nets and start sorting the fish the moment the boats touch the shore. The fish fall 'sap-sap' into the plastic bucket, round eyes wide open. The unwanted are thrown outside. A general murmur of low voices, rising now and then in flashes.

Dark hands. Wood-brown boats. White-bellied fishes through the meshes of the nets. Very close, the colours of the saris stroke the eyes softly, but firmly. Colourful buckets. Dry sands. An amazing melding of colours. On the shores of a vast sea. A vivid collage that gradually gets frozen in the mind.

A yellow fish falls with a plop on the sand.

Of that yellow seen before the leaves brown in autumn. With black spots. When I bend down to look, it sloshes around. The mouth gasps, keeps on gasping. In the hot sands, it twitches and tosses around. The sorting of the fish goes on briskly. That mouth opens and closes, again and again. Thirsting for water. Like Jalaja's mouth.

That hasty little Jalaja. Shoved and thrust her way into the world. A name for her had been chosen. The one who has risen from the waters. Jalaja. Lotus. They had kept her in the incubator. Standing outside the room, I kept looking at her. Tender pink lips. Round eyes. Opened and closed her mouth, now and then, as if she was sucking.

The ashes that Arun brought back from the electric crematorium were in a small urn. A miniature of those huge earthenware urns used for burial in the days of Mohenjodaro and Harappa. Its narrow mouth was tied with a cloth.

'Why is the mouth closed?'

'What mouth?'

'The mouth of that urn. Open it.'

'Anu, it just contains ashes.'

'I want to see it. Open it.'

'Anu…'

'Open the mouth… mouth… that mouth…'

Loud sobs. The cloth was removed to reveal the copper urn's tiny mouth. Her ashes… in this very sea.

The sea is just a little away. The yellow fish tries to leap, but fails. Its mouth open to the skies. When I pick it up from the hot sands, it slips and falls. Tossing round and round. As I try to lift it up with a leaf tossed ashore by the waves, it again slips away.

A fisherboy walks back after sloshing around in the sea.

When I call out in Marathi, 'Ikade ye,' he comes.

'Will you throw back this yellow fish in the sea?'

A gurgle of laughter. He quickly grasps it by the tail. Starts running towards the sea. I run after him. He places it on the tip of a gentle wave. It gulps the water yearningly. It flounders, like a drunk who has lost his way. Again and again, it opens its mouth and sucks in water. Then a swish of the tail. Then an audacious leap. Flapping its tail this way and that, it swims forward. The yellow can be seen far into the sea. Then disappearing into the blue-grey white of the sea.

Original title: Manjal Meen
1988

Ghee Stain

39

Na Muthuswamy

In our kitchen between two pillars hung a ghee chombu on a rope-net from the roof. I don't know through how many generations this age-old rope-net had passed to support our ghee vessel. I don't remember anything other than ghee being hung from it. Ghee, or sometimes butter. If there wasn't time or inclination to make ghee, only butter hung from it. There was always butter in our house. Our house was known for its buffaloes. Every couple of days they would churn the curd. I too would join in. In fact, everyone would. There was a kind of pleasure in it. The poet Kamban too had experienced it:

The churner tumbles along; the buttery curds splatter around…

And the delicate palms of the milkmaids turn crimson under the strain.

Our kitchen was huge. Not only ours, but everyone else's too. But the open courtyard inside our kitchen was really huge. I haven't seen one like it anywhere. If you had such a big courtyard, the kitchen would be well lit. In other houses it was strangely dark. Even in the height of day. But today we have driven away such darkness. Even in broad daylight we have accustomed ourselves to using artificial light. The old light which caressed our eyes and skin has brightened. A good thing, really. It's only now that we have started working for the entire community, shorn of justice so far. We need this much illumination for that.

The space between the two pillars from where the ghee chombu hung was rather narrow. The roof was supported by another pillar, used only for churning the curd. This pillar stood a little towards the east, near the main pillar at one corner of the courtyard, which stretched from east to west. It had its own special carvings. It looked as if the carving of the pillar was etched in such a way that the two ropes that hung from the pillar to the curd vessel never slipped off; the groove which held them formed a part of the carving.

The kitchen plan was a bit different. In the street stretching from east to west, the kitchens in the houses on either side of the road were also placed in the same direction but differed from one another. But, if by happenstance the houses weren't split into two, the most prominent feature in those kitchens was the open courtyards. These courtyards were usually surrounded by passages on three sides. But ours had only two. On the northern side a wall dominated instead of a passage. The western hall stretched a bit towards the north and turned to the east to join another inner passage, making way for the entrance of the second courtyard, dividing the front. In the passage adjoining the hall on the northern side was a low-roofed entrance to the kitchen. But a generous doorstep gave way to the second courtyard. Unlike today's tall doors, one had to bend to pass through these traditional doors. The kitchen doorway was even more low.

The rope-net from which hung the ghee chombu could be seen by outsiders through this door frame. If one crossed the passage from the main doorway of the house and reached the inner doorway and sat in the pial adjoining it on the eastern side, then one could see the rope-net and the curd being churned. But in the space between the pillars by the western roof and the northern one adjacent to the kitchen hung a closely woven screen of coconut fronds. So anyone sitting in the smaller pial could not directly see the kitchen. So the ghee chombu remained hidden from view.

If you say ghee chombu, old-timers would know that it was a lead one. And those from Tanjore would know that lead vessels were made in Mayavaram and Kumbakonam. These vessels were well known. If one visited Mayavaram one could see at the end of Pattamangalam Street near the Thula bath-square, on the eastern line facing the west, a few shops where these vessels were being hammered into shape. I knew this because Punjai, my village, was close to Mayavaram. I knew Kumbakonam only by name. I never had any reason to go there. Except for the festival of Maamaangam. In the month of Aipasi we would all go to Mayavaram for the ceremonial Thula dip. Now we all talk a lot about the environment being dirtied. Sixty years ago if one thought of the Thula Tank during the ceremonial dips, one would realise that the environment had been dirtied even then. It was only in the month of Aipasi that lead and stone vessels were bought in plenty. Only then more people visited Mayavaram. This ghee chombu must have been bought during one such auspicious month of Aipasi. The awareness of lead vessels has decreased. Why, even the chombu's awareness has waned. Their place has been usurped by plastic mugs. Chombu. Mug. Two types of lead, black and white. If you didn't know, they said that you could be cheated into buying the black for the white. If you stored foods with salt in them in the black lead, they would turn toxic. Nothing would happen if stored in the white one. Even to make rasam, the white one was more suitable. They used to say that you had to make rasam only in the white lead vessel. Perhaps lead was necessary for the body. Now they talk of lead poisoning. If beyond the required measure, maybe even medicines turn toxic. Must check with the doctor.

That lead chombu was the size of a head. Then it hung full of ghee. I was sitting below it, churning the curd in a big stone vessel. Today to the city folks you would have to mention that it would be morning if it was curd-churning time. It would have been about eight in the morning. Those were days when you could know the time by seeing the shadow on the courtyard and not by the clock. I think my mother was heating the milk to set the curd. There were stoves on the eastern and the northern end of the kitchen. Stoves lit by firewood. When I was churning the curd, Amma was near the stove at the eastern end.

My friend Palanivelu was perhaps sitting on the small pial in the courtyard. He called out, 'Kanna.'

I was immensely glad. 'Palanivelu,' I shouted excitedly. By the time I placed the churner aslant so that it wouldn't fall into the stone pot, he called out again, 'Kanna, I want some water.' That we remained hidden because of the screen in the courtyard should be kept in mind. I got up to fetch water. He was my dearest friend; I had to offer him only the water I myself drank. So I went to get the water stored in a pot placed on a small counter built in the corner of the passage that led to the shed behind. It was to the west of the corridor in the northern wall. Remaining in the kitchen, Amma called out looking at me, 'Ei, ei, here, da.' The meaning of that was that I ought to sprinkle some buttermilk to the water that I offered my friend. To cleanse it. He wasn't a Brahmin, but a Mudaliar. In Punjai, the Mudaliars were as influential as Brahmins. I didn't want to sprinkle buttermilk on the water. We were about ten years then I think. I was aware of such evils even then. So was he. Our non-Brahmin friends used to tease us about them. Hiding a little away from the banks of the Kaveri, the little cowherds had begun to jeer at the Brahmins bathing in the river,

'The Brahmins of the agraharam, won't they all croak,
On the banks of the river, won't they go up in smoke!'

Giving a hard stare, I took the tumbler without pouring the buttermilk. Amma ran out from the kitchen, dipped her hand into the churned buttermilk in the stone pot and sprinkled it on the tumbler. That was all. I was livid. I banged the tumbler on the wall. I kicked the stone pot into the courtyard and broke it. I snatched the ghee pot from the rope-net and smashed it against the wall. All over the wall, all over the courtyard, rivers of ghee and buttermilk. I, who attempted to run out in anger, banged my head, because I was tall and because the doorway was low.

'Ayyo, Amma.' I fell unconscious on the floor. This 'Amma' was not a wail to call out to my mother but a cry of pain. It was said that it was my friend who ran and lifted me, made me lie down, fetched a doctor, applied the medicine and bandaged me.

He would certainly have known why it all happened. Rising above all this, he remained my friend.

Even though it may have lost the reason and relevance of its origin, this ghee stain is still imprinted on the wall of the courtyard.

Original title: *Nei Chombu*
2004

The Opposite End 40

Sa Kandasamy

Vasudevan was the physical education teacher of Kaniyur High School. Around forty-five years. But was already bald since all his front hair had dropped off. Combing over the back hair, he hid the bald spot. Twisted moustache and red big eyes. He always looked testy, as if forever angry. His temper was evident even in his speech. Still he was a very capable teacher. The students liked him. It was only after he came that the school won three gold medals at the district level for volleyball, high jump and the two-hundred-metre dash.

The district collector who gave away the prizes called on to the stage and specially congratulated the principal Pon Dhanasekaran of the Kaniyur High School, which had won three gold medals at one go. In his speech he said that in this day and age books alone didn't constitute education, but sport did too. And no one knew this better than Kaniyur High School, which had done everyone proud. He wished that the school which had come first in the district, would get gold medals at the state, Indian and even the Olympic levels.

The principal wasn't happy with the district collector's speech. He had played no part in the students winning gold medals in this competition. To tell the truth, he was opposed to sports and games. To him education meant poring over books and earning good marks. Several times he snatched away hours meant for physical education for special classes.

Which was why Vasudevan entered the principal's room and shouted. He really shouted; the whole school could hear him. Students and teachers alike ran out of their classrooms to watch the spectacle. It was the first time there was such a fracas in the principal's room. Everyone stood frozen, not knowing what to do. In all the anger and humiliation, the principal became speechless.

Paarivallal, the Tamil teacher, hurriedly entered the principal's room. On seeing him, Vasudevan stepped a foot forward and yelled, 'See, saar, just because he is the principal, he has no right to steal the games periods.'

Paarivallal caught hold of his hand. 'What, saar, you are talking like this and all…'

'It's been going on for many days, saar. He is keeping on stealing. I'm not going to leave it. I'm going to take it up to the chief minister's level and put an end to this.'

'We'll see about all that. Come, saar.' Paarivallal pulled his hand and took him out.

The maths teacher Sivanandam said, 'Why, saar, all this unnecessary quarrel?'

'You shut your mouth and keep quiet. I can't keep quiet if they steal my time,' Vasudevan bellowed. Most of the time it was maths which was studied during the physical education hour, hence Vasudevan was extremely cross with the maths teacher. But not only the principal but also the Tamil teacher was shocked that Vasudevan used a word such as 'stealing'. But no one knew what to tell him. He wouldn't listen to anyone. He would pick a fight whichever school you put him in. He had never stayed in any one school for even two years.

The education officer of the district called Vasudevan over to his office and told him, 'You mustn't fight for at least three years in Kaniyur High School. The principal is a very nice man.'

'As if I'm a quarrelsome fellow. Games too is a period, like any other. If they keep snatching it away, how can I leave it, saar? I won't keep quiet if they snatch away my period, saar.'

The officer didn't say anything. But thought to himself that Vasudevan was a man who didn't know the world and didn't know how to survive. Education in school meant marks. Any subject without marks counted for nothing. Here he was, doing a job which carried no value, so how could he get respect?

He couldn't make Vasudevan understand all this and he wasn't sure if Vasudevan would ever understand. Besides, he had other work to attend to. Anyway, he sent him away with a smile. You couldn't say that he was like that only in school. He was worse at home. He and his younger brother had had a big fight and weren't on speaking terms. It was after his father's death, a fight over division of wealth.

When they were dividing the property, Vasudevan had accused that the brother hadn't shown the correct account for liquid cash. The brother had stiffly stood his ground. 'In which case you keep everything,' Vasudevan had said, and walked away.

After four months the brother sent someone, but Vasudevan didn't go. The elder uncle came to see him. After eating a sumptuous meal of crab and fish, the uncle washed his hands and said, 'I believe your younger brother is going to buy a house in Delhi. He is short of money. If you split the wealth, it will be helpful to him.'

'Maama, it's because it is you I'm speaking so politely. The day he tried to cheat me, he stopped being my younger brother. And I stopped being his elder brother. Let him keep everything, buy a house in Delhi and live like a king.'

'Do you think what you are saying is right?'

'Why is it not right? The fellow who tried to cheat me, let him take all the money and live happily.'

'You shouldn't speak like this, with your stomach burning with so much anger!'

'Whose stomach is burning?' he said, and slapped his Maama across the cheek. Rubbing his cheek, Maama looked at him. Hearing the noise, Rani came running from inside.

'I came running here because I wanted you to get a couple of rupees and live happily. And for that you stretched your hand out and slapped me. That hand will become numb and useless,' he said and walked down the steps.

Vasudevan pounced, 'What did you say?'

Rani grabbed his hand and pulled him back. Shrugging her away, he sat down on the sofa one leg over the other and looked at Maama going away.

'Everyone getting together and trying to cheat me, is it... What money...

Big thing it is… You all take it and be happy…' he screamed.

Rani stood there, just looking at him. He lifted his head.

'That's your money only. Why do you want to refuse it?'

Vasudevan shook his head.

'If we get that money, all our troubles will be over. We can build a small house; we can get a bicycle for our son.'

'Will give you one with the slipper now,' said Vasudevan and leapt up from the sofa. 'You have made all sorts of big plans for that money, is it? The day he tried to cheat me, he ceased to be my brother. I'm not a cheap fellow to live off my father's wealth. I have two hands and feet… I will toil happily, earn enough and build a mansion… What cycle, I will get a motorbike… If you speak about that money again, I will chop you into two, do you hear?'

Rani lifted her head, gave him a look and went inside.

One evening Vasudevan sat on a chair swinging his legs. He wasn't one to sit around at home in the evenings. As soon as school was over, it was to the playground he went. Then friends. He would park the motorbike in front of the house only at eight-thirty or nine. Why was he at home this hour, wondered Rani and offered him tea. He gestured her to leave it on the table; she left it and went in. He started drinking the tea while looking outside.

His son Sunderarasan, studying in the ninth standard, entered the house. He got a bit scared seeing his father. He stood still, lifted his head a bit and looked at his father.

'You are coming home only now after school, is it?'

'The maths teacher took a class, Appa.'

'Leave your bag and come quickly.'

Sunderarasan came inside quickly. Last week, as he was learning to ride a cycle in the mahua grove, his father had come by, stopped the motorbike under a peepul tree and watched him. As soon as he had seen his father, Sunderarasan had ridden the bike unsteadily in fear, hips shaking. Vasudevan had stood there, looking at him. When he had taken a second turn, as soon as he neared the peepul tree, he had looked at his father and jumped down hastily.

'Come here,' Vasudevan had gestured with his hand. Sunderarasan had stood fearfully in front of him.

'Why are you afraid? Ride without fear.'

Sunderarasan had stood there hesitantly. Vasudevan had held the cycle in his left hand, and Sunderarasan had climbed on to it. Vasudevan had given the cycle a push. The boy had pedalled, his body wobbling. Vasudevan had run in front and given him a slap on the hip. It wasn't a light tap. A slap Sunderarasan would remember till the end of his life. Even if he had wobbled a bit, he had somehow managed to straighten himself and ride the bike properly. Leaning against his motorbike, Vasudevan had watched him weave in and out of the trees.

Sunderarasan hung his school bag on a nail and went to the back of the house. His mother was winnowing the rice.

'Amma, Appa wants me to go out with him. I will go and come back.'

Vasudevan wasn't a man who normally took either wife or son out on the motorbike. Even if father and son went to the same school, the son walked three kilometres every day. Not only that, Vasudevan wasn't a man who informed them when he set out.

When they were newly married, Rani had said, 'Only if you tell me where you are going can I tell people where you have gone.'

'Hereafter to each and every place I go, I will seek your permission, is it.'

She couldn't understand a word. She had given him a look.

'Look here, I'm a man. I will go as I please. Come as I please. Don't have hopes and come stand behind me showing all your teeth, hoping that I'll tell you I'm going here, I'm going there.'

From that time Rani never asked about his coming and going. If someone came in search of him, she would only tell them, 'He's gone to school.'

Vasudevan kick-started his bike. The bike started at the first kick. He turned the accelerator once and sat himself down. Sunderarasan stood looking at his father. He gestured with his head, asking him to sit on the pillion. The boy sat down and looked behind. His mother was standing under the poovarasu tree.

The motorbike made its way across the Kaveri bridge, wove into the mahua grove, then on to the Periya Muni pathway and then halted in front of Anbuselvam bicycle shop. Anbuselvam, the man sitting in the shop, was his old student. As soon as he saw Vasudevan, he got up from the chair and welcomed him, 'Come in, saar... come in, saar...

Sunderarasan got down from the motorbike and stood staring at the different bikes on display.

Vasudevan shook his head, went and sat on the chair and asked, 'How's business… you only couldn't run properly… do your cycles run…'

'Not bad, saar.'

'Give me a good cycle.'

'For whom, saar? For the boy…' He looked towards Sunderarasan.

Vasudevan nodded.

'You should have bought one for him last year itself, saar. Poor boy… Daily he's been walking six kilometres…'

'Where's the money? Today I got the loan from the provident fund… I've come running immediately. Give me a good cycle…'

'Now it is all Hero these days, saar… All the boys seem to like that only… Lot of ads even on TV, saar…'

'Okay… Give me that only… What's the price?'

'Thousand three hundred rupees, saar. I will reduce hundred rupees for you, saar. Give me thousand two hundred rupees, saar.'

'No need for all that. Get a good cycle ready for me… Don't dump an inferior cycle on my head reducing hundred rupees.'

'Nothing like that, saar…' said Anbuselvam and signalled for a man to come. He went out wiping his hands.

Sunderarasan was waiting near a green bike that was getting fitted. A man brought three coffees on a plate. Anbuselvam offered Vasudevan a tumbler. He took a sip.

'Saar, I'm thinking of keeping a twenty-kilometre cycle race on Independence Day. You must only come and flag it off. Our district SP too has said he will come…'

'You remembered only now, is it, after I came to your shop?'

'Nothing like that, saar. I wanted to come and call you personally. But I couldn't leave the shop…'

'Why do you need to conduct a competition? You stay here and look after your shop…'

'What, saar, you're saying like this…'

'Then what, if you ask me in all sorts of odd places, I will say like this only…' Sunderarasan was seated on a stool, staring intently at the cycle.

The cycle was ready after fifteen minutes. Anbuselvam stretched out the bill to Vasudevan. He gave the cash, folded the bill, put it in his bag, and patted the cycle seat. Rang the bell. It resounded loudly. Then he straightened the pedal, turned the wheel and clasped the brake. Everything seemed to be all right.

Anbuselvam pushed the cycle out of the shop and gave it to Sunderarasan. The boy held on to the handle bar and looked at his father.

'It is your cycle only. Take it home.'

Sunderarasan nodded with happiness. He pushed the bike for a bit till the poovarasu tree, then got on to the bike. It was a mud path; the wheel wobbled, getting caught in the mud. He turned the handle bar this way and that and then straightened the bike and pedalled hard. The cycle seemed to fly. He kept pedalling harder.

'The boy seems to ride well,' said Anbuselvam.

Vasudevan got on to the motorbike without saying a word.

Sunderarasan got down from the cycle in front of the house and rang the bell. His mother came out and asked, 'Where is the bike from?'

He said Appa had bought it. Astonished, she ran in and hurriedly brought out vibhuti, camphor and all and did a pooja for the bike. She smeared vibhuti on his forehead and on the handlebar and then placed a dot of kumkumam.

'It must be very costly. Keep it carefully,' she said.

Sunderarasan was very careful with his bike. If the road was bumpy, he rode it along the edge. He often pressed the tyres to check if there was enough air in them. Before he started for school, he dabbed coconut oil and polished the cycle with a white cloth. The green of the bike twinkled brightly. Finding only one lock for the back wheel inadequate, he fixed one for the front wheel too. One day his father stood watching him wipe the bike.

After eating lunch on a Sunday afternoon, the father left on the motorbike. It would have been around four in the evening. Sunderarasan, who was working out some maths problems, had a sudden doubt. Mannur Narayanan of his class was a tiger in maths. He also willingly taught others. Telling his mother that he was going to visit Mannur Narayanan and would be back by six, he started on his bike.

'Quick. Come by six before Appa returns.' She came to the door and waved him off.

The mother looked at the clock now and then. The clock struck seven, but no sign of her son. Rani stood outside. At seven-thirty Vasudevan got down from his bike. When he saw Rani he got irritated.

'Why are you standing at the door at this hour…,' he raised his voice.

'Sunder said he would be back by six. Hasn't come back yet.'

'He has the cycle, no? No doubt he is roaming the streets. Let him come. If you give four tight slaps, everything will be all right.' The father went in, and so did the mother.

Vasudevan took off his pants, tied a veshti around himself, switched on the TV and sat on the chair. The mother kept restlessly walking to the door and back. The news had started on TV.

'Hasn't he come back yet?'

'No,' she said, and went hurriedly to the front. Sunderarasan was coming towards the house, head bent. She looked around, but no sign of the cycle.

'Sunder, Sunder,' she said, and went towards him. When he saw his father, he stood still with fear.

'Where's the cycle, Sunder?' asked the mother, coming close.

'I locked it in front of Mannur Narayanan's house and went in to study. I came after half an hour and found the cycle gone. We searched everywhere.' He squeezed his eyes and started weeping uncontrollably.

The father pushed the chair back and got up.

'Really, Appa. We locked the cycle, Appa, and then only studied. Here is the key too, Appa…' He showed the key.

His father reached out for his hand. 'What is there if the cycle is lost? Why are you crying for that?'

He started sobbing even more.

The father pulled him and folded him in an embrace. The mother stood still, astonished.

Original title: *Ethirmunai*
1995

He's Going to Tell Her... 41

Ramakrishnan

The summer heat was scorching. Even though it was four, it seemed like two in the afternoon. There weren't yet too many people on the streets. The emptiness of the long road and the heat wave that swept in since the sea breeze hadn't yet set in did something to the body and mind. The tar had melted in the heat and patches could be seen here and there on the road.

He folded his handkerchief, tucked it into the pocket of his shirt and stepped outside the house. He looked at both sides of the street. Screwing up his eyes, he lifted his arm and looked at the time. Only if he started now would he reach at five-thirty. He had to take two buses and walk to cover the distance.

That he was going to meet her for the last time didn't bother him at all, he thought. His heart wasn't eager. It would have been good if he didn't have to go. But how long to postpone it? He had to go some day. He had to tell her his decision.

'I'm not a puppet.' Puppet… puppet…He asked himself, 'How did I put up with it all this while?' He had danced to whatever she said. He even combed his hair the way she liked it. Even the watch strap he was wearing was chosen by her. It was she who decided whatever he did.

And now this realisation. Was it realisation? How? In the last six months, the feeling that he was moving away from her had deepened in his heart every moment and wiped away the traces of the past.

Nowadays the thought of her created only a blankness. The earlier feelings of comfort, happiness and excitement didn't arise at all. He could only think of her ordinarily, nothing special.

In a way this made him happy. Since the spell and the magic of her had left him, even the wind that surrounded him blew gently.

He came to the bus stop. There was no bus in sight, but he wasn't anxious.

'Mmm... What am I going to accomplish by going early?'

When he was in the bus, he went over once in his mind what he was going to tell her.

'I shall...'

Whenever he spoke to her he could only use English. He even fought with her in English. Why, more often than not he could only think in English. He believed that she could understand clearly only if she was spoken to in English. She too was like that, wasn't she?

'I shall have nothing to do with you!'

Yes, he would utter that clearly. Very clearly. Without fumbling and looking into her face (except her eyes, though...?), he could tell her that.

She had never respected him at all. Even if she hadn't noticed his mind's growth, couldn't she have at least noticed it of his body? It was foolish of him to have loved her when he was still young. She always thought of him as a little boy... *a little good friend...* She was older... by a few years or what?... no, by many years... had he always been a child to her?

For a moment his mind stirred.

It had become his nature to be attracted to older women. Even if it wasn't a love like this, his mind always went towards older women.

He laughed to himself. Strange... wasn't it?

Even when he was young he had had the same urge. Even when he was seven or eight. Always throbbed to be in the company of the women he saw. How this attraction had tormented him then! He didn't know when he had taken to daydreaming. He had had a tremendous crush on his teacher Miss Solomon. Every day she would hug him close and tell him all sorts of things. And he would be given something or the other – a chocolate, slate-pencil, pencil or a chalk piece. He could only remember the lush trees outside the room where he usually saw her. What did she ask… what did he reply? All he could see was the crowd of shadows outside the window and the spreading blooms of yellow and red.

He couldn't remember now what she looked like. All he felt was the comfort of her embrace and her hushed voice, as if he had heard it in his dreams.

What fantasies he'd had after he took leave of her! He in her room… in the staff room on one side of the first floor of the big school… on the big mattress spread on the tiny bed facing the vast sea on the east… Appa! What a soft bed that was!… Him sleeping next to her…

Earlier, even a few years ago, that he could dream all this in broad daylight overwhelmed his body and gnawed his heart.

Now he wasn't like that.

Putting his leg around her hip, hiding his face in her chest, he was drinking milk from her breast… her hands clasped him tight to her.

Often that dream appeared in his tender heart.

Many years later his sister had playfully asked him, holding a photo in her hand, 'Ade, can you spot your Solomon Teacher?' He couldn't place her at all. It was she who had pointed her out in the crowd.

'Oh god! Was this her…?' His mind had refused to believe. 'She was this ugly, was she?'

He had shaken his head again and again, tried to dredge up the hidden thought of her, her face… her body… hands… her breasts where he had suckled…but he hadn't succeeded.

He had thrown away the photograph.

Was his relationship with her the continuation of this feeling that was born in him? In the seven years of the relationship he had forgotten all about himself. He now often asked himself what it was in her that made her everything to him. He couldn't remember if she had ever considered his feelings at all. Of an age when he didn't understand anything clearly, it was all about her appearance and the scent of her… no, only the scent… he felt that it had drawn him to her. But to her, he always remained a small boy.

In the course of these seven years, at twenty-five, he understood many, many things clearly. As far as she was concerned, the new understanding and the urge to share it were irrelevant and meaningless.

He itched to display his new awakening to her. When he sat on the beach, when he walked along dark long roads, when he saw the crescent-shaped moon in the skies that peeped out of the trees, he felt overwhelmed. Did words always do him in? He would itch to say something. She would twitch her lips (though not in jest?), and after a few moments... 'Pchh, big Wordsworth you are!'

His mind would curl up, like a caterpillar, and he would feel an inexplicable anger within him. Lifting his leg, twisting his arms, ought he to have banged his body hard against the floor...?

'Careful... legs would hurt!' He would come back without speaking. Gasping, as if he had been unexpectedly pushed into water from behind.

'You know what Krishnakumari said looking at this sari...'

Her question pierced his ears. Why did he feel all this only now? Not that he didn't know all this earlier, but now that he was away from her he could see all her shortcomings clearly. Earlier he could put up with all this. Now he couldn't stand it.

She was really ordinary. He wasn't the first person to receive her love. She didn't have any special quality – except, among the world's ordinary women she had a special ordinariness. The changes in his heart, due to the passage of time, the awakening of his consciousness and the maturing of his intelligence – had she ever acknowledged all this? She didn't need all this.

Though he knew all this well enough, he couldn't leave her. Even when he thought about it over and over again, he couldn't fathom clearly what he got out of her. Maybe she was merely an outlet of female companionship for youthful male ardour, or perhaps it was the feeling of triumph when people looked at them while strolling gracefully on the streets, fashionably well-dressed, or perhaps it was just a feeling of vanity. While taking her leave after walking her home, embracing with his right hand her well-endowed hips (how such a big body yields so easily), putting his left hand on the back of her shoulder and touching her upturned face with his, letting time stand still. Besides the frenzied game of tasting her tongue to tongue under the dark trees, what else did he attain? Perhaps it was this pleasure of touch and its intense and fiery expectation that pulled him to her.

He shook his head swiftly. He felt as if an unbearable headache was burgeoning. It would be a relief to fling this head away. The pain increased every moment.

Why had she got so close to him? This question that had been in his mind for a long time reared its head again. She wasn't even the right age for him. It was surprising that he, so many years younger than she, had won her love. Did her earlier life and painful experiences push her towards him, he wondered. Losing her mother on the eleventh day of her life, burnt and beaten by a cruel grandmother, neglected in a girls' hostel for twenty-three years, she had finally landed a job and faced the world alone. Only to have fallen in love with someone for three years and been betrayed by him. She, who had been crying like a baby, he had befriended, comforted and showered with love, and whatever he had said to her reassuringly were all events of the past. He was also a witness to her past sorrows. He understood her well. He was happy when she laughed. When she shed tears, the smile which she gave when he wiped them away, he could drown himself in them. But her not having confidence in him pricked his heart. That she didn't have faith in him he realised concretely now. This doubt which he had within him, how could he have suppressed it during the time he was with her…

'No, No, No' – what a fruitless effort!

But why should he blame her, he wondered for a moment. Was she testing him?

He puckered his lips. How long could one test a person like this? He could not withstand it. When would life begin then after all this? He felt that she wasn't in a hurry. She was always in doubt.

'You are all the same lot. Will your ways ever change?'

'I know. You will run away from me one day.'

By turns playful, resolute, firm, nonchalant. How long would this game go on?

But she herself had given a shock that had thrown him. He, who had thought that he could take her anytime, was told by her clearly.

It seems her mind wasn't in it: even if he didn't give any importance to such a thing, to her it became important. It seems he had proved her fears right. It wasn't any use to blame him. Men were like that, weren't they? Something on the lips and something else in the heart.

It had seemed like a lull after a storm. Something had pricked his heart. He had looked up at her. She was looking somewhere far away.

Something had fallen off from his heart. He had searched for it. Should his longing and patience be withered away like this?

She hadn't stopped there. Had said all sorts of things. With every word, his heart had tightened.

Now he knew that his heart was completely hardened.

The bus stopped. He looked at the time when he got off. Fifteen minutes left. He crossed the road. It was a crossroad junction. If he walked across, he would reach her place in five minutes.

But the stream of vehicles prevented him from crossing. He stood there, confused. He felt a void in his heart. Couldn't understand anything.

Somehow he reached the other side of the road. He didn't know what to do for a moment. Couldn't even recollect why he had come. He stared blankly ahead. There was a hotel in front of him. As if with firm resolve, he entered through the high glass door and sat at a table near the window. Colourful curtains hung from the glass window on either side. He, who was staring outside the window for a while, sat up straight.

'Mm...What am I going to say?' His mind was muddled. He couldn't think beyond a line.

'I shall...'

Yes, that would do. He would say it clearly. He would say it to her face. He would not hesitate.

The waiter appeared.

'Black coffee...'

He stretched his legs and leant against the chair. He relaxed his arms. The fan above started to whir.

Original title: *Avalidam Sollapokiraan...*
1966

FARAWAY LAND... 42

K VITTAL RAO

Traffic was hotting up in GST Salai. The army was erecting poles with flags for a forthcoming parade in Mohite Maidan.

He was walking slowly from Mathias Nagar on the pathway adjoining the Military Signal building on the other side the road. He had looked up Thotharam in his newly opened pawn shop on Butt Road. Mindful of the dragging steps of his old Anglo-Indian companion, he too walked slowly. Since his pant always slipped off his waist and trailed the ground, he had rolled it up above his ankles. Only the straps of his well-worn hawai chappals were new. His boyish face revealed a squint. His arms, roasted to a pink in the sun, had the typical Anglo-Indian tattoos.

Arguing with the old Anglo-Indian lady, he quickly crossed the road, leaving her behind. Lighting a beedi, Mahmud Kaka, who ran a tea-stall adjoining the post-office wall, watched her.

She stood helplessly on the other side. She couldn't see properly. She would never be able to cross a busy street on her own. She had called him only to escort her to the post office. They both were neighbours.

'Hey, Mac, you've left me and gone, have you? I will kill you. Mac, come and take me across.' She, who was shouting at him, slipped into slangy English and called to account his dubious genealogy. In return he too shouted at her in much the same way. Mahmud Kaka was delighted with the swear words that were bandied about in the Anglo-Indian patois.

'What Maccu Dorai, you've left missy and come. Go and bring her, poor thing,' said the refreshment-stall owner.

'Hey, Mac Morgan...' A scooter sped by. Pleased and honoured that the scooterist had asked after him, a much-cooled-down Mac Morgan crossed the road again and went to the old lady. She, who had begun walking holding his hand and shouting at him, shrugged him away, put some distance between them and crossed the road. Yelling all the while, she reached the tea-stall, and ordered, 'Put some tea, man. Two. One with less sugar.' She handed over coins from her dirty Rexene purse even before she could have her tea.

Mahmud Kaka pulled Mac Morgan near him and said, 'A man came asking for old things. Gave him your address. He will come in the afternoon. You will be home only, no?'

Missy wanted to know what it was about.

Mac Morgan replied, 'I believe a man asked after Reuben Uncle's stuff.'

All Mahmud Kaka could make out from the quick exchange in slangy English were words such as 'London' and 'Australia'. Then they went into the post office.

The old lady took out a paper from an envelope which had come from her daughter in London.

'Only ten pounds?' Mac Morgan asked mockingly, and then continued with concern, 'Nowadays Marie doesn't look after you properly...' They were given to quick compassion after bouts of anger... They would invariably aim deadly missiles at each other, casting slurs on their births.

The old lady turned around and walked up when she heard, 'Good morning, Christina...' An aged, dark-complexioned Anglo-Indian couple was sitting on the wooden bench. The lady had elephantiasis in one leg. She would have been better off in a sari than in a frock.

'Good morning, Joan...' said the old lady.

'What, so early in the morning,' said Mac Morgan. The post-office clock began to strike ten.

'For the pension... Didn't get it last week since I had gone out of town...' said Joan.

Mac Morgan went near the man and asked him what had happened to his helping him to go to Australia. The man said that he had told his brother and would let Mac know when an opportune moment came by. At that time two Anglo-Indian girls, bewitchingly proportioned and clad, strolled in and asked for airmail envelopes. Joan called out to them, 'Hello.' The two girls feigned a smile and went away.

When Mac Morgan eyed the girls, he looked as if he was gazing at the telephone booth because of his squint.

Christina hissed, 'Mac, do your job…'

Through the window Mac Morgan stretched out the postal order which the old lady's daughter had sent from London.

'Where's the witness?' asked the clerk.

Mac Morgan turned his gaze into the office and looked for the postman who came to Mathias Nagar and shouted, 'Perumal… Perumal.'

'Don't shout like this. Learn to speak softly…' whispered the old lady.

'Go to hell…' he said and walked towards the postmen who were sorting out letters on either side.

When the postman had put his signature on the 'shilling paper', they collected the money in Indian currency and came out.

Mac Morgan asked her angrily, 'You are a useless thing. You never give Perumal money for coffee. Shouldn't you have given him something?'

'They don't give tips in London,' said the old lady.

'Talk about this country.'

'I said only in London.'

'You haven't even seen London.'

'So what, da? My daughter is there.'

'Your life itself runs on handouts here…'

'Mac, God will punish you.'

Then they walked a little silently. As they reached the compound wall of the post office, Mac Morgan bent down and asked in a low voice, 'Aren't you going to your daughter?'

'Yes. I'm going only. Everyone's belly in Mathias Nagar will burn when I go… Let the time come.'

'Huhmm… who cares about you? When really your time comes, you will be gone forever, once for all…'

The old lady stamped her foot on the ground and started crying loudly. When she calmed down somewhat she had come to GST Salai. When he saw them, Mahmud Kaka asked, 'Did you get money from abroad, missy?' The old lady murmured. After she crossed the Military Hospital, she half-heartedly gave Mac Morgan a ten-rupee note. He lifted it against the sun to check if it had tears or holes and then stuffed it into his shirt pocket.

She didn't need an escort anymore, so she started dragging herself towards Mathias Nagar. Mac went to Reuben Uncle's house.

Whenever there was a quarrel, people gossiped about Mac Morgan's lineage and about his mother who was living somewhere else. He hadn't studied much and didn't possess any skills. He would often be a packer or a watchman in some small company and then become unhappy and quit it. He would get food and clothes from the church, sponsored by missions abroad. He would inform Christina and others of the dates when they distributed food and clothes. That was how he had become close to the old lady.

Whenever anyone – Anglo-Indians or others – left the country, they would sell their furniture, fans, utensils and stuff cheaply. It was Mac Morgan's job to find customers for them. He would take a commission from both parties. And they would promise to call him over once they settled in Australia or Canada. He always believed them.

Christina's husband used to be a crane operator in the port. He had drunk himself to death. What was left the old lady frittered away at the races. It was a good thing that Marie was a girl. Her matter was settled quite easily. She, who was writing accounts in a clock shop, flew away to London with a smuggler named Syed, a British national.

The old lady couldn't stop talking about her daughter going away to England to the few remaining Anglo-Indians in St Thomas Mount area. She would visit their houses without being called and didn't care either if she wasn't welcome.

'What, Marie sent you money, did she?' asked a friend teasingly.

'Got ten pounds. That scoundrel Mac made such a fuss to come. He will learn only if he is left in the lurch. Don't know when my daughter will come and take me. If I go, he will die. Leave that aside, what happened to your going to Australia?' asked the old lady eagerly.

Her friend replied, 'Arrangements are being made, Christina. Mr Biggs went only now. He only is going to arrange everything...'

'I see,' said Christina.

After passing the entire day on frugal rasam-rice, she visited another house. There, in honour of some guests from Singapore, there was music, dance, liquor and great food. Not even a single dog there respected her. She looked intently and then left saying, 'Nothing, simply only,' without even anyone having asked her anything.

At the same time, Mac Morgan after finishing the business in Reuben's house, pocketed the commission from both sides and walked towards a hut in the foothills of Kurangu Kunram.

His visits to the hut in Kurangu Kunram and the old lady's preparations of meat every day emptied both their purses in only ten days.

Christina waited for yet another post from London. She had fought bitterly with Mac Morgan the previous day. So she didn't breathe a word about the post that came that morning.

Christina came to GST Salai muttering to herself, 'I will go by myself. As if there is no one else other than him… If I call out 'Ayya, Appa', I'm sure plenty will come running to help me.' This time Marie had sent twenty pounds. This time she would get rum from the Military Canteen. Go to Azharkhana to get beef. And call the Joneses over. And give the postman Perumal five rupees for coffee. And hereafter she wouldn't have anything to do with that cheap fellow Mac.

While she was thus imagining, she had inched along to the centre like a tortoise. Mahmud Kaka, busy with the morning business in his tea-stall, didn't notice her.

Christina broke into a sweat. Her bowels heaved as if she was coming down on a giant wheel. As if she was trapped between two archers of ancient times, flinging arrows at each other. All sorts of vehicles flew past, towards the airport and vice versa towards the city. Every moment was touch and go. A few cursed loudly in Tamil.

Fear rose within her that she wouldn't be able to cross the road on her own at this peak hour. There was no let-up in the traffic. Also she had forgotten to take her tablet for high blood pressure. Her head spun as if Mac Morgan was spinning a top on it.

Lorries, cars, buses grazed her and whizzed by – any minute a vehicle would run over her. She remembered what she had once said when Mac Morgan had given her a beer. 'Mac… what I wish for is to die in the land where Marie is. Near her, in the soil where she is, I must go.' For one of her age, she drank too much.

As she struggled, a hand held her tight. She looked to see who it was. It was Mac Morgan. He had hastily limped across.

'What, why didn't you call me?' he asked and shouted at her. But now she didn't shout at him in return. She walked under his care silently. When they neared Mahmud Kaka's shop, Mac said, 'Two teas, one strong with lots of sugar.'

'Mac, your pant is torn, frayed completely,' she said.

He replied, 'No princess is sending me cloth from England.'

'I will give you the money, buy it. Twenty pounds have come...' said the old lady.

Original title: *Dooradesam...*
1991

The Sound of Footsteps 43

Aadhavan

After waiting for more than ten minutes at the Motibhagh I bus-stand, Ramaa started walking. No sign of the bus to take her to Motibhagh II.

The time: nine forty-five, slightly chilly. She should have brought her sweater. Che, it was so late. He would be waiting. Would he have eaten? She had left only after cooking. She had asked him to eat if it got too late. He would have eaten; how long would he wait without eating? He would of course be worried that she hadn't yet returned. He would be peeping out from the balcony. He would be looking expectantly at any sari-clad woman turning into the street, only to be disappointed when the light revealed that it wasn't her face.

At eight itself she had tried to take leave of Raji. But would that Raji let her go? She had made her sit, saying, 'Wait for a while. What's the hurry, di?' In the end, by the time she had left her house it had been eight forty-five. When she had got the bus at Golmarket it had been nine-fifteen. Now when she was walking home in the dark and the cold, she thought of Raji angrily. Shouldn't she have thought of my problem? If she was that dear a friend, she ought to have found a house close by! Who asked her to live in Golmarket? Some friend she was!

Che… he would be so worried… Ramaa started walking fast. If only she had got Bus No. 7 at Golmarket, she could have got down at Motibhagh II itself. But she had got only No. 45, so she had had to get down at Motibhagh I.

Balakrishnan was a good-natured fellow, really. He would never get angry because she was late, wouldn't mutter, wouldn't show his displeasure through silence too. But didn't she have her own rules and discipline or what? To knock on the door at ten or eleven in the night when the husband was at home – che, che was that nice or what? Henceforth, one ought not to get caught like this. Today would be the last day. Like him, she was educated too, worked and went out on her own. All this was fine. She was proud of his trust in her and the freedom and rights he gave her. Because of that one must not start leaping from heaven to earth, is it not? She shouldn't fall down in his esteem, is it not? What he thought was as important to her as what he said. It was more important for her to know if his face was hiding something than what it was revealing.

'I'm sorry, please forgive me…' she begged forgiveness in her mind. 'I will never come so late hereafter. Mhmmm… I will never.'

Suddenly footsteps could be heard behind. She jumped. Who could it be? The sound of slippers could be heard, 'sarak sarak'. Was it a man or a woman? It sounded like a man. She was hesitant to look behind. Was someone following her or what? It was night time, and there was no one on the streets. The Ring Road was dark; no lights were burning, as usual. Her heart beat fast, 'tik-tik'; her stomach churned. Behind, footsteps. They seemed to be coming nearer, the footsteps.

She took longer strides. It was just a ten-minute walk, but now it seemed like a huge distance. Her chest heaved, her footsteps faltered. 'O god, please protect me. Please get me home. Enough of this distress, this mental trauma, this struggle… Enough, enough, please, god, somehow take me home! I'll never again go out in the night without a companion. I swear, I won't!'

The noise of a scooter – 'darr' – could be heard, drowning out the sound of the footsteps. Did her prayers reach god or what? The scooter went a little slowly as it neared her. The rider turned around, looked at her, recognised her instantly and stopped the vehicle. She too recognised him. He lived in her block; not only that, he worked in her office too. The two weren't friends, hadn't even spoken to each other; there hadn't been any occasion to. But they knew of each other. This was an interesting thing, wasn't it! How often we encounter people in our lives, at bus-stands, inside buses, on office verandahs, at cultural dos – people who aren't strictly our friends, but seem like friends anyway.

We never speak to such people while we are in our towns; but if we meet them out of town, we may end up speaking to them, she thought.

But now, the late hour and the lonely stretch of road turned the city into an alien town. It erased shyness and hesitation. He asked, 'You are going home, aren't you?' She nodded. 'Why don't you sit?' he said, pointing to the pillion. When she said 'thanks'... and sat behind, the scooter started.

She heaved a sigh of relief, 'appaada'. The footsteps came to mind and she turned for a second. But she couldn't see the face in the dark. She didn't even bother about it now. Her mind was filled with happiness, the happiness one experiences when one encounters good men and good deeds, filling life with new hope. 'Appaada, he came at good time; may he live long... all these days I thought he was a short-tempered fellow; must be a nice chap, after all. Poor thing! It's so wrong to judge by the face...'

When he dropped her by the gate, she muttered another 'thanks' and started climbing the stairs.

The front door was locked. She was surprised. She opened the door with the second key she had and went in. She thought to herself, 'Where could he have gone at this hour?' She opened the vessels. Balakrishnan had already eaten. Must have gone out for a cigarette.

She changed her sari, took out the dishes, and as she was about to sit down to eat, she heard a knock on the door. She opened the door. Balakrishnan came in. When his eyes took in the empty plate and the vessels, she said with a smile, 'I came only now.'

'I know,' he said. 'I came behind you, but before I could call out you got onto the scooter.'

She didn't know whether to laugh or cry. O Rama, had it been him behind?

'Ganapathy had come. Since you hadn't come back as well, I walked with him to Motibhagh I. When I returned, I saw you walking on the opposite side of the road. I crossed the road and came. But you, you walked so fast...'

'I was wondering who it was, I was scared...'

'Never mind. You got a jolly scooter ride. He's in your office only, isn't he?'

'Yes,' she said, mixing the rice. She wanted to see his face but was scared what it would reveal. She wanted to say, 'Before this, I've never even spoken to him.' But she didn't, because it would look as if she was needlessly trying to…

'I was walking there, right behind… Perhaps he didn't notice me.'

She didn't speak. She thought of how pleased she had been earlier with human kindness and helpful nature. Was this all it amounted to in the end? Did the scooter stop because she was a woman? Did he think it was an opportunity to introduce himself to her?

O god, o god! She would go mad if she started thinking like this, but what was Balakrishnan thinking now? What had taken seed in his mind now?

Suddenly another thought came to mind. A couple of days ago when she and Balakrishnan were in a bus, this scooter-chap too was sitting in the next seat. Would Balakrishnan be thinking, 'They didn't even say hello to each other. Had I not been there, would they have wished each other?'

Now it is likely that his scooter will be under repair and that he will stand next to me in the bus queue. Likely that he will travel in the bus with me. How can I not smile at him? What if he sees me in the evenings in the bus queue, stops the scooter? What will I do then?

Couldn't this fellow have been a little older? Ugly too? A married fellow?

He's young; a thirty-five-year-old youngster. Handsome. Unmarried. In my office, in my block…

O god, please save me. Hereafter…

Must never come alone at night.

Must wait till Motibhagh II bus comes.

Above all, most importantly, while you are walking, if you hear footsteps behind, turn around immediately.

Original title: *Kaaladi Osai*
1971

Ire

Poomani

44

'Aathi, do you have any brains at all?'

'What is this, HC ayya, asking me like this?'

'Then what? Sending me off to Chennai without any care, as if you've merely lost a strand of hair.'

'Ayyo, don't rake up my stomach burn! I went to Cuddalore, got withered like dried fish and have just come back!'

'What? The last-minute story, is it?'

'You are happy now, no?'

'Shit. We are cursed to go for both a corpse and a treasure.'

'You came only today, is it?'

'Don't ask! It's a big thing that I came back. For generations to come I won't sleep with my head in that direction!'

'Why, you were trapped in an awkward situation, is it?'

'Is there ever a tale of this Rasagovalu getting caught? What do you think of me?'

'As if I don't know about our HC ayya.'

'Listen to the story. I went and reached the city that day, no! It had turned really dark. I satisfied my hunger in a hotel and went to the place the Inspector said. Is that a place for a man to sleep? It was a stable for horses. Policemen were sleeping in rows.'

'So you too became a horse.'

'Sleep was very well there in my eyes. But I couldn't sleep.'

'What happened?'

'A battalion of mosquitoes came and started attacking me. They buzzed like trains around my ears. Each one the size of a giant grasshopper. If you are not careful, it will carry off a man even. If we had buffalo tails, we could have kept shooing them off and slept.'

'All those great lords who proclaim till their mouths tear that they will eradicate this and that, they don't have the know-how to eradicate this. And such types we have to guard like watchdogs.'

'Early in the morning I slept a bit. But by then everyone had woken up.'

'Sivaratri only then for you.'

'Things were getting done in such speed, as if they were sowing seeds in black soil. One fellow was putting polish for the boots. Another fellow was wiping the rifles…'

'Yes, yes, as if the minister from Delhi is coming only to see them.'

'I too pinched some for free and finished my work. We must also look neat, no?'

'What will happen to the pride of our station?'

'Exactly at six, all of us reached our respective spots.'

'Where were you assigned?'

'Go and stand by the beach, they said.'

'Nice place only, no? You can stand there gazing at the sea.'

'The cool breeze and all made me drowsy. I was so tired that I just wanted to lie flat on the sands.'

'Wonderful! You longed for that also, is it?'

'This side, government offices one after another in a row. That side, full of people, like herds of sheep on the beach. On the edge of the beach any number of buses, lorries, vans. In each one, all sorts of party flags flying. A cacophony of songs can be heard. The blessed fellows, from where did they drum up such crowds?'

'They are showing them the city, with food and wages. As if there will be a shortage of people then.'

'Lucky fellows.'

'Both of them.'

'Shouldn't simply say, aathi. It looks like a painting – daybreak squeezing out of the sea, looking like a little tomato, and we can keep on looking at it.

The waves look as if they are sprinkling the front yard of a house, removing the dirt and sweeping it all back into the sea – all this looks beautiful only, 'pa. Faraway, boats are roaming around, catching fish. Like ploughing the land in a vast, open field.'

'HC ayya, you have a taste for all this too?'

'When my mind was immersed in all this, I never felt tired.'

'You would have leant against the electricity post and slept off. To mask all that, this story-aa?'

'Brainless fellow. Can anyone sleep in that place?'

'As if you need a place. You can nod off and get up even before one can take a piss.'

'Next time when you snore, no, in the station. I will deal with you then.'

'Then what happened? You went to bathe in the sea, is it?'

'I wanted to bathe only. But who will allow it? I briskly shook off my languor, looked this-side, that-side. The traffic began to heat up the road. The policemen standing in rows everywhere became alert.'

'Time for the minister to come?'

'Who knew when he would come? Who knows – maybe he was bathing or eating in Delhi at that time.'

'You should have also eaten, no?'

'Hunger did begin to bite me a bit. But if I wanted something, I would have to go some distance away. By that time what if the minister went past? Our officials will jump up and down the sky and the earth, no?'

'So much drama for one big man swishing past like a bandicoot in the blink of an eye. For that so many people have to wait, putting aside all their work.'

'That you know, but do others?... One fellow came along selling coffee. I bought from him twice. Paying for it only.'

'Did I say anything now?'

'Your pop-eyed stare just doesn't seem right.'

'Is it a marble for me take it off and put something else in?'

'How long will coffee last? I looked around everywhere. I went into an office, drank water till my stomach was full, washed my face and came back and stood full of vim and vigour.'

'This is what I call bravery.'

'Even then my hunger didn't abate. I cajoled a young boy to get me four idlis and pushed it down my throat, all standing up. Again I drank water.'

'Now you are loaded, so no worry till afternoon.'

'Now only the story begins, 'pa.'

'What story now?'

'The belly started getting heavy.'

'The water you filled up came down.'

'At that moment only, our officials flew around, "sarr, sarr", in a flurry. One vehicle grumbled, one neighed.'

'The minister would have started.'

'Where? From Delhi?'

'You should have gone to the beach and sat behind the bushes.'

'In that crowd-aa? Is it possible? I could have done the job in the office garden, but no luck even for that. Men and women started streaming into the office. You should have seen the disgust on the bus drivers' faces when they crossed the road with great difficulty. No patience to wait even for a bit.'

'What happened to your patience?'

'It started getting heavier and heavier, as if there was a sea in my stomach. How long to cope just pulling the stomach in? If it had been dark, I would have stood against the pole and done my business.'

'Became a big problem, is it?'

'Didn't know at which moment the pot will break. I was scared. That rifle also was pressing against my shoulder.'

'So you were heavy up and down.'

'From the road a dog inside a car looked at me, tongue hanging out, as if making a face at me.'

'It also knew about the matter, is it?'

'No sign of the minister too. Here now, there now, like waiting for the delivery-time of a very old crone.'

'Wonder when your delivery-time came.'

'I thought, now if I stand like this, squeezing and pulling in my stomach, that's all…'

'Can't bear it if the sea breaks, no?'

'Let anything happen, I thought, and rushed straight into an office quickly. Will the minister come and go or what by the time I finish?'

'Even if he comes, so what?'

'Somehow I found a toilet and opened the pot. What comfort! Everything became light. Not for nothing they say that you can control your anger but not your bladder.'

'Yes, yes, who can bear that emergency?'

'Aathi, when I came out and saw, my heart stood still.'

'What happened in the meanwhile?'

'So many people gathered that even the road itself couldn't hold them. A big commotion. On either side, long lines of vehicles waiting. People were running from the office to the road.'

'Some trouble, is it?'

'My heart was in my mouth. I ran and fought my way through and what did I see – a woman lying on the road like a turmeric root.'

'O my god.'

'A woman who had crossed the road to reach the office, and the government-bus fellow hit her and chapter-close.'

'What a sinner.'

'Hair pins on one side, flowers on the other, all scattered. Bunches of hair ripped off with the flesh smeared on the road. Since she was hit face-down, by and by the trail of kumkumam turned into blood. Her book lay forlorn. This sight was more grisly than the wrapper of the book. Couldn't bear to see it.'

'Don't describe anymore.'

'Tears pushed into my eyes. But I suppressed them and somehow dispersed the crowd. The bus which had hit her was standing nearby. The driver and the conductor had run away, unable to bear the blows from the crowd.'

'And to think it all happened on the minister's route.'

'I was shaken, wondering what all will happen. Meanwhile three policemen who were doing bandobast duty appeared. We discussed again and again what to do. I thought we first had to make way for the vehicles and clear the traffic.'

'What did you do?'

'We marked the spot where the woman's body lay and where the bus stood. We took the body and placed it on one side. We turned the bus and parked it in a corner.'

'Who drove the bus?'

'I sent up a policeman only. In a while the bus started.'

'Still the minister didn't come?'

'We were afraid of that too. What all will happen when that big lord comes?'

'Yes, you can't say what will happen.'

'The crowd jostled in waves. The trade union leaders were in a huddle.'

'They too arrived, is it?'

'When we were talking, they rushed in, shouting something or the other and sat in the middle of the road. Ladies in front, and gents behind.'

'So the situation got worse again! What did they want, it seems?'

'It was wrong it seems to move the body. Everyone glared at me and abused me with all sorts of swear words. Didn't know what will happen. Okay, hospital only for me today, I thought, and stood like a dead stone.'

'Anyway the body was already moved. Instead of doing what needed to be done…'

'Meanwhile, big-big officials with battalions of policemen arrived.'

'Thank god you escaped.'

'The union leaders argued left and right with one of the officials. Even if a dog is hurt the police usually take a photo after marking. Why then was this treated so callously? We fight for you people too and get you benefits. And you are treating us worse than dogs. If a big minister comes, the small minister runs behind his arse. And the police run behind that fellow. Who is then worried about the general public? They started protesting about this and that. The officials agreed to go their way.'

'What way was that?'

'They asked to place the body back in the old spot and the bus too nearby. They asked us to take a photo of that. One policeman marked it well on the road. Then we removed both.'

'They were satisfied now?'

'Behaved as if they accomplished some great task. The road emptied bit by bit and in a while vehicles started moving. The blare of songs from the beach didn't seem to stop. We could see the corpse clearly now. It had dried up in the sun. Seven-eight women stood nearby and kept weeping. In a while an ambulance came, picked up the body and vanished.'

'Just look at the fate of human donkeys.'

'That official caught me. Such anger on his face. Who is the fellow who moved the body, he asked. I bowed my head and went and stood in front of him. He looked at me as if he would bite and tear into me.'

'He should also give vent to his anger, no.'

'"You make them into such big shots. First we must shut their mouths. After that, do you think they will bother what we do to the case? Think any fellow will come as witness? They will just shout till their throats are torn. After that they will go and have tea. If the minister knows, I only have to answer him, 'ya. Fellows like you who ought to be grazing buffaloes are coming here to take our life out." He spat at me like this and went off. I too listened without uttering a word.'

'Why won't they talk? They will realise only if they suffer like us. The minister didn't come, is it, till the end?'

'First, they were to take that route, it seems. Then they changed the route it seems and he went off to eat a feast somewhere.'

'I see.'

'I was livid. Such anger that I wanted to shoot someone. If you take the body they will shout, if you don't take it also they will shout. What do you say, aathi?'

'If we go in front they will bite us, if we go at the back they will kick us – that's only their job, no.'

'Others at least can shout. We can't even do that.'

'That is the boon we have got.'

'In fury I banged it against the iron grill. The lathi split into two. I threw it into the office garden and briskly made my way to the water tap.'

Original title: *Aathiram*
1998

Jackfruit 45

Vannanilavan

A jackfruit had arrived next door.

Chella Paapa turned around and lay down. It was her heavy stomach that first felt the cold of the floor, triggering a tingling sensation all over her body. The stove was burning with a hiss in a corner of the room. A good number of wicks had become stubby. They ought to be changed. Some never burnt at all. So it took a long time to cook anything. It was a small thing, to change the wicks. Yet she didn't do it.

Ever since she was a child, she liked lying down on the cement floor without spreading out a sheet. No matter what her problem, the coolness always lightened her heart. But now all these small, small things had moved far away and disappeared.

She looked intently at the wooden shelf nailed to the wall. The empty Horlicks bottle and the Glaxo tins that she had brought from her maternal home had blackened with smoke. A lot of bottles had nothing in them. One or two had god-knows-what right at the bottom. Her mind butted in. She turned around.

Sinivasan lay close to her. She played with his banian, rolling its ends at the shoulder again and again. There was dirt at the neck and the corners. Her hands turned sticky. Grazing her lower stomach, she pushed her belly and chest close to his back. She mussed his rough hair with her fingers. Tiring of that, she touched and played with the tiny hairs that grew at his nape. She wanted to put her hand down his neck and tickle him. She leant her head against his hip and settled down. Sinivasan woke up.

'Just come here, I tell you. Ei, Seetha, what's happening there? Because I've come back, you've just left the stove, is it?'

'No, 'ma... I want another jackfruit piece, 'ma.'

'For her alone another one, is it? I'm going to tell Appa...'

'Ei, you fat donkeys... Behaving as if you've never seen it before. The one who bought all this for you – it's all his fault!'

'Just one more, 'ma.'

'How you all take my life out! Just look at this Losu Kutty. Such a small child! Just told her she has fever and shouldn't eat all this. Just look, how quiet she is... And look at you people! You are big children in name only. Like monsters...'

Some quarrel between the children had certainly taken place. You could hear them banging themselves against the thin board of a wall which separated the two tenements. Besides, there were tearful cries as well.

Still clasping him tightly, Chella Paapa craned her neck – even if she couldn't see anything – towards the wooden partition. Under the impact of the banging, Sinivasan's shirt, which hung on the nail, had fallen down, and lay as if it had been rolled and flung down.

Suddenly, every now and then, the smell of jackfruit from the other side wafted in.

Sinivasan turned, and clasped her tight to his chest, like he always liked to do. There was the smell of tooth powder from her mouth. He asked when her heavy belly pressed against his, 'Chella Paapa, your stomach is not pressing, no, when you sleep like this? Is it painful?'

Chella Paapa laughed lightly without replying. The outer skin had peeled off a bit on her lips, looking prettily white. When she smiled, she looked even more pretty. Nowadays there was a kind of tiredness to her smile. He relished the extraordinary beauty the smile imparted to her face. If only she would smile like that again, he thought.

'Ei...ei...you cow! How many times I told you to spit out the seeds in one place! Don't know why you are taking my life out like this.'

'Yamma... See me, 'ma, I've collected all the seeds in one place. This Seetha monkey only has spat all over the place!'

'Yes, yes... blow your trumpet.'

'What cheek, di, for you!'

Some vessel toppled and rolled on the floor. The noise of screams and tears floated in, and over all that the distinct smell of jackfruit.

Sinivasan and Chella Paapa looked at each other while all this happened.

Chella Paapa asked, 'Haven't they given you the salary yet?'

Immediately Sinivasan's face changed. Perhaps I shouldn't have asked, she thought, staring at his hairy navel visible below his rolled-up banian. His comforting body heat soothed her.

'We've all decided not to take any salary. Only when the talks are over we'll know the decision.'

She didn't utter a word. The silence frightened them both. Each fervently yearned to say something.

Now the fruit smell was overpowering and filled the small room.

He asked about it. 'This smell is strange. Like palm fruit...'

'No, this is the smell of jackfruit,' countered Chella Paapa immediately. He was surprised by her quick answer. He looked intently at her.

Even now the tears and cries on the other side of the wooden partition hadn't abated. The smell of fruit too disappeared after a bit, but the crying never stopped. That Seetha, who was minding the stove while Amma cut the fruit, was the one who was crying. The mother was shouting at the boy. Whenever the words tumbled out fast, the voice turned hoarse, as if about to cry, and choked the throat. The note of desperation, of being unable to cope with the shenanigans of the children, could be heard in the voice. As the wails and cries increased, the fruit smell completely disappeared.

He spoke affectionately, 'Chella Paapa, are you finding it very difficult? Just make coffee alone. I'll go and buy idli or something from the hotel. Don't make anything.'

'Where's the money?'

'I have it. Yesterday I asked Harikrishnan for a rupee.'

'Which Harikrishnan?'

'That fellow only – the one who came once in the evening when we were newly married. Sat on the doorstep itself – chatted and had coffee and all and left... that chap.'

''Mhmmm...'

'I thought they'll give me the salary and I can take you to the doctor. I'm just not able to do it... Meghanathan said he'll give twenty rupees this evening.'

'The one you said studied with you and has a vessel shop?'

'Yes, that fellow only. He's fond of me. I have to go this evening. Saw him in the bazaar yesterday. He asked after you very much. Told him I have to take you to the doctoramma. Come 'condition-aa' this evening, he insisted.'

Looking at him, she tried to bring Meghanathan to mind. She couldn't remember him. She wondered how he would look. She very much wanted to see him. Every time he met Meganathan, he would come back and tell her that Meganathan enquired after her. Whenever he mentioned him, she wanted to see him. She had an image of him in her mind.

Chella Paapa added the coffee powder and put off the stove. Setting aside the stove in a corner, she said, 'All the wicks have become short, 'pa. They need to be changed.'

'All right, I'll buy some in the evening. Be ready in the evening. As soon as I come, we'll go to the doctor.'

'Why now, 'pa? We'll go after you get the salary… Let's give that house-owner aachi the rent money first.'

He got angry. Without replying, he lay down, looking the other side.

'What… are you angry? What have I said, 'pa?'

'What did you tell? You said clay and dust, nothing more…'

Chella Paapa sat, head bowed, one leg bent. Coffee-scented steam floated around.

Suddenly the smell of fruit blew in, even stronger than before. Perhaps the lady was sending her fruit through the children, she thought wishfully.

He felt sorry just looking at her sitting like that. He got up with a start, sat in front of her, held her by the chin and looked into her face. She looked yearningly at him with tear-filled eyes.

'What then, 'ma? If I say one thing, you say something else, is it? Won't a man get angry, tell me?'

'What was wrong in what I said, 'pa… after all?'

Someone knocked on the door. A voice was heard, 'Akka…Akka…'

Chella Paapa tried to get up slowly, pressing both her hands on the floor. He touched her shoulder and made her sit. He got up and went. It seemed like Seetha's voice. In her mind, she was happy that Akka remembered to send it.

He opened the door. It was Seetha. Without speaking to him, she looked at her through the gap. 'Akka, Amma wants to know if we can go to the Puttaarathi Amman temple this evening.'

Chella Paapa glanced at him and then replied, 'I can't come today, 'ma. Tell her akka cannot come.'

When Seetha turned Chella Paapa saw that a jackfruit fibre had stuck to her lip at the corner of her mouth.

Sinivasan didn't return in the evening as he had promised. He came very late. When the door was opened, he came in and sat, head hanging down. Lengthening the wick of the lamp hung on the wall, she placed it in front of him. She uncovered the plate kept for him and gave it to him. She went back and lay down immediately.

Suddenly the smell of fruit blew in. She got up with a start and sat up.

Sinivasan was eating slowly, head bent.

Original title: *Palaapazham*
1974

At a Standstill 46

Vannadasan

'Look after the house,' said everyone when Komu asked just as they were leaving, 'Where is the chariot coming, aachi?'

'It's turned the corner of Vagaiadi Street. We'll just take a look and be back. Don't wander off somewhere playfully, okay?'

When they closed the verandah door and left, Komu remained inside, looking at them. Through the grilled door, she saw them go into the street, one by one. From this corner one couldn't see the street. The street must be a wonderful sight today. A lot of people would pass through the street – people from the Big Street, West Street, Kambarezhi and Pettai. The balloon man, the coconut-flakes man, the javvumittai man selling sticky candy, the ice man, all of them would be there. The ice man would sell ice even in the night. The Bombay-sweet man too. Perhaps Appa too might go this way after leaving his cart at the firewood shop. It would be good if he came today and stood in a corner, like he usually did when he didn't have any money and asked, 'Is Komu there?' They always served Komu more food than a twelve-year-old child could eat. She would upturn the lead vessel that covered her plate and hand it over to Appa. After eating,

Appa was wont to leave without even telling her. It would be nice if Appa came today.

The house-front was quiet. The people from the two opposite houses too had gone to see the chariot festival. Snippets of cloth filled the verandah. The tailor had stitched some clothes for them in his hand machine. Even the striped cloth-mat on which the tailor had sat still remained spread out, littered with white and green bits of cloth. The child opposite went to school, not here, but in Palayamkottai. The tear in her long skirt had to be stitched tomorrow. Also the torn under-skirt that aachi had given her. Would this tailor mend old clothes? She wanted to open the verandah door and fetch the green bit of cloth. It wasn't dark green, it was a light shade. Like sprouted grass. Like unripe neem fruit. Like wet firewood, with the bark peeled off.

She could open the door and go but it would make a noise 'dang,dang', even more than the main door. It shouldn't wake up the big aachi who lay sick on the cot. There would be big trouble if she got up. She would keep on nattering. 'Have you filled water? Did you fetch the clothes from the clothesline? Has the flower-man brought enough strands for today's lamp-pooja? Why hasn't Ammukutty turned up to make the dung pats? How much rice and gram has been soaked for the dosai? When is full moon day? I can hear someone walking around in the house opposite – who's there?' Dawn would break by the time you answered all of aachi's questions. Moreover, how was Komu to know the answers to all her questions?

Komu didn't open the verandah door. She had heaps of work to do. She had to fill the good water let in from the river. Before that she had to round up the calf and tie it. Komu sat down in the passage leading to the cowshed and looked around. This wasn't like the doctor's house where she had worked earlier. There, all the floors were smooth, shiny and new. There were no stone-paved floors like these. Here room after room was paved with stone. This garden passage was even more pitted. It never dried immediately after being washed. Water filled the small holes dimpled all over floor like the surface of a grinding stone. They remained wet for a while. Cool.

Komu liked the garden more than the house. Even in this tiny space were small, small trees – curry leaf, drumstick tree and golden oleander. They were not big, no more than a man's height. They were like growing children. When guests came from out of town, Komu played with their kids and it was with the curry-leaf fruit and the oleander that they used to play 'house-house'.

When Komu had come to work here, the calf had been tiny. Komu had loved it when it gambolled away, kicking its legs in the empty garden after drinking milk or when it came running back to pull at the teats, suddenly remembering its mother and the next minute scampering away lifting its tail. Its reddish-brown colour had gone away, the baby hair had dropped off and its looks and behaviour had now changed. It had even turned sly. When it heard footsteps it always hid behind the cow near the fence. It could never be pulled and tied up; it stood motionless like an oil-press. Komu felt the day wasn't far off when it would snap the rope and suck away all the milk and earn her abuses.

Afraid that the calf would stamp her feet, she gave it a long rope and tied it on the other side of the shed. As if it would butt her, it came near and started to lick her forearm. When the smooth, blue-black tongue quivered on her arm, she felt tickled. She felt that it behaved very affectionately towards her today. Scratching the skin where the horn was sprouting through, she put an arm round it and tenderly hugged it, fondly giving it the name, 'Lakshm-ee'. Just as the calf shook its head and jerked loose, came the burst of firecrackers, once, twice, thrice.

Only if the chariot had neared, the hiss and the crackle of firecrackers would be heard like this. From wherever you looked, the sparkles and bursts of the firecrackers would be seen in the sky, billowing out smoke. Anyone would rush out to see the crackers, like they did when aeroplanes passed by.

Komu stepped out of the eaves and stood looking at the sky. Only a bunch of colour balloons floated around the blue and white sky. How many balloons, bit-notices of cloth shops and exhibitions would be flying around today. The green, red and yellow notices flung up in thc air would fall down so prettily, like claps of the batons in a kolattam dance. How Komu had scrambled to pick up the notices. How sad she used to feel when the brand-new notices were stamped at one end, pierced through with stone and gravel.

Now even the bunch of balloons had drifted away. Only the sky spread above, like a sea, like a swollen pond.

~

Perhaps they had turned on extra water for the chariot festival. Water continuously poured out of the taps. Even after the cauldron, the cistern, the mud pots and the ever-silver pitchers had been filled, the water overflowed in a rush into the filling pot. She didn't know what to do. She kept standing near the tap. The water spilled out from the vessel, rolling coolly beneath her feet.

'Are you all alone at home? Haven't you gone to see the chariot?' asked a voice from above.

'Look up! Here, here!' The akka from the house adjoining theirs called out from the terrace. Akka and a couple of others stood there and were looking at the chariot. She had seen this many times – in many such one-storey houses where there were young girls. Komu too had once seen the chariot from the rooftop. But she hadn't got the full view of the chariot. She couldn't see those pulling the chariot nor the great big rope. She had seen the decorated plating of the chariot, the spire on top, and the red flag. When it had turned the corner, she had seen the side of the chariot and the banana-tree festoon. Even that view had been beautiful. From wherever you looked, there had been terraces, chimneys, tiled roofs, and neem trees here and there. Beyond them, more red tiled roofs. In between the chariot had moved on, as though hiding and raising only its head – what a lovely sight that had been. She felt like going to that terrace to watch. But the way to that house was not on this side. You had to go around the street. You couldn't leave the house and go off just like that. She had to put away the buckets and pots inside and wait in the passage till everyone returned; she had no other choice.

As she sat down, it slowly turned dark. She didn't know how the darkness surrounded her. It was not only the chariot festival but also the full moon. Thank god both fell on the same day. Otherwise she would have had to mop the floors and wash the kitchen on two nights. By the time she swabbed the hearth after everyone had eaten, she felt so sleepy. If there was no water in the tap, then you had to pump the water as well.

Komu had never sat all by herself in this passageway like this. It was not yet seven; even then she was afraid to sit in this dark. Moonlight shone, but who could sit alone like this? Two smooth wooden pillars bore down on either side of her, as if menacingly trying to grab someone. Their shadows dug huge pits in front of the house, trapping Komu in the middle. The opposite house also had four stone pillars painted blue. In the dark, these huge pillars which enveloped her looked like monstrous beasts moving towards her, stamping their hind legs. If she moved even the slightest bit, she would be snapped up in one gobble. She had no choice but to chat with the ailing old aachi on the bed inside.

'Did you call me, aachi?' Even if she hadn't, Komu went near aachi's bed and put on the switch. Only when she took a big jump, she could reach it. In the glare of the light, aachi screwed up her eyes and got up. 'Who is it?' she asked.

The fear Komu had felt earlier had fully subsided. Komu started chatting with aachi. She informed her that everyone had gone out to see the chariot. A long while ago. And that it was time for them to come back. When aachi asked her, 'Is there a big crowd?' Komu replied, 'Yes, a terrible crowd. The streets are full and thousands of people are going up and down.' When aachi asked her, 'Didn't you go to see the chariot?' Komu felt very happy. 'Yes, I must,' she said, 'after everyone comes back… till now I had a lot of work.'

'O you poor thing. You too are a small child only, no? You too will feel like going. Go, go, go and come back. Let them come,' said aachi and went back to sleep.

Aachi's words made Komu even more happy. She asked aachi, 'Aachi, would you like a little hot water?' Even when aachi replied, 'I don't need anything,' Komu wasn't satisfied. The thought of aachi repeatedly saying, 'Go, go,' as if it were an order, thrilled Komu. Komu felt a little disappointed when aachi went back to sleep without saying anything more. Komu started pressing aachi's long bony legs, as if she were giving a gentle massage.

Komu heard the sounds of the giru-giru candy man. Even today he had come at the same time. Ever since she had come to work here, she heard him every night at the time she ground the dosai batter. She saw him go by. There wasn't enough light on this street. Even in this dimness, she could see him twirling 'gir-gir' and on the other hand hung a weighing-scale-like round wicker tray filled with brinjal-shaped candy, sugar candy, coconut flakes, and rock-hard tuck. The light from a chimney-less bottle lamp in the middle flickered and shivered, revealing a few coins in the middle of the tray. This man looked like Komu's father. Both wore veshtis, no shirts. But this man had a turban. Even if no one called him, he stopped by at every house, twirling 'gir-gir'. Well and good if they bought anything.

Here he always stood by the stone at the end of the street. When Komu stuck her face through the grilled door, he was still standing there. In the desolate entrance, the pillars still looked menacing, lifting their legs. But he stood there like a coin which had reached home in a game of dice. Komu yearned to buy the rose-coloured candy. They had given her four annas for the chariot festival. 'Don't spend everything,' they had warned her. Even if she bought for only five paise, she would get five candies. 'Should I buy?' Komu didn't know what to do. When she went to the wall-niche near the water tank and brought back very, very reluctantly the four annas, the gir-gir man was not to be found. But she could hear the twirling sound from the lane fading into the street. It was a good thing too that he went away. Otherwise she would have spent everything. Once you change the full coin for loose change, nothing will remain in your hands.

Everyone entered the house happily. Since they had started speaking in loud voices to be heard over the crowd, they continued to do so even within the house. Even the neighbours who had gone off separately came back together to keep company in the dark. Since everyone had switched on the lights at the same time, the entrances were well lit. The crisp swishing of the balloons and the whistle sounds, all passed Komu by.

This year the chariot had made the rounds and come to rest in a single day itself. Such a thing had happened only nine years ago. An overwhelming crowd. It seems there were plenty of people from the oppressed castes this year. There wasn't space even to move here or there. From the Lala Choultry corner to the Royal Talkies corner the chariot had sped along like a toddler. They had seen it from the terrace of Ambi Maama's place on the Theppa Kulam Street. What they said about the chariot gracefully swanning by seemed to be so true. It was a beautiful sight.

Komu stood listening.

Everyone stood around talking all this in front of their houses. When they entered in, Komu smilingly held out her hand for the infant.

'What were you doing all this while, di? Did you fill up the river water or what?' asked Deivu aachi.

'Yes, I did,' said Komu but no one heard her. They rushed into the house. Komu sat again by the entrance.

'We need the gram dal for the chutney. There isn't enough coconut either. Give the baby to someone else and go to the shop,' said a voice from inside.

After she bought the gram dal and the coconut, Komu stood staring at the chariot. It had come to its place of rest. Without any cars or buses, the road looked wide. The long ropes of the chariot lay curled like snakes right up to the sanctum of the goddess. The chariot with all its glorious decorations and banana festoons stood still in the moonlight, as if it had quarrelled with Komu. Three or four policemen sat on the ropes of the chariot around a gaslight. So sinful to rest one's bottom on the chariot rope. And smoking beedis on top of it. Komu was aghast. She was afraid to go near the chariot and see. But she wanted to go near. The oil-smell wafting out would be wonderful. But what if the policemen caught her?

Komu once again slung the bag over her shoulder and watched from afar. The newly painted four horses, their legs held high, looked as if they were about to leap. She liked only the white horse. If she leapt on to the white horse, she could go up to the skies. Like an airplane. Smiling, Komu drew near little by little. When she reached the spot where the ropes lay on the ground, like the trunk of a baby elephant wending its way through coconut fronds, she felt like pulling the chariot. Firmly tucking the bag under her armpit, Komu bent down and tried to lift the shredded ends of the heavy rope. She couldn't. She touched it, prayed and lifted her head.

From its resting place, the chariot gazed unwaveringly at Komu.

Original title: *Nilai*
1982

In a Town, Two Men 47

Prapanchan

Finishing his morning tiffin and wiping his washed hand, Krishnamoorthy came into the hall. Appa was sunk inside an easy chair in the corner. For several years now he had been like that. It seemed as if he couldn't remember Appa ever standing up. Amma wasn't at home. Must have gone to the neighbour's. Must have gone to borrow rice or money for the afternoon meal. He put on his shirt and came into the street.

His colony was well inside, away from the main road. The place linking this colony and the main road had remained barren for a long time. A place overgrown with weeds and cacti. A cinema theatre was coming up there. Bricks, cement bags and sand filled the street. He came to the main road. There too a cinema hall had been built, ready to open. Next to it was a hotel and beyond was the bazaar lined with pawn shops. Another street meeting the main road had yet another cinema hall. There used to be huts there. The huts were razed and they built a cinema hall there. No one knew where the hutment dwellers had disappeared. Perhaps they were living inside the cinema hall. In the shadows of that hall nestled a petty shop. Krishnamoorthy bought a Charminar cigarette there and lit it. Puffing on the cigarette, he contemplated where to go; he decided to see Rangasamy and walked towards the shops.

Nadar's shop was thickly crowded. He stood a little away, in the shade of a drumstick tree by the wall. When the branches swayed in the wind, the sun hit him. Under the aegis of the tree, Old Lady Kannama sat, selling tapioca. The previous month she had sold guavas.

On seeing him, she said, 'What, rice-merchant, it seems you shut tight the rice shop. What a fellow you are, 'pa. Every other fellow with a rice shop is scooping up money. You, on the other hand, have shut even what you have and are standing with nothing in hand.'

The branches swayed in the wind again and the heat struck him. Sweat dripped inside his shirt. The ends of the cigarette burnt his hand.

Krishnamoorthy retorted, 'If those who bought rice had paid the money correctly, why would I close the shop? Talking like a big honest one... You too owe me money.'

The old lady said, 'What, 'pa, talking such words! As if I don't want to give. Money should stay in the hand, no? I will give it within this week itself, raja.'

When Nadar's eyes fell on him, he asked, 'What, saar, you want to see Rangasamy?' He nodded. He shouted into the shop, 'Ade, Rangasamy, your old boss wants to see you... Go, go.' He flung away the sweat on his chest with his hand fan. The drops fell on the red gram dhal. Rangasamy jumped over the counter-planks and came outside.

'What, annen...?'

'That Gopalu hasn't yet given the money, da. That mill-worker fellow. It's okay if it had been five-ten rupees, but it is one hundred and eighty rupees. There's a crunch at home. Ask him if you see him.'

'When I shut shop at night, I will go and see him,' said Rangasamy.

'Will you drink tea, annen...?'

'No.'

A crow came and sat on the wall. It crowed twice and left.

'No plans to do any other business, annen? This Nadar is not okay for me – asking me to buy tea and all, as if I'm a small boy.'

'Let us see.'

The very next day itself Rangasamy gave Krishnamoorthy the news.

'Gopalu couldn't be found at home, annen. I went for the night show – there saar got caught tightly. He had come for the film with four or five people. I told him: "What, 'ya, so much for your integrity. You bought and ate rice on credit, did you bother to return it? You might as well pimp and eat, you dishonest fellow." Man stood there dumbstruck, you know. Didn't even watch the film. Got up and left before the interval.'

Whenever Rangasamy was excited, his one eye would always shut. He would punch his left palm with his right index finger.

Krishnamoorthy said, 'You shouldn't have humiliated him like that…'

'This is your problem, annen. You don't know how to survive. If you give these people respect and all, they'll reduce you to begging. This scoundrel got a bonus of one thousand one hundred rupees only last week, did you know that? And you want to give him respect!'

Two days after this happened, Krishnamoorthy accidentally saw Gopalu near the peanut stall. He was standing, picking his tooth with a stick, in front of the biriyani shop run by a man from Salem. Gopalu also saw him. But he walked away, pushing his bike, as if he hadn't noticed him. Since it was a one-way street, he couldn't ride his bike. Krishnamoorthy ran and tapped him.

'What, 'pa, Gopalu – you've completely forgotten, is it?'

Gopalu looked at the changing traffic signals, as if for the first time.

'Do you know how much troubles I have? As if I'm asking you for the entire thing? Can't you pay me back little by little? It will be convenient to me, and to you,' said Krishnamoorthy in a choked voice.

'Let that be, 'pa. How much do I owe you – a paltry hundred and eighty only, no? I can give back even if it is a thousand. I'm not a person without some wealth. When I quietly went to a cinema hall, you asked your shop boy to insult me in front of everyone. I didn't see the film at all.'

Gopalu's face twisted.

'I even started crying. Look here, I will give only when I can. Don't keep pestering me. Save your dignity.' Pushing his bike quickly, he walked off.

Krishnamoorthy ran behind him. 'Gopalu, Gopalu.' When Gopalu sped away, he stood in the middle of the road and looked from the corner of his eye to see if anyone had noticed him. He felt relieved. Looking at him, the traffic policeman shouted, 'Walk on the platform, 'ya. Why are you standing in the middle of the road and taking my life out.'

He got on to the platform. He bought and lit a Charminar cigarette from the petty shop at the corner. His heart was heavy. His mother asking when he started, 'Give me ten rupees if you have, 'pa,' came to mind. A flower-seller with a maroon pottu sitting on a stool asked him, 'Do you need flowers, saar?' He walked on without answering.

A week later, Krishnamoorthy saw Gopalu chewing betel leaves in front of the Iyer hotel. It was dusk. Calling out, 'Gopalu,' he went near him. As if he didn't know that a man named Krishnamoorthy existed on earth, Gopalu nonchalantly rubbed his lime-smeared finger on the pillar, hopped on to the bike and went away. As he sped away, he turned towards the left and spat out betel-stained spittle.

One day when Krishnamoorthy accidentally came across Rangasamy, he sadly related how Gopalu had sped away while he called out to him. Listening to everything, Rangasamy said, 'Annen, you mustn't get angry with what I'm going to say. If you remain like this, you will die without rice or water. You're giving respect to scoundrels like Gopalu. Unless you pull his shirt and ask, "You bastard, what about my money?", he's not going to give you any money. And you are not going to get the money.'

The next day happened to be a Sunday. Contemplating since morning, Krishnamoorthy finally decided to go and see Gopalu. When the entire neighbourhood of Kanattupettai was buried in darkness, he knocked on Gopalu's door. The door opened and a lady asked, 'Who is it?' In the dim light he made out that she was carrying.

'Is Gopalu there?'

'He's eating. Please sit down – who shall I say has come?'

'Krishnamoorthy – say rice-merchant Krishnamoorthy. He will know.'

She closed the door and went away. The light from inside spilled out in a long line from behind the shut door. He remained standing and finished three cigarettes. Wiping his hand, Gopalu opened the door and said, 'What, 'pa, at this hour?'

It was so dark that you could see the face only if you looked intently. Krishnamoorthy found this convenient. A whiff of fish sambar came from Gopalu. Krishnamoorthy hated it.

'Nothing. A little crunch at home. Money trouble. If you give something, it would be good.'

The lady opened the door and looked out. A little more light spilled out.

'I told you then itself, no. I will come and give you when I get some in my hands. Why are you simply pestering me?' he said in a low voice, looking the other way.

Krishnamoorthy looked at the lady. She seemed to be looking at him.

'You should understand my situation, Gopalu. I've given away most of my stuff on credit. Some crunch at home now. Akka has come for confinement. I'm finding it difficult to manage.'

'You may have several troubles. Should I cut my neck for all that?'

'The way you are talking, it looks as if I've come to borrow from you.' So saying, Krishnamoorthy lit a cigarette. He felt a little rejuvenated. His chest fluttered a little.

'Okay, I'm going to sleep.'

'I'm telling you one thing. You think I'm yielding to you. One musn't lose the respect between man and man. But it looks as if you are not going to keep it up.'

'Will you come here, please,' called out the lady.

'Ssh. You go in.' Turning to him, he said, 'What, 'pa, you're talking a little strangely.'

'You only made me talk like this. I'm giving you one week's time. By then you should give the money.'

'If I don't?'

'I'll kick you. You can go to the mill only past my house. I'll break your legs and arms. I'll snatch away your mill token. You can't then go for work. You know me. And my family. You also know who my friends are. Definitely I'll do what I say.'

The lady came out, away from the door. Krishnamoorthy stamped out his cigarette and walked away slowly.

Two days later, at the time when even the sun hadn't risen. Covered up against the cold, Krishnamoorthy lay curled. His mother came and woke him up.

'Somebody's come in search of you, da.'

He covered his chest with a towel and came out. Gopalu stood there with a muffler round his neck.

'What, Gopalu?'

'Here, there's hundred rupees here. That's all I could rustle up. Keep it. Within two days I will also give the remaining eighty. Don't get angry.'

Krishnamoorthy took the money.

'What happened to the bonus?'

'My loans were greater than what I got, 'pa.'

Krishnamoorthy found it difficult to count the money.

'It's all right. How much do you still owe – eighty only, no. Cut off thirty. It's enough if you give fifty. Give it after a week or ten days. If I said anything wrong, please don't be upset, Gopalu.'

'Cheche. The fault is all mine. I should have given you correctly. When I was in difficulty, you helped me out. But I didn't when you were in difficulty…'

Gopalu went away. He came back the third day.

'What, Gopalu?'

'See, 'pa, there's thirty here. That's all I got. I borrowed it from somewhere. In my house she had a ritual head-bath day before yesterday. I spoke to you and went away, no. Within hours she delivered. Expense after expense.'

'What child, 'pa?'

'This also female only.'

'So what – a child is a child!'

'Okay, shall I take leave? I'll give the balance within two days.'

'Wait. How much do you still owe – twenty only, no? Buy a dress for the child with that money on my behalf.'

'Please don't take anything to your heart, Krishnamoorthy.'

'Cheche.'

That evening, after tiffin at Iyer Hotel, Krishnamoorthy and Rangasamy went to see a film.

Original title: *Oru Ooril Irandu Manithargal*
1972

The Key 48

Rajendra Sozhan

He heard it with much happiness and joy. What an opportunity after so many years. Opening a lock without a key was an art in itself. An interesting task too. It was in his hostel days that he had opened his friends' locks like this. After that, where did one find a lock without a key?

'How did you lose it?' he asked with a laugh.

His wife replied, 'Didn't lose it. Forgot. Put it in and locked it away.'

He, who usually washed his legs and face whenever he returned home, went towards the box today.

'Bring that lamp.'

The wife brought the lamp.

He looked intently at the box and the bolt from which the lock hung. It was a lock that he looked at every day, but today he had to scrutinise it – the way the lock was fashioned, the keyhole, the system, everything.

It was a lock that locked if you pressed tight. A white lock. A sturdy one. He had opened several such locks. If you inserted a small nail, slanted it slightly towards the right and twisted it lightly, that would do it – click! It was a fine, deft job that awaited him.

'Bring a small nail.'

'Small one…!' his wife dragged on hesitantly.

'Yes. Something which will fit into this hole,' he replied. He too began to search.

The wife searched with the bedroom light. He searched with the lantern.

An old wooden box, assorted scrap, old iron rods, some junk, tin box – he searched everything. He couldn't find a small nail. Would there be anything nailed to the wall?

He investigated the walls. The coat stand, cloth bag, shelf, winnowing tray, sieve, the thin rod which held old letters. The place where the lantern was hung… All the nails were huge! A little irritated, he began inspecting again all the places he had searched. 'Che, there isn't even a small nail in this house!'

The wife came back with a tiny piece of tin. 'Take a look at this.'

He looked at it, then looked up at her. 'Will this fit? Don't you have a sense of proportion?'

She moved away dejectedly.

He looked around again and again. Not knowing what to do, he contemplated deeply. If only there was a small nail…

He once again surveyed all the nails. Nothing seemed to fit. He wondered if he should attend to it in the morning. As if this is such a big task… why should it wait till morning… he could open it right now.

He ransacked again the same old iron junk. Even if there wasn't a nail, a small rod would do. Rusty tin sheets, an unusable stove, useless cycle locks and latches and huge nails were heaped together haphazardly. He rummaged through them irritatedly. On the other side, she was riffling through something.

'What, didn't get anything? Still searching or what?'

'See if this will fit…' She came with an old umbrella rib.

He took it and flung it away on the floor.

'Shouldn't you have some sense… Will this thing ever fit into that? If it is a Godrej lock, you can open it with a calendar-rod. This stupid thing is a Tiger lock. A small nail…'

He opened the wooden box and rummaged through it. 'Why have you kept everything in such a mess… How many times to tell you… Can't you keep everything in order? Chee, is it like a box? All rubbish, in such a mess.'

Luckily, a small, thin rod. In the crevices of the box. A cycle spoke-rib. He picked it up with satisfaction. He turned it this way and that in the light. Both the ends looked the same; it would do if one end was flattened slightly.

He called out to his wife excitedly. 'Hold the lantern. Bring it here.'

He took out the small hammer from the wooden box and took it to the entrance. 'Hold it lower this way.'

He flattened the rod on the black stone paved on the floor. He peered at it against his face, banged it a couple of times again. He got up only when he was satisfied.

'Bring it here.'

The wife came along with the lantern. She sat on her haunches near the box and held the lamp so that the light fell brightly on the lock. He began to open.

He skilfully inserted the rod, tilted it slightly towards the right and very lightly a bit upwards, with a great knack... he started to twist... very carefully for a long time... very gently... this way and that, he twisted... the lock refused to open.

'Hold it high. Should I teach you how to hold a lantern too?'

With a lot of patience and tact, he tried to open, recalling the ways in which he had opened locks earlier. He stopped, then looked carefully at the lock, once again inserted it into the hole, gave it a slight twist upwards...

'Chee, is this any way to hold a lantern? Instead of holding it to one side, shaking it this way and that.' Once again, he attempted. He stopped, turned and glared at her.

'Don't you know which way I'm turning and which way you should hold? Are you a small child?' he asked.

He tried again and looked at her. 'You don't have to hold it. Just leave it and go,' he yelled.

Losing patience, he started poking around. This way and that. There was a rattling sound. But the lock refused to open.

'What wonderful forgetfulness this is, I don't know. Shouldn't you think a little bit before locking... where the key is and all.' With a frown and with his face in a rage, he fought with the lock.

'Che. After running here and there, when you enter home, is there any peace? Some problem or the other as soon one steps in. You must have some responsibility, no? Nicely gorging every few hours and idling away time with a storybook. Otherwise, if someone comes by, gossiping.'

He spluttered. He poked at the lock clumsily. Rattled it, creating a racket. 'Don't know how many years since the lock was bought. A bit of oil should have been dribbled, no. No time for all that I suppose. It's nicely rusted. That's why it is not opening…'

He threw away the rod and looked disgustedly at the lock, as if he would pound it. Only the lantern remained near him. 'You've gone off, is it, as soon as I told you off. Waiting to run away. Bring that coconut oil bottle here!'

'Where's the oil? This morning only you completely upturned it and oiled your head. Only if we buy in the morning…'

'Couldn't you tell this earlier? No habit of telling as soon as something gets over. Wonderful way of running a home. Okay, you locked the key inside. What precious thing is inside this that you must lock it away now and then – will someone come and rob it? Go and bring some gingelly oil, at least.'

'No, let it be. Just leave it. I'll try to open it myself in the morning. You get up…'

He took off his sweaty vest to hang on the clothesline. He grumbled, 'Yes, yes, never short of this kind of empty, boastful talk.'

Original title: *Saavi*
1973

BUSTING OF BRAVADO 49

BALAKUMARAN

'Our Vadivelu has died, saar!'

'Which Vadivelu, da?'

'Casual labour Vadivelu, saar. Works in the Heavy Section, saar. The dark and thin fellow, who comes drunk to work every day. That Vadivelu, saar.'

Putting on his shirt, Govindan got into the first auto he found and flew to the factory. Vadivelu had been a 'casual labour' for two years. Like him there were forty others who were 'casual labours' for many, many years. One of Govindan's main demands had been to make all the 'casual labours' permanent. He wondered if he could somehow rake up the issue today. If not today, at least this week or this month, he ought to call a meeting about this. But before all that it must be seen if they will declare a holiday today. They won't. They will cite rules saying that he is but a 'casual labour'. If you shake them up thoroughly, they will budge. Would they declare a holiday just like that? We have to demand that they pay respect with garland and all. You need money for that. Have to ask our own people to shell out eight annas each for this. All these fellows are only used to taking. If you ask for eight annas, they will pull a long face. Whatever it may be, the death of Vadivelu is a good opportunity.

It was only three months since Govindan had become a union leader. Though no great changes had occurred in these months, the management had begun to give in noticeably. The officers feared that Govindan would burst into their rooms at any time like Lord Narasimha, who had emerged ripping through from a pillar.

It wasn't easy to be the union leader of a private factory with one thousand one hundred labourers. You needed guts. A sharp tongue. A strong body. A brassy voice. A little education – no, that wasn't required. Govindan had very, very little education. He had been beaten up like a dog by his father when he failed the eighth standard for the third time. That came to his mind ever so often. 'You are killing me like this only because I'm not studying. You wait and see, I'll become a big man without this education. Before your death I will become a bigger shot than you.'

The vengeful streak that gnawed his mind had sprouted, grown into a sapling, a tree, and today it had started to bear fruit. Today, Govindan was the leader of a thousand one hundred men. The great leader Govindan. When he had won the union elections and rode with garlands on the shoulders of his friends, his father had come to mind. When the highly educated young engineers and managers trembled before him, his father came to mind. When a dozen comrades crowded around him and pleaded, 'Somehow you must solve the issue, boss,' his father came to mind.

The day after he had become a leader Govindan had bought a new pair of chappals. He learnt to walk rubbing the chappals forcefully on the floor. He felt that such a gait would announce his arrival and instil a kind of confidence within him. That apart, when once he had playfully told someone that he would slipper him, his father, who had been standing behind him, thumped him on his neck and said, 'Only if you have one, can you beat him.' The father had flung Govindan's chappals into the gutter and made him run away barefoot. This was a kind of protest to that too. Here no one dared ask Govindan, 'Why are you walking like this.' With every menacing step, he felt the comfort of trampling over his father's face.

Except in his house, Govindan was wont to walk like this everywhere else. He could try it at home too, but the old man would say something. Even if he didn't say it to his face, it would be within his earshot. There wasn't any point in needling the old man lying like a rag on the pial. After becoming the union leader of ten such companies, with a car at his disposal, Govindan could insist on wearing chappals even within the home. Such a time would surely come!

Before the factory was even open, the news of the death had been pasted on the front gate. Black ribbons had been bought and pinned on everyone's shirt as they entered. Even before Govindan could request, the management had given permission to leave for home an hour early. Even a donation box was allowed within the premises. In a way it was good that they hadn't declared a full holiday. Most of the fellows would say they were just going for a bite and take off for the cinema instead. Then he would be left alone to suffer at the house of mourning. If it was just one-hour permission, he could herd the entire lot. It would look good only if he went with a battalion. A donation box, tied with a black ribbon, was taken in a procession through every department.

'If anyone gives less than eight annas, I'll turn vicious' – Govindan's words had sufficient effect. When the overflowing box was upturned, there was four hundred and fifteen rupees. Garland for twenty rupees, rosewater bottle for twenty rupees, agarbathis for eight rupees, and other sundry items for fifteen rupees – after all this, the remaining amounted to three hundred and fifty-two rupees. He put it into a cover, wrote over it and put it into his pocket. He sent a man before him to Vadivelu's house to announce his arrival. At four, he stood at the gate and asked everyone to follow him in a silent procession.

A word to those who might be tempted to bunk – 'One day we too might face Vadivelu's situation: keep this in mind… '

The crowd obeyed and followed him like a flock of sheep. Buses stopped on the streets. At the sudden sight of a thousand men in procession, the bazaar trembled like a calf. Frightened and surprised faces peeped at Govindan through half-shut doors. A crowd swarmed around Vadivelu's house. When the procession neared, the crowd moved away, making way for Govindan. The gaggle of women, whose throats had become parched from all the wailing since morning, burst out again on his entrance. An old woman – who looked like the mother – with a nauseating stench of tobacco, hugged Govindan. She wailed in a variety of ways. Govindan gasped for breath. 'The blessed soul who had to go has gone. Why are you harassing people who have come to moan? Move away.' A young man shooed away the old lady.

When he placed the huge rose garland on Vadivelu's body, a few fellows clapped out of habit. When Govindan glared at them, they quietened down. When three bundles of agarbathis were lit at one go, there was a cloud of smoke. When Govindan dutifully sprinkled the rose water, the womenfolk looked at him with awe.

'Who is he? A friend?'

'Chee, chee. He is the leader.'

'The leader of what?'

'Where Vadivelu worked. He is a leader there.'

'Is he the one giving the salary?'

'Even above that. He has collected cash for Vadivelu, it seems, and brought it here.'

'Look, how he has come! Bringing with him such fragrance.'

'Chee, chee. That is the fragrance of agarbathis.'

'That's what I'm telling you, di. If you and I die, who will burn three bundles of agarbathis – this blessed one has arrived and it's full of the fragrance of agarbathis and rosewater.'

'Who is the head of the house, 'ma?' Govindan called out.

'Here, old lady. He's calling you.'

'No, no. Don't bother the old lady,' Govindan demurred.

'He's calling to give cash. Why are you disturbing the old lady? Ask the younger brother to come.' The thin-moustachioed younger brother appeared in a half-pant. Govindan counted out the notes in front of the crowd and placed them in the boy's hand.

'Long live our leader Govindan!'

'Long live comrade Vadivelu.'

The shouts of the crowd hit the roof and wafted out with the smoke of the agarbathis.

Govindan hushed them with his hand, looked outside and said, 'Dei, is there anyone there? Ask them to start the drums.'

'Drums, drums.' Someone shouted and others echoed.

'Ask them to take the body quickly… We have to leave.'

'The mother's brother hasn't come yet. That is why we are waiting.'

'Yes, yes, the uncle only is going to pay respects with garland and all! With so many big people around, you are talking back, is it?' A fat woman carped. She looked at Govindan and smiled.

'Please ask them to finish quickly, 'ma. Our men have to go very far.'

When Govindan came outside, they propped up a chair for him. Asked him to sit comfortably. Gave him a hand fan. Huddled in a circle at a distance. When he asked for a soda, they gave him an aluminium tumbler covered with cloth.

'Why all this, da?'

'Drink, boss! You have toiled since morning.'

'Drinking this only Vadivelu died, no?'

'If you drink a half or one, nothing will happen. In a house of mourning no one will mind. Drink it.'

Govindan drank and handed back the tumbler. He saw four or five people holding tumblers at the back. 'What, da? Brought the entire can?'

'Don't heed all this, boss. We were waiting for you only to finish.' The tumblers changed several hands in a flash.

In ten minutes Vadivelu's funeral started. The crowd jostled.

Govindan ordered his men to join hands and stand in a circle. Who should streamline the traffic, who should control the crowd, how many people in the front and how many at the back – he spelt out all this clearly. The procession started and wound its way slowly like a snake that had swallowed the prey.

'Vadivelu was a fellow with nothing. Look how grandly he is going.'

'The old lady is fortunate. Who has ever had a funeral like this in our street?'

'What did this old lady do – this big man is doing all this. Otherwise will there be such a crowd?'

Govindan felt as if he was floating. 'You keep going. I will go change into a veshti and come.'

He broke through the crowd and went towards his house with a few of his trusted men.

He sat in the pial opposite his father and shouted for a veshti.

'What a crowd, boss! You did an excellent job.' One of Govindan's sidekicks complimented him prudently.

'What is so great about this, brother? This is nothing. Wait and see next time. The collection will be thousand then.'

'Just the local drums won't do, boss. We have to have a band.'

'Why only band, 'pa? We'll call even the martial arts troupe. Next time we will definitely do it.'

'If you set your mind, you can do it, boss! It will be difficult only to rustle up the money.'

'I won't leave it – the next time won't I put my hand into the management's belly! Won't I tell them to shell out five hundred bucks! Wait and see. How grand it will all be next time…'

The old man who lay coiled up got up with a start. He banged the wooden plank near him on the floor.

'Get up and leave, you scoundrel! From then I'm listening, next time, next time. Waiting to see when the next fellow will die! This fellow is a great leader it seems. You broomstick, get out of here!'

Why did the old man hiss like this? Why did their leader Govindan run out without changing into a veshti? The comrades never understood.

Original title: *Mithappugal Muriyum*
1977

Fed Up with God 50

Subramanya Raju

When I got off the train it was chilly. Dawn hadn't yet broken fully. Perhaps because no one other than me got off at the Aazhiyur station, the train chugged on wearily. As I came out of the station, I could see the gopuram of the temple standing majestically at a distance. I would have to walk at least a mile. I remembered going in a jatka long ago with my wife when we were newly married.

I wasn't familiar with this town. Walking at this early-morning hour without slippers, looking at people not known to me and walking towards a faceless town filled me with pleasure. As I approached the town, the height of the gopuram increased, creating a child-like astonishment within me.

Nothing interesting had happened in my life so far. My tender years were spent growing up in a street in Thiruvallikeni, not knowing where life would take me. A distant uncle had educated me and had a daughter of marriageable age whom he couldn't marry off since he didn't have sufficient funds; hence I was contracted to marry her.

Chitra was a nice girl, really. Like all new brides, she was loving towards me. From the morning coffee when

I read the papers to a glass of milk when I lay down at night, she did it all perfectly.

One day, all of a sudden, she said that her back was paining and lay down. We woke up only when the pain spread in cosmic proportions through the body. We visited every doctor in town. In the end, one day they threw a big stone on our heads and announced it was TB. After that, Chitra never got up from the bed.

In the fourth month of my marriage itself all the joys of life had been interred. Chitra fumed at everything. Others walking about normally in front of her planted the seeds of envy within her. The seeds grew into a huge banyan and Chitra became a burden to me. It had been ten years now – since I ate well, slept well and lived well.

The town had shrugged off sleep; the freshly drawn kolams in all the houses seemed to welcome me. A crisp elderly man, vibhuti smeared across his forehead, appeared in front of me. I was a bit hesitant to ask him.

'Do you know the priest Vaidyanatha Gurukkal's house?'

'Yes. Have you arranged for a pooja to be done today?'

'No. But I know him. I just came to see him.'

'There, at the end, can you see a neem tree? That house only.'

I thanked him and walked towards the Gurukkal's house.

'Does Vaidyanatha Gurukkal…'

'Yes, it's me…'

'My name is Sankaran. I had come here ten years ago. I've come from Madras. I want to stay here and have the darshan of the Lord and go…'

'Besh! Besh! Welcome. Come in.'

It was an ancient tiled house. Even so, as soon as you entered the house, you got a sense of a peaceful refuge. You felt young at heart, as if you had shed off all your previous years.

The Gurukkal's wife was a woman who had been married for long. Radiantly graceful. She made coffee. Excellent coffee. Even if you searched the whole of Madras, you wouldn't get coffee like that. The Gurukkal came and sat in front of me.

'What did you say your name was?'

'Sankaran.'

'What do you do in Madras?'

'I am a supervisor in Thomson company.'

'You haven't brought your wife?'

'No. She's not well.'

The Gurukkal's wife peeped out. 'Do you want hot water? Or will you bathe in the pond?'

'In the pond only. And from there I will have the darshan of the Lord and come.'

I started for the temple with the Gurukkal. It was a biggish temple. A beautiful pond behind it. The kind which invited passersby to come and have a dip in it.

I bathed. The water was a sorrow-killer. Ambrosia. Full of peace. 'All your troubles are nothing but illusions. Your life is ephemeral. Only He is eternal. You were born to bathe here. To pray here.'

I came outside, made a paste of the vibhuti that the Gurukkal gave me and smeared it. I followed him into the temple and in the glow of the camphor he lit in front of every shrine, I realised their divine grace, and for the first time I prayed to god without begging for any favour.

I felt as if I'd shed my old skin. From today I'm a new being. All my old ties have snapped. From now on I have no bonds. I'm a liberated being. I have become a sanyasi without the aid of a guru. From now on, this Lord Nandikeswaran here is my guru, my friend, my everything.

The lunch was at the Gurukkal's house. His wife served us on banana leaves. After many days I was eating a meal with relish. When the Gurukkal's wife served me, I suddenly remembered my mother. Thank god my mother was no more. Had she been alive, she would have shed blood at my plight.

'What is wrong with your wife?' The Gurukkal started the conversation from where he had left off in the morning.

'They said it was TB. She hasn't got up from the bed. Now she is with her parents. I'm frustrated with life. It's ten years since I slept well. I applied for two months' leave and here I am. I came here not knowing where I was going. I really like this place. I have a little money. I'm thinking of settling here.'

'Nothing will happen to your wife. The deity of this town is very powerful. Pray to him. He won't ask for much. Just half a measure of salt and quarter measure of pepper – just make a vow that you will offer this in his shrine when she gets well. So many people have been cured of such serious illnesses. Just wait and see. Your wife will get well and the next year itself you will come here with her – just see. All right, eat now. When

He's there we don't have to worry about anything. Lakshmi, serve us rice and buttermilk.'

After lunch, I slept soundly on the pial under the shade of the neem tree. No terrible dreams, no nightmares. A really peaceful sleep. When I woke up, the temple bells chimed for the evening pooja.

I went to the backyard, washed my face and went to the temple. Today the temple was a bit crowded. There was a tourist bus outside. The Gurukkal was busy. I had a darshan of every shrine and came to the outer yard of the temple. The music of the nadaswaram mingled with the cool breeze. Moonlight shone on the top of the gopuram and scattered around.

The Gurukkal came along with someone, the archanai plate in hand. 'O, you are here? I've been looking for you. Today I will be late. You go home and eat. I've informed Lakshmi. Don't wait for me.'

'All right.'

Even after the Gurukkal left, I sat there for a long time. A thought slowly firmed up in my mind: that this is going to be my hometown from now on.

'Come, come. It will be late by the time he comes. You can eat.'

'I saw him at the temple. He told me.'

She spread out the leaf and brought water. As soon she served rice, I mixed it.

'Don't you perform the purification ritual?

'No. I've forgotten about all that. When trouble comes, everything disappears, maami.'

'What trouble do you have?

'I mentioned in the morning, no? The same thing.'

'You are fed up with your wife, and I am fed up with god.'

'What? Fed up with god?'

'Mmm… Do you know that my husband is not from a family of priests?'

'What do you mean by that?'

'We are not from this town. We are from Tanjore. I believe he had something like fits when he was young – his legs and arms became stiff. I believe his mother prayed to the deity of this town – that she would give away half her wealth to the temple if he became well. And he became well, it seems. He came to this town then. And just stayed put! He said that he would become a slave to the god that cured him. We should have more than ten acres there, the remaining half. Every year we receive rice, pulses, chilli, everything. Sent to our house itself. He has leased out our fields. The remaining – a little, the lessee gives in cash. The lessee is cheating him. He says, "He's poor, we shouldn't ask him anything. We should just take what he gives." '

'In this town, there's no way to pass your time. Can chat only with people like you who visit. I have never gone out. Must never, he says. He doesn't visit other temples. He says that this Nandikeswarar is enough for us. But that god is unable to give me even a child. He also has my husband firmly in his grasp. For twenty years, I've been all alone in this town. Half the people in the agraharam have left for the city. Every day I have to just sit at home staring blankly. That's why I said I'm fed up with god too.

'Now… have I run away from my husband? Or is it possible for us to leave? If you had the same illness, do you think your wife would have left you and come off like this?'

Without saying a word I washed my hands and went to the neem tree in the front yard. Words like a whiplash. How delicately she has put it – that I'm not renouncing, but just running away. Even if you don't like certain things in life, you have to face them – that's real courage.

When I thought about her, I was saddened. If she had remained in their native town, she would have turned the twenty acres to forty. She would have gone around majestically in a double-bullock cart. Though she had everything, she had nothing.

I didn't know when I slept off.

When I got up the next day, the Gurukkal, freshly bathed, a crisp vibhuti mark on his forehead, was starting off to the temple.

'Are you coming to bathe in the pond?'

'Wait a minute. I'm coming.'

'Never mind. Drink your coffee and come. I will wait for you.'

When I brushed my teeth, had coffee and came out, he was sitting on the pial chanting mantras.

'Shall we go?'

'Mmm… '

When we neared the pond I told him, 'I'm thinking of leaving this afternoon for Madras by the Day Express.'

'Why, what is the matter? I thought you will stay here for at least a week.'

'No, I have changed my mind. Where will I get salt and pepper here?'
'You'll get it in front of the temple itself. Why?'
'No, I'm thinking of making my offering in advance.'

Original title: *Saami Alutthu Pochu*
1979

Bonds of the Daytime

51

Jeyanthan

Nine in the morning. Locking the door behind them, they stepped into the street. At that instant, the contract between them came into effect. As it usually did.

He in terrycott pants, a terylene shirt, with cooling glasses and a trim gait, she in a ulli-ulli sari and a matching full-voile blouse, with slippers and a handbag. Their walk in tandem made an entertaining daily spectacle. For the past three years they had been leaving home and returning in the same manner. Even so, it unfailingly drew the attention of some people every day. A few were even envious of them. Particularly of her. Because she was a local. Some jeered, 'Ada, when she was a little girl… dripping nose, boils in arms and legs, couldn't bear to look at her!' Some said, 'Her mother toiled in the fields to bring her up!'

Both were government employees. They worked in the Muthupatti panchayat office, five miles away. He was a cashier, she a typist. They stayed here for the convenient housing and commuted by bus every day.

As they walked the street, some would smile. Some would ask, 'What, started already?' He would give a smart nod. That smartness was a bit much. It seemed to convey: I'm a big man, that's why you ordinary folks wonder about me like this. If anyone asked her the same question, she would give a half-smile. A beautiful smile. A smile that irritated him many a time: 'Showing your teeth to all and sundry…'

They were Christians. She a born Christian, he became one mid-way. In order to marry her.

They came to the bus stop by 9.10 itself. The bus was at 9.20. There was a crowd there, to the extent that you might not get a ticket. Each had a take on the unusual crowd. He grumbled about those who get married with fanfare and gather for temple fairs.

When she moved away to buy something from the nearby petty shop, Balaguruvar Reddiar asked him, 'What? 'they' are not here today?' This was the way of the village. Instead of wishing good morning, they usually asked something like this. He, in his usual stiff and proud fashion, said, 'they have come.' Whenever he spoke about her in public, he always used the respectful third person plural. She, in turn, always referred to him as 'our saar'. The 9.20 bus arrived at 9.40. Even as it came, you could make out through the window that there were plenty of people, even standing. The crowd, which until then had stood here and there, now gathered in a wave, anxiously trying to gauge where the bus would actually stop. As the bus stopped, people jostled to get in. When the conductor sternly ordered, 'No one get in,' the crowd hesitated and looked expectantly at the bus.

He and she too rushed forward. She stood behind Balaguru Reddiar, who held on to the bar, almost grazing the footboard. He was pushed back little by little and found himself at the end of the crowd.

Parthasarathy, a youngster who stood a little away from the crowd, shouted out, 'Conductor, give two tickets for saar. Office tickets!' He looked at her and she gave him her half-smile. He was boiling. Parthasarathy was just loitering there. If he was taking the bus, he would be the first one to hold on to the bar. Then, no 'saar' or 'mor' would come out of his mouth.

Four or five people got down from the bus. Immediately the conductor stretched out his left leg across the entrance, barring the way and said, 'No place.' Then he turned around and looked through the back windshield and asked, 'Are you done?' A man was getting down from the ladder at the back, after loading his bundles on top.

When the conductor caught her eye, with a half-smile she raised two fingers in a v-sign. The conductor grinned, 'No, I'm Rising Sun, madam.' Elections were two days away and the symbols of the main parties were the v-sign and the rising sun; hence everyone understood and laughed. Her half-smile turned into a three-quarter one. The conductor looked at her once again. After the man who got off the ladder got into the bus, the conductor looked at her and said, 'The two of you get in.'

The bus took off. Then, seat allotment became a problem for the conductor. Shuffling 'mother goats with kids and kids with mother goats', he somehow managed to make place for her. Finally, when she sat down, there was an empty seat beside her. There were no women standing in the bus. So someone suggested, 'Let saar sit there.' He, who was standing somewhere at the back, came and sat beside her. A few, always given to comparing couples, looked at them intently. Aware of this, he sat a little more stylishly and looked at the road through the bus window.

When they reached their office compound, a few employees were chatting on the verandah. When they saw them, they said something and laughed. Then they smiled at them. He got up the steps and asked, 'What?' Attender Krishnan said laughingly, 'Saar, we have a doubt. Now, are 'they' our office typist or Mrs Cashier?' The husband and wife just smiled. Depot clerk Jagannathan said, 'I will tell you. When 'they' are sitting in front of the typewriter 'they' are typist. Once they get up, 'they' are Mrs Cashier.' Establishment Mahalingam said, 'But at that time he must be sitting in his seat. Otherwise 'they' will become Mrs Rajamanickam.' Everyone laughed. Then they wondered that if a woman can be addressed Mrs So and So by the husband's name, why not a man be called Mr Philomena. They went in laughing. His smile seemed to indicate, 'Don't you have any work?', but hers seemed to say, 'I shouldn't chat merrily like you all. I can't.'

As they went in to sign in at the manager's desk, the manager too arrived. She went to her table and he to his room.

She sat in front of her typewriter, but didn't do anything useful for fifteen minutes. She just whiled away her time. Then she listlessly inserted a few sheets along with carbon paper into the typewriter.

Despatch Krishnan, who was sitting at the end of the hall, two tables away, looked at her a couple of times. For the past five years he had been the attender at the office. He wondered if she was the same Philomena of three years ago. He thought that even at the verandah, as she went in after her husband, just smiling. No, he was very sure. She wasn't the same Philomena of three years ago. Had she been the same person, she would have joked and laughed with all of them. In those days her face had a certain liveliness and cheer. A joke she once cracked in front of the same typewriter was still fresh in his mind.

At the time, Rajamanickam didn't work here. He was in the Sayakadu panchayat office. Only when he got transferred here did the two of them fall in love and get married. Before that, Sami Subramaniam, the social welfare worker in the office, moonlighted as a broker. He had brought a proposal for her. The boy was working in LIC, Madurai. In the initial stages, he was to come and 'see' her in the office one day. But twice, he couldn't make it. Once when the office was bustling with people, she had asked loudly to Sami Subramaniam, 'What saar, where is your bridegroom? When is he going to come? The next time you ask him whether he is going to come and see the girl or I should go there to see the boy.' The whole office had spluttered into laughter. She too had laughed heartily.

Two maternity assistants walked up to the manager's table, looking for someone in the hall. Philomena, who was typing, didn't notice them. Krishnan saw them. One was Povoor Mangalam. He recalled that three months ago she and Philomena had had a blazing row at the executive officer's hall. Rajamanickam too had joined in and it had all turned ugly.

One day Philomena had gone to the executive officer hall to drink water since there was no water in her room. There were always about ten people there. Since there were huge bureaus arranged haphazardly here and there, it was possible not to be aware of someone else's presence. When Philomena had entered, four or five maternity assistants were talking among themselves. Povoor Mangalam had been one of them. They hadn't noticed Philomena. Some travel allowance had been sanctioned and they had come to collect it.

In general Rajamanickam didn't give much respect to people. And that too when he was in his seat – why, he wouldn't even respect the commissioner then. Why would he? After all, he was the one who doled out money to everyone. Would he then respect these petty maternity assistants? When they had asked him for money, he had said, 'Later.' An assistant, who had joined in the conversation just then, had asked, 'Have you got the money?' To which Povoor Mangalam had replied, 'That low-caste fellow! Will he take out the money that quickly? It's his father's property, no?' They had sniggered covertly.

When Philomena had heard this, her face had turned red at once. 'Speak respectfully, di. Are you paying his salary for him to give you money as soon as you wish?' They had been shocked to see Philomena there. Even so, Mangalam wasn't a lightweight. Not for nothing she had earned the nickname Povoor Rowdy. She snacked on quarrels and brawls. She wasn't one to give in easily. She had said belligerently, 'No big deal. Even he, behind our backs, refers to us by saying, "call that thing, call this thing".'

A heated row had erupted. Hearing about it, Rajamanickam had rushed in. Without even enquiring about what had happened, he had burst out, 'Just knock her and give her a kick. All that rowdy title will fly away.' On hearing this, everyone had stood aghast. But Mangalam strode forward defiantly, 'Come on, da, just kick me. Let us see, da.'

Some women flashed this as a trump card. If you confront a man with a 'da', and also say, 'Come, da, hit me,' it was certainly a downright insult. Besides, they also knew that no one would really hit a woman because the very next day there would be four people to say, 'Whatever it may be, how can you hit a woman, no?' Most men would be aghast at such situations. Fuming, they would feel like doing something drastic, like drinking off their blood. But they couldn't do a thing.

When she had said that, Rajamanickam too had felt much the same for an instant. But the next moment he had recovered himself. The shame he would endure after hitting her would be no less than the humiliation of letting her off now. 'What will you do, di?' he had said, giving her a tight slap across her cheek.

Mangalam hadn't really expected this. For a moment she had been shell-shocked. But soon she had smeared both him and the entire office with filthy gutter language. 'Dei, you beat me, is it? Wait and see – I'll ask my brothers to break your arm. I'll complain to the police and break your knees.' She had spat out the choicest of lewd abuse.

To stop her, he had tried to hit her again. But the others had separated them somehow. The matter had been taken to the level of the commissioner, who, wanting to save the reputation of the office, had requested her not to go the police. The whole thing had ended with their being summoned to his room and being made to apologise to each other.

Recalling the harshness on Philomena's face throughout the incident, Krishnan looked at her, overcome by an urge to compare it with her present expression. By chance Philomena lifted up her head and caught him gazing at her. She asked, 'What are you looking at, saar?'

'Nothing,' he said, and went back to his work.

It was about three in the afternoon. The whole office was abuzz. Everyone slowly gathered outside the chairman's room. Except Philomena, who was sniffling, slumped over her typewriter. Rajamanickam could be heard shouting inside the chairman's office. Since the chairman spoke in a low tone, no one understood what the matter was. Besides, the chairman's clerk, Vedanayagam, stood outside the room and kept them at bay, saying, 'Don't crowd around!'

At one stage, Rajamanickam shouted. 'You should have at least remembered that she is my wife.' The chairman's loud reply too could be clearly heard, 'That's why she's been let off this easily. Otherwise, for what all she said, something else ought to have happened.' Then, heated challenges: 'I'll see to it.' 'Okay, see to it.'

His face was red when he came out. Muttering, 'Just because they got a few votes, they think they can speak whatever they want. Let him try all this with someone else,' he went to his room. In a while, the chairman sent for the manager.

They came to the bus stop at around six. They had met the commissioner – who had been out of town – at his residence and explained their version of the incident.

The bus was empty, as if to compensate for all the jostling and the standing that the passengers had to undergo in the morning. There were only four or five people inside. Both of them got in and sat down in a seat. When they reached their town, they walked together, as they did in the morning. They unlocked their door.

As the lock was undone, so too the contract of the morning. He took off his shirt, washed his face, doused half a tin of talcum powder on his body and came and stood menacingly on the threshold, arms akimbo, as if ready to hit anyone who came by. Then he paced up and down. She, without even changing her sari, went straight to the easy chair and closed her eyes. The two of them didn't speak a word for a long time. Between them there was not even the bond that would have normally resulted between two people who had battled a common enemy.

After half an hour the girl who delivered milk for them left the milk. It lay untouched for fifteen minutes.

He finally came in and asked her, looking elsewhere, 'Aren't you going to cook?'

She, without even opening her eyes, said, 'Yes, I'll cook.'

He looked at the clock and asked, 'When are you going to cook? And when are we going to eat?'

She said with the same listlessness, 'What am I to do? Are my arms and legs made of iron or what?'

His face tightened and he once again paced up and down.

After about ten minutes, she went towards the kitchen. She lit the stove, pumped it and placed the milk vessel on it. When the milk was done, she took it off and put the rice pot to boil. She started washing the rice. He came and stood there, expecting a cup of coffee. She continued to wash the rice and said, 'The milk is done. Make yourself some with Bru.' With a grimace he poured out a tumbler of milk and searched for sugar and coffee.

When she put the rice into the pot, she poured out a tumbler of milk and walked towards the entrance. He stood behind her, glaring, as if contemplating whether to punch her or hack her. He couldn't stop her. Earlier, he had tried once or twice, but it had only resulted in a crowd gathering outside his house.

Down the road, three houses away, her elder sister lived. She was sickly and had been recently hospitalised for a month. Her husband was managing with hotel food. She only took on the responsibility of giving him a tumbler of milk every night.

He had once shouted, 'Why can't you send it through someone?' To which she had shouted back, 'If I go, I will ask a couple of questions after my sister – Did you go and see her? How is she?'

She came back after fifteen minutes. Till then he sat spluttering like a rice grain on a hot pan. As she turned into the kitchen, he asked, 'Have you finished cooing with your secret husband?'

She turned around, deliberated for a minute and burst out with suppressed anger, insulting him by his caste name, 'Yes, da, you… fellow!' She found out recently that this was a strong weapon to deal him a severe blow.

He wasn't one to believe that there was no caste, nor was he one to raise his voice to pronounce that his caste was inferior to none. He believed that it was enough to hide under the shadow of something. That was why he had changed his given name Andi and called himself Rajamanickam. Later when he had had to change his religion for her sake, he had been immensely glad that he had found a permanent solution to his caste problem. That he was fair like one from the Reddiar caste pleased him and rankled him all at once. Whenever he met any relative who reminded him of his past, he was irritated. During a quarrel with him the previous week, it had suddenly occurred to her how he would feel if he were to be called by his old caste name, and that too by her. She had tried it out and had also scented victory.

He jumped up, pounced on her, grasped her hair and slapped her with his right hand. 'Do you dare to say it!'

She bore the slap that made blood rush into her face, lifted her head and looked at him straight. His face had reddened, betraying him. She knew that her blow too was not an ordinary one. So she used the same weapon again and said firmly and clearly, 'You… fellow!'

He pressed her head down and hit her on the back even more fiercely. 'Will you say it?'

'… fellow!'

He punched her.

'… fellow!'

He pulled her hair and jerked her around violently. He beat her again and again. With every punch, she steadfastly insulted him with the same word. This war of blows and words lasted for a few minutes. But it looked as if she wasn't intending to lose, come what may. Her voice rose, matching his every blow. In the end, he was the one who was frightened. There was no point anymore. She would bring the entire town and tell them everything. So, he retreated from the battlefield, pushed her into a corner and stood glaring at her. She staggered and collapsed on the floor. Yet, she managed to sit up and said once again, raising her head, '…fellow!' He wanted to run and trample upon her. But, as if someone had cautioned him that there was no point to all this, he suppressed himself and said, 'You wait and see. I'll deal with you in two days.' He went to the chair and sat in it for a long time.

After a while, she lay down in the same place. Her whole body hurt like a blistering wound. But that she wasn't the only one who got beaten up comforted her, like a cool poultice. The tears that hadn't flowed in this fight now drenched the floor.

The place was full of mosquitoes. As the thoughts of this incident gnawed their brains, the mosquitoes sucked their bodies. He got up and came to the kitchen. The stove with the rice pot had gone out on its own. He drank a tumbler of water, spread out the mattress, hung up the mosquito net and lay down.

For a long, long time, she couldn't sleep. Even when she thought that it could be one or two in the morning, she couldn't get sleep. Even when the thoughts of the incident faded away, interrupted by ordinary thoughts, she couldn't fall asleep. What the chairman asked and what happened thereafter came to mind. So did tomorrow's chores. And the abortion of the previous year. Everything came, but sleep never did. Now, even more than the blows, was the agony of sleeplessness. Along with several thoughts, the thought of sex too fleeted by. She was irritated with herself: 'That thing? After all this? And with him?' She firmly decided never to indulge in it, even if she had to die. But that such earlier resolutions had got broken too filled her mind. Even at times when rage and hatred had bubbled within them, and when the dying cinders had still smouldered, they had come together as man and wife in the nights as well. Even now it was a surprise to her that all this still happened. But now, some dim answer to that seemed to emerge faintly. At last her eyes slowly drooped.

However well you tie a mosquito net, a couple of mosquitoes always manage to slip in. Two mosquitoes which had flitted here and there peacefully settled on her body when she fell asleep.

Now they would suck blood, little by little. Only after that they would realise that there was no way out. Then they would bang themselves on the walls of the net. Finally, they would try to gnaw a corner on the top. Till the net was rolled up in the morning, they would be perched there, in penance, contemplating freedom.

Original title: *Pagal Uravugal*
1977

Mouse 52

Maa Aranganathan

When a life belonging to the species Homo sapiens passed away and was taken to the cremation ground, it was found that it wasn't a natural death but a murder. On his way back after the cremation, he felt nauseous. Not because he had seen a murdered body, but that such a raw instinct could have sprung in the mind of this species disgusted him.

But one ought not to harbour such ideas – he had been told that one ought to go along with the world; hence his strides hastened and he reached home quickly.

When he washed his feet and sat, as usual, on the easy chair, it jumped and ran across his feet. His wife appeared. It must have been chased away from the kitchen. She had a winnowing tray in hand. It was on the tip of his tongue to utter, 'Don't hit it.' But fortunately, he didn't.

After retirement, one couldn't order her about like this. He'd already been crowned 'the smart one'. But that was convenient too. No one asked him to do any chores for the house. It was also believed that sub-standard cloth and old vegetables in the shops waited only for him.

The mouse damages books, and clothes get spoilt too. It requires courage to tell one not to hit it. But the mouse is courageous. It doesn't do anything unjust. Even if you hit it, it only keeps doing what it knows.

Other than the fact that he had retired from government service, there wasn't much difference between Muthukaruppan and the mouse. When it jumped over the newly bought TV set and climbed into the loft, the chaos would begin in seconds. No one would tolerate books in the loft being nibbled at daily. Forget books, if it nibbled away newspaper, it would be a problem to get it weighed and sold. When wife and children got up on chairs and tried to thrash it with whatever they could lay their hands on, there would be silence for a few moments.

Perhaps Muthukaruppan knew where violence began. And knew that its extreme state was murder. Perhaps he also understood the hypocritical approach to life that fear begets. He considered more violent what is preached in religious discourses – that each one ought to do one's duty and get enlightened. More than war, he considered the voice of moral pontification more violent.

All this is total pretence – the mouse should not be killed.

Muthukaruppan's daughter got a call for a job. Surprisingly, his wife said, 'Go with her.' There was a reason. The company's manager was Muthukaruppan's childhood friend. His word would carry weight. True. They both were friends, so he had to go.

His outings had decreased after retirement. Once in a while he would meet former colleagues in his old office. When they were busy at work, a retired man's visit was always bothersome. It was a chore to feign small talk and smiles. A waste of time. Totally false and irritating. It was all fake, including meeting friends.

Filled with such thoughts, how could one lead a life? Thoughts were hindrances. Could we go along without the question, 'What do you want?'…

Yes, we could go along. But everyone else had to go along too. If not, it would be better if we went along, leaving them behind. We could go into forests, eat leaves and watch nature, like the Siddhars. This kind of violence would never do.

When he had visited the fair the previous year, he had bought a tricycle for the child. The acquaintances he had met there, the wonderment he had felt at the strange things he saw there, the hatred he had felt for the people queuing up for the bus on his return… was all this violence or madness, he had wondered when he had come home. The only meaningful thing that had happened that day was the tricycle. So, with great difficulty, he had sat on the tricycle and tried to ride it. When his wife had said, 'What is all this drama?' he had felt, 'This? A drama?'

When hypocrisy is twisted into intelligent code of conduct – that is where all violence begins, felt Muthukaruppan. Or was this too natural?

But he didn't know what was natural. The daughter attending the interview was also a 'natural' member of the Homo sapiens.

Muthukaruppan started after drinking water. They had to take the electric train.

A train was not like a bus. The journey was much easier. You could befriend other passengers. If you got used to them, they would become family. Even in the electric train, there could be mice scampering around.

He remembered that it was the week of the Vinayaka Chaturti festival. In the train, a few of them had mud figurines of Lord Vinayaka. A retired friend of his would say that it was wrong to conclude that Saint Paranjothi Nayanar was the one who brought Vinayaka to these parts. The temple in Vallam existed even before Paranjothi. Muthukaruppan had a poor knowledge of Tamil history. So he asked if there was also the mouse with the Vinayaka in Vallam. A silly question, remarked his friend.

He would have had to get down at Mambalam, reach the once-familiar Thiuvallikeni by bus, wait for the interview at the multi-storey building on the main road, wipe his sweat off and meet the office manager. In between, he would have to encounter the hateful gaze of the other applicants. Would the manager greet him with a 'hello'? Before that he would have to plead with the receptionist. To plead for one's self too was violence.

As he climbed the stairs, he saw colourful posters pasted on the walls. Red posters – blood red. Pictures of rats and insects – advertisements of the company's pesticide products.

The wordings of the posters:

'Kill!'

'Kill instantly!'

'It's dangerous – kill it today.'

Muthukaruppan felt like vomiting. Looking at his face, his daughter asked, 'What's wrong, Appa?' She knew that she couldn't change her father's views on certain matters. Wiping his face, he said that he would not see the manager. Since many people were around, his daughter didn't say anything. She knew now that she wasn't going to get any help from her father.

'I will wait down,' he gestured and ran down. The street was crowded. Standing in a corner, he saw coming from afar a big Vinayaka, followed by many small statues.

It was a mammoth statue. At the foot of Vinayaka, a big mouse. With its tail twirled upwards, it was biting on a modakam – it looked very happy.

He wiped his face. As his anxiety ebbed away, he walked along with the crowd to the corner of the Thiruvallikeni High Road. Nearby there was a beautiful mosque. There was a crowd there too.

He got trapped in the crowd.

Original title: *Eli*
1990

THRILLS 53

C R RAVEENDRAN

The moon was fading away behind the row of cupolas on the temple top. Seated on the platform of the temple yard, Sambu looked at it raptly, leaning against the northern wall of the Pillayar shrine, his left leg stretched out and the right folded. He found this relaxed posture very comfortable. Nearby a few vagabonds were curled up haphazardly, snoring away.

'Amma! O Mother! Amma…O Mother…'

He turned around. A man was babbling in his sleep. He laughed to himself, and fished out a smooth bottle tucked away under his banian. He lifted it to the light and found that there was half a bottle of arrack still remaining. He unscrewed the bottle, looked around and gulped down mouthfuls. His face contorted. He cleared his throat, closed the bottle and tucked it back inside the banian. He felt like eating a poovan banana. He got down slowly, groped for his slippers. He felt as if he was walking on air.

A few donkeys ran screaming around the sacred Garuda column. The donkey in front ran kicking its hind legs. Another who chased it was kicked on the face. The rest of the donkeys followed, shaking their tails. He laughed aloud derisively. They are right when they say 'a donkey's orchestra', he said to himself and walked towards the tea stall. He could see the people laughing in the stall.

At the south-east corner of the temple yard, Kuttappan had a tea stall, always open. In the nights, Kuttappan himself manned the stall because business was brisker then. There were two more such stalls, but this one was always bustling. Besides, people could always rest a bit here. The ones who played cards trickled in even after one in the morning. The ones who couldn't get sleep found it convenient to stop by for tea here and talk about this and that. Drivers waited around here for the 'women' to return from their business. A few pimps often stayed awake right through the night. For all this, the stall was only a thatched hut.

When he neared the stall, Sambu saw that the official's son was there too. His transistor on the table was spluttering out a song in a low volume. A few sat gossiping. He walked, staggering a bit. The Petromax lamp blinded his eyes. His legs gave way in front of the shop, but he managed to straighten himself.

'Some bastard has thrown a banana peel on the pathway. Dei, Kuttappa, couldn't you have asked that motherfucker to throw it aside?' shouted Sambu irritatedly as he entered the shop.

'What can anybody do? You only must walk carefully, saar,' Kuttappan said with a smile.

'You Malayali bastard. What cheek!'

Kuttappan stood silently by the boiler. Sambu's eyes had reddened. He looked around. He couldn't make out any face clearly. The people in the shop looked at him warily.

'Where's the official's son?' asked Sambu, looking around.

'The fellow is sleeping there,' said Kuttappan in Malayalam. He pointed to the chair in the corner, where the official's son slept huddled in a black blanket.

Sambu cleared his throat and said, 'Lucky prince! He's sleeping.' He pouted his lips.

He moved slowly towards the showcase. It was open. There were packets of mixture on the top shelf, varki biscuits and coconut buns in the second one and murukkus strewn carelessly in the third. A bunch of bananas hung from the thatched roof.

'How much for a fruit?' Sambu asked, plucking one.

'Twelve paise, saarey.'

'Hei… go, da. Ten paise. Will you dare ask more?'

'No, saarey. Whatever you give is okay.'

'Mmm... Good, you've come around. If you argue...' Swallowing the fruit, he mimed, as if squeezing his throat.

Kuttappan never got angry with him. He got a lot of things done out of Sambu. If he needed ten or twenty in a crunch, Sambu was the one who gave him.

Sambu plucked two more bananas. He peeled one and threw the skin away carelessly. Four or five people left the shop. The last settled the bill with Kuttappan. Sambu broke the banana, popped it into his mouth and sat on the bench.

On the bench opposite him sat Broker Raman. He slept leaning back, hands on his thighs. His lips were slightly parted. He was wearing a head-cloth. At the end of the bench slept Saamiyar, head bent over the table. He too was a broker. Everyone knew him only by the name Saamiyar. A few people were on the chairs outside, some smoking beedis, some cigarettes. They chatted in low tones.

Sambu felt like smoking a cigarette. Pushing his veshti aside, he took out a crumpled cigarette from the pocket of his underwear. He had just one cigarette left. He threw the empty pack outside.

'Dei, Kuttappa, give me a light,' he said, taking out the bottle from his banian. Kuttappa brought the light in an iron ladle from the boiler.

'Here! Keep this safely. Give it to me when I ask.' Kuttappan took the bottle, while Sambu stretched out his hand to take the light.

'No, saarey. Let me light it myself.'

'The motherfucker wants to light my pyre while I'm still alive. Okay, da, even when I die, you only light my pyre.'

He tucked the cigarette between his lips, and as Kuttappan lit it, he started puffing it.

'Enough, saarey?'

'Mmm, mmm...' He gestured to him to move away.

He perched his head on his knee and puffed away.

After a while, a taxi entered the yard. Kuttappan shook Broker Raman awake. 'Ramu... Taxi has come... taxi has come... Ramu...'

Raman woke up with a start, rubbed his eyes and looked towards the yard. The taxi was faintly visible; tying his veshti, he ran towards it. He had a word with the driver, got into the taxi and sped away. 'That man is in great demand,' Kuttappan griped.

In a few minutes six or seven people came from the eastern side. Alumilaan came inside and asked for six strong teas and one milk tea. Kuttappan gave them a murukku each and started preparing the tea. Munching, they spoke about spades, clovers, jack and queen. Kuttappan served them tea and Alumilaan settled the bill.

Just then an auto stopped in front of the stall. There was no one inside. The driver got down and sat on the bench. Kuttappan looked at him enquiringly.

'One coconut bun, two varkis and a light tea,' he ordered hastily.

Kuttappan brought a coconut bun and the varkis in a piece of paper. The driver munched on the varki noisily.

Hands folded across his chest, head bent, Ardhanari strode in from the direction of the temple car. Looking around, he said, 'What, Kuttappa? Who is this? Sambu? Why is he lying here today?' He shook Sambu, who was lying face down.

'Who is this motherfucker?' groaned Sambu. When he saw it was Ardhanari, he was overjoyed.

'Come, come, Maapillai! Do you have Apollo?' He stretched his hand towards Ardhanari's pocket.

'One rupee a shot. Can you give it?'

'Hm...hm... What one rupee. Take how much ever you want. Today only I got the money from the jaggery merchant.' He pushed aside the fold of his veshti, took out the money from his drawers and threw the notes on the table.

'I simply said, da. Here, take it,' said Ardhanari and gave the cigarette. Sambu inspected it; it was slightly short and an edge was folded.

'What, da? Have you filled it properly?'

'Ada, I filled it for myself!'

'Then give me the match.'

'Wait, da. Let me light it for you.'

'Do it fast, you motherfucker.'

Ardhanari lit the cigarette and Sambu took a puff hungrily.

'Dei, Kuttappa! Two hot milks with extra sugar,' Sambu ordered. Then putting the cigarette between his index finger and the middle one, he circled it with his thumb and took a puff. He felt as if he was floating in the skies.

'Here take this, da.' Ardhanari took out two orange candies from his pocket.

Sambu munched on the candies and took another puff. Kuttappan brought two foaming tumblers of milk and left them on the table.

'Here, da, you too take a puff,' said Sambu, passing him the cigarette. While Ardhanari smoked, Sambu drank the milk.

Taking the cigarette back from Ardhanari, Sambu blabbered, 'Apollo means Apollo! Nothing to beat it. I feel as if I'm flying.'

'I'll give an even better one tomorrow,' Ardhanari said, pampering him. He too drank the milk.

'Give me another one now.'

'I don't have, da. All over.' He said loudly, walking looking towards the north. 'Dei, Kannamma is coming.'

'Go da, let her be.'

'Why, da?'

'How many times will I sleep with that dark one?'

'If you don't have anything, even she will seem great.'

'Anyone new, da?'

'I believe there are four or five new ones in Pandu's "company". Kittan mentioned it in the evening.'

They fell silent as Kannamma entered the shop. Though dark, she had a great figure. She gave a flask to Kuttappan and asked for two teas. A few left the shop. Sambu and Ardhanari stared at her as if they would gobble her up. The pottu on the forehead was smudged and her faded green voile sari was crumpled. Her face was oily. Her tousled hair fell on her forehead.

'Ennadi Rakamma, Pallakku nadipu, en nenju kulungudadi – What, di, Rakamma, you're swaying like a palanquin, and my heart is thumping and jumping,' Sambu sang the popular Tamil song out of tune.

'What, 'ya, singing lustily and all?' Kannamma placed her hand on her forehead, to shield herself from the glare from the Petromax lamp.

'Who is to ask? I will sing as I please.'

'But who is to listen if you shout like this?'

'Ei, di? Is my singing like shouting?'

'Just ask four people how it sounds.'

'Just go, di. As if you're a great thing!'

'It's not your fault. It's all the fault of money.'

Kuttappan gave her the flask. She gave him eight annas and turned around.

'Why, di, who did you trap today? Jumping like this!'

'Get lost.'

'Wait, I'm coming.'

'Come, come there. And you can see it all.'

She started. The hooks of her bra peeped out from beneath her blouse.

Sambu gossiped about Kannamma for a while. Ardhanari left, saying that he was sleepy. Sambu took back the notes from the table and tucked it back into his underwear.

For a while now a desire dangled in his brain. Today it dangled even more fiercely. 'Today, somehow,' he kept telling himself from time to time. He kept thinking of Thangammal's daughter Parameswari. Parameswari was really fair, with a smooth and sculpted figure. Round face and a sharp nose. Any colour pottu on her perfect forehead looked good. She studied in college. Every morning he tailed her till she got into a bus. He unfailingly waited at the bus stop in the evenings. Whenever he saw her he eyed her lustily. Every day she came to the tank to bathe. He always tried to chat her up but she ignored him. Some days she would bring a bundle of clothes and wash them for a long time. At those times he enjoyed more than an eyeful. He relished her from the temple mandapam. He would climb up and down the tank steps to distract her, and sometimes even bathe in the river for a long time. He would circumambulate the Pillayar temple again and again. She never came alone, but always with her neighbour Radha, a small girl. When Parameswari readied herself to go home, rubbing her feet one after the other on the last step, he would stand mesmerised.

That day his frenzy heightened. His pocket too was heavy.

'Dei, Kuttappa, give me a beedi, da,' he asked, lifting his head.

Kuttappan placed a roll of beedis and a matchbox on the table and went back to the boiler.

'Where did you get the matchbox, da?'

'It was lying there.'

'Wonder who left it behind.' Sambu lit the beedi and smoked it.

Raman came hurriedly to the stall and asked for four strong teas. He said he had booked a room in Murugan Lodge for the men who brought 'goods' from the city. Kuttappan brought the teas in a metal carrier. Raman also asked him to pack eight buns. He handed him a five rupee note and said that he would collect the change later. He rushed back.

'I must have her today, that sisterfucker. Whatever it takes. Otherwise I don't deserve to be called a man,' he mumbled, looking at the thatched roof.

'How will you make it happen?' Kuttappan asked him in Malayalam.

'What is it to you, da? I will finish and come and tell you,' he said, lighting another beedi.

'Saarey, Thangammal herself is coming.'

Puffing away, Sambu turned around. He could make out someone approaching from the temple-car side. He realised it was Thangammal. He felt a little elated. He had been hesitant to go to her house.

Thangammal was a little portly. She walked in jauntily, but he could make out that she had difficulty in walking. She had wrapped her sari around her shoulder. She was fair, with a shiny, smooth face. She had black rings around her eyes. She had a big pottu in the centre of her forehead, just above her eyebrows. It glistened in the light of the Petromax lamp. The dog which accompanied her wagged its tail.

'What akka, at this time of the hour?' asked Sambu, coming outside.

'Just came to drink tea.'

'Why? Where has Sada gone?'

'I asked him to go to town. The fellow hasn't come back. Why don't you too have tea, thambi?'

'No, akka, I just drank.'

'Never mind, drink one more. Here, two strong teas with extra sugar.'

Kuttappan started washing the glass tumblers. The dog circled Thangammal.

'Kuttappa, bring two murukkus.'

He took out two from the display shelf. Taking it, she said, 'Give two to thambi too.' She broke one and fed the dog and ate the other.

'Don't want. I feel uneasy.' Sambu asked Kuttappan to take back the murukkus.

In a while Kuttappan brought the teas which they drank silently.

'What, thambi? It is so late. Why aren't you asleep?'

'Where do I get sleep, akka?'

Thangammal sighed. 'Kuttappa, how much?' she asked, taking out her drawstring bag.

'No, akka. You don't give. Kuttappa, put it into my account.'

Thangammal didn't demur. 'What, thambi, shall we go?'

'Why? Have you got new "goods" today?'

'Nothing, saami. That's why I sent that fellow. God knows what happened. Come, let's chat for a while. I also can't get sleep.'

'Dei, Kuttappa, I'm leaving.' Sambu staggered behind her, but he hadn't lost his mind.

The two of them walked back, chatting. The dog followed them. She complained about the police interference. She spoke enviously of Pandu and the way he conducted the Mariamman festival. She also mentioned her own inability to contribute to all this. They crossed the temple-car and went towards the temple tank.

There was a broken statue of a Nandi on the north-west side of the tank. The dog ran towards it. As they neared Mani Iyer's house, two bandicoots ran across, one after the other. Pigs grunted near the Saraswathi School.

The two of them entered a lane and stopped in front of a tiled house. A mat was spread on the pial; Thangammal pulled it and asked him to sit down. Leaning his left shoulder on the pial's pillar, he swung his legs down. Thangammal sat beside him. He asked for betel leaves. The door creaked as she went in.

Thangammal came back with a plate and sat near him. His right thigh rubbed against her left side. They folded the betel leaves.

It looked as if someone was going down the steps of the house. She turned around. It was Parameswari. Beaming the torch, she went behind the house. They munched on the betel leaves.

She asked him about his fields and lands. He answered measuredly. Parameswari went back into the house. Sambu eyed her in the dark.

'Why, thambi, why don't you get married and settle down? How long will you roam around like this?'

'Who will give me a girl, akka? My uncle is tired searching around for me. Even if someone comes forward I believe they say, "To that fellow? It's better to push her into the well".' He spat out the betel.

'No girl in your family circle?'

'Go, akka. What family? What relatives?'

'What, thambi? How will anyone give a girl if you keep roaming like this and all?'

'As if the others didn't play around. My mother has loads of tales to tell.'

She got down, spat out, came back and sat on the opposite pial. Both of them remained quiet for a long time.

'What, akka? So nothing for me?'

'No, saami. If I have, will I say no to you?'

'Akka?'

'What, thambi?'

'Nothing…'

'Just tell me!'

'If I tell you something, you won't get angry, no?'

She was pensive for a while. 'What is there between us? Tell me.'

'No...but...'

'Go on, just tell me.'

'Just for today... Parameswari... I have more than two hundred rupees. He mumbled hesitantly. Stung, she fell silent.

'Thambi, I'll tell you something. Will you listen?'

He felt encouraged. 'Just tell me, akka.'

'If I tell you...'

'Just tell me, akka. What is there between us?'

'I'm a sullied, shattered woman. Somehow with great difficulty I have managed to educate my daughter. I want to get her married off to someone far away. I have brought her up well till now without a blemish.' She spat out the betel leaf and continued, 'So, let's go to a temple. I will marry her off to you itself. You will also mend your ways. Then why do I need this profession, thambi? I will stay with you all and eat some gruel. That's enough till I die. What do you say, thambi?'

Thangammal lifted her head. He was already at the end of the street. She felt something slurping against her leg. She bent down. Only to see her dog licking her leg. 'Chee...' she kicked her leg. The dog whimpered and fled.

Original title: *Silirppugal*
1974

Daily, a Pandian Express 54

Gandharvan

When he heard the knock on the door, Annachi, half asleep, called out, 'Mani, think the train has arrived. See who it is.'

Mani, who was sleeping bare-bodied on the verandah, wrapped the lungi tightly up to his chest and opened the door. A middle-aged man, bag in hand, stood at the door. The day had almost dawned.

'Has the Pandian Express arrived?' Mani asked the man. As the man nodded 'yes', Mani opened the door. Mani had never seen him before. Even so, those who visited this house usually came by the Pandian. Those who came to Chennai from Annachi's town usually preferred the Pandian. It was convenient too.

On the man's face was worry and anxiety, and on his veshti and shirt, travel creases. 'Is Annachi there?' he asked fretfully. Mani replied, yawning, 'Don't worry. Annachi's here only. Sleeping.'

The visitor entered carefully. Colourful photographs on all the walls. In every one of them leaders, from those of yesteryears to ministers of today, stood with arms around Annachi's shoulders. In one of them Annachi was draping a ponnadai, the customary zari shawl, on a minister. In another a minister himself was garlanding Annachi.

The citations – almost the height of a man – awarded to Annachi hung on the walls in gold letters in glittering frames the size of a span. To the visitor, who looked at them intently in the quiet of the dawn, it appeared that all that was said about Annachi back home was true. A twinge of fear entered the respect he already had. Satisfied, he entered Annachi's room.

Annachi was an old hand at politics. Whichever party he was in, he had his men in plenty. There were crowds of men of his caste and clusters of villages willing to listen to him. The fishing rod in his hand may change, but the hook never did. He ought to have been an MLA or a minister ages ago.

Mani used to say, 'Annachi is a smart man. But doesn't know how to cleverly hold on to what he grasps. If a group is on the rise, you should run and stand in front, isn't it, be it gain or loss? But by the time Annachi slowly makes his way, the one before him will run to Annachi and tell him that he can become an MLA or a minister only with his help. Annachi still stands in the same place proudly.'

But west of Madurai it was believed that if you wanted anything done in Madras, it would be accomplished if you saw Annachi. That MLAs and ministers would never fail to heed Annachi's words was a deep-rooted belief among the bigwigs in that region.

When Annachi was practising politics from Madurai, he would come seven-eight times a month to Madras with someone or the other to get various things done for them through ministers. Coming to Madurai from his town, catching a train from Madurai to Madras, staying oftentimes in a lodge for a week or two, then going back home – at some stage all this became tiresome for Annachi. He took a house in Madras and remained there. With Mani as help.

He left his family behind in the village itself. A wife and kids around him wouldn't work with Annachi's ways. He restricted himself to sending money and visiting them once in a while.

Back home, when he had had influence and was deep in politics, his followers and caste men called him, 'Annen, Annen,' as they were wont to do with all political leaders. Once a witless fellow had audaciously addressed him as 'Annen' in front of everyone. Annachi had fumed and fumed and spluttered, 'Look here, all those fellows wandering around with round-round faces, same moustaches, same towels, and all looking like each other – go and call them Annen-Ennen. I'm not that kind of fellow. If you want to address me, call me “Annachi” respectfully and sweetly. Only that sounds nice.’ After that, everyone – including those at the top – initially fumbled a bit and started addressing him as ‘Annachi’. For the new acquaintances it was the name Annachi they knew him by.

The visitor came and sat beside Annachi’s bed. By now Mani had tied his lungi properly and put on a shirt. Annachi was awake but lay without opening his eyes. He was happy. The day had dawned well. The Pandian Express which had left Madurai the previous day had brought with it his share of men, as it usually did. Blissfully satisfied, he tried to open his eyes. But he couldn’t open them immediately. His eyes burned a lot. He opened his eyes with difficulty.

The visitor folded both hands and greeted Annachi. Annachi responded with his hands half-folded and said, ‘Ade! Is it Kasi? What brings you this far?’ He couldn’t bear the irritation in his eyes. Before the visitor could reply, he said, ‘Mani, bring a small pot of water.’ One had also to show that one was not overly excited by a visitor.

Kasi slowly started talking about his business. Annachi washed and wiped his face as he listened. ‘Mani, buy three coffees. We have a rare visitor from so far away.’ Mani came with a flask. When Annachi got up to fetch money, Kasi quickly held down Annachi and took out a five-rupee note from his pocket and gave it to Mani. When Mani left, Kasi started to talk about his business in detail.

Mani poured out the coffee and gave it to the two of them. After hearing him out while drinking the coffee, Annachi said, ‘It looks as if this must be attended to immediately. You ought to have come ten days earlier, Kasi. Our people never think of being alert as soon as they see a knife. Only when it touches their throat do they think of Annachi. Okay, okay, we’ll see the minister and ask him to call the collector.’

‘It’s to Annachi I’ve come. If I go back empty-handed, I cannot walk the streets with an upper cloth on my shoulder.’

‘Yes, yes, you’ve told me everything. Okay, get started. We’ll see the minister in his residence itself. You must bathe and get ready in half an hour.’

Kasi felt as if he had accomplished half the task. He got up and hurriedly went about his morning chores. Annachi’s eyes were still smarting. Brushing his teeth, he called out, ‘Mani, have to start to see the minister. See if a fresh veshti and shirt are there.’

Mani opened a box and came back with a chit. Kasi stood, freshly bathed, a wet towel around him.

Mani said, 'I'll get the "urgent" laundry I gave day before yesterday.' Brush in hand, Annachi went to take out money from the box. Kasi stopped him saying, 'Let it be,' and grabbed the laundry chit and took out twelve rupees.

In half an hour Annachi was at the door in a waft of fragrance, terry-cot veshti, cream silk jibba, powdered face and all. On the shoulder, a long white towel. A big diary in hand. Tucked inside it innumerable folded sheets of paper. Running hither and thither, Mani too readied himself, and was soon looking tip-top. Kasi carefully took out the records from the bag, put them in a plastic cover and came out.

Mani ran, fetched a taxi and opened the front door. Flinging his arm on the back of the seat and drumming his fingers, Annachi sat nonchalantly, as if he were the owner of a thousand cars. Kasi and Mani sat at the back.

Annachi told the taxi driver, 'Go to Udupi restaurant.'

Mani added, 'We have to go to the minister's house and all after eating. Till the evening we'll be using your taxi only.'

Sitting beside Annachi and eating his tiffin, Kasi continued to sketch out his business more and more. Annachi listened to him as he watched Mani, who sat opposite him, busy polishing off more than four plates.

When the bill arrived on the plate, Kasi took out the notes automatically, like a machine, and ran to the taxi, matching Annachi's pace.

The minister's compound looked like a huge playground. Taxis, cars and autos stood as if for a royal event. Kasi was slightly jittery but happy too. He thought, 'If I didn't have a man like Annachi, would it be possible for me to see the minister, competing with so many people?'

Kasi was proud that Annachi's jibba, veshti and demeanour matched those of the men who came there. He thought that he ought to honour Annachi in a big way the next time he came to their village.

Crossing the PA, the officials and the VIPs seated on sofas and benches, Annachi stood in front of the minister's room. That the PA, peon and the servant greeted Annachi transported Kasi to heaven. After the minister sat down, Annachi entered the room with Kasi after four-five men.

The minister looked at Annachi and greeted him with folded hands. Annachi greeted him even more respectfully, sat down in front of him and quickly started discussing, as if with a friend, his town's affairs, the minister's tour programmes and the minister's statement which appeared in the previous day's papers.

In the end, he also quickly summarised Kasi's problem.

'I must talk to the collector. That's all, no. I will do it,' said the minister. When Kasi got a bit emotional and suddenly tried to impress his problems directly on the minister, Annachi hushed him, 'I finished telling, no. And the minister too has promised to speak to the collector. Then why again?' Annachi turned to the minister and said, 'Our town-folk are only half interested in getting the work done. They are more interested in explaining to the minister from beginning to end. Total tactless fellows! Okay, I'll take leave.' He folded his hands reverently and led Kasi out. All in five minutes.

Kasi thought to himself, 'Annachi is really smart. He knows fully well how important time is to a minister and how much work he has. He conducts himself according to that. Otherwise can he come and go frequently like this, as he pleases?'

Annachi explained in detail to the PA all that he had spoken to the minister.

'Kasi, briefly write all the particulars and give it to saar,' he said. Kasi carefully consulted the records, wrote them down and gave it to the PA. With pleasing smiles and folded hands, Annachi took leave of the PA, peon and the servant and came outside.

Many taxi drivers got out and greeted Annachi respectfully with folded hands. Annachi responded casually, scarcely lifting and putting down his hands in quick succession, and got into the taxi.

The day was heating up. Annachi's jibba was drenched with sweat, sticking to his body here and there. He asked the taxi to halt near a petty shop. Mani ran and fetched two full glasses of soda, lime and salt for Annachi and Kasi. Taking the soda with one hand, Kasi took out the money from his pocket with the other and gave it to Mani.

Annachi asked for the taxi to be driven to Beach Road. He went to the fort and met several people. He stopped in several places and spoke to people. Then he went to four or five offices in Chepauk. And to two offices in Mount Road.

Wherever they went, before Annachi could put his hand in his jibba pocket, Kasi kept shelling out fives, tens, fifties and hundreds, as befitting the face and status of each one. Annachi's sweat only increased. Twice he handed the diary to Kasi and wrung out the small towel.

When it struck two in the afternoon, Annachi ordered the taxi to be driven home. When he got down, Annachi started pulling off his jibba in the verandah itself. Tying a lungi, he took off his veshti. Kasi took out big, big notes and settled the bill of the taxi which had taken them around the town since morning.

As he entered, Annachi said, 'Mani, go and give these clothes as "urgent".' Mani gathered Annachi's jibba, veshti, banian, underwear and all and went to the laundry.

Switching on the fan, Annachi sat bare-bodied on the chair, immensely satisfied and cheerful. Kasi asked Annachi softly, 'Shall we get the food, or shall we go out and eat it?'

'Leave the food. How did you find Madras, Kasi? Does Madras suit your Annachi? Sharp fellows you are, you Madurai fellows. Tell me.'

'Shouldn't be saying all this to your face, but since Annachi is asking, I'm telling. You are virtually walking all over Madras.' So saying, Kasi turned. Mani came back. Kasi continued, 'Mani, do you understand what this means? That means Madras is lying under Annachi's feet.'

Annachi laughed silently. He stretched out his legs even more and shook them. Suddenly he said, 'Mani, this is the first time Kasi has come to our house. Take out some money from the box and go and buy some "medicine".'

Kasi knew somewhat about these things. He knew 'medicine' meant whiskey, the term given by big men. He took Mani's hand which went in search of the box and pressed a hundred-rupee note from his pocket and said, 'Go buy Annachi's favourite.'

When it became dusk, everyone woke up. Kasi was the one who lay most awkwardly. Mani shook him awake and made him stand.

He said, 'You said you had to catch the Pandian Express and return home today itself.'

Everyone's eyes burned. They were red, like live charcoal. Kasi stuffed his clothes into his bag and called Mani. He took out a hundred-rupee note. 'Mani, get whatever Annachi likes for the night. I ought to stay back and do all this. But the enemy is at the door. So I have to leave today itself.'

Annachi sat, eyes scrunched up, as if in a dark room.

'Annachi, you must meet the minister once again tomorrow, please, and make sure that he spoke to the collector. I've troubled Annachi too much today. I'll see you, Annachi,' said Kasi and placed ten hundred-rupee notes on the table from his bag. To Mani he said, 'Mani, I think Annachi is a bit angry that I am leaving money like this. It's nothing – he has to go tomorrow for my sake only, no? It's for those expenses only.'

Annachi looked unconcerned. Kasi hurried Mani. 'Mani, go fetch an auto. If I start now only will I be able to catch the Pandian Express.'

That evening from Madurai another Pandian Express was readying itself to come to Madras. A worried and restless man was smoking a cigarette with trembling fingers. The passenger next to him asked, 'How far are you going?'

The man answered. 'Madras only. Our Annachi is there. I'm on my way to see him on an important matter.'

Original title: *Dhinam Oru Pandian Express*
1989

VOTE-GRABBERS 55

NANJIL NADAN

In that constituency there were one lakh twenty-three thousand voters. Including those who had passed away ten years ago or left the country. Of these around twenty thousand belonged to the Naadaar community. Approximately forty thousand were Harijans. People who belonged to communities such as Vannaar, Naavidar, Kuyavar, Kuravar, Maravar, Asaari, Poosaari, etcetera, would be around three thousand. The remaining sixty thousand belonged to either the Velaalar, Vellaalar or the Pillai communities.

Among the Velaalars, there were sub-divisions such as Saivar, Kaaniyalar, Makkal vazhi, Marumakkal vazhi, and Chetti pillaimar. But no inter-marriages. Other than the Marumakkal vazhi, the other Velaalars numbered very few.

Anyway, in this constituency, despite dinning in from Standard Five that this is a secular, egalitarian republic, no one other than a Velaalan who belonged to the Marumakkal community could ever win here. Not even Mahatma Gandhi. So all the political parties usually propped up only a Velaalar Marumakkal vazhi candidate. The political parties here – even going by their manifestos – were no different from each other. So one could never guarantee which party a candidate would be in, before and after the elections. Hence no one complained about the sewage mingling with the clear Kaveri waters.

It was only a small district. Only seven legislative assembly constituencies. In five of them only a Naadaar could win. In the sixth one adjoining the seaside, only someone from the fishing community could win. But a shrewd national politician, well versed in election machinations, reconstituted the five Naadaar constituencies into six. And the sixth fishing constituency, which ran along the five constituencies, was chopped into bits and redistributed to all the six. In such a way that only a Naadaar could win in all the six. These six together made for a Lok Sabha constituency. In that he himself would stand for elections. After all, one could always abolish caste after the elections, conveniently. God knows why, but he sliced this Velaalar constituency and combined it with the adjoining district's parliamentary constituency. Perhaps he segregated it because these cunning fellows might have spoilt the chances of the other constituencies too, much like a single bad measure that can devalue the rest of the ninety-nine good measures.

From the time the constituency was established, there was always a stiff fight only between two Velaalars. At times they even turned out to be uncle-nephew or father and son-in-law. But, unfailingly, they were wealthy.

In 1951 the tussle was between a hut and a banyan tree. In 1956 between the banyan tree and the elephant. In 1962 it was between the banyan and twin bulls. In 1967 it was the twin bulls and the rising sun. In 1971, the rising sun and the cow and its calf. In 1975, two leaves and the rising sun.

In this year of 1980, strangely enough three Velaalars had filed their nominations. Besides them, there were always independents for various reasons. But all that was no contest at all.

If only an influential Naadaar or Harijan contested independently, the veshtis of the Velaalars would be in tatters. But in this election no one was astute enough to see it.

Ayyappan Pillai's father, Adimoolam Pillai, was the Number One rich man in the constituency. He was a real big shot. His fields, orchards, lands, ponds, woods, stretched to eight to ten miles around. Wherever there were fields, there were harvest yards. Next to it, granaries for the paddy, black gram, etcetera. Besides, a small house, a shed for the bullocks used in the ploughing season.

If his cows were led to graze, the streets would be full. Eight to ten open carts and three fully covered ones. Besides all these, to go around a crane-white Ambassador car.

A simple man. Pure white khadi veshti, khadi shirt, khadi towel and a khadi loincloth. Neatly trimmed hair, well anointed with heated coconut oil. Before seven in the morning, he would be done with shaving and bathing. Then if he stepped into his car at seven-thirty after breakfast, he would return only at twelve.

The driver sat in the front seat of the big Ambassador car. In the back seat, diagonally opposite him, huddled by the window so that only his face was visible, sat Adimoolam Pillai. This was a familiar sight to all in the vicinity. All his four children held good positions. Each one had a car. So in his car, only he travelled. No one had seen him offer a lift to anyone.

Adimoolam Pillai's native village was tucked two miles inside from the highway. In between lay two villages. Every one and three-fourth hour, a bus packed with people would go by, leaving a trail of dust, like a cyclone. It had to go to the town and return. In the meanwhile, people who needed to travel either walked, went pillion on cycles, or used load-carts that happened to pass by. If the bus ever broke down, the day was finished. If the bus wasn't there, rain, heat or the dark, one had to walk alone or in twos or threes.

At such times when the townspeople saw the car, empty save for Adimoolam Pillai huddled in a corner, they passed by huffing and panting. Even if they belonged to his village – or why, even if they were his relatives – no one was allowed to step into the car.

It was for this reason that he didn't enjoy much goodwill in those parts. But somehow his children were well liked.

After his son Ayyappan Pillai filed his nomination, slowly people were offered lifts in Adimoolam Pillai's car. It started with acquaintances and relatives, but soon all sorts of people – people returning from shanties with small bundles; people with gunny bags who bought and sold tubers from the hills; people with wet spades; women with infants returning from government hospitals, medicine bottles in hand, accompanied by neighbours; people with brass vessels heaped with cashew visiting pregnant relatives; people with dirty bundles stuffed into the boot – travelled in the car.

Huddled in the same corner with the same expression, viewing the road outside, Adimoolam Pillai accompanied them.

Dr Parameswaran, MA Economics, MA History, MA Lit, PhD, was one of India's leading economists. For a few years he was the head of the department of Economics in a local college. Then he became a reader in the University of Madras. After that for two years he was in a German university engaged in research on the economy during the reign of the Chalukyas. After that, for seven to eight years, he was the Economic Advisor to one of the African countries.

To tumble around in the mire of this election, he left everything – his advisory position, his beautiful bungalow and other trappings – and returned to India. Only Elsie Mariammai Selvaraj, daughter of Francis Selvaraj, who had settled in Africa, came back with him, but as Elsie Mariammai Parameswaran since he had married her. First wife Isakkiammai Parameswaran, who lived in the village, wasn't at all perturbed by all this.

Dr Parameswaran was fifty-eight. Grey khadi pant. Grey half-sleeved khadi shirt. Since he didn't wear a veshti to reveal a tightly tied loincloth like Adimoolam Pillai, no one knew if his underwear was khadi too. Against the backdrop of grey hair, black-framed glasses. A President pen, the diameter of a flute.

From the looks of him, no one would doubt that he was an intelligent man. But many wondered about his wallowing like a pig in this caste-filth. A rumour floated around that he would be made the finance minister if he won this election. Even if he didn't win, knowledgeable sources believed that he would find a position in the planning commission, a public sector enterprise, or in one of the Indian embassies in a minor country.

In the hope that it would be useful to get a medical or an engineering seat or a job for their sons, the town's big shots descended to campaign for him.

Since Dr Parameswaran had been cut off from his roots for several years, he unwittingly took his wife Elsie Mariammai – Isakkiammai was not sophisticated enough – along with him when he canvassed door-to-door. Elsie Mariammai's awkward Tamil, cropped hair, sleeveless blouse, gold-framed glasses and sandals, evoked a frown on the faces of the real pure Velaalar households. The votes of the women seemed to already tilt to another side, and if this ignominy was to happen, then Dr Parameswaran Pillai would have no choice but to go back to the banks of the River Nile felt his advisors and hesitantly informed him.

From the next day, when they canvassed for votes Isakkiammai too was in the car. Her neck so full of chains – even if you knifed her it wouldn't pierce her skin – in pearls, gold coins, twisted ropes of gold, necklaces; eleven-stoned red earrings, seven-stoned nose-ring on either nostril; thick, heavy gold bangles; a maroon silk sari like the ones draped for goddesses; a big kumkumam pottu, the likes of which worn by Tamil cinema's 'family women'; a big hair bun redolent of jasmine.

When Isakkiammai walked with Dr Parameswaran in the Velaalar streets, they looked majestic.

'Should you be roaming around in this hot sun just for this, akka?' said the Velaalar women, as they greeted her hospitably.

After they were done with the Velaalar streets, when they ventured into the nearby Harijan settlements, Isakkiammai stayed back in the car. It was Elsie Mariammai who got down with Dr Parameswaran. She pulled out her chain with a cross from inside and displayed it over her sari. She spoke to the Christians with concern. Her large breasts weighing heavy, she bent down to pat the cheeks of little children who huddled around, without heeding their grime. She took little infants in her arms and kissed them.

Ever since he had come of age and wised up to the world, Kulasai Arivarasan loved his leader as much as he did his own life. Long, long ago he had pledged his life to the Tamil language and his body to the earth. He had been jailed for three months for protesting against price rise and two weeks for participating in the anti-Hindi agitation. But in the days of Emergency, out of fear of 'MISA' he developed a heart problem and was consigned to the intensive care unit. Otherwise he could have appended the honorific 'MISA' before his name.

Ever since his fourteenth year when he had joined the Vadaseri Weavers' Cooperative, every Friday he unfailingly attended the political meetings. His house was plastered with calendar pictures of his leader. Just as roaches flitting here and there enjoy the benefit of devotion when poojas are performed for Lord Padmanabha in the temple, so did the dancing and smiling cine queens embracing the leader in the photograph enjoy the honour of paper garlands and joss sticks meant for the leader. Arivarasan didn't seem to mind this at all.

By the time he had got down to weaving in the cooperative, he had already become the party's secretary in the local unit. When the Tamil Nadu political waters swirled muddily like the dramatic thunderstorms in films, Arivarasan somehow managed to become the party's district secretary.

After he became the secretary, he acquired a two-storey house in the heart of the town. Hundred and ten acres of rubber estate in Asambu Hill. In addition, the adjacent two hundred acres of government puramboke land that he had appropriated was the icing. Two Ambassador cars. Two lorries. A high-paid trustee's post in a temple under the Hindu Religious and Endowment Board. Managing director in the district Land Development Cooperative Bank. All this in just eight years. Where can all this be possible but in this country?

In an ordinary veshti, a sweat-soaked handloom shirt, and a towel slung over his shoulder as if it were a child, Arivarasan went door to door to catch votes.

'Akka, maini, aatha,' he beseeched, prostrating himself over and over again.

When he entered a house at lunchtime, the householder, vibhuti smeared on his forehead, was ready to eat. The aroma of tamarind curry wafted.

The lady of the house too came out to take a look at the candidate.

Feigning exhaustion, Arivarasan plonked himself on the steps.

'Amma, would you give me some drained rice water with a bit of salt. My head is spinning after going around in the sun…'

'Haven't you eaten yet?'

'No, 'ma. From the morning I have been running around. Is there a hotel in our town? I haven't even sipped a bit of tea…'

'You could eat in our house. But our curry today is too humble a fare,' said the householder hesitantly.

'Who needs curry? Give me some old rice with some salt and a green chilli… that's enough.'

The lady of the house looked tenderly at Arivarasan eating rice with just tamarind curry and a humble chutney. People from the neighbourhood filled the verandah of the house to look at this sight.

Elections were over in that constituency and counting was on. Of the three, one would definitely win.

Original title: *Vaakku Porukkigal*
1981

The Mind's a Boat and All That... 56

Dilip Kumar

He is sitting on the beach. Today is the last day of his life. He is going to commit suicide. Your guess is right, he is a poet.

You are of course aware that great poets never die of illness. They usually choose to kill themselves. But even if he isn't such a great poet, this act of suicide will surely confer greatness upon him. You can say that he possesses all the requisites of a great poet: a face dripping sorrow; eyes filled with fear and dismay; a meaningful smile that hides his teeth. What's more, no one ever understands his poems either. And only magazines with a print-run of no more than three hundred ever publish them. If he lives, it will only be on account of those three hundred people. But it could also be said that besides Rajakumari these three hundred people too are in a way responsible for his wanting to commit suicide.

You might want to know who Rajakumari is. Rajakumari is a simple girl, reasonably good-looking. Who has no taste, however, for poetry. But her not liking poetry doesn't worry him in the least. After all, there is no law which says that reasonably good-looking girls should like poetry. Anyway, it was Rajakumari only who told him that she loved him. But he never said that he returned her love. You can't, however, say that he doesn't like her. Or that he likes her either. His poetic mind is not used to taking decisions. He is of the belief that life's beauty lies in its uncertainty. Whoever said that the human mind is a decision-making machine?

But in the end, he was unfortunately forced to take a decision. He'd rejected Rajakumari's love (declared in as decisive a voice as possible). He didn't understand why he had done so. There is no big difference really between a decision taken with a clear head and one taken under pressure. Any decision, it has been proven, turns out to be sometimes right and sometimes wrong. You could also say that of this decision to commit suicide.

There have been many times he'd come to this very beach to commit suicide and returned alive. It can be said that he neither has the enormous guts nor the cowardice necessary to commit suicide. But that won't hold true today. Today he is determined to die.

He gets up and walks towards the sea. He sits at the edge of the beach, stretching out his legs so that the waves can gently stroke them. He will surely commit suicide after watching the waves for a bit.

O the sea! What an amazing thing it is. Brimming over even beyond where the eyes can see. Gigantic waves pouncing with such frenzy. Waves, big and small, rubbing against each other and breaking into pieces with such a noise at the edge – he likes all that very much. That crushing, big sound which evokes such a deep emotion in his heart is rather wonderful. The silence that prevails for a second when the waves retreat seems to him like the silence that visits after death. The sea in the end always reminds him of death. Nature's grandeur is always a nuisance to mankind. The moment you encounter it, it seems to ridicule man's helplessness.

A golden tinge spreads over the sky, marking the setting of the sun. Two boats can be seen far away. Fishermen are busy mending the dried nets spread across the sands. Beedi smoke and the smell of sweat waft around as they cross him to and fro. One of them, a slightly old man, luxuriant moustache, blazing eyes and all, smiles at him. When he smiles in return, he can't but help think of the smell of sweat the man emits.

In a way you can say that body odour too is one of the causes of the friction between Rajakumari and him. The first smile that she had flashed at him at Prince's Corner along with the smell of sweat that she had given out comes to his mind. Poor thing! Inexperienced girl. Wonder what she saw in him? He wants to shout out a theatrical laugh thinking of his worthless life. Opening his mouth wide, he laughs loudly into the sea.

Truth to tell, his life is abysmally worthless. His name is Rahul K Naik. Gujarati. Poor. Age twenty-four. Six feet one inch. Thin. Brown. A blunt long nose. The neck and head, of seemingly the same size, stretched out. In short, he is as attractive as a chameleon. Has studied till Class Eight. He neither knows English nor Gujarati well. Knows a little – very little, really – Tamil. It's this which gave him the temerity to write in it. Fortunately, his poetry did nothing to Tamil, a language which has been around even longer than stones and mud.

He had come to Chennai six months ago in the hope of becoming a great man by writing poems. But even as he had got down at Central Station he knew that his dream wouldn't come true. To date none of his dreams has ever come true. Back home he has a widowed mother, a sister who had run away with a tailor, tiny younger siblings – in such family backgrounds dreams remain but dreams.

Acquaintanceship with poverty is nothing new to him. In his thirteenth year itself he had experienced the kind of gnawing hunger which feels as if mice are running amok in an empty stomach. He'd never worn anything other than torn shirts and chappals. He took all this indignity as a matter of course. He knew very well that India's poverty is as boundless as her infinite spirituality.

He stayed at a relative's place and searched high and low for a job. On the side he wrote plenty of poems. After trudging up and down several shops, he finally found a job at Prince's Corner, a readymade shop at Pondy Bazaar. For two hundred and fifty rupees a month. Ten hours a day. He had met Rajakumari here only.

Besides Rajakumari, Jayakumar, Kaja, Ratnasingam and Venkatesan too worked at Prince's Corner. With the exception of Rajakumari, the rest of them worked there only because of straitened circumstances. Ratnasingam had come from Sri Lanka to write scripts for Tamil films. Jayakumar hadn't got a job at the fire service. Kaja couldn't become a corporation worker. Venkatesan ought to have cleared at least one thousand rupees at Ashok Leyland, but here he was sticking it out at Prince's Corner for a mere three hundred rupees.

Rajakumari alone sparkled, as if she was born to be a sales clerk at the readymade shop. She was a bit short. Only around four feet seven inches. Thick curly hair. But extremely fair. Attractive face. If only she had a few more inches, she would have been a great beauty.

Everyone took to him just within a few days of joining work. But Ratnasingam alone didn't think much of him. He thought he was a complete idiot. He believed that only intelligent beings could write Tamil film scripts. Anyway, those days passed delightfully. He wrote poems in Natesan Park on Sundays. He ate three square meals a day. Late at night, he strolled up and down Pondy Bazaar, where trees seemed to lock hands. He saw European films at foreign consulates. He went to literary meetings. He made a lot of friends. His poems got published. One of his poems on trees, particularly, caught everyone's interest.

In the dead of night
Trees have a singular beauty
(much like wives)
The banyan looks to the ground
The palm stretches upwards
Bending low, the coconut
Is ready to sieve the moon.
Eyes bargain with sleep
Trees
Refuse to fade in the dark
Revealing great beauty
In a deep shade of green.
Any time, any place,
Trees have a singular beauty
In the dead of night – much like wives.

But in Prince's Corner, no one, including Rajakumari, liked the poem. 'You call this a poem?' she laughed, squeezing her lips.

Then suddenly one day Rajakumari had decided to love him. That afternoon, he who usually ate at a hotel, was shepherded to Jeeva Park by her. There, after plying him with tamarind rice and curd rice brought specially from home, she declared her love for him. He was taken aback. That someone could actually bring herself to love him. But he gathered himself together quickly. A strange arrogance engulfed him, and in a voice laced with indifference and bluster he said: 'Look here, Rajakumari, your world and mine are far apart. You're an ordinary girl. I'm a poet. I'm not at all keen on love. It's only because of fate I've sunk so low, working in a cloth shop and all, but my goals in life are lofty. This thing called love will only be a burden while I'm leaping across to reach the peaks. Please forgive me.'

Rajakumari hadn't believed him and had smiled sarcastically.

He continued, 'Besides there is another problem in loving you. You sweat too much. The stench of your sweat stinks like garlic. I'll give you some advice: Before you fall in love with someone, take some medicine to get rid of your odour.'

Rajakumari's face had fallen.

From the very next day bad luck had descended on him. The old owner of Prince's Corner started on his case. If he was late by even five minutes he was scolded; if customers went away without buying anything he was taken to task; if he so much as relaxed for a bit after lunch he was abused; if he stood up he was shouted at; if he sat down he was cursed. It was all Rajakumari's doing, said the others (she wielded a lot of clout with the owner). Day before yesterday, a customer who had bought clothes worth three hundred and five rupees was given a discount of five rupees – this was considered a grave blunder. An altercation had taken place between the old man and him, and he had been sacked! Everything was over in just five minutes.

Losing the job was a severe blow. What was worse was the absurd manner in which he had lost it. He believed that it was Rajakumari's excessive love for him that had made her so maliciously spiteful. Till the previous week it had never occurred to him that life would deal with him so heartlessly. Today everything has gone beyond the limits, everything has completely dried up.

People have started to gather on the beach to enjoy the breeze. Boats have come ashore and the fishermen have left. Young lovers huddle in the dark. Stars flower in the sky.

He is sitting, watching the sea dazedly. He consoles himself that he, who is staring into the jaws of death, has nothing much to think about. From the morning he has made preparations to get into a suicidal frame of mind. He didn't speak with anyone for fear of shattering his resolute mind. Didn't smile at anyone either. Didn't even see his face in the mirror. Even if his face is not very interesting, he wonders how it will look now in the mirror. The human face does not reveal everything. It can heavily pat on, like cosmetic powder, straightforward emotions such as desire, love, affection and sorrow. But it cannot fathom deep-seated turmoil and perversities. Just as the pollen waits to be disturbed by the bee, the doors of the inner mind too wait to be slammed by the hands of death. The naivety of human life cannot be captured by the human face.

Facial expressions are not important to a person who is going to die. It's only the mind that matters. Anyhow death is a good thing. There is no big difference between dying with a reason and dying without one. Why, there is no big difference between even life and death. The proof of life itself is in death.

Lying on his back he looks at the sky. The moon, the stars, his youth, his mother, his poems, all toss around in his mind, only to come back to Rajakumari in the end. Coming to think of it Rajakumari is really a fine person. Perhaps I ought to have accepted her love. She certainly possesses the allure of a lover. Besides, I can see in her eyes the pure ardour of one possessed by love. What an idiot, I didn't understand that universal love and romantic love spring from the same source. What right do I have to mock her and her body odour? The beauty of youth sparkles only through the body. And the dignity of its mind too. Truly, Rajakumari is an exceptional girl. While the waves gently stroke his feet, he tightly squeezes his eyes shut and opens them again. The merry stars in the open sky delight him. He wants to wail loudly; he shuts his eyes again.

After a while he feels as if someone is walking towards him. He can hear the soft footfalls in the wet sand. He senses someone standing very close to him. He opens his eyes gently. It looks as if it is Rajakumari. He opens his eyes wide in astonishment. There is no doubt, Rajakumari it is. He gets up with a start. She looks beautiful in the moonlight. He smiles at her. Moving aside a little, he beckons her to sit near him. She sits down.

He: How come you're here?

Rajakumari: It was so humid. I just came.

He: Me too.

Ra Ku: It's summer.

He: Yes.

Ra Ku: Feeling sweaty? You!

He: I understand. Please forgive me. I shouldn't have spoken to you like that.

Ra Ku: It's ok. You only said the truth, after all.

He: I'm really upset.

Ra Ku: Well, you will feel like that.

He: I'm not such a lout as you believe.

Ra Ku: I know.

He: You won't believe me, I've actually come here today to commit suicide.

Ra Ku: O! Is that so?

He: Don't make fun of me. My heart is crushed already.

Ra Ku: You're an idiot.

He: Truly.

Ra Ku: You're a coward, a real scoundrel.

He: That's so true.

They remain silent.

Ra Ku: Have you ever loved anyone in your life?

He: No.

Ra Ku: Why, is it a crime to love someone?

He: No.

Ra Ku: Is it a crime for a girlfriend to sweat?

He: Not at all.

Ra Ku: Confess. You love me, don't you?

He: Yes. I admit. I love you.

Ra Ku: Then why all this drama?

He: That's what I too can't understand.

Ra Ku: What can't you understand?

He: Perhaps I don't like the fact that I love you.

Ra Ku: What nonsense are you talking?

He: Nothing. You're an inexperienced girl. You don't know anything about life. That emotion called love happens only by chance.

Ra Ku: So?

He: There's no chance for love now. At least, as far as I'm concerned, not even the smallest bit. I only wish to die now. I've even written my last poem.

Ra Ku: Don't talk rubbish.

He: Listen to this poem now. You might understand that I'm not spouting rubbish.

He begins to recite his poem.

Dawn in the month of Margazhi
From somewhere wafts in a soft bhakti song
The world trickles down, unchanging
Like a known face
Life dissolves and torments me
Like forms floating around in an artist's mind
They are spread all over my table – faces, expressions, voices

Whose face shall I see?
Whose voice should I hear?
Where do I begin?
Nests from
The withered leaves of dreams
Don't always take shape –
The heart
Like the sorrowful spring
That is drying up
Oozes out
The last drops with deep bitterness
In the torpid mid-afternoon sun
Entwined in the still aerial roots
Appears ancient life
I can feel the wings of desire
As also the way of love
In this world full of shadows
A spot of light
Like a child's first smile
Fills me,
No,
Mocks me.
The world trickles down, unchanging.

He smiles at her bitterly.

Ra Ku: I'm telling you again, you're talking utter rot. Pure unadulterated rot. There's no hope really for those who can make fun of a child's first smile.

He: Please forgive me. I just can't understand anything. I'll really be put through a lot of inconvenience by loving you.

Ra Ku: What inconvenience?

He: You don't know my mother. At your age she was already a widow with five children. She's an angry woman. Poor thing. She has a lot of hopes for me. I'm everything to her. Just looking at her bare forehead day in and day out has made me lose all faith in love, affection and attachment. Listen to me without frowning. Poverty dries up everything. There's nothing beyond basic needs for men. Their inner core is only full of needs. If you observe closely, you will know. Men are just bundles of needs… Even so, you're an extraordinary girl. You don't expect anything much from life or men. You have a lot of love to give and share with people. You've a lot of affection. But I, I've nothing to give. My life is loveless. Filled with bitterness and trouble. I'm not interested in the difference between truth and falsehood. I understood all this long ago. I'm not even aware if my sorrow is real or false. If you hitch yourself with me your life will be spoilt. Believe me, selling frocks in Prince's Corner is infinitely preferable.

Ra Ku: You talk too much rubbish.

He: It's true. But I can't bear to love you.

Ra Ku: You're totally crazy.

He: We're all crazy.

Ra Ku: I really hate you.

He: That's my humble request too.

Ra Ku: What will happen if you die?

He: Nothing will happen.

Ra Ku: Then what are you waiting for? Go and die then. There, the sea is waiting for you.

They fall silent once again.

He: It's really dark.

Ra Ku: Yes.

He: The stars are twinkling beautifully.

Ra Ku: Yes.

He: The full moon is shining brightly.

Ra Ku: Yes.

He: The waves are becoming big. They're roaring.

Ra Ku: Yes.

He: The cool breeze is delightful.

Ra Ku: Yes.

He: Your face looks beautiful in the moonlight.

Ra Ku:…

He: When your curly hair teased by the wind falls on your face, you look utterly beautiful.

Ra Ku:…

He: I can see the sea in your eyes.

Ra Ku:…

He: I like your long fingers.

Ra Ku:...

He: This is my first time. How warm your touch is.

Ra Ku:...

He: Can I pinch your palm?

Ra Ku:...

He: I want to take you on my lap and stroke you fondly.

Ra Ku:...

He: With your permission, I'd like to kiss your tiny lips.

Ra Ku:...

They hold each other tight. Time stands still. After a while they exchange sweet nothings in whispers.

Ra Ku: Can I ask you something?

He: Mm...

Ra Ku: Do you like me?

He: Mm...

Ra Ku: Do you like me a lot?

He: Mmm...

Ra Ku: What about my body odour? You don't mind that?

He: Mm...

Ra Ku: Am I beautiful?

He: Mm...

Ra Ku: Do you love me?

He: Mm...

Ra Ku: Do you really love me?

He: Mm...

Ra Ku: You're not confused?

He: Mm...hmm...

Ra Ku: Truly?

He: Truly.

Ra Ku: See, I knew that mine was true love.

He: You're a clever girl, aren't you?

Ra Ku: Enough. Don't choke me. How many more time times will you kiss me?

He: This is the last one.

Ra Ku: Chee! Lecherous fellow! You desire me so much and how you play-acted.

They both burst into a laugh.

Ra Ku: Ok, shall we start? It's getting late.
He: Mm…
Ra Ku: Ok, take off your hands.
They stroll towards the road.
He: When will I see you again?
Ra Ku: Don't know.
He: Tomorrow?
Ra Ku: No.
He: Next Sunday?
Ra Ku: Mm…

The road is empty. Just two or three people at the bus stop. Just as they cross the road, the bus arrives, as if they have ordered it to do so.

They fold themselves into a corner in the empty bus. 'Two, Pondy Bazaar,' he asks the conductor, signalling with two fingers. The conductor looks at him strangely, tears out only one ticket and gives it to him. He turns towards Rajakumari to say something. But she, who was sitting near the window, has suddenly disappeared.

The bus, which is hurtling along at breakneck speed, hits a pot hole and shudders. It then picks up the usual speed.

Original title: *Manam Enum Thoni Patri…*
1992

Their Separate Ways 57

Suresh Kumara Indrajith

Naganandan, who till then had enjoyed a comfortable, relaxed journey in his compartment, was irritated when he saw them boarding the train. Just across him his wife slept on the seats meant only for sitting. He had the corner window seat. A little away from him sat his daughter, poring over an English book. Very fair she was, almost bloodless. A woman, a young boy and a little girl got into his compartment and came near him. He asked his wife to get up. Annoyed, she got up and moved to the corner, near the window. Only after they sat down did he realise that it was Ranjini.

He adjusted his clothes and sat down properly. This unexpected meeting unsettled her countenance. Turning her eyes down, she straightened her blouse. Not knowing how to begin, he said, 'Do you remember?' She smiled faintly at his wife. 'She is from my town. My mother and her mother know each other well. She is in Coimbatore,' he said. 'No, Tirunelveli,' said Ranjini. His wife listened to all this, yawning lazily.

Ranjini's daughter was married. Her son was doing engineering. She had brought her granddaughter home for the holidays and was now taking her back to her daughter in Madurai. Her husband was busy with his business.

Naganandan had a daughter and a son. The son was studying catering in Chennai, despite being dissuaded from doing the course. The daughter was doing her MSc in Mathematics.

Beyond these enquiries they didn't know what to speak. Ranjini went to the bathroom, looked at herself in the mirror there and tidied up her hair. She washed her face and wiped it with the ends of the sari and straightened her pottu.

Naganandan looked out of the window. Time flew by. Naganandan and Ranjini had grown old. She had a granddaughter. Her son sat beside her, as big as a buffalo. His tiny daughter who he had once carried was now doing her master's. The past and the future seemed like an infinite sea of sorrow.

Ranjini sat down. Naganandan noticed that she had washed her face. She had greyed near her ears. Naganandan Thaatha and Ranjini Paati – these words surfaced in his mind. The train stopped. Through the window a banyan tree with aerial roots could be seen. Gypsies lived under it in tiny tents. How many men, how many women – with what all thoughts and moods they must have sat under this banyan tree. The train started.

Sitting opposite each other, it was impossible not to meet each other's eyes. But the meeting of the eyes roused memories and confusion in the mind. But looking out through the window the whole time gave him a crick in the neck.

She had long hair.

It didn't look as if Naganandan's wife possessed a neck. She was portly. She was busy asking Ranjini, 'Who did you get your daughter married to? How much gold did you give? What job? What has he studied?'

Naganandan had wondered how a man could ride a bike properly if a girl was on the pillion, touching his hip and shoulder. But when Ranjini had sat behind him, he had never fumbled when she touched his shoulder. Unusually enough, the motorcycle ran smoothly, and that was a surprise. Perhaps the government laid such bypass roads only to make it convenient for those who travelled like this.

Both had been sitting on a small bridge when Ranjini had said, 'They won't allow me to get married to you in my house. They won't like me marrying out of caste.'

He had retorted, 'In that case we have to run away on this motorbike and get married. That's why my father has bought it for me.'

'Just thinking of it scares me. We have to struggle a lot. Our friends will help us or what?'

'Only if you struggle will life be sweet.'

Two policemen had stopped their bike, come near them and asked menacingly, 'You've run away with her, is it? They took down their addresses. 'What does your father do? Where does he work?' They asked their castes. 'Will these two castes ever come together?' they said. 'Do you know what will happen if the father gives a complaint saying that this girl is lost?' They used all sorts of swear words against him.

Ranjini had gone home, scared. As she had feared, the situation at home had changed the very next day.

'Would it be twenty-five years since I saw you?' asked Naganandan. 'Perhaps,' said Ranjini. She flicked her plait to her front; it was thick. Her body had sagged, her face had wrinkled; but her hair, she hadn't lost it. Did she flick her thick plait in front to display her beauty?

He went and stood near the door by the bathroom and let the breeze blow on his body. It was soothing. The thought that life wasn't happy churned his mind.

Time neared for both the families to alight. Since he wanted to free himself from this mental turmoil, he wished that the station would come sooner. He thought he would go in and sit only when the train neared the station.

The station came close. He sat opposite her. She was looking out of the window. I have met you after so many years. The next time, will I ask after your death, or will I meet you after several years like this, me as an old man and you as an old lady? As such thoughts ran in his mind, the train halted.

He asked his wife and daughter to take their belongings and walk. He asked Ranjini's son to walk ahead. He then asked Ranjini to go. When she started walking, he tapped her lightly on her behind. She turned around and left space for him to go ahead of her. When he went ahead, she too tapped him lightly on his behind.

They got down from the train, took leave of each other and walked their separate ways.

Original title: *Avaravar Vazhi*
2006

The Flower Brought by the Little Girl

58

Vimaladhitha Maamallan

He lay for several hours in the night without any sleep. In the morning Suganchand Jain got up late. He sat on the bed with a blank stare, as if struck by a ghost. In front of him was an empty tumbler-dabara set. But he was under the illusion that someone else had drunk the coffee. Truth to tell, he didn't understand anything. All that had happened from noon the day before to now seemed like a magical tale.

He had come to the shop the previous day after his meal. He had lain against the bolster after sending the boy off for lunch. The heat outside was dull yet oppressive; there weren't too many clients. He reviewed the morning's accounts. Just two things had been redeemed, otherwise not much business. Things would hot up only as the month-end neared. For the first ten days of the month, everyone's hands would rustle with money, wouldn't it? With nothing to do, he looked vacantly at the street. The sky looked as if it would by turns close and open up. What was there to watch?

It was then that he saw her. Just lifting his face as he sat there. Standing across the road, she stood looking at his shop; she crossed the road and climbed the steps. He was amazed. She wore a short skirt with a top tucked into it. Two plaits folded up and tied with ribbons. What work would a school child have with a pawn shop? Perhaps she mistook it for Lala's sweet shop. The face, like that of an adult, had a stately glow, and didn't gel with the rest of the body. As he was thus contemplating, she began to speak.

'Take this and give me some money.' She stretched out her clenched right hand.

Older boys usually came by to pawn rings and chains. He would quiz them mercilessly, asking all kinds of questions – Is it yours? Are you studying? Working? Why didn't you bring an adult along? At the same time he wouldn't let go of the fellows. He would confuse them and clinch the deal for a lower figure. He couldn't utter anything to this small girl; he didn't know why. He stared at the girl's face without batting an eyelid. Seemed like a friendly, familiar face, but where and when he had seen it, he couldn't bring to mind.

'I have to leave quickly.'

It reminded him of his grandson's pestering. But it didn't have any of the pucker and the pleading; it looked like a boss's haste.

'What have you brought?'

'A flower.'

'Whaaat?'

'A flower. A blossom.'

He didn't understand head or tail. He quickly refused, shaking his head this way and that. 'We don't accept all that.' Really, he ought to have laughed at what she said. But he couldn't bring himself to do it.

Like an experienced magician she opened her fist slowly. Her lips seemed to be smiling slyly. Her demeanour seemed to convey without words that he was going to be astonished foolishly.

He really was astounded. What else? In the middle of the day a girl, as old as his granddaughter, wanted him to buy something. And when she opened her palm, there was a rose of gold. That it was pure gold, there was no room for doubt. An eye which could see without glasses even at sixty-three could never go wrong. The daze lasted for just a while. His senses came back to earth. His mind salivated and reflected in his shiny pupils. She quickly closed her hand. She took away the hand from the glass counter and stepped back.

'How much are you asking?'

'Thousand.'

'What?'

'Thoussaand.'

'I can't give so much.'

'If you can't, then I will go to another shop.'

'Let me rub it and see.'

'I only will hold the flower. You take the stone and rub it.'

He rubbed it two or three times. Didn't change his previous opinion at all. Still his inner mind cautioned him to test it again. Posing endless questions to a child who didn't even know to wash herself? His brain admonished him to not let this good fortune slip by.

It changed hands.

He placed it in the lower drawer of the short desk. She counted the money for the second time. He opened the drawer once again and shut it.

He wondered whose face he had got up to that such luck had come in search of him, beckoning him to catch it. Happiness filled his heart. There was nothing wrong with such happiness. No doubt at all. Truth to tell, no one cheated anyone. It was like walking on the street, stepping on something, bending down and picking up a wad of notes. We never went in search of it; it fell in our path. What else could one do? If we knew who it belonged to we would give it away. But was it that easy? These are times when owners mushroom merely looking at money. Everyone would lay claim to it. And the one who lost it would never be among them. What right did we have to refuse money given by god?

Since he had been sitting for a long time in the same pose, his legs had turned numb. He realised that he hadn't taken the girl's address. He managed to limp to the entrance, leant against the door and looked in both directions of the street.

The street looked like it always did. Spillage from the flour-machine shop, rickshaws under the shade of the temple tree, drunkards staggering under arrack, old women selling yam, boys playing marbles one foot in the gutter, squatting gamblers in a huddle, boys carrying pressed clothes from the 'mobile laundries', dung-dropping buffaloes ambling along, legs apart, priest collecting the urine of a poster-eating cow in a vessel; the sickly street in the suburbs looked like it always did.

No sign of the little girl.

So what if he didn't have the address? It was all for the good. Even if she brought someone, she wouldn't have any proof to show.

Judging by the weight, it looked to be about seven-eight sovereigns. If you discounted seven-eight grams of copper, the day's rate was one hundred and eighty rupees.

'Come in, 'ma.'

An old lady and a girl came in. He went back and sat in his place.

'Sit down, 'ma.'

She untied the drawstring bag she had tucked at her hip and took out a paper packet. She placed a pair of earstuds and a nose-ring on the glass table. He started examining them. He heard a whimper; he looked without lifting his head. The girl, unadorned except for the kumkumam on her forehead, was weeping, her cheeks and nose twitching. The old lady was consoling her. He weighed it on the scales, rubbed it to verify and then looked at the lady.

'How much do you want?'

'We need six hundred rupees, sait.'

'Altogether it is five sovereigns, seven grams. If you deduct the stone and copper, it is less than even five sovereigns. I can give four hundred,' he said, showing four fingers.

'Sait, sait, how can you say that? We have admitted the son-in-law in the hospital. We have so much expenditure – doctor, medicine. The company has given leave, but no salary. We have to run the house too. See what you can do, sait.'

'What can I do, 'ma?'

'We have come because we are in trouble. See what you can do, sait.'

'I'm saying I will give four hundred rupees. The shop there won't even give that.'

'No, sait, if you can do something, your children will prosper, sait.'

'Total five hundred I can give. You do what you think fit.'

His son came in. He asked him to make out a receipt and somehow managed to pack them off. It was time to switch on the lights. He adjusted his dhoti and went up to eat his evening meal.

He took a little rest and came back to the shop. It was totally dark and the lights had been switched on. They only made the place appear darker. He sent off his son and leant against the bolster. Still reclining, he pulled open the bottom drawer of the small desk. There was only a beautiful rose! He anxiously opened the upper drawer, found coin containers and notes under them. He put his hand under the table and groped awkwardly. He opened the iron safe in a twitter. The laundry boy stretched out a hundred-rupee note and asked for change. He shut the iron safe and spluttered at him, 'No, no, go away.' After he left, he opened and looked. The things, all safe inside. After locking it, he opened the bottom drawer. The rose bloom lay there majestically.

Placing his hand on the floor, he heaved himself up and went to the shop front. Looking upstairs, he called out to his son. When the son came down he asked him about it. The son said, 'You had taken the key with you. I didn't want to disturb you while resting. So I managed the business with whatever money I had on hand.' Again he bent down and searched. The rose seemed to say: even if you open and shut a hundred thousand times, it's only me, me alone. He asked his son to look after the shop and went down to the street, tightening his belt around his waist.

He was not one to walk on the street. If at all he had to, he would lift the ends of his dhoti and walk carefully, not stepping on the shit of both animal and man. But he wasn't in a state to notice all that then. In his mind, there was a girl, and in her hand, a gold flower. He took it eagerly in his hand; the next moment it turned into an ordinary flower and burnt his hand.

The streets lamps lit the streets dimly. The windows let out very little light. He kept looking intently at the children reading aloud in many voices. He wandered the streets with searching eyes. Smoke and a stomach-churning odour began to fill the air. He knew that he was nearing the Cooum River. She wasn't likely to be in these places; so he turned into one of the streets. It butted into a house. He turned the way he came and entered another street. Every little girl he spotted looked like the one who had brought him the flower. He was about to return to the shop when he thought he would visit the temple and turned towards the temple tank.

The mercury lamp of the gopuram shone like a solitaire nose-ring. The waterless tank was silent. In the central mandapam a single flame shone faintly. The lamp on the steps of the Hanuman shrine seemed to say that it would be better if it had been put out, so dimly it flickered. Even though he had walked this route a few times earlier, the bank of the tank seemed to stretch endlessly now.

In front of the main entrance stood the elephant. A gaggle of tonsured heads surrounded it. What was in it to peer so eagerly? As if that were not enough, a pack of tourists as well. Irritated, he circled the crowd and went in. He went to every shrine. There weren't too many children around.

All this wandering around hurt his legs. He sat down on the steps of the prasadam stall. A family of shaven heads were munching on something noisily. Leaves and grains of rice littered the floor. There was more crowd here than in front of the shrines.

Flicking away his sweat and tying up packets with demonic speed, the Iyer from the temple kitchen asked him, 'What sait-saar? What's up? To occasion such a rare visit? We have mysore pak and thenkuzhal. What would you like to eat?' He just mumbled something and left.

His heart palpitated. What injustice. Daylight robbery it was. But could he report it to the police? Or even tell someone and weep? Who would believe him? But it was the truth. Neither dream nor delusion. 'A chit of a girl, of schoolgoing age, in a skirt and two plaits, cheated me. When she gave it, it was gold, no doubt about that. I rubbed it carefully and only then took it. No place for any doubt that someone else would have stolen it. Only I had the key. Was it some trick or magic? And was the girl herself real or an illusion? But he was a thousand rupees short, that was for sure.

When he was about the girl's age, he had come to Madras. It was a trade he had learnt step by step, sitting beside his grandfather. A trade he had learnt playfully, which came to him like child's play. Even when he had started out, such a thing had never happened to him. His grandfather used to encourage him. So proud was he of his grandson's prowess. Only his father would shout at him for the smallest of mistakes. If the key hung from the box after locking, he was finished. He had rapped him on the knuckles several times with the shop key itself. His father would often tell him that one should be able to judge by merely looking at the face. Only such a one was the seasoned trader. 'What was the deal? Would it be ever redeemed? Or could it be considered as one's own from this very instant? One should judge all this correctly.' A drunk or a gambler would never redeem the thing he pawned. One should never bargain too much with such characters. Enough if you said 'that's all' firmly a couple of times. They needed money. And that too immediately. One had to finish with them fast. If you tarry, they would go to another shop. This was how he picked up his grandfather's wisdom, his father's cleverness and his own experience – all these nuances had come to nought now.

He felt cold. He could see the mist descending clearly by the light of the single street lamp. They were shutting down several shops near the chariot. The pushcarts were being covered with plastic sheets after the day's remaining fruits were sifted from the rotten ones. It seemed as if it was past ten. He had wandered the entire area. No hope now. Exhaustion and tiredness had consumed him, as if they had fallen down from the skies. Even though he had found it difficult, he walked a bit quickly.

The servant boy took the coffee-dabara. His train of thought abruptly nicked, he looked out. He could feel the heat rising, just by the feel of the breeze. He had to anyhow open the shop. The next day was Friday, the weekly holiday. It was already late. Even though he was tired, he started the motions of the day.

His son had already opened the shop. He inwardly applauded his conscientiousness. But he didn't show it and sent him off for the morning tiffin. Reclining on the bolster, he took out the key from his waist and pondered for a moment. He foolishly hoped that the thing would have taken its original form. Craning his neck, he turned and looked up at the nude Mahavira above his head, prayed and opened the lower drawer. The rose appeared pure and fresh, as if it had just been plucked.

His eyes burned with no sleep. His body ached and his head was heavy. He wished his son would appear soon. His mind and body urged him to lie down. His youngest grandson entered the shop, holding on to the stairs and climbing over. Had it been any other time, he would have picked up the child and hugged him to his chest. Deep in thought, he stared at him. The child leant his hand on the small table and climbed it. When he saw the flower in the open lower drawer he babbled something joyfully and reached out his hand. He shooed away the child's hand in irritation and chased him upstairs. With anger he flung the flower away. It fell into the gutter.

Lifting the heavy ledger, he drowned himself in work.

Original title: *Sirumi Kondu Vanda Malar*
1986

The Wheel of Time 59

Thoppil Mohamed Meeran

The house resounded with silence for a week. There was no cheer on anyone's face, faces that were crestfallen with the worry of how to pay the exam fees for Najib's final year. The evening that we came to know that we had to pay seven hundred and twenty-five rupees, I was shattered.

How could I rustle up such a big amount?

Since my efforts drew a blank, I spent a sleepless week. I had just sat down after roaming around the entire morning. I hadn't even rested my feet for a moment when my wife started nagging. Unable to bear her words, I set off on my regular route. As usual, my head was crowded with the thoughts of my downfall.

That I couldn't even rest for a moment added to my irritation. She was forever badgering me – to get fish. There were heaps of them it seems. Very cheap. It had been a long time since she had eaten fish. Twenty sardines for a rupee!

It was pre-noon. I hadn't taken my umbrella. Not that I didn't want to, but I forgot along with several other things too, thanks to her nagging. I just wanted to escape from her.

As soon as I turned the corner to the beach, fragrant smells wafted everywhere. I couldn't walk without savouring them. I was choked by the foreign smells. This choking was recent, after the unemployed of the town crossed the seas.

My wife and children yearned for someone to gift them a soap or perfume from abroad. But that they couldn't afford it themselves was also there at the back of their minds.

'I want to bathe with "Persia" soap.'

Silence was the answer whenever my wife voiced any desire.

Any answer to her nagging, spilling out of the silence, was not enough to satisfy her.

'Just wait. If some of our relatives' children come from abroad, they might bring one.'

'Write a letter to your nephew. Six bars of soap and a quarter dozen sprays.'

'What else?'

'A hair dye for me.'

'I don't want to write to anyone asking for anything. Be patient. My nephew might give you when he comes down.'

She turned her face away, as if I was denying her something that I possessed. Knowing that I wouldn't budge, she didn't insist on my writing a letter. That was a relief for me.

Whenever she saw someone with an eye-catching sari or wearing a perfume, eyeshadow or lipstick, her voice would quiver.

'If only I had a sibling abroad.'

I was tired of listening to such talk.

But I had to. And every time I did, I was pained and reduced to a silent creature. I couldn't get over my financial downfall, the reason for all this, out of my mind. This helplessness was an additional punishment for people fallen on bad times.

The house around the corner belonged to a relative of ours. The man was in Kuwait or Bahrain. The well was at the back of the house. Since there was no drain near the well, the water snaked out through a hole from the wall. Even the water draining off was fragrant. You had to step on it.

When I was contemplating how to cross without stepping on the water, a glittering wrapper of an imported Camay soap fell on my shoulder. It didn't fall into the water. I couldn't resist smelling the wrapper that I picked up.

I could understand the desire of my wife and children. The smell could captivate even me, who didn't have the means for the next day's food! The one who ought not to think of such desires.

When a wet finger from my dark recesses incited me, I put the wrapping into the 'asafoetida bag' and moved away. Without stepping on the water, I walked on my toes and somehow crossed the corner. To think of it now, it was somewhat demeaning to shift the wrapping from the bag to my waist as I made my way to the beach.

My wife wasn't wrong. Heaps of fish lay around. Every buyer had but one answer: 'It is cheap. Twenty sardines for a rupee.'

My tongue twitched at the thought of eating a fish curry at least in this season when it was cheap.

Seeing the fish on the big tray, I asked for the price.

Before quoting the price, the fisherwoman sized me up. I saw her nostrils flaring.

She said the price: 'One sardine for a rupee.'

I trembled.

Everyone had said it was dirt cheap. But why was she quoting this exorbitant price?

'Why are you hesitating? Don't bother about the price. Buy it and eat.'

As I stood wondering about the flaring of her nostrils, she dropped a bombshell.

'The foreign-returned ones will never ask for the price.' The fragrance from my waist had made me a big man in her eyes, but I felt small within me.

That I didn't have the means to match her flaming price anguished me. Even today it had to be rasam and chutney, as usual. I had no other go but to walk away.

As I returned disappointedly, those who had ignored me till yesterday hailed me with claps now on the road and enquired, 'How is your son doing abroad?' I didn't get the sarcasm, and in my ignorance I got caught in the web.

When I climbed the steps empty-handed, my wife tucked the ends of her sari into her waist. As if she were drawing a sword. The edge of her under-skirt touched her knees.

'What, you've come empty-handed?' Her question seemed like a blow. When her angry countenance suddenly changed into a smile I was befuddled.

'Give it,' she said, stretching out her hand.

'Didn't buy the fish. Too costly.'

'Never mind. Give me the "Persia" soap.'

'Soap?'

I remembered the wrapping at the waist. I didn't know what to say. When she saw the empty wrapping her face turned beastly. Her look burned me.

I couldn't help appreciating the work of the creator who bestowed on a woman's face such beauty and also such aggression.

'Today too eat just plain rice then.'

She unhitched the sari and walked away, as if renouncing the world. Maybe she was off to a river or a well.

Despite all this, I couldn't bring myself to throw away the wrapping. I straightened out the wrinkles and put it away in the broken, empty glass showcase. I wanted to sniff the fragrance.

When my sister's son had come to ask for blessings before leaving for Bahrain, the hall in the big house had been furnished with chairs and glass teapoys. Now this rented hovel contained only an old coir cot for guests to sit on. Whenever I sat on it, my ruin, poverty and the difficulties of educating Najib all came to mind, transforming night into day and day into night.

When I sat cross-legged on the cot, the coconut grove in front of my house that once belonged to me could be seen through the window. As my eyes gazed over the ripe bunches of coconut, Najib came and stood in front of me.

'Tomorrow is the last day. If I don't pay up, I won't be allowed to write the exam.' Najib's face filled with both disappointment and expectation.

When I turned toward Najib, my own face betrayed my mortification and made him downcast. I couldn't bear to look at his drooping face.

'You didn't get it…?'

I couldn't bring my tongue to utter 'no'. Instead, I nodded to convey my inability. He stood still like a statue, wrenching my guts.

'Tried everywhere. Don't know who else to ask…' I returned my gaze to the coconut tree.

He broke the silence and said, 'It's been a week it seems since Rashid Uncle came back from abroad.'

'Has he?'

I was pleased. It seemed as if God had shown a way to a man who had roamed like a dog.

'Ask him. Tomorrow is the last day.'

When I saw Najib's anxiety, I couldn't remain passive.

'Let me not leave him. I will ask him too.'

When I was about to start, my wife asked me to drink some gruel. Since I wanted to leave early so that I could return by the eight-thirty bus, I didn't wait for the gruel.

When I picked up the umbrella, my wife reminded me, 'Ask for soap, sari and spray. After all, he is our own boy.'

Half-hearing her, I unfolded my umbrella and hastened my steps to catch the one-fifteen bus.

If Najib somehow managed to take the exam, I could get him a job somewhere. That would be a little helpful.

When trees and houses whizzed by, thoughts filled my mind: of how I gave money for my nephew's education, of how I bought him new clothes for every festival, of how I helped him when he was unemployed, of how I procured the 'no-objection certificate' for his trip to Bahrain.

It had been six years since he was away and this was his first trip back. There were bound to be several changes. He would have come back with the intention of getting married. After he'd left, he had written several letters asking after our welfare. In his last letter he had mentioned that he would be bringing us an air conditioner for the office, a fridge for his aunt and also a washing machine.

He had promised many other modern gadgets, keeping in mind my high financial status. I never failed to reply to every letter, though I didn't mention my downfall. I wanted my troubles to remain only with me. In this rented chicken coop of a house where one couldn't even stretch one's legs, where was the space to fit a fridge and a washing machine?

Soon he relocated his parents from the tiny village to a two-storey house in a busy town. I never envied his good fortune. I prayed to god to only give him more.

The house was far away from the bus stop, at a corner of a long street, where no buses plied. If I took an auto, there wouldn't be enough in my pocket to get back.

Since the sun was down and the breeze was cool, it was pleasant to walk. Since I had walked the route several times when I was well off, I was familiar with the neighbourhood. I didn't have to ask for directions.

Even though my sister greeted me warmly with a smile, I couldn't say that I was cheered. But the watery tea and the tiny piece of cake that wetted my dry stomach was a relief.

My worry prevented me from even noticing the Dubai artefacts that filled the house.

Cushioned chairs and glass teapoys stuffed the entire hall. I realised that I had lost the privilege to sit on such chairs when my sister brought a wooden stool with the tea and the cake and yet another one for me to sit on. But Najib stood in front of my eyes. He was the future of my family. I had to somehow lead him to the shore. Even a bed of thorns wouldn't deter me.

I got up with a sense of guilt from the chair and sat on the stool. When a nail poked my behind, I carefully lifted my veshti so that it wouldn't get torn.

When we were young I used to play the horse that crawled on all fours. For a sister who had ridden happily on my back, I was now a stranger. Or so it seemed to me. I fervently prayed to god that it shouldn't be true.

That Najib would waste a year was the fear in my heart.

Since this was the first time I was visiting them after they had settled in the city, she asked about our welfare. She asked after the education of Najib and the other children. And about our daughter's marriage and also about the business.

That everything was okay was my reply.

As I was talking, my nephew landed grandly in a car, as if he were a minister. At first I couldn't recognise him. There were so many changes – in his walk, dress, physique and behaviour.

Time's artistic hands had wrought such changes in the six long years.

'Maama, when did you come?' He greeted me with pleasure.

The same voice! Time had not changed his voice. Nor his dimples.

'How are you, 'pa?'

'I'm fine. I was just about to visit you.'

'When I heard that you had arrived, I myself decided to come.'

'How are Maami and the children?'

'Okay.'

'Is Najib in medical or engineering college?'

'No, 'pa. Final year BA.'

'Why didn't you join him in medical… giving eight or ten lakhs.'

Perhaps he didn't understand the meaning of the silence behind my smile.

'This is a kind of a big investment only no, Maama. If you couldn't rustle up money all of a sudden, you should have written to me. I would have immediately sent.'

'Yes, you would have…'

I couldn't help remembering that Najib had been offered a payment seat in an engineering college. And a five-thousand-rupee capitation seat for BSc Computers. The echoes of those difficult days when everyone shunned me in the fear that I would approach them ran in my mind.

'I brought an AC and a fridge for you, Maama. But I met Kaliyal Estate owner Peerkannu Sahib in Savera hotel. He has built a new house and said there was a housewarming function.'

'Do you know him well?'

'No. He asked if I was your nephew. When he asked what I was doing I said I was in Bahrain. That's when he invited me for the function. How could I go empty-handed? He's a big shot. He's a big estate owner, no? We have to give something to suit his status. I gifted away the AC and the fridge to him. I am just returning from there.'

'Yes, you must give him.'

'As soon as I go back, I will send one to you. And a watch for Najib.'

When he said that he was going to send expensive things, I didn't know how to ask him for a piddling amount. He was a little perturbed by my silence.

'What, Maama, you are so quiet. Are you upset that I didn't come to see you?'

'No, 'pa. If I was angry, would I come to see you?'

'How's the business? Doing any export?'

When I saw his face, I couldn't answer. So I turned away.

'Why are you not saying anything?'

'No business now. Big loss. I sold the shop and the house to pay the creditors. I don't have any income now. I'm not doing anything.'

'So much loss?'

'Yes, so much that I can't even lift my head.'

I didn't want to see the changing expression on his face.

'Are you bankrupt?'

Even though the question was humiliating, I couldn't help replying. 'I'm completely broken.'

My sister was standing in the passage. No one said a word. It seemed as if something was frothing in their hearts.

'So what brings my uncle here?' The warmth in his voice had dried up.

I first wanted to hide the real reason, but my tongue slipped and the words in my mind slid out.

'A small help...'

'What help?' The coarseness in his voice was now evident.

'Only if Najib pays the money tomorrow, will he be able to write the exam. Final year. If we don't pay, his education will all go waste. He has to finish and join some work.'

'What will he gain by studying? Why don't you join him in some shop...?'

Shocked, I didn't know what to say. For the sin of educating him, I now stood, head bowed, like an accused facing interrogation.

'What help do you need?' He sounded like a stern police officer.

'If I get seven hundred and twenty-five rupees...'

Perhaps unable to reply, my nephew sat on the cushioned chair stretching out his boots on the glass teapoy and biting his nails.

It seemed to me that he was perhaps upset by his uncle's sudden misfortune.

'Don't be upset. Ups and downs in life is all god-given. If he takes away what he has given, what is there to be upset?'

I tried to pacify him.

'Maama...'

'What, 'pa...' I lifted my head.

I pretended as if I didn't see his mother secretly speaking with her eyes to him. Was this the reason that I had several times blown away the dust and grime in her eyes when we were young?

'It's not like before now, the Arab countries. Only if you slog like a dog in the hot sun can you send some money home. No salaries like earlier. They've cut them all down.'

When my nephew finished telling me his sorry tale, my sister pulled the curtain and went away inside.

I now knew that the darkness within my heart had even spread outside.

'Did you eat anything?'

'Your mother gave some tea and cake. My hunger has gone.'

'The last bus is at 8.30.'

'Yes, I had enquired about the bus timing even as I came, 'pa.'

I got down from the bus and made my way through the dark. Through the window, the flickering light from the lantern fell on the courtyard, revealing the thin, grass-laden nerve-like pathway.

Hearing my footsteps, Najib himself came to open the door. Behind him stood my wife. 'What all did our son give?'

'Did he give money?'

The string of questions pierced my heart. Seeing only the umbrella that I had taken, my wife looked disappointed.

'Vaappa…!' Najib's pathetic voice sounded like a cry of help from a deep pit.

'You don't know that your father had to stop his college education because he couldn't pay the exam fee of sixty rupees. What happened to me is also happening to you. Tomorrow it could happen to your son too. Never be dejected. It's all time's game.'

I didn't know if my wife or son slept. Or were they awake, crushed by the disappointment?

Anyway let the dawn break. My sleepless eyes travelled to the broken glass show case. There, the shiny wrapper, my tormentor, glistened.

Original title: *Kaalatthin Aavardhanam*
1995

THE CUSHIONED CHAIR AND FOUR GENERATIONS 60

THILAKAVATHI

Amma asked for flowers. To get them one had to go to the end of the street. In her excitement, Thavamani's feet didn't touch the ground. The doctor's house was at the corner. That was the only house on the street that was always clean and whitewashed like a freshly laundered veshti. If you climbed nine steps, you would reach a pial so inviting that you felt like having a sumptuous meal there, served on banana leaves. Beyond it, if you went in, a spacious hall. Polished wooden chairs with fluffy cushions, meant for guests. Thavamani loved looking at the chairs to her heart's content.

Whenever her mother sent her on an errand to the end of the street, the first thing she would do was to leap over the steps, enter the hall, stand near the chairs and trace snake-like patterns over the cushions with her middle finger. She stroked the chair too, as if patting the coffee-brown calf in her house. Whenever she did that, the calf would wriggle with excitement. Like the water in a pond which rippled when a stone is flung into it, so did the back, belly and the entire body of the calf. But the chair never jiggled. Instead Thavamani did.

'Who is that, di?' asked the doctor's wife, coming out. 'Who is it? O, Aayamma's daughter? Did she send word for something?'

'No, athai. I came simply… just like that, to see the chairs…' The words dissolved in shyness.

When the doctor's wife looked at Thavamani stroking the chair with the tip of her finger, eyes bubbling with eagerness, she said, 'My goodness! Are you that fond of the chair? Why don't you sit and see for a while?'

Thavamani gently pressed her palms on the cushion and sat on it. The chair nestled her. It was as pleasant as dipping into a pond. She thought: 'I could sit on this the whole day! How soothing it will be for the whole body.' Had athai gone in, she would have enjoyed it even more. In her presence, she felt coy.

'Okay, okay! Get up! Go and get what Amma wanted.'

Thavamani got up and came out, her heart filled with joy.

When she visited the doctor's house with her mother, she often sat on the chairs without hesitation. Like a mother nestling her infant on the lap, the chair cuddled Thavamani. She would keep her hands on the arms of the chair, barely touching them. They felt cool, like chilled water. When the thrill slithered over her skin, she would be totally mesmerised.

She wanted such cushioned chairs all for herself in her house. One for herself and the other for her friends. Lounging comfortably on those chairs, they could talk about the fairytale of the prince who crossed seven seas to reach the summit of a huge mountain. There, he found the parrot inside an iron box, guarded by poisonous snakes and black ghosts. Then he would tear open the belly of the parrot to kill the monster. But she wouldn't allow that rat-tailed Kamala to sit on the chair. She was the one who said she wouldn't give the golden bee, wasn't she?

She asked her mother, 'Why don't you buy a chair like the one in the doctor's house for our house too?'

Stroking her cheek, her mother laughingly said, 'My dear one, I'm just an aaya… You study like them, become a doctor and fill the whole house with chairs. Who is stopping you?'

If you want to buy a cushioned chair, then you must become a doctor. Thavamani decided to become a doctor.

~

Thavamani could only become a nurse. A crisp starched gown with frills like a palm frond. A white half-sleeved shirt. Knee-high stockings like fluorescent tubes. And white shoes like daintily moving doves. Falling in love with this uniform, many young girls joined this profession.

She choked when she took the first salary in hand. It was the first time she saw such a lump sum. She too was a working woman now, a woman who stood on her own feet. She felt grand, as if she had taken a vishwaroopam, spanning the earth and the sky. Whenever she felt happy, it was the image of the cushioned chair that came to mind. She wanted to immediately buy the chair with the first salary and put it in the drawing room. She walked towards the shops. Four shops in a row adjoined the hotel Komala Vilas. Several cane and wooden sofa sets in different sizes and varieties were on display. She felt that she could gaze at them for an entire day. Glistening wood, the colour of jam-plums, honey and gold. They looked even grander than what she had imagined. To buy one sofa set, she would have to shell out her whole salary plus a little more. But how would she then survive the entire month? She also had to buy medicines for her ailing mother. But one didn't have to pay for window-shopping. She went to the next shop. There too she found a wide range and she looked at the price tags intently. They were even more costly than the previous shop. Of course the prices matched the material. She left the shops with a heavy heart. She resolved to somehow rustle up the money the next month, or even borrow, to buy a sofa set. She would place the sofa set in the drawing room – there was no such room, of course; you had to assume the passageway to be the drawing room. Maybe the cracks in the wall would have to be covered and whitewashed. Dignified people like Dr Arumainathan, who lived in the next street and often popped in to exchange a few words when he passed by on his walk, must be entertained on the sofa. She didn't want anymore the indignity of pulling a dusty stool or a steel chair for them to sit on.

Rita was her friend. Often they had the opportunity to work together in the same ward. Thavamani had visited Rita's house once. In the drawing room, under the images of Jesus and Virgin Mary, there were antique chairs. Broad, wide chairs. One could even squat on them. Embroidered cushions with floral designs on the cane backs. Elegant curved armrests like a snake in hood, edged with decorative wooden motifs in the shape of tiny rosewater sprinklers. The chair was comfortable. She didn't want Rita to visit her home for at least two more months. How could she make Rita sit on a mat?

Thavamani asked Rita's advice. 'In this town Navabharatam Company is the biggest. They have all the latest models. Of good quality too. The owner is a relative of ours. If you like, you can pay some advance and buy a sofa set. The rest you can pay in two or three instalments.'

She felt as if all the flowers of a tree-jasmine had suddenly drizzled on her when she took refuge under it for shade. The very next day she rustled up half the amount and brought the sofa home.

It was ten minutes past six then. A sofa, as if two chairs had been joined together. Besides that, two other chairs. The entire set stood majestically in the drawing room. Shiny wooden frames like a freshly bathed child. She slowly came near and sat on one end of the long sofa. She imagined Gopal sitting on the other side. She felt like calling him immediately and asking him to sit there. This thought grew like a forest within her, held her by the nape and pushed her forward. She locked the door and hurried to the telephone booth at the end of the street and called Gopal in the hospital.

'What is it?' asked the voice at the other end in surprise.

'Please come home for ten minutes...please...'

'Just now I put on my uniform. How can I go and ask the doctor for permission?'

'Please...please... don't say no.'

'What's the matter? Tell me.'

'I will tell all that only in person.'

She sped home and stood looking for his cycle lamp to appear at the end of the road. He came in ten minutes.

'Come, come,' she invited him and made him sit on the place where she had imagined him sitting.

'What is the matter?'

'Wait,' she said and went into the kitchen and returned with a stainless-steel cup. A spoon stuck out of it like a cock's comb.

'What is it?'

'Payasam.'

'Ai! What... what is this? What's the occasion? Is it your birthday?'

'In a way, yes. But, not for me...'

'Then whose is it?'

Shyly she pointed to the sofa. 'You must do one thing for me. This coming Sunday, we must sit on the sofa and take a photo... you and me together...'

Smiling, he said, 'Yes.'

'We must make our children too sit on the sofa and take a photo,' she said to herself.

And they did take a photo. They made the elder girl Sushila and the younger boy Guna sit on the sofa on their birthdays and took photographs. They framed them and hung them on the wall.

Rita, who was visiting Thavamani after many months, wondered at the way the photographs were hung. 'What is this, Thavamani? You have hung the photographs of you and your husband side by side. Why didn't you hang the photographs of your children on the side? Why did you hang them one below the other?'

'There's a reason. This one was taken on Sushila's first birthday. One will be taken when she will wear her first long skirt. One when she wears a half-sari. One when she graduates with a black robe. After that one with her husband, garlands and all. After that she standing with her children. All this must be hung in a row one beside the other. Don't you need space for all that? It will be the same for Guna too. Till he becomes a doctor and opens his own clinic, a steth in hand.'

Rita struggled to contain her tears. How many dreams, desires and hopes in a mother's heart.

But her husband never understood her and neither did he comport himself suitably. 'Tell me, how is Gopal now? Is he the same like before?' enquired Rita about their married life, which had withered like a dried garland, become thorny like a parched branch.

'Same, as usual. Even last week there was a problem in the hospital. A staff had stolen medicines. I had already warned him once or twice. This time he was caught red-handed. They suspended him. Thinking that I was the reason behind his suspension he came home to ask for forgiveness. Gopal was eating at the time. We heard a knock on the door. When Gopal opened the door, that fellow sobbed to him.

'"Have you come to straighten this universe or what? You think you are a great revolutionary? Why can't you do your job and keep to yourself? Why are you unnecessarily creating problems? Because of you I feel so ashamed. Because of your arrogance you have been deliberately shunted here on transfer. Because of you I was also forced to get a transfer here. So much problem because of you. Can't you be a good girl, get a light ward and be happy – instead you have started creating trouble here too." For the past one week he has been torturing me like this with words. Now my children are my only hope,' said Thavamani to Rita.

Even Thavamani's children didn't live up to her hopes. She thought her elder daughter would study well, be intelligent and stand on her own two feet. Instead, when she was in the tenth standard, she ran off with a boy who hadn't even finished his tenth. Within eight months of her marriage, she delivered a plump child. Love won't feed hunger, will it? When she got into deep trouble, she could have come to her mother. But that obstinate girl drank the pesticide meant for the chilli plant and ended her life. When her daughter's only child was handed over to Thavamani, she was devastated. Her only last hope was Guna. She spent her days dreaming he would become a doctor. Enamoured by cinema stars, he hung around the film studios of Kodambakkam, hoping to become a star himself. She broke to pieces like a shattered mirror.

In the previous night's rain, the shed at the back which had housed all the junk, had collapsed. She went to see the damage. With help, she cleared the crushed roof and looked over her things.

She got a start. A symbol of her happy days, the sofa set bought with her first salary, now lay in a heap, dusty and grimy. To her the sofa set suddenly looked like a mark of misfortune, as if a consequence of a curse. She immediately sent off the sofa set to be repaired.

When the freshly upholstered sofas came home, she felt as if twenty-five years had rolled back. The sofa set looked like a fresh bloom. The armrests, wooden frames and the upholstery looked the same as they had when the set had been bought twenty-five years ago. She stood aside, gazing at it lovingly.

Suddenly the sofa seemed to mock at her. Waves of images tossed in her mind, one after another – she and he sitting for the first time, enjoying, taking a photo… Would it ever be possible to restore and renew her heart like the sofa? But hadn't that become frayed and threadbare now? Ruined hopes, destroyed aspirations and crushed dreams burdened her chest and filled her eyes with tears. If hope is life, and hope about hope itself is lost, life becomes nothing but a millstone – what was she to do? When her heart was mired in frustration, a tender hand plucked her little finger. Thavamani looked… it was her granddaughter Sudha.

'What is it, my darling?'

'Paati! Will you make me also sit on the sofa and take a photo and hang it there…?'

Her heart surged like an untrammelled flood. A tinge of dampness spread gradually over the arid, cracked expanse of her heart.

'Of course, my darling.' A desire to hang a row of at least Sudha's photos sprouted in her heart.

Original title: *Naarkaaliyum Naangu Thalaimuraigalum*
1990

Seven Seventy Times 61

A Egbert Sachidanandam

S Albert Gnanam, who worked as a sexton in our church from 1 Sept. 1979, has given in writing to this commission that during the tenure of the 1982-84 Pastorate Committee he had embezzled Rs 4820.50 collected as donation, given to him to be deposited in the bank. Further, he has also admitted that he never returned the Christmas advance of Rs 1000.00 that he received from the Pastorate on 10.12.83. It has also come to light that when Reverend Stanley Rajasekhar questioned him concerning this matter, Albert, his wife Yesammal and his daughter Esther abused the Reverend in very foul language and also cast aspersions for other reasons too. Besides, he has also failed to carry out his other duties such as maintaining the garden, keeping the church premises clean and returning the subscription envelopes to the congregation.

Owing to the above reasons, many activities of the church were disrupted and it has brought disrepute to the Pastorate. Hence, members of the commission are of the opinion that Albert Gnanam may not be allowed to continue as sexton. This commission recommends that Albert Gnanam be dismissed from his post with immediate effect.

Reverend	Mr R John Yesupadam (Head)
Stanley Rajasekhar	Mr M S Johnson

Pastor — Mr K Simon Rajendran
Date: 12.6.84 — Mrs R Lilavathi Moses

Samuel closed the file and kept it back in the box. The stench of corpses from the hospital mortuary across the road curdled his innards. He closed the window. Only the rays of the sun streaming through the broken tiles lit his one-room tenement. The walls that had never seen lime paste were an eyesore. It had been four months since he put in a submission to the Pastorate to change the window to the east. His dark-skinned children played on the church verandah, bare-bodied.

He put the subscription covers and notices for Brother Sam Jebaraj's special prayer meeting the next day into a cloth bag, slung it across his shoulder and set off from home.

His wife was standing by the cycas tree. 'What did the pastor say?'

'Tomorrow, the committee is meeting, it seems.'

Avoiding her face, he looked at the cycas tree. The tall tree planted by the Reverend Mclean. It stood still.

When he reached the cement road on his cycle, tears filled his eyes to the extent he couldn't see the road.

'Here, Samuel, the pastor is calling you.'

He turned, hearing Albert's voice. Albert was standing with Yesammal in front of the pastor's house.

He parked his cycle and went into the newly built room with an attached bathroom in the pastor's house. He felt that he should give another submission to replace the tiles and change the window of his house.

'Get the secretary's signature in this circular and show it to everyone. Decorate the church for the wedding in the evening.' Thomas and Viswasam were still there. But no sign of Sigamani.

'Viswasam, find out when the interview is in Gnanodayam. Reverend Wilson only is the chairman, no? We'll tell him! In our Pastorate I'm going to recommend your son only. Thomas. I'll give you a letter for Reverend Diraviyam. You and Sigamani go there and see what he says. It's enough if he tells CMC, Vellore…'

He came out. Albert and Yesamma were standing in the porch, hands folded.

When he neared the post office, he saw the slushy buffalo pond. At the end of the slope by the road he could see Albert's hut. There was no door. He knew that after the decision of the commission, when he was dismissed from the church, Albert was living here. He remembered that the pastor had asked him to allow Yesammal and Esther to sleep in the church verandah at night. After that, his own family had stopped sleeping in the breezy verandah and huddled in the room to the stench of the corpses.

How did the Albert family reconcile with the pastor – when he thought about this, the morning's incident came to mind and gnawed his heart.

'Do you know that girl Grace from Ambedkar Colony?' asked the pastor. Sigamani, Thomas and Viswasam were with him.

'Yes, I know.'

'Do you talk to her?'

'Yes, I do.'

'Have you ever gone there when no one else was at home?'

'Yes, I have… to give the covers, and show the circulars.'

'Then you would laugh and joke with her, no?'

Samuel looked at the others.

'Only if her father is not there, I would speak to her.'

'So you would chat and laugh and say naughty things, no?'

'Nothing like that.'

'Don't lie. You have spoken inappropriately to her.'

'She's like my…'

'A fellow like you, why wouldn't he have said nasty things about the pastor's wife?'

'Ayya…'

'What ayya, ayya? You said nasty things about the ayya's wife. What is the point of this "ayya"?'

'God promise, I didn't say any such thing. Who told you, saar?'

'Mercy, ask Esther to come.'

Wiping her hands on the ends of her half-sari, Esther came in from the kitchen. He could see the pastor's wife hiding in the kitchen.

'Esther, what did he say about ayya's wife?'

'"Is that fatso all alone?"'

'Ayya, she's telling lies. I swear I never speak much to these people. Two months ago, you yourself told me not to have anything much to do with these people.'

'Shut up. Why should Esther lie? One who has a relationship with Grace, where is the surety that he wouldn't have said this?'

'I swear on the Bible. I've never misbehaved with Grace. And I never said anything about ayya's wife.'

'Look here, this is my personal matter. You are not agreeing. I will take whatever action I want.' The pastor's hands shook. Through his tears Samuel could see the pastor's lips twitching behind the closely trimmed beard. The images of his wife and three children also kept flashing through the tears.

'Ayya…' Samuel grasped his feet. 'Please don't sack me. I promise I didn't say anything about ayya's wife.'

The pastor removed his feet from Samuel's clutches and went in saying, 'I will call the Pastorate Arbitration Board tomorrow itself and take a decision.'

He could see Esther watching from the kitchen. Her eyes seemed to be smiling.

Viswasam and Sigamani didn't say anything. Thomas got up and came.

'Look here, Samuel. Why are you making this a big matter? You've done wrong, no, so ask for pardon!'

He went by the cement road, and sped along the mud road next to the market. The secretary had built a new house in the State Bank Colony only last year.

When he crossed the municipality garbage dump, he could see coffin maker Ellappan's house. A few months ago when he had come here along with the pastor to make a coffin for Magdelammal, he had found Yesammal standing there.

'What ayya? Like those hospital girls, you thought I was also your wife, is it? You sinner, you threw out my husband. Will you ever prosper? Besides, wearing a robe and all, big preaching you are doing! Dei, Samuel, you've thrown mud into our food, and grabbed this job… I'll see how you'll continue. If not today, some day we only will get back the job.'

Through the Chetty Street, he crossed the Perumal Koil toll gate and reached the State Bank Colony. Freshly bathed, the secretary came with damp hair.

'You ought to have come at six-thirty. Why have you come at eight-thirty? What's the matter? Samuel… Ei, look here…'

Samuel wiped his eyes and looked up.

'Ayya, you know what all atrocities that old sexton Albert's family committed in the church. They beat my children. They abused my wife whenever they saw her. What all they said about the pastor. But now suddenly, the pastor himself has asked them to sleep on the church verandah. And Esther is working in his house.'

'She spoke ill of me too. So what? They asked for the pastor's pardon, and he pardoned them. He's asked them to sleep only on the verandah, no? Leave it. Since he's also the chairman of the pastorate, he's allowed it.'

'He said that Esther mentioned that I spoke nasty things about ayya's wife. So he's questioning me. Why would I say anything about her? Not only that. My uncle's daughter is in Ambedkar Colony. Her mother is the Bible-woman in the Thiruvallur Pastorate. So I usually ask her about our village matters. And the pastor is suspicious about all this.'

'Let that be, 'pa. Okay, why did you go to old secretary Arulanandam fellow's house yesterday?'

'I went to give a birthday card to his son. Why are you asking, ayya?'

'No, I believe you go there often. Only in his time that Albert fellow sprouted guts. They nicely looted the Pastorate. Don't go to his house and all.'

'For a sexton, all houses are the same. I've gone to his house only for church matters.'

'Bloody scoundrels.'

'Ayya… the committee is meeting tomorrow to discuss my matter.' Samuel gave the circular. The secretary read it and signed.

'Okay, get the signatures from all the nine members. Distribute the Convention notice to all. Clean the church premises for the evening wedding. Tomorrow night buy fifteen biriyani packets. I'll see to everything.'

Samuel gave the subscription covers and the convention notices to all the houses. He got the signatures of all the nine in the circular. When he returned home, it was three. He wasn't hungry. Since none of the youth association members turned up, he himself decorated the church with plastic flowers. He placed four bamboo arches twisted with plastic flowers in the aisle. He swept the church clean. He polished the cross and lamps with Brasso. He could see Esther carrying something in a bag to the pastor's house next door. Yesamma was plucking drumsticks.

The wedding that ought to have started at four-thirty started only at five-thirty. As the hymn 'Mangalam Sezhikkave' (Let us all prosper, blessed be thy grace) was sung, the pastor rushed into the vestry.

'Where is the marriage register?'

'It's in your house only, ayya.'

'Don't you know you have to bring it, you idiot?'

He ran and brought the fat register. He tucked in the jutting torn pages and kept the register on the table.

'You know it is torn? Shouldn't you have bound it?'

The bride and the groom arrived. He didn't say a word. After they signed, an elderly man gave a hundred rupee note to the pastor. He took out a receipt book from his pocket and wrote out. He gave fifty rupees to Samuel. 'Give this today itself to the treasurer. Tonight there is all-night prayer, no? Don't sleep off. Be awake till everyone leaves.'

When the marriage party left the church and went outside, one of them gave Samuel five rupees. He removed the plastic flowers and kept them in the room. He swept away the flowers that had dropped off and went to the treasurer's house to give him the money.

The prayer group came at ten in the night. They prayed for Sam Jebaraj's convention the following day. Thomas and Sigamani were there. Thomas prayed for a long time. Yesammal and Esther were kneeling in front of Thomas. At two, Samuel bought tea for everyone. When everyone left at four, he locked the church and went to lie down. His whole body ached.

He got up at five in the morning and put on the cassette of 'Palaivana Solai' by Padma Nataraja Mudaliar. On Fridays and Wednesdays when people heard new gospel songs on the loudspeaker, they usually asked him about the singers. This 'Palaivana Solai' cassette was given to him by Johnson Ayya. He was to keep it for a week and return it. When the song 'Pothum Kripaye' (My grace is sufficient for thee) was being played, Esther filled water from the tap behind the cycas tree and went inside the pastor's house. He realised that from now on he wouldn't get the water allowance.

At eight he bought a cloth banner from Mano Arts, tied it across two casuarina poles at the entrance of the church. He felt the word 'Avikuria' in the banner was somewhat small. The name could have been written in blue... He took the subscription covers and the notices and left. He distributed all the subscription covers of the last fortnight and came back at three-thirty.

He ate the previous day's rice and lay down on the mat. At four he got up with a start, put on his shirt and hastened outside to get milk for the pastor's house. He saw Yesammal and Esther coming down the road with a milk can.

He washed his face and opened the door and the windows of the church. He set the mikes on the altar and the pulpit. The Bible stand's Ahuja mike was under repair. He watered the plants around the church, including the cycas. He plucked the fat, round yellow cones within arm's reach from under the matted fronds. There were plenty of worms. There was a cycas in the high school. It was also a male tree. Reproduction was not at all possible.

His wife had tidied the guest room. He fetched two buckets of well water. Esther was playing with the pastor's son with a rose plucked from the flower pot.

Sam Jebaraj came at six. The pastor, the secretary, the treasurer and the members of the pastorate committee chatted with him. He bought bondas, multicoloured boondi and coffee for them. Sam Jebaraj drank only the coffee. The convention began at six-thirty. Sam Jebaraj talked about the second coming of the Christ. Samuel sat near the amplifier. The pulpit mike gave a bit of trouble. Perhaps the lead wire had snapped off somewhere. The pastor glared at him from the altar. He had already complained to him that many people walked around stamping the lead wire. Sam Jebaraj asked those who accepted Jesus as a personal saviour to raise their hands. No one should look at the other. Samuel looked from the corner of his eye. A lot of people raised their hands – Thomas, Sigamani, the secretary, Albert… Yesammal, Esther… The church reverberated with the sounds of people chanting 'hallelujah', 'praise the lord', 'bless the lord' and 'Amen'. A few spoke in tongues. Some clapped. Some shook their heads vigorously. Some trembled, as if with cold. Yesammal was one of them.

When the convention was over at eight-thirty, Sam Jebaraj went to the guest room with people who wanted a special prayer. He said that he didn't want any food.

Samuel locked all the doors of the church. He placed three chairs under the cycas tree for the pastor, the secretary and the treasurer. In front were nine chairs in a half-circle. The cycas shone in the tubelight from the verandah.

He bought fifteen biriyani packets from Muniandi Vilas. By nine, Johnson, Gnanayya and Thomas arrived. After a few minutes Sigamani, Viswasam and the secretary came from the pastor's house. At nine-fifteen the pastor arrived and the meeting began.

'Let us pray. Our dear Lord, who is the wellspring and the reason for everything on earth, we have assembled here to discuss matters relating to the church which bears your name. Benevolent father, may you bless us to take the right decision…'

Samuel placed the biriyani packets on the long bench in the vestry and sat in a corner. He could see that the pastor had finished praying. The secretary got up.

'In the name of the Lord, we have gathered here today to decide on an important issue concerning our sexton Samuel. Our pastor will speak on the matter.'

When the pastor got up to speak, the frond of the cycas stroked his face.

'Precious children of the Lord, as you all know, at the recommendation of the commission in July last year, we tried to discharge Albert from his duties. At the instigation of some members of the church, we faced impediments. And you also know that it became a police case and we finally managed to remove him and his family from the church. Only in these troubled circumstances, we appointed Samuel as a sexton last August. Within six months, we confirmed his job and started paying him a salary of three hundred and fifty rupees.'

'Pardon me for interrupting you, pastor,' Gnanayya said in a hoarse voice, stroking his moustache. Samuel remembered that he was the uncle of the pastor.

'What the pastor says is hundred per cent true. I too questioned him, "What is this, from 1972 onwards we have been paying only two hundred rupees for the sexton. Why have you raised it to three hundred and fifty rupees…"'

'Many members of the congregation too asked me the same question… I raised it because he was the servant of the Lord… Okay… last month, pastors and bishops from our diocese went to Ooty for the clergy retreat. Before leaving, I instructed the sexton to take care of my wife and children and get them whatever they needed. My wife called him twice through Esther. Once to buy rice and another time to go to the post office… At the time, he spoke vulgarly about my wife…'

'What did he say?' asked the treasurer.

'Should all those vulgar things be repeated?' rebuked the secretary.

'Once an enquiry is conducted, it has to be told. On both occasions he told Esther, "Is that fatso all alone? I will come and squeeze her."'

'Dirty rascal! What is the need for an enquiry? Just fire him immediately!'

'Mr Gnanayya, be patient.' Johnson held up his hands.

'He is right to get angry,' said Sigamani.

'Today if he says this about the pastor's wife, tomorrow won't he say the same thing about other women?' asked Viswasam.

Samuel wiped with his hands the sweat drops that gathered on his face. The needle-like leaves of the cycas lifted up in the breeze, as if aiming straight at his face.

'Pastor, who told you that he said all this?' asked Johnson.

'Albert's daughter, Esther.'

'Please don't mistake me. If Albert's family is the witness, it is like Beelzebub's daughter being the witness. What all they did against the church! Esther is their daughter. To what extent will this be true?'

'Mr Johnson, don't you know the Christian doctrine – When King David said to Nathan, "I have sinned against the Lord," Nathan said, "The Lord also hath put away thy sin. Thou shall not die. When we also confess our sins, we too will be forgiven." Read Samuel 1: 1-9. The Albert family has confessed that they had sinned against the Lord and asked for forgiveness. "Each one of you confess your sins to each other," says Jacob 5:16, isn't it? What do we say when we pray to the Lord – Like we forgive those who sin against, please forgive us our sins too, don't we? Last month, Albert, Esther and Yesammal, all of them stood at the altar of our church and asked for my pardon. I forgave them. After that Esther started working in my house. What's wrong? Albert's got a job in Vandavasi. Because they are women, I allowed Esther and Yesammal to sleep on the verandah of the church. What is wrong with this?'

'The pastor is setting a good example by this,' said Sigamani.

'Yes,' said Thomas and the treasurer.

'I'm glad that you forgave them, pastor. But the question is whether the Albert family has really reformed itself. After pardon, there should be reformation, no? If they had really reformed themselves, Yesammal wouldn't have spoken so insultingly to the sexton.'

'Who is the witness to that?'

'Ask Samuel himself.'

'He will lie now because he is angry with Esther,' said the pastor.

'Some members in our congregation can even needle him not to confess to his mistakes,' said the secretary. Johnson laughed.

'Why are you laughing? The people who don't like this Pastorate Committee, why won't they do this to create trouble? Ayya, please remain in your house for a while.'

They called Samuel. Everyone looked intently at his face. His gaze held the cycas tree. 'Let me ask you straight. Tell me, didn't you speak vulgarly about the pastor's wife to Esther?' asked the secretary.

'I swear I didn't say any such thing.'

'What such thing?'

'That is…'

'No problem, come on, tell us.'

'The pastor's wife… that is… "is that fatso alone… I will come and squeeze her" – I didn't say all this.'

'What, 'pa? How did you know that we were going to ask you this only – that you said it?' asked Sigamani.

'I was listening to what you all were saying.'

The secretary looked at the others.

Sigamani approached Samuel. 'Samuel, think carefully. You must have said something about the pastor's wife sometime casually. Never mind, 'pa. Tell the pastor and ask for his forgiveness. What do you say? I'll see to it that you don't lose your job.'

'Yes, 'pa, Samuel. Don't be afraid, tell,' said Viswasam.

'No, ayya. If I had said it, I would have asked for forgiveness. Without having said…'

'Dei, now you are going to get a kick from me. You broomstick, agree that you said it. She is the wife of an anointed man. She is like your mother, da, you dirty scoundrel.'

'Gnanayya! Gnanayya! Hold him.'

'Leave me, leave me.'

'Please sit down, Gnanayya. Don't get angry.'

'After having said it, he's also lying… Ungrateful rascal!'

Johnson held Gnanayya. 'Ask for forgiveness, 'pa. Think of your family…'

'Ayya, let the committee members say whatever they want, I'm not bothered. Even if I lose my job, I will not ask for forgiveness…' He looked at the cycas tree and said this, without looking at anyone's face. His chest heaved.

For a few minutes no one spoke.

The secretary cleared his throat and said, 'Okay, 'pa, you go.'

Samuel walked towards the vestry. The pastor came back from his house. Samuel was standing by the entrance of the vestry.

'In the Lord's Holy Mountain, Lucifer, who had lived a blemishless life, lost his wisdom on account of his proud heart. He went against the Lord. The Lord didn't forgive him. He threw him away from the Holy Mountain into the devouring flames. Samuel has also started working against me. He thinks he is equal to me. If he remains the sexton here, I will ask the bishop to transfer me to another pastorate. I can't bear the shame.'

When the pastor finished speaking, the committee members turned emotional. They jumped up, gesticulated with their hands and shouted at the top of their voices that Samuel should be thrown out.

Samuel entered the church and stood in front of the altar. The crucifix shone in the night lamp. He knelt down, prayed and through the vestry walked towards his home.

Original title: *Yezhu Ezhuvathu Tharam*
1986

THE SAGA OF SAROSADEVI 62

SHENBAGAM RAMASWAMY

When Sarosadevi tried to peep into the outside world from her mother's belly, her mother Bhagyam was watching a film. When she gave her breathless mother's belly a hard kick, the mother shouted out, 'Oon.'

'Bhagyam Akka! Has the pain started?' asked Ponnamma anxiously.

'Think so, di,' said Bhagyam, screwing her face and slowly getting up.

It was the time when actor Sarojadevi was mouthing the song sung by the playback singer P Susheela: 'Thangathile Oru Kuraiyirundalam (Even if there is a flaw in the gold…)'

A stern voice ordered from the back, 'Sit down, di.'

'Move your feet. Make way for this akka. She's got labour pains.' Ponnamma had to announce this loudly in the dark of the cinema hall.

The women in the hall who understood the import of the words started to grumble: 'Wretched woman! Look at her coming to watch a film at the time of labour!' 'Such a craze for films, is it?' 'Perhaps she thought that if she delivers in the cinema hall she'll get fame.' Hearing the words from the unseen faces, Bhagyam and Ponnamma made their way out with difficulty, grazing the knees of a line of women.

When Ponnamma realised that Bhagyam wouldn't last till she reached the hospital, she sent for midwife Paapa.

By the time Sivaji Ganesan and Sarojadevi were united with their child in the film, Bhagyam had given birth to a girl.

'Ei, di, the child was born when you saw a Sarosadevi film! So keep that name itself for her!' suggested Ponnamma. Since Bhagyam didn't have any reason to oppose this, she started calling the child by that name.

Just as Bhagyam was deprived of nutritious food and vitamins, so too the child. By the time she turned a month old, she had suffered and survived many a fever and diarrhoea.

After Bhagyam resumed her work at the construction site, the child's condition turned even more pathetic. The child's only caretaker was Bhagyam's grandmother, Old Woman Appayi. Shrunk and wizened, with skin like the bark of a neem tree and a gait like a lopsided weighing scale, Appayi herself needed someone to tend to her. Since her deaf ears couldn't hear Sarosadevi's soft moans and cries and heard only the high-pitched screams, most of the time Sarosadevi kept bawling.

Other than that, Appayi looked after the child with whatever affection she could muster.

Whenever the hunger-ridden child cried for food, the old woman would feed the tiny mouth two conchfuls of coffee that she bought from the Nadar Coffee shop. Three-fourths of Appayi would be satisfied with this, but one fourth of her would lament, 'The belly of this bitch will never get filled.' Hence Sarosadevi got into the habit of drinking coffee in the third month itself.

Since her body always touched the floor through the tattered mat and she was always covered with damp, soiled sheets, Sarosadevi was prone to cold. Even when the child struggled to breathe, whining 'gar-gar', the two women didn't have the means to take her to the doctor. At such times Appayi would resort to a crude treatment. Rolling the end of her dirty sari, she would take out her snuff packet from her waist, dip the cloth into the snuff and fearlessly put it into the two holes of Sarosadevi's tiny nose. Sarosadevi survived these life-and-death moments. So Sarosadevi got into the habit of taking snuff from the fourth month itself. Her strong resistance to snuff slowly weakened and at one stage it became just a nod and a mild sneeze.

Unable to bear the moaning and groaning of Sarosadevi, Appayi took a decision: she bought a five-paisa biscuit from the Pandi petty shop, mixed it with coffee and fed the soggy stuff to the child.

Though this was in contradiction to what the childcare books advised, it agreed very well with Sarosadevi.

The old woman kissed the child with an unwashed mouth and loads of bad breath. Though WHO might not agree to all of this, Sarosadevi was in no position to disagree; she had to endure and also survive.

Life is nothing but a cluster of cells thirsting to survive and Sarosadevi was a living proof of this. Appayi, on the other hand, firmly believed that life could not be so easily wiped away. Between them, they pushed time like this and Sarosadevi soon turned two and a bit. Fearing that the evil eye would befall her emaciated, pot-bellied granddaughter, Appayi always said when anyone asked, 'She is three going on four.' Clutching the pots and pans, holding on to the backs of her mother and grandmother and grasping the walls, Sarosadevi learned to walk and even run. By this time Appayi had become more decrepit and found it difficult even to walk.

Now only in her dreams could Appayi carry Sarosadevi. So whenever the child pestered her, she pinched, beat and punched her with her bony fingers, showing her helpless irritation.

One day, as Appayi was walking, biscuit from the Pandi shop in one hand and the grandchild in the other hand, a cycle that looked amorphous to her dim eyes, turned true and solid and hit her; in a snap she relinquished her life.

By the time this news reached Bhagyam – who was working at a hospital construction site far away – and she hurried back, Sarosadevi had bawled her lungs out and finally fainted.

After the funeral rites were over and as Bhagyam contemplated going back to work, Sarosadevi lay on her lap.

She thought of her husband, who had eloped with the girl Renuka who lived in the third house and was now working in town. 'Send the girl if you want. We'll bring her up,' he had said to Ponnamma who had seen him in town and berated him.

'Scoundrel! As if the one who ran away with a loose woman will look after a child.' In the next instant itself, Bhagyam had flung aside the idea.

When she enquired around, she came to know that there was a woman who would tend to the child if she was given food and twenty-five paise per day.

When she went to see her, she found out that this was her profession. Ten to twelve tots crowded around her and she greeted Bhagyam with an assured air.

'May you live well! How well you've understood the problems of women like me.' Bhagyam praised her wholeheartedly and set off for work. But Sarosadevi kicked up a racket in protest against this new arrangement.

'You leave, 'ma. On the first day they will usually cry. Then she will get used to the other children. You go,' she said firmly and Bhagyam left.

The fever that Sarosadevi got that night never abated. The next day her body swelled. She neither ate anything nor opened her eyes. Moaning, she lay, and on the third day, even the moaning stopped.

'O my princess, my princess, my little parrot.' Bhagyam leant against the wall and wailed. Not knowing how to rationalise her sorrow and whom to blame, the women who visited her could only say, 'Don't cry. Enough. Have some coffee.'

When she returned for work at the hospital site, the mason said, 'I heard that you lost a child.' She stood crying.

He said in a kind of philosophical tone, 'Even if the child lived, what comforts would she have seen? No father. A mother who is struggling even for gruel. She realised that this world is difficult. So she left. All this is god's deed. What is in our hands?' He sneakily looked around.

'Don't cry, girl… If you want another child, you can always beget one. You've still got years.' When he uttered this in a low voice, Bhagyam stood, head bowed.

Yet another experience of rearing a child without a father seemed to approach her from afar like a very, very faint shadow.

But somehow she wasn't afraid.

Original title: *Sarosadeviyin Kathai*
1981

In the Hours that Remain... 63

Subrabharathi Manian

As if discarded in a corner, Mallikarjunan had to forever sit down. A corner that he was fed up with. The dulling of the paint and the oil stains silhouetting an image on the wall always looked as if someone was sitting, even if one wasn't. Though he sat like this for ten years, he didn't get sores, boils or piles. Piles and diabetes only visited people who ate three times a day... if one gets piles, one is doomed to pick and prod now and then with one's hand...

There was no sound from the hosiery machines in the neighbouring godown. Nowadays, it was only for a week in a month that one heard the machines and the noise. Earlier there was at least noise that reached one's ears. With no noise it was sheer torture. If there was noise, it seemed as if someone was proclaiming that there wouldn't be any dearth of two meals a day.

A yellowing veshti was drying out in the sun. It would be enough to wear if one stepped out. Today there was a wedding in Thirumalaisamy's family. It would have been good had the veshti been a little whiter for the function. At least when one sat around with people, one needed to look white and bright.

It was in this corner that the old lady's life had been snuffed out. And after that he too had to silently confine himself to that corner. Earlier, a haphazardly written board would hang outside – 'Mallikarjunan Chettiar: Turban Tied Here'. Don't know who threw it away. It could have remained there. But it would have been of no use simply remaining there.

In earlier times, whenever there was a wedding in town, even if relatives and community members were invited or not, Mallikarjunan would be the first to be invited. Because who could bear looking at a groom without a turban? Time was when Mallikarjunan used to sit like a crownless king amid at least ten colourful turbans hanging around him. Then there was a value for caste. And respect for elders. At a wedding, even if one small ritual was missed out, they could dare to chase them away, saying, 'Cannot give you the girl.' On the wedding day, would a groom without a turban be able to visit a Ganesha temple?

Mallikarjunan was immensely respected. One got a turban only on 'advance booking'. People would come to remind him the day before the wedding, taking him away for the night's food. Even so they would again return in the morning either in a cycle or on foot and knock on the door, 'Have you got up...' They would wake him up at three in the morning for a six o'clock muhurtam. Only if one reached the groom's place at four, could the ten-yard cloth be folded and tucked into the groom's head so that fold by fold was visible, with one end hanging down. Only when he had fixed the fanned-out jewel called 'seepu' and taken a look at the groom did Mallikarjunan feel satisfied that his task was done.

You could charge by the demand. Could ask for fifty to two hundred, depending on the status of the family. A wedding could take place without a comb. But not without a turban from Mallikarjunan.

It had been a mistake to remain on a single livelihood such as this till the age of forty-five. Ten painful years had passed by like weddingless lazy months. It had been many years since the community had formed an association. When they had revelled in their own building, mikes, etcetera, Mallikarjunan had been happy too. 'Our community people are inferior to no one. First they should become big shots...' Then a wedding hall for the community. When they had bought all the paraphernalia required for the wedding ceremony, someone had suggested a turban too. He had almost fainted when he saw silk ready-made turbans in ten different colours. 'Ada, you sinners... in the end, you have brought my ruin...'

All the pomp had vanished from a community wedding. At muhurtam time, instead of tying the ten-yard turban till the groom felt breathless, they now simply plopped a readymade one, as if by magic.

At the time of a wedding, even close relatives wriggled away, saying, 'Our association is giving the turban free. If Uncle feels that he alone should tie the turban, then he can come and do it for free.' When he saw the turbans in any community wedding Mallikarjunan felt like weeping. When he was handed the rice grains to bless the couple, where else would he look but at the turbaned groom. 'Instead of doing things for free, it is better that the turbans are eaten away by insects,' felt Mallikarjunan and bundled away all the cloths. When the old lady lay incontinent, they used two moth-eaten turbans to cover her. The old thing was lucky. She was covered in silk. From then on, now and then the daughter-in-law tore up pieces to wipe the children, while the son used up the rest to make loincloths for himself. When he had searched the previous month, he had found a white turban cloth, not so badly damaged. Thinking that it might be used at least as a veshti, he had washed and dried it out. He was afraid that it might give way when worn and cause a scene. He hadn't gone out ever since he folded it away carefully.

Times had changed even more. A few said that marriages were taking place without turbans. It was Kali Yugam. Otherwise would they say that they were shy to wear a turban on their heads? It was a time when boys thought that it was enough to get hold of any woman and roam around. As if this were not enough, there were inter-caste marriages too. You didn't have to ask about the boys working in the banian factories. What's more, girls too were everywhere in the factories, sticking labels, ironing and cutting cloth. Uncaring of castes, they easily got into relationships based on employment.

His son had never faced such hard times in the past four or five years. No export orders at all. From four days of work a week, it had now tapered off to four days a month. Boys from decent weaving communities who had joined the banian factories were now in dire straits. Some had returned to weaving. A few had found opportunities in power looms. Still others who remained in the banian factories also took up jobs in power looms and weaving whenever they were out of work. Thinking it would be futile to be a labourer in the weaving industry, Mallikarjunan's son had sold off his wife's jewels, bought up panties, bras and underskirts and gone to the neighbouring town. The thought of his spreading out bras and underskirts on some platform and calling out to ladies who pass by brought a smile to Mallkarjunan. 'Only in name he belonged to the Mysore Maharajah's clan,' he moaned and straightened up. When he was young, in his hometown in Karnataka, everyone would only come to school wearing a turban. The colour and the shape of the turban differed from person to person. The style of the turban revealed the person's family, profession and status. In royal families, they would change a turban a day. Now the lineage itself had vanished.

Had the banian companies run properly, there would at least be two rupees a week for beedis. If he mentioned to his son that the mouth gnawed and dried up, he would get some money to visit Konaar's shop. Now he had to wait for the daughter-in-law to bring the plate of rice. But the regularity of that too had decreased. Yesterday, he had got only one meal.

When the old lady was alive, whenever he left for a muhurtam, she would see him off cheerfully, whatever their quarrel. 'Tie the turban with a good heart and bless them with rice grains,' she would say. It was good that she wasn't around to see the turbans being torn bit by bit, used as a bedsheet for the cold or to wipe shit. When he had come to know that his brother's son had sold off a beige turban for ten rupees and bought arrack, he had felt humiliated. Since he didn't want it to be known, he had fumed inside. If it came to light, people would mock: can a turban turn to arrack? There were plenty to gossip.

What was the point of sitting idle? Might as well go to the wedding in Thirumalaisami's family, he decided, and got up clutching the wall. There was both pain and a kind of pleasure when he scratched his beard. Thirumalaisami was a bit decent, bothered about elders. When it came to a wedding, he would distribute the cards only to the big shots, the upper castes and the turban community. People would remark that this was how our community wedding ought to be conducted. Thirumalaisami was a man of old values. That was why he had remembered to invite him. It was a comfort to know that people still didn't forget him. Whether the board 'Mallikarjunan Chettiar: Turban Tied Here' had been there or not, Mallikarjunan would always be held in esteem. After his turban-tying days were over, if anyone called him 'Chettiar', he started to get angry. 'What is the need for the title 'Chettiar' now? Not only is my livelihood gone, but the satisfaction in doing something for the community is also lost. When community members themselves have packed me off, what big community title? I'm not born to a Chettiar, go!' he would rant furiously.

He touched the faded veshti that was drying. It wasn't wet. It could be worn. Had he whitened it with 'blue' every time he had washed it, it wouldn't have faded so much. It was a thin veshti. The thigh bones, the stick-like legs, the sunken buttocks, all would be visible. Had there been something better than this, it would have been good. He ought to ask his son for one for such festive occasions, he thought.

The old silk turban cloth came to mind. It was only last month that he had taken it out to wash it and wear it. Now the daughter-in-law wasn't at home. She wouldn't find out if he rummaged here and there. He tried opening the lid of the wooden box. It was quite heavy. Even a month before he wouldn't have had the strength to open and close it. So there was no chance of it being there. Beside the box were cardboard boxes and strings of banian cloth. When he tapped them with his foot, he could hear the hollow sound of the empty boxes. There was one box that didn't make that kind of a sound. Inside it was the turban cloth.

Even though it had been washed, there were a few wrinkles. It didn't matter if there were wrinkles in a silk cloth. But what could be done with ten yards? Now no one wore even eight yards. Measuring by hand, you could tear it into two. He could even give his son one. He would be happy that his father's last turban was being put to such use.

How could he tear a turban? He could put it away as a keepsake… But what was the use? Only tears and the life he had lived would come to mind. If he preserved it, it would only be used like the one that had been used to wipe the old lady's urine. This too would be used and thrown damply in a corner. No need…

It was a wrench to tear it.

It seemed as if it was the end of his life. Won't tears come at such moments? Tears didn't appear as he was thinking about how to cut it. The vegetable cutter came to mind. When he pressed an end, he could tear it. When he pulled it slowly, it split in a line. He could tuck the uneven torn ends inside and wear it.

As he neared, he could hear the sounds of the wedding instruments. The muhurtam was at ten or something. In the earlier days it would be over before dawn. Nowadays it stretched even up to noon. One good thing. There was no breakfast, but straightaway meals. If there was food after the muhurtam, it was always lunch.

Bent over the walking stick, he made his way to a place from where he could see the stage. It was convenient that there were chairs for everyone. Otherwise one had to sit down fearfully, balancing on the hand.

He looked at the man sitting next to him. It was Sonachalam. It was Mallikarjunan who had tied the turban for the weddings of all his five sons. Sonachalam smiled at him. A dull smile. 'Long time since I saw you,' he said. 'Who cares to invite me?' said Mallikarjunan to himself. The bridal stage looked dim. The decorations as dull as a clumsily repainted wall. It was his eyes that were dim. Nothing else.

The turbaned head must be the groom. Screwing his eyes, keeping his hand over the brow, he peered. He couldn't see the turban.

'Is the groom wearing a turban?'

'Now only the ones who are scared of the parents agree to wear a turban, even if they feel shy. It's only because of the fear of the family. Otherwise who is willing? Caste and honour have all gone...'

Mallikarjunan felt sad. Boys were getting married without a turban? Had life come to this now?

'All that was only in our times...'

He looked around to see if enough crowd had gathered for the first round of lunch.

Original title: *Innum Meethamirukkira Pozhuthugalil...*
1985

REVENGE 64

PAAVANNAN

It was not an easy thing to wipe from memory the image of the maker of the dolls of folk deities, popularly known as the doll-maker. The statues made by him were all over the village. Anna's statue at the village hall. A few paces away the Gandhi statue in the Gandhi park. Kamarajar. Nehru. Nearby Lord Ayyappa at the top of the eighteen sacred steps. Plenty of small statues in the compound wall of Draupadi Amman's temple – gods, saints in penance, Lord Shiva, Goddess Parvathi, Lord Brahma, Arjuna, Krishnan as a charioteer, yalis at the gateway. All fashioned by him. They might even fool one into thinking that they were ancient sculptures given a fresh coat of painting. With just cement paste he managed to capture the perfection and beauty of stone statues. In the beginning they would all look like chipped stones heaped one on top of the other. It was only after ten or fifteen days they revealed themselves to be Goddess Lakshmi or Saraswathi. Moulding and blending the cement, his hands fashioned the images that were in his heart. Like repeating again and again to a slow-learning child, he would slowly work on the image. It looked like magic. Whether I was bewitched by the magic, or it was my fascination for colours, or a secret desire to become like him, I haunted him. That was a long time ago.

If I close my eyes even now, I can see him clearly. I can see him seated on the scaffolding, engrossed in a statue, a single light above him. Standing a few paces away, tea in hand, he would review the statue, eyes flashing in his dark face. Specks of cement on his hair and jibba. Occasionally, he would hum a tune: 'The debts and deeds of my previous births will all be settled in this birth.'

My father took me to him: 'The boy draws somewhat well. Only you have to show him the way in your free time.' It was the distressing period when he had suffered deep humiliation and had distanced himself from everyone. His wife had eloped with the young man next door. Everyone laughed at him. Respecting him to the face, they mocked him behind his back. Under the pretext of commiserating with him, they further cut open his wound. The doll-maker would stare at them, eyes moist. As far as I know he had never quarrelled with his wife. Never raised his voice. This ought not to have happened to such a person, I thought. I prayed fervently that she should return home soon. Kumarasami, the boy down my street, shocked me: 'That athai won't come back home, da.' 'Why are you saying that?' I asked. I wondered how he could say this with such conviction. 'She won't come means she won't come,' he smiled. In our standard VIII A, Kumarasami was the only one who smoked. When he leant on the tamarind tree overlooking the lake and puffed away, we all stood around looking at him. He was well informed in matters that we didn't know about.

'He doesn't have "it". That's why athai went away, da...'

'"It" means?'

'"It" means the thing a man should have. He doesn't have it.'

I didn't know what 'it' was. In my view he looked like a full man. Strong arms, legs, firm shoulders, tousled hair. Dark face. Sharp nose. I didn't think he fell short in anything. I didn't know which part he was referring to as an emblem of manliness.

When I lay down after dinner, my mind was mulling over the same thing. It looked as if I wouldn't get sleep if I didn't learn the answer. Trying to unravel this mysterious tangle, my innocent mind tired. As I closed my eyes, my mother who was serving food to my father, started speaking. First I thought it was all about some debt. Later I realised that it was about the doll-maker. Suddenly I perked up and listened to the entire thing.

'That lady was too hasty. She waited for so many years, couldn't she have waited for a few more? As if people don't beget children when they are a little older. My maama in Villayanur had his eldest son at the age of forty-eight. It's all god's wish. Was my aunt as hasty as this one? They waited for thirty years after marriage, you know. Why she thought that that doll-maker could never give her a child, I don't know. Poor thing, that man cannot lift his head now and walk. He cringes, as if he has been stripped in the middle of the street. A hundred gods have been born from his hands, but not a single one of them has shown grace towards him.'

I didn't hear Appa's voice for a long time. Perhaps his silence betrayed his empathy.

'Not everyone can be like your aunt. Some people are in a hurry. This girl must be of that type…'

'The fellow she's gone with now, how can she be sure that she'll get a child through him? There also there could be the same problem.'

'Chee, chee. Why should we think like that? Come, just serve me some rice.'

My father raised his voice. My mother didn't speak after that. I didn't understand all this business of 'manliness'. Still, I think I half understood that it was to do with the business of getting children. I felt comforted that I learnt all this without Kumarasami telling me about it.

After two-three weeks the doll-maker was back to normal. He immersed himself in completing the half-finished statues in the garden. A big politician from Vikravandi had given a hefty advance for an Anna statue. Halfway through, not happy with it, the doll-maker had flung it away. A messenger from Vikravandi reminded him. Starting again for the third time, he somehow completed it to satisfaction.

My job was to sweep and clean the house. And to fetch water and bring food from the hotel.

The doll-maker corrected my sketches. He straightened my lines around the curves of the face, shoulders and hips. He got me the job of drawing god pictures in the freshly whitewashed Draupadi Amman temple, which was being readied for the fire festival. I first drew the sketches in pencil. After he made the corrections, they looked beautiful. I would be surprised how his eyes would immediately home in on the flaws in the figures. I was immensely proud after I painted the corrected figures. When people applauded, I silently thanked the doll-maker. My schoolmates were proud of being my friend. They pestered me to sketch god Vinayaka or Muruga in their notebooks. Only Kumarasami fumed at my fame. He challenged me: 'Don't want all this business of drawing god pictures. I'll stand in front of you. Draw me. Then we'll know if you are a great artist or not.' I hated speaking to him and avoided him. But he still came after me. 'Okay, don't draw me. Can you draw another simple picture?' I was forced to prove my prowess to him. He took me alone to the backyard of the school. He took out a picture from his pant pocket. It was a nude picture of a man and a woman. My limbs trembled and I felt like peeing. My throat too was parched. In the next instant I flung the picture on his face and ran away. Behind my back I heard the laughter of his gang. Their jibe attacked my neck: 'Your guru doesn't have 'it' and neither do you.'

When I entered the doll-maker's house, Rice Mill Gounder and a few others were talking to him.

Gounder said, 'Who else is there in these parts but you to make statues of deities? You only must accept and complete this temple job.'

The doll-maker hesitated, 'No, no… I just want to finish all the work I have on hand and pack up. At this time you are…'

'You are the one with the skill. How can you say such things? It is said that only one in a lakh is fortunate enough to build a temple. Only your large heart can make that possible. I will give you whatever you ask.'

'I'm not talking about money. It's my mind…'

'Put all the burdens of your mind on Goddess Mariatha and begin the work.'

When the others too persuaded, the doll-maker relented. I also felt happy.

The work at the new temple was getting done gradually. The doll-maker drew sketches for the sanctum sanctorum and the walls around. His speed and swirls astonished me. Since it was the summer holidays I was always with him. Not a day I took off. He worked even on Sundays. The idol of Mariamma for the sanctum sanctorum was readied first. When he did the face, he didn't allow anyone to hang around. Not even me. When he saw my disappointment, he said, 'There is a reason for everything. As time goes, you will understand.' When the face was finished, he covered the idol with a cloth. He said that it could be uncovered only at the time of painting the idol. Everyone agreed. Even Gounder looked at it from a distance. One by one, all the statues came to life. All the statues – a big Vinayakar on the temple tower, Parvathy, Paramasivan, Murugan, the devas worshipping the goddess on the compound walls – all of them were covered with cloth. In the nights, in the dim light of a single bulb, they looked like scarecrows.

Work came to a standstill the following day. I went to his house and found it wide open. I waited, presuming that he had gone to the lake or the bazaar. As usual, I swept the house and fetched the water. I sat in a corner and started drawing. I was hungry. It was the time to fetch him food. I could go only if he gave me the money. I thought I would buy him the food when he came and then leave. But he never came. Only my mother came in search of me. That evening, the following day, the day after that. He never came back at all. Men from the rice mill came looking for him.

'Where is your doll-maker, da?'

'Don't know.'

'The deadline is nearing. And there are hundred and eight jobs to finish. And this man has disappeared for weeks together – what does he mean?'

People started saying all kinds of things in the village. That he had gone to get a new wife. That he had gone in search of his wife – 'It was a body he was used to sleeping and getting up with, how could he do without it,' they smirked. One person wondered if he had committed suicide. Another said, 'He should have hanged himself on the day that she ran away. You think he'll have the guts to do it today?'

After waiting patiently for a long time, Gounder finally called a doll-maker from a neighbouring village. The job of painting the statues still remained. On an auspicious day the work began again. In the first rays of the sun, the new doll-maker reverently touched and prayed to the goddess and lifted the cloth. The cloth had got stuck to the statue in several places. He carefully moistened those places and prised the cloth away. He was happy with the perfect beauty of the idol. 'No doubt at all. A very experienced hand, this,' he praised. He started to keenly examine from the bottom to the top. His eyes went to the goddess's face. He looked terror-struck. Sweat gathered on his face and neck. He rubbed his eyes and looked again. 'Ayyo,' he exclaimed. His tongue slurred. Gounder asked, 'What, annachi?' He too looked nervous.

'Inside... goddess... for the goddess... no eyes.'

The shocked Gounder and his men rushed inside. A perfect idol, but with no eyes. Everyone looked scared. They wondered if what they were seeing was true. One man struck a matchstick to see even more clearly. The empty sockets hit you in the face. The doll-maker hurried to uncover the other idols. Ganapathy, Murugan, Parvathy, Paramasivan, no god had eyes, only holes. Everyone froze. Baffled, each one suggested something.

Gounder and his men asked the new doll-maker, who was trembling, to fix the eyes for the idols. With trembling folded hands he quavered, 'Please let me go. This is some kind of sin against god. I want none of it.'

Gounder called doll-makers from several villages and begged them to finish the work. After seeing the statues, each one of them refused. The date for the opening of the temple passed by. The broken-hearted Gounder finally gave up. Without ever being opened, the temple lay ruined. At first, everyone was scared to go that side. But as the years went by, emboldened, people bustled around.

Whenever I passed by, the doll-maker came to mind. He seemed to be standing near the temple, sniggering at the abandoned gods.

Original title: *Pazhi*
1995

The Scar

65

Cho Dharman

He heard someone clapping out for him. Velsami looked back. In the dim yellow street light he saw a couple of men hastening towards him, waving their hands. He stood by the lamp post at the corner shop and peered southwards. Only when they neared, he made out who they were – Soliappan and Innasi from Urulakudi. When they stood in front of him, he carefully put down the bundle of chisels, wedges and hammers, taking care not to tear the gunny sack. Only then he lifted his head. He forcefully plunged into the earth the crowbar balanced horizontally across his shoulder so that it stood upright.

'What annen, again and again we are calling you and you are walking away as if you never heard us?'

'It's not like before. Everyone changes like this once their value goes up.'

'What is this value and all that you are yapping about? First tell me why you called me.'

The three stood against the wall in front of the shop and lit their beedis. The crowbar glittered in the light of the passing vehicles.

'Nothing really… The Pongal festivities in our village have begun. So we thought we'll just come and see you.'

'So? For Pongal, pray nicely to the gods, cook meat-peat and all and nicely eat, what else?'

'As if we don't know how to eat, you rascal. As if you must give us permission to eat!'

'Then what do you want?'

'We want two cans of "goods".'

'If you want goods, you must go to Vannakudi, tell Savanaan to fetch donkey's urine… why only two, you can get even four cans.'

'What annen, don't act so smart. Here, take the money. Even if you want empty cans, we will provide you. But if you already have cans, we'll come for the goods.'

'Yey… Who does this bundle belong to? Here, shove it aside. Dumped it in the middle of the road and yapping away! Can't you see the lorry coming behind?'

The rebuke from the lorry cleaner prompted Velsami to shift the bundle near himself.

'What are you saying now, annen? If you keep quiet like this, what is the meaning?'

'Get lost, you mad fellows… It's five months since I did fermentation or set the pot on boil. I'm drinking kanji now, breaking rocks and digging earth. You want goods, it seems. Why are you wandering around like this, hanging your tongues out? There are three shops in every corner, no? Go, buy and drink that.'

'Whatever we buy and make, nothing like your goods, annen.'

'Every fellow says that. I said I didn't want anything to do with that trade and moved off, no? Just get lost, you dogs.'

'Annen, promise on my head that you no longer make.'

'What promise? I'll take off the veshti wrapped around my bum and step over it here itself. It's five months since the pots have been washed and upturned.'

'Ok, agreed. But what are you doing about your drinking?'

'Why, will someone come and beat you up if you don't drink? Or will they hold your mouth tight and pour it in through a funnel? Why are you wandering around like this, clicking your tongue?'

Velsami bent down and lifted his bundle on to his head. One of them prevented him from lifting the crowbar.

'Ok, we'll do one thing. Tell us what all stuff has to be bought. We'll buy it now itself. Before Pongal, you yourself come one day and do it for us. We'll give how much ever you want.'

'Even if you heap up lakhs and lakhs, and even if the sun rises in the west, I will not light the stove, I tell you. I swear on Goddess Marithai.'

He jerked the crowbar off the ground, slung it across his shoulder and walked away. They watched him go for a while and then turned and went away. A heavily loaded lorry growled past, spitting out fumes.

In that entire district, Pandavamangalam Velsami's goods had special value. On Pongal and other festival days, crowds would crash in like waves. They would wait for hours to buy.

'Motherfucker, if it is goods, then Velsami's goods only can be called goods. Even if you belch after you drink, the aroma of bananas, dates and babool will linger in your mouth… Even if you drink a tiny bit, you will feel as if you are sleeping on a silk-cotton mattress and floating in the air. These days the fellows who make the goods, boil dry batteries, thorn-apple leaves, urea and salt, and as if this isn't enough, they also throw in sleeping tablets and chunks of jaggery and call it arrack. As soon as people down this, thirsting for water, eyes tucked upwards and legs wobbling, they plop down with a thud on the street, reeking and lying for hours like a corpse, not even aware of peeing or shitting.'

'Last year, during Pongal, on a challenge, he had stuffed his goods into a tube, much like a chicken's intestines, and dropped it from above, the height of a man. Throughout the night, it had kept bouncing like a rubber ball and never settled on the ground. That's the kind of stuff he makes…'

When Velsami stood in front of Arumuga Aasari's workshop, Aasari was hunched over in the dark, blowing the bellows in one hand and tossing and turning the chisels with the tongs in the other in the hissing fire. The beedi stuck to the edge of his lips glittered like a blood spot in the dark. He peered at Velsami.

'Who is it… Velsami… why so late? Thank god you came now. Otherwise I would have put out the fire.'

'Don't ask… Two useless fellows accosted me on the way. Holding my hand, they wouldn't let me go. Still thinking of old times, they were after me for goods, running after me like dogs.'

'Why didn't you bring them here… could have nicely roasted the rod and branded them across the lips…'

'Hereafter must do that only so that no fellow comes near me. I can also mind my business quietly.'

'Even if you leave the wretched thing, that wretched thing is circling your feet and doesn't seem to leave you – that's your lot.'

'Daily, this is the drama, saami. Somehow at least four fellows come after me. Okay, get my things done quickly. Only if I go fast I will be able to catch the cart-men. Otherwise, they will leave, thinking I'm not coming. Then it is a big problem to catch hold of them and get the money. Flatten the edge a bit more. For the past two days the rock has been quite hard.'

Velsami hastened, took a short cut and went beyond the south bazaar to the market corner. He saw a crowd of cart-men, masons, labourers and contractors on their way from work. He identified the cart-men and made quick calculations.

'Pichayya Devar's cart – four trips of stones, two trips of small stones. For Senbaga Velar, three trips of gravel, two trips of stones, fine sand-dust, one. Four threes are twelve, five twelves are sixty. Sixty plus eight, sixty-eight…'

'Look here, 'pa, Velu, tomorrow we need four extra cartloads of stones. The mason came and informed, it seems. Finish the trips early morning itself. Don't delay the work; even if the stones are slightly big, it's okay. We can't bring the cart and wait here and all. I'm telling you now itself, then don't blame me. If you're late, I will go to Muthvel.'

'You first bring the cart, rasa. The stones will be ready. Why are you in such hurry now itself?'

As he counted the notes, he walked towards the ironsmith's workshop. He bought eatables for his son and wife from the shop on the way.

'What, Velsami, like magic you have returned?'

'What other work I have. By grace of which god I don't know, I found all the cart-men in one place. I quickly collected the cash and hastened back.'

Arumugan Aasari was beating the nicely heated chisel with a hammer and lengthening it. To cool the chisels, he dunked them into a shallow, rectangular stone basin with just enough water so that only the hot ends lay immersed. Each time he carried a chisel with his tongs and dipped it into the water, it smoked with a hissing sound. When he placed the next chisel in the fire and went to hold the bellows, Govind Aasari entered and worked the bellows.

'Who is it? Velsami? Come, come. You're never to be seen… How is the stone-quarrying going? You're doing well, no?

'Somehow doing okay with your blessings.'

'We only are stuck inside this heat and wasting away, melting like wax. Look how all sorts of people make money in all sorts of ways. Let them do what they want and say what they want. If you go back to your old profession, you can make good money – why are you toiling away like this day and night?'

'Only other fellows are talking like this. What, saami, should you also talk like this? Even if I fill only one-fourth of my stomach with kanji, I'm drinking it with dignity, saami.'

'How can you be like this in this day and age?'

'Maama, please blow gently. The coal-dust is hitting my face.'

'Not like that, saami. They think that a fellow who makes arrack will do anything, so they are treating me lightly.'

'Are all five fingers the same? Like that when four people gather, they will say four different things. So what? Let the donkeys say what they want. They are just speaking – are they beating us? Let the words go with the breeze. You should take it in one ear and leave it through the other.'

'Saami, you are talking without knowing the real story.'

'What story – big story, Velu? If you complain, you can't do the business, you very well know. But the money you get there, can you get it from anything else? Look at Pithukaal Raakan. Rings on all five fingers, a bunch of gold chains round the wife's neck... he's strutting around like a king.'

'It's all right for him and his wife. But I can't survive like that. Shameless existence.'

Velsami walked slowly, a load on his head. The mind mulled over the events of that day...

Velsami is sitting on a string-cot in front of his house. His son is sleeping on a mat spread out on the floor. Women are sitting under the street lamp posts, sticking labels on matches. Velsami's wife Chinna Madathi is fetching water from the street hand-pump. Two cycles stop in front of his house. Velsami gets up to make place on the cot for the two of them. The two are local policeman, who come and go here pretty often. The two have downed arrack up to their neck. They ask for a packet of cigarettes. They demand money. They stuff it into their pockets.

'Dei, Velsami, the new head constable will come now, da.'

'Okay, let him come.'

'He needs stuff.'

'There's plenty. He can drink how much ever he wants.'

'Not that stuff, da. He doesn't drink.'

'Then which stuff?'

'What he needs is woman stuff.'

'…'

'What, da, you're keeping quiet. Set it up quickly. He will come anytime now.'

'You very well know about me, no?'

'Yes, very well.'

'Then what?'

'"Then what" means what can we also do? If the head constable asks for it, how can we say no?'

'…'

'Look here, listen, Velsami. He is new. You certainly need his support. Otherwise you can't do business. It's only for today, no. Let it be, just set up your own wife for today. If he asks again, we'll somehow set up another item before that.'

The way Velsami yelled, the two fled, rolling away their cycles. He shouted at them furiously. Chinna Madathi too joined in. 'Month after month, without fail, on the exact day you have to grease the palm. Every time they come and go, you have to give them free arrack to drink. If they want to take it away, that also free. Cigarette, beedi, all free. And mutton and eggs too for these lords. And every couple of months, they cook up cases and we have to pay fine to the courts. As if all this is not enough, they want a prostitute now. Would you dare ask these things if you had elder and younger sisters, you rascals?'

The whole night both husband and wife didn't sleep. With the child lying between them, they spoke through the night. When it dawned, they flung the remaining arrack away into the gutter. They washed the pots and put them away in the lofts. Taking the crowbar, spade and basket, they made their way to the stone quarry. They bought a wedge, chisel and hammer…

The sun was going up. Under Velsami's hammering, the wedges that had been sharpened the previous day split open the rocks. With a spade, Chinna Madathi sorted out the splintered stones, rubble and sand. With a rod, Velsami's son scraped out from a pit the clayey soil to dry it out. The last five-six months bullocks had dragged up the loads from the pit the three had created. As the carts ferried up and down, crunching the gravel and sand under the wheels, the midday sun steadily rose.

Velsami's body glistened with sweat, as if he had rubbed castor oil over it. He hammered away, heaving noisily. When he heard a loud yell, he thought that a lorry had arrived. Two police vans halted on top of the quarry. For the first time Velsami quaked on seeing the police. Four-five policemen came running down towards him.

'Get into the vehicle.'

'Why should I get into the vehicle?'

'Oho, we have to tell the reason, is it? Otherwise you won't get into the van…?'

'Rascal, a big mouth for a dog who makes illicit arrack… just get into the van!'

Two fellows caught him and the other two tied him up and threw him into the van. Chinna Madathi started cursing them loudly, flinging fistfuls of sand.

The head constable shouted from the van, 'Ei, you whore, keep quiet. Or shall I tear your thing…'

As her son climbed into the loft and handed down the huge pots one by one, Chinna Madathi slowly stacked them. After all the pots had been taken down, the crowbar, rod, wedge, hammer, sledgehammer, etcetera, were handed over one by one, and after placing them in the same spot as the pots, the son climbed down. She dusted off the cobwebs sticking to his head.

'Here, da, keep this chit carefully in your pocket. On the way, stop by in Kittnan Maama's house, explain everything to him and hire a pushcart. Then go straight to Thirukotti Nadar shop and give the chit. Load all the stuff carefully and bring it back. On the way back, without fail ask the firewood fellow for two hundred kilos of firewood. Tell him that you want well-dried wood, which breaks easily. He will know if you tell your father's name. Tomorrow you and Kittnan Maama should go and scrape some babool barks. Today itself we must start soaking. Tell him to give good jaggery. See that it has an aroma. Keep the bananas right on top. Otherwise they will get crushed.'

Velsami's son took the old chit from his mother and walked briskly. Chinna Madathi bent low to wash the dust-laden pots. Not wanting the soot to soil the sari, she tucked the ends into her hip.

Original title: *Thazhumbu*
1995

Scorched Hearts

66

Dhamayanthi

Waves were flapping around. Sebastian was sitting on the rocks, body stinging with salt. Beads of sweat glittered on his forehead. It would take a while for the heat to abate. It was too late for the boats to be readied. Even the net was hanging down from the roof of the house, in the western corner. In the dark of the night it flapped around like the skeleton of a ghost, setting the mind aflutter.

Like a ghost, it too had lost its life. It seemed as if it would be of no use at all for anything. When the thermal plant began to take shape near the port area, Savariaandi had clearly said, 'Yesuvey, what is this? Won't our livelihood be spoilt?'

'What are you saying, Annen?'

'All the fish will die, Seba.'

In the dark, Sebastian lifted his veshti, groped for his beedi in the pocket of his drawers and lit it. The beedi glittered in the night like a firefly.

Within a few days they laid the foundation of the thermal plant. The bricks too piled up quickly. With masons and labourers buzzing around, the place came alive. Even though Muyal Theevu didn't bustle with people, it was a place where fish, shrimps and crabs were found in plenty.

If you cast the net, you didn't know what you would catch. But whatever you netted would earn you profit.

Once Grace's brother who had come from Cuddalore went with them on the boat. When the net was spread in a while, he was surprised. 'Let's go a little further in, Annen,' he told Savari.

'All that's in your place, Machan. Don't forget, this is Thoothukudi.'

That day they got good lobsters, sardines and fat 'full-moon' crabs. That night Grace made hot rice and crab kuzhambu with fried lobster. They sat outside the hut, drinking arrack. As they kept drinking, the aroma of crab mixed with ginger and garlic and the fry tormented them. With great happiness they munched on sardine fry with the drinks. The old lady didn't approve of all this. She screwed up her lined face and glared at them. The ends of her sari were draped across her chest anyhow, just for form's sake.

'Ei, di, Grace, are you making crab kuzhambu?'

'Yes, Athai, kuzhambu only. It's not enough if you just fry, it won't go down their throats. Annen's also come, no? Have to make something tasty, no?'

'Yes, yes, make. Five-thousand-rupee sari, gold waist-chain, all that he has scooped up and brought specially for you, this great lord.'

This is what Grace didn't like. If you told her, the old lady wouldn't understand. If you said, 'Just leave Grace. It's her house. Let her cook what she wants,' the old lady would reply, spit falling from her mutton-stench mouth, 'How can that be? I'm the elder.'

Grace whispered to her husband who came to pick up the mat to sleep outside, 'Go and leave the old lady in your brother's house. She just keeps on talking. I don't know how long my patience will last.'

'Okay, okay, why all that now?'

'My brother didn't scoop up anything and bring. But he came, no? When your brother comes, when we make seela and uzhi fish, teeth and all sprout in her toothless mouth. Will your brother give her kanji even for a couple of days? Will that merciless woman make kanji?'

Since all she said was true, Sebastian would just keep silent. Only that silence would ease the tension. But nowadays Grace didn't let go. The old lady too never kept quiet. She couldn't swallow her spit if she didn't belittle Grace on some pretext or the other. 'What is this, drying the fish like this. Not enough salt at all,' she would say, kicking the seasoned fish. 'You've washed this plate or what, you bitch? You want me to die of diarrhoea or what, that's why you are handing me the soiled plate of yesterday?' Earlier there was always cash on hand, so he had the strength of mind to put up with such talk. But nowadays Sebastian only got angry. He shouted, 'If you want, you eat. Otherwise, go to Yesudas's house.' The old lady would be shocked and hurt. She would sob as if a skeleton was rattling.

'Yes, I'm a homeless wretch. I will go away. The sea is there, 'pa, wide and vast. Either I go, or you shove me into it.' She would blow her nose, sniffing.

It was only after the ash-dyke was set into the sea that the catch had lessened. The ash-ridden effluence from the power plant mingled with the waters in the Thoothkudi seaside and the Mannar bay. It was through the ash-dyke that the effluence filtered out. Since lumps of ash hardened like rocks, no fish floated around. Last week they had held a meeting with big, educated folks. After the procession and all, his legs had swelled. Some fellow next to him had spoken about ash-dyke in detail. Sebastian thought that he hadn't really seen the ash-dyke, but was talking about it from what he had heard. Because he talked of ash-dyke as if it was Alibaba's 'anda-ka-kasam' door. But Sebastian had seen it.

The first ash-dyke stretched from Muyal Theevu to the port. A protective wall of about ten to fifteen feet was built from the ground, and the ash-dyke looked like a monstrous beast on the surface of the sea, stretching to ten square kilometres. Stumps of waste ash had hardened like rocks, firm as a concrete surface.

Only when the second dyke was being built did all the fishermen come together. Protests and meetings filled the days. The catch dwindled. Sticky wastes of ash were let into the waters. Unable to breed, a number of fishes were either wiped out or lessened. The fisheries department found traces of copper, aluminium, lead, mercury and cyanide in the waters. Not only that, the sea water used to cool the boilers was let back into the sea. However, they recorded in pristine sheets of paper the temperature variations of the sea waters.

'What is the point in doing anything, Seba? Anyhow we don't seem to ever get the lion shrimp here,' said Savari wearily. The lion shrimp was a gold mine, exported to foreign countries. The paucity of that crustacean considerably reduced the bulge of the purse.

Many ideas cropped up and vanished. The proposals to use imported coal to cut down the waste and even build concrete blocks sprouted, but they disappeared just as quickly.

The stock of not only fresh fish depleted at home, but also dried ones. Days of quarter- and half-empty stomachs went by; now they even got used to hunger. It was a torment to sleep on an empty stomach which seemed like a raging wind-blown sea. Drinking plain water induced acidic belches. The old lady didn't have the strength to put up with such hunger. Grace made millet gruel at least for her. As she stirred the gruel, her own stomach growled. As she flicked the gruel from the ladle on to her hand and put it into her mouth to test if it was done, the single drop which made its way into her stomach made her quiver. She was tempted to drink up the whole thing. But Seba would shout at her. He didn't want the old lady to go hungry. She smacked her tongue again. Her eyes blurred immediately. She angled the pot and furiously gulped down the water.

'Grace.'

Sebastian stood; his eyes too were blurred. He stretched out his hand. As if she was waiting for this, she nestled in his arms and wept copiously.

'Drink if you want, Grace. We'll give the old lady something else.'

'No need!'

Moving away from him, she poured the gruel into the old lady's plate. If she served on another plate, she would yell. On seeing the gruel, the old lady tutted.

'Don't have even nethli dried fish to go with it?'

'No, Athai.'

'Who can eat this?' The old lady turned her face away.

'Eat, Athai. It's not like before. We don't get much fish these days. Bear with it, there's some problem.'

'Yes, yes, bear it, it seems. Then go and give this to someone who can bear it.'

This time round the old lady pushed the plate away. The gruel splattered out and lay in puddles on the floor. The old lady spat 'thoo'. Grace wept, beating her head.

'Don't cry, you wretch.' The old lady shouted in anger. Then god knows what she thought, she came and pushed Grace. She hissed like a python.

'Can't give anything tasty to eat. You must have eaten it all, you dog.'

Sebastian came in. 'Don't talk, you old thing. She hasn't eaten a thing for three days.'

'Expect me to believe it? You think I'm mad?'

She threw the rolled-up mat on Grace; it scratched her face.

'Ei, old thing! Go, go away. You are staying in my house and hitting me itself?' Grace shouted.

There was a heavy silence. Then Sebastian said, 'Get ready tomorrow. I will leave you in Yesudas's house early in the morning.'

The old lady started crying. The torture meted out by Yesudas's wife all came to mind and made her quiver. The wretched hag. Even the handful of rice that she served she would fling, as if feeding a dog.

The old lady moaned, 'Seba, Seba.'

'What?'

'I'm not coming to Yesu's house. Sesuvey, she will trouble me no end, that wretch.'

'The way you are troubling Grace here! Enough of all this.'

However, even Sebastian had his doubts about what Yesudas would say. The minute they removed their slippers, Margaret would peep out. If she saw the old lady, she would immediately begin, 'If you have any shame of at all, leave immediately.'

When Grace came to sleep that night, Sebastian said, 'I told the old lady that we will start in the morning.'

'That's right. What income do we have? Let that wretch also keep her for a little while.'

'That's what I'm thinking about. She won't keep her. Yesudas will have no say.'

'Ah! So, I only always get caught, is it? I can't look after her anymore. Either you keep me or her.'

Grace didn't say anything beyond that. What was there to say? She had said clearly what she wanted to say.

He took the first bus in the morning to Virudunagar with the old lady. As expected, the moment Margaret saw the old lady she began, 'Tell me, with what face have you come here to stay? Okay, the old thing doesn't have any sense only, what about my brother-in-law?'

After that it was humiliating to even sit there.

His heart melted when the old lady followed him with her bundle of clothes. It would be catastrophic if he went home too. It wouldn't be a catastrophe that would abate either, like before. Because there are no solutions in hard times.

He climbed into the bus to Thirunelveli along with the old lady. He bought her biscuits and coffee. The old lady wolfed it down hungrily.

Because she had thrown away the gruel the night before, her hunger was evident in the way she slurped on the coffee. They got down at Kovilpatti.

The old lady screwed her eyes and asked, 'What, da? Have we arrived in our town?'

'No, we have to change the bus. Wait here.'

'Where are you going?'

'I'll go and ask where the bus to Thoothukudi will arrive,' he said. Conveniently, as he moved away, a bus for Thoothukudi was just leaving the bus stand.

He hopped into it.

Original title: *Anal Min Manangal*
1999

A Long Train Journey 67

Sivakami

The train started, chugging out tiny sighs in a chain. She ran and caught the train. As she was searching for her seat, the ticket examiner asked, 'No. 52 Jaya?' She nodded.

'The passenger has arrived,' he announced and moved ahead, circling No. 52 in his notebook. A man who had pursued him for the seat went and stood by the toilet.

Unaware that a passenger had come to occupy the window seat, Kamini was busy saying 'tata', sticking her head out of the window. When she turned, a sliver of a moon glittered on her nose.

Kamini looked at Jaya and said, 'Just sit there for a bit, please?'

Only for a little while. After that the person who will occupy the seat is me, she seemed to say. Jaya sat down gingerly on the edge.

The train's speed steadied into a soothing rhythm. The sizzling heat spread a golden hue outside. The second-class passengers folded their legs, stretched them or just reclined. A languid drowsiness, the effect of the morning meal, consumed a number of passengers.

Kamini's four-year-old boy occupied the place near the window. Jaya leant behind, realising fully well that it would take a while before she took possession of it.

Within half an hour, the little boy's arms and legs were caked with dirt and he looked around eagerly for new mischief to accomplish. He kept twisting the lid of the water jug, downing water and shutting it. His mother Kamini looked relaxed, as if the whole compartment belonged to her. Diamonds dazzled in her ears. A thick chain circled her neck. Eight slim bangles on her arm. Her hair was loosely tied, a string of slightly wilted jasmine around it. Faint scratches on her thumb from cutting vegetables. Turmeric added to the glow on her face.

Her not-so-old father sat next to Kamini. When she asked now and then, 'Appa, do you want to eat anything?' he merely gestured with his hand and shut his eyes.

A couple sat beside Jaya. The wife leant her face against the window, looked out lazily, a paper cone of fried groundnuts in her left hand. Now and then, her husband put his hand inside the packet and scooped out some nuts; each time he did that, she kept inspecting the amount of nuts left over in the packet.

Her husband's head – either naturally or as a result of his crop – was like a squashed papaya. He reclined, spreading his legs out. His rubber chappals had slipped off and lay near the feet of the older man. Not wanting to ask him to sit properly, the old man sat folding his legs on the seat.

The wife cautioned him, 'Don't look now,' and whispered something in his ears. But he immediately looked at Kamini's diamonds and the twisted rope-chain round her neck and nodded meaningfully. Realising that they were speaking about her, Kamini pulled out the ends of her sari from her waist and wrapped it gently around her shoulders.

Because he had looked immediately the wife pinched him sharply. The next time the wife tried to tell him something, he dismissively asked her not to say anything, gesturing to her that he knew everything.

The old man who appeared to be sleeping took in all this through half-opened eyes.

No one spoke to anyone, but they seemed to be enjoying within themselves all the petty goings-on around.

Jaya was desperate for the window seat. The train sped along with a thunderous noise, throwing up waves of hot air. In her haste, Jaya had forgotten to buy either a book to read or a packet of food. She curled up on the upper berth, feeling sticky and uncomfortable.

When the train neared a big station, Kamini took out from a shining tiffin carrier, tamarind rice and curd rice, redolent of asafoetida, and portioned them neatly on clean plastic plates for the three of them. Crisp chips, ladoos on the side, and the three of them began to eat. Their eating became the green signal for everyone in the compartment to begin eating and soon you could hear the noise of packets opening and water being poured.

The couple opposite took out two big packets, snapped the string used for wrapping, 'pat pat', since they didn't have the patience to unwind it carefully. Then they turned their backs to everyone, and without even opening the packets fully, they held them curled in their hands like a nest and gobbled huge mouthfuls, 'avak avak', without even revealing what they were eating.

The train slowed down gradually and came to a halt. Jaya got down, bought poori-potato and some fruit, and made a dash for the empty seat by the window. Even though it was her seat, she felt a little uncomfortable since Kamini was bound to be surprised to find her sitting there.

'Amma, ten paisa, amma... ten paisa... ten paisa...' A dirty young boy nagged Jaya to the point of snatching her purse. When Jaya took out her handbag, he stopped shouting, held out his hand, looking around for the next prey. Without even checking how much she gave, he pounced on the next passenger. She turned aside, fearing another attack from a beggar.

Jaya suspected that the look Kamini gave her was unduly admonitory. 'Don't go near the window. Just stay here like a good boy.' Kamini stopped the child who ran for the window.

Kamini secretly sized up Jaya. Who was this person who never uttered a word, where was she going?

Jaya avoided Kamini who was trying to gauge her.

The more Jaya avoided her, the more necessary it became for Kamini to strike up a conversation with her.

'Is this sari a Kanchipuram?'

Jaya just nodded her head, as if to say 'yes'.

'Cotton?'

'Mmm...'

'Looks like silk... You from Kanchipuram?'

'No, Cuddalore. I'm Jaya.'

'My name is Kamini.'

'I know. I heard your father calling you.'

'You working?'

'Yes, nurse.'

'My husband's a doctor.'

'Oho...'

As the train started Jaya looked out of the window. She thought it would be good if the conversation stopped here. Another two hours left. She wanted to get off without getting upset.

'Which hospital are you working in?'

Jaya wasn't sure if Kamini used the respectful form of 'you' or tried to muffle the ending with the upper-caste lingo. Jaya realised with a strange feeling that as a nurse her esteem fell down in the eyes of a doctor's wife. She mentioned the name of the hospital.

'You a Christian?'

She couldn't still take in her stride the embarrassing situations of long train journeys. 'No, why?'

'No, because you don't have a pottu on your forehead.'

Jaya searched in her sari for the stick-on bindi which had dropped off and pressed it on her forehead.

Knowing very well that there wasn't much time before the next question, Jaya started thinking of how to counter it.

The old man, husband, wife, everyone started sleeping in their berths.

The young boy pestered Kamini for a banana. Jaya plucked one from her bunch. The boy took it with Kamini's permission.

Kamini held out a plate of chips and ladoos. When Jaya first refused, Kamini urged her to eat the chips at least if she didn't like sweets. Jaya took the plate.

'You a Pillai?'

At last she had asked. 'Mmm... what did you say?' Jaya asked again.

'No, I asked if you were from the Pillai caste?'

'No.'

Jaya thought she could have ended the conversation by saying 'yes'. But why did she have to lie?

That one lie about the caste issue, which had led to ever so many lies in one of the earlier train journeys, came to mind.

In fact, she thought that this question was put to her by ever so many people either at the beginning, middle or end of every train journey. Her answer elicited discomfort and unease, transforming her into a child and the other into a powerful being. The tone usually changed... and then heated arguments against reservation and in the end she would find herself cast aside.

She clearly remembered the very first person who had asked her this question.

When she had gone to drink water from her classmate Tamilarasi's house at recess when she was in primary school, a white-sari-clad old lady had asked, 'What caste?' Not knowing, she had blinked. 'Father's name?' She had said, 'So and so.' That was all. The old lady had chased her on to the verandah with a stick. That was the first time her backbone had been broken, she remembered painfully.

When she and her friends had gone for the 'puberty function' when her classmate Rojarani had come of age, only she had been made to eat on the pial under the pretext of no space inside...

When she had been eating in the centre hall in Akilandam's house, Akilandam's mother, with a tonsured, covered head, had raised the question of her caste. Akilandam herself had managed the situation with a lie... When they had come out, Jaya had cautioned herself never to tell the truth about her caste...

The train stopped.

Combing out the knots with her hand from her windswept hair which fell about in threads in front, she finished the ladoo nonchalantly, held out the plate and asked, 'What did you ask? The caste?' Ascertaining the question, she composedly revealed her caste. Relishing Kamini's discomfort, she got off the train.

The train started, chugging out tiny sighs in a chain.

Original title: *Oru Rayilin Neenda Payanam*
1991

VOICES 68

SA TAMILSELVAN

After everything, he said he wanted to take a photograph. Immediately all the children were excited. Pushing one another, me-first you-first, and shouting one after another, 'Here, don't push me… Ei, Valli-Kolli, why are you shoving me,' they stood in front of the camera that hung down from saar's neck. The town's elders who were watching the spectacle yelled at the children, 'Stand without making noise, you donkeys!'

But when the saar said, 'Not everyone. It's enough if these three boys stand,' the children felt cheated. Cowed by the scoldings from the elders they stood to one side and looked at the three boys – Kaliappan, Rangasami and Mari – with disappointment and envy. When Kaliappan and Rangan said they would run home and wear a shirt, the saar refused to let them go. He said they had to stand shirtless. Of the three, the youngest one Mari (who had dropped out last year halfway through the sixth standard) found it strange, 'What is this? All the three saars who came in the last ten days wanted us only shirtless, as if it was pre-planned, for the photo.'

After taking a photo of the three of them, god knows what the saar thought, he also clicked the children standing aside after herding them together.

After putting away the things in his hand into the 'schoolbag' that slung on his shoulder, he asked the person who had come with him, 'Shall we leave?' Mari had seen the man who accompanied him. He would often come on a motorbike to the 'fire' office where Mari worked.

As they were leaving, Maadathi's voice could be heard from the crowd, 'Starting, is it? No rupee-gipee and all, is it?' A loud cackle arose; Mari too laughed. Maadathi was always like this. She would cheekily ask something or the other and everyone would laugh.

Folding his palm to everyone in general, he sat on the pillion and they sped away hastily. A few kids chased the bike for a distance and then returned.

Had it been some other time, Mari too would have run like that. But these last ten days all his playfulness had vanished. A fright consumed his mind, always. He was even more scared when he was alone. Besides, since big-big people came in cars and bikes one after the other and questioned him, he felt that he ought not to run around like that.

After the bike left, the elders and the womenfolk who were returning home discussed among themselves in other ways the same question that Maadathi had asked. 'They are writing down and all... will they go back and arrange for some money?'

'Ada, you are another! These are all newspaper fellows. They'll write everything and put it in their papers. That's all. No notes, no coins,' replied a few mockingly.

Mari too had thought at first, 'They've come on the bike and all... will they give something?' But when this saar, like the others who had come yesterday and the day before, opened his notebook and started asking questions, Mari realised, 'Okay, nothing will come of it.'

There was reason enough for everyone to talk about money. In the last ten days cars and bikes had come into town five or six times. And at least four times money had been distributed. That's why on seeing vehicles people began to expect money.

The first time, about ten days ago, four cars together came into the village. It was about three in the morning. It was quite dark. The wind blew strongly with a whizz, frightening everyone. The thought of it even now frightened Mari. It was from one of those cars that Kali, Rangan and Mari had got off. His boss, other owners of fireworks, a few village elders and politicians got down from the other cars.

As soon as he had come, Mari's mother had come running, scooped him up against her breast and started weeping uncontrollably. She could neither speak nor wail aloud. But Kaliappan's mother, hugging him, burst into an oppari, a lament. A few other women beat their chests and bellies and moaned aloud. None of their children had arrived in the car. Immediately, two cars had picked up the women and started for the town. All the big shots had sat down in the village hall and called for a village meeting.

Mari hadn't understood anything. Dazed with fear, he had been tongue-tied. Hugging his mother, he had huddled in a corner.

They spoke for a long time. They gave hundred rupees each to every house in the village and two thousand rupees to the affected sixteen families. They promised not only to give even more to the victims but also to deepen the village well and build a tank. In return, the elders had to tell anyone who came that only three people had died from their village and the other three who had gone on night shift had escaped totally unscathed. Extracting such a promise, they had left in the cars.

Keeping to their word, within four days they had given three thousand rupees each to the sixteen families. And the well with good drinking water? Well, they had already detonated to deepen it. They also promised to extend even more help to the affected sixteen families.

There was talk in the town: 'What for him… to dole out… if he sends two loads of fireworks to the north he'll sweep up one lakh flat. Will business folks be ever short of money?'

Mari had escaped unscathed, so his family had received only hundred rupees. He was rather disappointed.

But when the minister had visited the previous week, Mari had received new shorts and a shirt. Both were of polyester, which made him happy. He kept them carefully to wear for the Panguni festival. But his mother gathered him up to herself now and then and wept, 'No need of any money or cash, saami. If you are healthy with all your limbs intact and stay with us, that's enough for us, ayya.'

Like they had now, they would have taken at least ten photographs of him. But none of them had even shown him a photo. Mari badly wanted to see a photo of himself. All the journalists said they were from the weekly magazines. Still, Mari somehow wanted to see it.

He didn't feel like going home now. He wanted to sit like this in the hall or watch the well being dug till his mother returned from the fields.

If he went home now, he would have to be all by himself. He was scared to be alone. He would only think again and again of what happened. One by one, it all came back – going to the town for the night shift, buying and eating karasev on the way, polishing off the rice in the food-container at half-time with Kali, going to the water tap to wash his hands, Kali splashing water on him placing his finger on the spout of the tap… then, then a big blast from behind the screen and the screams, how they ran in – smoke, fire, wails, noise of crackers. Che, he shook his head. Tears started. He went home. Till his mother came, he sat on the grinding stone, shaking his leg, thinking of this and that.

After his mother came and made food, they ate and slept off. His mother smeared the vibhuti that the village priest had given her on Mari's forehead and chest and prayed. It was silent, not a sound anywhere, enveloped in darkness.

Suddenly Kaliappan put a finger on the tap and splashed water on him. 'Ei, keep quiet. Listen to me. Or else I will smear you with my soiled hand. Listen, don't splash water. Or I'll spit on you.' But Kaliappan didn't stop.

Mari turned over. There was smoke everywhere. The blackness and smoke. Piercing wails and screams could be heard with loud coughs, 'kak-kak'. Plaintive human cries like the bleating of goats whose necks were being sliced. Mari ran.

Agitated, he ran helter-skelter. Again he turned over. Mari, who was running on a long, neat road, fell down suddenly, his limbs giving way. He tried to get up, but couldn't. He felt something pulling him down. He tried to shake it off, but couldn't. It stuck to his body. A chunk of pale flesh, half cooked, as if scooped out. Someone came and peeled off the burnt corpse, tearing off the flesh bit by bit… Mari screamed with fear. His mother, who was sleeping near him, woke up with a start, shook him awake and gathered him close, stroked him and said, 'Ayya, my prince, my darling…' Closing his eyes tightly shut, gritting his teeth, his limbs shivering, he howled, 'ooooo'. Hugging him close, Mari's mother thought of her husband who had died of jaundice ten years ago and wept loudly, 'O god, why are you torturing me like this?'

It was like this every night. They said that his fear would vanish in a few days. Some said it would never go. In the beginning, the neighbours used to come, stay for a while and console him. Now, when they heard him, they turned over in their sleep and murmured, 'Poor thing.' His poor mother.

She smeared vibhuti whenever he shuddered and shouted, and she herself moaned and groaned. She took a vow to tonsure his head for Goddess Maariatha. She prayed to all sorts of gods. Once or twice, she took him to the government hospital in town too, only to be shouted at by the nurses and the compounders there.

His howls and her wails pierced the nights every day. Even though these voices never reached the fringes of the village.

Original title: *Kuralgal*
1987

Kittunan

69

Ma Kamuthurai

Kittunan was dead.

After I had served fifteen years in the army and come rushing back to the village he was the first person I beheld. At the time itself he must have been forty years old. Neither thin nor fat, his body was just right. A hardy body, they said. Bald with one or two grey hairs. Even now it was like that, but the hair was whiter. Clad in a sleeved vest of mull and a single-fold veshti, he could forever be seen munching on betel leaves.

My wife too used to remark, 'Even when Kittunan dies, he will lie there with one cheek puffed up.' He used to reply with a faint smile, 'What, aayi, you don't like even this harmless habit.'

Even the news of his death, spread by the girls playing hopscotch, reached the village through young boys wielding the catapult, without the services of the cobbler who usually brought such tidings.

To tell the truth, his death saddened everyone. When there wasn't a barber in this village, they had fetched Kittunan's father from another town. From that day onwards Kittunan remained in this village. Now, even if seven-eight barber families are to be found in the village, more often than not the oldies would look for Kittunan. 'Ask that Kittunan to come,' they would say.

As for the Big Naicker, even to trim his nails Kittunan had to come. In those days itself the villagers had allotted a place for him to set up shop at the bank of the river. Earlier, he lived with his wife in the hut where his father stayed.

He begot a child too there. Later a few other families came to the village, and the East Street was formed. The first house there was Kittunan's. He had earned that much goodwill in the village. Though his house was here, the shop was on the riverbank, as always.

The villagers had settled him there so that he could shave them before they had a dip in the water. But more often than not, they never allowed him to work in the shop; they always took him home.

The Big Naicker had not gone even once to his shop to get a shave. He used to say, 'Tell me, army-man, who will go there just for a shave? Go inside his shop and all and sit on the coconut frond spread on the mud floor?' From that day till today he would get a shave by his cowshed under the gulmohar tree.

Kittunan had a separate barber's knife for him. After giving a shave, he had to wash the knife with cow dung, oil it and leave it behind. Big Naicker would say that he would break into a rash if a common knife was used, so clean he was.

Kittunan's death would have affected Big Naicker more than anyone else. Only yesterday he had remarked, 'Tell me, who is there like Kittunan today, so good at his job? I swear that he is the only one who shows the respect expected of his profession… how many barbers have followed after him… they have all set up big shops in the Bazaar Street… only the shops are big, but does anyone know how to respect people… These fellows, they speak to you, looking you straight in the face.'

So true.

No one in the village had seen him walking head held high. The knife, cup and other paraphernalia of his profession tucked in a bundle on his hip, he would walk, head bowed low. He wouldn't look up till someone called out to him. I remember teasing him once, 'What, Kitna, what have you lost that you are searching for years and years…' He said, 'If you don't tease me, you can never get sleep.'

Truly, a day wouldn't go by without my seeing him at least once. If it did, it always seemed as if I had forgotten something. Or he would come to see me, cooking up some excuse or the other. If he didn't have work, he would simply come and ask, 'Give me a betel leaf, saami… just give me a tiny bit of tobacco, saami…' Chewing on something, he would listen open-mouthed to my tales of the army. In much the same way, he wouldn't forget to spill the affairs of his house.

If he picked up his knife, he would keep talking till he finished his job. Even then he wouldn't take out the wad of betel from his mouth. The one in front of him would always fear that the spittle would fall on him. But he would speak without even spilling a drop, skilfully tucking the wad into the sides of his mouth. He would also gurgle with laughter.

Fearing this, Big Naicker would also instruct him not to speak while doing his job. But somehow Kittunan would have his way with him too and force him to give ear to his conversation.

That Kittunan was dead.

On hearing the news, I couldn't do anything other than sit on the pial in shock.

'Bboo…ooo.' I could hear the loud sound of the conch, but it trailed off quickly. Had it been Kittunan, he would have blown the conch in full breath for a full minute and a half, perfectly without any let-up. Somehow whatever I saw or heard today only seemed to echo his memory.

Poor fellow! For how many people he had blown the conch. Today someone is blowing it for him.

Once, I clearly remember it… It was at the obsequies for Subbiah Pillai, I think. Yes, it was. After coming back from the graveyard, and after the food, when they were disbursing money for the pandal, cooking and all, Kittunan was found in a corner, the conch in hand. When the man disbursing the money searched for Kittunan and asked, 'Where is Kittunan? I don't find him here.' Kittunan got up respectfully, 'I am here, ayya.'

At the time an interesting thing happened. It was like teasing a cricket (one never killed it since it was believed that one wouldn't beget children then), which everyone liked to do. Even at that instance Manickam Pillai who was distributing payments wanted to tease him.

'Come here Kitna… what are your wages…?' Counting the notes, he looked at him from the corner of his eye.

Kittunan had never named his wages to anyone, whether he gave a shave or a haircut or did any funeral jobs. He accepted whatever was given. So he blinked when Manickam Pillai asked him to name a sum.

After a while he said, 'Give me, saami…' He stood, hands folded, as was his wont, without even stretching out his hand.

Manickam Pillai wouldn't let him go. 'Le, Kitna, ask how much ever you want. Unless you name the amount, I won't give.' The others around who had finished their meal watched the fun happily. Big Naicker was also there. He was the most keen. When Kittunan remained silent for a while, Big Naicker pleaded on his behalf.

'Ei, Pillai… Nice fellow you are, 'pa… bargaining with him… Give him something… He has left his work and stayed here the whole day… He also came to the graveyard. Keeping all this in mind, give him something, whatever you usually give…'

But Manickam Pillai remained firm. 'Keep quiet, Naickerey… Let us see how much he asks.'

Big Naicker didn't believe that he would name a sum. He had never done so, had he, haircut or shave! He had never asked till given. He would heap up the cut hair and wait. Naicker would go inside the house and fetch whatever he could find. He would hand it over, saying that was all he could lay his hands on. I have never heard it said that he laid hands on anything bigger than four annas, not even once.

Whenever Big Naicker spoke of Kittunan, he would say this of him, 'I generally never count what I give Kittunan. I give whatever I can lay my hands on. He too will take whatever is given and leave with folded hands. Army-man, no one can be like him… His father too was like that… But those fellows who have shops there… they have a rate for each and everything… written down too.'

If you asked him, 'What, da, taking without a word whatever is given to you. How are you going to survive?' he would reply, 'What, saami, you have given me this life. As if you'll allow it to starve… Till I have something, I will cook and eat. If not, I will come and stand in front of your houses. As if you'll say "no".'

That day I came to a conclusion. 'This fellow will never learn.'

That day Kittunan thought for a long time and said finally, 'Give me three rupees, saami.' Everyone laughed aloud, forgetting that it was a house of mourning.

Immediately Big Naicker said, 'Lei, you've asked, all right, but couldn't you have asked for ten or twenty? Manickam Pillai himself had mentioned that he would give you five rupees…'

'Why do I need ten or twenty! Till now you have fed me kanji. Now I have to think only of tomorrow. Three rupees is enough for me…'

When he said that I felt like hugging him. In just a second he seemed to be asking without questioning, 'Why do you need to amass wealth for seven generations?'

There was some food left over. Even when they said, 'Ask your wife to come and take kanji,' he demurred.

'Why do I need so much food, saami? We are just two oldies and one small fellow. At least if you keep it, it will be of use to four people. Why should it turn stale at my place?' When he said that everyone called him a cussed fellow. But somehow I thought that those people weren't even worth the dust on his feet.

That Kittunan was dead now.

The wind from the south blew strongly on my face, scattering my thoughts. I spat out the dust from my mouth and removed my glasses. My eyes had misted. Was it the wind or Kittunan? When I put on my glasses and leant against the pial, I saw a couple of urchins chattering away in the deserted street.

One fellow asked, 'Lei, Kittunan is dead it seems. Shall we go and see?'

The other explained, 'I believe he went to the temple to tonsure someone's head. Said his chest was paining and slept there. Then he died like that only. Poor thing!'

True. He came last evening and said, 'They are calling me at Maariamman Koil to tonsure people's heads. I'll go and come back.' So saying he pinched some betel leaves and tobacco from me and went munching away. Only to never return today.

Poor thing. Even these young ones will miss him. Even the most wilful brat will get his hair cut quietly from Kittunan. Because he would tell fox tales, cat tales and what not while cutting hair. Heaven knows where he read all those stories. Once when I asked him, 'Where did you read all these stories, 'pa?' he replied sheepishly, 'Where will I read, saami? For you I tell the tales of the village. Them, they are children only, no, so I just tell them whatever comes to mind.' When he said that I realised that to him everyone in the village was a child.

I could hear the sounds of the conch again. I closed my eyes and leant against the wall. When I made up my mind to see him one last time, Kulandaivel Pillai of East Street came by and asked, 'What, army-man, aren't you going to see your friend? They are going to take the body away it seems… Come, let's go and take a look.' I got up and said, 'Shall we go?' Yes, it had gone to the extent that the whole village thought of him as my friend.

I went inside the house, slung an upper cloth over my shoulder and started.

'Pcha… Poor fellow, such a nice chap… It's a loss to people like us… Even if we don't have money, he will adjust…'

As Kulandaivel Pillai was chattering away, I said, 'Since we are going anyway, let us also take Big Naicker along.'

'Mmm… let's go. He was like a right hand to him… Call him, let's go together…'

When we entered his house, Big Naicker was eating. Chicken feathers lay scattered in the garbage. He said that his son-in-law had come. When I gave him the news, he clucked his tongue and said sadly, 'Heard about it… Nice chap…Only yesterday he came and shaved me…'

'They are going to take the body away, it seems. Shall we go and see…?' He thought for a while and said, 'Do we need to go?'

It was fifteen days after everything was over. When we were chatting away, as usual, in Big Naicker's pial, he said that he had asked Kittunan's son to come.

Of course. It had been decided at the village meeting three days ago. When Big Naicker had said emphatically, 'Though there are several barber families in the village, there should be at least one descendent of Kittunan. It is our duty to patronise him,' the crowd had concurred.

When Big Naicker was prattling away about this and that, including Kittunan, suddenly he stopped and looked sharply at Kittunan's son coming down the road.

'What, army-man… His gait seems kind of odd…Not like Kittunan at all…He's walking with his head high…'

Original title: *Kittunan*
1985

TRESSES 70

JEYAMOHAN

Now your eyes are slowly getting drowsy. A pleasant breeze is wafting over you. You are hearing soft music from afar. Yes, now you are asleep. You are hearing my voice only in your dreams. Now there is just the two of us. No one else. Actually, even I'm not there. In fact, it's just my voice you are hearing. Listen carefully. Do you hear my voice through your ears? Or is it your own voice from deep within? Can you hear it?

Yes, it is all very pleasant…

What is your name?

Nila, Nilayadatchi.

Mrs Nila, where are you now?

My husband's place in Kesavapuram.

Why is it so quiet?

Everyone has gone to sleep. It's past midnight. Now you can hear only the buzz of the cicadas, the bells jingling in the cowshed and the rustling of the coconut fronds…

Aren't you asleep yet?

Normally I go to sleep early. But I wake up in the middle of the night. After that for a long time I can't get sleep.

What does your husband do?

I'm a widow.

I see. Any children?

One son. Padmanabhan, whom we called Paddu. He'd always be with my father-in-law. They wouldn't even allow me to touch him.

How did your husband die?

He had a congenital heart problem. Doctors advised him not to get married. Afraid that he would be consigned to a hell called 'buth', my father-in-law got him married to me. My father was a poor kitchen-help in the temple. I had three younger sisters.

So you stayed back in your father-in-law's place?

Yes, we didn't have enough to eat in my house. My father-in-law was a big landlord. He was also an astrologer. Very orthodox.

Mrs Nila, in this cold, lonely night, what are you thinking about?

As usual, about my hair only.

What about it?

Every week, without fail on Friday, the barber's wife Shanmugathammal will come to shave off my head. Tomorrow is Friday. I keep touching my hair again and again. She will be waiting tomorrow in the firewood room near the cowshed in the backyard. The very thought of that room scares me. Disgusts me. I never go there for anything else. Just looking at Shanmugathammal, my mother-in-law would start shouting, 'You wretch, go get your head shaved and then come and cry.' Not even a single day she had spoken to me kindly. From the day we got married, she kept guard, making sure that her son never got too close to me. She believed that he died because of my carelessness – it was my excessive desire that turned into death-god Yaman for him. 'What kind of lust is this? Are you a family woman or a prostitute?' she would scold.

Did they beat you?

A lot. She would keep giving me work non-stop. Worse than that, she would never give me enough food. If you eat more food, your body will start craving, she would say. No salt, no tamarind, nothing. Yearning for coffee with milk, I would hang around when she made coffee just to get a sniff of the aroma. Shanmugathammal would tightly hold my head between her knees and shave my head with a blunt knife. When she was done, my head would burn, as if it was on fire. When I was done with my bathing, I would go into the storeroom and sit and weep in its dark corner.

Did you have lots of hair as a young girl?

Everyone in my house had long hair. My plait used to hang like a python. My neck would pain if I tied my hair into a bun. My mother too had long hair. At times my father would pull her hair playfully. My mother would shy away saying, 'Ayyo, the children are looking.'

Has anyone pulled your plait?

He used to say that with so much hair you will catch a cold.

When you were young?

Mmm… no.

Mrs Nila, you can't tell even me? After all, it's going to remain only with you.

Appu.

Who was he?

The Nair boy from next door.

What did he do?

He… after his studies, he became a lawyer. At that time he was still studying. He once asked me if I would wait for him. I wept.

Mrs Nila, what all would you think about your hair?

My hair always grew fast. Even as Shanmugathammal left, my head would start itching, as if it was sprouting hair. I would keep touching it. In the night, I could even feel it grow in the dark. When I touched it in the morning, it would prick like thorns. The day after, like weeds in the harvest field, it would be soft. And the next day it would feel like a rug. I would cover my hair with the ends of my sari. But somehow my mother-in-law would always notice. According to the aesthetics of beauty, only prostitutes have long hair. It is harmful to the family. In the beginning, I too believed it. I would curse my hair. But later on when I touched it, I began to feel secretly thrilled. In the night, when I gently stroked my head in the dark, my body would tingle.

What would go through your head then?

All sorts of thoughts. Incoherent bits of images. Absurd doubts. How shall I say?

Never mind, tell me…

For example, where does all this hair come from? Is my head and body filled with dark hair? There in those dark places it sprouts, grows, lays coiled and finally bursts through the head since there is no space. Doesn't this sound crazy?

Yes, but when you are alone, all these thoughts will appear.

Yes. What fantasies! I am Kannagi from *Silapadikaram*. Hair all spread out, I have come to Madurai. I pluck off my breast, fling it and burn the entire city. Houses in smoke and flames. People screaming, getting scorched. The smell of burnt flesh. Then I become Panchali from Mahabharata. In the battle of Kurukshetra… heaps of corpses… Pandavas… Kauravas… Krishnan…

Everyone?

Yes, everyone. Ponds of raw blood. Thick red liquid bubbling over like in a payasam cauldron. I dip into it and bathe. I fan out my hair and wash it. It spreads like seaweed.

Then?

Then a different fantasy. I'm a princess. I stand in the palace balcony. A handsome prince walks below. I hang my hair loose, he holds it and climbs and embraces me. Then we unite…

Okay…

At that time my tresses cover us like a black sheet. When he tries to get up, it has tightened into the cocoon of a silkworm. I dig my teeth into his neck and drink his warm, sweet blood. After my hair drops off, I kick his shrivelled body, and tearing open the cocoon I come out. I realise I have sprouted wings now.

Wings?

Yes. The wings of a butterfly. On both sides they flutter like sari ends. I can now fly. The town, the agraharam, the Perumal temple, even the hills, appear tiny below my feet. Do you know that when you reach high above, light becomes a sweet potion. The clouds, a delicate feast.

Then?

There are plenty. But how much can I tell? I fantasise about my hair in many different ways. Whatever catches my attention on that day. I spin a cobweb with threads of hair and then sit like a spider in the middle waiting for the prey. My hair descends into the earth like aerial roots all over and I stand like a banyan, spreading out my branches. Above my head, thousands of birds chatter in thousands of languages. My tresses become creepers in a forest, twining over fat tree trunks and reaching above. Then they clasp the rocks and spread over.

Then I took a cloth, put it on my head and started plaiting it like hair. My mother-in-law saw it. That day I was beaten up and branded. But as the pain subsided, I recalled the panic-stricken face of my mother-in-law and suddenly I burst into a laugh.

You started doing this daily, didn't you?

It became a good way to take revenge on her. So I started doing it every day. The moment I start plaiting the cloth, laughter would splutter out. They tried beating me. Then they packed me off to my house. There too if I thought of my mother-in-law, I would tie my hair. Nobody troubled me. I would tie my hair, and looking at the changing expression on everyone's face would make me beam with pleasure… But one day, when I was sleeping, my hair came to life.

Is that so?

Yes. Seeing it move, I woke up startled. Slithery and warm like a snake, it raised its hood. No one cared when I screamed. They looked through the window and went away.

Had they locked you in?

Yes. I had a separate room. Cosy and dark.

What did the snake do?

It squeezed me in a tight embrace. My body got crunched, my bones broke. My innards crushed and oozed out, with blood splattering all over. But like a ripe boil about to burst, it gave an amorous pleasure.

Yes, I understand.

After that nothing happened. Perhaps I had died.

Mrs Nila, then shall we press forward in time? See how easy it is. We are moving on, like a gentle breeze. Beyond buildings, roads… beyond time… a totally different place, a different city… isn't it? Mrs Nila, where are we?

Chennai, my great granddaughter's house.

That is?

Paddu's son Narayanan's second daughter. Her name too is Nila. She looks exactly like me. She's married and has a son.

What about her hair?

Like me, she too has very thick, long hair. Now as she is reclining on the cot, her plait is lying on the bed like a black chariot rope.

Do you come here often?

Yes, she has one of my possessions with her. A tall oil-lamp which my mother bought from Vadaseri for my marriage.

In the pooja room?

No, it's a different kind of house. It's a big flat on the sixth floor. There is no pooja room here. She has kept it as a showpiece. When she is troubled, she will come and sit in front of it. I too come and sit with her. I stroke her forehead.

What is her problem?

For her too it's her hair which is the problem.

But she has long hair, no?

Yes, that is the problem. She was always good at studies, even as a young girl. She doesn't believe in dolling up. Washing, drying and grooming her hair every day was a problem for her. She always said that it was like looking after a retarded child. But, for her father, a woman's hair was a symbol of Indian culture. He considered short hair in women as grossly overstepping the limits. Like one holding a flying kite in strings, her father kept hold of her through it, she would tell her friends.

What does her husband say?

He holds a high post. Mesmerised by her hair, he followed her home and asked for her hand in marriage. For him her hair is the object of lust and love. In the night, he likes to spread it out on the pillow and sleep on it... In the early days of marriage all this thrilled her. But when she too became an important official her hair became a burden. He wouldn't allow her to cut her hair. Every day arguments, fights, tears...

Mrs Nila, what is she doing now?

She is crying. Her husband has just quarrelled with her and left. She has got a promotion. The managing director of the company himself suggested that she adopt a more modern look. The fashion consultant said that her hair wouldn't suit modern attire. To which her husband suggested that she then resign her job. Again and again he asks if her job is more important than him.

He doesn't like her going for work?

Yes. Both of them live a harried life. When he returns home, she is not there. And when she is at home, he is never there. It's very rarely that the two of them talk to each other leisurely. He says that his income is enough for both of them. For her, her job is not just an income, but an independence and an identity. She needs a channel to showcase her talent, earn recognition and succeed. He can never understand this. To him it's arrogance and indifference on her part. The cell phone is ringing now. It is him.

What are they talking?

He is conveying his final decision. She has to resign. Otherwise, divorce, he says. She tries to say something, but is unable to, and falls on the bed crying, head down. After a while, as if she has made up her mind, she leaps out of the bed and stands in front of the mirror with a pair of scissors. She puts her hair in front and looks at it with disgust. Once or twice she looks at the scissors and then quickly chops it off. Thick, heavy hair. Her hand aches. Biting her lips, her veins bulging at the neck, she cuts her hair. She lifts with two fingers her chopped plait, as if it is a loathsome, strange object. It looks like a lopped-off cow's tail. She takes a manila cover from the table, puts it in, seals it and comes back to the bed. She picks up her cell phone and calls her husband. When she hears his voice, her face looks as if she is gasping. She purses her lips firmly. He says hello, hello, loudly a few times. It's me, she says in a soft voice, holding her chest. I won't be there in the morning. There is a cover on the dressing table. That is my answer. That's all. She switches off the phone.

Is she crying?

No, propping a pillow under her back, she sits up and looks at the fan. After a long time, when she turns, she looks at her hair with a start. She runs her fingers through her short hair. Switching off the lights, she lies down and once again riffles through her hair. Unable to sleep, she tosses and turns. She heaves a big sigh. She gets up, opens the drawer, takes out two Calmpose tablets, pops them in her mouth and drinks water from the jug. She lies on the bed, curling herself up tightly.

What are you doing?

I gently walk towards her and pat her forehead and hair affectionately.

Mrs Nila, are you sad?

No. Not happy either. But in a way I feel relieved.

Relieved, Mrs Nila?

Yes, relieved. As if all the burden has lifted off my mind. You could call it even happiness.

Really, Mrs Nila? Are you sure?

Yes. I've never been this peaceful.

Mrs Nila, I will now take leave of you. After I leave, you will wake up. You will forget all that we spoke. I am clapping my hands. You will wake up at the third clap.

One…two…

Doctor?

Yes, Mrs Nila. You can get up. How do you feel?

I'm fine. What did I say? I feel I was talking in a dream.

Even if I tell you, you won't understand, Mrs Nila. Come, sit here.

Will I have to come again? I won't be free for two months. Only after the general body meeting is over, I will find some time.

Never mind. It's enough if you do the mental exercises that I will show you. Insomnia is common with people like you who hold high posts. The dosage of your tablets is the issue. We will gradually reduce it. Look at this doll.

It's marble, isn't it? It looks so beautiful and delicate.

Did you notice what it is?

It looks as if a hair has been stuck on it.

Look at it more carefully. It's a crack.

Yes, the doll is coming apart.

Yes. It's two dolls put together. You keep one. Let the other half be here. You should always keep it near your bed. Before you sleep, look at it keenly for a few minutes.

Why?

It's a mental exercise. You will remember the other half that is here. Think of this and that, alternatively. It's an experiment I want to try. Okay, then, Mrs Nila.

Doctor, what did I say?

I can't tell you. Nothing coherent. Lots of childhood memories. Goodbye, Mrs Nila.

Original title: *Koonthal*
2002

DARKNESS 71

KONANGI

A broken chimney it was. Even so, it was perfect for that lamp.

It was a chimney only in name; it blocked all the light from the lamp.

Though it poured out only very little of the light, it spluttered out fumes in plenty from its upper mouth.

That lamp, along with the broken chimney, was on the western wall. Forgetting when it came into being, the 'black trail' resided in the western wall. The lamp was placed on the rusty nail four and a half feet off the ground.

Our Chinnapappa could reach only up to four and a half feet. There wasn't anyone younger than Chinnapappa in our house. So there it was on the wall, the lamp, to spread light on the floor, within the reach of everyone's hands, to be used as and when needed.

Earlier, ever so many chimneys had been used on that lamp. One by one, all of them broke. Each time they broke, you heard a crackling sound. They would shatter to pieces.

Only Chinnapappa and Mariappan used to be afraid when they broke. Whoever broke it would get blows and the one who broke it the previous time would be heaped with abuse. The pain from previous slaps would come to mind. Mariappan had earned a lot of prizes and good wishes from Ayya for breaking the chimney.

Who hadn't broken a chimney at home? Amma… Ayya… Periapappa, everyone had broken one.

There was no end to it; in the end it was Amma who took a decision. 'Dei… you lot… hereafter let this lamp burn without a chimney. It's become a regular nuisance. If it burns, let it, or let it die out… all right,' she said. From the day she said that, the lamp was without a chimney.

As she said, the lamp would die out within a few minutes of being lit. The lamp was scared of the wind. Poor thing, once the wind blew, it would limp along, shivering!

Chinnapappa was very fond of the house lamp. She loved it when it burned in the night.

If it looked like the wind would blow, Chinnapappa would try to shield the lamp, her little hands cupped. She would worry about it getting snuffed out in the wind.

As if the wind didn't know how to fool one! It would fool her stealthily. The wind, of course, knew all the directions. Beyond the thatch-screen, beyond the verandah, beyond the reach of Chinnapappa's hands, the wind would slowly climb the wall and put off the lamp with a 'gup' sound. The rascally wind!

Once Chinnapappa had sobbed heart-rendingly. Mariappan couldn't bear it. His eyes too glistened. Even Amma must have been troubled by her tears. But, for the sake of Chinnapappa, how could she wash her hands off the vow of 'never buying a chimney'?

If they bought a chimney just once for Chinnapappa's sake, wouldn't the lamp burn steadily, without flickering? Mariappan tried to persuade his mother, but to no avail. 'Dei… Mariappa, what do you know of the situation at home? You are still like a playful child. Without the rains, there's no way even to fill our stomachs. What, da? As if you can't live without a chimney?'

It looked as if one had to befriend darkness from that day onwards. But Chinnapappa was scared of the dark. In the night, if she woke up suddenly, she would howl loudly. But nowadays the house was always dark. Even during the day it was dark.

As days went by one became used to the dark. Only Chinnapappa knew well enough how dark it would turn and when. But she was afraid of the dark. Even so, by and by, she learnt to peer through the darkness.

It was Chinnapappa who became smart at manoeuvring through the dark, even more so than Amma. Mariappan would often trip and fall, bang against the front step. Whenever he fell, Chinnapappa would click her tongue. She would hold her brother and rub the spot where he had hurt himself. If the foot was bruised, she would blow on it.

Amma too made kanji sitting in the dark. The burning fire would then light up the whole house brightly. Every nook would be seen clearly.

The lamp on the western wall… Above it the black trail, which looked as if it was holding up the entire roof, seemed magnified.

When the stove was lit in the night, the black trail would clamber up the wall, like Saduka Bhootham, the guardian-ghost in the Tamil lesson in Class Eight. It would laugh at Chinnapappa. It would shake its head when everyone drank kanji. You couldn't see it at all in the dark of the night. Suddenly in the dead of the night Ayya would appear like a fire-spitting demon, his beedi-end glowing. He always had a matchbox. Even if he didn't have a beedi, he would always have a matchbox.

Ayya always lay down smoking a beedi. When the lit beedi moved from hand to mouth, this way and that, you wondered if the eyes of the bogeyman-thief looked like this.

Ayya often lit the beedi in the night and whenever he struck the match, 'sarr', the whole house would fill up with light. Even in that momentary flash, the wall and the black trail would appear monstrous. This trail had been there ever since they were children. How many years at the time of Pongal in the month of Thai they had whitewashed the place; yet it never disappeared. In the house of Mariappan's friend, Munusamy of Nine B, the black trail faced the east on the eastern wall.

Whenever the Tamil teacher asked a question about the guardian-ghost, it was the black trail that came to Mariappan's mind.

At the times when the teachers didn't ask questions or take any lessons, Mariappan lost himself in the thoughts of bathing in the lake and frolicking in the pond. When he suddenly thought of his house, it was the black trail that appeared first. Only then would Amma, Chinnapappa and others come to mind.

The black trail didn't come to Chinnapappa's mind often enough. All she thought of was the chimney that was needed for the lamp. The broken chimney that now fitted well was patched up with the last page of Mariappan's maths notebook; the red line in the middle revealed that it was from a maths notebook.

It was Chinnapappa who had picked up the broken chimney from the undergrowth of the plant that fenced the lake.

She put it carefully in her little full-skirt, carried it and showed it joyfully only to Mariappan.

Mari too was ecstatic when he saw Pappa's broken chimney. Immediately he hit upon an idea. He tore out a leaf from his Maths book, cut it to fit the crack that ran along the chimney and stuck it with cooked millet paste. The chimney got set.

Now it looked nice when the lamp was lit. The light was a bit dim in the place where the Maths page was stuck. Half the head of the 'man', which he had drawn with the numbers one to nine a long while ago, could be seen on the page.

That night Amma didn't put anything on the stove. In the pot was some rice-water and grains of rice. Amma said she would give kanji only when Ayya came. Chinnapappa was very hungry. She slowly inched across from where she was leaning against the wall and buried her face in her mother's lap. Years ago Mariappan used to sleep like that on his mother's lap.

Ayya arrived. He said that they had to catch the train that night itself. Ayya and Amma spoke between themselves – that they would get daily-wage jobs and also rice three times a day if they went to Thanjavur.

Should they stay back here, they wouldn't even have anyone to give them the last drops of water in the mouth. In the lamp's light Ayya was counting, one by one, the notes that he had got for the travel after pawning Chinnapappa's anklets. They had to leave without the neighbour being aware of it. Chinnapappa couldn't sleep. Mariappan gathered his books and notebooks together, stuffed them inside a cloth bag and readied himself.

After the bustle of the town died down, Amma got ready, bags, bundles and all.

Carrying Chinnapappa on his shoulder, Ayya walked briskly without looking back. But as Amma walked, she kept turning and looking at the house again and again. Periapappa walked silently behind Ayya. Mariappan walked carrying the small sack full of vessels and his book-bag.

Only when he sat down in the train did Ayya find the courage to let out a sigh. He put away the odds and ends of the luggage under the seat. The train started in a little while. Chinnapappa slept off, putting her head on Amma's lap.

Mariappan too was sleepy. The breeze on train journeys was always comforting. He woke up when the train started again from one of the stations on the way.

Everyone seemed to be asleep when he got up. The train's light appeared before his eyes. He was troubled that they had left behind Chinnapappa's chimney-lamp burning at home. He looked at Chinnapappa's face and clicked his tongue, as she always did. He couldn't forget the black trail that stood on the western wall. The dark trail too stalked him stubbornly, leaping and hopping over everything.

Original title: *Iruttu*
1981

SCRIBE

72

IMAYAM

Just opposite the tahsildar's office, at a little distance away, stood a huge neem tree. Under its shade, five-six people had spread out date-palm mats and sat facing the east. In front of each one was a wooden writing board. The first man in the row was immersed in the lottery section of the day's newspaper. Sivaraman, sitting to the right of him, had plastered lines of vibhuti across his forehead. His face drooped, as if he had forsaken something. Like the other scribes, he too asked – without being requested – the few heading towards the tahsildar's or the sub-registrar's office, 'Do you need to write a petition?'

Sivaraman looked at the tahsildar's office. Even though it was after eleven, there was not much crowd. Neither was there any in the sub-registrar's office. There was not a soul in front of the scribes sitting under the neem tree in front of that office. That not a single person had given him an opportunity to write since morning made Sivaraman angry. If a Monday itself was like this, what was one to do, he lamented. Perhaps he would feel better if he smoked a cigarette or a beedi, he thought. He asked Chinnasami, who was to the left of him, 'Do you have a cigarette?' Without even opening his mouth to utter a 'no', Chinnasami simply signalled, pouting his lips, and started looking out, as earlier, for someone who might need a petition to be written.

When Sivaraman said, 'From the morning, no earnings, not even for tea and beedi,' Chinnasami, replied dispiritedly, 'That is how it will be in lean times,' and started picking up and flinging away the neem leaves fallen on the mat.

Looking at the woman making her way to the tahsildar's office, all of the five-six of them called out at the same time, 'Come here, 'ma.' No sooner than the woman, bewildered, looked at them with a start, they all asked her persistently, using her gaze as an excuse, 'What do you want, 'ma? Do you need to write some petition-kitition? Come here, 'ma, sit down on the mat.' Who would she ask, how would she ask, thought the woman, and when she took a few steps towards Sivaraman seated directly in front of her, he urgently said, 'Come 'ma, come 'ma,' fearing that the others would deter her from coming to him. And then, as if welcoming someone important, he fanned the mat with his towel and said with undue familiarity, 'Sit, 'ma, sit. Tell me what you want. Why are you standing? Come, sit, 'ma.' When he saw the baffled woman taking a few more steps hesitantly, Sivaraman firmly persuaded her, 'Come 'ma. I'm a bear or a tiger or what for you to get scared? Come and sit on the mat first.'

When the woman said, 'To admit my son in a government hostel, they asked us to write the caste and community in this form and get a signature,' Sivaraman replied before she could complete, 'That's all, no. Why are you hesitating for that? Come sit,' and gave a little laugh. The woman took a step or two more towards him.

'They won't put their signature right away on this form. For that you must first give an application. They will put their signature on that. You must take that and get the signature of the village official or the RI, only then will the tahsildar put his signature,' Sivaraman explained, afraid that the woman would give him the slip.

The woman asked like a little child, 'You can get the signature, no?'

Sivaraman said, laughing a little, 'We can get it, 'ma. First you come and sit on the mat. You must run around for one or two days. That's all. Why are you worried about that?' He explained clearly how to get the caste, income and proof-of-residence certificates. He then asked in the end, 'Shall I write out the application?'

'You will be blessed, saami. Please write it out. Our village deity Kulla Karuppan only has brought you here. If you were not here I would be roaming around not knowing where there is a pathway and where there is a waterway. May your son, daughter, everyone, live well,' said the woman, and looked up at the sky, folded her hands and prayed. And then sat down on the ground near the tip of the mat, despite Sivaraman's entreaties to sit on it. Without his urging she began, 'I have four children. The eldest is a girl, the next is a boy. The last too is a girl child. The first boy, I tried my level best to beat and kick him, but he wouldn't even sleep with his head pointing to the school! But the second boy is keen and intelligent. He is only saying, 'Don't call me to work in the fields, I want to go to school only.' Should we spoil such a boy? That's why I've brought this form.'

After asking the woman information such as her native place, caste and income, Sivaraman took out a sheet of paper, placed it on the writing pad and started writing. A small smile bloomed on his lips. He looked at Chinnasami sitting next to him from the corner of his eye and gave a mocking smile. And pretended as if he hadn't seen the disappointment on Chinnasami's face. When he began to write out the application itself, his mind started calculating. First, he would drink tea and then buy a packet of beedis, came the thought again and again. Besides, what Valli said when he left home in the morning also came to mind: 'Come in the evening a little early. Only after you come can I buy rice to cook.' The thought angered him and he started writing fast.

That woman kept gazing at Sivaraman. She couldn't believe it. She was astonished that he himself had called her and started writing with so much care on his own sheet of paper. Had she known it was going to be this easy, she would have come three days earlier when the boy had brought home the application form. She had tried but couldn't get away for three days.

There wasn't a person in the village she hadn't asked for twenty rupees for the bus fare and five or ten rupees in case she had to grease someone's palm. She had roamed around for two days; in the end she had to pawn the only lamp they had at home. In her efforts to pawn the lamp, she hadn't even had the time to down kanji in the morning. But when she saw Sivaraman writing away, she forgot everything – how she had pawned the lamp, the fatigue from walking, and how she hadn't drunk anything since morning. Her face bloomed with joy. Brimming with curiosity, she looked at him writing. She was fascinated by the twists and turns of his pen. A doubt suddenly appeared: would he ask money for writing? Going by his face, she felt he wouldn't ask. If at all he did, she would give him money to drink tea.

Sivaraman assumed the look of someone writing with great care. He lifted his head up once and looked at the woman. Both her demeanour and her words 'saami, saami' increased his faith in her. Perhaps he ought to ask for a rupee or two more, he wondered. It would be a sin to ask more from someone who looked like a beggar. At that very moment a crow on the tree shat and it plopped right on his shoulder. Abusing the crow, he wiped away the shit and started to read what he had finished writing. Then he asked her, 'Fingerprint or signature?' When she said, 'Fingerprint, saami,' he held her thumb to the stamp pad, pressed it and then imprinted her fingerprint on the application. He once again read the application. Her gave it to her, and then hastily scribbled a couple of lines on another sheet of paper, lifted his head and said, 'Go, take this straight to the office, to a man who is called DT. He will sign on it. Then take that to the officer in your village. He will look after everything.' He began to write again.

Overjoyed, the woman said, 'You are like god, saami. If you hadn't been here, I would have suffered like anything. For your good heart, god will keep you well, without any wants.' She folded her hands, paid her respects to him and got up. Sivaraman asked her casually, 'Give me five rupees, 'ma.' Wondering if he had asked her, she questioned him doubtfully, 'Did you ask me, saami?'

'Mmm,' he replied, nodding his head, and continued to write.

The woman asked, 'Why are you asking for money, saami?'

'For what-aa? Writing labour, 'ma.'

'Money for writing? You are asking money for this? And that too without any inkling of shame, five rupees?'

Just to write on a piece of paper if this fellow asks for five rupees, how much will others ask, she thought with fear.

'Don't keep on talking. Just take out the money, 'ma.'

'What only have you written for you to ask five full rupees, like a whole big vadai? Wages just to write which village, whose son? Ada, my god, which place will tolerate this injustice?'

'Just give the money and go quietly, 'ma.'

'You are asking like this, do you think it is fair? Is it false that he is my son? Is it false that I am his mother? And for generations we have been living in that village only. Moreover, I was born in that village, got married in that village and got four children in that village. We are paying taxes in three corners of the village. You are asking for money for writing what is true? Where will I go and talk about this robbery? If I had gone to the teacher in our village and just asked, he would have written hundred-thousand such letters for free. Just because I look slightly unkempt and not very neat, you are talking like this or what?'

'You are giving me dialogues, is it? When you take this form and run after the village officer, revenue inspector or tahsildar, then you will know. Go, give them all these dialogues. Give me the money quietly, close your mouth and go.'

'Just four words. Don't even know if you wrote them properly. For that you are asking for five rupees, justifying it in your heart. Just try telling this to any villager and then you will see! I'm seeing only now someone asking for money for scribbling four words on a sheet of paper for a schoolboy. Because of people like you only, even the sky is refusing to give rains. What will you do? The world has become like that. God, it has become a world where people wander about, waiting to grab and eat from gullible people. Just because someone is new to the place, you think you can talk anything?'

'Don't simply keep on talking. Take out the money. Saniyan, you've come first thing in the morning,' said Sivaraman. The next instant she started fighting with him. Her face changed colour. She started shouting like one possessed. 'Who are you calling sani?' she repeated over and over again. Sivaraman too shouted, trying to keep pace with her. But his voice didn't match up. On his behalf, the other scribes too started quarrelling with her. They argued the she ought to pay the writing fee. She tried to answer all of them at the same time. A crowd began to gather there.

'Who did he call saniyan? I don't want anybody's labour. Some story it has become – like they say, a Brahmin's money for rites, a Muslim's money for meat and a peasant's money for waste. You opened your mouth and asked. If I refuse, I will have the sins of seven villages heaped on me. Here, this is what you deserve for writing this,' she said and stretched out a rupee note which she took out from a betel-bag she had tucked into her waist.

When he saw everyone watching the spectacle he thought he would die of shame. He puckered his face and he shouted disgustedly, 'Go, 'ma, go far away.' Not paying any attention to his screaming, the woman said, 'Ayyo, sins will dog me. Here take your money.' She threw the coin on the mat and started walking towards the tahsildar's office.

Sivaraman looked at the other scribes. When he saw their pitying looks, he shrank. And down drooped his head.

Original title: *Ezhutthukkaaran*
2005

BIRDS THAT LIVE ON A WILTING TREE 73

SU VENUGOPAL

Mahendran peeped into the tank by the well after scooping out the earth to make a plant-bed. Three-fourths of the tank was full. He didn't feel like going home. Wouldn't he get the news at least by the evening, he wondered, bubbles of anguish rising inside him. He shook the dust off his feet with the head-towel. When he sat on the tank he could picture his father lying on the bed, mouth agape, eyes closed.

Five years ago, the second day he had succumbed to dysentery, when he had lain unconscious in Chinnasamy Devar's farmland, Ratnasamy had carried him home. His mother Mayilthai had been more anxious than Mahendran. The entire village had been in the grip of dysentery. In the hope that he would get well in two days, Mahendran's father Kumarasamy had foolhardily refrained from telling anyone at home. High noon had felled the man; had Ratnasamy not spotted him the man would have been dead and gone.

Tongue twisted, unable to speak, Mahendran had run towards the taxi standing outside, beating his chest 'ayyayo', making a grab on the way for a bedsheet and a couple of lungis and stuffing them in. Tears had plopped down. Kumarasamy's face had been enveloped in pity as he had sat in the taxi. Stupefied, Mayilthai had clutched him close. Nothing had run in her mind: which hospital? How to admit him? Mahendran's maama had said to Mahendran as he sat in front: 'Go to Ramamurthy Hospital, I'll come there after rustling up the money. How much do you have on hand?'

'Have four hundred, maama.'

'Okay, go. I'll get it from my clients.'

When the taxi had started, Mayilthai's lips had trembled. 'Doesn't matter how much ever it takes,' she had mumbled. A fear, that she would lose something that was truly her own, had shadowed her face.

That Kumarasamy had got up and sat immediately after being given glucose had surprised Mayilthai. The daughters had come rushing in, crowded around the father and wailed. Though Mayilthai had wept along with her daughters, she actually had been happy. Lying on the floor, shaking his leg, Mahendran had listened to their chatter. When she had come to know that it wasn't a dangerous illness, Mayilthai had felt sheepish about her anxiety. There had been a thrill in speaking to visitors, sitting on the bed, chewing betel. Whenever she had bustled around the bed, jasmine flowers strung around her bun, the distinct look of a married woman had shone brightly.

His wheezing had never before been so intense. Even if he had lain on the sofa the whole night gasping for breath, it never surprised either Mayilthai or the children when he got ready for school the next morning. It was something of a second nature to the father. Perhaps it was because of old age or something, the man who had fallen sick a couple of days ago couldn't get up. The day before Mahendran's maama had said, 'Let us take him to the hospital, Akka.' When his aunt had reminded Mayilthai to let the daughters know, she had said, 'No need for all that. They'll come rushing, thinking this and that.' Mahendran had been relieved when he had heard that.

Couldn't it all end on its own in the dead of the night, wondered Mahendran. The previous afternoon Kumarasamy had drunk two glasses of barley kanji. In the night when he had asked, 'Mayil, will you make gruel with ragi flour?' no one had been around. She had replied, 'If you eat, the bedsheet will get soiled. Only if you starve your stomach one time, will it turn solid.' 'No, Mayil, I'm feeling very hungry.' Even if Mahendran knew that his mother had done right in not replying and sleeping off, the palpitations of his heart reached his ears. How terrible it would be if, in the morning, his father told about this to someone. When he had tossed and turned, Mahendran couldn't sleep. What if we shut only the nostrils? He had perspired. He had got up and put the switch on. Kumarasamy had been lying down, pressing his hands, one or the other, on his stomach and taking deep breaths. Thin frame. Grey hairs on hollow cheeks. Shifting aside the flask, covering him well with the sheet, Mahendran had switched off the light and lain down on his back. Snapping his fingers, Mahendran had steepled his hands and looked into the darkness, eyes wide open.

'Can't get sleep, Appa?'

'Yes.'

'Sleep, Appa.'

'…'

'Don't keep thinking about this only.'

'Mmm… Only eight months to retire. If god himself takes me away, it will be good.'

Couldn't stay there. Mahendran jumped off the ledge of the tank, walked through the plant-bed. Without his knowing, his speed increased. The happiness hidden inside the deep of his heart kept vigil. When his mother had sought a girl for him from among her relatives through a mediator, they had refused: 'How can we give a girl to a man who is doing nothing. He should somehow try and get a job, no? Without a job, how can one…' Mayilthai had tried in two or three places without Mahendran's knowledge, but without any success. She was scared to ask anyone, head held high.

It had been certain that he would somehow get a job in Zamindarini High School. They had had strong hopes since they had already given fifty thousand rupees to the founder. Kumarasamy had assured them of the rest of the money once Mahendran joined work. When Mahendran suddenly heard that another chap, who had given one and a quarter lakhs had joined, he had been shattered. The advance given on trust – without earning any interest whatsoever for two years – was also gone. But that wasn't such a big matter. Because such hopes had been dashed at least four times before. But it was the age bar which caused the shock. He was running thirty-three.

As soon as he was back from school, Kumarasamy would rush off to pour water over the construction. As the house had slowly taken shape at the northern edge of the village, the entire family had been proud. There hadn't been any houses around in those days. If they had to build such a house today, it would take at least four lakhs. It had taken only sixty-five thousand eighteen years ago; yet it was a house built in stages. When Mahendran, Kavitha and Paranjothi used to run up the stairs to pour water after the concrete was set, Kumarasamy too would compete like a child with them but would soon become breathless.

When he crossed the bridge, Manikanda Bawa, cycling from the opposite side, stopped him. 'What Mahesh? Appa is unwell, is it? Ramu told me this morning only.'

'Yes, Bawa.'

'Then take him to a doctor, no?'

'That's where I'm going. Thought I'd finish the field-work…'

'Going to Kadiresan's clinic?'

'Should go back and decide. Usually, we take him to Dr Ramamurthy…'

'I'll go to the farm and come back.'

'Mmm…'

The cycle left. Mahendran was overcome by exhaustion. He wanted to run away somewhere. His walk slowed down.

It was when Mahendran had been in the final year of MSc that an EB clerk had fallen in love with Kavitha. Kumarasamy had wanted to get her married off only after a year. But when he saw that Paranjothi too was quickly filling out, he had decided to complete his 'duties' one by one. Five years later when they decided to buy twenty-five sovereigns of gold for Paranjothi, as they had done earlier for Kavitha, Kumarasamy who had gone into the bank leaving Mahendran, Mayilthai and Paranjothi behind at the entrance, didn't come out till noon. When Mahendran, losing all patience, went in, he could see him arguing with the manager. Kumarasamy, who had been sure that he would get the loan, had been disappointed. Since he had already gone fifteen times and had been sure of getting it, he had gone with the family, but look what had happened. The next day he had taken only the mother, leaving behind the son and daughter. They had come back with three boxes of necklaces and nose-rings. Paranjothi had shown them off to her relatives.

When Mahendran turned the corner of the street, he could see his younger aunt climbing the steps. Visitors never kept their mouth shut. 'What is this, simply watching him lying on the bed for so long? Shouldn't you have quickly gone and put some injection-kinjection or something and made him okay?' Mahendran burned with irritation. 'Mind your own business.' Though he wanted to retort, it died down in the hollow of his throat.

When he entered, he could see him lying down, propped up by a pillow against his back. When his aunt asked him, 'Is it enough?', Kumarasamy replied, 'Just a while ago I drank coffee.' A weak, squeaky voice was heard. 'Dei, what is this farm and field and all? Shouldn't you have gone at once and showed him to a doctor?'

As if nodding, he went inside. Mayilthai felt uneasy with all this crowd. If one more day could be pushed off, you could take him off the bed and stretch him out. When the relatives who came said, 'What, 'ma, it is one forty-five. Shouldn't you be giving him something to eat?', Mayilthai was forced to reluctantly enter the kitchen saying, 'Yes, must give.'

Wiping his face, Mahendran sat on the verandah. He could see cobwebs spun on the photographs. Once every six months Kumarasamy would dust them off, climbing on a high stool. For the past year he hadn't done much work. In the photograph where the young Kumarasamy was carrying Mahendran and kissing him, he was wearing a coat. It was taken in Bharat Studio. But the photo playing with Kavitha was taken with a hand-held camera. Then a photo of a banian-clad, thin Kumarasamy head-to-head with his granddaughter, playing the game 'dee dee dee'.

Of late, whenever Kavitha came home asking five hundred or thousand rupees for this or that, it always ended in a fight. 'Dei, you mind your own business. Who else will my daughter ask if not me?' The laughter that accompanied would shatter the argument. It wasn't only for Kavitha. When the mess bill had to be paid on the sixth of every month, it was Kumarasamy's wont to stand at the gate of the college on the fifth evening itself. Sometimes when he handed over to Mahendran the snacks made at home, it would be evident that he was troubled by breathlessness.

It was only when the headmaster who had come to enquire about Kumarasamy's health shouted at them that a taxi was hurriedly called for. Mayilthai was on the verge of tears when she saw Mahendran standing in the middle of the doorway, head hanging down. Packing Kumarasamy's clothes, she called out to Mahendran. When she went in, she pushed the door shut and turned, 'What 'pa, what do you think?'

'What about you, Amma?'

'If people don't keep coming and going, something may happen. What if people start talking?'

'Mmm, mmm.' The room was enveloped in a deathly silence.

When the taxi arrived, the headmaster helped Kumarasamy to stand up. Kumarasamy's legs shook. Mahendran gathered his breathless father close and got down the steps with him. When Mayilthai got in, Kumarasamy leant against her. Mahendran sat in the front, turned around and said, 'Make him sit properly, Amma.' Mayilthai was not perturbed.

Why are all these people wagging their tongues at our business? Did we call them? She was irritated. Every time she cleaned him up, she was repulsed. But she had to grit her teeth and show a caring face to others.

When they entered the hospital the doctor was out on a case. It took half an hour for him to return. He asked Kumarasamy to lie down on a bench and take deep breaths. He went about his business, as usual. Placing the stethoscope on the chest, he examined carefully. Then placed it on Kumarasamy's back. He took his pulse, asked him to stretch out the tongue and checked his eyes… Kumarasamy's throat dragged out the breath noisily.

'Since when has he been unwell?'

'Since day before…'

'What, 'ma, you've left him to lie like that since day before? Okay, he has to be admitted. 'Roshini…' He called out to the nurse.

'Just give him some injection. We'll take him home in the evening.'

'Are you joking? Just take him out of this place then. Did you bring him here for the sake of "formality"? If you just wanted an injection, why didn't you call one of the two RHMPs who are always roaming around in your town?'

'No, sorry. You admit him…'

Circumstances forced Mahendran to speak. Mayilthai was ashamed when the doctor shouted at her with her husband nearby. Kumarasamy looked at the two of them intently. He made an effort to say something but closed his eyes.

No one thought that Kumarasamy would recover so much by the evening. He propped up pillows for his neck and sat up, stretching out his legs. The wheezing had come down and his breath had stabilised. 'Don't tell anything to Kavitha and Paranjothi. I'm fine, 'pa. It becomes like this only in the cold season. I feel like getting up and walking, Mayil.' He shook out his hands and snapped his fingers.

When Mahendran got ready to leave the hospital, Mayilthai looked at him with depressed eyes. They moved restlessly and seemed to say, 'Even this last chance for a government job on compassionate grounds has slipped from your hand.' His face tightened. When he turned and looked at his father, Kumarasamy smiled. Was it out of gratitude? Or was it a knowing smile which implied, 'I know you all'? In return, Mahendran didn't smile, and walked into the street.

Original title: *Veezhndha Maratthil Vaazhndha Paravaigal*
1998

THE CROW 74

PERUMAL MURUGAN

It was on a full moon day in the month of Maasi that the crow with a glistening neck started chasing him. It was the festival of Goddess Maariamman in his aunt's village. Children were playing in the generous shade of the neem tree in front of the house. The ruckus they created drowned out all the other noises. At first no one noticed the screechy cawing from the branches. Crowing, it descended branch by branch. Tilting its head, the crow looked down. A girl who came out from the house shooed it away with her hand saying, 'Why is this crow screeching like this?' Ignoring her, the crow continued to caw, jumping up and down the branches. Its voice seemed to be filled with confusion and sorrow. At moments it seemed full of excitement, as if it had spotted a prey. 'The house is full of guests. Who else has to come for this crow to shout like this?' said a voice from inside. Unmindful, the children were caught up in the frenzy of the game.

Suddenly, the crow swooped down like an eagle, without flapping its wings. Of all the children, it picked him and pecked him on the head, aiming its sharp beak. It circled above his head, ready to strike him again. The children scattered in fright. It was only after a while that he felt the pain. He pressed his hand to where he had been pecked. His eyes couldn't control the tears. By that time, another peck landed on his closed hand. The skin split and blood was visible. He plopped down with a terrifying scream. His bawling prompted everyone who was eating in the pial to come out rushing. Looking at the crowd, the crow flew back up into the sky from the shadows of the tree and faded into a dot. They pacified him and fed him some snacks. His mother, who kneaded his head hard, abused the crow non-stop. After that, he didn't go back to play. Weeping, he fell asleep. They shook him awake in the night and took him to the temple.

They left for their hometown the day after the festival was over. As the bullock cart made its way, the crow suddenly appeared in the sky and dived down, aiming for his head among the crowd. In a flash it pecked him and flew away. No one had expected this. They tried to shoo away the vicious crow with their hands and the whip. Though it floated up a bit, it didn't change its spot. It was clear that it was aiming for his head again. His mother covered him with the ends of her sari and tucked him into her lap. Her face had darkened, drained of all the joy of the festival. Her eyes were stuck to the sky. Any bird, even the ones which appeared like a speck, appeared to her like the crow that had pecked him. Till they reached home, she didn't lift the ends of her sari. She wondered if this was an omen of some misfortune that awaited him.

Nothing happened after they reached home. He too looked at crows very carefully. No sign of that crow. Even if everything had happened only in a moment, he knew the crow quite well. It was a big-headed crow with jet-black wings and a bleached beak. He had noticed that the tiny feathers on its neck glistened in flashes like white stone. The aggression in its eyes was imprinted on his mind. The astrologer that his mother consulted asked her to observe fasts for eleven Saturdays, offer sesame seeds, light lamps with gingelly oil, and do a pooja for Lord Sanisvaran. He also said that it would be a good thing if they went to the temple on all Saturdays. His mother took him every Saturday to the temple that was ten miles from his home. He always looked at the black stone statue of the crow at the entrance of the temple. There wasn't anything unusual about it. From whichever side he looked, its neck didn't glisten. When he said that to his mother, she said, 'Don't worry. All crows are the vehicles for Lord Sanisvaran.' Even if he didn't like it, he continued to visit the temple.

It was only after a few months that he visited his aunt's place again. When he went to see his aunt who was grazing goats in the forest, the crow from the tamarind tree flew down. Even when he covered his head with his hand and pelted stones at it, it didn't fly away very far. Feigning to fly away, it came back again and again. He ran back home without seeing his aunt. He didn't say anything, but everyone guessed what had happened. The whole day he remained imprisoned at home and it was only in the night that he started out for his town.

This happened to him countless times. Whenever he went there, the crow came out, as if waiting for him. Even if there was a bunch of crows, he could easily identify it. Not even once Lord Sanisvaran came to his rescue. As he grew, it seemed as if the aggression of the crow too increased. He didn't visit his aunt's place for almost a year. When his aunt lamented, 'How fond this boy used to be of me. Because of the crow, he has stopped coming,' he started visiting her again. But the crow never changed. Its chasing and its cruel pecking became even more violent. Perhaps its anger had increased because he hadn't gone for a long time.

It was only a few days after Deepavali. His aunt had a suggestion: she gave a gun used for firecrackers and asked him to shoot at the crow. At the sound of the cracker, the crow would fly away. This was a trick used to shoo away birds in the fields at harvest time. He went with the toy gun. When the crow came towards his head, he fired at it. Since it was a rolled firecracker, it burst out continuously. The frightened crow flew away. But in the time he took to change the roll, the crow found its target. It didn't allow him to change the roll. It pecked him again and again. It wasn't scared anymore of the outstretched gun. By the time he escaped, his head was bruised and swollen. It wasn't possible to always keep wandering around with a toy gun. He tried many other tricks. Instead of walking, he tried to zip past on a bicycle. But the crow's wings were stronger than his feet. He walked, twirling a big stick around his head. But after a little while, his hands started aching. But the crow knew when he changed the stick to his other hand. Every method seemed useless.

A long time went by. He was engrossed in studies to the point of forgetting about the crow. Even his aunt wasn't very much upset that he never came. Perhaps she thought it was better that he didn't come at all than getting hurt all the time. He had to go there for a wedding. Everyone thought about the crow. But he wasn't afraid at all. Actually he had become curious – would that crow still be alive… would it be as strong and vicious… would its neck still glisten… He was dying to know all this. When he said, 'I will also come,' no one protested. Only his mother was apprehensive. But when she saw the excitement on his face, she didn't object.

Now one could take a bus to the town. As soon as he got down from the bus, he looked at the sky. The sky was empty. A patch of a black cloud very far above. He walked normally towards the wedding hall. But his eye and attention were above. Nothing happened. The crow must have died. How long did a crow live? More than ten years? He couldn't remember the number of years it had chased him. Could be more than ten years. When he was chatting around outside after the wedding was over, he felt the black patch in the sky descending on his head. He quickly lifted his head. The peck landed on his forehead. Along with the burning sensation, a little gash. He ran and took shelter inside the pandal. The caw of a lone crow echoed at a distance, but what it signified wasn't very clear.

Since the wedding hall was abuzz with this talk, he hid himself in a room in embarrassment. Only when it turned dusk and grew dark he returned to his town. From its peck he felt that the crow had become a little sore and exhausted. Of all the pecks he had endured, this was the lightest. Since he had tilted his head, the tip of the beak had pierced his forehead. Had it landed on his head, it would have been but a mere tap through his hair. Later on, when he had to be there on urgent work a few times, he left at night and returned too at night. When his yearning to see the town by day increased, he stopped visiting the place altogether.

Another time his uncle himself came to invite him. He said that the Kurava community had pitched a settlement in his town and that they were experts at catching crows. He also assured him that they had trapped the big-headed crow. He asked if it was the one with the glistening neck. 'I've been seeing that crow for years. As if I can't identify it.' His uncle said that it was the same crow without a hint of a doubt. He felt as if he had lost something. His face drooped. He felt uneasy to go to his uncle's place. But what reason could he give? So without any enthusiasm he accompanied him. As soon as he entered the town, his eyes went to the sky, as usual. Clear skies everywhere. Not a spot of black to be seen. He lowered his eyes. He, who was looking firmly at the ground and walking, suddenly looked up, sensing something. That crow flew in from a neem tree, wings spread out. Since his uncle sensed the danger, he unfurled the umbrella and protected him. The crow's beak pierced the umbrella in many places. With a lot of difficulty, they managed to make it home. His uncle felt awkward to look at him. Though he felt bad, he was relieved in a way. As always, he returned home in the dark. That was the last time he was attacked by the crow.

The next few years he was busy with his higher studies and seeking a job, so his aunt's place and the crow crossed his mind only fleetingly. When he was alone and depressed, he thought of the crow. If he closed his eyes, he could see it flying, black wings spread out. When it slowly descended towards his head, he would reflexively cover his head with his hands. He would be filled with laughter and excitement. He was never able to fathom why it had chased him like this. Troubled, he thought of many probable reasons. But all of them were easily wiped away and only the questions remained. So instead of pondering over it, he would fill his mind with the image of the crow. As it flew, he would rejoice for a long while in the glimmer on its neck that could be seen from an angle. Like a playful game, it was also a means to lighten his heart.

He got a job and his marriage too got fixed to a colleague. He took the invitation to his aunt's place. He hadn't taken any precautions to face the crow. He was told that his aunt was in the fields. He walked on the furrow edging the field. On the way, the motor of a well was chugging away. Water flowed copiously. His eyes combed the skies. He was disappointed. He noticed it while crossing the water channel. A crow was flapping its wings in the running water, dipping its head, like a woman taking a bath after visiting a house of death. He looked at it suspiciously. It dipped its neck again and again in the water. He looked at it with utmost curiosity. Oblivious to everything other than its bath, the crow didn't even give him a glance.

Original title: Kaakkai
1997

THE JUDGEMENT 75

BAMA

The children of Classes Three, Four and Five were terribly excited. Only they were to be taken to see a film in a theatre in the neighbouring town. So delighted were they that they couldn't concentrate on their studies; they just kept wondering when tomorrow would arrive. The headmaster had announced that they each had to bring five rupees. He also sent them away with a whole lot of instructions: they all had to come in uniform, those who had chappals had to wear them, and those who had water bottles had to bring water. The children were thrilled, and why wouldn't they be? They all thought that they were off on a tour to the city.

Even though the Kattur Primary School had existed for over fifty years, there was no evidence of any kind of development in the village. No bus, water, or hospital facilities, nothing. No tea shop or provision store. Not even a petty shop to quench thirst-ridden mouths with soda-geeda. You had to trudge three kilometres away to Uthukottai for anything. That was a somewhat biggish town. You could buy all sorts of things there. That's where you could find not one but two cinema halls. It was in one of those theatres that the children were going to see a children's film. It didn't matter what film it was; going to Uthukottai was joyous enough.

The next day, breaking routine, they came to school at seven itself. After the assembly, they were made to stand in a line and were packed off with the teachers; the headmaster then got into his vehicle and went ahead of them. Uncontrollably eager and happy, the children walked very fast. They had to walk three kilometres, more or less. Half-walking, half-running, they arrived. Children of another school were already seated in the theatre. Counting the heads one by one, they let our children inside. There was such a din inside the theatre that you thought you would go deaf. By the time all the children had settled down and the film began, it was after ten. There was a hush of silence once the screening started. Even if it was an English film, 'Baby's Day Out', the children were deeply engrossed and enjoyed the film thoroughly. They totally identified with the little child. During the interval, they bought this and that to eat, whatever their eyes settled on, till all the money they had on hand dwindled away.

After the film was over, again the children stood in a line, and walked back somehow, in the unbearable heat. Once they crossed the main road all the line-kine broke up. The feet burned in the midday heat. Many children didn't have chappals. Tongues curled up in thirst. Somehow they ran along. The children had finished all the water in the theatre itself. Sweating and puffing, they eagerly headed back to school, wondering when they'd be able to drink water.

On the way back, just a kilometre away, was a village named Pallatthur. As soon as they reached it, all the children drank water, pumping it from the street tap. So thirsty were they. A big boy from the fifth class pumped water for all of them. Everyone crowded around, shoving and pushing, wanting to get ahead. It was a tremendous task, ordering them to stand in a queue to drink water. Magalakshmi from Class Three eagerly filled up her bottle. But her sister Vijayalakshmi from Class Five wouldn't allow her to drink it – she snatched the bottle away, slapped her soundly on the back and said angrily, all the while emptying the water to the ground: 'You're going to drink water from a tap in the Cheri Street, is it? Wait… I'll tell Appa. You'll get tight slaps.'

'I'm so thirsty, please don't tell Appa, Akka. I'll drink very little,' begged Magalakshmi.

Vijayalakshmi wouldn't allow her to drink. Magalakshmi howled loudly. Hearing her, Mary Teacher asked, 'What Magalakshmi, why are you crying? You can't walk? It's only a little further away. See, there's our school… we can even see your class.'

Shanthi, who was walking along, said, 'No, Teacher, Maga's thirsty – that's why she's crying.'

Teacher replied, 'Now only everyone drank water from the water-pump. How can you be thirsty already? All right, come, come, let's go and drink in school.'

'She didn't drink water from the tap, Teacher. Her sister said she shouldn't drink and dragged her away.'

'Why didn't she allow her to drink?'

'That's a Cheri tap, Teacher. If they drink that water, I believe their Appa will beat them.'

'Who said that?'

'Magalakshmi's Akka, Teacher.'

Mary Teacher was shocked. At this young age itself they are conscious of all these differences… Anger and pain filled the teacher's heart… They're all together in the class… They mix with each other… In this school all of them drink water from the same tap… What is this Cheri tap that she is talking about now… How did such ugly thoughts enter the subconscious mind… If her father will beat her up, then they've taught all this at home… With such thoughts in her mind, Mary Teacher walked on without saying a word.

After a while, she called Vijayalakshmi and asked her: 'What will happen, Vijayalakshmi, if you drink water from this tap? Only clean water comes out of it, doesn't it? I believe you told her not to drink that water?'

'Yes, Teacher, we've been told so at home, Teacher. Don't mix with the Cheri children. Don't eat anything they give. They said don't go near the Cheri Street, Teacher.'

'How can you behave like that? It's wrong, isn't it?' said Teacher. Vijayalakshmi walked on without saying a word. After which even Teacher didn't ask anything else. Dizzy with hunger and exhausted from the heat, the other children hurried towards the school. The teachers too made haste.

Mary Teacher was greatly troubled by the conversation. All that I taught all these days –'There are no castes, child, it's a sin to say upper caste – lower caste' – it's all a complete 'waste'… This Vijayalakshmi was my student last year in Class Four… I remember how I explained in detail Bharatiar's Murasu song which was part of the Tamil lesson… how, by taking the kitten as an example, I taught them that all men are equal till my voice dried up… all that's a big 'waste'… It's of no use at all… More than what is taught at school, it is what is taught at home these children pick up fast… What's the use… As soon as the headmaster comes, I'm going to ask him to question that child… Mary Teacher picked at her lunch half-heartedly and waited for the headmaster.

The headmaster came around two in the afternoon after finishing his lunch at home. Teacher slowly started, 'Saar… the children suffered while coming back, saar. The heat made them so thirsty… It's a good thing we came to Pallatthur – only after drinking water there the children started walking a little briskly, saar. But even in that thirst some children refused to drink water from that tap, saar.'

'Wh… Why, what happened?'

Mary Teacher gave a detailed account of what happened on the way and finished by saying that the child ought to be questioned. They immediately sent a child to fetch the two sisters.

After the two children came, the headmaster said casually: 'There's nothing wrong with drinking water from a street tap. It's only from the houses of these Cheri people you mustn't drink water. Did the elders in your house tell you not to drink water from that street tap also? Ok, ok, go back to class.' Emphasising forcefully the words 'only from the houses', Headmaster Varadarajulu went to the class.

Original title: *Theerppu*
2003

THE ASCENT

76

UMA MAHESWARI

With the ease that comes from long years of practice, Ramaa poured out the batter on the heated griddle and smoothened it carefully into a circle. Then she watched it intently, in readiness to catch the perfect moment to flip it over. In a few moments a murmur emanated from her: 'Come on, come on, get cooked quickly.' Ramaa was always like that: while cutting tomatoes, she would keep a frightened watch over the dripping juice, as if it were blood. She would admonish the whistling cooker: 'Coming, coming, don't simply scream.' She would put a lid on the vessel in which the sambar bubbled, smear it with vibhuti and kumkumam and pray loudly to Lord Ganesha: 'O Pillayaarappa, only you can save me!'

Through the dingy kitchen window you could see a mountain which appeared to loom so close, as if it were within touching distance. The peaks, glowing brightly with swirls of blue, green and yellow, stood tall, jutting into the sky. After looking at the hill fondly for a while, Ramaa began in a low voice: 'The hill is very far from here, isn't it, Kalpana? We can't ever reach the top.' As Ramaa's fingers swished the soaking rice, her eyes swept over the peaks of the mountain. I burst out in a loud voice to contradict her: 'What far, Ramaa? Big distance… Nothing is so far that we can't reach it. Shall we climb it today?' My question lay between us like an unopened package. Anxious that she might refuse, I pushed and prodded her, giving her no chance to come up with any argument.

Ramaa conceded: eatables in a small bag, towels, water bottles. I kept aside everything except the water. 'Even the most important, absolutely necessary things, will be a burden. They will just be a big hindrance to our climbing.' It gave me great pleasure to see the meek acceptance in Ramaa's eyes to whatever I said.

We started. When we firmly locked the doors I had a strange feeling that we might not come back.

The mountain loomed at a distance, a manifestation of resoluteness. Its solidity, majesty, firmness, chilling silence, and rugged hardness didn't instil in us the confidence that we could ever reach it. Yet the mountain seemed to invite us openly and loudly. The blue rims glowed temptingly. The sun sharply lit the edges, giving the mountain a metallic sheen.

The rows and rows of houses, the lacklustre streets, we put them behind us as we walked on. The tar road lay crushed like a charred dream under the wheels of vehicles. The tall lamp-posts looked orphaned. We saw questions on the faces framed within the windows. We walked on, without uttering a word, yet it wasn't an empty silence that lay between us.

Crossing the well-trodden tar road, we reached the grassland where no pathway had ever criss-crossed. Suddenly the town came to an end. The trees burst into the sky with great liberty. The shadows huddled together, whispering with intimacy. The broad expanse of nature was immensely attractive: the lush greenery, the fine red earth, the tiny nose-ring-like flowers. Ramaa plucked the long stem of a small plant: 'Remember how we used to play this game – "Thaatha, Thaatha, off with your head!"' The thumbai flowers hung like white drops, the bright yellow flowers covered the grass, and the seeds of the 'snappy-tomato' plants crackled. Even in this solitude, the distant railway tracks seemed to script the stirrings of life.

From a certain point the untrodden earth assumed a frightening newness. An immense expanse, not cleaved even by a solitary foot-track. The velvety grass, soft as the fur of a pet animal, gently tickled the foot. At first we hesitated to crush the plants; later we walked on, burying our guilty conscience. Even when Ramaa let go of my hand, a suggestion of togetherness remained, and we walked on singly, leaving enough space between us.

As we neared the mountain, its majesty, in contrast to our insignificance, took our breath away. Its colossal physique, which seemed to firmly shut out all pathways, not allowing anything to violate it in any way, frightened us. Surprisingly enough, the mountain was not as elegantly sculpted as it appeared from a great distance. It had a more rugged appearance, the profile in slim folds, which didn't look deep or wide enough to hold footsteps.

The ends of our saris fluttering, and with a spring and fervour in our step, we ran to touch the base of the mountain, as if we were little girls once again. Gasping, we rested for a while. We then made our way towards the foot of the mountain, taking soft, slow steps, as if gently rocking the cradle of a child in deep sleep. Our bodies thrilled when our feet touched the still, cool beatific edifice. We gently walked on, and as if disturbed by our footsteps, the sleeping mountain leapt awake. Hating to be encroached upon, it let us down when we least expected it. As we helped each other up, we heard its soundless laugh. Obstinacy, detachment, bitterness, heaps of stones and flowering plants, what all melded together and became the mountain! Its secret softly spread all around us. Two magic hands seemed to have torn the level ground apart, heaped it and flattened it. The straight corners were sharply etched. The mound, it seems, ambitiously wished for more and more height. The upright mountain stared with very little friendliness.

In our next phase we were hesitant yet determined. The wind initially swirled around our feet and intimidated us. Later, as if surprised by our firm, hard legs, it mellowed down and whistled. As we went on, the wind at our backs pushed us helpfully towards the top.

The rocks majestically rose skywards. Deep brown in colour. A scaly body. An uneroded face, though endlessly battered by the wind. An amorphous appearance which couldn't be grasped. Slimy, slithery moss spread everywhere. Rocks of different shapes. The wind gushed around me. I dashed against the rocks and then somehow, catching hold of either a rock or a plant, scrambled up. Tying us up with magic ropes, the mountain pushed us here and there at its whim. It also made us jump and crawl. Ramaa once lost her balance. Gasping for breath, she struggled, splaying her hands open, as if she were under water. I too, who was in front of her and saw her slipping down, was pulled down by the wind. Like a wily enemy it toppled my foot.

I tried to overcome my helplessness and willed myself to go on, but she floundered around helplessly. Deep down, small stones, big rocks.

And sloping bunches of green grass. As I followed her, I realised that she had slipped behind the rocks and screamed. Small cuts and bruises. When I held her and gave her water to drink, she stammered: 'Enough, stop. We can't climb anymore.' Cutting short her groans and flinging them aside without thinking even a little, I said: 'Come, come, just a little more to go.' I clasped her by the shoulder and started going towards the top. Our speed may have slowed down somewhat, but our steps were determined. Ramaa must have seen me as a manifestation of her own thoughts. In a while she gained strength, moved away from me and started walking alone. The warmth of the sun brimmed over like liquid. The scenic beauty spread everywhere. Green knots blossomed. The wind was loaded with the scent of roots. Roots cracked the rocks. They burst forth like nerves on the surface of the rocks. Walking past them one by one, we came across a hollow piece of land. Like the lap of the mountain. Yes, the lap. Soft flesh in the form of plants. Splitting into two, the warmth of the lap nestled us. A gentle slope. Small streams with stagnant pools of water. Not wanting to disturb the glassy blanket-like surface and its purity, we hesitantly touched it; its compassion welled up and quenched our thirst in a gush. We dangled our feet, depleted our exhaustion, enjoyed its essence and then were able to walk.

As we climbed on, the mountain turned affectionate and yielded to us. As we went up a span, we slipped down a foot, but the mountain looked at us with compassion, we who persisted. With great acceptance the mountain's body became one with our feet. Like a father allowing himself to play the 'elephant game' with a child, getting on and getting off, it stooped, bowed under our feet, lay down and laughed.

We climbed on. Leaving behind all our bonds, we resolutely set our eyes on the heap at the top. On and on. Our feet stumbled, as if we were climbing a magic ladder, the steps of which were invisible. Small stones shone like stars. Even as they pierced our palms and drew out blood, we were intoxicated enough to climb. Higher and higher, the wind's power consumed me. Clothes dishevelled, skin bare, the wind pierced the flesh, and the body lost weight. It became a feather. The initial struggles all disappeared; I watched with astonishment my body losing control, swirling around and flying high. I was lifted up by the waves of the wind, as if on the top curve of a giant wheel. I could see everything below. Patches of land, swaying grass, rivers burning with silver wicks, feet-piercing thorn-bushes, what all we had passed by! Weariness and wonderment. In an unexpected fraction of a moment, our feet slipped into the palm of the mountain. The mountain playfully threw us up into the sky. We turned dizzy. An unknown experience, almost orgasmic, consumed us; the nerves in our thighs tingled and tightened, sending goosebumps through our entire body. So far the peak that could only be seen was now under our feet.

A peak is not really the highest point as one would imagine. Besides, it's not so high that everything else is down below. It's absolutely even. A poise, in which the high, the low, aggression, submission, joy, sorrow, are all contained. It's a vacuum. It's utter stillness. It's nothingness. Once you comprehend this, fulfilment and disappointment engulf the mind. The wind ballooned out our clothes, mussed up our hair and shook our legs. A dangerous urge to jump to the ground far below consumed us. There is a helpless urge to come up when you are down and to go down when on top.

Exhausted, we returned with such ease. How simple it was to climb down. The birds looked at us with amazement. The sky, which had been tilted over our heads, pulled back its blue walls. The sun was now a faded yellow. We didn't really walk; like pieces knocked off in a board game we simply rolled down. The mountain swallowed us and spat us out, and like little bubbles we flew around. It kicked us out, as if proclaiming that the game was over. The ease and speed with which we came down choked us with sorrow. That's all it was. Fatigue. Exhaustion. And the end. Our steps lengthened, and we didn't speak, didn't see anything. When we turned back and looked at the mountain, its derisive laugh burst out in the wind. As we edged closer and closer home, the void which the mountain created within us widened. Our faces, which betrayed neither the pride of victory nor the disappointment of failure, were tinged with the glow of a novel experience.

The street turned narrow, posing no challenge in crossing it. It was a short way home. The calm house, waiting for us, opened out and swallowed us silently.

Ramaa and I entered the kitchen. She opened the windows. Swaying crotons, the mullai creeper, rows and rows of houses, high walls, and beyond all that, the mountain too was framed within the window.

Original title: *Malai Yettram*
2002

MEAT

77

VELA RAMAMOORTHY

Like bees swarming around a honeycomb, people crowded the bus stop.

It was the eighteenth of the month of Chittirai, the annual Solaisami Temple Festival.

People brimmed over, like a flood. Ever so many buses came by and scooped them up; yet the crowds didn't thin. The police had to resort to a 'lathi charge' to bring in some sense of order. The entire lot had come to eat meat – yes, they had travelled by car and bullock cart, and some had even trudged, craving for meat.

Was it just one or two? No, three hundred to four hundred goats were sacrificed.

He was a spirited, yet strict sort of god, this Solaisami. An offering of one goat for headache, stomach ache and the like. Two for court and police cases. Three-four for acquittal in a murder case.

Head, legs, intestines, blood, everything had to be cooked. Even the skin had to be roasted over fire, stripped of hair, and made into a special kuzhambu, a spicy, tangy gravy. Even if you were not a relative, and just strayed into a family feast, a leaf had to be placed in front of you. And the meat had to be served in heaps. But be warned: if you so much as pocket even a ten-paisa coin from the temple premises, you could be sure that you'd never get home sound of limb and mind. You would keel over vomiting, purging and feeling giddy. Why, some have even been known to die!

Such a powerful god was Solaisami.

Angamma's son Muthupandi had a squint in the right eye. He was just a boy, only twelve. If within Angamma's earshot, even if only in jest, his friends called him 'one-and-a-half eyes', she would take a broom.

'It'll break, this broom'll break, I tell you… Useless fellows, just who are you calling "one-and-a-half eyes"? My son is Indran, lord of the heavens! Even if you searched seven generations in your family, you won't find anyone to match my son's beautiful curly hair.'

Such a fond mother was she, the one who now chased her son all over the temple premises to give him tight slaps. All those waiting for the bus watched the fun.

'You blind idiot… why you came? For what you came? I told you not to come, no? Is this your father's bus which is running or what? They're going to take you free or what? I need two rupees for the ticket. What will I do? Who can I borrow the money from in this place?'

Her heavy earrings drooped to her shoulders.

With a smile filling his mouth Muthupandi dodged his mother, weaving in and out of the ever so many arms and legs.

Angamma was livid. 'Cross-eyed fellow… Just see how he's embarrassing me in this town?' So angry was she that she might have digested the meat she ate.

There was only two rupees left in her little drawstring purse. A 'full ticket' to her place cost two rupees. It was enough for her. But what about the son? Even if she lied about his age and asked for a 'half ticket', it would still cost a rupee. 'Even if I want to borrow money, I can't see a single familiar face. What will I do now?' She wrung her hands.

Muthupandi's tummy jingled violently, 'ginuk ginuk'. But how long could he run without getting caught with a stomach that had stuffed itself with chunks of meat? He finally fell into his mother's grasp.

She gave him two on his back, 'vatak vatak'.

'You walked here without telling me, no? Just go back walking then… you son of a blind fellow…'

Muthupandi howled. His mother's slaps didn't hurt him. That she, his own mother, had called him a 'blind fellow' choked his heart. 'I came to eat the meat. Aatha, I won't come again…'

An elderly man from the crowd stopped her, shouting angrily: 'Why, 'ma, he's only a little fellow… he came only because of the meat. Why don't you let him be? Beating a son born to you like this! People like us see one-two pieces of meat only for Aadi or Deepavali. Only by the grace of this Solaisami on one day of the year we can eat meat to our heart's content… Let that be. You're scolding this little boy, but why did you come? To eat the meat only, no?'

Angamma let go of her son. She straightened his hair. She pulled the end of her sari and wiped his face. How could she get the money for the bus? Angamma hit upon an idea. She pulled him close and whispered something to him.

Muthupandi nodded: 'All right, Aatha.' Spit gathered in his tongue. His stomach squeezed in pain. He trudged on uncomfortably, his belly jutting out. 'I ate so much meat.' He was so happy. His tummy ached.

The bus arrived. The mother and son shoved and pushed their way in.

Muthupandi slipped effortlessly under Angamma's seat, and curled himself up, his face directly in front of her legs.

There was such a mob. People were perched even on the roof of the bus. Muthupandi could hardly breathe.

A couple of old things on the roof were scared stiff. They tightly caught hold of the support on the side, gazed nervously and chattered on, about this and that. The young ones were making merry. They didn't care if it was hot or cold.

The bus tilted dangerously to the left, grazed the ground, and started. The young girls inside didn't know if they were alive. What a crowd! The vehicle would any minute just turn over.

People clutched on to whatever they could.

Muthupandi, lying under the feet of his Aatha, perspired profusely. The driver didn't even think to press the horn, so intent was he in keeping his gaze fixed directly on the road in front of him.

The conductor squeezed himself through the crowd, shouting angrily: 'Ticket, ticket…'

Angamma let down her sari, fanned it around, and spread her legs wide to hide her son.

'If only I had a rupee… I would have made my son sit up and spoken with such authority. Only because I don't have money for the bus I put him under my feet. How shameful it will be if everyone comes to know.' Her heart thudded.

'Ticket... ticket...'

Muthupandi gasped for breath. In a small voice, he called out to his mother: 'Aathov.'

Angamma didn't look down. She gazed outside, spreading her legs even wider.

People were pressed together, one falling over the other. The conductor's khaki shirt turned dark with sweat.

'Aathaaoi...' he scratched her feet. Angamma was livid. Muthupandi's tummy rumbled. The conductor was getting crushed, just a few hand spans away.

'Aathov...' he gazed unblinkingly

'May you die of loose motions... wretched fellow, why don't you keep quiet for a while...' she cursed under her breath. She loosened her sari.

'Ticket...ticket...' Just three hand spans away.

'Aathov...' he scratched.

'Blind fellow...' she stamped him hard with the back of her foot.

'Ticket... ticket...' two hand spans away.

'Eaathov...'

Again she stamped him.

'Ticket... ticket...' Just a hand span away.

'Eaathov...' he pinched her.

She furiously stamped him again, again and again. After that there was no noise from below.

The crowd got off as soon they reached the town.

'Ei... Muthupandi... get up...' she called out softly. There was no response. She peered down.

'Aathadi... what's this... my son has fainted. My child... Muthupandi... my prince... she lifted him up – his eyes had turned up, the spit drooled from his mouth, and he was sweating profusely. 'Ayya, Muthupandi, saami...' she called out going down the steps.

Muthupandi vomited as soon as he tottered down. The meat pieces which he had devoured spewed out of his mouth in spurts. A crowd gathered. Sitting on his haunches, hand on head, he vomited over and over again.

Angamma stroked her son's chest. 'What a sinner I am? What will I do now? What's happened to my son?' She moaned, beating herself on the chest.

The crowd retorted: 'Angamma, it's nothing but this. Your son has stolen something from the temple premises. Even if he did it unknowingly... Solaisami is a strict god. He's paying for it. Anyway, you'd better pray that you'll sacrifice two goats next Chittirai. The vomiting will then stop.'

Angamma looked at her son.

Mouth dripping, eyes full of tears, he said, 'Aathaa...' He wiped his mouth with the back of his hand.

She hefted her son over her shoulder and walked through the crowd.

The crowd gathered behind her.

Muthupandi, hanging over the shoulder, lifted his head and turned his mother's head towards him, 'Aatha... I swear on that Solaisami... I promise on your head... I didn't steal anything, Aatha.' He placed his hand on his mother's head.

'Muthupandi, my prince... I know, I know... if only this sinner had had money for the bus, why, you wouldn't have vomited or got a stomach-ache... let this stupid town say what it wants...' Clasping him by the neck, she folded her son close, and marched on firmly, the ground shaking beneath her feet.

Original title: *Kari*
1995

Sultriness 78

G Murugan

She watched him from afar. He was readying the patch next to the kanakambaram flower bed to sow some greens. The sounds of the hoe against the bund dissolved in the muggy heat.

The day was steadily climbing. Thick, winding palmyra trees and an arid, burning stretch thirsting for water. Deeply embedded rocks. Only here and there, patches of green, either near solitary houses or pump-sets. Water trickled into wells in some corner or the other and people drew it, drop by drop.

She stood in the shade of the pump-set shed and looked at him. 'In this heat… why, you can do it later. What is the hurry?'

Only then he realised she was there and looked up.

'I have only a little more to finish…' Rubbing off the mud on the hoe, he smiled.

He had a slim, dark body. Ready-made drawers hung up to his knees. It was years since he had joined as a farmhand. He had been a small boy when he came. But now he had the sheen of a young man. Had sprouted a moustache.

He bent again and dug with the hoe.

'You had a brother, no? Has he got married?'

'Only last month.' He kept digging.

'Where is he now?'

'He's gone away to Bangalore after marriage.'

She sat down, leaning against the wall.

Dried kanakambaram plants and parthenium weeds were heaped separately.

Beyond the palmyra trees you could see Khaderbhai's sugarcane field. A little ahead of that Munasami Gounder's cotton field. Unlike them, her father never had the guts to borrow money and use dynamite to deepen the well. He had thought that the income from the fields would be just enough to pay off the interest, so he had let it be. He felt that whenever it rained and the wells filled, the saplings could be planted. The two plough-bulls had been sold off and only a cow remained. They could barely manage to find fodder for it. They had to pay for the hay. Her brother, who had failed in his higher secondary class, was working in the town now. A job in the wine shop. It looked as if he also drank, like their father. She felt that his ways were not right at all.

Saitoo was still digging away. Perhaps because he had done manual labour from a young age, his muscles were tight and hard. Veins popped from his long legs.

'Okay, when are you getting married?'

He smiled shyly.

'Aren't there any girls in your family for you?'

'Why, my sister's daughter is there…'

'Won't they give her to you?'

'They want a groom from the town, it seems. I believe their daughter can't take this kind of sowing and digging in the heat…'

'Has she studied?'

'Umm… Tenth or something.'

He finished digging and wiped clean the hoe in the dried grass.

'As if there is no other girl. Let them be,' she said. 'Does the girl like you?'

'She likes me only. But only my sister is adamant.'

He placed the hoe in the bund, put his hand into his pocket and took out a matchbox. He sat near the heaped plants, lit them, cupping his hand around the flame. The dried kanakambaram plants and the weeds caught fire immediately. The smoke thickened and the shrivelled weeds perished in the flames.

How much ever you pull out these weeds, why was it never enough, she wondered. Like a thousand demons springing up from a single drop of blood, these weeds too sprouted profusely.

He picked up a palmyra frond lying nearby, lit it and set fire to the other heap. The flames danced like waves on the heaps. He gathered the unlit plants and threw them in.

She kept looking at him with an unexplainable interest. In the dripping sweat, his body shone. It seemed to her that in the mirage-laden expanse, against the backdrop of the erect palm trees, he stood embraced by the fire. It looked as if body was enveloped by the fire. His body and soul, everything seemed to melt and ooze out from the fire. Afraid, she got up. She felt giddy. She walked away.

Unable to bear the mugginess, she got up. Her whole body was in a sweat. The fan didn't work. The sweaty palms of her son lay on her stomach. She ought to have slept on the pial itself. It was an error sleeping in the room, believing that the fan would spin. She brought a cardboard sheet and fanned her son.

Even though the window was open, no breeze came in. Though the wind whirled outside, why didn't it come into this room, she wondered. Through the window, she looked at the sky wearily. Today the heat was scorchingly muggy. It might rain in the evening or night, but it wasn't a certainty. For the past two or three days the skies had played tricks like this.

She loosened the ends of her sari and let it fall on her lap. As she fanned her son, she fanned her busts too. It wasn't enough. She unhooked the top button of her blouse. Her fair body, so far constricted, popped out, glistening sweat. She had big breasts. Before, she used to be shy and also proud of them. But now they seemed like a burden. It was two years since her son had been weaned. The husband, who had lusted after them, was never going to come back.

He had primed her body, as one would a bow, to shoot an arrow at the fastest speed. Soaring to uninhibited heights, he made her body blossom. He was never satiated. Even that last night, at two in the morning he had woken her up. 'Selvi, Selvi…'

She had woken up. He had pulled her on top of him.

'Don't you have any time or place?'

'It will take two or three days for me to come back…'

'So…'

'Selvi…' He had pleaded.

'Shall I also come with you?'

'Won't I take you if I can?'

He had chomped on her lips and rolled her down. 'The child…' she had said to abate his ardour.

That had been the last. He had left at four in the morning. By seven she had heard the news of his death in an accident.

She had lived with him only for a few years, and so quickly everything was over. Like she had slept and woken up, like a sweet dream…

She leaves her bed and comes outside. All her relatives are standing there. Aren't they the ones who had come for her wedding? Why are they still hanging around shamelessly? Earlier they looked happy; why are they sad now? What is this farce?

Only yesterday, just yesterday, it seems, I married him. I tossed around with him on the bed when the night was young. And in the late hours, when my hand searched for him, it found only a void.

He has got up and gone. To a place from where he will never come back. He entered through the front door and disappeared through the back door. With this, it is all over. Is it really over? How many years would she have to live now? If each day passes like this, a yuga, when will old age come, and when will the heat in her loins be extinguished…

Like one nailed and pegged in a dilapidated house, she hung in the scorching heat. Overcome with lassitude, she had no strength to unpeg the nail and get down. Pain, heat, sultriness, the burden of the body, the longings – if she were to burn to ashes and wither away at this moment, what a liberation it would be. Appearing from nowhere and spreading all over my body, the fire, with its merciless tongue, is lapping me all over. My moans unheard, my limbs unable to move… am I in my grave? Has the earth swallowed me?

The strand of sleep that had snapped earlier and the giddiness of the heat pushed her back into slumber.

Her mother couldn't be seen outside. She must have gone to the shop with her son for a rusk. She walked towards the sugarcane field. It was difficult to ease oneself here. It was okay in the dark, one could go somewhere nearby. If this sugarcane field wasn't there, one had to go very far, to the riverside. It was a year since the river too had dried. One had to come back home for water.

The heat hadn't abated yet. The grass on the hilly slope in the distance had charred away.

From the palmyra pathway she got down to the bund. It was several days since the sugarcane had matured. They hadn't yet got the 'cutting order' from the cooperative mills. If you let them be like this, in a month they would get dried up and turn into firewood. Except for four or five husks with flowers, all of them had dried below. So much heat blew out that it seemed as if a spark could burn the entire thing to ashes.

In the centre of the field, she walked on a small bund, looking this way and that and crossed the swaying sugarcanes. She took care to see that the husks didn't cut her feet. She could see a cave-like path some distance away. If she went through that, she would find a secluded place to ease herself.

She entered in and looked for a place a little less dense. There, the rats had chewed up the sugarcane.

Unable to walk further, she stood there, shocked. In a small canal in the middle, he sat there, dark bodied, his back to her.

In the next instant, she hastily walked back the way she came. Behind her, she could hear the noise of the husks being trampled over. He must have seen her too.

She came out of the field. The sultry landscape once again spread before her frighteningly. Unperturbed, the palmyra trees stood erect. Unable to go further, she sat on the bund. Afraid to see anything outside, she buried her face in her lap.

All alone… secretly… pleasuring oneself with one's own hands… Yes, it was him… she couldn't believe it. Was it rage, frustration or sorrow; unable to fathom what had come over her, she started to weep.

Original title: *Vemmai*
2003

The Bird

79

Gokula Kannan

The boy sitting in his garden, a bird in hand, would have been no more than five. He was plunging the bird into the heap of wood by the lawn.

He had never seen the boy before. By the look of him he seemed like a Mexican. How could the boy have come to his house? And why? Had any elders accompanied him?

The house had surely been locked when he had returned home. She hadn't yet returned from office. Because he had a splitting headache, he had decided to come home early.

The boy who was sitting with a light blue bird wasn't perturbed on seeing him. He was half inserting the bird into a gap between the logs. In a while the bird disappeared completely into the logs.

The right fence had been bent in last year's tornado. The fence between his house and John Goodman's belonged to both of them. John had been without a job for several years now. Ages ago his job had been outsourced from Silicon Valley to China. After that he sustained himself doing carpentry work in his garage. He was excellent with his hands. He himself had replaced the fallen wooden fence with a brand new one. It was those logs that he had heaped in the garden so that they could be used as firewood in winter. A number of rusty nails jutted out of the wood pieces.

This boy must have surely lost his way. What idiocy to allow such a small boy to wander the streets unaccompanied! Where and to whom would he have to take the boy? If he rang 911, in a trice the police would be at his door, flashing red and blue lights. He would then have to spend the next hour saying the same thing again and again in different ways to the two policemen.

Yes, he was alone at home. He had a headache. A migraine. Yes, no medicine helped. No, he hadn't seen the boy before. Even his wife wouldn't know him. She hadn't yet returned. The doors were locked. The French door… that was never locked. It was always kept open for the gardener. Yes, even the gardener was Mexican. It couldn't be his son. He was an old man. But you could never say. No, no, the gardener wasn't Mexican; he was Vietnamese.

He came outside. He said 'hello' to the boy. Then in a friendly tone he also said 'hola' in Spanish. The boy didn't heed him. The bird peeped out of a gap from the other side.

Its face and bead-like eyes were visible. The boy gingerly parted the logs that were hiding its body.

'Careful, careful! It's full of nails. They will scratch the bird,' he shouted anxiously.

'Look here, first take the bird away from it. If the logs slide down, they will crush the tiny bird. Then it will die,' he shouted again. He ran and stood beside the boy.

By that time the bird had freed itself from the wood pile. The boy lifted it in his hands and moved back. A slight fear shone in his eyes. Looking at the plump-cheeked frightened boy, he wanted to hug him.

'Where is your mother, father?'

Stubbornly refusing to answer, the boy moved back. Now that he looked at the bird in the boy's hand closely, he made out that it was a parakeet.

'Okay, this is a parakeet, isn't it?'

No answer for that too.

'We too had a parakeet. My daughter called it Blue. Yes, it was blue like the sky. But it died within a week.

'Do you see that orange tree there… we buried it under that.'

The boy looked to where he pointed. After a few seconds, he looked up at his face.

'It wasn't ill at all. We had kept it in a cage. The reason it died was because we didn't hang it from the roof. We had planned to buy a high table and place it on it. Till then we had placed the cage on the floor. After it died, the man who sold it to us said that a bird not placed at a height wouldn't live long.

'You also carefully place it in a cage at a height and take care of it, okay.'

He went slowly near the boy. He stood there without moving.

'My daughter was really sad when Blue died. What a terrible thing it is to rear a bird, to whom the sky is the home, in an ordinary house. That too at ground level. Even a slight ignorance can have such grave consequences!

'All right, tell me where your house is. What is your name? Your parents will be searching for you, won't they? It's not very wise to enter a stranger's house like this. Bad people live in this town too.'

He took the boy's hand. Soft fingers tucked into his hands. The boy came along without a protest, not saying a word.

Where would he take him now? He stood at his entrance, looking to see if someone was searching for the boy. No one in sight.

It was time for her to come home. She would be home in half an hour. He must finish this business before that. She hated facing any problem when she came back. It would spoil the rest of the evening. The more he looked at the bird, the more he felt that it was like the one they had had. If his wife and daughter saw this, certainly bitter memories would surface.

The mid-afternoon sun still lurked outside. There were one or two cars. The quietness of Santa Clara now seemed incongruous. It would be good if a couple of police cars screamed past with flashing lights and loud sirens.

Only then he remembered. At the corner of the street, which curved in a half-circle, he had seen a Mexican family. They had moved in only a few months ago. Their things had arrived in a pick-up truck. They were the first Mexicans on this street. Richard, the neighbour, had said, 'Hereafter there's going to be a lot of merrymaking in the first week of May. On 5 May Mexicans celebrate their culture – Cinco de Mayo.'

Taking the boy, he walked towards that house. He asked, 'Isn't that your house?' Even to that the boy didn't reply. Even though his face displayed the same expression for everything, there was something charming about the boy.

There was an empty pick-up truck in front of that house. Toys lay scattered on the lawn that stretched from the doorway of the house to the street. When he saw a cage in the middle, he felt a little relieved.

The boy shook off his hand and ran to pick up a ball from the lawn.

When he rang the bell, an old lady opened the door. She didn't know any English. A young lady came up behind her. She was quite plump. Thick black hair. She had wide eyes that constantly darted here and there.

He introduced himself and pointed to the boy. In Spanish-accented English, she replied, 'Yes, that's my son.'

He briefly tried to explain all what had happened. He was always confused about what to include and what to leave out. Had he only mentioned about the boy coming to his house, she would have immediately understood. But when he kept repeating about the bird, the logs, the nails, the dead parakeet, she lost her patience. She constantly looked inside the house. He expected her face to brim with emotion and gratefulness. He was disappointed. She shouted at the boy in Spanish. Ignoring her, the boy ran, pushing a hoop on the lawn. From inside the house, a child's sharp wail was heard. The woman ran inside. Not knowing what to say to the old woman, he hesitated for a moment. 'Isn't the boy's father there?' he asked. She said something in Spanish. When she saw his perplexed gaze, she mimed a gun and said, 'Iraq…'

He simply nodded and came out. Before turning home, he looked back at the boy for a moment. Without paying any heed to him, the boy was playing. A clear light shone in the sky. When a pleasant breeze blew in, the cherry tree nearby shed its leaves on the lawn. He felt the old woman's gaze on his back. In the late afternoon, a chill entered his body and shook him.

That was when he noticed that the bird was not in the boy's hand.

The cage in the lawn too was empty.

Original title: *Paravai*
2010

The Proofreader's Wife

80

S Ramakrishnan

It had been several years now since she had begun to hate printed pages. They had grown even more loathsome than the cockroaches hidden in the crevices of the bathroom wall. Sometimes she would tear the pages up till her anger was spent. But the pages never protested. Unlike cockroaches, they never scampered away or attempted to escape, giving up their whiskers in the bargain.

Other than the soft rustle when they were being torn, the pages never raised a noise. Even that she couldn't bear. So she soaked the pages in water. As far as she was concerned, this was the worst punishment you could mete out to them. If she dunked them in the iron bucket as she started to cook in the morning, by evening they would turn to pulp.

As the pages disintegrated, where did the printed words go? Like salt dissolving in water, did they also disappear? She would stare intently at the bucket. Sometimes when she thought about it, she would wonder: What was the relationship between words and paper? Did the pages agree to have lines printed on them? Was there a gulf between the pages and the words? When her mind began to travel like this, she would often get angry with herself for entertaining such wasteful thoughts.

Her house overflowed with printed pages. Until seventeen, when she had got married to Mandiramurthy and come to Chennai, she had never seen anything other than textbooks. Also since there was no girls' high school in her village, she had stopped at the fifth standard.

For six or seven years she had worked, either sticking labels on matches or breaking lumps of rubber. There had been a radio in the match factory. She had loved the film music that was aired on it. In those days she had so badly wanted to own a radio that she had joined a chit fund. But whenever she got the funds, there were always other expenses. So at the time of her marriage she had insisted on getting a radio. But Mandiramurthy didn't like the radio, so it was always kept switched off.

When she came to Chennai as a new bride, she used to be scared of Mandiramurthy. At the time he was working in Royal Printing Press. There was always a pencil and an eraser in his pocket. Sometimes a red pen too could be found.

She didn't know anything about proofreading. Sometimes at night when Mandiramurthy propped himself on a pillow on the floor and marked the pages with a pencil, she would watch him intently. He would look as if he was speaking to himself. Sometimes she could even hear him laugh out loud. Till late in the night, he would proofread. Then he would open the back door, take a piss and come back to lie down.

Even when his fingers roamed over her body, the thought of proofreading would unnecessarily come to her mind. He wasn't much interested in sex. He would do it as a ritual, and after his body was spent, he would turn his face away and fall asleep – all this irritated her. Even in sleep, she had sometimes noticed his fingers moving, his face in tight concentration.

Mandiramurthy never spoke much to anyone. From six in the morning, he would proofread. When he started for work, he would put the corrected pages along with his lunchbox into his yellow bag. His office was in the Royapettah area. He didn't have many friends. He never went out either. His only habit was chewing betel leaves. He had a small leather pouch for that. Every ten minutes, he would take out a couple of leaves, pinch off the stalks and pop them into his mouth.

Once he had taken her to his office for a function. She had been awestruck when she saw a huge machine rolling out reams of paper, which slid off endlessly, as if the skin of an onion was being peeled again and again. The whole roll of paper would be printed upon. He would have to proofread the entire lot, wouldn't he? When she asked this, her husband had told her not to be silly and had taken her off to the binding section.

Four or five women of her age had been stacking the paper and sticking them. She had asked about their salary. Without replying to the question, Mandiramurthy had said that it wouldn't suit her. When she had gone to the toilet at the end of the press, she had found pages strewn everywhere. Everyone seemed to be stomping around on them.

To the south, she had found a small iron door, open. When she had peeped in, she had found it to be full of waste paper. She had been frightened. Were pages bubbling over, as if from a spring? What would happen to all this paper? Even after she went to the toilet, she couldn't wipe out the thought.

She never understood why Mandiramurthy was the lone proofreader in the office. One day she had picked up the pages that he had corrected. Every other line had mistakes, circled and corrected. When she had looked at the pages, they had seemed like the doodles of children. Sometimes she felt as if her husband was more intelligent than all the writers. Perhaps it was she who didn't understand him well enough. She had placed back the papers with trepidation and started to serve his meal.

How did Mandiramurthy's eyes spot even the smallest error? Was this trait of his confined only to paper, or did the scrutiny extend to her too? In the early days, she would sit out in the evening and watch the goings-on on the road. She had noticed his face hardening as he walked home. As soon as he entered, he would take out the pages and sit down to proofread. She never knew when he drank the coffee and ate the snacks she gave. Why he was so sunk in words puzzled her.

Mandiramurthy didn't much care about food either. Sometimes he would start for work in a wet veshti. Whenever she asked hesitantly about looking for a different job, he would reply with a glare: what was wrong with this job? She never could explain.

Mandiramurthy hadn't missed a day's work. Even when she was ill, he would make kanji for her and leave for the office. She would lie on the mat, gritting her teeth. Why had she got married to a person like this? She fumed – how could this man, who was so concerned when a single letter was misprinted, forget to look after her?

He never gave much thought to all this. Once in a blue moon he himself would offer to take her for a film. She would then hastily change her sari and come out. She had seen him look intently at the billboards and even the wrappings of groundnuts and his lips would often murmur the errors to himself.

She had never heard him laugh in a cinema hall. His face was always frozen in thought. He was always anxious to return home the minute the show ended. He never touched her the nights they saw a film. She never understood why.

It was over fifteen years since they had got married. To date they didn't have a child. She was used to staying home alone. Once in a while she would take a lime and set off to have a darshan of Lord Dakshinamurthy. She would even forget what to pray for and stand still in front of the deity. On the days when she was livid, she would ask the lord to wipe out printed paper from the whole world. Her anger soon began to include pencils, erasers and so on.

A couple of years ago, when she had nothing to do, she had torn up, one by one, all the printed pages at home. In the evening, when Mandiramurthy had come home to a room littered with paper, he had scolded: 'Thangamma, if you like tearing paper up, then go to the dustbin. You'll find plenty there. Don't do this again.' He had gone straight to his table and started to correct the pages from his bag. She had wailed loudly. He hadn't seemed to have heard her cries at all. He had gathered the proofread pages. She hadn't slept that night. She had felt as if the words had dropped off the pages and stuck to her arms, legs and all over her body.

Soon after, Mandiramurthy had taken her to the doctor. With a confused look, she had said she was scared. The doctor had given her medicines for a week to sleep. Even when she slept, her eyes tightly shut, she could faintly see him proofreading. Unable to even cry, she would fall asleep.

For a year she had to be taken every week to the general hospital. She would walk silently on the streets. Neither would utter a word till they reached the hospital. He would sit her down in the outpatient ward and would go off to gaze at the vagai tree on the opposite side.

The minute they returned home with the white and yellow capsules he would set off to his press. Even the capsules had words printed on them. She would look intently to figure out if they were proofread or not. A thought usually surfaced: as the capsules dissolved in her stomach, would the words too dissolve? She would close her eyes and swallow the capsules.

Paper too increased her hatred and anger. She became obsessed with wiping out all the printed pages in the world. So she stopped talking to him. Even when he asked for water, she just stared at him, pretending she had not heard. He himself would get up and drink the water.

At night, even if he noticed her sitting still on the mat, not wanting to sleep, he wouldn't stop working. One day she stood behind him and watched him work. Like an enraged beast mauling its prey, he kept on striking out and correcting the words with his pencil.

Incensed, she asked: 'What is there only in this paper?' Without turning around, he said, 'I don't know.' When she looked intently at the papers, words seemed to split and break away and dance. Suddenly she embraced him and started to weep. The pencil fell from his hand and the lead broke. He prised her arms away, picked up the pencil and started sharpening it carefully. There was a one-thousand-page novel in front of him, waiting to be proofread. Thangammal's sobs rolled down, filling the entire house.

Original title: *Pizhai Thirutthubavanin Manaivi*
2006

ALMS

81

AZHAGIYA PERIYAVAN

Startled by the raucous crow that grazed her on the head, Chinuvu Paati stood trembling. The bird flew low from the coconut tree in the middle to the drumstick tree in the backyard. A coconut bud dropped from the tree. Looking up at the sky, she tapped her hands on her cheeks and prayed, 'Muruga.'

'Who is going to come and see me?'

Weaving through the coconut-frond screens in the backyard, she scooped out water from the pot and washed her feet. She locked the door, stuffed the key into a drawstring purse and went into the street.

In earlier days old man Subbaya would come home. It always flustered her when she had to leave the key in a place where he could easily find it. Nowadays the old man never came home. It had been quite some time now since Chinuvu allowed him at home. She never fed him either. Nor let him sleep there. Besides, the old lady kept to herself all the money the son – who lived away – regularly sent; hence old man Subbaya took to begging.

For a while the old man kept coming and going. Now he had stopped completely. The old lady was not bothered. One burden less, she felt. Whatever the townsfolk said, she blew it all away with a single curse. There wasn't a soul in town who wasn't scared of her tongue. Once she opened her mouth, it was difficult to stop her. She herself didn't know when to stop.

Old lady Chinuvu's hut was in the western corner of a huge plot. The remaining land was her front yard. The low compound wall had crumbled here and there. If you crossed her house, you could reach the next street; hence her house served as a shortcut for all. Whenever the old lady was home, no one dared to cross it. She wasn't afraid or shy of anyone. On some days, she would bathe naked right in the middle. Cursing and carping, she never allowed any children near her home.

Chinuvu slowly reached the bylane at the end of the street and plonked herself in the pial of a double-storey building. She looked around and picked up a black stone. Blowing away the dust in the pial, she placed her betel leaves and nuts. She flattened the nut and started munching, keeping a lookout for Postman Kanakasabai.

'What, Chinuvu? You've come in the morning itself and plopped yourself on the steps of the post office. What's the matter?'

'Nothing, Yasoda. Today I will receive money from my son. That's why.' She spat out the betel leaf noisily and wiped the corner of her mouth.

'Go on, only you speak so proudly of your son. Can't he come and see how you are – the one who begot him? It's been seven or eight years since he came home. What are we to think? Is it enough to just send money? Is he throwing alms?'

'Why are you cursing him? He's doing what he can. He thinks of his mother and at least sends this, no?'

'How much per month? Twenty-five? What can you do with this pittance? Tell him at least to send more.'

The old lady patted her stomach. 'He went from here. How can I beg from him? Let him send what he can. This is enough for this single person.'

'Yes, you'll never let your son down.' As Yasoda started to leave, Postman Kanakasabai appeared.

'Even I can't remember the day and all. How do you know exactly the day he will send money?'

Chatting away, Kanakasabai opened the room at the left end of the verandah.

Kanakasabai called the old lady in after an hour. He smeared some ink onto her left thumb, pressed it against two places on the money order form and then handed her twenty-five rupees. She took the notes devotedly and pressed them to her eyes. As if it was a bundle, she counted the two ten-rupee notes and the five-rupee note four to five times. Satisfied, she folded them into four, tied them in the ends of her sari, which she then tucked into her hip.

'I'll take my leave, saami.'

'Wait, wait. There's a letter for you.'

The old lady couldn't believe it. A letter for her? In all these years, nothing had ever been scribbled even on the money order forms.

'Read and tell me what it is, 'pa.'

'I don't have time for all that now. Go and come in the evening. The officer will come now. I have to finish my accounts.'

Nonplussed, she took the letter and walked towards the eastern street that led to the river. What could be inside the blue inland letter? Kanakasabai had said that it was from her son. As if her son himself was locked away inside the letter, she yearned for someone to release him and make him speak to her. But who was educated enough in this town? Only the son of Chinnasami from East Street and one or two others in the West Street came to mind. The boy was there in Chinnasami's house. He patiently read out the letter to her. As if listening to an oracle, she reverently listened to him, sitting down.

Dear Amma,

I think you are receiving the money I send every month. With that you and Appa take care of your food. There's a problem here with my job. So I want to come to our place, sell our house and see if I can do something with the money. I'm coming there this week with the family.

Your son,

Ambrose

Tension and anxiety gripped the old lady. Her son was coming. After seven years. Looking at the letter, her eyes blurred. Though she had had five children, all had died, leaving only this boy, Velusami. Chinuvu and Subayya didn't stint on anything since he was the only child. After finishing his PUC, Velusami had suddenly converted to Christianity, at the behest of a few friends. Outraged that Velusami had become Ambrose, Chinuvu had wept. Ignoring her tears, Ambrose had left town and gone away to Nagercoil. A fellow who visited every year suddenly wrote a letter to say that he was married. And stopped coming. After that, this was the second letter.

There was a long queue at the ration shop. It was always like this on the days when rice was distributed. Chinuvu stood, cursing. She couldn't stand for long.

'I cannot stand. Please make way for me.'

Pleading, she jumped the queue and bought the rice.

'Measure it out properly, saami,' she kept saying, till the bag was filled. As soon as she came home, she sat out with the winnowing trays. She poured out the rice, little by little, and picked out the chaff, stones, bran and broken bits of rice. This rice would have to last till the next instalment of money came from her son. A handful in the night. Wasn't this quantity enough for this thin, withered body? Even old man Subbaya wasn't there. Even if he were, she wouldn't feed him. Thinking that for a single person this was more than enough, she winnowed the rice.

The expectation of her son's arrival kept her awake through the night. Like this, she spent three of four nights anxiously. Four days had passed after the date mentioned by her son. She was worried.

How many grandchildren, she wondered. How would his wife be? Was her son still stocky? Had he thinned? Was she taking care of her son properly? She felt as if she had forgotten even his face. Stone-hearted fellow. How could he not have come for so many years like this? He was born, after all, to a stubborn fellow; so how else would he be?

Every time the crows cawed, Chinuvu kept looking into the street. In the evenings, she would go to the main road and return dejected. For two days she managed with kanji. One day the neighbour gave her some sambar. Today she made a tamarind gravy with the four pods of tamarind she found on the way. What would she do tomorrow? What her son sent wasn't enough even for the rice. Earlier she used to sell steamed bean pods. Now she had left all that. She didn't have a paisa in her hand.

As the sun set behind her back, the old lady locked the house. She slowly made her way towards the town. When she reached the railway station, her legs ached. Though she had walked slowly, she was satisfied that she had reached on time. It was at the time that four or five trains came and went.

Not only passengers, but a lot of people bustled about. Chinuvu sat among the line of beggars outside the station. She took to this only because she couldn't work any further. At first, she hesitated because of her son, but hunger soon forced her to stretch out her hand. The last four days she hadn't come this side out of fear of her son's arrival. Every day, from the railway station she went to the nearby bus terminus and then up to the bazaar to beg. Once she crossed the bazaar, she would stop asking. She would wash her face from the tap by the river, have a cup of tea and have enough time to just go home and light the fire.

'Why haven't you come for four or five days, paati?' asked the leper near her and Peruma who came from four villages away.

'Wasn't well. No train has come, no?'

'Not yet. It's time though. It will come.'

When a train arrived, there was a buzz of passengers.

'Amma…' 'Appa…' 'Thambi…' 'Yeppa…' The beggars' voices pleaded pathetically.

The gloom that settled tearfully on their eyes was enough to move the onlookers. In each stretched-out hand was a heart begging for money.

Chinuvu looked up when the first coin dropped into her hands. A family passed her by. The man who gave the money resembled her son. Her heart tried to leap out from her withered skeleton. She got up and ran behind them. He was trying to hire an auto. As she neared, her joy grew. It was her son. So what if he was in a crowd? So what if several years had gone by? When a mother sees a son, wouldn't her blood throb?

'Eppa, Velusami, my prince.'

He, who was talking to the auto man, was startled for a moment and turned towards the old lady. His face which had softened for a moment quickly retreated and grew stiff, leaving no ripples of emotion.

'What, paati? I gave you the money then itself, no?' Hastening, he piled his wife and the two children who kept looking at the old woman into the auto. The auto sped away spitting smoke into Chinuvu's face. Chinuvu choked. She clutched her chest. Her hand stroked her stomach. Tears rolled down her bony face.

Chinuvu stood still for a long time. A heavy sigh rose from deep within. She started walking. Her feet refused to tread the path towards her home.

Original title: Picchai
1999

DHAVAMANI 82

KANMANI GUNASEKARAN

Dhavamani plonked down, shattered. Water poured down in cascades from eyes that looked vacantly into the open cowshed. She hadn't smeared cow dung in front of the house. Hadn't swept the floor. Hadn't washed the vessels. Everything lay abandoned. It looked like a house in mourning.

As time went by, the four legs of the cow that lay in the shed had stiffened and the stomach had bloated as if it would burst. Red ants and flies vied with one another to bore into the staring eyes of the cow. Dung jutted out of the stretched-out anus of the animal.

Her elder son, who had come out of the house, went into the street, folding up the sleeve of his shirt. Uncontrollable anger surged out from Dhavamani. 'Dei, you've started out, is it, with your full-sleeved shirt? Go, da, go. It's all happening like the way you all wish. You all keep saying that I shout all the time. Look, it's all over. Hereafter Dhavamani will never trouble you, will never shout at you. Go wherever you wish.'

He stared at her. Dhavamani's sharp tongue lashed like a slap across his face. 'Why are you staring, da? If I pick up the broom, I will break your ribs. What did I tell you yesterday and what did you do? You thought let this useless broomstick say what she wants. Why should we listen to her? You didn't tie the cow. It was tied by the fence to the groundnut shrub. God knows what bit it or what happened – look there it is, lifeless. Go, go and come back. This Dhavamani would have cooked for you and you can come fill your belly. The cow is dead and he is walking off without a care. Go. That family man too went off and is yet to be seen. When he went to shit, perhaps the lake swallowed him up… Go, you also go…'

'Just because the cow is dead, you want me to die too is it, along with it?' He callously said this and walked away.

'Go, 'pa, go. As if I'm asking you to die. Go, go. It's all my fault, you see. After so many years I went and got a cow. I must beat my brains only with a slipper!'

'Beat yourself, beat yourself…' He walked on.

When Dhavamani started her married life, there wasn't even a bit of dung to smear in the front. Such a house it was. When her father saw her plight he gifted her a calf for Pongal.

Everyone tittered. 'What, di. Instead of giving the customary offerings for Pongal, your father seems to have a sent a calf instead…'

On the day of the Cow-Pongal, she decorated it with garlands and offered it festive food. Her husband, Kadirvel, was very happy. Only after Pongal was offered to a calf did it seem like a festival.

She herself had grazed it initially. Then she gave it to the cowhands. At the right time, it became pregnant. First it had a heifer. It came from a good line of milch cows. In four to five years, the open cowshed was full of animals. There wasn't a day when there was no milking. There were also two pairs of bullocks for ploughing. Dhavamani sold curd, buttermilk and milk and ran the house. Kadirvelu, who had the habit of taking a sip now and then, always found notes and coins when he groped inside the pots and pans.

There was no dearth of milk for the children. And for him too. As days went by, when the money kept in the pots started disappearing, she warned him. Cautioned him. He usually retorted with words, but one day he lifted his hand. She spluttered in pain: 'You dog, you didn't even have a jot of dung to smear in front and didn't have the means to buy a calf. Today when I have reared, milked, sold and made money, you not only take that to drink but you also have the guts to kick me, you scoundrel!'

It pricked him sharply. 'It's only because of these four calves and the diluted milk you sell, you are able to tuck a few rupees into the ends of your sari. That is why you are acting so high-handed. I will sell these things and clip your arrogance.'

'Why don't you sell it all and stand like a barren tree? As if I'm stopping you. When I leave the world, as if I'm going to gather it all up and go away,' she said angrily.

It happened just as he wanted. The cowhand stopped grazing. The children too showed no desire to look after the cows and calves. She couldn't run around herding the animals. Even so, she tried her best, roaming over fields and mounds and toiling away at home. Finally, exhausted, it came out of her own mouth: 'Look, no one seems to be coming. And you're also just waiting and watching to see how far I can go. So what now – as if I'm going to graze these things, make money and take it all away to the Uthimakulam burial ground when I die. Just sell it off somewhere and do what you want – it's your funeral!'

Like they say, the 'lame tumbled and the race ended', Kadirvelu used it as a handy excuse and sold the entire lot. She adamantly kept behind a calf.

Used to an entire herd around it in the cowshed, the calf now stood forlorn, mooing and creating a big racket. Turning round and round, it tightened the rope. Lonely, it screamed, refused to eat and became emaciated. The millet-grass and other fodder just lay there, untouched. Even a newborn calf would forget the mother's milk if it saw the millet-grass and dhara plant. God knows what bad times these were, it just managed to subsist, too weak and feeble even to walk. It stood shivering in the cold of the month of Marghazhi. It just collapsed and never got up.

Kadirvelu said, 'This is not going to get any better. If we sell it now, at least the butcher will give something.'

It was the festive Pongal season. Dhavamani was reluctant. 'Whatever it may be, let it remain till Cow-Pongal festival at least,' she tried to convince her husband.

When it looked as if it would die on the main Pongal festival itself, Kadirvelu said, 'In this auspicious time, tomorrow it shouldn't die. So we'll ask them to somehow pick it up today itself.'

'If it has to die, let it die in the cowshed. Let tomorrow go,' she said firmly.

On the Cow-Pongal day, she caught the writhing calf and put an avaaram-flower garland round its neck and sprinkled some turmeric water. By the time the camphor flame died down, life was snuffed out of it.

Dhavamani was completely shattered. Along with the Cow-Pongal, Lakshmi, the goddess of wealth, too vanished. After that, how much ever she tried, she couldn't buy a calf and tie it in the shed. For seven or eight years the shed remained empty. The husband and children felt relieved and free.

In the sowing season, when there was no bullock, she needled them pointedly. 'Two pairs of bullocks stood like hardy zebras. In a day, they could plough two measures of land. Your evil eyes were always on that. You sold them off. Now to hire, you're going from house to house. If only we had them… for ploughing and manure you wouldn't have to beg a single fellow.'

All this never pricked Kadirvelu. That too after he became a 'panchayat member', he didn't bother about house or field. If he left in the morning, he would come back only in the evening. Even for the most trivial of things, they would have a 'panchayat meeting'. However, there was no shortage of 'drinks'.

When her schoolgoing sons asked for three or four rupees, she would fume at them. 'As if I'm now milking eight or ten cows and selling the milk for me to have money tucked away in my sari. Go and ask that man sitting in the centre of the village who is all the time only concerned with "panchayat-panchayat".'

But for how long could she keep on telling this to her children? And for how long could she struggle to buy small things like salt, pepper and cumin? She plotted to buy a calf somehow. She had about ten to fifteen hens. She sold them and bought a 'ripe' goat-kid from Janaki. The goat came from a stock which produced triplets every time. In a single season itself she sold them and got a female calf.

The calf grew up, became pregnant. And then all this happened.

'Ei, Nalluvan, get up. You dumb-faced dog – just like your father. Get up, da,' she said angrily.

Pulling the sheet tightly over him, he said sleepily, 'Yesterday you packed me off to buy the Thanjavur pill and some such thing and did not let me sleep. Leave me in peace at least now.'

'Sleep, da, sleep tightly. This whole family will die sleeping one day. Otherwise, why would a well-tied cow die?'

Yesterday when she had left for the cashew field, she had told her sons: 'Ei, tie the animal in the shade, pluck two measures of groundnut shrub, drop them in front of it and then leave. Ask your father to give it some water in the afternoon. That itself will be too much for your father.'

'Who will go and get that creeper from that heap? I will tie it there itself,' said the elder boy.

Placing the water-pot on her head, she had said, 'Don't go and tie it by the heap. He won't think of home or animal and it will remain tied there itself. It will just keep on eating. Without any water it will become parched. So tie it here, bring some groundnut shrub, put it and go…'

When she came back after sunset, she saw it as soon as she turned eastwards. The cow was tied by the heap…

'You murderous sinners…' She came running with big strides. The animal, which usually turned round and round to welcome her, stood still like a statue. She put down the pot and ran to the makeshift stand on which the groundnut creeper grew. The cow was tied to the fodder-stand and she pulled it. The cow didn't move. It shivered, as if it was going to collapse. Dhavamani was totally shattered. 'Something has happened to the cow…'

She looked intently at the animal. On its front leg, just above the knee, a spot of blood had dried, as if bitten by a giant fly. She hunched down. There was a wound, as if a bamboo thorn had got stuck. It wasn't bitten by a giant fly. She felt its ears. Boiling heat spread to her hands. She was afraid.

She ran, and cursed as she ran: 'Are these children or what, born to me? They are gods of death, like Yama. They must be chopped up, or die of dysentery…'

Old man Sembulingam was at home. She brought him along. He checked the leg and pressed the stomach. Felt the ear. Then looking at the spot of blood, he said, 'Some poisonous creature has bitten it.'

Dhavamani choked. Sembulingam inspected the place where it was tied. It looked as if it had passed urine and motion hours ago.

'If it passes urine or motion freely, then no need to fear. But it doesn't look as if it has done it for a while. The creature is also trembling. Anyhow buy the Thanjavur pill for two rupees, fold it in a betel leaf and give it. It will help it pass urine and motion.' He asked for a few broomsticks. 'Let me chant some mantras and try to cure it. If there is poison and all, it will go off…'

She ran and brought four sticks from the broom. He knelt down, looked up and down, murmuring something to effect a cure.

The boys who came back from school, dropped their bags down and came near the cow. That was all – she caught them: 'Why are you coming and looking, da? To check if it is still not dead, is it? What did I tell you… And what have you done? You two who are born to me are like this! And that fellow who was destined for me is also like that! It's a pregnant cow, da. Don't you have the tiniest bit of compassion?'

The three fellows who studied in Aladi High School scratched their heads.

'Look at the way you all are standing! Like thieves who have stolen a goat! Go, he'll be squatting in the centre of the village. Go and ask him for food. Why should this Seetayyan's daughter Dhavamani alone care? That she alone should toil at home and field and rot.' She blew her nose.

Sembulingam got up. 'Here, you woman. Go and see what's to be done next. Standing there and yapping! And sniffling here.'

'No, maama. If he only is like that, can't these fellows at least care a little about the animals? If they had, why would this innocent animal be standing like this, trembling?'

'Okay, okay. Tell them to go and buy the Thanjavur pill.'

She looked at her middle son and said, 'Ei, take five rupees from the mustard box and go and buy the Thanjavur pill for two rupees. Buy betel leaves for fifty paisa. Go and come back quickly. Otherwise sit like that fellow somewhere and come back whenever you want. It's all written on my forehead that I have to suffer under you all.'

The middle son ran. The elder son pulled the cow towards the entrance. It tottered, as if it would fall down.

Sembulingam rolled four Thanjavur pills in the betel leaf, opened the cow's mouth, pulled its tongue and pushed it down its throat. But it didn't go in. He pressed its horns forcefully so that it would tilt its head and the medicine would go in. But with the force with which he pressed, the animal stumbled and fell down. Dhavamani was utterly shattered.

The elder son straightened its legs.

'The medicine has gone in. Let it lie there for some time. Anyhow grind some dried chillies into a ball and put it in. May be it had eaten the groundnut shrub and didn't have water, and it all didn't get digested properly…'

Dhavamani started grinding the chillies in a frenzy. The middle son ran to the street and came back with Sadavisam, Arunachalam and Selvaraj.

They lifted up the cow and stuffed the chilli ball inside. Even when it was propped up against them, it slid down. They gently laid it down and straightened its legs. 'Let it lie like this for a while.'

When everyone was about to leave, Kadirvelu bustled in, having just heard the news. Arunachalam jeered, 'What, maama, the cow is lying like this and you are coming only now?'

'Yes, which of you fellows in the town is letting me go? A big collector's job I have. The moment I became a member, I'm always called here and there – someone got beaten up here, someone pulled some girl's hand there. I have time only to settle all these. Who's allowing me to think of my own home…' Kadirvelu said wearily.

'Why did you come even now? You could have eaten in someone's house and slept in another,' Dhavamani retorted stingingly.

Kadirvelu didn't say a word, but knelt by the cow, lifted its head and felt its ears. And with the other hand pressed its belly.

Kadirvelu tittered commiseratingly, 'This won't survive.'

'What only will survive in this house? For this to survive now!'

Only at eight she lit the stove. She didn't feel like cooking at all. She cooked something, fed everyone, took the lantern and went to see the cow.

In the light of the lantern she could see that the gaze was still. She touched it. It had died and felt cold.

The middle son stretched his limbs and came out.

'Ei, go and see where he is. The fellow left in the morning…'

'Who…'

'Lord Ayyanar or what! Your father only!'

'Why?'

'You scoundrel! What all happened in this house last night – didn't you see? The cow has fallen in a heap. And this fellow is asking questions!' She ground her teeth and spat out, almost crushing him.

He went off muttering and didn't come back for a long while. Unable to control herself, Dhavamani went near the cow. The belly had bloated to bursting. She pressed it. It was rock hard.

It had become pregnant three months ago. How hopeful she had been. She had dreamt that the calf would be spotted with a white forehead and would be roly-poly like a real bull's offspring. How much she had pleaded with the fellow who owned the stud bull so that it could get pregnant immediately. 'See that it gets pregnant. This is not an animal that has roamed around. This house was full of animals. With your blessings, it should again become full. You would have done a good thing.'

She could still remember what he had said as he tucked away the twenty-five rupees, 'This is the first cow since this morning. If a bull like this doesn't stand in your shed, then ask me…'

The middle son came back and said, '"Go… I'm coming", he said.'

'It took him this long to say this, is it? The cow is dead here. And what great thing is he doing there?'

As he stood listening, the youngest boy studying in the sixth standard asked her, 'Amma, give me some rice.'

'Yes, I have tied the rice pot to my stomach! Just eat something and get lost. If you are here, I'll ask for this and that. That is why even before the sun can prick your buttocks, you want to eat, take your bag and run away. If you come in the evening, you are again going to put your hands into food. What do you care, what dies or goes? If your hunger goes, that's enough.'

The oldest boy went in, saying the same thing that the middle one said. They served themselves and ate. Dhavamani went inside and raged, 'There the cow is lying dead. And here you all are stuffing yourselves. Are you all my children or what?'

They didn't utter a word. They kept eating. Sadasivam came from the northern side of the street. She stood at the doorway and asked him, 'What, is the man of this house still yapping there? Here the cow is lying dead, staring. Instead of coming here, he is saying, "I'll come, I'll come, you go", it seems.'

'That is what they are discussing there, aachi. Earlier when "their" man stood for the leader's post, it seems none of us voted for him. So they won't do what they usually do – lift the cow, beat the drums. He is asking for that only for this cow.'

For a minute Dhavamani stood nonplussed. Anger and rage surged within her. She hastened towards the temple. When she neared the crowd itself, she could hear what was being said.

'Then… what are you saying?'

'What is there to tell? We won't do any chores in the village. We will work for wages in the fields, that's all…'

Kadirvelu, who was about to give a sharp retort, stopped himself when he saw Dhavamani. Dhavamani questioned, 'The cow is dead there. What are you doing here, holding a meeting and all…'

'That's what we are discussing here…' he dragged out.

She burst out, 'Our cow is dead. And four of you are there like hardy sticks, big and strong. We can dig a pit in the garden and bury it. And plant a jackfruit which will flourish. Instead of doing that, he has called for a panchayat meeting, it seems. Panchayat, it seems, panchayat. If we bury it ourselves, will they cast us away from our caste or what… Chee, get up and come home. What a householder you are…!'

Original title: *Dhavamani*
2001

Governor Pedda 83

Meeran Maideen

'Salaam-alaikum! It is with great pleasure that we announce that the governor of Tamil Nadu, Her Excellency Fatima Beevi, is visiting our dargah at about nine in the morning. We humbly request everyone to participate and grace the occasion.'

Everyone heard this announcement over the radio after the morning azaan, mingled with the early-morning wind. Peerma Pedda who was on the prayer mat was overwhelmed. She itched to go to the dargah immediately. Lifting out a roughly fashioned bamboo ladder lying in the attic, she propped it aslant and climbed up, and looked east, at the sky which lay somewhat reddened, like a faded sari. The dargah's minaret, which seemed to touch the sky, came into her view. A flag fluttered on the decorated minaret. She looked at the street. No one was around. Peerma Pedda was really angry.

'Che. What creatures. The governor is coming – won't they get up early! Undisciplined lot! Che, che…'

'Shall I go down to the street?' The moment the thought came she knew that her son or grandson was bound to comment.

They would surely shout: 'Where do you think you are going? Can't you sit still in one place in this old age?'

Peerma Pedda was not worried about what her son or grandson would say. But her daughter-in-law would surely make fun.

Though there had been a buzz in the village even ten days ago that the governor was coming to the dargah, it hadn't reached Peerma Pedda's ears. It was Mariam Pedda, who had gone to see an English play in her grandson's school, Amla Convent, who showed off to Peerma Pedda.

'Ei, Peerma, just see, they are going to lay the road in Dargah Street… do you know anything about it?'

'What do I know…'

'I believe the police were around the dargah in the afternoon…'

'Why did those useless creatures come here?'

Peerma Pedda didn't know the answers to any of Mariam Pedda's questions, so she simply kept asking counter-questions. Mariam Pedda, who had actually come to glean some information from Peerma Pedda, was disappointed. Peerma Pedda, who peered into Mariam Pedda's face, saw the chagrin and didn't wish to send Mariam Pedda back with such a look.

She would then tell the whole world, 'I went to ask that Peerma. But that idiot didn't know anything.' What a blow that would be to Peerma's pride, so she called out to Mariam who was already on her way: 'Ei, Mariam, wait. Let's ask my grandson.' She called out to him.

'Ley, come here. I believe they are going to put road and all near the dargah… the police and all came it seems.'

'That's right.'

'What for?'

'Oh that… it seems our governor Fatima Beevi is coming to our dargah.'

'Fatima? Muslim?'

'Then what…' The grandson nodded.

The smile that swept across their faces wafted in the wind and crept into the faces of all women their age within half an hour.

'I believe she was a big judge before this. A Malayali it seems. How she looks, you know, head covered and all… they have put it in the papers…'

On Saitoon Pedda's pial sat Noor Beevi and Senamma, bursting with news. It must be mentioned that Subramani Annachi's mother Vadivaachi was there too.

Saitoon Pedda brought the paper over to Peerma. The information about being a judge was there along with a photo. Everyone scrutinised the photo. Peerma didn't know how to read. Mariam too. Saitoon and Senamma could barely string letters to make out the words. All of them knelt before that bit of paper and peered into it, saliva dribbling down.

Even though they appeared faded in the black and white photograph, the governor's smiling face and neat glasses, the shine of her silk sari, the way a part of it covered her head regally, gave goosebumps to Peerma. She looked intently, a lot of questions in her gaze.

She felt she should immediately meet Fatima Beevi, pay her salaams, hold hands and say, 'How are you?'

The governor saga spread to several of the town's houses. In the streets, around shops, in the ponds, everywhere some talk about the governor would spring up. And if people happened to see each other face to face:

'Only eight days left.'

'For what?'

'For the governor to come.'

'Oh god, I forgot.'

Butcher Maheen went from house to house. 'I'm going to butcher three goats for the governor's visit. If you need some mutton, tell me…'

Two kilos for one house, one kilo for another, orders piled up. Maheen went to the market, bought three more goats and tied them to a coconut tree in front of his house.

All the little boys crowded round a goat and bleated like it. One fellow beat the goat soundly with a coconut frond. The goat raised its foreleg and tried to butt him.

'Trying to butt me uh! I'll smash you into bits. He went far away and aimed a stone at it perfectly.

Hearing the 'mai…mmai…' Butcher Maheen sprang out of his house. The boys scattered in all four directions. Mastan Pillai who happened to pass by said, 'What… driving away small boys…'

'Then what! They are throwing stones at governor's goat…' After that every one named all the six goats 'governor goats'.

Just five days left for the governor's visit. Meanwhile, they fixed lights on five-six shabby electric posts on the road. The street light spread far and wide.

Avusaan Pillai looked up and praised the street lamps, 'Long live governor. With her blessings, we got light…'

In the light boys played 'patto-idiyanto'. Girls played 'cycle pandi'. The eyes of the governor goats in front of Butcher Maheen's house shone like fireflies.

Peerma, who was sitting on the pial patting out betel leaves, felt like buying a silk-bordered outfit and a top. She went in to find her son reclining in the easy chair. Her eyes searched for her daughter-in-law; she was busy in the kitchen. She used the opportunity to ask her son, 'My son…'

He looked up.

'Please make me an outfit with a silk border and a top.'

'Why now…'

'I want it.'

'We just bought one for the festival. Why again?'

Peerma didn't know what to say. She kept silent; her son just kept looking at her.

'Governor… it seems she is coming to the dargah. That's why…' As she said this hesitantly, her daughter-in-law appeared.

'Yes, yes. As if the governor is going to come straight to you and shake your hand.'

Everyone spluttered into laughter. Peerma's face fell. Her son shook with laughter till tears poured out of his eyes. Tears came to Peerma's eyes.

Peerma didn't sleep properly the whole night. The black-and-white photo of the governor in the papers flashed several times before her eyes. Her daughter-in-law's words spattered again and again in her mind.

In the morning half a dozen arches were found on the road near the dargah. Work was being speedily done on the arch in front of the street. Little children and the elderly, why, even youngsters, stood around, watching it all. One or two houses near the dargah were freshly whitewashed. Officials whizzed in and out in jeeps. After the Friday prayers, the peels of the fruits distributed in the mosque were given to Butcher Maheen. Maheen collected them all in a plastic packet and fed them to the governor goats tied in front of his house.

The governor was to arrive the next day. The dargah radio blared from the previous day itself. The string of lights in the dargah twinkled.

Peerma looked at the street from the doorstep of her house. She would have asked at least six-seven passersby, 'What time is she coming in the morning?'

'Nine.'

'Must go to the dargah by eight. Must be the first person,' she thought to herself, her heart fluttering the more she pondered about it.

It was about ten when Peerma spread out the mat to sleep. She was restless that night. She wished dawn would break in a minute, like magic.

She counted her rosary beads. Though she wanted to nod off, sleep just wouldn't come.

She heard the cock crow half a dozen times. The goats made a noise – must be the governor goats. When she heard the morning azaan she jumped up from the mat.

After prayers, she opened the front door and looked at the street from the pial. The light was dim. She heard the dargah radio announcing the governor's visit. She looked at the street again. The governor goats tied in front of Butcher Maheen's house were not to be seen.

When the day broke brightly, she wore the silk-border outfit and top that she had bought for the festival and went to Mariam Pedda's pial. Mariam Pedda, who had stretched out her legs on the pial, made place for Peerma.

'I believe they have tightly tied casuarinas sticks. No one can go near, it seems. I believe only officials will surround her. Also the police with their rifles reached there even before early morning. I'm scared to see those rifles…'

Peerma listened to Mariam in disbelief. 'Who said all that?'

'They went early in the morning… that Mukoot fellow and that grandson of Karichatti were talking and going after the prayers. I called them inside and asked them. It will be nine it seems by the time she comes. She will go to Pappanapuram Palace and Susindram temple and then only come here…'

'She's going to temple-aa?' Peerma was astonished.

'She's a governor, no?'

When Peerma started to speak, reaching out for Mariam's betel box, Asma appeared. In a little while Paaku Pedda joined them and started to give some fresh bit of news. She was always like that; she had to tell someone if she heard something. If it was night-time, she wouldn't sleep; if it was day, she wouldn't eat. Only if she broadcast the news to five-six ears would she be pleased. Many said only trouble visited when Paaku Pedda came to their house.

'Ei, you know something?' As soon as Paaku Pedda uttered those words everyone looked expectantly at her.

'She will speak only English, it seems. Doesn't know Tamil…'

'But in the newspaper, it is mentioned in Tamil only, no?' countered Asma.

'Who knows all that! She will speak only English, it seems, so said my son-in-law…'

That what she said didn't create such a buzz disappointed Paaku Pedda.

At eight-thirty itself they walked down the road. Peerma walked ahead. At the corner of the street, boys made fun of them. Policemen lined the stretch on either side, from the main road to the dargah. Mariam got frightened.

'My stomach curdles just looking at these wretched fellows…'

'Just shut up and come…' Senamma tried to be brave.

Casuarina sticks were packed all around, just allowing a kind of path in front and around the dargah. Peerma walked swiftly ahead, chose a vantage point in front and made herself comfortable. As time went by, plenty of women piled in, behind and by the side of Peerma. All the men were on the opposite side.

The morning heat fell brightly on Peerma's face. Even then she didn't move away, merely pulled her head scarf and covered her face. The border lining the head scarf twinkled in the sun.

There was a great buzz. Uing…uing… cars whizzed in and out; officials and policemen walked briskly here and there. Whenever there was a flutter, Peerma's face was plastered with expectation.

Paaku Pedda and Mariam Pedda were irritated. They moaned and groaned in the crowd. Senamma grumbled and cursed that someone had stamped her foot, 'Curse her, only as soon as she saw my foot she felt like jumping up and down, is it?'

A few ladies laughed loudly when they heard Senamma, and pushed and squeezed her. Senamma cursed even louder. The laughter too turned louder. The crowd grew even more and a few women fell against Peerma too and pushed her. A good thing that there was a casuarina stick in front of her, so she didn't fall down. Even then she turned around and cursed them.

After nine, behind a convoy of cars, the governor arrived. Officials surrounded her and one unfurled an umbrella. Governor Fatima Beevi walked regally, head covered, looked at the crowd all around and waved and smiled.

The Jamaat chief welcomed her with a 'shawl'. When the governor walked to the front with a smile and turned beaming towards the ladies, Peerma brightly stretched out her hand. Governor shook Peerma's hand. Soon many hands were stretched out. Governor smilingly let go of Peerma's hand and went inside.

There was noise in the crowd.

'Ei, Governor Pedda…'

She puffed up.

In twenty minutes the governor left. It became news in the town that the governor had shaken Peerma's hand. Many thronged to Peerma. Peerma's daughter-in-law even fainted. A few looked at Peerma with envy. Peerma came to be called Governor Pedda.

When they came back from the dargah, Peerma said to Mariam, 'Curse them… they didn't make us study. She is like us only. That mother of mine was stupefied – when I asked if I could go to school. She said, "You, a female brat, is going to study and become a big governor, is it…"'

Original title: *Governor Pedda*
1998

SHARDS 84

VIZHI PA IDAYAVENTHAN

It was with great faith that he set up his shop. He had an inkling that he would somehow be able to corner customers here. Today's survival depended on this spot. His anxieties vanished and he bustled about briskly.

He had tried setting up shop in two other places. No one had come. A lot of bullock carts usually stopped by around the Hanuman temple's tank. Carts from out of town. To procure vegetables and provisions for smaller towns.

Bilur Munusami's horseshoe shop was well liked by both the locals and the cartmen from out of town. Whether his work was up to the mark or not, his talk was clean and smooth. He could sway the entire town.

As if to attest to this, whenever anyone brought a bull for a shoe he said, 'Look here, Munusami, last time because I was in a hurry I asked that useless Govindan to fix the shoe. Only if there is strength in the body can it be nailed hard, no? Just look, the nail has come loose and the shoe has fallen off. The bull is limping.'

'Don't worry. I will do the job perfectly. Take a look, the shoe and the nails are from Madras. For me it's the work that is important, not the money. Money will come today and be gone tomorrow. People should come in search of me, that's what matters. What do you say?'

As if in evidence, the shoes and nails of various sizes spread out on the sack glistened… Others would buy the cheap shoes and nails procured by the local dealer to somehow finish the day's job.

But Munusami wasn't like that. If at all he had to buy locally, even if it cost a little more, he bought good-quality shoes. His nails too never broke that quickly. How much ever the bulls sped along or charged around, the nails would hold the shoes to the hoofs tenaciously like a monitor lizard. He would put to use imaginatively the nuances taught by his father and perform the job flawlessly, all the while chatting convincingly with the customers.

That day he was upset that no one came his way.

'What, Gopalu, it's been a long time. What is your bull telling?'

'O Munusami, is it? How are you? What can the bull say? The cost of living being what it is, I can't even feed it. Better to sell it and look for a daily-wage coolie job.'

'All right, all right. But your bull doesn't seem brisk like before.'

'How do you say that?'

'You can tell by seeing itself. Look at the legs. Like sticks.'

'What to do? I have to make a living with this creature only.'

'Yes. But when did you last fix a shoe? Six months ago?'

'More than that. You only fixed it. It's all come off now.'

'Shall we fix it now?'

'No, 'pa. Too much expense this month. Can't manage.'

When he spoke about his problems, Munusami didn't know to whom to tell his own problems. If he could fix shoes for just two animals, he could buy rice and vegetables and eat something for the night. His son had asked for fried peas and rusks. He wanted to fulfil his wish. 'Buy some mango and dried fish. I will make you some nice kuzhambu,' said his pregnant wife, covertly conveying her own yearning.

'Okay, Gopalu. Give what you have. I will fix the shoe. The rest I will take tomorrow. Where will the money go?' Munusami tried to trap him.

'How much do you charge now for a pair?'

Munusami was elated. It looked like Gopalu was relenting.

'I've increased by a little bit. Twenty rupees. The price of shoes and nails have gone up, you know, no?'

'What, 'pa? Last time you did for fifteen rupees. Now you are saying twenty.'

'Okay, Gopalu, what's the problem between us? Give me one rupee more. Shall I bring the tools?'

'No, no, wait. I will get it done tomorrow.'

Munusami's voice dulled. His eyes searched elsewhere.

'In those days if you gave a rupee, your father would do such a fine job. Do you know that?'

'Whose cart is that in front?'

'That one? That's the Koliyanoor fellow's cart.'

'Who? Chinappan's son?'

'Mmm... He's gone to get stuff from the bazaar.'

Munusami went to the next cart. He pulled out the bull's folded legs. The animal got up with a start. The shoes were completely worn down. There was a fellow sleeping in the tilted cart. He woke him up cautiously.

'Thambi, thambi.'

'What?'

'Shall I fix the shoe?'

'No need. I will get it done later.'

'The bull won't be able to walk properly.'

'Why only walk? With me any animal will even run.'

'Is that so?'

'Mmm...'

'How?'

'If you give it four at the right place, won't it run?'

'Poor things. They are dumb creatures.'

'Because it is a dumb creature only we give it water and feed it.'

'Is that enough? We have to bathe it often, sharpen its horns, fix the shoes. Only then it will be brisk. Otherwise it will get sick, do you know that?'

'We can't even treat our own sickness. And you are talking about this...'

'Don't say that, thambi. It's only with these creatures we earn our livelihood.'

'Look here, I've no money now. Shall see to it later,' he said sharply and went back to sleep.

How much ever Munusami tried to persuade, he didn't bite. Even though there were a line of carts, there wasn't anyone around. His cycle was parked near the tank and he checked to see if his tool-sack at the back was intact. He pushed the cycle and reached the place where he wanted to set up shop.

Vans for hire were parked in the lane near the park. He parked his cycle under a tree and stood looking at the vehicles passing by on the main road.

At a distance he could see a tyre-cart laden with bricks. The cartman was known to him. It was a fierce bull. It had kicked him on the chest when he had fixed a shoe earlier. That he had been out of work for nearly a month after that came to mind.

'What, 'pa, shall we fix it?'

He understood.

'I have to unload this urgently.'

'I will do it in ten minutes. See how the animal is staggering in the heat.'

'No, people will be waiting at the building site. This has to reach. We'll see to it tomorrow.'

Since morning, unable to buy even a glass of tea, Munusami was in a half stupor. Each cart fellow had a sob story to relate. The nails and shoes that he had bought with the twenty-five rupees borrowed from the moneylender lay unused. He had to give him an answer too. Otherwise he would abuse him in filthy language. It was dusk and till now he hadn't yet got a single customer. He suddenly got an idea and feeling a little uplifted, he started to push his cycle.

He was given to pushing his bike rather than riding it. The front tyre had burst and had been patched up. The back tyre that had torn when pumped with excessive air bulged awkwardly. He went near the Market Committee. Farmers had unloaded cotton, peanuts, etcetera, and it was time for them to return with money. It would be enough if he got two carts. He could get by today and even manage to pay something to the moneylender. With this goal in mind he pushed his cycle quickly. And arrived at the spot.

There was a line of lorries in front of the Committee. A little away, near the wall, was an open space. He stopped the cycle and untied the sack. An x-like log, hammer, shoes, nails, he separated them and spread out his shop.

He hailed a cart coming out of the Committee. The man sped away twisting the tail of the bull, as if he didn't hear Munusami. He approached the next cart.

'Shall we fix the shoe?'

'How much?'

The cartman's query cheered his heart.

'Give what everyone gives. Take the cart to the side. Untie the bull.'

Munusami tied his veshti tightly and tucked his head cloth firmly.

'Look here, tell me correctly. I don't want any quarrel after the shoe is fixed.'

'Between us what quarrel? You are also a labourer and I'm also a labourer. Twenty rupees for both the bulls. Bring them here.'

'Don't want. Just a couple of months ago I got them fixed by the fellow in Kolathur and he charged only fifteen rupees. Why are you asking so much?'

'Look here, my job will be perfect. If you shave the hoof evenly and fix firmly, it will last for six months. If you want good-quality shoe, look, it's here. It won't wear out that quickly.'

'Forget all that. I will give only fifteen rupees. What do you say? It's already dark. I have to go back to my village.'

Munusami hesitated a bit and said, 'Okay, okay,' He asked him to bring the bulls.

He went through the drill of placing the log, picking the hammer and choosing the right shoe. He took a rope and tied a noose around the front legs and without the help of the cartman he gently pushed the animal and made it fall on the side. Then he tied all the four legs and placed them on the log and examined the hoofs as a veterinarian would. When he turned towards his tools he heard the sound of a motor engine. He looked up.

Munusami got up with folded hands.

'Clear the place first,' he said and kicked Munusami. The man on the pillion got down and gave him a few hard slaps. The bull jerked, trying to get up.

'Untie it. Is this your cart? Remove it. Dei, why are you staring?' He flung the shoes on the road and kicked the cycle with his boot.

'We'll go and come back. If it is still here, then we'll clap you behind bars.' The vehicle hissed away.

Untying the bull, the cartman made good his escape.

Munusami stood staring at the path of the motorcycle beyond the line of lorries. In the dark he could only hear its noise.

He turned his attention to the cycle and his wares.

His eyes turned dark.

Original title: *Sidharalgal*
1993

The Days

85

Sudhakar Ghatak

She was lying down in the last room on the first floor of that lodge. She had simply closed her eyes. She wasn't sleepy. Even if she tried, sleep just wouldn't come. She thought it would be nice if she had someone to chat with at times like this. Being alone wasn't something new to her. Every month she had to be alone on such days. She felt happy that she was alone, only to feel irritated the very next minute thinking of how long she would be cooped up like this. The other girls here always had two others with them at times like this. Why, last month, there were three of them. They would chat and giggle softly. She never had the opportunity to be with them. However much she calculated the number of days, she never found company so that she could be cheerful in this room. The girls were happy, but there would be no smile on owner Subbarayalu's face if they were together.

'Gone. No cash for four days!' Subbarayalu would lament. Let him also stew for a while, she would think. Her back pricked from sleeping on a bare mat. She had seen a cot in this room earlier. But it was gone now. When the girls used this room, they weren't able to earn money. So, what was the need for a cot for simply lying down? That must have been Subbarayalu's contention. She turned around, stretched her legs and slept with her face towards the door. Once she entered this room, everything would come in search of her, from tea to meals. On other days, she had to go to Subbarayalu's room for every little thing. Whenever they all ate together the hard grains of rice from the brass tiffin carrier with the engraving 'Stolen from Rajavilas Hotel', her throat would choke with inexplicable sorrow. Sometimes, at such moments, someone would come, asking for a 'room'. They would never say, 'Let them finish their meal.' Even if they did, Subbarayalu wouldn't allow it. 'It's our customers who are important,' he would say. Only if someone took them out, they would see good food. That too only if the customers wished to do so.

Since morning no one had come this way. Mostly, they wouldn't come. If there was one person less, the other girls would vie to earn more. Subbarayalu too would be keen to do so. He would demand more from those who wished to take them out. If they shelled out more cash, they were newbies. If they refused, you knew they were old hands.

She could hear footsteps behind the closed door. It would be Esther. Visiting the bathroom. Earlier, when she had stood near the door, she had seen Esther going to Room No. 5 with a fellow. An hour must have gone by. She would certainly have earned twenty or thirty as tips. Of all the ones here, Esther was the smartest and boldest one. But if we said anything, she would burst into tears easily. She would use the foulest of language. If newbies either hesitated or wept, it was Esther who consoled and advised them. In a day at least twenty times she uttered 'O Jesus!' If you looked at her she seemed a bit old, but it was she who knew a lot of customers.

'What! Haven't seen you for days!' she would say with familiarity. And the customers would be flattered – it could be seen on their faces. Even the policemen who came for raids seemed to speak to Esther politely. She was the only one who stood up to Subbarayalu. Often, she would even quarrel with him.

The door opened slightly. She peeped out. It was Esther only. Wiping her wet feet on the bit of gunny rag, she smiled at her. Standing by the door, she asked, 'What? Sleepy?'

'No. Where does sleep come?'

'I'm going to ask for tea. Do you want some?'

'No. How much did you get from him?'

'Tell me, who pulls out and gives it?' He said, 'Already given there. Here too, is it?' he asked. I said, 'Only if you shell out, things will happen. He gave twenty.' As far as she was concerned, twenty was a lot of money. But Esther's face revealed that it was too little for her. She wasn't smart enough to wrest money out of those who came to her. If they themselves gave her, she took it. She would never ask for it. The others felt that she was too innocent in these money matters. But she never gave it much thought. Coming to think of it, no one had ever left without giving her money.

Girls from all sorts of towns somehow managed to land up in establishments like these. In the beginning, new places and new faces would make them hesitant. Initially, they wouldn't speak to each other. Not even a smile would be seen. As days went by, they would mingle. But they would hardly stay for two-three months. They would leave for another town. They would enquire from each other where such establishments existed and where they were previous to coming here. No one had even spoken to her easily when she had first come. One afternoon, when they were all huddled in Room No. 4, it was Esther who had spoken to her. She, who was sitting a little aside, leaning against the green distempered wall, came forward.

'From which town?' asked Esther.

'Thanjavur.'

'Where in Thanjavur?'

'Flower Bazaar Street.'

'Really?' she asked, her eyes widening.

'What is there to lie in this?'

'No. Some of them lie about their towns, names, everything. That's why I asked,' said Esther.

She thought that Esther too must be the sort to be truthful. All the others too spoke to her. She felt that all of them were keen on hiding their past. Everyone had a look of weariness about them. Why, for what, and because of whom – one couldn't clearly say because they were so battered.

Esther closed the door and left. She could hear Subbarayalu's voice downstairs. Looking at him, no one would say that he was into making money out of girls. He seemed so meek. Always wore only a white veshti and shirt. A wonder that he picked up such stiff white clothes. Besides, he would always get them starched and ironed. His room was adorned with pictures of gods. On seeing Subbarayalu, she realised that there was a wealth of difference between his appearance and his deeds. Thinking of this god-loving Subbarayalu, an instance in Room No. 2 came to mind.

Looking at a calendar with a god's picture, the customer had remarked with a laugh: 'What is god doing here?'

When you are idle, a chain of thoughts usually followed.

'It will come to you tomorrow morning,' you could hear Subbarayalu saying in a loud voice. The voice which replied was even louder. It was the voice of the constable who usually came. He had come for his cut.

'Look here, Subbu. The new sub-inspector has arrived. Your aisa-paisa dodging business and all won't work. Otherwise, only raid. I'm warning you.'

The constable's voice lowered. In fact, you couldn't hear a sound. Subbarayalu must have plied him with coffee or cool drinks.

Earlier she used to be afraid of raids. But now she was used to them. If they spotted a girl who they hadn't seen before, they would beat her up. They would lift the lathi and begin slowly with the calf, shoulder, buttocks, and then speed it all up. The blows which fell on the clothes slapped, 'sath sath'. Foul language accompanied the blows. It looked as if there were no foul words that the police didn't know. Earlier, they beat up the girl from Salem like this only. But the next time at the station after the raid, the way they ogled them lustily and spoke slyly was astonishing.

She got up and came to the window. The heat wasn't much. Two men passed by, looking at the first floor. After they walked a bit, they looked up again. In a while they might even come here. She wondered if she could go down and speak to Esther. Esther would be asleep by now. Because she would have to be awake during the night. It was she who stayed awake longer than anyone else did. It was Esther who coped with men who came at odd hours. The tales she related about them were funny, even dirty. Even so, the way she related them made you ask for more. 'Whatever you say, this Esther is incorrigible,' the others would remark.

Like Esther, she too wished to gossip about the people who came there. It remained nothing but a thought: she didn't reveal anything to anyone. There were so many, who would she talk about? Even so, one person stayed in her mind. Always, the customers were more keen. She never was. But that day, when he came, she herself went to him fondly. She could remember his face distinctly. Till today, he had never come back. Even though she had seen him only once, his face was imprinted in her mind. He had come at seven one evening last month. He had come up with Subbarayalu and had a look at all of them. He was definitely younger than her. When he looked at Esther's disarranged half-sari, he bent his head. Lifting his head slightly, he pointed at her. They went to Room No 3. She, who was only used to veshtis and lungis, liked the fashionable look of his striped shirt tucked into his pant. He was hesitant. And shy. One must say that women like shy men. The moment she saw him she knew he was different.

'You must be elder to me,' he said, addressing her respectfully in the second person plural. He was the only one who addressed her thus.

She was more than eager to reply to this. 'So what if I am older?' she said, surprising herself.

'I'm not very experienced,' he said.

'I can see that from your face,' she said. For her, he was easy. She went close to him as he fumbled like a lost child. It was she who made all the moves. When, with a soothing embrace, he whispered into her ear, 'What is your name?' she thought she would burst into tears. She mentioned her name. He said that one of his relatives too had that name. That comforted her even more. At that moment she felt that he was the only one who loved her.

'What if your parents get to know about this?'

'Only if they are alive, no?'

She felt that the question was rather childish. She grasped him, bending his back. When she saw his girlish hairless legs, she laughed. He wondered why. It was a joy to look at his perplexed face.

She always closed her eyes. Not wishing to look at anyone's face, she concentrated on the darkness within. The nights at odd places, the hotels, the dirty beds, the bug-ridden pillows, the policemen who beat her up, would all come to mind. The thoughts disappearing, she would feel a certain emptiness. But that day she didn't close her eyes. He kissed her eyelids. So many men – the ones in a hurry, in fear, in stinking sweaty clothes, stripping as they entered the room, the ones who wore no underwear, the ones who groped for flesh… he was completely different from them all.

'Please stretch your legs. My knees are hurting,' he said softly. His demand pleased her. How softly he said it. She very much wanted his embrace. When he tried to disentangle himself slightly, she didn't let him go. She softly plucked his thin lower lip and kissed him. When he lay in her arms exhausted, she hugged him like a little lamb. When the body and mind yearned for affection, what did it matter who it was? He left her in silence. She lay weeping for a long time. She didn't know why.

Even if he came now, she could chat with him in this room. Why didn't he ever come back? Had he turned fat, she could have asked him why. She wondered what his reply would be.

She heard footsteps outside the door. She came out. The others were on their way to wash their faces. She felt like drinking tea. The room boys were near the staircase.

'Dei, Murugesu.'

'What, akka?'

'Will you buy some tea?'

'Mmm… Strong or light?'

'Anything.'

'Then I'll get light.'

He went happily down the stairs. She wondered if he bounded down the steps thinking of her ten-paisa tip. What would he do once he grew up? Would he be a lorry cleaner? The one with soiled half pants, talking nineteen to the dozen about the places he had seen. Or would he land up like Subbarayalu in this profession? Who knew?

The tea arrived.

'Why, akka, you didn't go to rooms for the past two days?'

'Chee, get lost, you cheeky fellow,' she admonished. Could she tell him the actual reason? What would he understand! As if making up for the rebuke, she gave him the glass and the tip with a smiling face. Wanting to wash her face, she crossed the door. But what use was it washing her face today? Esther stood by the staircase, all dolled up. That Esther would always wear a half-sari – even if she turned into an old crone, she thought. She came back to the room and sat near the mat.

It was well and truly dark now. She would have her ritual bath tomorrow. Subbarayalu would definitely be a bit happy. Like Esther, she too would doll up with care. But she would wear a sari, not a half-sari and skirt. On hearing footsteps on the stairs, she would stand by the door and show her face. She would look disdainfully at the ones who said 'no' to her. But the naked men who fell on her – she would feel their weight along with the burden of her own mind. She would then definitely close her eyes. In the darkness of her closed eyes, she would grope for the face of the young man who had come that day. The rest of the time, whenever she thought about what all she would have to undergo, she felt weary and exhausted. The thought flashed through her mind: that everyone ought to have parents with them right till the end.

She felt as if she loved this room. The light from the lamp-post outside, which leapt through the window and pierced the darkness, scattered its rays. Not wanting to put on the switch, she watched the gleaming rays. She slowly stretched her body and then curled herself up again.

Original title: *Naatkal*
1990

Easter Hen 86

Kumaraselva

Thambi woke up a little late. He had stayed awake the whole night with his friends and decorated the lorry in which they would go around to announce the resurrection of Christ. He eagerly enquired about the places they would visit. Not because he loved Christ, but because he was very fond of going to different places. These opportunities arose only on such occasions or when there were weddings in the family. He came home to sleep only when the first bell rang for the five o'clock service. His father tried to keep him awake. Five- and ten-paise coins – exchanged for a rupee the previous day itself – meant for offering lay on the table. His father went ahead, taking his elder brother who had just then put a ten-paisa coin in his pocket. 'Don't let the fellow sleep. Shake him awake and bring him along,' he told his mother. But his mother who was dolling herself up – rolling up her hair in a bun with a ring the size of a palmyra palm, using pins and all – had no time at all for him. In the meanwhile, even the second bell rang. Mumbling, 'If he wants, let him come,' she locked the door. Clutching the Bible to her chest and covering herself fully with the ends of her sari, she walked on, her gait proclaiming, 'See how piously I'm going to church.'

The father realised that Thambi hadn't come to church. Thambi was usually attentive even during the last prayer of the service. Even as the priest began the final blessing, they would start singing, 'Amen.' Though most enjoyed this tuneless cacophony, it irritated Deacon Vedamuthu. As the service drew to a close, he would make his way forward and quietly slip in among the children. He would pinch the boys who were noisy. In return, the children hid themselves at street corners and teased him, shouting out 'Sepoy!' whenever he passed by. In the old days when Deacon Vedamuthu was a teacher, without rhyme or reason a student wrote on his answer sheet: 'We will stage a sepoy mutiny!' After that he realised that apart from his given name he had earned this nickname on account of his 'jubba', pronounced as 'sippa' by the boys, and the 'sepoy' being a contortion of it.

Thambi got up and came to the kitchen sleepily. The sight there shocked him. His father was holding the hen that he had raised so lovingly and his mother was plucking it. Feathers parted, the bird hung down lifeless, head slumped. This brought to mind the paintings in the church. He was reminded of the passage from the Bible recited by the assistant pastor at the three-hour passion worship on Friday:

'He was oppressed and He was afflicted, yet He opened not His mouth; He is brought as a lamb to the slaughter, and as a sheep before her shearers is dumb, so He openeth not His mouth.'

When Thambi had gone to a tapioca field, a kite out of nowhere had gone past him, holding a chick. He had run behind it for a distance. The kite had placed the chick on a morinda tree and had tried to peck it. He had thrown a palmyra palm fruit at it and chased it away. He had applied some medicine and nurtured it in a basket. Because it didn't have feathers at the bottom, he couldn't make out whether it was male or female. Whenever he looked at it, he thought of his little sister who had died very young. He called it by her name: Elizabeth. Whenever it heard his voice, it would come running.

Looking at him standing, his mother was overcome with guilt. His father's face remained unchanged.

His mother took half a coconut, shook off the ants stuck to it onto the fire and gave it to his brother. He got busy extracting coconut milk out of it.

'It's really fat,' said the father.

'It's a cock, no,' said the mother. She laughed slyly while she said this.

'You call this thing a bird? Does it allow us to plant one banana tree? Or allow one coconut sapling to sprout?'

'Even that's okay. But it crows only after dusk!'

'In a Naicker household, if a cock crows after six in the morning, they will twist its neck and fling it on the roof.'

Thambi didn't like to stand there. He fell on to his bed, his eyes full of tears. When a girl had appeared in a house of two boys, it was Thambi who had been more excited. When she had often taken ill and become skin and bone, the happiness had turned to disappointment. When she had been hospitalised for typhoid, his father had cursed, 'This female corpse has come to ruin me.' He'd also heard his mother saying, 'Don't know why such a child was born to me.' Thambi was the only one who had loved her dearly. Whenever they went to the hospital or church, it was he who had carried her. He would often buy her ice-sticks without anyone knowing.

'This corpse of a cock has ten heaps of fleas on it.' Stretching his limbs, the father got up. He went outside, made a torch out of the palm fronds and burnt the small feathers of the cock. The mother plucked the charred feathers and scraped off the ones that couldn't be removed. She smeared turmeric, washed it and wiped it, sliced off the head and the legs. The father brought a banana leaf from the front yard. He sharpened the chopper on the mortar. As he cut through the neck of the bird, its chest fell to one side and the liver and the intestines fell to the other. The blood splattered on the banana leaf; the mother searched for its bile-duct and cut it out carefully. Had it got it mixed up, the meat would have turned bitter. The father upturned the outer flesh and started chopping it with a big knife. Using the kitchen chopper, the mother cut into small bits. The children rejoiced only when a female bird was chopped up. The mother would take out the ovary, cook it with the gruel and give it to the children. She put the vessel with the meat soaked in coconut milk on the fire and got ready to grind the spices.

Thambi's father had got married to the mother saying that he owned a workshop. Only later it came to be known that he worked in a workshop. He never went to work regularly. He would go to the pond with a fishing rod in the morning. Even if he caught one fish, it was enough. He'd roast it and take it with him to the toddy shop. It was the mother who sewed and stuck matchbox labels and ran the family. Sometimes there wouldn't be anything to eat in the afternoons. Thambi would come from school and nod off. If he stayed awake, he would only feel hungrier. After dark, the mother would borrow some embers in a coconut shell from the neighbour and stoke the kitchen hearth. The elder brother, who would have nodded off with a book open, his head dangling, would become suddenly alert on sniffing the sardines and start reading hurriedly. Salivating, he would go to the kitchen and stand scratching his head. They never had books or notebooks. By the time half the year was over, their second-hand books would be in tatters. The brother helped the family by failing twice – the same books could be used by both the brothers. When Thambi had collected all the old loose sheets and made an eighty-page notebook, the teacher had remarked, 'What is this? Is this your father's loincloth?' Thambi had felt humiliated.

The teachers in Thambi's school were heartless. The English teacher's son loafed around, not studying properly. So the teacher would often tell the students: 'My son himself is not studying. Why do you need to study?' The maths teacher would heap marks on students who came for private tuition and paid him a hefty sum month after month. During exams he would allow only them to copy. During the final exams the answer sheets of the bright students would be given to the teachers' children.

As if they had descended from the skies, the teachers would mock students from poor families. Shortie Aruldas's drawers always yearned for freedom from his hips. Like a make-do wedge chipped from the shavings of a tree you cut, he would produce a gunny twine borrowed from the ration shop and tie his drawers into place. In front of everyone, the science teacher would ask him to lift his shirt and humiliate him. Looking at the hole in Thambi's drawers, he had once asked, 'What is this? A bullet hole fired by a Pakistani?'

When the grandmother was alive, she would often come to see her daughter. Nobody had ever seen the old lady staying put in one place. Moving from one market to another – Karunga market, Monday market, Kaliakavilai market – she sold vegetables. As soon as the children spotted her, they would be delighted. Thambi would ask, 'Did you bring the catfish that is carrying eggs, Paati?' Everyone loved crabs. So the old woman would bring giant-sized green crabs and butterfish too. Once she had even bought a thick-skinned trigger fish that seemed to have on a shirt and knickers. Mother had complained that peeling its skin took her life out. The next day Thambi had wolfed down tapioca, old gruel and the fish before going to school. When the richer kids had complained, the teacher had made him wash his smelly hands with soap.

Thambi's mother loved to rear hens. She would collect the eggs and keep them in the rice pot. When they had annual vacations, she would let the eggs hatch. Only if she did that she would be able to sell the chicks one by one and use the money to buy clothes and books for the children. His father hated hens. He thought that they were troublesome creatures. Their climbing the roof, shitting right in the middle of the house even if they were shooed – all this he didn't like one bit. He would roar looking at the mother, 'Finish off everything. Tomorrow I shouldn't see a single one here.' He was against hens but had nothing against their flesh. He would eat all kinds of meat. When Thambi got chicken pox, they went to Polliadi and got pork to keep him cool. While eating, the image of the snout-nosed beast disturbed Thambi. The others in the family too felt so. But his father had no problem. Wasn't he the one who had snatched even a dead cock about to be buried and cooked it with tender mango? Would he stop at anything at all? The mother would often taunt, 'The crow eats all kinds of shit. Who would eat crow shit?'

When Thambi's father was in a jolly mood, he would call his mother 'little one'. On the days when a hen was cut or meat was bought, this endearment could be heard even more. Without going anywhere, he would be around and help her from the morning itself. All this lasted only till noon. As the meat was almost cooked, he would bring a bowl and say, 'Here, just give me a tiny bit, little one.' That would be the last time he would address her so. The mother would lament, 'Ayye, I'm tired of forever pouring from the cooking pot, kicking pot and all.' Heaping into the bowl how much ever he could cajole out of her, he would walk straight to the arrack shop near the tapioca field. When he returned, he sometimes brought a friend or two. Without even leaving the tiniest bit for the children, they would polish off everything. Even before the father crawled into the house, the mother ought to have laid the mat. Otherwise he would scream murder. As they squatted, she had to bring everything that was cooked for the day. When she had once forgotten to get the mango pickle, he had shattered all the pots in the front yard. When the mother had tried to stop him, he had pulled her hair and banged her head against the pillar, saying, 'Trying to eat without giving me, is it, you thief!' The mother too hadn't let go. 'I cooked a delicious feast for a gargantuan ghost. And you are beating me, is it, you lout! Worms will crawl out of your hands!' Sometimes, looking at the pillar, she wailed, 'There's no one to ask on my behalf nor anyone to protect me.'

Even at ordinary moments, if someone spoke in support of the father, she would always retort, 'Just married, I hadn't even stepped into this house and he removed my jewels and weighed them. This cunning fellow from Kayankulam.' After having his fill, he would go into the kitchen and pop a piece of ginger into his mouth without even peeling it. Grating it in his mouth noisily, he would squeeze out the juice and let out a huge belch. If there was anything left over, the others could help themselves. In earlier days, in an inebriated state, when he splattered the food around, the mother would eat the crumbs, gritting her teeth. But now she wouldn't even touch it. He would feign sleep till they all finished food and ask, 'Aren't you going for the afternoon prayers?' When the children said, 'There's no meeting today,' he would shoo them away, 'Then go to the neighbour's house and play!' Then he would pull the mother's hands and shut the door. The next day he would be a good boy. But only till ten in the morning. He would ask the mother to heat up the remaining meat in the pot and wash it down with the leftover arrack till the last drop. Cursing, 'The jackal always likes to feed only on stale food stashed away,' the mother would do all what he asked.

The elder brother possessed almost all of the father's qualities. The mother always said that he would become 'another father'. The old grandmother didn't like him at all. She would exclaim, 'Do you ever need a big barrel of poison? Isn't this one enough?' He would catch crabs in the fields, tie them to the ends of a frond and smash them on the ground where the old woman had spread out her sari to dry. The stench of the raw flesh would make her nauseous. As he ran away from her clutches, the old woman would curse, 'We shouldn't wait for a good day to sacrifice you. You should be burnt alive here and now.' She would then take the sari to the pond and wash it again. Thambi had seen his father beating the elder brother only once. Noticing smoke billowing out from the bushes and a hand jutting out with a rope tied to the cow, the father had dragged him out and hit him again and again. 'Will you smoke again, you fellow!' The father had a tamarind twig in one hand and a burning cigarette in the other.

The memory of Elizabeth flashed like a dream in front of Thambi's eyes. He hadn't realised what was happening till they placed her in a coffin, shut it and nailed it. He'd thought she was peacefully sleeping. The chain on her neck, the menacing smell of the incense and light of the candle had terrified him. Only when the pastor had sung a grim song as they carried the coffin, he had started weeping. Heaving, he sobbed. Not knowing what, he had felt as if something dear within him was being snatched away.

When the mother chopped vegetables, the three of them always sat around her. He would take the trimmed end of the ladies' fingers and stamp a 'pottu' on his sister's forehead. Tying a towel around her like a sari, he would say, 'Look, the new bride is coming.' As if justifying it, Elizabeth too would sashay this way and that. She would ask the mother for her chain. Her mother would reply, 'You can't take off the thaali chain.'

One day, Elizabeth had asked her mother, 'When will you die?' The mother had replied, 'Why, girl, you don't like me being alive, is it?'

'After you die, I'll take your wedding sari and wear it,' Elizabeth had said happily, clapping her hands.

'But when I die, they will place the sari in the coffin and bury it along with me, no?'

The child had thought for a while and said, 'I will say "please give it to me" and take it.'

One day Elizabeth had held her father's hand and said, 'Look at your hand… how black it is. Who will work in a workshop these days?'

The father said, 'Little one, with this hand only I'm going to give you away.'

The child had become sad. Jumping from his lap, she had rolled on the floor and wept, 'You should not give me away.'

Thambi couldn't stop crying, even though he tried to control it. The mother looked at him. 'Dei, are you crying? Stop it this minute and come and eat your food.' His sobs reached a pitch. Even when they consoled him saying that they would get him another hen, his tears didn't abate. As the father touched the food on his plate, Thambi let out a wail, 'O Elizabeth, my dear little sister…'

The mournful voice pierced the father through his drunken stupor.

Original title: *Easter Kozhi*
1988

The Story Told by Crane 87

Kanchana Thamodaran

The storytellers had gathered round the table. One of them had introduced himself as 'Crane'.

No one had heard about this Crane. Nor had anyone read his stories. For over an hour, in silence, he had carefully listened to what the others were saying.

The laughter that had spluttered at the end of a narration had just died down. Crane suddenly sat erect. And started talking. Firmly, but in a tone without a hint of criticism.

'Your stories brim with incidents, strangling the very voice of the story. Like a tiny stream swamped with reeds. Stories shouldn't be like that. May I tell you a story? Nothing will happen in it. It will be empty, like my life.'

'It's to fill the emptiness in the lives of our readers that we fill our stories with incidents,' said one of the storytellers.

Crane smiled at him. 'You must understand one thing. When I say that my life is empty, it only means that there are no incidents. But it is full of drama.'

Each one's face revealed a different emotion. Some looked at him pityingly. Some were irritated with his pseudo intellectualism. Some felt that had he written the words that he had uttered, they would have made a stronger impact. Yet all of them urged him to narrate the story that had no incidents at all.

Crane looked around for a moment. After everyone had quietened down, he began his tale.

'At the foothills of a blue-green mountain, in a tiny village, lived an old lady. With her daughter and son-in-law. Every evening, with her three ducks she would set off to the pond at the end of the village…'

One storyteller interrupted, 'A fox or a wolf will pounce from the dark of the forest and carry away a duck. Or the drunk son-in-law will beat up her daughter. Looking at it, the old lady will shed tears of blood.'

'Nothing like that happened. The daughter and son-in-law were busy with work. When they didn't have work, they stared at the walls. The ducks waddling in a row one behind the other and drinking water was a peaceful incident. If the old lady found someone on the way, she would stop and speak a sentence or two. There weren't too many people left in that tiny village now. Lots of riots…'

Another storyteller grew impatient. 'Riots are incidents too! You're trying to fool us!'

'O, all that happened long, long ago. After the riots there was famine and starvation. The entire village was half ravaged, in a decrepit state. Those who survived the riots were swallowed by the famine. Some fled, looking for better prospects…'

'You said it was a story without incidents and now you are talking of so many incidents…' another storyteller hesitantly drawled. Where was this story heading – anxiety was writ large on his face.

'No, I'm simply narrating all this now, as a matter of course. Actually, all I'm talking about is a wizened old woman taking her three ducks to drink water in the pond every evening.'

'One day, definitely these ducks will run away, won't they?' The voice sounded confident.

'Ducks are intelligent and friendly by nature. They enjoyed their evening walk and their dips in the pond without getting wet, splashing water on each other joyfully. Why would they run away? Every day they returned behind the old woman, and laid as many eggs as they could.'

'Ayyo, I can't bear the thrill and the pace of the story!' Frustration had turned into scorn.

'There are as many kinds of stories as there are readers. As much as we learn from incidents, we must also learn from the absence of incidents. You must learn to experience the lack of incidents and the silences in a story.'

Crane looked around calmly. The silence was piercing. Everyone wriggled uncomfortably in their seats.

Crane suddenly changed track. 'You could compare this old duck-woman's life with another person's life. To the life of a prince who lived nearby. They were both born in the same year.'

'Aha, one more protagonist! The story is withering, petering out, so you need different characters in emotional conflict.' The one who said it looked around the table, victoriously proud. His heart brimmed over.

'Not at all. The old woman and the prince had met only once. They must have been twenty then. The prince was on his way to his palace beyond the village. She suddenly ran across the path of the chariot. The prince had admonished her kindly, yet sternly: 'Do you know the worth of your life?' The old woman never forgot those words. She repeated them several times to her husband, daughter and neighbours. She had been utterly overwhelmed. Not only because the prince had spoken to her, but also because she who toiled in the fields had never thought that her life too had value. In a way, his question was like a riddle.'

'Remember all this is in the past,' said one of the listeners, waking from his half sleep. His job over, he contemplated yet another shut-eye.

'If there is such a thing as peace, then it perhaps existed only in the past,' Crane continued. 'Every day, when the old woman stood at the pond with her ducks, she would silently stare at the huge, closed gates of the palace. Even when the village was shaken by riots, droughts and famines, not even once did the gates open.

'One day when the old lady stood by the water, a huge bell tolled. Before the reverberations subsided, the gates of the palace opened. The old lady was surprised. The unoiled hinges of the gates moaned loudly. The prince himself came out and stood on the pathway. The old lady bowed to him, from five hundred feet away.'

'Was the old lady's head immediately chopped off?' asked the optimist eagerly.

'Sorry, no. In this story there is no dismembering, bloodshed and all. You must imagine this situation carefully. On the one side, stood an old woman, shrivelled and thoroughly ravaged. She had lost her parents one after the other in the riots and her husband in an epidemic. On the other, stood a prince who never knew troubles, born only to rule countries, destined to lead a high life. Unlike the old woman, he had the power to decide how to live his life…'

'All right, enough. As if we don't know the differences between the haves and the have-nots. What does it have to do with your story is the question.' One of them interrupted curtly.

Crane said, 'Nothing at all. I said that I would tell a story without incidents and I've said it. The prince had changed beyond recognition. Even his well-tailored silk outfits couldn't hide his bloated body and his caving legs that couldn't bear the weight. He looked around once at his decrepit lands with a frown. Then, without saying a word, he went back into the palace. The huge gates closed again.

'The old lady herded her ducks back home. That night, they ate duck-egg fry, spiced with onion and green chillies, along with their gruel.'

There was a stunned silence in the room. The one who recovered first asked, 'Do you mean to say that the old woman and the prince didn't exchange a single word? Couldn't she have asked at least one question in protest? Or, you could have made the prince recognise the old woman and take her into the palace. I must say that this is a very, very disappointing story.'

'It is not in keeping with the character of my woman to ask a question in protest. Likewise, the prince recognising the old woman too would hardly be true. But don't you understand that this is about a story without incidents. Life's tragedies need not only happen around epic-like incidents. The void created by lack of connection and empathy can also lead to such sorrows,' sighed Crane.

'Please explain a bit.' It was better to listen to Crane's tale than to worry about elusive catnaps. He suddenly felt that he should also know more about this Crane.

'The prince did not fulfil his duties. Behind the closed gates, he lived in his own world. His job was to cuddle several princesses in the harem. A life with no sense of history. But, because of his indolence many historical events and downfalls occurred. Riots, petty wars, and many such things turned the entire kingdom into a theatrical farce.'

The storytellers round the table looked at one another. One of them cleared his throat and started to speak, his voice reflecting concern and good intention. 'Couldn't you have written some interesting stories about those wars? Or some stories about the people involved in the wars? Or at least the tales in the harem?'

Without replying, Crane shook his head in disagreement.

The only picture he had in mind was an old woman walking with three ducks in a decrepit village against the golden rays of the setting sun. An old woman who was asked once, 'Do you know the worth of your life?' To which she would never know the answer.

Original title: *Naarai Sonna Kathai*
2000

The Ones Who Jumped Into Wells

88

N Shriram

In these parts there weren't many who jumped into the well. Even if they did, it wasn't known that anyone actually died. All the wells had this one characteristic: they never guzzled any lives. They also believed it was god's wish. Ever since he was old enough to understand, it was very rarely that anyone jumped into wells.

He could still remember the face of the person who he had seen jumping into the well for the first time. He had been a young boy then. At the time, Renganna Gounder of Poosarikadu was getting a well dug in his field. Master Well-Digger's family was the one doing it.

In those times Master Well-Digger was known for his expertise. All the wells in the neighbouring villages had acquired their depths by the pounding of his sledgehammer. If Master dug, water would gush out in a surge. The farmers in the upper lands believed that Ganga herself would stream in.

That day too the summer winds blew gustily. The day was beginning to fade. Suddenly the village folk ran toward Renganna Gounder's fields. Renganna Gounder too ran with the crowds. Even as they neared the fields, a few were coming back from the opposite end, talking loudly.

'Now he won't survive…'

'God knows from how many families they had taken advance and eaten it?'

They had pulled out Master with a string-cot and laid him at the head of the well. He looked pitiful. He lay curled up like a fully plucked chicken. Bruises all over his bare body. His limbs lay lifeless. He was gasping.

Master's wife wept loudly in a lament. Her wails melted the entire village. The womenfolk who had helped in the digging dragged her away. Renganna Gounder alone stood at the head of the well and fumed. 'It's okay if the man drinks. But if the woman drinks along, will they ever prosper…'

It could be that Gounder was unhappy that the work had stalled midway. The month of Aadi was almost coming to an end. The skies were readying themselves to pour down monsoon rains. When Master was carried away in a hooded cart to the Darapuram hospital, it was already very dark.

Two to three months went by. Suddenly one day Master was found sitting under the peepul tree near the village well, puffing away at his beedi. No one knew when he had come back to the village.

The man looked like his old self, majestic and robust. A rolled-up gunny bag lay near him. A faint smell of dynamite sticks wafted out. The village folk were startled to see Master back. No one had thought he would survive. Renganna Gounder wasn't convinced at all. He went near and touched him to make sure. His broken bones had mended well.

After that for a long time no one jumped into the well. By then, he had sprouted a moustache. That year it rained abundantly in the summer and the monsoons. All the wells brimmed over. At cock's crow itself, when it was still dark, the farmers set up the kapilai, the device to draw out the water. The slapping sounds of the water containers hitting against the inner walls of the well could be heard non-stop.

Till the sun reached the height of the palm tree, Ayya, my father, worked on the kapilai. It was he who was watering the fields. Krishnasami Konaar of the neighbouring field had a share of the kapilai too. Besides this, Konaar had three other fields as well. He had left them under the care of his son, Devaraj. He had hired men to work the kapilai.

On that day too Krishnasami Konaar sat at the head of the well, like he always did. He kept chivvying his men along. When they were done with the kapilai, it was high noon. When the men untied the bulls and were about to feed them, Devaraj appeared from the village track. Konaar went up to him and started speaking. No one knew about what. But it soon turned out to be a heated quarrel. The farmhands stood at a distance and watched the spectacle.

There was a fight at home too that night. It took a turn for the worse. Devaraj shouted so loudly that the whole village could hear him. The womenfolk stood by the pillars of the hall and wept. The next night a meeting was held at the pial of the village headman in front of the entire village. Talks went on well into the night. But nothing got resolved. People dispersed, commenting among themselves.

'Have you ever heard the tale of a fox stealing away ghee hung from a rope-net? This Devaraj doesn't seem to know that a father's wealth will only come to the son… why is the wretched fellow in such a hurry…'

Ayya talked about Devaraj to him. When dawn broke, Krishnasami Konaar set off for Darapuram. He came back after staying at his daughter's place for two days. Somehow the village got to hear of it. It reached Devaraj's ears too. When he set up the kapilai, Ayya said, 'Look where Konaar's brains are going in his old age… He seems to have willed two fields to his daughter…'

Around afternoon Devaraj was seen sharpening his huge chopper on the stone by the head of the well. He saw it and went and informed them at home. The women were afraid. But Konaar was unperturbed.

In the evening, Devaraj came to Konaar's home itself, chopper in hand. Only then did Konaar get afraid. He opened the inner door and ran through the backyard. Devaraj wasn't one to let go. He gave chase. Konaar wove through the small lanes by the river bank. Devaraj ran after him, shouting. Ayya and he ran behind them. Others too ran behind, hoping to separate the two. A mad chaotic chase.

After running for about half a mile, Devaraj managed to catch up with Konaar. The gap between the two of them was fast narrowing. The villagers running behind called out to them loudly. Devaraj, who suddenly looked back, tripped over a stone. Before he could straighten himself, Konaar jumped on to the side. In front of him an abandoned well. He turned back. Devaraj was within an arm's length, the chopper raised in his hand. Not thinking even for a moment, Konaar jumped into the well.

Devaraj flung the chopper away there itself. Without turning back, he fled through the small lanes. The village folk gave chase for a bit and then came back.

He peeped into the abandoned well. It was pitch-dark deep down. There was no sign that Konaar had fallen in. There was no sign of water either.

In a loud voice Ayya said to the village folk, 'Konaar's chapter is closed… Go into the village and tell them all… Bring back a rope and a string-cot… Hurry, hurry…'

He stood there, frightened. Ayya shouted again. A few started running back to the village. The western skies had dimmed.

In a little while the villagers gathered around the well in a circle. Everyone looked sorrowful. The women of Konaar's family beat their breasts. The youngsters who got into the well with ropes laughed. The ones outside the well wondered why. The ones who held the ropes in the four corners of the well tugged at the ropes, little by little. The cot floated up, like a chariot. They lifted the cot and placed it by the head of the well.

Krishnasami Konaar got up and started walking. Then need you ask – only the sounds of laughter and teasing.

At night when the whole village had quietened down, Devaraj came home. He screamed when he saw Konaar lying on a cot in the hall. 'Ghost… ghost…'

The days that followed were equally unforgettable.

Ayya took him to Kathapullipatti to see a girl. The hired cart was driven by none other than Renganna Gounder. He doubled as a broker too. People in the village joked that he did it only so he could eat sumptuous rice meals. It was high noon. Tired after running the kapilai, the bulls trudged along slowly. The branches of the balsam tree on either side cupped the Bank Road. The thorns grazed the hood of the cart. The cowherds standing at the edge of the grazing fields looked on. Ayya and Renganna Gounder drove along, talking loudly. By the time they untethered the bulls in the girl's field, it was already evening.

The girl was grazing goats in the field. It was the time when eight-yard saris were worn, pleats at the back. And with no blouse. Only castor oil for the hair. Besides, all the girls wore two nose-rings.

The girl's brothers were working the evening kapilai. Two kapilais went back and forth. The girl's father was watering the millet fields. The millet ears glinted. The place was thick with weaver birds. There were even more on the fence. He couldn't even see the girl properly. He guessed that she must be dark. A drooping face too. Renganna Gounder asked him to be patient.

At the time there was a sudden commotion by the well. The stone pulley of the kapilai collapsed and fell into the well. Along with it the elder brother too. Mud and stones heaped over him.

He and Renganna Gounder felt as if they were in a fix. It appeared that something drastically unfortunate had happened. The seasoned rescuer that he was, Ayya ran towards the well, shouting. The younger brother went towards the village, screaming as he ran. The light too was fading. When the women in the fields came to know about it, laments and wails filled the air.

Then a sobbing voice could be heard. Suddenly the girl alone came running towards the well. 'What a time… they came to view me… my brother has gone…Wretched fellow, O goddess Mahamayi…'

She beat her chest, as if possessed. Suddenly, when no one expected, the girl too jumped into the well.

People came running from the village. After that things started happening fast. First they pulled out the girl. Must say it must have been god's grace only. The girl wasn't hurt at all. Not even the slightest graze. The whole village was astonished.

They removed the stones to pull up the brother. The chorus of 'ailasa' could be heard. Hitting the walls, it reverberated. Every one of the stones that had fallen in was huge.

In a while they tugged out the brother, covered in slush. Along with the girl's father the village women too started to cry. An old woman burst into a long lament. Yet another surprise awaited the villagers. The brother got up and walked. He got into the tank and started to bathe. A sound of laughter wafted from the women. Renganna Gounder was narrating in detail how the brother had fallen in and been rescued.

That night by the time they lay down in the front hall, it was past midnight. Renganna Gounder started the talk of marriage. Ayya got up and spat out in disgust on the street. Since evening Ayya's face had been dull. When everyone had fallen asleep, Renganna Gounder talked to him once again about the girl.

'I like the girl very much, maama… Talk to Ayya about the marriage in the morning…'

Even before he could finish the sentence, a slap fell on the nape of his neck. It was Ayya who had given him the sharp slap.

'Look at the family he took us to… Thoo…'

Once again Ayya spat out. Even Renganna Gounder was sharply scolded.

Three years went by and the days passed without his getting married. No sooner had he viewed a girl than she found another groom. Almost immediately. Renganna Gounder too untiringly took him to see girls. Even girls who had been on the shelf for several years quickly found grooms once he viewed them. Such were the lucky stars in his horoscope!

In the neighbouring villages, they often called him to view girls who were unmarried for several years just so they would get married quickly. Without considering their status or class, he too obliged them. The very next instant the girls got hitched. To well-placed grooms.

Whenever they went on such trips, Renganna Gounder never said they were going to see girls. 'We will goad things into action and be back,' he would say jokingly.

He too kept doing this as an act of propitiation. Meanwhile his brother fell in love with a girl in the village and got married. Ayya lost all hope. He gave up on him. The villagers made fun of him behind his back: 'What an unlucky dog!' He too was shattered. And he decided to take his life.

The lanes leading to the bank were lined with abandoned wells. All of them had sprouted thorny trees and were without rims. If a man peeped in, owls would hoot. Pigeons would flutter up noisily. Not a drop of water, even for form's sake. The floor of the well could be seen. The mounds in the depths crawled with ants. He chose a deep abandoned well, from which grew a sirissa tree. The slanting steps were overgrown with agave. The late afternoon lumbered on. Mirage-inducing heat waves loomed everywhere. The wind blew weakly. No sign of humanity as far as the eyes could see. All that was left was for him to jump. At that very instant, the image of the girl who had jumped into the well came and perched on his mind. After that he couldn't bring himself to jump. When he returned home, he told Renganna Gounder about the girl.

After that everything happened quickly. After he got married to her and came back, several changes took place in the village. Electricity arrived. The kapilai slowly disappeared. A school was built. It was in the year Ayya died that his son was born. The boy went to the city for higher studies. As soon as he finished, he got a government job. And he settled down in the city itself.

Time was wreaking more and more changes. The face of the village was getting transformed. But jumping into wells never ceased. The night Krishnasami Konaar died, Devaraj's eldest daughter threw her three children into the village well and she too jumped in. It was midnight then. The whole village had retired. She must have been destined for a long life. Master Well-Digger was sleeping on the cement platform of the village well. Age had drooped him. He raised a weak cry. But his voice floated to every corner.

The children too survived. Even at that midnight hour Renganna Gounder joked loudly: 'If only the legendary Nallathangal had jumped into a well in our village, there wouldn't be any legend at all...'

Afterwards, the daughter-in-law of the Kerala man, Latchmi Paati of the big house, 'justice' maama, Paapaathi of the high-beamed house – all of them jumped into the well. What was surprising was that every one of them survived, as expected. As each one of them was lifted up the well, the village got a new tale. For a long time, the villagers regaled each other with the stories and laughed heartily. The people of this village were overly fond of jumping into wells.

Last month, suddenly one day his old lady died. Without jumping into the well. The son came only after the last rites were over. He then said, 'What are you going to do living here in your old age... our fields touch the main road... the mill owners are keen to buy... a cent is likely to fetch more than a thousand... looks like a good price... if we miss this chance, people say we may not be able to sell again...'

He looked at the son intently and said, 'What's the hurry, da... let it remain till I live...'

The son left in a huff. The next day the mill-owners inspected the fields. He was troubled. Once, in between, he went to the city and spoke to his son and daughter-in-law. The son didn't listen at all and shouted at him. He too got angry.

'They are my fields... I bought them with my earnings... what right have you got to sell it... I won't allow you to sell it to anyone...'

He and his son had a heated argument. Even when he got back home, his anger hadn't abated.

A week later the son came and spoke to him softly, 'The agreement is all over... they are giving the money tomorrow... you must sign it off and come and live with me... do you understand what I'm saying... don't keep on saying fields and all, tie yourself to it and rot... at least live comfortably in your old age...'

He couldn't bear that the fields were sold. Now he couldn't stop his son. Even if he tried, his son wasn't in a mood to listen. The son arrived hastily on the eve of the market day. The milch cow, the goats, the hens and chickens – he sold everything to the local merchant at a cheap rate. He also gave away the hen coop to someone.

When the son was about to leave, someone came on a moped bike. He removed the pumpset from the well and took it away. The mill-owners also arrived. The coconut trees were cut. A bulldozer was brought in. They said they were going to fill up the well tomorrow.

The fields that he had nurtured and safeguarded for years and years were getting ravaged. He couldn't bear it at all. They didn't even take his signature. His heart was shattered. The whole night he lay awake thinking. Only when the cock crowed, this idea flashed. Kept swirling in his mind. He sat up and watched the dark fade away.

When he stood at the head of the well, the heavy stone pressed his back. The thick rope, tied so that the stone wouldn't slip, pierced his belly. The day was breaking in in the east. There was no one around. When he peeped into the well, the water shone clearly. Even the summer clouds were clearly visible. He thought that if he hesitated some more, somebody might see him. Taking a deep breath, he jumped in. Drenched, his body began to slip deep into the waters. From within, bubbles started floating up.

From now on, it will be said that people who jump into wells die in these parts too.

Original title: *Kinattril Kudhitthavargal*
2003

GLOSSARY

aachi	a form of address for an elderly woman/grandmother/lady of the house
aatha	mother
aayi	a term of address for an elderly woman denoting respect
abhishegam	pouring substances such as water, honey, etc., over an idol in a temple
ada, adada, adade	a term used to express surprise, boredom, annoyance or regret
adei	a familiar way of calling a man
adiye	a familiar way of calling a woman
agraharam	the area of a village or town, normally leading off a temple, where Brahmins traditionally lived
akka	elder sister, also used to address a slightly older woman
ammaadi	expression used in wonderment
ammami	a term for maternal uncle's wife, also used to address other women acquaintances
angavastram	an ornamental upper cloth worn formally over the shoulder by men
anna/annan/ annen/annachi	elder brother literally, but also used to address a slightly older man
annadhaanam	charitable distribution of food to the poor, usually in fulfilment of a vow
archanai	a form of worship with flowers, etc., in a temple
athai	father's sister; also mother-in-law
ayya	a term of respect used for men
ayyo, ayyayo	a term used to express sorrow, pity or frustration
bai	reference to an older woman in many parts of North India
bale	a term of appreciation
besh	a term of appreciation

chembu/chombu	a vessel with a narrow neck
cheri	the part of the village where the oppressed castes live
cycle pandi	hopscotch
dabara	a small, flat-bottomed vessel used along with a tumbler for serving hot drinks
dakshinai	offering made to a priest
da/di/dei	terms of familiarity used between equals or to those younger than oneself
dharma	the religious and moral law governing individual conduct
dwadasi	the twelfth day from the new/full moon, on which the fast is broken
EB	Electricity Board
ekadasi	the eleventh day from the new/full moon, on which fasting is observed by the religious
elei	a familiar way of calling someone
gopuram	a temple tower
Gounder	a caste name
gurukkal	a Brahmin priest
japa	silent recitation of mantras
jatka	a horse-drawn cart
jibba	a loose-fitting long shirt pulled over the head
kaavadi	a wooden rod joined by a semi-circular wooden strip on either end. Devotees make their way to the temple in rhythmic steps, carrying it on the shoulder with offerings for the deity
kali yugam	the last of the four ages (according to the Puranas) in which atrocities and evils abound
kanji	gruel
Kannagi	the central female protagonist of the Tamil epic *Silapadikaram*, revered for her virtuous character
karagam	an acrobatic folk dance; the dancer usually balances a decorated brass pot filled with water on the head
karmam/karmame	a term of condemnation, disapproval or curse
kolam	decorative designs drawn on the front courtyard, floor, etc., with rice flour or flour paste

kolattam	a baton dance. Girls in long skirts dance in circles, clicking their short wooden batons rhythmically against their partners' batons
Kuchelar	a poor childhood friend of Lord Krishna, who meets him after several years, to seek help to support his family. Though he never asks for anything, Krishna rewards him bountifully
kutti	affectionately referring to a little girl
kuzhambu	a spicy gravy usually eaten with rice
lathi	baton
maama	maternal uncle, also a term of address for an older man
maami	maternal uncle's wife, also a term of address for an older woman
maangalyam	cord or gold chain tied around the bride's neck by the groom during the marriage ceremony. It is considered the essential symbol of marriage
maapillai	bridegroom/son-in-law; also a term of address used between friends in banter
machan	brother-in-law, also a term of address used between friends in banter
madi	observance of ritual purity, especially of clothes, food, etc. A madi sari, for example, is a ritually washed sari, untouched by others
madini	sister-in-law
mai	kohl
mandapam	a pillared structure open on all sides, especially in a temple
matham	a monastery-like religious institution
melam	a two-sided drum, usually played on auspicious occasions
mirasdar	a prestigious landowner
modakam	steamed sweet dumpling, considered a favourite of Lord Ganesha
mridangam	a South Indian percussion instrument
muhurtam	auspicious hour in a wedding ceremony
mundu	cloth worn by men, wrapped around the waist
Mysore pak	sweet made with chickpea flour and sugar
nadaswaram	a wind instrument with a long pipe

Naicker	a caste name
naina	term for father, generally used by Telugu-speaking people; also a term of address used between friends in banter
nei appam	spongy delicacy made of sweetened rice flour and ghee
neivedyam	the ritualistic offering of cooked food, fruits, etc., to a deity
nyaya	fairness, justice
ollock	one-eighth of a measure
paapaathi	pejorative term for a Brahmin woman
paati	grandmother, also a term of address for a very old woman
paavaadai	a long skirt worn by young girls
padi	a measure, approximately a litre
palam	measure of weight used before the metric system was introduced, roughly equal to 40 grams
panchamritam	a combination of banana, honey, ghee, sugar or jaggery, and raisin used for anointing the idol in a temple
patto-idiyanto	game of hide and seek
payasam	a sweet preparation, generally made of milk, on auspicious occasions
peramboke	unregistered government land
periappa	father's elder brother
pial	a short raised verandah or balcony, usually found on either side of the front door of a traditional house. It is the ideal place to chat with friends, take a nap, or even watch the world go by
Pillaiyaar	Lord Ganesha or Ganapati, the remover of obstacles, worshipped often at roadside shrines
pongal	a harvest festival; also a dish made from freshly harvested rice in a new pot
pottu	bindi
prasadam	sacred offering to a deity, which is distributed to devotees
purohit	Hindu priest
raga	melody in Indian classical music
Rayarvaal	respectful form of address of a Marathi in Tamil Nadu
RHMP	Rural Health Medical Practitioner
saami	god or deity; also a respectful term of address for a man

saamiyaar	an ascetic
saar/ saare	derived from 'sir', a term of respect for a man/male teacher
sait	reference to a North Indian in Tamil Nadu
samaaradhanai	a thanksgiving ceremony performed at home or in a temple during auspicious occasions, followed by a feast where Brahmins are fed
sani/saniyan	term of abuse conveying irritation towards someone or something
seemandham	a ceremony performed during the eighth month of the first pregnancy in the husband's house
shanthi muhurtam	auspicious time of consummation of marriage (after the wedding)
siddhar	a yogi who doesn't believe in religion or rituals
Silapadikaram	a classical Tamil epic
Sivaratri	a night in the month of Maasi when one keeps awake and offers prayers to Lord Siva
sumangali prarthanai	a ceremony in memory of a woman who died while her husband was alive. Saris, bangles, etc., are distributed to married women during the feast
tala	rhythmic cycles in Indian classical music
thaali	same as maangalyam
thambi	literally younger brother; but also used to address a youngster with affection or familiarity
thaatha	grandfather, also a term of address for a very old man
thenkuzhal	deep-fried snack made of rice and lentil flour
thirumanjanam	the ritual bathing of the image of a deity with milk, curd, honey, coconut water, sandal, turmeric and water
thuvaram paruppu	red gram dal
vadai	South Indian deep-fried lentil snack
vaidyar	practitioner of traditional medicine
vanakkam	a term of respectful greeting
vaappa	father in the dialect of Tamil Muslims
veshti	a white cloth worn by men. Usually wrapped around the waist, it is sometimes folded up at the knees. On formal occasions, and by Brahmin priests, a longer veshti is brought up between the legs and tucked at the waist

vibhuti	sacred ash. A mark of Saivaite worship, it is worn on the forehead and smeared on the chest, arms, etc.
vishwaroopam	the cosmic, gigantic form of god
yaazh	an ancient stringed musical instrument
Yali	a mythical animal with the face of a lion and the trunk and tusks of an elephant
Yama/Yaman	god of death
Yeppa	a familiar way of calling someone

BIO NOTES

A Egbert Sachidanandam (1950-) is a retired teacher. He has published a collection of short stories. Though not prolific, he has won acclaim for his nuanced portrayals of Christian life in Tamil Nadu.

Aa Madhavaiah (1872-1925), one of the pioneers of modern Tamil writing, also wrote in English. He successfully melded his reformist ideals into his immaculate prose. His *Padmavathy Charithram* was one of the earliest novels written in Tamil. His concerns, particularly relating to women and caste, are still relevant today.

Aa Madhavan (1934-) is an established novelist and short-story writer who has been writing for more than five decades. He has published three novels and six collections of short fiction. He has also translated two novels from Malayalam into Tamil. He has several awards to his credit.

Aadhavan (1942-1987), whose real name was K S Sundaram, started his literary career writing children's stories. His works have even been translated into Russian to much critical acclaim. He was an editor at the National Book Trust. He was awarded the Sahitya Akademi award posthumously for his collection of short stories.

Ambai (1944-) is the nom de plume of C S Lakshmi, a historian and a creative writer, whose stories have been published and translated to much critical acclaim. A PhD from Jawaharlal Nehru University, New Delhi, she has been an independent researcher in Women's Studies for the last thirty-five years. She is the director of SPARROW (Sound & Picture Archives for Research on Women).

Ammani Ammal's story 'Expectation and the Event' appeared in the journal *Viveka Bodhini* in March 1913. Unfortunately, nothing much is known about either her background or her literary output.

Ashokamitran (1931-) is the pseudonym of J Thyagarajan. He is one of the most revered writers today. Deemed the ultimate modernist, his spare, nuanced prose explores a vast terrain, deftly bringing to light the concerns of contemporary Tamil society. In a period of sixty years of writing, he has published more than sixty books in Tamil and English. A recipient of the Sahitya Akademi award, he has also won several regional and national awards.

Azhagiya Periyavan (1968-), one of the important Dalit writers, is a poet, short-story writer, essayist and novelist. A teacher by profession, he has more than fifteen books to his credit. He has received many awards, including the Tamil Nadu Government Award.

Balakumaran (1946-), one of the most popular writers in Tamil today, has written more than two hundred books, including novels, short stories and essays. Many of his novels have been serialised in popular weeklies. He is also an accomplished screenplay writer. He has won the Raja Sir Annamalai Chettiar award and the Ilakkia Chinthanai for his contributions to literature.

Bama (1957-) is the pen name of S Faustina Soosairaj. An important Dalit voice, her short stories and novels have been widely translated into several languages. She has won several important awards, including the Crossword award.

C N Annadurai (1901-1969) was popularly known as Arignar Anna. The most influential of all Dravidian writers, he wrote novels, short stories, plays, poems and essays. Immensely loved by the people of Tamil Nadu, he launched the political party Dravida Munnetra Kazhagam (DMK) and served as the chief minister of Tamil Nadu for two years.

C R Raveendran (1945-) is a novelist and a short-story writer, known for his faithful depiction of the rural communities in the Coimbatore district. An MA in English Literature, he has authored fourteen novels and eight collections of short stories. He has won the Bharatiya Bhasha Parishad Award.

Cho Dharman (1953-), who started writing in 1980, has published five short-story collections and two novels. He also has a monograph on villupaatu (bow songs) to his credit. He has won many awards, including the Tamil Nadu state government and the Katha awards.

Ci Su Chellappa (1912-1998) belonged to the *Manikodi* literary movement along with Pudumaippittan, Mauni and Ku Pa Ra. He founded the literary magazine *Ezhuthu*, which ushered in modern criticism in Tamil. He wrote several novels, short stories and critical essays. He was conferred the Sahitya Akademi award posthumously.

Devan (1913-1957) is the pseudonym of R Mahadevan. A hugely popular humorist, he wrote novels, travelogues, short stories and articles under several pen names. He edited the popular Tamil weekly *Ananda Vikatan* for several years.

Dhamayanthi (1975-), an important woman writer who emerged in the 1990s, has published six short-story collections and one novel. A media professional, she has won many awards, including the Ilakkia Chinthanai.

Dilip Kumar (1951-) whose mother tongue is Gujarati, is a well-known short-story writer and editor in Tamil with several awards to his credit. He has published three short-story collections and a critical work on the late Mauni, a pioneer of

Tamil short stories. He has also translated poems, short stories, etcetera, from Hindi, Gujarati and English into Tamil.

G Murugan (1966 -), a short-story writer and poet, is known for his experimental works set against the rural backdrop. He has more than five books to his credit. He works as a sub-editor in the Tamil daily *Dinamani.*

G Nagarajan (1929-1981), who defied convention, wrote evocatively about the lives of the marginalised. He has a collection of short stories, a novel and a novella to his credit. Though his output was slim, his works, refreshingly earthy and daring, are considered classics.

Gandharvan (1944-2004), an important writer of the progressive movement, started writing in the 1970s. He has many collections of short stories and poems to his credit. He worked as a government official.

Gokula Kannan (1969-) is the pen name of Gokul Ramaswamy, a computer professional by vocation. One of the finest prose writers among the younger generation, he has published poems, short stories and novels.

Imayam (1964-) is the nom de plume of V Annamalai, a school teacher. An important writer of the 1990s, he has published three novels and two short-story collections and many essays on literary and cultural issues. He has won many awards.

Indira Parthasarathy (1930-), popularly known as Ee Pa, is the pen name of R Parthasarathy. An award-winning novelist, short-story writer and playwright, he has published more than fifty books. Among the many prestigious awards that have been conferred on him are the Sahitya Akademi, the Sangeet Natak, the Saraswati Samman and the Padma Shri.

Jayakanthan (1934-2015) has about forty novels, nearly two hundred short stories and fifteen collections of essays to his credit. He has won both the prestigious Jnanpith and the Sahitya Akademi awards.

Jeyamohan (1962-), one of the most prolific Tamil writers today, has published several novels, short stories, plays, children's books and essays. Perfectly bilingual, he also writes in Malayalam. He is a sought-after screenplay writer in both Tamil and Malayalam. He has won several awards, including the Sanskriti Sammaan.

Jeyanthan (1937-2007), a well-known progressive writer with many short-story collections and plays to his credit, was a veterinary doctor by profession. He won the prestigious Ilakkia Chinthanai award for his experimental plays.

K Vittal Rao (1942-) has been writing in Tamil since 1967. His stories, novels and non-fiction have earned praise from readers and critics alike. Recipient of the prestigious Kusumanjali Sahitya Samman, he is also an accomplished painter and photographer.

Ka Naa Subramanyam (1912-1988), a noted Tamil writer and critic, was popularly known by his Tamil initials Ka Naa Su. He has published more than twenty novels, and hundreds of short stories, poems and essays. His translations of European literary works into Tamil helped shape the awareness of modern literary sensibilities across generations of writers. He also edited several important literary magazines, valiantly championing the cause of modern Tamil literature.

Kalki (1899-1954) was the pen name of R Krishnamurthy. He was a famous writer known for his humorous short works and nationalist and historical novels which were serialised in popular magazines and are still cherished by generations of readers. A nationalist and freedom fighter, he was jailed thrice. He launched and edited the popular magazine *Kalki* after having worked in *Ananda Vikatan*, another popular weekly, for several years.

Kanchana Thamodaran (1958-), an alumnus of IIT-Madras, started writing fiction in the late nineties. The author of five books, she has won Tamil literary awards such as Kalki, Kanaiyazhi and Shakti. She lives in the US.

Kanmani Gunasekaran (1971-), a well-known Dalit writer, works with the Government Transport Department. He has written seven books, which include novels, short-story collections and a dictionary of the South Arcot dialect. He has won several awards.

Ki Rajanarayanan (1922-), an important senior writer and folklorist, started writing in the late 1950s. He is known for his deft use of dialect in his novels and short stories. He has over thirty books to his credit. He has won the Sahitya Akademi award.

Konangi (1958-) is the nom de plume of S Ilangovan. Always open to experiment, he has carved a niche for himself in the contemporary Tamil literary milieu through his unconventional postmodern writings. He has published ten books.

Krishnan Nambi (1931-1975) was the pen name of Azhagiya Nambi. He began writing when he was at school. He is also famous for his stories and poems for children. His stories are known for their humour and precision.

Ku Azhagirisamy (1923 -1970), a journalist and writer, was known for his compact short stories. His abiding interest and erudition in classical Tamil literature was evident in his non-fiction. A winner of several awards, he was given the Sahitya Akademi award posthumously in 1970.

Ku Pa Rajagopalan (1902-1944), popularly known as Ku Pa Ra, was an accomplished author, journalist and translator. One of the famous trio of *Manikodi* writers (Pudumaippittan and Mauni being the other two), who shaped the modern Tamil short story, he is known for his compassionately etched portraits of women. His brilliant career was cut short by an untimely death.

Kumaraselva (1964-) is the pen name of Selva Kumar, a professor of Tamil. He is particularly known for his deft use of dialect. He has to his credit two short-story collections, a novel and an anthology of poems.

Kumudhini (1905-1986) was an autodidact, proficient in Tamil, Sanskrit and English. Though married off at the age of ten, she was encouraged to write by her family. Known for her nuanced stories laced with humour, she was also an able translator. Apart from stories and novels, she also has a book on child psychology to her credit. A true Gandhian, she even corresponded with Gandhi.

La Sa Ramamrutham (1916-2007), who was popularly known as La Sa Ra, was a doyen of Tamil literature known for the poetic and mystical sensibilities in his writing. He has written three hundred short stories, six novels and ten collections of essays. Funnily enough, as a young man he wrote in English, and only later switched to Tamil. He won the Sahitya Akademi award in 1989.

Ma Kamuthurai (1960-) brings his rich work experience, which straddles a spectrum of widely varying jobs from selling pesticides to footwear, to his nuanced stories and novels. He has published more than ten books and received many awards.

Maa Aranganathan (1932-) is a senior novelist, short story writer and essayist. Almost all his stories are based on the protagonist Muthu Karuppan, lending them an unusual charm and coherence. He has so far published fourteen books.

Mauni (1907-1985), the pen name of S Mani, was dubbed a 'writer's writer'. He was one of the most important figures of the *Manikodi* era. Though his output was meagre, he has remained an enduring influence through generations of writers. His metaphysical and symbolic landscapes and motifs lend a lyrical allure to his writings.

Meeran Maideen (1968-), a businessman by profession, is an award-winning writer. His skilfully sketched narratives, laced with humour, bring to life the Muslim community of southern Tamil Nadu. He has published three collections of short stories and two novels. He works in the field of Tamil cinema.

N Shriram (1972-) is an important short-story writer who emerged in the 1990s. He has published three volumes of short stories and a collection of novellas. He has won important literary awards such as Ilakkia Chinthanai and Kanaiyaazhi.

Na Muthuswamy (1936 -), the pioneer of experimental theatre in Tamil, is also an accomplished short story writer. Most of his stories are centred on his native village

Punjai. He founded the theatre group Koothu-p-Pattarai, which has created a new idiom for the contemporary stage, inspired by traditional folk theatre. He has been honoured with the Sangeet Natak Akademi Award and the Padma Shri.

Na Pichamurthy (1900-1976) was an important voice of the 1930s, known for his evocative short stories and poems. A lawyer by profession, he published many short-story collections, novels and poems. Known for his bold experiments with the blank verse, he was rightly named the father of the new poetry movement in Tamil.

Nanjil Nadan (1947-) is the author of six novels, two poetry collections, nine essay collections and hundred and twenty-two short stories. He has won many awards, including the Sahitya Akademi award, the Kalai Mamani from the Government of Tamil Nadu and the Literary Garden from Canada. His stories have been made into films. He wrote the screenplay for the award-winning Tamil film *Paradesi*.

Neela Padmanabhan (1938-), an engineer by profession, is a bilingual writer who is equally proficient in Tamil and Malayalam. He has to his credit twenty works of long fiction, five collections of short stories, and four volumes of poems. Widely translated into many languages, he has won several awards, including the Sahitya Akademi award.

Paavannan (1958-) is the pen name of B Baskaran. A short-story writer, novelist, poet, essayist and translator, he has dozens of books to his credit. He has won many state- and national-level awards for his writings, including the Sahitya Akademi award for translation.

Perumal Murugan (1966-), professor of Tamil, is a well-known Tamil writer. His works include novels, short stories, poems and essays. He has also compiled a dictionary of the dialect in the Coimbatore region of Tamil Nadu. A recipient of important awards, his novels have also been translated into English.

Poomani (1947-) is the pen name of P Manickavasagam. A distinguished writer, he has published six novels, six short-story collections and one collection of essays. He has also scripted a film and directed it. His works have been translated into several languages. His latest novel *Angnaadi* has won several awards, including the Sahitya Akademi award in 2014.

Prapanchan (1945-), the pseudonym of S Vaidyalingam, is an important novelist and short-story writer. Trained in classical Tamil literature, he was influenced by the self-respect movement and progressive ideology. A prolific and popular writer, he has won several awards, including the Sahitya Akademi award.

Pudumaippittan (1906-1948), the pseudonym of C Viruthachalam, is rightly recognised as the pioneer of the Tamil short story. A maverick, he broke conventions and taboos and ushered in a renaissance in Tamil writing. Though his productive years barely amounted to fifteen, he left behind a remarkable corpus of short stories, essays, poems and translations, which are revered even today.

R Chudamani (1931-2010), one of Tamil's important women writers, started writing in the late 1950s. Well known in both the world of literary journals and popular magazines, her felicitous and earnest writings made a significant contribution to contemporary Tamil literature. Winner of several awards, she also wrote novels and novellas.

Rajam Krishnan (1925-2014), one of the most important women writers, successfully intertwined progressive ideas and perspectives into her writings. Her well-researched novels reflect the trials of women from various communities and backdrops. A recipient of several awards, she has won even the Soviet Land Nehru Award in 1975. She was awarded the Sahitya Akademi award in 1973.

Rajendra Sozhan (1945-), a retired teacher, is an important short-story writer, novelist and playwright. He is also known for his articles and essays on contemporary social and literary issues.

Ramakrishnan (1944-), known as Cre-A Ramakrishnan, began his career writing short stories. He is a well-respected Tamil publisher today. Known for ushering in professionalism in Tamil publishing, he has published several pioneering modern works of all genres. The *Cre-A Dictionary of Contemporary Tamil* is a landmark publication in Tamil.

Rasikan (1893-1982), was the pen name of N Raghunathan. A doyen of English journalism, he was a profound scholar in Tamil, English and Sanskrit. His short stories and plays are highly acclaimed. He was also known for his outstanding translations from classical Tamil and Sanskrit into English.

S Ramakrishnan (1966-) is a prolific, popular writer. His works include short stories, novels, essays, plays and children's stories. Deeply interested in cinema, he has written several screenplays. He is the recipient of several awards, including the Iyal Award from Canada and the Sangeet Natak Akademi award.

S V V (1880-1950) was the popular name of S V Vijayaraghavachariar, a noted writer of the 1930s. His humorous writings full of human warmth and love were immensely popular. His writings in both Tamil and English brought much joy and cheer to his readers.

Sa Kandasamy (1940-), one of the most established writers in Tamil, has been writing for the past fifty years. He has written over two hundred short stories, fourteen novels and two works of non-fiction. He is also a documentary and short-film maker. His novels have been translated into English. He has won the Tamil Nadu state literary awards and the Sahitya Akademi award.

Sa Tamil'selvan (1954-) comes from a family of litterateurs. He is the state president of the Tamil Nadu Progressive Writers' and Artists' Association. He has written over twenty books. Deeply committed to the propagation of literacy, he has written several books for neo-literates. He also served in the Indian army.

Saarvaagan (1929-) is the pseudonym of Dr H Srinivasan, a leading specialist in leprosy rehabilitation. Though his output is slim, his well-etched stories have earned him a legion of followers. He has also written perceptive novellas, poems and essays. He was awarded the Padma Shri in 1984 for his contribution to the field of medicine.

Selvakesavarayar (1864-1921) was a Tamil scholar who taught at Pachiappa's College, Madras. One of the earliest practitioners of the Tamil short story, he brought out a significant collection titled *Abhinava Kadaigal.* Adhering strictly to the grammar of the short story, he was one of the first few to write about the world around him.

Shenbagam Ramaswamy (1940-1998), a professor of Tamil, was steeped in both classical and contemporary literature. She attempted to translate classics from Greek – in which she was proficient – into Tamil, but unfortunately she passed away before she could.

Sivakami (1957-) is known for her novels and short stories dealing with Dalit and feminist themes. Her novels and poems have been translated into English and other languages. She was with the Indian Administrative Service till 2008, when she quit to join politics. She is the founder editor of the Dalit journal *Pudiya Kodangi.*

Sivasankari (1942-), a popular writer, is known for her short stories and novels that deal with social evils. Her works have been translated into many languages. Her significant contribution is 'Knit India through Literature', a compilation of interviews and translations of works of writers from eighteen Indian languages.

Su Venugopal (1968-), a professor of Tamil literature, comes from a family of agriculturists. He has several collections of short stories and awards to his credit. His works have been translated into English and Malayalam. He is also trained in the various folk forms of Tamil Nadu.

Subrabharathi Manian (1960-) is a novelist and short story writer, who has published more than forty books. His works have been widely translated into several Indian languages. He is the editor of the Tamil literary journal *Kanavu.*

Subramania Bharati (1882-1921) needs no introduction. A freedom fighter, social reformer, translator, editor and, above all, a great poet, he pioneered every genre of modern literature. His timeless expressions indelibly mark Tamil phraseology; any discourse on modernity has no recourse but to take refuge in them. His prodigious output – poems, songs, essays, journalistic articles, translations and children's writings – is too vast to enumerate.

Subramanya Raju (1948-1987) was an accomplished short-story writer and critic. He has two anthologies of short stories to his credit. His well-crafted stories deftly capture the angst of the urban youth. He died tragically in an accident.

Sudhakar Ghatak (1967-) is an assistant engineer in the Public Works Department. Deeply influenced by the famous Bengali filmmaker, he appended the name 'Ghatak' to his own. An important Dalit voice, he has an acclaimed collection of stories to his credit.

Sujatha (1935-2008), whose real name was S Rangarajan, was a hugely popular, prolific writer. An engineer by profession, he has written hundreds of novels, short stories and essays. Known for his intelligent humour and stylistic prose, he has also written successful plays and screenplays for popular Tamil films. He demystified arcane scientific concepts for the layperson through his popular columns.

Sundara Ramaswamy (1931-2005) was one of Tamil's most influential writers. His literary career, which spanned fifty-odd years, included short stories, novels, translations, poetry and criticism. He published poetry under the name Pasuvayya. Much of his writing has been translated into other Indian and European languages.

Suresh Kumara Indrajith (1953 -) is a retired officer from the Revenue Department. His writing career began in the 1980s. He has published five collections of short stories.

T K Seenivasan (1924-1979), writer and politician, was one of the important ideologues of the Tamil Dravidian movement. He published three novels, three short-story collections and an anthology of essays. He also served as a member of parliament.

Thi Janakiraman (1921-1982), an immensely gifted novelist and short-story writer, was a media professional. Even today his novels, which are nuanced depictions of life in the district of Thanjavur, are considered classic examples of lyrical prose. His short stories, laced with wit, compassion and dignity, are flawless masterpieces. He won many awards, including the Sahitya Akademi.

Thilakavathi (1952-), the first IPS woman officer from Tamil Nadu, wrote fiction right through her career. A winner of many prestigious awards, including the Sahitya Akademi, she has more than fifteen books to her credit. She now runs a Tamil socio-literary journal, *Amrutha*.

Thoppil Mohamed Meeran (1944-) is known for his authentic portrayal of the rural Muslim world. Many of his novels and short stories have been translated into other languages. He is a recipient of the Sahitya Akademi award.

Uma Maheswari (1971-) has been writing from the 1980s. She is an accomplished novelist, short-story writer and poet. She has over half a dozen books to her credit. She has won several important literary awards.

V Visalakshiammal (1884-1926) accomplished a lot in her short life. Widowed at an early age, she was fluent in Tamil, English, Sanskrit and Kannada, besides being knowledgeable in music. She joined V. Nataraja Iyer's *Lokobakari* as assistant editor in 1902, thereby becoming the first woman to ever be on the editorial board of a Tamil journal. She became its editor in 1906. She also edited the monthly *Hitakarani*. She wrote about thirty novels. Her first two novels *Lalithangi* and *Jalajakshi* were published in the name of V. Nataraja Iyer. The truth was revealed only when he disclosed it when *Jothishmathi* was published.

Va Ve Su Iyer (1881-1925), a revolutionary who fought the British in the freedom struggle along with the nationalist poet Subramania Bharati and Bengali rebel Aurobindo Ghosh, is considered the father of the modern Tamil short story. Widely read and travelled, his only collection of short stories is hailed as a classic by critics and readers alike.

Vaasanthi (1941-) is the nom de plume of Pankajam. A popular Tamil writer who has been writing for fifty years, she has authored over forty books, which include novels, short stories, journalistic articles and travelogues. Her works have been translated into several languages, both Indian and foreign. She also writes in English.

Vannadasan (1946-) is the pen name of Kalyana Sundaram S, a retired bank officer, who has been writing since 1962. He writes poetry under the name Kalyanji. He has published short-story collections, poems, essays and even a collection of personal letters. He has won the Saaral award.

Vannanilavan (1949-) is the pen name of U Ramachandran. An important novelist, short-story writer, essayist and poet, he has several publications to his credit. The social milieu of his native Thirunelveli district unfolds in his poignantly perceptive fiction. He has won awards such as the Ilakkia Chinthanai and more recently, the Saaral.

Vela Ramamoorthy (1953-), an ex-army man, is both a novelist and a short story writer. His works have been widely translated into both Indian and foreign languages. He has also directed several street plays. He is currently an actor and a screenplay writer.

Vimaladhitha Maamallan (1960-) is the pen name of C Narasimhan, whose mother tongue is Marathi. A student of Tamil literature, he started writing in the 1980s. He is also a theatre person and a screenplay writer. He has published three volumes of short fiction. He participated in Baba Amte's Knit India Movement and cycled over five thousand kilometres across the length and breadth of India.

Vizhi Pa Idayaventhan (1962-) is the pen name of P Annadurai. A prolific Dalit writer, he has over twenty-two books to his credit. He has won several literary awards.